O

DIANA GABALDON is the   by
Outlander nove.

She says that the Outlander series started by accident: 'I decided to
write a novel for practice in order to learn what it took to write a
novel, and to decide whether I really wanted to do it for real. I did –
and here we all are trying to decide what to call books that nobody
can describe, but that fortunately most people seem to enjoy.'

And enjoy them they do – in their millions, all over the world.
Published in 42 countries and 38 languages, in 2014 the
Outlander novels were made into an acclaimed TV series starring
Sam Heughan as Jamie Fraser and Caitriona Balfe as Claire.
Seasons three and four are currently in production.

Diana lives with her husband and dogs in Scottsdale, Arizona,
and is currently at work on her ninth Outlander novel.

Praise for Diana Gabaldon

'Gabaldon is a born storyteller'
Los Angeles Daily News

'The writing is superb'
Library Journal

'History comes deliciously alive on the page'
New York Daily News

'Triumphant'
Publishers Weekly

'A blockbuster hit'
Wall Street Journal

Also by Diana Gabaldon

Outlander Series

Dragonfly in Amber
Voyager
Drums of Autumn
The Fiery Cross
A Breath of Snow and Ashes
An Echo in the Bone
Written in my Own Heart's Blood

Lord John Series

Lord John and the Hellfire Club
Lord John and the Private Matter
Lord John and the Succubus
Lord John and the Brotherhood of the Blade
Lord John and the Haunted Soldier
The Scottish Prisoner
Lord John and the Hand of Devils (Collection)

DIANA GABALDON

OUTLANDER:
CROSS STITCH

arrow books

9 10 8

Arrow Books
20 Vauxhall Bridge Road
London SW1V 2SA

Arrow Books is part of the Penguin Random House group of companies
whose addresses can be found at global.penguinrandomhouse.com

Penguin
Random House
UK

First published in Great Britain by Century in 1991 as *Cross Stitch*
(First published in the US by Delacorte Press in 1991)
First published in paperback by Arrow Books in 1994 as *Cross Stitch*
Dragonfly in Amber extract first published in the US by Delacorte Press in 1992
This TV tie-in edition published in 2014

www.penguin.co.uk

A CIP catalogue record for this book
is available from the British Library

ISBN 9780099599531

Printed and bound in Great Britain by Clays Ltd, St Ives plc

Penguin Random House is committed to a sustainable future
for our business, our readers and our planet. This book is made
from Forest Stewardship Council® certified paper.

To the Memory of My Mother
Who Taught Me to Read
Jacqueline Sykes Gabaldon

Acknowledgements

The author would like to thank ...

Jackie Cantor, Editor par excellence, whose 'boundless enthusiasm' had so much to do with getting this story between covers;

Perry Knowlton, Agent of impeccable judgement, who said, 'Go ahead and tell the story the way it should be told; we'll worry about cutting it later.'

My husband, Doug Watkins, who, despite occasionally standing behind my chair, saying, 'If it's set in Scotland, why doesn't anybody say "Hoot, mon"?' also spent a good deal of time chasing children and saying 'Mummy is WRITING! Leave her alone!'

My daughter Laura, for loftily informing a friend, 'MY mother writes BOOKS!'

My son Samuel, who, when asked what Mummy does for a living, replied cautiously, 'Well, she watches her computer a lot.'

My daughter Jennifer, who says, 'Move over, Mummy; it's MY turn to type!'

Jerry O'Neill, First Reader and Head Cheerleader, and the rest of my personal Gang of Four – Janet McConnaughey, Margaret J. Campbell and John L. Myers, who read everything I write, and thereby keep me writing.

Dr Gary Hoff, for verifying the medical details and kindly explaining the proper way to reset a dislocated shoulder;

T. Lawrence Tuohy, for details of military history and costuming;

Robert Riffle, for explaining the difference between betony and bryony, listing every kind of forget-me-not known to man, and verifying that aspens really do grow in Scotland;

Virginia Kidd, for reading early parts of the manuscript and encouraging me to go on with it;

Alex Krislov, for co-hosting with other systems operators the most extraordinary electronic literary cocktail-party-cum-writer's-incubator in the world, the CompuServe Literary Forum . . .

AND . . . the many members of LitForum: John Stith, John Simpson, John L. Myers, Judson Jerome, Angelia Dorman, Zilgia Quafay . . . and the rest – for Scottish folk songs, Latin love poetry, and for laughing (and crying) in the right places.

People disappear all the time. Ask any policeman. Better yet, ask a journalist. Disappearances are bread and butter to journalists.

Young girls run away from home. Young children stray from their parents and are never seen again. Housewives reach the end of their tether and take the grocery money and a taxi to the station. International financiers change their names and vanish into the smoke of imported cigars.

Many of the lost will be found, eventually, dead or alive. Disappearances, after all, have explanations.

Usually.

PART ONE

Inverness, 1946

1

A New Beginning

It wasn't a very likely place for disappearances, at least at first glance. Mrs Baird's was like a thousand other Highland bed-and-breakfast establishments in 1946; clean and quiet, with fading floral wallpaper, gleaming floors and a coin-operated water heater in the bathroom. Mrs Baird herself was squat and easygoing, and made no objection to Frank lining her tiny rose-sprigged parlour with the dozens of books and papers with which he always travelled.

I met Mrs Baird in the front hall on my way out. She stopped me with a pudgy hand on my arm and patted at my hair.

'Dear me, Mrs Randall, ye canna go out like that! Here, just let me tuck that bit in for ye. There! That's better. Ye know, my cousin was tellin' me about a new perm she tried, comes out beautiful and holds like a dream; perhaps ye should try that kind next time.'

I hadn't the heart to tell her that the waywardness of my light brown curls was strictly the fault of nature, and not due to any dereliction on the part of the permanent-wave manufacturers. Her own tightly marcelled waves suffered from no such perversity.

'Yes, I'll do that, Mrs Baird,' I lied. 'I'm just going down to meet Frank. We'll be back for tea.' I ducked out of the door and down the path before she could detect any further defects in my undisciplined appearance. After five years as an army nurse, I was enjoying the escape from uniforms by indulging in brightly printed blouses and long skirts, totally unsuited for rough walking through the heather.

Not that I had originally planned to do a lot of that; my thoughts ran more on the lines of sleeping late in the mornings, and long, lazy afternoons in bed with Frank, not sleeping. However, it was difficult to maintain the proper mood of languorous romance with Mrs Baird industriously hoovering away outside our door.

'That must be the dirtiest bit of carpet in the entire Scottish Highlands,' Frank had observed that morning as we lay in bed listening to the ferocious roar of the vacuum in the hallway.

'Nearly as dirty as our landlady's mind,' I agreed. 'Perhaps we should have gone to Brighton after all.' We had chosen the Highlands as a place to holiday before Frank took up his appointment as a history professor at Oxford, on the grounds that Scotland had been somewhat less touched by the physical horrors of war than the rest of Britain, and was less susceptible to the frenetic postwar gaiety that infected more popular holiday spots.

And without discussing it, I think we both felt that it was a symbolic place to re-establish our marriage; we had been married and spent a two-day honeymoon in the Highlands, shortly before the outbreak of war seven years before. A peaceful refuge in which to rediscover each other, we thought, not realizing that, while golf and fishing are Scotland's most popular outdoor sports, gossip is the most popular indoor sport. And when it rains as much as it does in Scotland, people spend a lot of time indoors.

'Where are you going?' I asked as Frank swung his feet out of bed.

'I'd hate the dear old thing to be disappointed in us,' he answered. Sitting up on the side of the ancient bed he bounced gently up and down, creating a piercing rhythmic squeak. The hoovering in the hall stopped abruptly. After a minute or two of bouncing he gave a loud, theatrical groan and collapsed backwards with a twang of protesting springs. I giggled helplessly into a pillow, so as not to disturb the breathless silence outside.

Frank waggled his eyebrows at me. 'You're supposed to moan ecstatically, not giggle,' he admonished in a whisper. 'She'll think I'm not a good lover.'

'You'll have to keep it up for longer than that if you

14

expect ecstatic moans,' I answered. 'Two minutes doesn't deserve any more than a giggle.'

'Inconsiderate wench. I came here for a rest, remember?'

'Lazybones. You'll never manage the next branch on your family tree unless you show a bit more industry than that.'

Frank's passion for genealogy was yet another reason for choosing the Highlands. According to one of the filthy scraps of paper he lugged to and fro, some tiresome ancestor of his had had something to do with something or other in this region back in the middle of the eighteenth – or was it seventeenth? – century.

'If I end up as a childless stub on my family tree, it will undoubtedly be the fault of our untiring hostess out there. After all, we've been married almost seven years. Little Frank will be quite legitimate without being conceived in the presence of a witness.'

'If he's conceived at all,' I said pessimistically. We had been disappointed yet again the week before leaving for our Highland retreat.

'With all this bracing fresh air and healthy diet? How could we help but manage here?' High tea the night before had been herring, fried. Lunch had been herring, pickled. And the pungent scent now wafting up the stairwell strongly intimated that breakfast was to be herring, kippered.

'Unless you're contemplating an encore performance for the edification of Mrs Baird,' I suggested, 'you'd better get dressed. Aren't you meeting that parson at ten?' The Reverend Mr Reginald Wakefield, minister of the local parish, was to provide some rivetingly fascinating baptismal registers for Frank's inspection, not to mention the glittering prospect that he might have unearthed some mouldering army dispatches or somesuch that mentioned the notorious ancestor.

'What's the name of that six-times-great-grandfather of yours again?' I asked. 'The one who mucked about here during one of the Risings? I can't remember if it was Willy or Walter.'

'Actually, it was Jonathan.' Frank took my complete disinterest in family history placidly, but remained always on guard, ready to seize the slightest expression of inquisitiveness as an excuse for telling me all facts known to date about the early Randalls and their connections. His eyes assumed the fervid gleam of the fanatic lecturer as he buttoned his shirt.

'Jonathan Wolverton Randall – Wolverton for his mother's uncle, a minor knight from Sussex. He was, however, known by the rather dashing nickname of "Black Jack", something he acquired in the army, probably during the time he was stationed here.' I flopped face down on the bed and affected to snore. Ignoring me, Frank went on with his scholarly exegesis.

'He bought his commission in the mid-thirties – 1730s, that is – and served as a captain of dragoons. According to those old letters Cousin May sent me, he did quite well in the army. Good choice for a second son, you know; his younger brother followed tradition as well by becoming a curate, but I haven't found out much about him yet. Anyway, Jack Randall was highly commended by the Duke of Sandringham for his activities before and during the 45 – the second Jacobite Rising, you know,' he amplified for the benefit of the ignorant amongst his audience, namely me. 'You know, Bonnie Prince Charlie and that lot.'

'I'm not entirely sure the Scots realize they lost that one,' I interrupted, sitting up and trying to subdue my hair. 'I distinctly heard the barman at that pub last night refer to us as Sassenachs.'

'Well, why not?' said Frank equably. 'It only means "Englishman", after all, or at worst, outsider and we're all of that.'

'I know what it means. It was the tone I objected to.'

Frank searched through the chest of drawers for a belt. 'He was just annoyed because I told him the beer was weak. I told him the true Highland brew requires an old boot to be added to the vat, and the final product to be strained through a well-worn undergarment.'

'Ah, that accounts for the amount of the bill.'

'Well, I phrased it a little more tactfully than that, but

only because the Gaelic language hasn't got a specific word for drawers.'

I reached for a pair of my own, intrigued. 'Why not? Did the ancient Gaels not wear undergarments?'

Frank leered. 'You've never heard that old song about what a Scotsman wears beneath his kilt?'

'Presumably not gents' knee-length step-ins,' I said dryly. 'Perhaps I'll go out in search of a local kilt-wearer whilst you're cavorting with vicars and ask him.'

'Well, do try not to get arrested, Claire. The dean of St Giles College wouldn't like it at all.'

In the event, there were no kilt-wearers loitering about the town or patronizing the shops. There were a number of other people there, though, mostly housewives of the Mrs Baird type, doing their daily shopping. They were garrulous and gossipy, and their solid, tweedy presences filled the shops with a cosy warmth; a buttress against the cold mist of the morning outdoors.

With as yet no house of my own to keep, I had little that needed buying – there was little to buy yet, in truth; supplies were still short – but enjoyed myself in browsing among the sparse shelves of the shops.

My gaze lingered on a shop window containing a scattering of household goods – embroidered tea cloths, a set of jug and glasses, a stack of homely pie tins and a set of three vases.

I had never owned a vase in my life. During the war years I had, of course, lived in the nurses' quarters, first at Pembroke Hospital, later at the field station in France. But even before that we had lived nowhere long enough to justify the purchase of such an item. Had I had such a thing, I reflected, Uncle Lamb would have filled it with potsherds long before I could have got near it with a bunch of daisies.

Quentin Lambert Beauchamp. 'Q' to his archaeological students and his friends. 'Dr Beauchamp' to the scholarly circles in which he moved and lectured and had his being. But always Uncle Lamb to me.

My father's only brother, and my only living relative, he had been landed with me, aged five, when my parents were killed in a car crash. Poised for a trip to the Middle East at the time, he had paused in his preparations long enough to make the funeral arrangements, dispose of my parents' estates and enrol me in a proper girls' boarding school. Which I had flatly refused to attend.

Faced with the necessity of prying my chubby fingers off the car's door handle and dragging me by the heels up the steps of the school, Uncle Lamb, who hated personal conflict of any kind, had sighed in exasperation, then finally shrugged and tossed his better judgement out of the window along with my newly purchased round straw boater.

'Ruddy thing,' he muttered, seeing it rolling merrily away in the rear-view mirror as we roared down the drive in high gear. 'Always loathed hats on women, anyway.' He had glanced down at me, fixing me with a fierce glare.

'One thing,' he said, in awful tones. 'You are *not* to play dolls with my Persian grave figurines. Anything else, but not that. Is that clear?'

I had nodded, content. And had gone with him to the Middle East, to South America, to dozens of study sites throughout the world. Had learned to read and write from the drafts of journal articles, to dig latrines and boil water, and to do a number of other things not suitable for a young lady of gentle birth – until I had met the handsome, dark-haired historian who came to consult Uncle Lamb on a point of French philosophy as it related to Egyptian religious practice.

Even after our marriage Frank and I led the nomadic life of junior faculty, divided between continental conferences and temporary flats, until the outbreak of war had sent him to Officer's Training and the Intelligence Unit at MI6, and me to nurse's training. Though we had been married nearly eight years, the new house in Oxford would be our first real home.

Tucking my handbag firmly under my arm, I marched into the shop and bought the vases.

I met Frank at the crossing of the High Street and the Gereside Road and we turned up it together. He raised his eyebrows at my purchases.

'Vases?' He smiled. 'Wonderful. Perhaps now you'll stop putting flowers in my books.'

'They aren't flowers, they're specimens. And it was you who suggested I take up botany. To occupy my mind, now that I've no nursing to do,' I reminded him.

'True.' He nodded good-humouredly. 'But I didn't realize I'd have bits of greenery dropping out into my lap every time I opened a reference. What was that horrible crumbly brown stuff you put in Tuscum and Banks?'

'Comfrey. Good for haemorrhoids.'

'Preparing for my imminent old age, are you? Well, how very thoughtful of you, Claire.'

We had promised to drop in on the Carsons, round the corner. We pushed through the gate, laughing, and Frank stood back to let me go first up the narrow front steps.

Suddenly he caught my arm. 'Look out! You don't want to step in it.'

I lifted my foot gingerly over a large brownish-red stain on the top step.

'How odd,' I said. 'Mrs Carson scrubs the steps down every morning; I've seen her. What do you suppose that can be?'

Frank leaned over the step, sniffing delicately.

'Offhand, I should say that it's blood.'

'Blood!' I took a step back into the entryway. 'Whose?' I glanced nervously into the house. 'Do you suppose the Carsons have had an accident of some kind?' I couldn't imagine our tidy neighbours leaving bloodstains to dry on their doorstep unless some major catastrophe had occurred, and wondered just for a moment whether the parlour might be harbouring a crazed axe-murderer, even now preparing to spring out on us with a spine-chilling shriek.

Frank shook his head. He stood on tiptoe to peer over the hedge into the next garden.

'I shouldn't think so. There's a stain like it on the Collinses' doorstep as well.'

'Really?' I drew closer to Frank, both to see over the hedge and for moral support. The Highlands hardly seemed a likely spot for a mass murderer, but then I doubted such persons used any sort of logical criteria when picking their sites. 'That's rather ... disagreeable,' I observed. There was no sign of life from the next residence. 'What do you suppose has happened?'

Frank frowned, thinking, then slapped his hand ' iefly against his trouser leg in inspiration.

'I think I know! Wait here a moment.' He darted out to the gate and set off down the road at a trot, leaving me stranded on the edge of the doorstep.

He was back shortly, beaming with confirmation.

'Yes, that's it, it must be. Every house in the row has had it.'

'Had what? A visit from a homicidal maniac?' I spoke a bit sharply, still nervous at having been abruptly abandoned with nothing but a large bloodstain for company.

Frank laughed.. 'No, a ritual sacrifice. Fascinating!' He was down on his hands and knees in the grass, peering interestedly at the stain.

This hardly sounded better than a homicidal maniac. I squatted beside him, wrinkling my nose at the smell. It was early for flies, but a horde of the tiny, voracious Highland midges circled the stain.

'What do you mean, "ritual sacrifice"?' I demanded. 'Mrs Carson's a good church-goer, and so are all the neighbours. This isn't Druid's Hill or anything, you know.'

He stood, brushing grass-ends from his trousers. 'That's all you know, my girl,' he said. 'There's no place on earth with more of the old superstitions and magic mixed into its daily life than the Scottish Highlands. Church or no church, Mrs Carson believes in the Old Folk, and so do all the neighbours.' He pointed at the stain with one neatly polished toe. 'The blood of a black cock,' he explained, looking pleased. 'The houses are new, you see. Pre-fabs.'

I looked at him coldly. 'If you are under the impression that that explains everything, think again. What difference

20

does it make how old the houses are? And where on earth is everybody?'

'Down at the pub, I should expect. Let's go along and see, shall we?' Taking my arm, he steered me out of the gate and we set off down the Gereside Road.

'In the old days,' he explained as we went, 'and not so long ago, either, when a house was built it was customary to kill something and bury it under the foundation, as a propitiation to the local earth spirits. You know, "He shall lay the foundations thereof in his firstborn and in his youngest son shall he set up the gates of it." Old as the hills.'

I shuddered at the quotation. 'In that case, I suppose it's quite modern and enlightened of them to be using chickens instead. You mean, since the houses are fairly new, nothing was buried under them, and the inhabitants are now remedying the omission.'

'Yes, exactly.' Frank seemed pleased with my progress, and patted me on the back. 'According to the minister, many of the local folk thought the war was due in part to people turning away from their roots and omitting to take proper precautions, such as burying a sacrifice under the foundation, that is, or burning fishes' bones on the hearth – except haddocks, of course,' he added, happily distracted. 'You never burn a haddock's bones – did you know? – or you'll never catch another. Always bury the bones of a haddock instead.'

'I'll bear it in mind,' I said. 'Tell me what you do in order never to see another herring, and I'll do it forthwith.'

He shook his head, absorbed in one of his feats of memory, those brief periods of scholastic rapture where he lost touch with the world around him, absorbed completely in conjuring up knowledge from all its sources.

'I don't know about herring,' he said absently. 'For mice, though, you hang bunches of Trembling Jock about – "Trembling Jock i' the hoose, and ye'll ne'er see a moose", you know. Bodies under the foundation, though – that's where a lot of the local ghosts come from. You know Mountgerald, the big house at the end of the High Street? There's a ghost there, a workman on the house who was killed as a sacrifice for the foundation. It was some time in the eighteenth century; that's really fairly recent,' he added thoughtfully.

'The story goes that by order of the house's owner, one wall was built up first, then a stone block was dropped from the top of it on to one of the workmen – presumably a dislikable fellow was chosen for the sacrifice – and he was buried then in the cellar and the rest of the house built up over him. He haunts the cellar where he was killed, except on the anniversary of his death and the four Old Days.'

'Old Days?'

'The ancient feasts,' he explained, still lost in his mental notes. 'Hogmanay, that's New Year's Eve, Midsummer Day, Beltane and All Hallow's, Druids, Beaker Folk, early Picts, everybody kept the sun feasts and the fire feasts, so far as we know. Anyway, ghosts are freed on the holy days, and can wander about at will, to do harm or good as they please.' He rubbed his chin thoughtfully. 'It's getting on for Beltane – the Celtic May Day festival. Best keep an eye out next time you pass the kirkyard.' His eyes twinkled, and I realized the trance had ended.

I laughed. 'Are there a number of famous local ghosts, then?'

He shrugged. 'Don't know. We'll ask Mr Wakefield, shall we, next time we see him?'

We saw Mr Wakefield that evening, in fact. He, along with most of the other inhabitants of the neighbourhood, was in the hotel lounge, having a lemonade in celebration of the houses' new sanctification.

He seemed rather embarrassed at being caught in the act of condoning a paganism, as it were, but brushed it off as merely a local observance with historical colour, like the Wearing of the Green.

'Really rather fascinating, you know,' he confided, and I recognized, with an internal sigh, the song of the scholar, as identifying a sound as the call of a cuckoo. Harking to the sound of a kindred spirit, Frank at once settled down to the mating dance of academe and they were soon neck-deep in archetypes and the parallels between ancient superstitions and modern religions. I snagged a passing waitress and secured a couple of cups of tea.

Knowing from experience how difficult it was to distract Frank's attention from this sort of discussion, I simply picked up his hand, wrapped his fingers about the handle of the cup and left him to his own devices.

I found our landlady, Mrs Baird, on a loveseat near the window, sharing a companionable plate of digestive biscuits with an elderly man whom she introduced to me as Mr Crook.

'This is the man I tell't ye about, Mrs Randall,' she said, eyes bright with the stimulation of company. 'The one as knows about plants of all sorts.

'Mrs Randall's verra much interested in the wee plants,' she confided to her companion, who inclined his head in a combination of politeness and deafness. 'Presses them in books and such.'

'Do ye, indeed?' Mr Crook asked, one tufted white brow raised in interest. 'I've some presses – the real ones, mind – for plants and such. Had them from my nephew, when he came up from university over his holiday. He brought them for me, and I'd not the heart to tell him I never use such things. Hangin's what's wanted for herbs, ye ken, or maybe to be dried on a frame and put in a bit o' gauze bag or a jar, but why ever you'd be after squashing the wee things flat, I've no idea.'

'Well, to look at, maybe,' Mrs Baird interjected kindly. 'Mrs Randall's made some lovely bits out of wood anemone, and violets, same as you could put in a frame and hang on the wall, like.'

'Mmmphm.' Mr Crook's seamed face seemed to be admitting a dubious possibility to this suggestion. 'Weel, if they're of any use to ye, Missus, you can have the presses, and welcome. I didna wish to be throwing them awa', but I must say I've no use for them.'

I assured Mr Crook that I would be delighted to make use of the plant presses, and still more delighted if he would show me where some of the rarer plants in the area could be found. He eyed me sharply for a moment, head to one side like an elderly kestrel, but appeared finally to decide that my interest was genuine, and we fixed it up that I should meet him in the morning for a tour of the local shrubbery. Frank, I knew, meant to spend the morning consulting records in the town hall, and I was pleased to have an excuse not to accompany him. One record was much like another, so far as I was concerned.

Soon after this Frank prised himself away from the minister and we walked home in company with Mrs Baird. I was reluctant to mention the cock's blood we had seen on the doorsteps, myself, but Frank suffered from no such reticence, and questioned her eagerly as to the background of the custom.

'I suppose it's quite old, then?' he asked, swishing a stick along through the roadside weeds. Fat hen and cinquefoil were green in the ditches, and I could see the buds of sweet broom just starting to show.

'Och, aye.' Mrs Baird waddled along at a brisk pace, asking no quarter from our younger limbs. 'Older than anyone knows, Mr Randall. Even back before the days of the giants.'

'Giants?' I asked.

'Aye. Fionn and the Feinn, ye ken.'

'Gaelic folktales,' Frank remarked with interest. 'Heroes, you know. Probably from Norse roots. There's a lot of the Norse influence around here, and all the way up the coast to the West. Some of the place names are Norse, you know, not Gaelic at all.'

I rolled my eyes, sensing another outburst, but Mrs Baird smiled kindly and encouraged him, saying that was true, then; she'd been up to the north, and seen the Two Brothers stone, and that was Norse, wasn't it?

'The Norsemen came down on that coast hundreds of times between AD 500 and 1300 or so,' Frank said, looking dreamily at the horizon, seeing dragon-ships in the wind-swept cloud. 'Vikings, you know. And they brought a lot of their own myths along. It's a good country for myths. Things seem to take root here.'

This I could believe. Twilight was coming on, and so

was a storm. In the eerie light beneath the clouds even the thoroughly modern houses along the road looked as ancient and as sinister as the weathered Pictish stone that stood a hundred feet away, guarding the crossroads it had marked for a thousand years. It seemed a good night to be inside with the shutters fastened.

Rather than staying cosily in Mrs Baird's parlour to be entertained by stereopticon views of Perth, though, Frank chose to keep his appointment for sherry with Mr Bainbridge, a solicitor with an interest in local historical records. Bearing in mind my earlier encounter with Mr Bainbridge, I elected to stay at home.

'Try to come back before the storm breaks,' I said, kissing Frank goodbye. 'And give my regards to Mr Bainbridge.'

'Umm, yes. Yes, of course.' Carefully not meeting my eye, Frank shrugged into his overcoat and left, collecting an umbrella from the stand by the door.

I closed the door after him but left it on the latch so he could get back in. I wandered back towards the parlour, reflecting that Frank would doubtless pretend that he didn't have a wife – a pretence in which Mr Bainbridge would cheerfully join. Not that I could blame him, particularly.

At first, everything had gone quite well on our visit to Mr Bainbridge's home the afternoon before. I had been demure, genteel, intelligent but self-effacing, well groomed and quietly dressed – everything the Perfect Don's Wife should be. Until the tea was served.

I now turned my right hand over, ruefully examining the large blister that ran across the bases of all four fingers. After all, it was not my fault that Mr Bainbridge, a widower, made do with a cheap tin teapot instead of a proper crockery one. Nor that the solicitor, seeking to be polite, had asked me to pour. Nor that the potholder he provided had a worn patch that allowed the red-hot handle of the teapot to come into direct contact with my hand when I picked it up.

No, I decided. Dropping the teapot was a perfectly normal reaction. Dropping it on Mr Bainbridge's carpet was merely an accident of placement; I had to drop it somewhere. It was my exclaiming 'Bloody fucking hell!' in a voice that topped Mr Bainbridge's heartcry that had made Frank glare at me across the scones.

Once he recovered from the shock Mr Bainbridge had been quite gallant, fussing about my hand and ignoring Frank's attempts to excuse my language on grounds that I had been stationed in a field hospital for the better part of two years. 'I'm afraid my wife picked up a number of, er, colourful expressions from the Yanks and such,' Frank offered, with a nervous smile.

'True,' I said, gritting my teeth as I wrapped a water-soaked napkin about my hand. 'Men tend to be very "colourful" when you're picking shrapnel out of them.'

Mr Bainbridge had tactfully tried to distract the conversation on to neutral historical ground by saying that he had always been interested in the variations of what was considered profane speech through the ages. There was 'gorblimey' for example, a recent corruption of the oath 'God blind me'.

'Yes, of course,' said Frank, gratefully accepting the diversion. 'No sugar, thank you, Claire. What about "Gadzooks"? The "Gad" part is quite clear, of course, but the "zook" . . . '

'Well, you know,' the solicitor interjected, 'I've sometimes thought it might be a corruption of an old Scots word, in fact – "yeuk". Means "itch". That would make sense, wouldn't it?'

Frank nodded, letting his unscholarly forelock fall across his forehead. He pushed it back automatically. 'Interesting,' he said, 'the whole evolution of profanity.'

'Yes, and it's still going on,' I said, carefully picking up a lump of sugar with the tongs.

'Oh?' said Mr Bainbridge politely. 'Did you encounter some interesting variations during your, er, war experience?'

'Oh, yes,' I said. 'My favourite was one I picked up from a Yank. Man named Williamson, from New York, I believe. He said it every time I changed his dressing.'

'What was it?'

' "Jesus H. Roosevelt Christ," ' I said, and dropped the sugar lump neatly and deliberately into Frank's cup.

After a peaceful and not unpleasant sit with Mrs Baird, I made my way upstairs to ready myself before Frank came home. I knew his limit with sherry was two glasses, so I expected him back soon.

The wind was rising and the very air of the bedroom was prickly with electricity. I drew the brush through my hair, making the curls snap with static and spring into knots and furious tangles. My hair would have to do without its hundred strokes tonight, I decided. I would settle for brushing my teeth, in this sort of weather. Strands of hair adhered stickily to my cheeks, clinging stubbornly as I tried to smooth them back.

No water in the ewer; Frank had used it, tidying himself before setting out for his meeting with Mr Bainbridge, and I had not bothered to refill it from the bathroom tap. I picked up the bottle of L'Heure Bleue and poured a generous puddle into the palm of my hand. Rubbing my hands briskly together before the scent could evaporate, I smoothed them rapidly through my hair. I poured another dollop on to my hairbrush and swept the curls back behind my ears with it.

Well. That was rather better, I thought, turning my head from side to side to examine the results in the speckled looking glass. The moisture had dissipated the static electricity in my hair so that it floated in heavy, shining waves about my face. And the evaporating alcohol had left behind a very pleasant scent. Frank would like that, I thought. L'Heure Bleue was his favourite.

There was a sudden flash close at hand, with the crash of thunder following hard on its heels, and all the lights went out. Cursing under my breath, I groped in the drawers.

Somewhere I had seen candles and matches; power failure was so frequent an occurrence in the Highlands that candles were a necessary furnishing for all inn and hotel rooms. I had seen them even in the Royal Edinburgh, where they were scented with honeysuckle and elegantly presented in frosted glass holders with shimmering pendants.

Mrs Baird's candles were far more utilitarian – plain white household candles – but there were a lot of them, and three boxes of matches as well. I was not inclined to be fussy over style at a time like this.

I fitted a candle to the blue ceramic holder on the dressing table by the light of the next flash, then moved about the room, lighting others, till the whole room was filled with a soft, wavering radiance. Very romantic, I thought, and with some presence of mind I pressed down the light switch so that a sudden return of power shouldn't ruin the mood at some inopportune moment.

The candles had burned no more than half an inch when the door opened and Frank blew in. Literally, for the draught that followed him up the stairs extinguished three of the candles.

The door closed behind him with a bang that blew out two more, and he peered into the sudden gloom, pushing a hand through his dishevelled hair. I got up and relit the candles, making mild remarks about his abrupt methods of entering rooms. It was only when I had finished and turned to ask him whether he'd like a drink that I saw he was looking rather white and unsettled.

'What's the matter?' I said. 'Seen a ghost?'

'Well, you know,' he said slowly, 'I'm not at all sure that I haven't.' Absentmindedly he picked up my hairbrush and raised it to tidy his hair. When a sudden whiff of L'Heure Bleue reached his nostrils, he wrinkled his nose and set it down again, settling for the attentions of his pocket comb instead.

I glanced through the window, where the lime trees were lashing to and fro like flails. It occurred to me that we ought perhaps to close our shutters, though the carry-on outside was rather exciting to watch.

'Bit blustery for a ghost, I'd think,' I said. 'Don't they like quiet, misty evenings in graveyards?'

Frank laughed a bit sheepishly. 'Well, I daresay it's only Bainbridge's stories, plus a bit more of his sherry than I really meant to have. Nothing at all, probably.'

Now I was curious. 'What exactly did you see?' I asked, settling myself on the dressing-table seat. I motioned to the whisky bottle with a half-lifted brow, and Frank went at once to pour a couple of drinks.

'Well, only a man, really,' he began, measuring out a tot for himself and two for me. 'Standing down in the road outside.'

'What, outside this house?' I laughed. 'Must have been a ghost, then; I can't imagine any living person standing about on a night like this.'

Frank tilted the ewer over his glass, then looked accusingly at me when no water came out.

'Don't look at me,' I said. 'You used up all the water. I don't mind it neat, though.' I took a sip in illustration.

Frank looked as though he were tempted to nip down to the bathroom for water, but abandoned the idea and went on with his story, sipping cautiously as though his glass contained vitriol rather than the most expensive product of the local illicit stills.

'Yes, he was down at the edge of the garden on this side, standing by the hedge. I thought' – he hesitated, looking down into his glass – 'I rather thought he was looking up at your window.'

'My window? How extraordinary!' I couldn't repress a mild shiver, and went across to fasten the shutters, though it seemed a bit late for that. Frank followed me across the room, still talking.

'Yes, I could see you myself from below. You were brushing your hair and cursing a bit because it was standing on end.'

'In that case, the fellow was probably enjoying a good laugh,' I said tartly. Frank shook his head, though he smiled and smoothed his hands over my hair.

'No, he wasn't laughing. In fact, he seemed terribly unhappy about something. Not that I could see his face well; just something about the way he stood. I came up behind him, and when he didn't move, I asked politely if I could help him with something. He acted at first as though he didn't hear me, and I thought perhaps he didn't, over the noise of the wind, so I repeated myself, and I reached out to tap his shoulder, to get his attention, you know. But

29

before I could touch him he whirled suddenly round and pushed past me and walked off down the road.'

'Sounds a bit rude, but not very ghostly,' I observed, draining my glass. 'What did he look like?'

'Big chap,' said Frank, frowning in recollection. 'And a Scot, in complete Highland rig-out, complete to sporran and the most beautiful running-stag brooch on his plaid. I wanted to ask where he'd got it from, but he was off before I could.'

I went to the chest of drawers and poured another drink. 'Well, not so unusual an appearance for these parts, surely? I've seen men dressed like that in the village now and then.'

'Nooo . . .' Frank sounded doubtful. 'No, it wasn't his dress that was odd. But when he pushed past me I could swear he was close enough that I should have felt him brush my sleeve – but I didn't. And I was intrigued enough to turn round and watch him as he walked away. He walked down the Gereside Road, but when he'd almost reached the corner, he . . . disappeared. That's when I began to feel a bit cold down the backbone.'

'Perhaps your attention was distracted for a second and he just stepped aside into the shadows,' I suggested. 'There are a lot of trees down near that corner.'

'I could swear I didn't take my eyes off him for a moment,' muttered Frank. He looked up suddenly. 'I know! I remember now why I thought he was so odd, though I didn't realize it at the time.'

'What?' I was getting a bit tired of the ghost, and wanted to go on to more interesting matters, such as bed.

'The wind was cutting up like billy-o, but his drapes – his kilt and his plaid, you know – they didn't move at all, except to the stir of his walking.'

We stared at each other. 'Well,' I said finally, 'that is a bit spooky.'

Frank shrugged and smiled suddenly, dismissing it. 'At least I'll have something to tell the minister next time I see him. Perhaps it's a well-known local ghost, and he can give me its gory history.' He glanced at his watch. 'But now I'd say it's bedtime.'

'So it is,' I murmured.

I watched him in the mirror as he removed his shirt and reached for a hanger. Suddenly he paused in mid-button.

'Did you have many Scots in your charge, Claire?' he asked abruptly. 'At the field hospital, or at Pembroke?'

'Of course,' I replied, somewhat puzzled. 'There were quite a few of the Seaforths and Camerons through the field hospital at Amiens, and then a bit later, after Caen, we had a lot of the Gordons. Nice chaps, most of them. Very stoic about things generally, but terrible cowards about injections.' I smiled, remembering one in particular.

'We had one – rather a crusty old thing really, a piper from the Third Seaforths – who couldn't stand being stuck, especially not in the hip. He'd go for hours in the most awful discomfort before he'd let anyone near him with a needle, and even then he'd try to get us to give him the injection in the arm, though it's meant to be intramuscular.' I laughed at the memory of Corporal Chisholm. 'He told me, "If I'm goin' to lie on my face wi' my buttocks bared, I want the lass *under* me, not behind me wi' a hatpin!"'

Frank smiled, but looked a trifle uneasy as he often did about my less delicate war stories. 'Don't worry,' I assured him, seeing the look, 'I won't tell that one at tea in the Senior Common Room.'

The smile lightened and he came forward to stand behind me as I sat at the dressing table. He pressed a kiss on the top of my head.

'Don't worry,' he said. 'The Senior Common Room will love you, no matter what stories you tell. Mmmm. Your hair smells wonderful.'

'Do you like it then?' His hands slid forward over my shoulders in answer, cupping my breasts in the thin nightdress. I could see his head above mine in the mirror, his chin resting on top of my head.

'I like everything about you,' he said huskily. 'You look wonderful by candlelight, you know. Your eyes are like sherry in crystal, and your skin glows like ivory. A candlelight witch, you are. Perhaps I should disconnect the lamps permanently.'

31

'Make it hard to read in bed,' I said, my heart beginning to speed up.

'I could think of better things to do in bed,' he murmured.

'Could you, indeed?' I said, rising and turning to put my arms about his neck. 'Like what?'

Some time later, cuddled close behind bolted shutters, I lifted my head from his shoulder and said, 'Why did you ask me that earlier? About whether I'd had anything to do with any Scots, I mean – you must know I had, there are all sorts of men through those hospitals.'

He stirred and ran a hand softly down my back.

'Mmm. Oh, nothing, really. Just, when I saw that chap outside, it occurred to me he might be' – he hesitated, tightening his hold a bit – 'er, you know, that he might have been someone you'd nursed, perhaps . . . maybe heard you were staying here, and came along to see . . . something like that.'

'In that case,' I said practically, 'why wouldn't he come in and ask to see me?'

'Well,' Frank's voice was very casual, 'maybe he didn't want particularly to run into me.'

I pushed up on to one elbow, staring at him. We had left one candle burning, and I could see him well enough. He had turned his head and was looking oh-so-casually off towards the chromolithograph of Bonnie Prince Charlie with which Mrs Baird had seen fit to decorate our wall.

I grabbed his chin and turned his head to face me. He widened his eyes in simulated surprise.

'Are you implying,' I demanded, 'that the man you saw outside was some sort of, of . . .' I hesitated, looking for the proper word.

'Liaison?' he suggested helpfully.

'Romantic interest of mine?' I finished.

'No, no, certainly not,' he said unconvincingly. He took my hands away from his face and tried to kiss me, but now it was my turn for head-turning. He settled for pressing me back down to lie beside him.

'It's only . . .' he began. 'Well, you know, Claire, it *was*

32

six years. And we saw each other only three times, and only just for the day that last time. It wouldn't be unusual if . . . I mean, everyone knows doctors and nurses are under tremendous stress during emergencies, and . . . well, I . . . it's just that . . . well, I'd understand, you know, if anything, er, of a spontaneous nature . . .'

I interrupted this rambling by jerking free and exploding out of bed.

'Do you think I've been unfaithful to you?' I demanded. 'Do you? Because if so, you can leave this room this instant. Leave the house altogether! How dare you imply such a thing?' I was seething, and Frank, sitting up, reached out to try to soothe me.

'Don't you touch me!' I snapped. 'Just tell me – *do* you think, on the evidence of a strange man happening to glance up at my window, that I've had some flaming affair with one of my patients?'

Frank got out of bed and wrapped his arms around me. I stayed stiff as Lot's wife, but he persisted, caressing my hair and rubbing my shoulders in the way he knew I liked.

'No, I don't think any such thing,' he said firmly. He pulled me closer and I relaxed slightly, though not enough to put my arms around him.

After a long time he murmured into my hair, 'No, I know you'd never do such a thing. I only meant to say that even if you ever did . . . Claire, it would make no difference to me. I love you so. Nothing you ever did could stop my loving you.' He took my face between his hands – only four inches taller than I, he could look directly into my eyes without trouble – and said softly, 'Forgive me?' His breath, barely scented with the tang of whisky, was warm on my face, and his lips, full and inviting, were disturbingly close.

Another rumble of thunder heralded the sudden breaking of the storm, and a thundering rain smashed down on the slates of the roof.

I slowly put my arms around his waist.

' "The quality of mercy is not strainéd," ' I quoted. ' "It droppeth as the gentle rain from heaven . . ." '

Frank laughed and looked upwards; the overlapping

stains on the ceiling boded ill for the prospects of our sleeping dry all night.

'If that's a sample of your mercy,' he said, 'I'd hate to see your vengeance.' The thunder went off like a mortar attack, as though in answer to his words, and we both laughed, at ease again.

It was only later, listening to his regular deep breathing beside me, that I began to wonder. As I had said, there was no evidence whatsoever to imply unfaithfulness on my part. *My* part. But six years, as he'd said, was a long time.

2

Standing Stones

Mr Crook called for me, as arranged, promptly at seven the next morning.

'So as we'll catch the dew on the buttercups, eh, lass?' he said, twinkling with elderly gallantry. He had brought a motorcycle of his own approximate vintage, on which to transport us into the countryside. The plant presses were tidily strapped to the sides of this enormous machine, like fenders on a tugboat. It was a leisurely ramble through the quiet countryside, made all the more quiet by contrast with the thunderous roar of Mr Crook's cycle, suddenly throttled into silence. The old man did indeed know a lot about the local plants, I discovered. Not only where they were to be found but their medicinal uses, and how to prepare them. I wished I had brought a notebook to get it all down, but listened intently to the cracked old voice and did my best to commit the information to memory as I stowed our specimens in the heavy plant presses.

We stopped for a packed luncheon near the base of a curious flat-topped hill. Green as most of its neighbours, with the same rocky juts and crags, it had something different: a well-worn path leading up one side and disappearing abruptly behind an outcrop.

'What's up there?' I asked, gesturing with a cheese and pickle sandwich. 'It seems a difficult place for picnicking.'

'Ah.' Mr Crook glanced at the hill. 'That's Craigh na Dun, lass. I'd meant to show ye after our meal.'

'Really? Is there something special about it?'

'Oh, aye,' he answered, but refused to elaborate further, merely saying that I'd see when I saw.

I had some fears about his ability to climb such a steep path, but these evaporated as I found myself panting in his wake. At last Mr Crook extended a gnarled hand and pulled me up over the rim of the hill.

'There it is.' He waved a hand with a sort of proprietorial gesture.

'Why, it's a henge!' I said, delighted. 'A miniature henge!'

Because of the war it had been several years since I had last visited Salisbury Plain, but Frank and I had seen Stonehenge soon after we were married. Like the other tourists wandering awed among the huge standing stones we had gaped at the Altar Stone ('where ancient Druid priests performed their dreadful human sacrifices,' announced our sonorous cockney guide).

Out of the same passion for exactness that made Frank adjust his ties on the hanger so that the ends hung precisely so, we had even trekked around the circumference of the circle, pacing off the distance between the Z holes and the Y holes, and counting the lintels over the Sarsen Circle, the outermost ring of monstrous uprights.

Three hours later, we knew how many Y and Z holes there were (fifty-nine, if you care; I didn't), but had no more clue to the purpose of the structure than had the dozens of amateur and professional archaeologists who had crawled over the site for the last five hundred years.

No lack of opinions, of course. Life among academics had taught me that a well-expressed opinion is usually better than a badly expressed fact, so far as professional advancement goes.

A temple. A burial ground. An astronomical observatory. A place of execution (hence the aptly named Slaughter Stone that lies to one side, half sunk in its own pit). An open-air market. I liked this last suggestion, visualizing Megalithic housewives strolling between the lintels, baskets on their arms, critically judging the glaze on the latest shipment of red-clay beakers and listening sceptically to the claims of stone-age bakers and vendors of deer-bone shovels and amber beads.

The only thing I could see against that hypothesis was the presence of bodies under the Altar Stone and cremated remains in the Z holes. Unless these were the hapless remains of merchants accused of short-weighting the customers, it seemed a bit insanitary to be burying people in the marketplace.

There were no signs of burial in the miniature henge atop this hill. By miniature I mean only that the circle of standing stones was smaller than Stonehenge; each stone was still twice my own height, and massive in proportion.

I had heard from another guide at Stonehenge that these stone circles occur all over Britain and Europe – some in better repair than others, some differing slightly in orientation or form, all of purpose and origin unknown.

Mr Crook stood smiling benignly as I prowled among the stones, pausing now and then to touch one gently, as though my touch could make an impression on the monumental boulders.

Some of the standing stones were brindled, striped with dim colours. Others were speckled with flakes of mica that caught the sun with a cheerful shimmer. All of them were remarkably different from the clumps of native stone that thrust out of the bracken all around. Whoever built the stone circles, and for whatever purpose, thought it important enough to have quarried, shaped and transported special stone blocks for the erection of their testimonial. Shaped – how? Transported – how, and from what unimaginable distance?

'My husband would be fascinated,' I told Mr Crook, stopping to thank him for showing me the place and the plants. 'I'll bring him up to see it later.' The gnarled old man gallantly offered me an arm at the top of the trail. I took it, deciding after one look down the precipitous decline that in spite of his age he was probably steadier on his pins than I was.

I swung down the road that afternoon towards the town, to fetch Frank from the manse. I happily breathed in that heady Highland mix of peat and evergreen, spiced here and there with woodsmoke and the tang of fried herring. Those houses near the road were nice. Some were newly painted and even the manse which must be at least a hundred years old, sported fresh maroon trim around its sagging window frames.

The minister's housekeeper answered the door, a tall, stringy woman with three strands of artificial pearls round her neck. Hearing who I was, she welcomed me in and towed me down a long, narrow, dark hallway, lined with sepia engravings of people who may have been famous personages of their time, or cherished relatives of the present minister, but might as well have been the Royal Family, for all I could see of their features in the gloom.

By contrast the minister's study was blinding with light from the enormous windows that ran nearly from the ceiling to floor in one wall. An easel near the fireplace, bearing a half-finished oil of black cliffs against the evening sky, showed the reason for the windows, which must have been added long after the house was built.

Frank and a short, tubby man with a dog collar were cosily poring over a mass of tattered paper on the desk by the far wall. Frank barely looked up in greeting, but the minister politely left off his explanations and hurried over to clasp my hand, his round face beaming with sociable delight.

'Mrs Randall!' he said, pumping my hand heartily. 'How nice to see you again. And you've come just in time to hear the news!'

'News?' Casting an eye on the grubbiness and typeface of the papers on the desk, I calculated the date of the news in question as being around 1750. Not precisely stop-the-presses, then.

'Yes, indeed. We've been tracing your husband's ancestor, Jack Randall, through the army dispatches of the period.' The minister leaned close, speaking out of the side of his mouth like a gangster in an American film. 'I've, er, "borrowed" the original dispatches from the local Historical Society files. You'll be careful not to tell anyone?'

Amused, I agreed that I would not reveal his deadly secret, and looked about for a comfortable chair in which to receive the latest revelations from the eighteenth century. The wing chair nearest the windows looked suitable, but as

I reached to turn it towards the desk I discovered that it was already occupied. The inhabitant, a small boy with a shock of glossy black hair, was curled up in the depths of the chair, sound asleep.

'Roger!' The minister, coming to assist me, was as surprised as I. The boy, startled out of sleep, shot bolt upright, wide eyes the colour of moss.

'Now what are you up to in here, you young scamp?' the minister scolded affectionately. 'Oh, fell asleep reading the comic papers again?' He scooped up the pages and handed them to the lad. 'Run along now, Roger, I have business with the Randalls. Oh, wait, I've forgotten to introduce you – Mrs Randall, this is my son, Roger.'

I was a bit surprised. If ever I'd seen a confirmed bachelor I would have thought the Reverend Mr Wakefield was it. Still, I took the politely proffered paw and shook it warmly, resisting the urge to wipe a certain residual stickiness on my skirt.

The Reverend Mr Wakefield looked fondly after the boy as he went off towards the kitchen.

'My niece's son, really,' he confided. 'Father shot down over the Channel, and mother killed in the Blitz, though, so I've taken him.'

'How kind of you,' I murmured, thinking of Uncle Lamb. He, too, had died in the Blitz, on his way to the British Museum, where he had been lecturing. Knowing him, I thought his main feeling would have been gratification that the bomb had not hit the museum.

'Not at all, not at all.' The minister flapped a hand in embarrassment. 'Nice to have a bit of young life about the house. Now, do have a seat.'

Frank began talking even before I had set my handbag down. 'The most amazing luck, Claire,' he enthused, thumbing through the dog-eared pile. 'The minister's located a whole series of military dispatches that mention Jonathan Randall.'

'Well, a good deal of the prominence seems to have been Captain Randall's own doing,' the minister observed, taking some of the papers from Frank. 'He was in command of the garrison at Fort William for four years or so, but he seems to have spent quite a bit of his time harassing the Scottish countryside on behalf of the Crown. This lot' – he gingerly separated a stack of papers and laid them on the desk – 'is reports of complaints lodged against the Captain by various families and estate holders, claiming everything from interference with their maidservants by the soldiers of the garrison to outright theft of horses, not to mention assorted instances of "insult", unspecified.'

I was amused. 'So you have the proverbial horse thief in your family tree?' I said to Frank.

He shrugged, unperturbed. 'He was what he was, and there's nothing I can do about it. I only want to find out. The complaints aren't all that odd, for that particular period; the English in general, and the army in particular, were rather notably unpopular throughout the Highlands. No, what's odd is that nothing ever seems to have come of the complaints, even the serious ones.'

The minister, unable to keep still for long, broke in. 'That's right. Not that officers then were held to anything like modern standards; they could do very much as they liked in minor matters. But this is odd. It's not that the complaints are investigated and dismissed; they're just never mentioned again. You know what I suspect, Randall? Your ancestor must have had a patron. Someone who could protect him from the censure of his superiors.'

Frank scratched his head, squinting at the dispatches. 'You could be right. Had to have been someone quite powerful, though. High up in the army hierarchy, perhaps, or another member of the nobility outside the army.'

'Yes, or possibly – ' The minister was interrupted in his theories by the entrance of Mrs Graham, the housekeeper.

'I've brought ye a wee bit of refreshment, gentlemen,' she announced, setting the tea tray firmly in the centre of the desk, from which the minister rescued his precious dispatches in the nick of time. She looked me over with a shrewd eye, assessing the twitching limbs and faint glaze over the eyeballs.

'I've brought but the two cups, for I thought perhaps

40

Mrs Randall would care to join me in the kitchen. I've a bit of – ' I didn't wait for the conclusion of her invitation, but leapt to my feet with alacrity. I could hear the theories breaking out again behind me as we pushed through the swinging door that led to the manse's kitchen.

The tea was hot and fragrant, with bits of leaf swirling through the liquid.

'Mmm,' I said, setting the cup down. 'It's been a long time since I tasted Earl Grey.'

Mrs Graham nodded, beaming at my pleasure in her refreshments. She had clearly gone to some trouble, laying out handmade lace doilies beneath the eggshell cups and providing real butter and jam with the scones.

'Aye, I save it special for the readings. Better than the Indian stuff, ye know.'

'Oh, you read tea leaves?' I asked, mildly amused. Nothing could be further from the popular conception of the gypsy fortune-teller than Mrs Graham, with her short, iron-grey perm and triple-stranded pearl choker. A swallow of tea ran visibly down the long, stringy neck and disappeared beneath the gleaming beads.

'Why, certainly I do, my dear. Just as my grandmother taught me, and her grandmother before her. Drink up your cup, and I'll see what you have there.'

She was silent for a long time, once in a while tilting the cup to catch the light, or rolling it slowly between lean palms to get a different angle.

She set the cup down carefully, as though afraid it might blow up in her face. The grooves on either side of her mouth had deepened, and her brows pressed together in what looked like puzzlement.

'Well,' she said finally. 'That's one of the stranger cups I've seen.'

'Oh?' I was still amused, but beginning to be curious. 'Am I going to meet a tall dark stranger, or journey across the sea?'

'Could be.' Mrs Graham had caught my ironic tone, and echoed it, smiling slightly. 'And could not. That's what's odd about your cup, my dear. Everything in it's contradictory. There's the curved leaf for a journey, but it's crossed by the broken one that means staying put. And strangers there are, to be sure, several of them. And one of them's your husband, if I read the leaves aright.'

My amusement dissipated somewhat. After six years apart, my husband *was* still something of a stranger. Though I failed to see how a tea leaf could know it.

Mrs Graham's brow was still furrowed. 'Let me see your hand, child,' she said.

The hand holding mine was bony, but surprisingly warm. A scent of lavender water emanated from the neat parting of the grizzled head bent over my palm. She stared into my hand for quite a long time, now and then tracing one of the lines with a finger as though following a map whose roads all petered out in sandy washes and deserted wastes.

'Well, what is it?' I asked, trying to maintain a light air. 'Or is my fate too horrible to be revealed?'

Mrs Graham raised quizzical eyes and looked thoughtfully at my face, but retained her hold on my hand. She shook her head, pursing her lips.

'Oh no, my dear. It's not your fate is in your hand. Only the seed of it.' The birdlike head cocked to one side, considering. 'The lines in your hand change, ye know. At another point in your life, they may be quite different than they are now.'

'I didn't know that. I thought you were born with them, and that was that.' I was repressing an urge to jerk my hand away. 'What's the point of palm reading, then?' I didn't wish to sound rude, but I found this scrutiny a bit unsettling, especially following on the heels of that tea leaf reading. Mrs Graham smiled unexpectedly and folded my fingers closed over my palm.

'Why, the lines of your palm show what ye are, dear. That's why they change – or should. They don't, in some people; those unlucky enough never to change in themselves, but there are few like that.' She gave my folded hand a squeeze and patted it. 'I doubt that you're one of those. Your hand shows quite a lot of change already, for one so

42

young. That would likely be the war, of course,' she said, as though to herself.

I was curious again, and opened my palm voluntarily.

'What am I, then, according to my hand?'

Mrs Graham frowned, but did not pick up my hand again.

'I canna just say. It's odd, for most hands have a likeness to them. Mind, I'd no just say that it's "see one, you've seen them all", but it's often like that – there are patterns, you know.' She smiled suddenly, an oddly engaging grin, displaying very white and patently false teeth.

'That's how a fortune-teller works, you know. I do it for the church fête every year – or did, before the war; suppose I'll do it again now. But a girl comes into the tent – and there am I, done up in a turban with a peacock feather borrowed from Mr Donaldson, and "robes of oriental splendour" – that's the minister's dressing gown, all over peacocks it is and yellow as the sun – anyway, I look her over while I pretend to be watching her hand, and I see she's got her blouse cut down to her breakfast, cheap scent, and earrings down to her shoulders. I needn't have a crystal ball to be tellin' her she'll have a child before the next year's fête.' Mrs Graham paused, grey eyes alight with mischief. 'Though if the hand you're holding is bare, it's tactful to predict first that she'll marry soon.'

I laughed, and so did she. 'So you don't look at their hands at all, then?' I asked. 'Except to check for rings?'

She looked surprised. 'Oh, of course you do. It's just that you know ahead of time what you'll see. Generally.' She nodded at my open hand. 'But that is not a pattern I've seen before. The large thumb, now' – she did lean forward then and touch it lightly – 'that wouldn't change much. Means you're strong-minded and have a will not easily crossed.' She twinkled at me. 'Reckon your husband could have told ye that. Likewise about that one.' She pointed to the fleshy mound at the base of the thumb.

'What is it?'

'The Mount of Venus, it's called.' She pursed her thin lips primly together, though the corners turned irrepressibly up. 'In a man, ye'd say it means he likes the lasses. For a woman, 'tis a bit different. To be polite about it, I'll make a bit of a prediction for you, and say your husband isna like to stray far from your bed.' She gave a surprisingly deep and bawdy chuckle, and I blushed slightly.

The elderly housekeeper pored over my hand again, stabbing a pointed forefinger here and there to mark her words.

'Now, there, a well-marked lifeline; you're in good health and likely to stay so. The lifeline's interrupted, meaning your life's changed markedly – well, that's true of us all, is it not? But yours is more chopped-up, like, than I usually see; all bits and pieces. And your marriage-line, now' – she shook her head again – 'it's divided; that's not unusual, means two marriages . . .'

My reaction was slight and immediately suppressed, but she caught the flicker and looked up at once. I thought she probably was quite a shrewd fortune-teller, at that. The grey head shook reassuringly at me.

'No, no, lass. It doesna mean anything's like to happen to your good man. It's only that if it did' – she emphasized the 'if' with a slight squeeze of my hand – 'you'd not be one to pine away and waste the rest of your life in mourning. What it means is, you're one of those can love again if your first love's lost.'

She squinted nearsightedly at my palm, running a short, ridged nail gently down the deep marriage line. 'But most divided lines are broken – yours is forked.' She looked up with a roguish smile. 'Sure you're not a bigamist, on the quiet, like?'

I shook my head, laughing. 'No. When would I have the time?' Then I turned my hand, showing the outer edge.

'I've heard that small marks on the side of the hand indicate how many children you'll have?' My tone was casual, I hoped. The edge of my palm was disappointingly smooth.

Mrs Graham flicked a scornful hand at this idea.

'Pah! After ye've had a bairn or two, ye might show lines there. More like you'd have them on your face. Proves nothing at all beforehand.'

'Oh, it doesn't?' I was foolishly relieved to hear this. I was going to ask whether the deep lines across the base of my wrist meant anything (a potential for suicide?) but we were interrupted at that point by the Reverend Mr Wakefield coming into the kitchen bearing the empty teacups. He set them on the draining board and began a loud and clumsy fumbling through the cupboard, obviously in hopes of provoking help.

Mrs Graham sprang to her feet to defend the sanctity of her kitchen and pushing the Reverend adroitly to one side, set about assembling sherry and biscuits on a tray for the study. He drew me to one side, safely out of the way.

'Why don't you come to the study and have sherry with me and your husband, Mrs Randall? We've made really the most gratifying discovery.'

I could see that in spite of outward composure he was bursting with the glee of whatever they had found, like a small boy with a toad in his pocket. Plainly I was going to have to go and read Captain Jonathan Randall's laundry bill, his receipt for boot repairs or some document of similar fascination.

Frank was so absorbed in the tattered documents that he scarcely looked up when I entered the study. He reluctantly surrendered them to the minister's podgy hands, and came round to stand behind him and peer over his shoulder, as though he could not bear to let the papers out of his sight for a moment.

'Yes?' I said politely, fingering the dirty bits of paper. 'Ummm, yes, very interesting.' In fact, the spidery handwriting was so faded and so ornate that it hardly seemed worth the trouble of deciphering it. One sheet, better preserved than the rest, had some sort of crest at the top.

'The Duke of . . . Sandringham, is it?' I asked, peering at the crest with its faded leopard couchant, and the printing below, more legible than the handwriting.

'Yes, indeed,' the minister said, beaming even more. 'An extinct title, now, you know.'

I didn't, but nodded intelligently, being no stranger to historians in the manic grip of discovery. It was seldom necessary to do more than nod periodically, saying 'Oh, really?' or 'How perfectly fascinating!' at appropriate intervals.

After a certain amount of deferring back and forth between Frank and the minister, the latter won the honour of telling me about their discovery. Evidently, all this rubbish made it appear that Frank's ancestor, the notorious Black Jack Randall, had not been merely a gallant soldier for the Crown, but a trusted – and secret – agent of the Duke of Sandringham.

'Almost an agent provocateur, wouldn't you say, Dr Randall?' The minister graciously handed the ball back to Frank, who seized it and ran.

'Yes, indeed. The language is very guarded, of course . . .' He turned the pages gently with a scrubbed forefinger.

'Oh, really?' I said.

'But it seems from this that Jonathan Randall was entrusted with the job of stirring up Jacobite sentiments, if any existed, among the prominent Scottish families in his area. The point being to smoke out any baronets and clan chieftains who might be harbouring secret sympathies in that direction. But that's odd. Wasn't Sandringham a suspected Jacobite himself?' Frank turned to the minister, a frown of inquiry on his face. The minister's smooth, bald head creased in an identical frown.

'Why, yes, I believe you're right. But wait, let's check in Cameron' – he made a dive for the bookshelf, crammed with calf-bound volumes – 'he's sure to mention Sandringham.'

'How perfectly fascinating,' I murmured, allowing my attention to wander to the huge notice board that filled one wall of the study from floor to ceiling.

It was covered with an amazing assortment of things; mostly papers of one sort or another, gas bills, correspondence, notices about the General Assembly, loose pages of novels, notes in the minister's own hand, but also small items like keys, bottle caps and what appeared to be small car parts, attached with tacks and string.

I browsed idly through the miscellanea, keeping half an ear tuned to the argument going on behind me (the Duke of Sandringham probably *was* a Jacobite, they decided). My attention was caught by a genealogical chart, tacked up with special care in a spot by itself, using four tacks, one to a corner. The top of the chart included names dated in the early seventeenth century. But it was the name at the bottom of the chart that had caught my eye: 'Roger W. (MacKenzie) Wakefield', it read.

'Excuse me,' I said, interrupting a final sputter of dispute as to whether the leopard in the Duke's crest had a lily in its paw, or was it meant to be a crocus? 'Is this your son's chart?'

'Eh? Oh, why yes, yes it is.' Distracted, the minister hurried over, beaming once more. He detached the chart tenderly from the board and laid it on the table in front of me.

'I didn't want him to forget his own family, you see,' he explained. 'It's quite an old lineage, back to the sixteen hundreds.' His stubby forefinger traced the line of descent almost reverently.

'I gave him my own name because it seemed more suitable, as he lives here, but I didn't want him to forget where he came from.' He made an apologetic grimace. 'I'm afraid my own family is nothing to boast of, genealogically. Ministers and curates, with the occasional bookseller thrown in for variety, and only traceable back to 1762 or so. Rather poor record-keeping, you know,' he said, wagging his head remorsefully over the lethargy of his ancestors.

It was growing late by the time we finally left the manse, with the minister promising to take the letters to town for copying first thing in the morning. Frank babbled happily of spies and Jacobites most of the way back to Mrs Baird's. Finally, though, he noticed my quietness.

'What is it, love?' he asked, taking my arm solicitously. 'Not feeling well?' This was asked with a mingled tone of concern and hope.

'No, I'm quite well. I was only thinking . . .' I hesitated, because we had discussed this matter before. 'I was thinking about Roger.'

'Roger?'

I gave a sigh of impatience. 'Really, Frank! You can be so . . . oblivious! Roger, the Reverend Mr Wakefield's son.'

'Oh. Yes, of course,' he said vaguely. 'Charming child. What about him?'

'Well . . . only that there are a lot of children like that. Orphaned, you know.'

He gave me a sharp look and shook his head.

'No, Claire. Really, I'd like to, but I've told you how I feel about adoption. It's just . . . I couldn't feel properly towards a child who's not . . . well, not of my blood. No doubt that's ridiculous and selfish of me, but there it is. Maybe I'll change my mind in time, but now . . .' We walked a few steps in a barbed silence. Suddenly he stopped and turned to me, gripping my hands.

'Claire,' he said huskily, 'I want *our* child. You're the most important thing in the world to me. I want you to be happy, above all else, but I want . . . well, I want to keep you to myself. I'm afraid a child from outside, one we had no real relationship with, would seem an intruder, and I'd resent it. But to be able to give you a child, see it grow in you . . . then I'd feel as though it were more an . . . extension of you, perhaps. And me. A real part of the family.' His eyes were wide, pleading.

'Yes, all right. I understand.' I was willing to abandon the topic – for now. I turned to go on walking but he reached out and took me in his arms.

'Claire. I love you.' The tenderness in his voice was overwhelming, and I leaned my head against his jacket, feeling his warmth and the strength of his arms around me.

'I love you too.' We stood locked together for a moment, swaying slightly in the wind that swept down the road. Suddenly Frank drew back a bit, smiling down at me.

'Besides,' he said softly, smoothing the windblown hair back from my face, 'we haven't given up yet, have we?'

I smiled back. 'No.'

He took my hand, tucking it snugly beneath his elbow, and we turned towards our lodgings.

'Game for another try?'

'Yes. Why not?' We strolled, hand in hand, back towards

the Gereside Road. It was the sight of the Clach Mhor, the Pictish stone that stands at the corner of the road there, that made me remember things ancient.

'I forgot!' I exclaimed. 'I have something exciting to show you.' Frank looked down at me and pulled me closer. He squeezed my hand.

'So have I,' he said, grinning. 'You can show me yours tomorrow.'

When tomorrow came, though, we had other things to do. I had forgotten that we had planned a day trip to the Great Glen and Loch Ness. It was after nine when we arrived at Lochend and the guide Frank had called for was awaiting us on the edge of the loch with a small sailing skiff.

'An' it suits ye, sir, I thought we'd take a wee sail down the loch-side to Urquhart Castle. Perhaps we'll have a wee bit and sup there, before goin' on.' The guide, a dour-looking little man in weather-beaten cotton shirt and twill trousers, stowed the picnic hamper tidily beneath the seat and offered me a calloused hand down into the well of the boat.

It was a beautiful day, with the burgeoning greenery of the steep banks blurring in the ruffled surface of the loch. Our guide, despite his dour appearance, was knowledgeable and talkative, pointing out the landmarks that rimmed the long, narrow loch.

'Yonder, that's Urquhart Castle.' He pointed to a picturesque stone ruin above the loch. 'Or what's left of it. 'Twas cursed by the witches of the Glen, and saw one unhappiness after another.'

He told us the story of Mary Grant, daughter of the laird of Urquhart Castle, and her lover, Donald Donn, poet son of MacDonald of Bohuntin. Forbidden to meet because of her father's objection to the latter's habits of lifting any cattle he came across (an old and honourable Highland profession, the guide assured us), they met anyway. The father got wind of it, Donald was lured to a false rendezvous and thus taken. Condemned to die, he begged to be beheaded like a gentleman, rather than hanged as a felon.

This request was granted, and the young man led to the block, repeating 'The Devil will take the Laird of Grant out of his shoes, and Donald Donn shall not be hanged'. He wasn't, and legend reports that as his severed head rolled from the block, it spoke, saying, 'Mary, lift ye my head'.

I shuddered, and Frank put an arm around me. 'There's a bit of one of his poems left,' he said quietly. 'Donald Donn's. It goes:

> Tomorrow I shall be on a hill, without a head.
> Have you no compassion for my sorrowful maiden,
> My Mary, the fair and tender-eyed?'

I took his hand and squeezed it lightly.

As story after story of treachery, murder and violence was recounted, it seemed as though the loch had earned its sinister reputation.

'What about the monster?' I asked, peering over the side into the murky depths. It seemed entirely appropriate to such a setting.

Our guide shrugged and spat into the water.

'Weel, the loch's queer, and no mistake. There's stories, to be sure, of something old and evil that once lived in the depths. Sacrifices were made to it – kine, and sometimes even wee bairns, flung into the water in withy baskets.' He spat again. 'And some say the loch's bottomless – got a hole in the centre deeper than anything else in Scotland. On the other hand' – the guide's crinkled eyes crinkled a bit more – ' 'twas a family here from Lancashire a few years ago, cam' rushin' to the police station in Fort Augustus, screamin' as they'd seen the monster come out o' the water and hide in the bracken. Said 'twas a terrible creature, covered wi' red hair and fearsome horns, and chewin' something, wi' the blood all dripping from its mouth.' He held up a hand, stemming my horrified exclamation.

'The constable they sent to see cam' back and said, weel, bar the drippin' blood, 'twas a verra accurate description' –

50

he paused for effect – 'of a nice Highland cow, chewin' her cud in the bracken!'

We sailed down half the length of the loch before disembarking for a late lunch. We met the car there and motored back through the Glen, observing nothing more sinister than a fox in the road, who looked up startled, a small animal of some sort hanging limp in its jaws, as we zoomed around a curve. It leaped for the side of the road and swarmed up the bank, swift as a shadow.

It was very late indeed when we finally staggered up the path to Mrs Baird's, but we clung together on the doorstep as Frank groped for the key, still laughing over the events of the day.

It wasn't until we were undressing for bed that I remembered to mention the miniature henge on Craigh na Dun to Frank. His fatigue vanished at once.

'Really? And you know where it is? How marvellous, Claire!' He beamed and began rattling through his suitcase.

'What are you looking for?'

'The alarm clock,' he replied, hauling it out.

'Whatever for?' I asked in astonishment.

'I want to be up in time to see them.'

'Who?'

'The witches.'

'Witches? Who told you there are witches?'

'The minister,' Frank answered, clearly enjoying the joke. 'His housekeeper's one of them.'

I thought of the dignified Mrs Graham and snorted derisively.

'Don't be ridiculous!'

'Well, not witches, actually. There have been witches all over Scotland for hundreds of years – they burnt them till well into the eighteenth century – but this lot are really meant to be Druids, or something of the sort. I don't suppose it's actually a coven – not devil-worship, I don't mean. But the minister said there was a local group that still observes rituals on the old sun-feast days. He can't afford to take too much interest in such goings-on, you see, because of his position, but he's much too curious a man

51

to ignore it altogether, either. He didn't know where the ceremonies took place, but if there's a stone circle nearby, that must be it.' He rubbed his hands together in anticipation. 'What luck!'

Getting up once in the dark to go adventuring is a lark. Twice in two days smacks of masochism.

No nice warm car with rugs and Thermoses this time, either. I stumbled sleepily up the hill behind Frank, tripping over roots and stubbing my toes on stones. It was cold and misty, and I dug my hands deeper into the pockets of my cardigan.

One final push up over the crest of the hill, and the henge was before us, the stones barely visible in the sombre light of pre-dawn. Frank stood stock-still, admiring them, while I subsided on to a convenient rock, panting.

'Beautiful,' he murmured. He crept silently to the outer edge of the ring, his shadowy figure disappearing among the larger shadows of the stones. Beautiful they were, and bloody eerie too. I shivered, and not entirely from the cold. If whoever had made them had meant them to impress, they'd known what they were doing.

Frank was back in a moment. 'No one here yet,' he whispered suddenly from behind me, making me jump. 'Come on, I've found a place we can watch from.'

The light was coming up from the east now, just a tinge of paler grey on the horizon, but enough to keep me from stumbling as Frank led me through a gap he had found in some alder bushes near the top of the path. There was a tiny clearing inside the clump of bushes, barely enough for the two of us to stand shoulder to shoulder. The path was clearly visible, though, and so was the interior of the stone circle, no more than twenty feet away. Not for the first time I wondered just what kind of work Frank had done during the war. He certainly seemed to know a lot about manoeuvring soundlessly in the dark.

Drowsy as I was, I wanted nothing more than to curl up under a cosy bush and go back to sleep. There wasn't room for that, though, so I continued to stand, peering down the steep path in search of oncoming Druids. I was getting a crick in my back and my feet ached, but it couldn't take long; the streak of light in the east had turned a pale pink, and I supposed it was less than half an hour till dawn.

The first one moved almost as silently as Frank. There was only the faintest of rattles as her feet dislodged a pebble near the crest of the hill, and then the neat grey head rose silently into sight. Mrs Graham. So it was true, then. The minister's housekeeper was sensibly dressed in tweed skirt and woolly coat, with a white bundle under one arm. She disappeared behind one of the standing stones, quiet as a ghost.

They came quite quickly after that, in ones and twos and threes, with subdued giggles and whispers on the path that were quickly shushed as they came into sight of the circle.

I recognized a few. Here came Mrs Buchanan, the postmistress, blonde hair freshly permed and the scent of Evening in Paris wafting strongly from its waves. I suppressed a laugh. So this was a modern-day Druid!

There were fifteen in all, and all women, ranging in age from Mrs Graham's sixty-odd years to a young woman in her early twenties, whom I had seen pushing a pram round the shops two days before. All of them were dressed for rough walking, with bundles beneath their arms. With a minimum of chat they disappeared behind stones or bushes, emerging empty-handed and bare-armed, completely clad in white. I caught the scent of laundry soap as one brushed by our clump of bushes, and recognized the garments as bedsheets, wrapped about the body and knotted at the shoulder.

They assembled outside the ring of stones, in a line from eldest to youngest, and stood in silence, waiting. The light in the east grew stronger and the line of women began to move, walking slowly between two of the stones. The leader took them directly to the centre of the circle and led them round and round, still moving slowly, stately as swans in a circular procession.

The leader suddenly stopped, raised her arms and stepped into the centre of the circle. Raising her face towards

53

the pair of easternmost stones, she called out in a high voice. Not loud, but clear enough to be heard throughout the circle. The still mist caught the words and made them echo as though they came from all around, from the stones themselves.

Whatever the call was, it was echoed again by the dancers. For dancers they now became. Not touching, but with arms outstretched towards each other, they bobbed and weaved, still moving in a circle. Suddenly the circle split in half. Seven of the dancers moved clockwise, still in a circular motion. The others moved in the opposite direction. The two semicircles passed each other at increasing speeds, sometimes forming a complete circle, sometimes a double line. And in the centre, the leader stood stock-still, giving again and again that mournful high-pitched call, in a language long since dead.

They should have been ridiculous, and perhaps they were. A collection of women in bedsheets, many of them stout and far from agile, parading in circles on top of a hill. But the hair prickled on the back of my neck at the sound of their call.

They stopped as one and turned to face the rising sun, standing in the form of two semicircles with a path lying clear between the halves of the circle thus formed. As the sun rose above the horizon its light flooded between the eastern stones, knifed between the halves of the circle and struck the great split stone on the opposite side of the henge.

The dancers stood for a moment, frozen in the shadows to either side of the beam of light. Then Mrs Graham said something in the same strange language, but this time in a speaking voice. She pivoted and walked, back straight, iron-grey waves glinting in the sun, along the path of light. Without a word the dancers fell in step behind her. They passed one by one through the cleft in the main stone and disappeared in silence.

We crouched in the alders until the women, now laughing and chatting normally, had retrieved their clothes and set off in a group down the hill, headed for coffee at the manse.

'Goodness!' I stretched, trying to get the kinks out of my legs and back. 'That was quite a sight, wasn't it?'

'Wonderful!' enthused Frank. 'I wouldn't have missed it for the world.' He slipped out of the bush like a snake, leaving me to disentangle myself while he cast about the interior of the circle, nose to the ground like a bloodhound.

'Whatever are you looking for?' I asked. I entered the circle with some hesitation, but day was fully come and the stones, while still impressive, had lost a good deal of the brooding menace of dawn light.

'Marks,' he replied, crawling about on hands and knees, eyes intent on the short turf. 'How did they know where to start and stop?'

'Good question. I don't see anything.' Casting an eye over the ground, though, I did see an interesting plant growing near the base of one of the tall stones. Myosotis? No, probably not; this had orange centres to the deep blue flowers. Intrigued, I started towards it. Frank, with keener hearing than I, leaped to his feet and seized my arm, hurrying me out of the circle a moment before one of the morning's dancers entered from the other side.

It was Miss Grant, the tubby little woman who, suitably enough in view of her figure, ran the sweets and pastries shop in the High Street. She peered nearsightedly around, then fumbled in her pocket for her spectacles. Jamming these on her nose, she strolled about the circle, at last pouncing on the lost hair-clip for which she had returned. Having restored it to its place in her thick, glossy locks, she seemed in no hurry to return to business. Instead she seated herself on a boulder, leaned back against one of the stone giants in comradely fashion and lighted a leisurely cigarette.

Frank gave a muted sigh of exasperation beside me. 'Well,' he said, resigned, 'we'd best go. She could sit there all morning, by the looks of her. And I didn't see any obvious markings in any case.'

'Perhaps we could come back later,' I suggested, still curious about the blue-flowered plant.

'Yes, all right.' But he had plainly lost interest in the circle itself, being now absorbed in the details of the ceremony. He quizzed me relentlessly on the way down the path, urging me to remember as closely as I could the exact wording of the calls and the timing of the dance.

'Norse,' he said at last, with satisfaction. 'The root words are Ancient Norse, I'm almost sure of it. But the dance – ' He shook his head, pondering. 'No, the dance is very much older. Not that there aren't Viking circle dances,' he said, raising his brows censoriously as though I had suggested there weren't. 'But that shifting pattern with the double-line business, that's . . . hmm, it's like . . . well, some of the patterns on the Beaker Folk glazeware show a pattern rather like that, but then again . . . hmm.'

He dropped into one of his scholarly trances, muttering to himself from time to time. The trance was broken only when he stumbled unexpectedly over an obstacle near the bottom of the hill. He flung his arms out with a startled cry as his feet went out from under him and he rolled untidily down the last few feet of the path, fetching up a clump of cow parsley.

I dashed down the hill after him but found him already sitting up among the quivering stems by the time I reached the bottom.

'Are you all right?' I asked, though I could see that he was.

'I think so.' He passed a hand dazedly over his brow, smoothing back the dark hair. 'What did I trip over?'

'This.' I held up a sardine tin, discarded by some earlier visitor. 'One of the menaces of civilization.'

'Ah.' He took it from me, peered inside, then tossed it over one shoulder. 'Pity it's empty. I'm feeling rather hungry after that excursion. Shall we see what Mrs Baird can provide in the way of a late breakfast?'

'We might,' I said, smoothing the last strands of hair for him. 'And then again, we might make it an early lunch instead.' My eyes met his.

'Ah,' he said again, with a completely different tone. He ran a hand slowly up my arm and up the side of my neck, his thumb gently tickling the lobe of my ear. 'So we might.'

'If you aren't too hungry,' I said. The other hand found its way behind my back. Palm spread, it pressed me gently towards him, fingers stroking lower and lower. His mouth opened slightly and he breathed, ever so lightly, down the neck of my dress, his warm breath tickling the tops of my breasts.

He laid me carefully back in the grass, the feathery blossoms of the cow parsley seeming to float in the air around his head. He bent forward and kissed me softly, and kept on kissing me as he unbuttoned my dress, one button at a time, teasing, pausing to reach a hand inside and play with the swelling tips of my breasts. At last he had the dress laid open from neck to waist.

'Ah,' he said again, in yet another tone. 'Like white velvet.' He spoke hoarsely, and his hair had fallen forward again, but he made no attempt to brush it back.

He sprang the clasp of my brassiere with one accomplished flick of the thumb, and bent to pay a skilled homage to my breasts. Then he drew back, and cupping my breasts with both hands, drew his palms slowly down to meet between the rising mounds, and without stopping drew them softly outwards again, tracing the line of my rib cage clear to the back. Up and again, down and around, until I moaned and turned towards him. He sank his lips on to mine and pressed me towards him until our hips fitted tightly together. He bent his head to mine, nibbling softly around the rim of my ear.

The hand stroking my back slipped lower and lower, stopping suddenly in surprise. It felt again, then Frank raised his head and looked down at me, grinning.

'What's all this, then?' he asked, in imitation of a village bobby. 'Or rather, what's *not* all this?'

'Just being prepared,' I said primly. 'Nurses are taught to anticipate contingencies.'

'Really, Claire,' he murmured, sliding his hand under my skirt and up my thigh to the soft, unprotected warmth between my legs, 'you are the most terrifyingly practical person I have ever known.'

*

Frank came up behind me as I sat in the parlour chair that evening, a large book spread out on my lap.

'What are you doing?' he asked. His hands rested gently on my shoulders.

'Looking for that plant,' I answered, sticking a finger between the pages to mind my place. 'The one I saw in the stone circle. See...' I flipped the book open. 'It could be in the Gentianaceae, the Polemoniaceae, the Boraginaceae – that's most likely, I think, forget-me-nots – but it could even be a variant of this one, the Anemone patens.' I pointed out a full-colour illustration of a Pasque flower. 'I don't think it was a gentian of any kind; the petals weren't really rounded, but – '

'Well, why not go back and get it?' he suggested. 'Mr Crook would lend you his old banger, perhaps, or – no, I've a better idea. Borrow Mrs Baird's bicycle, it's safer. It's a short walk from the road to the foot of the hill.'

'And then about a thousand yards, straight up,' I said. 'Why are you so interested in that plant?' I swivelled around to look up at him. The parlour lamp outlined his head with a thin gold line, like a medieval engraving of a saint.

'It's not the plant I care about. But if you're going up there anyway, I wish you'd have a quick look around the outside of the stone circle.'

'All right,' I said obligingly. 'What for?'

'Traces of fire,' he said. 'In all the things I've been able to read about Beltane, fire is always mentioned in the rituals, yet the women we saw this morning weren't using any. I wondered if perhaps they'd set the Beltane fire the night before, then come back in the morning for the dance. Though historically it's the cowherds who were supposed to set the fire. There wasn't any trace of fire inside the circle,' he added. 'But we left before I thought of checking the outside.'

'All right,' I said again, and yawned. Two early risings in two days were taking their toll. I shut the book and stood up. 'Provided I don't have to get up before nine.'

It was in fact nearly eleven before I reached the stone circle. It was drizzling and I was soaked through, not having thought to bring a mac. I made a cursory examination of the outside of the circle, but if there had ever been a fire there, someone had taken pains to remove its traces.

The plant was easier to find. It was where I remembered it, near the foot of the tallest stone. I took several clippings of the plant and stowed them temporarily in my handkerchief, meaning to deal with them properly when I got back to Mrs Baird's bicycle, where I had left the plant press.

The tallest stone of the circle was cleft, with a vertical split dividing the two massive pieces. Oddly, the pieces had been drawn apart by some means. Though you could see that the facing surfaces matched, they were separated by a gap of two or three feet.

There was a deep humming noise coming from somewhere near at hand. I thought there might be a beehive lodged in some crevice of the rock, and placed a hand on the stone in order to lean into the cleft.

The stone screamed.

I backed away as fast as I could, moving so quickly that I tripped on the short turf and sat down hard. I stared at the stone, sweating.

I had never heard such a sound from anything living. There is no way to describe it, except to say that it was the sort of scream you might expect from a stone. It was horrible.

The other stones began to shout. There was a noise of battle, and the cries of dying men and shattered horses.

I shook my head violently to clear it, but the noise went on. I stumbled to my feet and staggered towards the edge of the circle. The sounds were all around me, making my teeth ache and my head spin. My vision began to blur.

I do not know now whether I went deliberately towards the cleft in the main stone, or whether it was accidental, a blind drifting through the fog of noise.

Once, travelling at night, I fell asleep in the passenger seat of a moving car, lulled by the noise and motion into an illusion of serene weightlessness. The driver of the car took a bridge too fast and lost control, and I woke from my floating dream straight into the glare of headlights and the sickening sensation of falling at high speed. That abrupt transition is as close as I can come to describing the feeling I experienced, but it falls woefully short.

I could say that my field of vision contracted to a single dark spot, then disappeared altogether, leaving not darkness but a bright void. I could say that I felt as though I were spinning, or as though I were being pulled inside out. All these things are true, yet none of them conveys the sense I had of complete disruption, of being slammed very hard against something that wasn't there.

The truth is that nothing moved, nothing changed, nothing whatever appeared to *happen* and yet I experienced a feeling of elemental terror so great that I lost all sense of who or what or where I was. I was in the heart of chaos, and no power of mind or body was of use against it.

I cannot really say I lost consciousness, but I was certainly not aware of myself for some time. I 'woke', if that's the word, when I stumbled on a rock near the bottom of the hill. I half slid the remaining few feet and fetched up on the thick tufted grass at the foot.

I felt sick and dizzy. I crawled towards a stand of saplings and leaned against one to steady myself. There was a confused noise of shouting nearby, which reminded me of the sounds I had heard, and felt, in the stone circle. The ring of inhuman violence was lacking, though; this was the normal sound of human conflict, and I turned towards it.

3

The Man in the Wood

The men were some distance away when I saw them. Two
or three, dressed in kilts, running like the dickens across a
small clearing. There was a far-off banging noise that I
rather dazedly identified as gunshots. I was quite sure I was
still hallucinating when the sound of shots was followed by
the appearance of five or six men dressed in red coats and
knee breeches, waving muskets. I blinked and stared. I
moved my hand before my face and held up two fingers. I
saw two fingers, all present and correct. No blurring of
vision. I sniffed the air cautiously. The pungent odour of
trees in spring and a faint whiff of clover from a clump near
my feet. No olfactory delusions.

I felt my head. No soreness anywhere. Concussion
unlikely then. Pulse a little fast, but steady.

The sound of distant yelling changed abruptly. There
was a thunder of hooves, and several ponies came charging
in my direction, kilted Scots atop them, yodelling in Gaelic.
I dodged out of the way with an agility that seemed to prove
I had not been physically damaged, whatever my mental
state.

And then it came to me, as one of the redcoats, knocked
flat by a fleeing Scot, rose and shook his fist theatrically
after the ponies. Of course. A film! I shook my head at my
own slowness. They were shooting a costume drama of
some sort, that was all. One of those Bonnie-Prince-in-the-
heather sorts of things, no doubt.

Well. Regardless of artistic merit, the film crew wouldn't
thank me for introducing a note of historic inauthenticity
into their shots. I doubled back into the wood, meaning to
make a wide circle around the clearing and come out on
the road where I had left the bike. The going was more

difficult than I had expected, though. The wood was a young one, and dense with underbrush that snagged my clothes. I had to go carefully through the spindly saplings, disentangling my skirts from brambles as I went.

Had he been a snake I would have stepped on him. He stood so quietly among the saplings as almost to have been one of them, and I did not see him until a hand shot out and gripped me by the arm.

Its companion clapped over my mouth as I was dragged backwards into a grove, thrashing wildly in panic. My captor, whoever he was, seemed not much taller than I, but rather noticeably strong in the forearms. I smelled a faint flowery scent, as of lavender water, and something more spicy, mingled with the sharper reek of male perspiration. As the leaves whipped back into place in the path of our passage, though, I noticed something familiar about the hand and forearm clasped about my waist.

I shook my head free of the restraint over my mouth.

'Frank!' I burst out. 'What in heaven's name are you playing at?' I was torn between relief at finding him here and irritation at the horseplay. Unsettled as I was by my experience among the stones, I was in no mood for rough games.

The hands released me, but even as I turned to him I sensed something wrong. It was not only the unfamiliar cologne but something more subtle. I stood stock-still, feeling the hair prickle on my neck.

'You aren't Frank,' I whispered.

'I am not,' he agreed, surveying me with considerable interest. 'Though I've a cousin of that name. I doubt, though, that it's he you have confused me with, madam. We do not resemble one another greatly.'

Whatever this man's cousin looked like, the man himself might have been Frank's brother. There was the same lithe, spare build and fine-drawn bones; the same chiselled lines of the face; the level brows and wide hazel eyes; and the same dark hair, curved smooth across the brow.

But this man's hair was long, tied back from his face with a leather thong. And the gypsy skin showed the deep-baked tan of months, no, years of exposure to the weather, not the light golden colour Frank's had attained during our Scottish holiday.

'Just who are you?' I demanded, feeling most uneasy. While Frank had numerous relatives and connections, I thought I knew all the British branch of the family. Certainly there was no one who looked like this man among them. And surely Frank would have mentioned any near relative living in the Highlands? Not only mentioned him but insisted upon visiting him as well, armed with the usual collection of genealogical charts and notebooks, eager for any tidbits of family history about the famous Black Jack Randall.

The stranger raised his brows at my question.

'Who am I? I might ask the same question, madam, and with considerably more justification.' His eyes raked me slowly from head to toe, travelling with a sort of insolent appreciation over the thin sprigged cotton dress I wore, and lingering with an odd look of amusement on my legs. I did not at all understand the look, but it made me extremely nervous, and I backed up a step or two until I was brought up sharp by bumping into a tree.

The man finally removed his gaze and turned aside. It was as though he had taken a constraining hand off me, and I let out my breath in relief, not realizing until then that I had been holding it.

He had turned to pick up his coat, thrown across the lowest branch of a sapling. He brushed some scattered leaves from it and began to put it on.

I must have gasped, because he looked up again. The coat was deep scarlet, long-tailed and without lapels, frogged down the front. The buff linings of the turned-back cuffs extended a good six inches up the sleeve, and a small coil of gold braid gleamed from one epaulette. It was a dragoon's coat, an officer's coat. Then it occurred to me – of course, he was an actor, from the company I had seen on the other side of the wood. Though the sword he proceeded to strap on seemed remarkably more realistic than any prop I had ever seen.

I pressed myself against the bark of the tree behind me and found it reassuringly solid. I crossed my arms protectively in front of me.

'Who the bloody hell are you?' I demanded again. The question this time came out in a croak that sounded frightened even to my ears.

As though not hearing me, he ignored the question, taking his time in the fastening of the frogs down the front of his coat. Only when he finished did he turn his attention to me once more. He bowed sardonically, hand over his heart.

'I am, madam, Jonathan Randall, Esquire, Captain of His Majesty's Eighth Dragoons. At your service, madam.'

I broke and ran. My breath rasped in my chest as I tore through the screen of alder, ignoring brambles, nettles, stones, fallen logs, everything in my path. I heard a shout behind me but was much too panicked to determine its direction.

I fled blindly, branches scratching my face and arms, ankles turning as I stepped in holes and stumbled on rocks. I had no room in my mind for any form of rational thought; I wanted only to get away from him.

A heavy weight struck me hard in the lower back and I pitched forward at full length, landing with a thud that knocked the wind out of me. Rough hands flipped me on to my back, and Captain Jonathan Randall rose to his knees above me. He was breathing heavily and had lost his sword in the chase. He looked dishevelled, dirty and thoroughly annoyed.

'What the devil do you mean by running away like that?' he demanded. A thick lock of dark brown hair had come loose and curved across his brow, making him look even more disconcertingly like Frank.

He leaned down and grasped me by the arms. Still gasping for breath, I struggled to get free but succeeded only in dragging him down on top of me.

He lost his balance and collapsed at full length on me, flattening me once more. Surprisingly enough, this seemed to make his annoyance vanish.

'Oh, like that, is it?' he said, with a chuckle. 'Well, I'd be most willing to oblige you, Chuckie, but it happens you've chosen a rather inopportune moment.' His weight pressed my hips to the ground and a small rock was digging painfully into the small of my back. I squirmed to dislodge it. He ground his hips hard against mine and his hands pinned my shoulders to the earth. My mouth fell open in outrage.

'What do you . . .' I began, but he ducked his head and kissed me, cutting short my expostulations. His tongue thrust into my mouth and explored me with a bold familiarity, roving and plunging, retreating and lunging again. Then, just as suddenly as he had begun, he pulled back.

He patted my cheek. 'Quite nice, Chuckie. Perhaps later, when I've the leisure to attend to you properly.'

I had by this time recovered my breath, and I used it. I screamed directly into his earhole, and he jerked as though I had run a hot wire into it. I took advantage of the movement to get my knee up, and jabbed it into his exposed side, sending him sprawling into the leaf mould.

I scrambled awkwardly to my feet. He rolled expertly and came up alongside me. I glanced wildly around, looking for a way out, but we were flush up against the foot of one of those towering cliffs that jut so abruptly from the soil of the Scottish Highlands. He had caught me at a point where the rock face broke inwards, forming a shallow stony box. He blocked the entrance to the declivity, arms spread and braced between the rock walls, an expression of mingled anger and curiosity on his handsome dark face.

'Who were you with?' he demanded. 'Frank, whoever he is? I've no man by that name among my company. Or is it some man who lives nearby?' He smiled derisively. 'You haven't the smell of dung on your skin, so you haven't been with a cottar. For that matter, you look a bit more expensive than the local farmers could afford.'

I clenched my fists and set my chin. Whatever this joker had in mind, I was having none of it.

'I haven't the faintest idea what you are talking about, and I'll thank you to let me pass at once!' I said, adopting my very best ward-sister's tone. This generally had a good effect on recalcitrant orderlies and junior doctors, but appeared merely to amuse Captain Randall. I was resolutely repressing the feelings of fear and disorientation that were flapping under my ribs like a panicked flock of hens.

He shook his head slowly, examining me once more in detail.

'Not just at present, Chuckie. I'm asking myself,' he said conversationally, 'just why a whore abroad in her shift would be wearing her shoes? And quite fine ones, at that,' he added, glancing at my plain brown flatties.

'A what!' I exclaimed.

He ignored me completely. His gaze had returned to my face, and he suddenly stepped forward and gripped my chin in his hand. I grabbed his wrist and yanked.

'Let go of me!' He had fingers like steel. Disregarding my efforts to free myself, he turned my face from one side to the other, so the fading afternoon light shone on it.

'The skin of a lady, I'll swear,' he murmured to himself. He leaned forward and sniffed. 'And a French scent in your hair.' He let go then, and I rubbed my jaw indignantly, as though to erase the touch I still felt on my skin.

'The rest might be managed with money from your patron,' he mused, 'but you've the speech of a lady too.'

'Thanks so much!' I snapped. 'Get out of my way. My husband is expecting me; if I'm not back in ten minutes, he'll come looking for me.'

'Oh, your husband?' The derisively admiring expression retreated somewhat, but did not disappear completely. 'And what is your husband's name, pray? Where is he? And why does he allow his wife to wander alone through deserted woods in a state of undress?'

I had been throttling that part of my brain that was beating itself to pieces trying to make sense of the whole afternoon. It now managed to break through long enough to tell me that however absurd I thought its conjectures, giving this man Frank's name, the same as his own, was only likely to lead to further trouble. Disdaining therefore to answer him, I made to push past him. He blocked my passage with a muscular arm and reached for me with his other hand.

There was a sudden whoosh from above, followed immediately by a blur before my eyes and a dull thud. Captain Randall was on the ground at my feet, under a heaving mass that looked like a bundle of old tartan rags. A brown rocklike fist rose out of the mass and descended with considerable force, meeting decisively with some bony protuberance, by the sound of the resultant crack. The Captain's struggling legs, shiny in tall brown boots, relaxed quite suddenly.

I found myself staring into a pair of sharp black eyes. The sinewy hand that had temporarily distracted the Captain's unwelcome attentions was attached like a limpet to my forearm.

'And who the hell are you?' I said in astonishment. My rescuer, if I cared to call him that, was some inches shorter than I and sparely built, but the bare arms protruding from the ragged shirt were knotted with muscle and his whole frame gave the impression of being made of some resilient material such as bedsprings. No beauty, either, with a pock-marked skin, low brow and narrow jaw.

'This way.' He jerked on my arm, and I, stupefied by the rush of recent events, obediently followed.

My new companion pushed his way rapidly through a scrim of alder, made an abrupt turn around a large rock, and suddenly we were on a path. Overgrown with gorse and heather, and zigzagging so that it was never visible for more than six feet ahead, it was still unmistakably a path, leading steeply up towards the crest of a hill.

Not until we were picking our way cautiously down the far side of the hill did I gather breath and wit enough to ask where we were going. Receiving no answer from my companion, I repeated 'Where on earth are we going?' in a louder tone.

To my considerable surprise he rounded on me, face contorted, and pushed me off the path. As I opened my mouth to protest he clapped a hand over it and dragged me to the ground, rolling on top of me.

Not again! I thought, and was heaving desperately to and fro to free myself when I heard what he had heard, and suddenly lay still. Voices called back and forth, accompanied by trampling and splashing sounds. They were unmistakably English voices. I struggled violently to get my mouth free. I sank my teeth into his hand, and had time only to register the fact that he had been eating pickled herring with his fingers, before something crashed against the back of my skull, and everything went dark.

The stone cottage loomed up suddenly through a haze of night mist. The shutters were bolted tight, showing no more than a thread of light. Having no idea how long I had been travelling, I couldn't tell how far this place was from the hill of Craigh na Dun or the town of Inverness. We were on horseback, myself mounted before my captor with hands tied to the pommel, but there was no road, so progress was still rather slow.

I thought I had not been out for long; I showed no symptoms of concussion or other ill effects from the blow, save a sore patch on the base of my skull. My captor, a man of few words, had responded to my questions, demands and acerbic remarks alike with the all-purpose Scottish noise which can best be rendered phonetically as 'Mmmphm'. Had I been in any doubt as to his nationality, that sound alone would have been sufficient to remove it.

My eyes had gradually adapted to the dwindling light as the pony stumbled through the stones and gorse, so it was a shock to step from near-dark into what seemed a blaze of light inside. As the dazzle receded I could see that in fact the single room was lit only by a fire, several candlesticks and a dangerously old-fashioned-looking oil lamp.

'What is it ye have there, Murtagh?'

The weasel-faced man grabbed me by the arm and urged me blinking into the firelight.

'A Sassenach wench, by her speech.' There were several men in the room, all apparently staring at me, some in curiosity, some with unmistakable leers. My dress had been torn in various spots during the afternoon's activities, and

I hastily took stock of the damage. Looking down, I could see the curve of one breast clearly through a rip, and I was sure the assembled men could too. I decided that making an attempt to pull the torn edges together would only draw further attention to the prospect; instead I chose a face at random and stared boldly at him, in hopes of distracting either the man or myself.

'Eh, a bonny one, Sassenach or no,' said the man, a fat, greasy sort with a black beard, seated by the fire. He was holding a chunk of bread and didn't bother to set it down as he rose and came over to me. He pushed my chin up with the back of his hand, shoving the hair out of my face. A few breadcrumbs fell down the neck of my dress. The other men clustered close around, a mass of tartan and whiskers, smelling strongly of sweat and alcohol. It was only then that I saw they were all kilted – odd, even for this part of the Highlands. Had I stumbled into the meeting of a clan society, or perhaps a regimental reunion?

'C'mere, lass.' A large, dark-bearded man remained seated at the table by the window as he beckoned me. By his air of command, he seemed to be the leader of this pack. The men parted reluctantly as Murtagh pulled me forward, apparently respecting his rights as captor.

The dark man looked me over carefully, no expression on his face. He was good-looking, I thought, and not unfriendly. There were lines of strain between his brows, though, and it wasn't a face one would willingly cross.

'What's your name, lass?' His voice was light for a man of his size, not the deep bass I would have expected from the barrel chest.

'Claire . . . Claire Beauchamp,' I said, deciding on the spur of the moment to use my maiden name. If it were ransom they had in mind, I didn't want to help them by giving a name that could lead to Frank. And I wasn't sure I wanted these rough-looking men to know who I was, before I found out who they were. 'And just what do you think you're – ' The dark man ignored me, establishing a pattern that I was to grow tired of very quickly.

'Beauchamp?' The heavy brows lifted and the general

company stirred in surprise. 'A French name, it is, surely?' He had in fact pronounced the name in correct French, though I had given it the common English pronunciation of 'Beecham'.

'Yes, that's right,' I answered in some surprise.

'Where did ye find this lass?' he demanded, swinging round on Murtagh, who was refreshing himself from a leather flask.

The swarthy little man shrugged. 'At the foot o' Craigh na Dun, Dougal. She was havin' words with a certain captain of dragoons wi' whom I chanced to be acquent',' he added, with a significant lift of his eyebrows. 'There seemed to be some question as to whether the lady was or was not a whore.'

Dougal looked me over carefully once more, taking in every detail of cotton print dress and walking shoes.

'I see. And what was the lady's position in this discussion?' he inquired, with a sarcastic emphasis on the 'lady' that I didn't particularly care for. I noticed that while his Scots was less pronounced than that of the man called Murtagh, his accent was still broad enough that the word was almost, though not quite, 'leddy'.

Murtagh seemed grimly amused; at least one corner of the thin mouth turned up. 'She said she wasna. The Captain himself appeared to be of two minds on the matter, but inclined to put the question to the test.'

'We could do the same, come to that.' The fat, black-bearded man stepped towards me grinning, hands tugging at his belt. I backed up hastily as far as I could, which was not nearly far enough, given the dimensions of the cottage.

'That will do, Rupert.' Dougal was still scowling at me, but his voice held the ring of authority, and Rupert stopped his advances, making a comical face of disappointment.

'I don't hold wi' rape, and we've not the time for it, anyway.' I was pleased to hear this statement of policy, dubious as its moral underpinning might be, but remained a bit nervous in the face of the openly lascivious looks on some of the other faces. I felt absurdly as though I had appeared in public in my undergarments. And while I had

70

no idea who or what these Highland bandits were up to, they seemed bloody dangerous. I bit my tongue, repressing a number of more or less injudicious remarks that were bubbling towards the surface.

'What d'ye say, Murtagh?' Dougal demanded of my captor. 'She doesna appear to care for Rupert, at least.'

'That's no proof,' objected a short, squint-eyed man. 'He didna offer her any siller. Ye canna expect any woman to take on something like Rupert without substantial payment – in advance,' he added, to the considerable hilarity of his companions. Dougal stilled the racket with an abrupt gesture, though, and jerked his head towards the door. Squint-eye, still grinning, obediently slid out into the darkness.

Murtagh, who had not joined in the laughter, was frowning as he looked me over. He shook his head, making the lank fringe across his forehead sway.

'Nay,' he said definitely. 'I've no idea what she might be – or who – but I'll stake my best shirt she's no whore.' I hoped in that case that his best was not the one he was wearing, which scarcely looked worth the wagering.

'Weel, ye'd know, Murtagh, ye've seen enough o' them,' gibed Rupert, but was gruffly hushed by Dougal.

'We'll puzzle it out later,' said Dougal brusquely. 'We've a good distance to go tonight, and we mun' do something for Jamie first; he canna ride like that.'

I shrank back into the shadows near the fireplace, hoping to avoid notice. The man called Murtagh had untied my hands before leading me in here. Perhaps I could slip away while they were busy elsewhere. The men's attention had shifted to a young man crouched on a stool in the corner. He had barely looked up through my appearance and interrogation but kept his head bent, hand clutching the opposite shoulder, rocking slightly back and forth in pain.

Dougal gently pushed the clutching hand away. One of the men pulled back the young man's plaid, revealing a dirt-smeared linen shirt blotched with blood. A small man with a balding head came up behind the lad with a single-bladed knife, and holding the shirt at the collar, slit it across the breast and down the sleeve, so that it fell away from the shoulder.

I gasped, as did several of the men. The shoulder had been wounded; there was a deep ragged furrow across the top, and blood was running freely down the young man's breast. But more shocking was the shoulder joint itself. A dreadful hump rose on that side, and the arm hung at an impossible angle.

Dougal grunted. 'Mmph. Out o' joint, poor bugger.' The young man looked up for the first time. Though drawn with pain and stubbled with red beard, it was a strong, good-humoured face.

'Fell wi' my hand out, when the musket ball knocked me off my saddle. I landed with all my weight on the hand, and *crunch!* there it went.'

'Crunch is right.' The bald man – a Scot, and educated, to judge by his accent – was probing the shoulder, making the lad grimace in pain. 'The wound's no trouble. The ball went right through, and it's clean – the blood's runnin' free enough.' The man picked up a wad of grimy cloth from the table and used it to blot the blood. 'I don't know quite what to do about the disjointure, though. We'd need a chirurgeon to put it back in place properly. You canna ride with it that way, can you, Jamie lad?'

Musket ball? I thought blankly. *Chirurgeon?*

The young man shook his head, white-faced. 'Hurts bad enough sitting still. I couldna manage a pony.' He squeezed his eyes shut and set his teeth in his lower lip.

Murtagh spoke impatiently. 'Well, we canna leave him behind noo, can we? The lobsterbacks are no great shakes trackin' in the dark, but they'll find this place sooner or later, shutters or no. And Jamie can hardly pass for an innocent cottar, wi' yon great hole in 'im.'

'Dinna worry yourself,' Dougal said shortly. 'I don't mean to be leaving him behind.'

The bald man sighed. 'No help for it, then. We'll have to try and force the joint back. Murtagh, you and Rupert hold him; I'll give it a try.'

I watched in sympathy as he picked up the young man's

arm by wrist and elbow and began forcing it upwards. The angle was quite wrong; it must be causing agonizing pain. Sweat poured down the young man's face but he made no sound beyond a soft groan. Suddenly he slumped forward, kept from falling on the floor only by the grip of the men holding him.

One unstoppered a leather flask and pressed it to his lips. The reek of the raw spirit reached me where I stood. The young man coughed and gagged but swallowed nonetheless, dribbling the amber liquid on to the remains of his shirt.

'All right for another go, lad?' the bald man asked. 'Or maybe Rupert should have a try,' he suggested, turning to the squat, black-bearded ruffian.

Rupert, so invited, flexed his shoulders as though to toss a caber, and picked up the young man's wrist, plainly intending to put the joint back by main force; an operation, it was clear, which was likely to snap the arm like a broom-stick.

'Don't you dare to do that!' All thought of escape submerged in professional outrage, I started forward, oblivious to the startled looks of the men around me.

'What do you mean?' snapped the bald man, clearly irritated by my intrusion.

'I mean that you'll break his arm if you do it like that,' I snapped back. 'Stand out of the way, please.' I elbowed Rupert back and took hold of the patient's wrist myself. The patient looked as surprised as the rest, but didn't resist. His skin was very warm, but not feverish, I judged.

'You have to get the bone of the upper arm at the proper angle before it will slip back into its joint,' I said, grunting as I pulled the wrist up and the elbow in. The young man was sizable; his arm was heavy as lead.

'This is the worst part,' I warned the patient. I cupped the elbow, ready to whip it upwards and in.

His mouth twitched, not quite a smile. 'It canna hurt much worse than it does. Get on wi' it.' Sweat was popping out on my own face by now. Resetting a shoulder joint is hard work at the best of times. Done on a large man who had gone hours since the dislocation, his muscles now swollen and pulling on the joint, the job was taking all the strength I had. The fire was dangerously close; I hoped we wouldn't both topple in, if the joint went back with a jerk.

Suddenly the shoulder gave a soft crunching *pop!* and the joint was back in place. The patient looked amazed. He put an unbelieving hand up to explore.

'It doesna hurt any more!' A broad grin of delighted relief spread across his face, and the men broke out in exclamations and applause.

'It will.' I was sweating from the exertion, but smugly pleased with the results. 'It will be tender for several days. You mustn't extend the joint at all for two or three days; when you do use it again, go very slowly at first. Stop at once if it begins to hurt, and use warm compresses on it daily.'

I became aware, in the midst of this advice, that while the patient was listening respectfully the other men were eyeing me with looks ranging from wonder to outright suspicion.

'I'm a nurse, you see,' I explained, feeling somehow defensive.

Dougal's eyes, and Rupert's as well, dropped to my bosom and fastened there with a sort of horrified fascination. They exchanged glances, then Dougal looked back at my face.

'Be that as it may,' he said, raising his brows at me. 'For a wetnurse, you'd seem to have some skill at healing. Can ye stanch the lad's wound, well enough for him to sit a horse?'

'I can dress the wound, yes,' I said with considerable asperity. 'Provided you've anything to dress it with. But just what do you mean by "wetnurse"? And why do you suppose I'd want to help you, anyway?'

I was ignored as Dougal turned and spoke in a tongue I dimly recognized as Gaelic to a woman who cowered in the corner. Surrounded by the mass of men, I had not noticed her before. She was dressed oddly, I thought, in a long, ragged skirt and a long-sleeved blouse half covered by a sort of bodice or jerkin. Everything was rather on the grubby side, including her face. Glancing around, though, I could see that the cottage lacked not only electricity but also indoor plumbing; perhaps there was some excuse for the dirt.

The woman bobbed a quick curtsy, and scuttling past Rupert and Murtagh, she began digging in a painted wooden chest by the hearth, emerging finally with a pile of ratty cloths.

'No, that won't do,' I said, fingering them gingerly. 'The wound needs to be disinfected first, then bandaged with a clean cloth, if there are no sterile bandages.'

Eyebrows rose all round. 'Disinfected?' said the small man carefully.

'Yes, indeed,' I said firmly, thinking him a bit simpleminded, in spite of his educated accent. 'All dirt must be removed from the wound and it must be treated with a compound to discourage germs and promote healing.'

'Such as?'

'Such as iodine,' I said. Seeing no comprehension on the faces before me, I tried again. 'Dilute carbolic? Or perhaps even just alcohol?' Looks of relief. At last I had found a word they appeared to recognize. Murtagh thrust the leather flask into my hands. I sighed with impatience. I knew the Highlands were primitive, but this was nearly unbelievable.

'Look,' I said, as patiently as I could. 'Why don't you just take him down into the town? It can't be far, and I'm sure there's a doctor there who could see to him.'

The woman gawped at me. 'What town?'

The big man called Dougal was ignoring this discussion, peering cautiously into the darkness through the shutter's crack. He stepped quietly to the door, and the men fell quiet as he vanished into the night.

In a moment he was back, bringing the squint-eyed man and the cold sharp scent of dark pines with him. He shook his head in answer to the men's questioning looks.

'Nay, nothing close. We'll go at once, while it's safe.'

Catching sight of me, he stopped for a moment, thinking. Suddenly he nodded at me, decision made.

'She'll come with us,' he said. He rummaged in the pile

75

of cloths on the table and came up with a tattered rag; it looked like a neckcloth that had seen better days.

The bald man seemed disinclined to have me along, wherever they were going.

'Why do ye no just leave her here?'

Dougal cast him an impatient glance, but left it to Murtagh to explain. 'Wherever the redcoats are now, they'll be here by dawn, which is no so far off, considering. If this woman's an English spy, we canna risk leaving her here to tell them whicn way we've gone. And if she should not be on good terms wi' them' – he looked dubiously at me – 'we certainly canna leave a lone woman here in her shift.' He brightened a bit, fingering the fabric of my skirt. 'She might be worth a bit in the way of ransom, at that; little as she has on, it's fine stuff.'

'Besides,' Dougal added, interrupting, 'she may be useful on the way; she seems to know a bit about doctoring. But we've no time for that now. I'm afraid ye'll have to go without bein' "disinfected", Jamie,' he said, clapping the younger man on the back. 'Can ye ride one-handed?'

'Aye.'

'Good lad. Here,' he said, tossing the greasy rag at me. 'Bind up his wound, quickly. We'll be leaving directly. Do you two get the ponies,' he said, turning to weasel-face and the fat one called Rupert.

I turned the rag round distastefully.

'I can't use this,' I complained. 'It's filthy.'

Without seeing him move, I found the big man gripping my shoulder, his hazel eyes an inch from mine. 'Do it,' he said.

Freeing me with a push, he strode to the door and disappeared after his two henchmen. Feeling more than a little shaken, I turned to the task of bandaging the musket wound as best I could. The thought of using the grimy neckrag was something my medical training wouldn't let me contemplate. I tried to bury my confusion and terror in the task of trying to find something more suitable, and, after a quick and futile search through the pile of rags, finally settled on strips of rayon torn from the hem of my slip. While hardly sterile, it was by far the cleanest material at hand.

The linen of my patient's shirt was old and worn, but still surprisingly tough. With a bit of a struggle I ripped the rest of the sleeve open and used it to improvise a sling. I stepped back to survey the results of my impromptu field dressing, and backed straight into the big man, who had come in quietly to watch.

He looked approvingly at my handiwork. 'Good job, lass. Come on, we're ready.'

Dougal handed a coin to the woman and hustled me out of the cottage, followed more slowly by Jamie, still a bit white-faced. Unfolded from the low stool, my patient proved to be quite tall; he stood several inches over Dougal, himself a tall man.

The black-bearded Rupert and Murtagh were holding six ponies outside, muttering soft Gaelic endearments to them in the dark. It was a moonless night, but the starlight caught the metal bits of the harness in flashes of quicksilver. I looked up and almost gasped in wonder; the night sky was thick with a glory of stars such as I had never seen. Glancing round at the surrounding forest, I understood. With no nearby city to veil the sky with light, the stars here held undisputed dominion over the night.

And then I stopped dead, feeling much colder than the night chill justified. No city lights. 'What town?' the woman inside had asked. Accustomed as I was to blackouts and air raids from the war years, the lack of light had not at first disturbed me. But this was peacetime, and the lights of Inverness should have been visible for miles.

The men were shapeless masses in the dark. I thought of trying to slip away into the trees, but Dougal, apparently divining my thought, grabbed my elbow and pulled me towards the ponies.

'Jamie, get yourself up,' he called. 'The lass will ride wi' you.' He squeezed my elbow. 'You can hold the reins, if Jamie canna manage one-handed, but do ye take care to keep close wi' the rest of us. Should ye try anythin' else, I shall cut your throat. D'ye understand me?'

I nodded, throat too dry to answer. His voice was not particularly threatening, but I believed every word. I was the less tempted to 'try anythin' ', in that I had no idea what to try. I didn't know where I was, who my companions were, why we were leaving with such urgency or where we were going, but I lacked any reasonable alternatives to going with them. I was worried about Frank, who must long since have started looking for me, but this didn't seem the time to mention him.

Dougal must have sensed my nod, for he let go of my arm and stooped suddenly beside me. I stood stupidly staring down at him until he hissed, 'Your foot, lass! Give me your foot! Your *left* foot,' he added disgustedly. I hastily took my misplaced right foot out of his hand and stepped up with my left. With a slight grunt, he boosted me into the saddle in front of Jamie, who gathered me in closely with his good arm.

In spite of the general awkwardness of my situation I was grateful for the young Scot's warmth. He smelt strongly of woodsmoke, blood and unwashed male, but the night chill bit through my thin dress and I was happy enough to lean back against him.

With no more than a faint chinking of bridles we moved off into the starlit night. There was no conversation among the men, only a general wary watchfulness. The ponies broke into a trot as soon as we reached the track, and I was jostled too uncomfortably to want to talk myself, even assuming that anyone was willing to listen.

My companion seemed to be having little trouble, in spite of being unable to use his right hand. I could feel his thighs behind mine, shifting and pressing occasionally to guide the pony. I clutched the edge of the short saddle in order to stay seated; I had been on horses before, but was by no means the horseman this Jamie was.

After a time we reached a cross track, where we stopped a moment while the bald man and the leader conferred in low tones. Jamie dropped the reins over the pony's neck and let it wander to the verge to crop grass, while he began twisting and turning behind me.

'Careful!' I said. 'Don't twist like that or your dressing will come off! What are you trying to do?'

'Get my plaid loose to cover you,' he replied. 'You're shivering. But I canna do it one-handed. Can ye reach the clasp of my brooch for me?'

With a good deal of tugging and awkward shifting we got the plaid loosened. With a surprisingly dexterous swirl he twirled the cloth out and let it settle, shawl-like, around his shoulders. He then put the ends over my shoulders and tucked them neatly under the saddle edge, so that we were both warmly wrapped.

'There!' he said. 'We dinna want ye to freeze before we get there.'

'Thank you,' I said, grateful for the shelter. 'But where are we going?'

I couldn't see his face, behind and above me, but he paused a moment before answering.

At last he laughed shortly. 'Tell ye the truth, lassie, I don't know. Daresay we'll both find out when we get there, eh?'

Something seemed faintly familiar about the section of countryside through which we were passing. Surely I knew that large rock formation ahead, the one shaped like a rooster's tail?

'Cocknammon Rock!' I exclaimed.

'Aye, reckon,' said my escort, unexcited by this revelation.

'Didn't the English use it for ambushes?' I asked, trying to remember the dreary details of local history Frank had spent hours regaling me with over the last week. 'If there is an English patrol in the neighbourhood . . .' I hesitated. If there was an English patrol in the neighbourhood, perhaps I was wrong to draw attention to it. And yet, in case of an ambush, I would be quite indistinguishable from my companion, shrouded as we were in one plaid. And I thought again of Captain Jonathan Randall, and shuddered involuntarily. Everything I had seen since I had stepped through the cleft stone pointed towards the completely irrational conclusion that the man I had met in the wood was in fact Frank's six-times-great-grandfather. I fought stubbornly against this conclusion, but was unable to formulate another that met the facts.

I had at first imagined that I was merely dreaming more vividly than usual, but Randall's kiss, rudely familiar and immediately physical, had dispelled that impression. Neither did I imagine that I had dreamed being knocked on the head by Murtagh; the soreness on my scalp was being matched by a chafing of my inner thighs against the saddle, which seemed most undreamlike. And the blood; yes, I was familiar enough with blood to have dreamed of it before. But never had I dreamed the scent of blood; that warm, coppery tang that I could still smell on the man behind me.

'*Tck.*' He clucked to our mount and urged it up alongside the leader's, engaging the burly shadow in quiet Gaelic conversation. The ponies slowed to a walk.

At a signal from the leader, Jamie, Murtagh and the small bald man dropped back, while the others spurred up and galloped towards the rock, a quarter mile ahead to the right. A half moon had come up, and the light was bright enough to pick out the leaves of the bluebells growing on the trackside, but the shadows in the clefts of the rock could hide anything.

Just as the galloping shapes passed the rock, a flash of musket fire sparked from a hollow. There was a bloodcurdling shriek from directly behind me, and the pony leaped forward as though jabbed with a sharp stick. We were suddenly racing towards the rock across the heather, Murtagh and the other man alongside, hair-raising screams and bellows splitting the night air.

I hung on to the pommel for dear life. Suddenly reining up next to a large gorse bush, Jamie grabbed me round the waist and unceremoniously dumped me into it. The pony whirled sharply and sprinted off again, circling the rock to come along the south side. I could see the rider crouching low in the saddle as the pony vanished into the rock's shadow. When it emerged, still galloping, the saddle was empty.

The rock surfaces were cratered with shadow; I could

hear shouts and occasional musket shots, but couldn't tell if the movements I saw were those of men, or only the shades of the stunted trees that sprouted from cracks in the rock.

I extricated myself from the bush with some difficulty, picking bits of prickly gorse from my skirt and hair. I licked a scratch on my hand, wondering what on earth I was to do now. I could wait for the battle at the rock to be decided. If the Scots won, or at least survived, I supposed they would come back looking for me. If they did not, I could approach the English, who might well assume that if I were travelling with the Scots I was in league with them. In league to do what, I had no idea, but it was quite plain from the men's behaviour at the cottage that they were up to something which they expected the English strongly to disapprove of.

Perhaps it would be better to avoid both sides in this conflict. After all, now that I knew where I was, I stood some chance of getting back to a town or village that I knew, even if I had to walk all the way. I set off with decision towards the track, tripping over innumerable lumps of stone, the bastard offspring of Cocknammon Rock.

The moonlight made walking deceptive; though I could see every detail of the ground, I had no depth perception; flat plants and jagged stones looked the same height, causing me to lift my feet absurdly high over nonexistent obstacles and stub my toes on protruding rocks. I walked as fast as I could, listening for sounds of pursuit behind me.

The noises of battle had faded by the time I reached the track. I realized that I was too visible on the way itself, but I needed to follow it, if I were to find my way to a town. I had no sense of direction in the dark, and had never learned from Frank his trick of navigation by the stars. Thinking of Frank made me want to cry, so I tried to distract myself by trying to make sense of the day's events.

It seemed inconceivable, but all appearances pointed to my being in some place where the customs and politics of the mid-eighteenth century still held sway. I would have thought the whole thing a fancy-dress show of some type, had it not been for the injuries of the young man they called

Jamie. That wound had indeed been made by something very like a musket ball, judging from the evidence it left behind. The behaviour of the men in the cottage was not consistent with any sort of play-acting, either. They were serious men, and the dirks and swords were real.

Could it be some secluded enclave, perhaps, where the villagers re-enacted part of their history periodically? I had heard of such things in Germany, though never in Scotland. *You've never heard of the actors shooting each other with muskets, either, have you?* jeered the uncomfortably rational part of my mind.

I looked back at the rock to check my position, then ahead to the skyline, and my blood ran cold. There was nothing there but the feathered needles of pine trees, impenetrably black against the spread of stars. Where were the lights of Inverness? If that was Cocknammon Rock behind me, as I knew it was, then Inverness must be less than three miles to the southwest. At this distance I should be able to see the glow of the town against the sky. If it were there.

I shook myself irritably, hugging my elbows against the chill. Even admitting for a moment the completely implausible idea that I was in another time than my own, Inverness had stood in its present location for some six hundred years. It was there. But, apparently, it had no lights. Under the circumstances this strongly suggested that there were no electric lights to be had. Yet another piece of evidence, if I needed it. But evidence of what, exactly?

A shape stepped out of the dark so close in front of me that I nearly bumped into it. Stifling a scream I turned to run, but a large hand gripped my arm, preventing escape.

'Dinna worry, lass. 'Tis me.'

'That's what I was afraid of,' I said crossly, though in fact I was relieved that it was Jamie. I was not so afraid of him as of the other men, though he looked just as dangerous. Still, he was young, even younger than me, I judged. And it was difficult for me to be afraid of someone I had so recently treated as a patient.

'I hope you haven't been misusing that shoulder,' I said in

82

the rebuking voice of a hospital matron. If I could establish a sufficient tone of authority, perhaps I could persuade him into letting me go.

'Yon wee stramash didna do it any good,' he admitted, massaging the shoulder with his free hand.

Just then he moved into a patch of moonlight and I saw the huge spread of blood on his shirt front. Arterial bleeding, I thought at once; but then, why is he still standing?

'You're hurt!' I exclaimed. 'Have you broken open your shoulder wound, or is it fresh? Sit down and let me see!' I pushed him towards a pile of boulders, rapidly reviewing procedures for emergency field treatment. No supplies to hand, save what I was wearing. I was reaching for the remains of my slip, intending to use it to stanch the flow, when he laughed.

'Nay, pay it no mind, lass. This lot isna *my* blood. Not much of it, anyway,' he added, plucking the soaked fabric gingerly away from his body.

I swallowed, feeling a bit queasy. 'Oh,' I said weakly.

'Dougal and the others will be waiting by the track. Let's go.' He took me by the arm, less as a gallant gesture than a means of forcing me to accompany him. I decided to take a chance and dug in my heels.

'No! I'm not going with you!'

He stopped, surprised at my resistance. 'Yes, you are.' He didn't seem upset by my refusal; in fact, he seemed slightly amused that I had any objection to being kidnapped again.

'And what if I won't? Are you going to cut my throat?' I demanded, forcing the issue. He considered the alternatives and answered calmly.

'Why, no. You don't look heavy. If ye won't walk, I shall pick you up and sling ye over my shoulder. Do ye want me to do that?' He took a step towards me, and I hastily retreated. I hadn't the slightest doubt he would do it, injury or no.

'No! You can't do that; you'll damage your shoulder again.'

His features were indistinct but the moonlight caught the gleam of teeth as he grinned.

'Well then, since ye don't want me to hurt myself, I suppose that means as you're comin' with me?' I struggled for an answer, but failed to find one in time. He took my arm again, firmly, and we set off towards the track.

Jamie kept a tight hold on my arm, hauling me upright when I stumbled over rocks and plants. He himself walked as though the stubbled heath were a paved road in broad daylight. He has cat blood, I reflected sourly; no doubt that was how he managed to sneak up on me in the darkness.

The other men were, as advertised, waiting with the ponies at no great distance; apparently there had been no losses or injuries, for they were all present. Scrambling up in an undignified scuffle, I plopped down in the saddle again. My head gave Jamie's bad shoulder an unintentional thump, and he drew in his breath with a hiss.

I tried to cover my resentment at being recaptured and my remorse at having hurt him with an air of bullying officiousness.

'Serves you right, brawling round the countryside and chasing through bushes and rocks. I told you not to move that joint; now you've probably got torn muscles as well as bruises.'

He seemed amused by my scolding. 'Well, it wasna much of a choice. If I'd not moved my shoulder, I wouldna have ever moved anything else again. I can handle a single red-coat wi' one hand – maybe even two of them,' he said, a bit boastfully, 'but not three.

'Besides,' he said, drawing me against his blood-encrusted shirt, 'ye can fix it for me again when we get wherc we're going.'

'That's what you think,' I said coldly, squirming away from the sticky fabric. He clucked to the pony and we set off again. The men were in ferocious good spirits after the fight, and there was a good deal of laughter and joking. My minor part in thwarting the ambush was much praised, and toasts were drunk in my honour from the flasks that several of the men carried.

I was offered some of the contents but declined at first on the grounds that I found it hard enough to stay in the saddle sober. From the men's discussion I gathered it had been a small patrol of some ten English soldiers, armed with muskets and sabres, the same patrol they had tangled with earlier.

Someone passed a flask to Jamie and I could smell the hot, burnt-smelling spirit as he drank. I wasn't at all thirsty, but the faint scent of honey reminded me that I was starving, and had been for some time. My stomach gave an embarrassingly loud growl, protesting my neglect.

'Hey, then, Jamie-lad! Hungry, are ye? Or have ye a set of bagpipes with ye?' shouted Rupert, mistaking the source of the noise.

'Hungry enough to eat a set of pipes, I reckon,' called Jamie, gallantly assuming the blame. A moment later, a hand with a flask came round in front of me again.

'Better have a wee nip,' he whispered to me. 'It willna fill your belly, but it will make ye forget you're hungry.'

And a number of other things as well, I hoped. I tilted the flask and swallowed.

My escort had been correct; the whisky built a small warm fire that burned comfortably in my stomach, obscuring the hunger pangs. We managed without incident for several miles, taking turns with both reins and whisky flask. Near a ruined cottage, though, the breathing of my escort gradually changed to a ragged gasping. Our precarious balance, heretofore contained in a staid wobble, suddenly became much more erratic. I was confused; if *I* wasn't drunk, it seemed rather unlikely that *he* was.

'Stop! Help!' I yelled. 'He's going over!' I remembered my last unrehearsed descent and had no inclination to repeat it.

Dark shapes swirled and crowded around us, with a confused muttering of voices. Jamie slid off headfirst like a sack of stones, luckily landing in someone's arms. The rest of the men were off their ponies and had him laid in a field by the time I had scrambled down.

'He's breathin',' said one.

'Well, how very helpful,' I snapped, groping frantically for a pulse in the blackness. I found one at last, rapid but fairly strong. Putting a hand on his chest and an ear to his mouth, I could feel a regular rise and fall, with less of that gasping note. I straightened up.

'I think he's just fainted,' I said. 'Put a saddlebag under his feet and if there's water, bring me some.' I was surprised to find that my orders were instantly obeyed. Apparently the young man was important to them. He groaned and opened his eyes, black holes in the starlight. In the faint light his face looked like a skull, white skin stretched tight over the angled bones around the orbits.

'I'm all right,' he said, trying to sit up. 'Just a bit dizzy though.' I put a hand on his chest and pushed him flat.

'Lie still,' I ordered. I carried out a rapid inspection by touch, then rose on my knees and turned to a looming shape that I deduced from its size to be the leader, Dougal.

'The musket wound has been bleeding again, and the idiot's been knifed as well. I think it's not serious, but he's lost quite a lot of blood. His shirt is soaked through, but I don't know how much of it is his. He needs rest and quiet; we should camp here at least until morning.' The shape made a negative motion.

'Nay. We're farther than the garrison will venture, but there's still the Watch to be mindful of. We've a good fifteen miles yet to go.' The featureless head tilted back, gauging the movement of the stars.

'Five hours, at the least, and more likely seven. We can stay long enough for ye to stop the bleeding and dress the wound again; no much more than that.'

I set to work, muttering to myself, while Dougal, with a soft word, dispatched one of the other shadows to stand guard with the ponies by the track. The other men relaxed for the moment, drinking from flasks and chatting in low voices. The ferret-faced Murtagh helped me, tearing strips of linen, fetching more water and lifting the patient up to have the dressing tied on, Jamie being strictly forbidden to move himself, despite his grumbling that he was perfectly all right.

'You are not all right, and it's no wonder,' I snapped, venting my fear and irritation. 'What sort of idiot gets himself knifed and doesn't even stop to take care of it? Couldn't you tell how badly you were bleeding? You're lucky you're not dead, tearing around the countryside all night, brawling and fighting and throwing yourself off horses . . . hold still, you bloody fool.' The rayon and linen strips I was working with were irritatingly elusive in the dark. They slipped away, escaping my grasp, like fish darting away into the depths with a mocking flash of white bellies. Despite the chill, sweat sprang out on my neck. I finally finished tying one end and reached for another, which persisted in slithering away behind the patient's back. 'Come back here, you . . . oh, you goddamned bloody bastard!' Jamie had moved and the original end had come untied.

There was a moment of shocked silence. 'Christ,' said the fat man named Rupert. 'I've ne'er heard a woman use such language in my life.'

'Then ye've ne'er met my Auntie Grisel,' said another voice, to laughter.

'Your husband should tan ye, woman,' said an austere voice from the blackness under a tree. 'St Paul says "Let a woman be silent, and – " '

'You can mind your own bloody business,' I snarled, sweat dripping behind my ears, 'and so can St Paul.' I wiped my forehead with my sleeve. 'Turn him to the left. And if you' – addressing my patient – 'move so much as one single muscle while I'm tying this bandage, I'll throttle you.'

'Och, aye,' he answered meekly.

I pulled too hard on the last bandage, and the entire dressing scooted off.

'Goddamn it all to hell!' I bellowed, striking my hand on the ground in frustration. There was a moment of shocked silence, then, as I fumbled in the dark for the loose ends of the bandages, further comment on my unwomanly language.

'Perhaps we should send her to Ste Anne's abbey, Dougal,' offered one of the blank-faced figures squatting by the road. 'I've not heard Jamie swear once since we left the coast, and he used to have a mouth on him would put a sailor to shame. Four months in a monastery must have had some effect. You do not even take the name of the Lord in vain any more, do ye, lad?'

'You wouldna do so either, if you'd been made to do penance for it by lying for three hours at midnight on the stone floor of a chapel in February, wearing nothin' but your shirt,' answered my patient.

The men all laughed as he continued, 'The penance was only for two hours, but it took another to get myself up off the floor afterwards; I thought my . . . er, I thought I'd frozen to the flags, but it turned out just to be stiffness.'

Apparently he was feeling better. I smiled, despite myself, but spoke firmly nonetheless. 'You be quiet,' I said, 'or I'll hurt you.' He gingerly touched the dressing, and I slapped his hand away.

'Oh, threats, is it?' he asked impudently. 'And after I shared my drink with ye too!'

The flask completed the circle of men. Kneeling down next to me, Dougal tilted it carefully for the patient to drink. The pungent, burnt smell of very raw whisky floated up, and I put a restraining hand on the flask.

'No more spirits,' I said. 'He needs tea, or at worst, water. Not alcohol.'

Dougal pulled the flask from my hand, completely disregarding me, and poured a sizable slug of the hot-smelling liquid down the throat of my patient, making him cough. Waiting only long enough for the man on the ground to catch his breath, he reapplied the flask.

'Stop that!' I reached for the whisky again. 'Do you want him so drunk he can't stand up?'

I was rudely elbowed aside.

'Feisty wee bitch, is she no?' said my patient, sounding amused.

'Tend to your business, woman,' Dougal ordered. 'We've a good way to go yet tonight, and he'll need whatever strength the drink can give him.'

The instant the bandages were tied, the patient tried to

sit up. I pushed him flat and put a knee on his chest to keep him there. 'You are *not* to move,' I said fiercely. I grabbed the hem of Dougal's kilt and jerked it roughly, urging him back down on his knees next to me.

'Look at that,' I ordered in my best ward-sister voice. I plopped the sopping mass of the discarded shirt into his hand. He dropped it with an exclamation of disgust.

I took his hand and put it on the patient's shoulder. 'And look there. He's had a blade of some kind right through the trapezius muscle.'

'A bayonet,' put in the patient helpfully.

'A bayonet!' I exclaimed. 'And why didn't you tell me?'

He shrugged, and stopped short with a mild grunt of pain. 'I felt it go in, but I couldna tell how bad it was; it didna hurt that much.'

'Is it hurting now?'

'It is,' he said shortly.

'Good,' I said, completely provoked. 'You deserve it. Maybe that will teach you to go haring round the countryside kidnapping young women and k-killing people, and ...' I felt myself ridiculously close to tears and stopped, fighting for control.

Dougal was growing impatient with this conversation. 'Well, can ye keep one foot on each side of the pony, man?'

'He can't go anywhere!' I protested indignantly. 'He ought to be in hospital! Certainly he can't – '

My protests, as usual, went completely ignored.

'Can ye ride?' Dougal repeated.

'Aye, if ye'll take the lassie off my chest and fetch me a clean shirt.'

4

I Come to the Castle

The rest of the journey passed uneventfully, if you consider it uneventful to ride fifteen miles on horseback over rough country at night, without benefit of roads, in company with kilted men armed to the teeth, and sharing a pony with a wounded man. At least we were not set upon by highwaymen, we encountered no wild beasts and it didn't rain. By the standards I was becoming used to, it was quite dull.

Dawn was coming up in streaks and slashes over the foggy moor. Our destination loomed ahead, a huge bulk of dark stone outlined by the grey light.

The surroundings were no longer quiet and deserted. There was a trickle of rudely dressed people, heading towards the castle. They moved to the side of the narrow road to let the ponies trot past, gawking at what they plainly thought my outlandish garb.

Not surprisingly it was misting heavily, but there was enough light to show a stone bridge, arching over a small stream that ran past the front of the castle, down to a dully gleaming loch a quarter of a mile away.

The castle itself was blunt and solid. No fanciful turrets or toothed battlements. This was more like an enormous fortified house, with thick stone walls and high, slitted windows. A number of chimney pots smoked over the slick tiles of the roof, adding to the general impression of greyness.

The gated entrance of the castle was wide enough to accommodate two rough carts side by side. I say this without fear of contradiction, because it was doing exactly that as we crossed the bridge. One was loaded with barrels, the other with hay. Our little cavalcade huddled on the bridge, waiting impatiently for the carts to complete their laborious entry.

I risked a question as the ponies picked their way over the slippery stones of the wet courtyard. I hadn't spoken to my escort since hastily re-dressing his shoulder by the roadside. He had been silent, too, aside from an occasional grunt of discomfort when a misstep by the pony jolted him.

'Where are we?' I croaked, my voice hoarse from cold and disuse.

'The keep of Leoch,' he answered shortly.

Castle Leoch. Well, at least now I knew where I was. When I had known it, Castle Leoch was a picturesque ruin. It was considerably more picturesque now, what with the sheep huddling under the walls of the keep and the pervasive smell of raw sewage. I was beginning to accept the impossible idea that I was, most likely, somewhere in the eighteenth century.

I was sure that such filth and chaos existed nowhere in the Scotland of 1946, bomb craters or no. And we were definitely in Scotland; the accents of the people in the courtyard left no doubt of that.

'Ay, Dougal!' shouted a tattered stable lad, running up to grab the halter of the lead pony. 'You're early, man; we hadna thought to see ye before the Gathering!'

The leader of our little group swung down from the saddle, leaving the reins to the grubby youth.

'Aye, well, we've had some luck, both good and bad. I'm off to see my brother Callum. Will ye summon Mrs Fitz to feed the lads? They'll need their breakfasts and their beds.'

He beckoned Murtagh and Rupert down to accompany him, and together they disappeared through an archway.

The rest of us dismounted and stood steaming in the wet courtyard for another ten minutes before Mrs Fitz, whoever she might be, consented to show herself. A cluster of curious children gathered around us, speculating on my possible origins and function. The bolder ones had just begun to get up enough courage to pluck at my skirt when a large, stout lady in dark brown linen and homespun bustled out and shooed them away.

'Willy, my dear!' she cried. 'How good to see ye! And Neddie!' She gave the small balding man a hearty buss of

welcome that nearly knocked him over. 'Ye'll be needin'
breakfast, I expect. Plenty in the kitchen; do ye go and feed
yerselves.' Turning to me and Jamie, she started back as
though bitten by a snake. She looked open-mouthed at me,
then turned to Jamie for an explanation of this apparition.

'Claire,' he said, with a brief tilt of his head towards me.
'And Mistress FitzGibbons,' he added, with a tilt the other
way. 'Murtagh found her yesterday, and Dougal said we
must bring her along wi' us,' he added, making it clear it
was no good blaming *him*.

Mistress FitzGibbons closed her mouth and looked me
up and down with an air of shrewd evaluation. Apparently
she decided that I looked harmless enough, despite my odd
and scandalous appearance, for she smiled – kindly, despite
several missing teeth – and took me by the arm.

'Well then, Claire. Welcome to ye. Come wi' me and we
shall find ye somethin' a bit more . . . mmm.' She looked
over my short skirt and inadequate shoes, shaking her head.

She was leading me firmly away when I remembered my
patient.

'Oh, wait, please! I forgot Jamie!'

Mistress FitzGibbons was surprised. 'Why, Jamie can
fend for himself. He knows where to get food and someone
will find him a bed.'

'But he's hurt. He was shot yesterday and stabbed last
night. I bandaged the wound for riding, but I didn't have
time to clean or dress it properly. I must care for it now,
before it gets infected.'

'Infected?'

'Yes, that is, I mean, inflamed, you know, with pus and
swelling and fever.'

'Oh, aye, I know what ye mean. But do ye mean to say
as ye know what to do for that? Are ye a charmer then? A
Beaton?'

'Something like that.' I had no notion what a Beaton
might be, nor any wish to go into my medical qualifications,
standing out in the chilly drizzle that had set in. Mistress
FitzGibbons seemed of a like mind, for she called back

Jamie, who was making off in the opposite direction, and taking him also by an arm, towed us both into the castle.

After a long trip through cold narrow corridors, dimly lit by slitted windows, we came to a fairly large room furnished with a bed, a couple of stools and, most importantly, a fire.

I ignored my patient temporarily in favour of thawing my hands. Mistress FitzGibbons, presumably immune to cold, sat Jamie on a stool by the fire and gently got the remains of his tattered shirt off, replacing it with a warm quilt from the bed. She clucked at the shoulder, which was bruised and swollen, and poked at my clumsy dressing.

I turned from the fire. 'I think it will need to be soaked off, and then the wound cleansed with a solution for . . . for preventing fevers.'

Mistress FitzGibbons would have made an admirable nurse. 'What will ye be needin'?' she asked simply.

I thought hard. What in the name of God had people used for preventing infection before the advent of penicillin? And of those limited compounds, which might be available to me in a primitive Scottish castle just after dawn?

'Garlic!' I said in triumph. 'Garlic, and if you have it, thyme. Also I'll need several clean rags and a cauldron of water for boiling.'

'Aye, well, I think we can manage that; perhaps a bit of comfrey as well. What about a bit o' camomile tea? T'lad looks as though it's been a long night.'

The young man was in fact swaying with weariness, too tired to protest about our discussing him as though he were an inanimate object.

Mrs FitzGibbons was soon back, with an apron full of garlic bulbs, gauze bags of dried herbs and torn strips of old linen. A small black iron cauldron hung from one meaty arm and she held a large pitcher of water as though it were so much goosedown.

'Now then, m'dear, what would ye have me do?' she said cheerfully. I set her to boiling the water and peeling the cloves of garlic while I inspected the contents of the herb packets. There was the thyme I had asked for, camomile, comfrey for tea, and something I tentatively identified as willow bark.

'Painkiller,' I muttered happily, recollecting Mr Crook explaining the uses of the barks and herbs we found. Good, we'd need that.

I threw several cloves of peeled garlic into the boiling water with some of the thyme, then added the cloth strips to the mixture. The comfrey and willow bark were steeping in a small pan of hot water set by the fire. The preparations had steadied me a bit. If I didn't know for certain where I was, or why I was there, at least I knew what to do for the next quarter of an hour.

'Thank you . . . ah, Mrs FitzGibbons,' I said respectfully. 'I can manage now, if you have things to do.' The giant dame laughed, breasts heaving.

'Ah, lass! There aye be things for me to do! I'll send a bit o' broth up for ye. Do ye call oot if ye need anything else.' She waddled to the door with surprising speed and disappeared on her rounds.

I pulled the bandages off as carefully as I could. Still, the rayon pad stuck to the flesh, coming away with a soft crackling of dried blood. Droplets of fresh blood oozed around the edges of the wounds, and I apologized for hurting him, though he hadn't moved or made a sound.

He smiled slightly, with a hint perhaps of flirtation. 'Don't worry, lass. I've been hurt much worse, and by people much less pretty.' He bent forward for me to wash the wounds with the boiled garlic decoction, and the quilt slipped from his shoulder.

I saw at once that, whether meant as a compliment or not, his remark was a statement of plain fact; he had been hurt much worse. His upper back was covered with a criss-cross of faded white lines. He had been savagely flogged, and more than once. There were small lines of silvery scar tissue in some spots, where the welts had crossed, and irregular patches where several blows had struck the same spot, flaying off skin and gouging the muscle beneath.

I had, of course, seen a great variety of wounds and

injuries, doing field nursing, but there was something about these scars that seemed shockingly brutal. I must have drawn in my breath at the sight, for he turned his head and caught me staring. He shrugged his good shoulder.

'Lobsterbacks. For escape and theft.'

I didn't know what to say to this, so said the first thing that came to mind.

'What were you escaping from?'

'The English,' he said, with an ironic lift of his brow. 'If ye mean where, Fort William.'

'I rather gathered it was the English,' I said, matching the dryness of his tone. The shock of the sight was beginning to fade. 'What were you doing in Fort William in the first place?'

He rubbed his brow with his free hand. 'Oh, that. I think that was obstruction.'

'Obstruction, escape and theft. You sound a right dangerous character,' I said lightly, hoping to distract him from what I was doing.

It worked at least slightly; one corner of the wide mouth turned up, and one dark blue eye glinted back over his shoulder at me.

'Oh, I am that,' he said. 'A wonder you think yourself safe in the same room wi' me, and you an English lassie.'

'Well, you look harmless enough at the moment.' This was entirely untrue; shirtless, scarred and blood-smeared, with stubbled cheeks and reddened eyelids from the long night ride, he looked thoroughly disreputable. And tired or not, he looked entirely capable of further mayhem, should the need arise.

He laughed, a surprisingly deep, infectious sound.

'Harmless as a setting dove,' he agreed. 'I'm too hungry to be a threat to anything but breakfast. Let a stray bannock come within reach, though, and I'll no answer for the consequences. Ooh!'

'Sorry,' I muttered. 'The stab wound's deep, and it's dirty.'

'It's all right.' But he had gone pale beneath the coppery

95

stubble of his beard. I tried to lead him back into conversation.

'What exactly is obstruction?' I asked casually. 'I must say it doesn't sound like a major crime.'

He took a deep breath, fixing his eyes resolutely on the carved bedpost as I swabbed deeper.

'Ah. Well, I suppose it's whatever Captain Randall chose to say it is.'

'Randall!' I couldn't keep the shock from my voice. Cold blue eyes fixed suddenly on mine.

'You're familiar with the man?'

'No! No . . . I . . . used to know a family of that name, a long time, uh, a long time ago.' Randall? *Captain* Randall? Could this possibly be Frank's gallant ancestor, the soldier with the sterling battle record, recipient of commendations from dukes? And if so, could anyone related to my sweet, gentle Frank conceivably have inflicted the horrifying marks on this lad's back?

In my nervousness I pressed harder than I had intended. He sighed, moving his shoulder uneasily under my ministrations. He was tired, too, and I was undoubtedly hurting him, gentle as I tried to be. He set his teeth for a moment, then went on as though trying to distract himself.

'In my case it meant defending my family and my property and getting myself half killed in the process.' He pressed his lips together, clearly meaning to say no more, but after a moment he closed his eyes and began to talk again, seeking to focus his attention on anything other than his shoulder.

'It was near to four years ago. There was a levy put on the tacksmen about Fort William – food for the garrison, ponies for transport and suchlike. I wouldna say many liked it, but most would yield what they had to. Small parties of soldiers would go round with an officer and a cart or two, collecting the bits of food and things. And one day in October, yon Captain Randall came along to L – ' he caught himself quickly, with a glance at me – 'to our place.'

I nodded encouragingly, eyes on my work.

'We'd thought they'd not come so far; the place is a good distance from the fort, and not easy to get to. But they did.'

He closed his eyes briefly. 'My father was away – gone to a funeral at the next farm. And I was up in the fields wi' most of the men, for it was close to harvest, and a lot to be done. So my sister was alone in the house, except for two or three of the women servants, and they all rushed upstairs to hide their heads under the bedclothes when they saw the red coats. Thought the soldiers were sent by the Devil – and I'll no just say they were wrong.'

I laid down my cloth. The nasty part was done; now all we needed was a poultice of some kind – lacking iodine or penicillin, it was the best I could do for infection – and a good tight dressing. Eyes still closed, the young man did not appear to notice.

'I came down towards the house from behind, meaning to fetch a piece of harness from the stable, and heard the shouting and my sister screaming inside the house.'

'Oh?' I tried to make my voice as quiet and unintrusive as I could. I wanted very much to know about this Captain Randall; so far, this story had done little to dispel my original impression of him.

'I went in through the kitchen and found two of 'em riflin' the pantry, stuffin' their sacks wi' flour and bacon. I punched one of them in the head and threw the other out the window, sack and all. Then I burst into the parlour, where I found two of the redcoats with my sister, Jenny. Her dress was torn a bit, and one of them had a scratched face.'

He opened his eyes and smiled, a bit grimly. 'I didna stop to ask questions. We were going round and about, and I wasna doing too poorly, for all there were two of them, when Randall came in.'

Randall had stopped the fight by the simple expedient of holding a pistol to Jenny's head. Forced to surrender, Jamie had quickly been seized and bound by the two soldiers. Randall had smiled charmingly at his captive and said, 'Well, well. Two spitfire scratchcats here, have we? A taste of hard labour'll cure your temper, I trow, and if it doesn't, well, there's another cat you'll meet, name of nine-tails. But there's other cures for other cats, aren't there, my sweet pussy?'

Jamie stopped for a moment, jaw working. 'He was holdin' Jenny's arm behind her back, but he let go then, to bring his hand round and put it down her dress, round her breast, like.' Remembering the scene, he smiled unexpectedly. 'So,' he resumed, 'Jenny stamped down on his foot and gave him her elbow deep in the belly. And as he was bent over choking, she whirled round and gave him a good root in the stones wi' her knee.' He snorted briefly with amusement.

'Weel, at that he dropped the pistol, and she went for it, but one of the dragoons holding me got to it first.'

I had finished the bandaging and stood quiet behind him, a hand resting on his good shoulder. It seemed important he should tell me everything, but I was afraid he would stop if he were reminded of my presence.

'When he'd got back enough breath to talk with, Randall had his men haul us both outside. They bound me to the wagon tongue, and Randall struck me across the back with the flat of his sabre. He was in a black fury, but a wee bit the worse for wear, ye might say, so he couldna keep it up for long.'

The brief spurt of amusement had vanished now, and the shoulder under my hand was hard with tension. 'When he stopped, he turned to Jenny – one of the dragoons had hold of her – and asked her did she want to see more, or would she rather go into the house with him, and offer him better entertainment?' The shoulder twitched uneasily.

'I couldna move much, but I shouted to her that I wasna hurt – and I wasn't, too much – and that she was not to go with him, not if they cut my throat before her eyes.

'They were holding her behind me, so I couldna see, but from the sound of it, she spat in his face. She must have done, because he grabbed a handful of my hair, pulled my head back and set his knife against my throat.'

'I've a mind to take you at your suggestion,' Randall had said through his teeth, and dug the point just beneath the skin, far enough to draw blood.

'I could see the dagger close to my face,' Jamie said, 'and a small spot of my blood in the dust under the wagon.' His tone was almost dreamy, and I realized that, from fatigue and pain, he had lapsed into something like a hypnotic state. He might not even remember that I was there.

'I made to call out to my sister, to tell her that I'd much prefer to die than have her dishonour herself wi' such scum. Randall took the dagger from my throat, though, and thrust the blade betwixt my teeth, so I couldna call out.' He rubbed at his mouth as though still tasting bitter steel. He stopped talking, staring straight ahead.

'But what happened then?' I shouldn't have spoken, but I had to know.

He shook himself, like a man rousing from sleep, and rubbed a large hand tiredly across the back of his neck.

'She went with him,' he said abruptly. 'She thought he would kill me, and perhaps she was right. After that, I dinna ken what happened. One of the dragoons hit me in the head wi' the stock of his musket. When I woke, I was trussed up in the cart wi' the chickens, jolting down the road to Fort William.'

'I see,' I said quietly. 'I'm sorry. It must have been terrible for you.'

He smiled suddenly, the haze of fatigue gone. 'Oh, aye. Chickens are verra poor company, especially on a long journey.' Realizing that the dressing was completed, he hunched the shoulder experimentally, wincing as he did so.

'Don't do that!' I said in alarm. 'You really mustn't move it. In fact – ' I glanced at the table, to be sure there were some strips of dry fabric left – 'I'm going to strap that arm to your side. Hold still.'

He didn't speak further, but relaxed a bit under my hands when he realized that it wasn't going to hurt. I felt an odd sense of intimacy with this young Scottish stranger, due in part, I thought, to the dreadful story he had just told me, and in part to our long ride through the dark, pressed together in drowsy silence. I had not slept with many men other than my husband, but I had noticed before that to sleep, actually *sleep* with someone did give this sense of intimacy, as though your dreams had flowed out of you to mingle with his and fold you both in a blanket of unconscious knowing. A throwback of some kind, I thought. In older, more primitive times (*like these?* asked another part of my mind) it was an act of trust to sleep in the presence of another person. If the trust was mutual, simple sleep could bring you closer together than the joining of bodies.

The strapping finished, I helped him on with the rough linen shirt, easing it over the bad shoulder. He stood up to tuck it one-handed into his kilt, and smiled down at me.

'I thank ye, Claire. You've a good touch.' His hand reached out as though to touch my face, but he seemed to think better of it; the hand wavered and dropped to his side. Apparently he had felt that odd surge of intimacy too. I looked hastily away, flipping a hand in a think-nothing-of-it gesture.

My gaze travelled around the room, taking in the smoke-blackened fireplace, the narrow casement windows and the solid oak furnishings. No electric fittings. No carpeting. No shiny brass knobs on the bedstead.

It looked, in fact, like an eighteenth-century castle. But what about Frank? The man I had met in the wood looked disturbingly like him, though Jamie's description of Captain Randall was completely foreign to everything I knew about my gentle, peace-loving husband. But then, if it were true – and I was beginning to admit, even to myself, that it might be – he could in fact be almost anything. A man I knew only from a genealogical chart was not necessarily bound to resemble his descendants in conduct.

But it was Frank himself I was concerned with at the moment. If I was, in fact, in the eighteenth century, where was he? What would he do when I failed to return to Mrs Baird's? Would I ever see him again? Thinking about Frank was the last straw. Since the moment I stepped into the rock and ordinary life ceased to exist, I had been assaulted, threatened, kidnapped and jostled. I had not eaten or slept properly for more than twenty-four hours. I tried to control myself, but my lip wobbled and my eyes filled in spite of myself.

I turned to the fire to hide my face, but too late. Jamie took my hand, asking in a gentle voice what was wrong. The firelight glinted on my gold wedding band, and I began to sniffle in earnest.

'Oh, I'll . . . I'll be all right, it's all right, really, it's . . . just my . . . my husband . . . I don't – '

'Ah lass, are ye widowed, then?' His voice was so full of sympathetic concern that I lost control entirely.

'No . . . yes . . . I mean, I don't . . . yes, I suppose I am!' Overcome with emotion and tiredness, I collapsed against him, sobbing hysterically.

The lad had nice feelings. Instead of calling for help or retreating in confusion he sat down, gathered me firmly on to his lap with his good arm and sat rocking me gently, muttering soft Gaelic in my ear and smoothing my hair with one hand. I wept bitterly, surrendering momentarily to my fear and heartbroken confusion, but slowly I began to quiet a bit, as Jamie stroked my neck and back, offering me the comfort of his broad, warm chest. My sobs lessened and I began to calm myself, leaning tiredly into the curve of his shoulder. No wonder he was so good with horses, I thought blearily, feeling his fingers rubbing gently behind my ears, listening to the soothing, incomprehensible speech. If I were a horse, I'd let him ride me anywhere.

This absurd thought coincided unfortunately with my dawning realization that the young man was not completely exhausted after all. In fact, it was becoming embarrassingly obvious to both of us. I coughed and cleared my throat, wiping my eyes with my sleeve as I slid off his lap.

'I'm so sorry . . . that is, I mean, thank you for . . . but I . . .' I was babbling, backing away from him with my face flaming. He was a bit flushed, too, but not disconcerted. He reached for my hand and pulled me back. Careful not to touch me otherwise, he put his hand under my chin and forced my head up to face him.

'Ye need not be scairt of me,' he said softly. 'Nor of anyone here, so long as I'm with ye.' He let go and turned to the fire.

'You need somethin' hot, lass,' he said matter of factly,

'and a bit to eat as well. Something in your belly will help more than anything.' I laughed shakily at his attempts to ladle broth one-handed, and went to help. He was right; food did help. We ate broth and bread in a companionable silence, sharing the growing comfort of warmth and fullness.

Finally, he stood up, picking up the fallen quilt from the floor. He dropped it back on the bed and motioned me towards it. 'Do ye sleep a bit, Claire. You're worn out, and likely someone will want to talk wi' ye before too long.'

This was a sinister reminder of my precarious position, but I was too exhausted to care much. I uttered no more than a token protest at taking the bed; I had never seen anything so enticing. Jamie assured me that he could find a bed elsewhere. I fell headfirst into the pile of quilts and was asleep before he reached the door.

5

The MacKenzie

I woke in a state of complete confusion. I vaguely remembered that something was very wrong, but couldn't remember what. In fact, I had been sleeping so soundly that I couldn't remember for a moment who I was, much less where. I was warm, and the surrounding room was piercingly cold. I tried to burrow back into my cocoon of quilts but the voice that had wakened me was still nagging.

'Come then, lass! Come now, ye must get up!' The voice was deep and genially hectoring, like the barking of a sheepdog. I pried one reluctant eye open far enough to see the mountain of brown homespun.

Mistress FitzGibbons! The sight of her shocked me back to full consciousness, and memory returned. It was still true, then.

Wrapping a quilt about me against the chill, I staggered out of bed and headed for the fire as fast as possible. Mistress FitzGibbons had a bowl of hot broth waiting; I ate it, feeling like the survivor of some major bombing raid, as she laid out a pile of garments on the bed. There was a long yellowish linen chemise with a thin edging of lace, a petticoat of fine cotton, two overskirts in shades of brown and a pale lemon-yellow bodice. Brown-striped stockings of wool and a pair of yellow slippers completed the ensemble.

Brooking no protests, the dame bustled me out of my inadequate garments and oversaw my dressing from the skin out. She stood back, surveying her handiwork with satisfaction.

'The yellow suits ye, lass; I thought it would. Goes well wi' that brown hair, and it brings out the gold in your eyes. Stay, though, ye'll need a wee bit o' ribbon.' Turning out a pocket like a mealsack, she produced a handful of ribbons and bits of jewellery.

Too stunned to resist, I allowed her to dress my hair, tying back the sidelocks with primrose ribbon, clucking over the unfeminine unbecomingness of my shoulder-length bob.

'Goodness, my dear, whatever were ye thinkin', to cut your hair so short? Were ye in disguise, like? I've heard o' some lasses doin' so, to hide their sex when travellin', so as to be safe from the redcoats. 'Tis a fine day, says I, when leddies canna travel the roads in safety.' She ran on, parting me here and there, tucking in a curl or arranging a fold. Finally I was arrayed to her satisfaction.

'Weel now, that's verra gude. Now, ye've just time for a wee bite more, then I must take you to Himself.'

'Himself?' I said. I didn't care for the sound of this. Whoever Himself was, he was likely to ask difficult questions.

'Why, MacKenzie to be sure. Whoever else?'

Who else indeed? This was Castle Leoch; Himself was therefore plainly MacKenzie of Leoch, chieftain of one of the large septs of Clan MacKenzie, and as such a person of some power.

I had no appetite for the parritch that Mrs FitzGibbons brought next for my breakfast, but pretended to eat in order to gain some time for thought. By the time she came back to conduct me to MacKenzie of Leoch, I had cobbled together a rough plan.

The laird received me in a room at the top of a flight of stone steps. It was a tower room, round, and rich with paintings and tapestries hung against the curving walls. While the rest of the castle seemed comfortable enough, if somewhat bare, this room was luxuriously crowded, crammed with furniture, bristling with ornaments and warmly lit by fire and candle against the drizzle of the day outside. While the outer walls of the castle had only the high slit windows suited to resisting attack, this inner wall had been more recently furnished with long casement windows that let in what daylight there was.

As I entered, my attention was drawn at once by an enormous metal cage, cleverly engineered to fit the curve of the wall from floor to ceiling, filled with dozens of tiny birds: finches, buntings, tits and several kinds of warblers. Drawing near, my eye was filled with plump smooth bodies and bead-bright eyes, set like jewels in a background of velvet green, darting among the leaves of oak, elm and chestnut, carefully tended trees rooted in mulched pots set on the floor of the cage. The cheerful racket of conversing birds was punctuated by the whir of wings and rustle of leaves as the inhabitants flitted and hopped about their business.

'Busy wee things, are they no?' A deep, pleasant voice spoke from behind me, and I turned with a smile that froze on my face.

Callum MacKenzie shared the broad planes and high forehead of his brother Dougal, though the vital force that gave Dougal an air of intimidation was here mellowed into something more welcoming, though no less vibrant. Darker, with dove-grey rather than hazel eyes, Callum gave that same impression of intensity, of standing just slightly closer to you than was quite comfortable. At the moment, though, my discomfort arose from the fact that the beautifully modelled head and long torso ended in shockingly bowed and stumpy legs. The man who should have topped six feet came barely to my shoulder.

He kept his eyes on the birds, tactfully allowing me a much-needed moment to gain control of my features. Of course, he must be used to the reactions of people meeting him for the first time. It occurred to me, glancing around the room, to wonder how often he did meet new people. This was clearly a sanctuary; the self-constructed world of a man to whom the outer world was unwelcome – or unavailable.

'I welcome ye, mistress,' he said, with a slight bow. 'My name is Callum mac Gibbon MacKenzie, laird of this castle.

I understand from my brother that he, er, encountered you some distance from here.'

'He kidnapped me, if you want to know,' I said. I would have liked to keep the conversation cordial, but I wanted even more to get away from this castle and back to the hill with the standing stone circle. Whatever had happened to me, the answer lay there – if anywhere.

The laird's thick brows rose slightly, and a smile curved the fine-cut lips.

'Well, perhaps,' he agreed. 'Dougal is sometimes a wee bit . . . impetuous.'

'Well.' I waved a hand, indicating gracious dismissal of the matter. 'I'm prepared to admit that a misunderstanding might have arisen. But I would greatly appreciate being returned to . . . the place he took me from.'

'Mm.' Brows still raised. Callum gestured towards a chair. I sat reluctantly, and he nodded towards one of the attendants, who vanished through the door.

'I've sent for some refreshments, Mistress . . . Beauchamp, was it? I understand that my brother and his men found ye in . . . er, some apparent distress.' He seemed to be hiding a smile, and I wondered just how my supposed state of undress had been described to him.

I took a deep breath. Now it was time for the explanation I had devised. Thinking this out, I had recalled Frank's telling me, during his officer's training, about a course he had taken in withstanding interrogation. The basic principle, insofar as I remembered it, was to stick to the truth as much as humanly possible, altering only those details that must be kept secret. Less chance, the instructor explained, of slipping up in the minor aspects of one's cover story. Well, we'd have to see how effective that was.

'Well, yes. I had been attacked, you see.'

He nodded, face alight with interest. 'Aye? Attacked by whom?'

Tell the truth. 'By English soldiers. In particular, by a man named Randall.'

The patrician face changed suddenly at the name. Though Callum continued to look interested, there was an

106

increased intensity in the line of the mouth, and a deepening of the creases that bracketed it. Clearly that name was familiar. The MacKenzie chieftain sat back a bit and steepled his fingers, regarding me carefully over them.

'Ah?' he said. 'Tell me more.'

So, God help me, I told him more. I gave him in great detail the story of the confrontation between the Scots and Randall's men, since he would be able to check that with Dougal. I told him the basic facts of my conversation with Randall, since I didn't know how much the man Murtagh had overheard.

He nodded absorbedly, paying close attention.

'Aye,' he said. 'But how did you come to be there in that spot? It's far off the road to Inverness – you meant to take ship from there, I suppose?' I nodded and took a deep breath.

Now we entered perforce the realm of invention. I wished I had paid closer attention to Frank's remarks on the subject of highwaymen, but I would have to do my best. I was a widowed lady of Oxfordshire, I replied (true, so far as it went), travelling from Edinburgh by sea to distant relatives in France (that seemed safely remote). The ship in which we had embarked had been blown to the north in a violent storm, in which it had been damaged. Frightened by the severe listing of the vessel and the gallons of brine pouring through the leaking sides, I had insisted on being put ashore at first sight of land, as the crippled vessel limped into the firth. Heading for Inverness to find a new ship, we had been set upon by highwaymen, and my servant had either been killed or had run off. While I had myself succeeded in escaping from the bandits by dashing into the woods, I had to abandon all my baggage. And, while wandering lost in the wood, I had run afoul of Captain Randall and his men.

I suddenly recognized that I was enjoying this dramatic recounting, and realized abruptly the danger of excessive invention.

'Er, that's all,' I said. 'I don't know what happened to

our ship; there was a heavy fog, and we lost sight of it almost at once.'

I sat back a little, pleased with the story. Simple, neat, true in all checkable details. Callum's face expressed no more than a polite attention. He was opening his mouth to ask me a question when there was a faint rustle at the doorway. A man, one of those I had noticed in the courtyard when we arrived, stood there, holding a small leather box in one hand.

MacKenzie of Leoch excused himself gracefully and left me studying the birds, with the assurance that he would shortly return to continue our most interesting conversation.

No sooner had the door swung shut behind him than I was at the bookshelf, running my hand along the leather bindings. There were perhaps two dozen books on this shelf; more on the opposite wall. Hurriedly I flipped the opening pages of each volume. Several had no publication dates; those that did were all dated from 1720 to 1742. Callum MacKenzie obviously liked luxury, but the rest of his room gave no particular indication that he was an antiquarian. The bindings were new, with no sign of cracking or foxed pages within.

Quite beyond ordinary scruples by this time, I shamelessly rifled the olivewood desk, keeping an ear out for returning footsteps.

I found what I supposed I had been looking for in the central drawer. A half-finished letter, written in a flowing hand rendered no more legible by the eccentric spelling and total lack of punctuation. The paper was fresh and clean, and the ink crisply black. Legible or not, the date at the top of the page sprang out at me as though written in letters of fire: 3 May 1743.

When he returned a few moments later Callum found his guest seated by the casement windows, hands clasped decorously in her lap. Seated, because my legs would no longer hold me up. Hands clasped, to hide the trembling that had made it difficult for me to stuff the letter back into its resting place.

He had brought with him a tray of refreshments: mugs

of ale and fresh oatcakes spread with honey. I nibbled sparingly at these; my stomach was churning too vigorously to allow for any appetite.

After a brief apology for his absence he commiserated with me on my sad misfortune. Then he leaned back, eyed me speculatively and asked, 'But how is it, Mistress Beauchamp, that my brother's men found ye wandering about in your shift? Highwaymen would be reluctant to molest your person, as they'd likely mean to hold ye for ransom. And even with such things as I've heard of Captain Randall, I'd be surprised to hear that an officer in the English army was in the habit of raping stray travellers.'

'Oh?' I snapped. 'Well, whatever you've heard about him, I assure you he's entirely capable of it.' I had overlooked the detail of my clothing when planning my story, and wondered at what point in our encounter the man Murtagh had spotted the Captain and myself.

'Ah, well,' said Callum. 'Possible, I daresay. The man's a bad reputation, to be sure.'

'Possible?' I said. 'Why? Don't you believe what I've told you?' For the MacKenzie chieftain's face was showing a faint but definite scepticism.

'I did not say I didn't believe ye, mistress,' he answered evenly. 'But I've not held the leadership of a large sept for twenty-odd years without learning not to swallow whole every tale I'm told.'

'Well, if you don't believe I am who I say, who in bloody hell do you think I am?' I demanded.

He blinked, taken aback by my language. Then the sharp-cut features firmed again.

'That,' he said, 'remains to be seen. In the meantime, mistress, you're a welcome guest at Leoch.' He raised a hand in gracious dismissal, and the attendant near the door came forward, obviously to escort me back to my quarters.

Callum didn't say the next words, but he might as well have. They hung in the air behind me as clearly as though spoken, as I walked away:

'Until I find out who you really are.'

PART TWO

Castle Leoch

6

Callum's Hall

The small boy Mrs FitzGibbons had referred to as 'young Alick' came to fetch me to supper. This was held in a long, narrow room outfitted with tables down the length of each wall, supplied by a constant stream of servants issuing from archways at either end of the room, laden with trays, platters and jugs. The rays of May's late sunlight came through the high, narrow windows; sconces along the walls below held torches to be lighted as the daylight failed.

Banners and tartans hung on the walls between the windows, plaids and heraldry of all descriptions splotching the stones with colour. By contrast, most of the people gathered for supper were dressed in serviceable shades of grey and brown, or in the soft brown and green tartan of hunting kilts, muted tones suited for hiding in the heather.

I could feel curious glances boring into my back as young Alick led me towards the top of the room, but most of the diners kept their eyes politely upon their plates. There seemed little ceremony here; people ate as they pleased, helping themselves from the serving platters. There were some forty people sat to eat, and perhaps another ten to serve. The air was loud with conversation, most of it in Gaelic.

Callum was already seated at a table at the head of the room, stunted legs tucked out of sight beneath the scarred oak. He nodded graciously at my appearance and waved me to a seat on his left, next to a plump and pretty red-haired woman he introduced as his wife, Letitia.

'And this is my son, Hamish,' he said, dropping a hand on the shoulder of a handsome red-haired lad of seven or eight, who took his eyes off the waiting platter just long enough to acknowledge my presence with a quick nod.

I looked at the boy with interest. He looked like the other MacKenzie males I had seen, with the same broad, flat cheekbones and deep-set eyes. In fact, allowing for the difference in colouring, he might be a smaller version of his uncle Dougal, who sat next to him. The two teenage girls next to Dougal, who giggled and poked each other when introduced to me, were Dougal's daughters, Margaret and Eleanor.

Dougal gave me a brief but friendly smile before snatching the platter out from under the reaching spoon of one of his daughters and shoving it towards me.

'Ha' ye no manners, lass?' he scolded. 'Guests first!'

I rather hesitantly picked up the large horn spoon offered me. I had not been sure what sort of food was likely to be forthcoming, and was somewhat relieved to find that this platter held a row of homely and completely familiar smoked herrings.

I'd never tried to eat a herring with a spoon, but I saw nothing resembling a fork, and dimly recalled that runcible spoons would not be in general use for quite a few years yet.

Judging from the behaviour of eaters at other tables, when a spoon proved impracticable the ever-handy dirk was employed, for the slicing of meat and removal of bones. Lacking a dirk, I resolved to chew cautiously, and leaned forward to scoop up a herring, only to find the deep blue eyes of young Hamish fixed accusingly on me.

'Ye've not said grace yet,' he said severely, small face screwed into a frown. Obviously he considered me a conscienceless heathen, if not downright depraved.

'Er, perhaps you would be so kind as to say it for me?' I ventured.

The cornflower eyes popped open in surprise, but after a moment's consideration he nodded and folded his hands in a businesslike fashion. He glared round the table to ensure that everyone was in a properly reverential attitude before bowing his own head. Satisfied, he intoned,

'Some hae meat that canna eat,
And some could eat that want it.
We hae meat, and we can eat,
And so may God be thankit. Amen.'

Looking up from my respectfully folded hands I caught Callum's eye, and gave him a smile that acknowledged the sangfroid of his offspring. He suppressed his own smile and nodded gravely at his son.

'Nicely said, lad. Will ye hand round the bread?'

Conversation at table was limited to occasional requests for further food, as everyone settled down to serious eating. I found my own appetite rather lacking, partly owing to the shock of my circumstances and partly to the fact that I really didn't care for herring, when all was said and done. The bannocks were freshly baked, though, and served with honey.

I looked around the room but didn't see the red head of my erstwhile travelling companion. James MacTavish, he had said his name was.

'I hope Mr MacTavish is feeling better,' I offered, during a momentary pause for breath. 'I didn't see him when I came in.'

'MacTavish?' Letitia's delicate brows tilted over round blue eyes. I felt, rather than saw, Dougal look up beside me.

'Young Jamie,' he said briefly before returning his attention to his food.

'Jamie? Why, whatever is the matter wi' the lad?' Her full-cheeked countenance creased with concern.

'Naught but a scratch, my dear,' Callum soothed. He glanced across at his brother. 'Where is he, though, Dougal?' I imagined, perhaps, that the grey eyes held a hint of suspicion.

His brother shrugged, eyes still on his plate. 'I sent him down to the stables to help auld Alick wi' the ponies. Seemed the best place for him, all things considered.' He raised his eyes to meet his brother's gaze. 'Or did ye have some other idea?'

115

Callum seemed dubious. 'The stables? Aye, well . . . ye trust him so far?'

Dougal wiped a hand carelessly across his mouth and reached for a loaf of bread. 'It's yours to say, Callum, if ye dinna agree wi' my orders.'

Callum's lips tightened briefly but he only said, 'Nay, I reckon he'll do well enough there,' before returning to his meal.

I had some doubts myself as to a stable being the proper place for a patient with a musket wound, but was reluctant to offer an opinion in this company. I resolved to seek out the young man in question in the morning, just to assure myself that he was as suitably cared for as could be managed.

I refused further food and excused myself, pleading tiredness, which was in no way prevarication. I was so exhausted that I scarcely paid attention when Callum said, 'Goodnight to ye, then, Mistress Beauchamp. I'll send someone to bring ye to Hall in the morning.'

One of the servants, seeing me groping my way along the corridor, kindly lighted me to my chamber. She touched her candle to the one on my table, and a mellow light flickered over the massive stones of the wall, giving me a moment's feeling of entombment. Once she had left, though, I pulled the embroidered hanging away from the window and the feeling blew away with the inrush of cool air. I tried to think about everything that had happened but my mind refused to consider anything but sleep. I slid under the quilts, blew out the candle and fell asleep watching the slow rise of the moon.

It was the massive Mrs FitzGibbons who arrived again to wake me in the morning, bearing what appeared to be the full array of toiletries available to a well-born Scottish lady. Lead combs to darken the eyebrows and lashes, pots of powdered orrisroot and rice powder, even a stick of what I assumed was kohl, though I had never seen any, and a delicate lidded porcelain cup of French rouge, incised with a row of gilded swans.

Mrs FitzGibbons also had a striped green overskirt and bodice of silk, with yellow woollen stockings, as a change from the homespun I had been provided with the day before. Whatever 'Hall' involved, it seemed to be an occasion of some consequence. I was tempted to insist on attending in my own clothes, just to be contrary, but the memory of fat Rupert's response to my 'shift' was sufficient to deter me.

Besides I rather liked Callum, despite the fact that he apparently intended to keep me here for the foreseeable future. Well, we'd just see about *that*, I thought as I did my best with the rouge. Dougal had said the young man I had doctored was in the stables, hadn't he? And stables presumably had horses or ponies upon which one could ride away. I resolved to go looking for Jamie MacTavish as soon as Hall was over with.

Hall turned out to be just that; the dining hall where I had eaten the night before. Now it was transformed, though; tables, benches and stools pushed back against the walls, the head table removed and replaced by a substantial carved chair of dark wood, covered with what I assumed must be the MacKenzie tartan, a plaid of green and blue with a faint red and white over-check. Sprigs of holly decorated the walls, and there were fresh rushes strewn on the stone flags.

A young piper was inflating a set of small pipes behind the empty chair, with numerous sighs and wheezes. Near him were what I assumed must be the intimate members of Callum's staff: a thin-faced man in trews and smocked shirt, who lounged against the wall; a balding little man in a coat of fine brocade, clearly a scribe of some sort, as he was seated at a small table equipped with inkhorn, quills and paper; two brawny kilted men with the attitude of guards; and to one side, one of the largest men I have ever seen.

I stared at this giant with some awe. Coarse black hair grew far down on his forehead, nearly meeting the beetling eyebrows. Similar mats covered the immense forearms, exposed by the rolled-up sleeves of his shirt. Unlike most of the men I had seen, the giant did not seem to be armed, save for a tiny knife he carried in his stocking top; I could barely make out the stubby hilt in the thickets of black curls that covered his legs above the gaily checked hose. A broad leather belt circled what must be a forty-inch waist, but carried neither dirk nor sword. In spite of his size the man had an amiable expression, and seemed to be joking with the thin-faced man, who looked like a marionette in comparison with his huge conversant.

The piper suddenly began to play, with a preliminary belch followed at once by an ear-splitting screech that eventually settled down into something resembling a tune.

There were some thirty or forty people present, all seeming somewhat better-dressed and groomed than the diners of the night before. All heads turned to the lower end of the hall where, after a pause for the music to build up steam, Callum entered, followed at a few paces by his brother Dougal.

Both were clearly dressed for ceremony, in MacKenzie kilts and well-cut coats, Callum's of pale green and Dougal's of russet, both with the plaid slung across their chests and secured at one shoulder by a large jewelled brooch. Callum's black hair was loose today, carefully oiled and curled upon his shoulders. Dougal's was still clubbed back in a queue that nearly matched the russet satin of his coat.

Callum walked slowly up the length of the hall, nodding and smiling to faces on either side. Looking across the hall I could see another archway, near where his chair was placed. Clearly he could have entered by that doorway instead of the one at the far end of the room. So it was deliberate, this flaunting of his twisted legs and ungainly waddle on the long progress to his seat. Deliberate, too, the contrast with his tall, straight-bodied younger brother, who looked neither to left nor right but walked straight behind Callum to the wooden chair and took up his station standing close behind.

Callum sat and waited for a moment, then raised one hand. The pipes' wailing died away in a pitiful whine, and Hall began.

It quickly became apparent that this was the regular

118

occasion on which the laird of Castle Leoch dispensed justice to his tacksmen and tenants, hearing cases and settling disputes. There was an agenda; the balding scribe read out the names and the various parties came forward in their turn.

While some cases were presented in English, most of the proceedings were held in Gaelic. Just as I had decided that one man, a rather moth-eaten specimen with a goatskin pouch at his belt, was accusing his neighbour of nothing less than murder, arson and wife-stealing, Callum raised his eyebrows and said something quick in Gaelic that had both complainant and defendant clutching their sides with laughter. Wiping his eyes, the complainant nodded at last, and offered a hand to his opponent, as the scribe scribbled busily, quill scratching like a mouse's feet.

I was fifth on the agenda. A placement, I thought, carefully calculated to indicate to the assembled crowd the importance of my presence in the castle.

For my benefit English was spoken during my presentation.

'Mistress Beauchamp, will ye stand forth?' called the scribe.

Urged forward by an unnecessary shove from Mrs Fitz-Gibbons' meaty hand, I stumbled out into the clear space before Callum and rather awkwardly curtsied, as I had seen other females do. The shoes I had been given did not distinguish between right foot and left, being in either case only an oblong of formed leather which made graceful manoeuvring difficult. There was a stir of interest through the crowd as Callum paid me the honour of getting up from his chair. He offered me his hand, which I took in order not to fall flat on my face.

Rising from the curtsy, mentally cursing the shoes, I found myself staring at Dougal's chest. As my captor, it was apparently up to him to make formal application for my reception – or captivity, depending on how you wanted to look at it. I waited with some interest to see just how the brothers had decided to explain me.

'Sir,' began Dougal, bowing formally to Callum, 'we pray

your indulgence and mercy with regard to a lady in need of succour and safe refuge. Mistress Claire Beauchamp, an English lady of Oxford, finding herself set upon by highwaymen and her servant most traitorously killed, fled into the forests, where she was discovered and rescued by myself and my men. We beg that Castle Leoch might offer this lady refuge until' – he paused, and a cynical smile twisted his mouth – 'her *English* connections may be apprised of her whereabouts and due provision made for her safe transport.'

I didn't miss the emphasis laid on English, and neither did anyone else in the hall, I was sure. So, I was to be tolerated, but held under suspicion. Had he said French, I would have been considered a friendly or, at worst, neutral intrusion. It might be more difficult than I had expected to get away from the castle.

Callum bowed graciously to me and offered me the unlimited hospitality of his humble hearth, or words to that effect. I curtsied again, with somewhat more success, and retired to the ranks, followed by curious but more or less friendly stares.

Until this point the cases seemed to have been of interest chiefly to the parties involved. The spectators had chatted quietly among themselves, waiting their turns. My own appearance had been met with an interested murmur of speculation and, I thought, approval.

But now there was an excited stir through the hall. A burly man stepped forward into the clear space, dragging a young girl by the hand. She looked about sixteen, with a pretty, pouting face and long yellow hair tied back with blue ribbon. She stumbled into the space and stood alone, while the man behind her expostulated in Gaelic, waving his arms and occasionally pointing at her in illustration or accusation. Small murmurs ran through the crowd as he talked.

Mrs FitzGibbons, her bulk resting on a sturdy stool, was craning forward with interest. I leaned forward and whispered in her ear.

'What's she done?'

The huge dame replied without moving her lips or taking her eyes from the action.

'Her father accuses her of loose behaviour, consortin' improperly wi' young men against his orders,' muttered Mistress FitzGibbons, leaning her bulk backwards on the stool. 'Her father wishes MacKenzie to have her punished for disobedience.'

'Punished? How?' I hissed as quietly as I could.

'Shhh.'

In the centre, attention now focused on Callum, who was considering the girl and her father. Looking from one to the other, he began to speak. Frowning, he rapped his knuckles sharply on the arm of his chair, and a shiver ran through the crowd.

'He's decided,' whispered Mrs FitzGibbons unnecessarily. What he had decided was also clear; the giant stirred for the first time, producing and flexing a leather strap in a leisurely manner. The two guards took the terrified girl by the arms and turned her so that her back was to Callum and her father. She began to cry, but made no appeal. The crowd was watching with the sort of intent excitement that attends public executions and road accidents. Suddenly a Gaelic voice from the back of the crowd rose, audible over the shuffle and murmur.

Heads turned to locate the speaker. Mrs FitzGibbons craned, even rising on tiptoe to see. I had no idea what had been said, but I thought I recognized that voice, deep but soft, with a spiky way of clipping the final consonants.

The crowd parted, and Jamie MacTavish came out into the clear space. He inclined his head respectfully to MacKenzie, then spoke some more. Whatever he said seemed to cause some controversy. Callum, Dougal, the little scribe and the girl's father all seemed to be getting into the act.

'What is it?' I muttered to Mrs Fitz, as I thought of her. My patient was looking much better than when last seen, though still a bit white-faced, I thought. He'd found a clean shirt somewhere; the empty right sleeve had been tucked into the waist of his kilt.

Mrs Fitz was watching the proceedings with great interest.

'The lad's offering to take the girl's punishment for her,' she said absently, peeking around a spectator in front of us.

'What? But he's injured! Surely they won't let him do something like that!' I spoke as quietly as I could under the hum of the crowd.

Mrs Fitz shook her head. 'I canna say, lass. They're arguin' it now. See, 'tis allowable for a man o' her own clan to offer for her, but the lad is no a MacKenzie.'

'He's not?' I was surprised, having naively assumed that all the men in the group that had captured me came from Castle Leoch.

'O' course not,' said Mrs Fitz impatiently. 'Do ye no see his tartan?'

Of course I did, once she had pointed it out. While Jamie also wore a hunting tartan in shades of green and brown, the colours were different from those of the other men present. It was a deeper brown, almost a bark colour, with a faint blue stripe.

Apparently Dougal's contribution was the deciding argument. The knot of advisers dispersed and the crowd hushed, falling back to wait. The two guards released the girl, who ran back into the crowd, and Jamie stepped forward to take her place between them. I watched in horror as they moved to take his arms, but he spoke in Gaelic to the man with the strap, and the two guards fell back. Amazingly, a wide, impudent grin lighted Jamie's face briefly. Stranger still, there was a quick answering smile on the face of the giant.

'What did he say?' I demanded of my interpreter.

'He chooses fists rather than the strap. A man may choose so, though a woman may not.'

'Fists?' I had no time to question further. The executioner drew back a fist like a ham and drove it into Jamie's abdomen, doubling him up and driving his breath out with a gasp. The man waited for him to straighten up before moving in and administering a series of sharp jabs to the ribs and arms. Jamie made no effort to defend himself, merely shifting his balance to remain upright in the face. of the assault.

The next blow was to the face. I winced and shut my eyes involuntarily as Jamie's head rocked back. The executioner took his time between blows, careful not to knock his victim down or strike too many times in one spot. It was a scientific beating, skilfully engineered to inflict bruising pain, but not to disable or maim. One of Jamie's eyes was swelling shut and he was breathing heavily, but otherwise he didn't appear too badly off.

I was in an agony of apprehension lest one of the blows re-damage the wounded shoulder. My strapping job was still in place, but it wouldn't hold for long against this sort of treatment. How long was this going to go on? The room was silent except for the smacking thud of flesh on flesh and an occasional soft grunt.

'Wee Angus'll stop when blood's drawn,' whispered Mrs Fitz, apparently divining my unasked question. 'Usually when the nose is broken.'

'That's barbarous,' I hissed fiercely. Several people around us looked at me censoriously.

The executioner apparently now decided that the punishment had gone on for the prescribed length of time. He drew back and let fly a massive blow; Jamie staggered and fell to his knees. The two guards hurried forward to pull him to his feet, and as he raised his head I could see blood welling from his battered mouth. The crowd burst into a hum of relief and the executioner stepped back, satisfied with the performance of his duty.

One guard held Jamie's arm, supporting him as he shook his head to clear it. The girl had disappeared. Jamie raised his head and looked directly at the towering executioner. Amazingly, he smiled again, as best he could. The bleeding lips moved.

'Thank you,' he said, with some difficulty, and bowed formally to the bigger man before turning to go. The attention of the crowd shifted back to MacKenzie and the next case before him.

I saw Jamie leave the hall by the door in the opposite wall.

Having more interest in him now than in the proceedings, I took my leave of Mrs FitzGibbons with a quick word and pushed my way across the hall to follow him.

I found him in a small side courtyard, leaning against a wellhead and dabbing at his mouth with his shirt tail.

'Here, use this,' I said, offering him a kerchief from my pocket.

'Unh.' He accepted it with a noise that I took for thanks. A pale, watery sun had come out by now, and I looked the young man over carefully by its light. A split lip and badly swollen eye seemed to be the chief injuries, though there were marks along the jaw and neck that would be black bruises soon.

'Is your mouth cut inside too?'

'Unh-huh.' He bent down and I pulled his lower jaw, gently turning down the lip to examine the inside. There was a deep gash in the glistening cheek lining, and a couple of small punctures in the pinkness of the inner lip. Blood mixed with saliva welled up and overflowed.

'Water,' he said with some difficulty, blotting the bloody trickle that ran down his chin.

'Right.' Luckily there was a bucket and horn cup on the rim of the well. He rinsed his mouth and spat several times, then splashed water over the rest of his face.

'What did you do that for?' I asked curiously.

'What?' he said, straightening up and wiping his face on his sleeve. He felt the split lip gingerly, wincing slightly.

'Offer to take that girl's punishment for her. Do you know her?' I felt a certain diffidence about asking, but I really wanted to know what lay behind that quixotic gesture.

'I ken who she is. Havena spoken to her, though.'

'Then why did you do it?' He shrugged, a movement that also made him wince.

'It would have shamed the lass, to be beaten in Hall. Easier for me.'

'Easier?' I echoed incredulously, looking at his smashed face. He was probing his bruised ribs experimentally with his free hand, but looked up and gave me a one-sided grin.

'Aye. She's verra young. She would ha' been shamed

before everyone as knows her, and it would take a long time to get over it. I'm sore, but no really damaged; I'll get over it in a day or two.'

'But why you?' I asked. He looked as though he thought this an odd question.

'Why not me?' he said.

Why not? I wanted to say. Because you didn't know her, she was nothing to you. Because you were already hurt. Because it takes something rather special in the way of guts to stand up in front of a crowd and let someone hit you in the face, no matter what your motive.

'Well, a bayonet cut through the trapezius might be considered a good reason,' I said dryly.

He looked amused, fingering the area in question.

'Trapezius, is it? I didna know that.'

'Och, here ye are, lad! I see ye've found your healer already; perhaps I won't be needed.' Mrs FitzGibbons waddled through the narrow entrance to the courtyard, squeezing a bit. She held a tray with a few jars, a large bowl and a clean linen towel.

'I haven't done anything but fetch some water,' I said. 'I think he's not badly hurt, but I'm not sure what we can do besides wash his face for him.'

'Och, now, there's always somethin', always somethin' that can be done,' she said comfortably. 'That eye, now, lad, let's have a look at that.' Jamie sat obligingly on the edge of the well, turning his face towards her. Pudgy fingers pressed gently on the purple swelling, leaving white depressions that faded quickly.

'Still bleedin' under the skin. Leeches will help, then.' She lifted the cover from the bowl, revealing several small dark sluglike objects, an inch or two long, covered with a disagreeable-looking liquid. Scooping out two of them, she pressed one to the flesh just under the brow bone and the other just below the eye.

'See,' she explained to me, 'once a bruise is set, like, leeches do ye no good. But where ye ha' a swellin' like this, as is still comin' up, that means the blood is flowin' under the skin, and leeches can pull it out.'

I watched, fascinated and disgusted. 'Doesn't that hurt?' I asked Jamie. He shook his head, making the leeches bounce obscenely.

'No. Feels a bit cold, though.' Mrs Fitz was busy with her jars and bottles.

'Too many folk misuses leeches,' she instructed me. 'They're verra helpful sometimes, but ye must understand how. When ye use 'em on an old bruise, they just take healthy blood and it does the bruise no good. Also ye must be careful not to use too many at a time; they'll weaken someone as is verra ill or has lost blood already.'

I listened respectfully, absorbing all this information, though I sincerely hoped I would never be asked to make use of it.

'Now, lad, rinse your mouth wi' this; 'twill cleanse the cuts and ease the pain. Willow-bark tea,' she explained in an aside to me. I nodded; I recalled vaguely from a long-ago botany lecture hearing that willow bark in fact contained salicylic acid, the active ingredient in aspirin.

'Won't the willow bark increase the chance of bleeding?' I asked. Mrs Fitz nodded approvingly.

'Aye. It do sometimes. That's why ye follow it wi' a good handful of St John's wort soaked in vinegar; that stops bleedin', if it's gathered under a full moon and ground up well.' Jamie obediently swilled his mouth with the astringent solution, eyes watering at the sting of the aromatic vinegar.

The leeches were fully engorged by now, swollen to four times their original size. The dark wrinkled skins were now stretched and shiny; they looked like rounded, polished stones. One leech dropped suddenly off, bouncing to the ground at my feet. Mrs Fitz scooped it up deftly, bending easily despite her bulk, and dropped it back in the bowl. Grasping the other leech delicately just behind the jaws, she pulled gently, making the head stretch.

'Ye don't want to pull too hard, lass,' she said. 'Sometimes they burst.' I shuddered involuntarily at the idea. 'But if they're nearly full, sometimes they'll come off easy. If they don't, just leave 'em be and they'll fall off by themselves.' The leech did, in fact, let go easily, leaving a trickle of blood where it had been attached. I blotted the tiny wound with the corner of a towel dipped in the vinegar solution. To my surprise the leeches had worked; the swelling was substantially reduced and the eye was at least partially open, though the lid was still puffy. Mrs Fitz examined it critically and decided against the use of another leech.

'Ye'll be a sight tomorrow, lad, and no mistake,' she said, shaking her head, 'but at least ye'll be able to see oot o' that eye. What ye want now is a wee bit o' raw meat on it, and a drop o' broth wi' ale in it, for strengthenin' purposes. Come along to the kitchen in a bit, and I'll find some for ye.' She scooped up her tray, pausing for a moment.

'What ye did was kindly meant, lad. Laoghaire is my granddaughter, ye ken; I'll thank ye for her. Though she had better thank ye herself, if she's any manners at all.' She patted Jamie's cheek, and padded heavily off.

I examined him carefully; the archaic medical treatment had been surprisingly effective. The eye was still somewhat swollen, but only slightly discoloured, and the cut through the lip was now a clean, bloodless line, only slightly darker than the surrounding tissue.

'How do you feel?' I asked.

'Fine.' I must have looked askance at this, because he smiled, still careful of his mouth. 'It's only bruises, ye know. I'll have to thank ye again, it seems; this makes three times in three days you've doctored me. Ye'll be thinking I'm fair clumsy.'

I touched a purple mark on his jaw. 'Not clumsy. A little reckless, perhaps.' A flutter of movement at the courtyard entrance caught my eye; a flash of yellow and blue. The girl named Laoghaire hung back shyly, seeing me.

'I think someone wants to speak with you alone,' I said. 'I'll leave you. The bandages on your shoulder can come off tomorrow, though. I'll find you then.'

'Aye. Thank ye again.' He squeezed my hand lightly in farewell. I went out, looking curiously at the girl as I passed. She was even prettier close up, with soft blue eyes and rose-petal skin. She glowed as she looked at Jamie. I left the courtyard, wondering whether in fact his gallant gesture had been quite so altruistic as I supposed.

Next morning, roused at daylight by the twittering of birds outside and people inside, I dressed and found my way through the draughty corridors to the hall, now restored to its normal identity as a refectory. Enormous cauldrons of porridge were being dispensed, together with bannocks baked on the hearth and spread with honey. The smell of steaming food was almost strong enough to lean against. I felt still off balance and confused, but an ample breakfast heartened me enough to explore a bit.

Finding Mrs FitzGibbons up to her dimpled elbows in floured dough, I announced that I was looking for Jamie, in order to remove his bandages and inspect the healing of the shoulder wounds. She summoned one of her tiny minions with the wave of a massive flour-smeared hand.

'Young Alick, do ye run and find Jamie, the new horse-breaker. Tell 'im to come back wi' ye to ha' his shoulder seen to. We shall be in the herb garden.' A sharp fingersnap sent the lad scampering out to locate my patient.

Turning the kneading over to a maid, Mrs Fitz rinsed her hands and turned to me.

'It will take a while yet before they're back. Would ye care for a look at the herb garden? It would seem ye've some knowledge of plants, and if you've a mind to, ye might lend a hand there in your spare moments.'

The herb garden, valuable repository of healing and flavours that it was, was cradled in an inner courtyard, large enough to allow for sun, but sheltered from spring winds, with its own wellhead. Fennel and mustard bordered the garden to the west, camomile to the south, and a row of blackberry brambles marked the north border, with the castle wall itself forming the eastern edge, an additional shelter from the prevailing winds. I correctly identified the green spikes of late crocus and soft-leaved French sorrel springing out of the rich dark earth. Mrs Fitz pointed out foxglove, sweet violet and fumitory, along with a few I did not recognize.

Late spring was planting time. The basket on Mrs Fitz's arm carried a profusion of garlic cloves, the source of the summer's crop. The plump dame handed me the basket along with a digging stick for planting. Apparently I had lazed about the castle long enough; until Callum decided about me, Mrs Fitz could always find work for an idle hand.

'Here, m'dear. Do ye set 'em here along the south side, between the thyme and foxglove.' She showed me how to divide the heads into individual buds without disturbing the tough casing, then how to plant them. It was simple enough, just poke each clove into the ground, blunt end down, buried about an inch and a half below the surface. She got up, dusting her voluminous skirts.

'Keep back a few heads,' she advised me. 'Divide 'em and plant the buds single, one here and one there, all round the garden. Garlic keeps the wee bugs awa' from the other plants. Onions and yarrow will do the same. And pinch the dead marigold heads, but keep them, they're useful.'

Numerous marigolds were scattered throughout the garden, bursting into golden flower. Just then the small lad she had sent in search of Jamie came up, out of breath from the run. He reported that the patient refused to leave his work.

'He says,' panted the boy, 'as 'e doesna hurt bad enough to need doctorin', but thank ye for yer consairn.' Mrs Fitz shrugged at this not altogether reassuring message.

'Weel, if he won't come, he won't. Ye might go out to the paddock near noontide, though, lass, if ye've a mind to. He may not stop to be doctored, but he'll stop for food, if I ken young men. Young Alick here will come back for ye at noontide and guide ye to the paddock.' Leaving me to plant the rest of the garlic, Mrs Fitz sailed away like a galleon, young Alick bobbing in her wake.

I worked contentedly through the morning, planting garlic, pinching off dead flower heads, digging out weeds and carrying on the gardener's never-ending battle against snails, slugs and other pests. Here, though, the battle was waged bare-handed, with no assistance from chemical compounds. I was so absorbed in my work that I didn't notice the reappearance of young Alick until he coughed politely to attract my attention. Not one to waste words, he waited barely long enough for me to rise and dust my skirt before vanishing through the courtyard gate.

The paddock to which he led me was some way from the stables, in a grassy meadow. Three young ponies frolicked gaily in the meadow nearby. Another, a clean-looking young bay mare, was tethered to the paddock fence, with a light blanket thrown across her back.

Jamie was sidling cautiously up along one side of the mare, who was watching his approach with considerable suspicion. He placed his one free arm lightly on her back, talking softly, ready to pull back if the mare objected. She rolled her eyes and snorted, but didn't move. Reaching slowly, he leaned across the blanket, still muttering to the mare, and very gradually rested his weight on her back. She reared slightly and shuffled, but he persisted, raising his voice just a trifle.

Just then the mare turned her head and saw me and the boy approaching. Scenting some threat, she reared, whinnying, and swung to face us, crushing Jamie against the paddock fence. Snorting and bucking, she leapt and kicked against the restraining tether. Jamie rolled under the fence, out of the way of the flailing hooves. He rose painfully to his feet, swearing in Gaelic, and turned to see what had caused this setback to his work.

When he saw who it was, his thunderous expression changed at once to one of courteous welcome, though I gathered our appearance was still not as opportune as might have been wished. The basket of lunch, thoughtfully provided by Mrs Fitz, who did in fact know young men, did a good deal to restore his temper.

'Ahh, settle then, ye blasted beastie,' he remarked to the mare, still snorting and dancing on her tether. Dismissing young Alick with a friendly cuff, he retrieved the mare's fallen blanket, and shaking off the dust of the paddock he gallantly spread it for me to sit on.

I tactfully avoided any reference to the recent contretemps with the mare, instead pouring ale and offering chunks of bread and cheese.

He ate with a single-minded concentration that reminded me of his absence from the dining hall the two nights before.

'Slept through it,' he said when I asked him where he had been. 'I went to sleep directly I left ye at the castle, and didna wake till dawn yesterday. I worked a bit yesterday after Hall, then sat down on a pile of hay to rest a bit before dinner.' He laughed. 'Woke up this morning still sitting there, wi' a pony nibbling at my ear.'

I thought the rest had done him good; the bruises from yesterday's beating were dark, but the skin around them had a good healthy colour, and certainly he had a good appetite.

I watched him polish off the last of the meal, tidily dabbing stray crumbs from his shirt with a moistened fingertip and popping them into his mouth.

'You've a healthy appetite,' I said, laughing. 'I think you'd eat grass if there was nothing else.'

'I have,' he said in all seriousness. 'It doesna taste bad, but it's no verra filling.'

I was startled, then thought he must be teasing me. 'When?' I asked.

'Winter, year before last. I was livin' in the woods with the . . . with a group of lads, raidin' into the Lowlands. We'd had poor luck for a week and more, and no food amongst us left to speak of. We'd get a bit of parritch now and then from a cottar, but those folk are so poor themselves there's seldom anything to spare. They'll always find something to give a stranger, mind, but twenty strangers is a bit much, even for a Highlander's hospitality.'

He grinned suddenly. 'Have ye heard – well, no, ye wouldna. I was goin' to say had ye heard the grace they say in the cottar-houses.'

'No. How does it go?'

He shook his hair out of his eyes and recited,

> *'Hurley, hurley, round the table,*
> *Eat as muckle as ye're able.*

131

Eat muckle, pooch nane,
Hurley, hurley, Amen.'

'Pooch nane?' I said, diverted. He patted the sporran on his belt.

'Put it in your belly, not your bag,' he explained.

He reached out for one of the long-bladed grasses and pulled it smoothly from its sheath. He rolled it slowly between his palms, making the floppy grain-heads fly out from the stem.

'It was a late winter then, and mild, which was lucky, or we'd not have lasted. We could usually snare a few rabbits – ate them raw, sometimes, if we couldna risk a fire – and once in a while some venison, but there'd been no game for days, this time I'm talkin' of.'

Square white teeth crunched down on the grass stem. I plucked a stem myself and nibbled the end. It was sweet and faintly acid, but there was only an inch or so of stem tender enough to eat; hardly much nourishment there.

Tossing the half-eaten stalk away, Jamie plucked another and went on with his story.

'There was a light snow a few days before; just a crust under the trees, and mud everywhere else. I was looking for *fungas*, ye know, the big orange things that grow on the trees low down, sometimes – and put my foot through a rind of snow into a patch of grass, growing in an open spot between the trees; reckon a little sun got in there sometimes. Usually the deer find those patches. They paw away the snow and eat the grass down to the roots. They hadn't found this one yet, and I thought if they managed the winter that way, why not me? I was hungry enough I'd ha' boiled my boots and eaten them, did I not need them to walk in, so I ate the grass, down to the roots, like the deer do.'

'How long had you been without food?' I asked, fascinated and appalled.

'Three days wi' nothing; a week with naught more than drammach – a handful of oats and a little water. Aye,' he said, reminiscently viewing the grass stalk in his hand, 'winter grass is tough, and it's sour – not like this – but I didna pay it much mind.' He grinned at me suddenly.

'I didna pay much mind to the thought that a deer's got four stomachs, either, while I had but one. Gave me terrible cramps, and I had wind for days. One of the older men told me later that if you're going to eat grass, ye boil it first, but I didna know that at the time. Wouldn't ha' mattered; I was too hungry to wait.' He scrambled to his feet, leaning down to give me a hand up.

'Best get back to work. Thank ye for the food, lass.' He handed me the basket, and headed for the stables, sun glinting on his hair as though on a trove of gold and copper coins.

I made my way slowly back to the castle, thinking about men who lived in cold mud and ate grass. It didn't occur to me until I had reached the courtyard that I had forgotten all about his shoulder.

7

Davie Beaton's Closet

To my surprise, one of Callum's kilted men-at-arms was waiting for me near the gate when I returned to the castle. Himself would be obliged, I was told, if I would wait upon him in his chambers.

The long casements were open in the laird's private sanctum, and the wind swept through the branches of the captive trees with a rush and a murmur that gave the illusion of being outdoors.

The laird himself was writing at his desk when I entered, but stopped at once and rose to greet me. After a few words of inquiry as to my health and well-being, he led me over to the cages against the wall, where we admired the tiny inhabitants as they chirped and hopped through the foliage, excited by the wind.

'Dougal and Mrs Fitz both say as you've quite some skill as a healer,' Callum remarked conversationally, extending a finger through the mesh of the cage. Well accustomed to this, apparently, a small grey bunting swooped down and made a neat landing, tiny claws gripping the finger and wings slightly spread to keep its balance. He stroked its head gently with the calloused forefinger of the other hand. I saw the thickened skin around the nail and wondered at it; it hardly seemed likely that he did much manual labour.

I shrugged. 'It doesn't take that much skill to dress a superficial wound.'

He smiled. 'Maybe not, but it takes a bit of skill to do it in the pitch-black dark by the side of a track, eh? And Mrs Fitz says you've mended one of her wee lads' fingers as was broken, and bound up a kitchen-maid's scalded arm this morning as well.'

'That's nothing very difficult, either,' I replied, wondering what he was getting at. He gestured to an attendant, who quickly fetched a small bowl from one of the drawers of the secretary. Removing the lid, Callum began scattering seed from it through the mesh of the cage. The tiny birds popped down from the branches like so many cricket balls bouncing on a pitch, and the bunting flew down to join its fellows on the ground.

'No connections to Clan Beaton, have ye?' he asked. I remembered Mrs FitzGibbons asking at our first meeting, *Are ye a charmer, then? A Beaton?*

'None. What have the Clan Beaton to do with medical treatment?'

Callum eyed me in surprise. 'You've not heard of them? The healers of Clan Beaton are famous through the Highlands. Travelling healers, many of them. We had one here for a time, in fact.'

'Had one? What happened to him?' I asked.

'He died,' Callum responded matter of factly. 'Caught a fever and it carried him off within a week. We've not had a healer since, save Mrs Fitz.'

'She seems very competent,' I said, thinking of her efficient treatment of the young man Jamie's injuries. Thinking of that made me think of what had caused them, and I felt a wave of resentment towards Callum. Resentment, and caution as well. This man, I reminded myself, was law, jury and judge to the people in his domain – and clearly accustomed to having things his own way.

He nodded, still intent on the birds. He scattered the rest of the seed, favouring a late-coming grey-blue warbler with the last handful.

'Oh, aye. She's quite a hand with such matters, but she's more than enough to take care of already, running the whole castle and everyone in it – including me,' he said with a sudden charming grin.

'I was wondering,' he said, taking swift advantage of my answering smile, 'being as you've not a great deal to occupy your time at present, you might think of having a look at the things Davie Beaton left behind him. You might know the uses of a few of his medicines and such.'

'Well ... I suppose so. Why not?' In fact, I was curious to see what the late Mr Beaton had considered useful in the way of paraphernalia.

'Angus or I could show the lady down, sir,' the attendant suggested respectfully.

'Don't trouble yourself, John,' Callum said, gesturing the man politely away. 'I'll show Mistress Beauchamp myself.'

His progress down the stairs was slow and obviously painful. Just as obviously he didn't wish for help, and I offered none.

The surgery of the late Beaton proved to be in a remote corner of the castle, tucked out of sight behind the kitchens. It was in close proximity to nothing save the graveyard, in which its late proprietor now rested. In the outer wall of the castle, the narrow, dark room boasted only one of the tiny slit windows, set high in the wall so that a flat plane of sunlight knifed through the air, separating the darkness of the high vaulted ceiling from the deeper gloom of the floor below.

Peering past Callum into the dim recesses of the room I made out a tall cabinet equipped with dozens of tiny drawers, each with a label in curlicue script. Jars, boxes and vials of all shapes and sizes were neatly stacked on the shelves above a counter where the late Beaton evidently had been in the habit of mixing medicines, judging from the residue of stains and a crusted mortar that rested there.

Callum went ahead of me into the room. Shimmering motes disturbed by his entry swirled upwards into the bar of sunlight like dust raised from the breaking of a tomb. He stood for a moment, letting his eyes grow used to the dimness, then walked forward slowly, looking from side to side. I thought perhaps it was the first time he had ever been in this room.

Watching his halting progress as he traversed the narrow room, I said, 'You know, massage can help a bit. With the pain, I mean.' I caught a flash from the grey eyes, and wished for a moment that I hadn't spoken, but the spark disappeared almost at once, replaced by his usual expression of courteous attention.

'It needs to be done forcefully,' I said, 'at the base of the spine, especially.'

'I know,' he said. 'Angus Mhor does it for me, at night.' He paused, fingering one of the vials. 'It would seem you do know a bit about healing, then.'

'A bit.' I was cautious, hoping he didn't mean to test me by asking what the assorted medicaments were used for. The label on the vial he was holding said PURLES OVIS. Anyone's guess what *that* was. Luckily, he put the vial back and drew a finger gingerly through the dust on a large chest near the wall.

'Been some time since anyone's been here,' he said. 'I'll have Mrs Fitz send some of her wee lassies along to clean up a bit, shall I?'

I opened a cupboard door and coughed at the resulting cloud of dust. 'Perhaps you'd better,' I agreed. There was a book on the lower shelf of the cupboard, a fat volume bound in blue leather. Lifting it, I discovered a smaller book beneath, this one bound cheaply in black cloth, much worn along the edges.

This second book proved to be Beaton's daily log book, in which he had tidily recorded the names of his patients, details of their ailments and the course of treatment prescribed. A methodical man, I thought with approval. One entry read: '2nd February, AD 1741. Sarah Graham MacKenzie, injury to thumb by reason of catching the appendage on edge of spinning reel. Application of boiled pennyroyal, followed by poultice of: one part each yarrow, St John'swort, ground slaters and mouse-ear, mixed in a base of fine clay.' Slaters? Mouse-ear? Some of the herbs on the shelves, no doubt.

'Did Sarah MacKenzie's thumb heal well?' I asked Callum, shutting the book.

'Sarah? Ah,' he said thoughtfully. 'No, I believe not.'

'Really? I wonder what happened,' I said. 'Perhaps I could take a look at it later.'

He shook his head, and I thought I caught a glimpse of grim amusement showing in the lines of his full, curved lips.

'Why not?' I asked. 'Has she left the castle, then?'

'Ye might say so,' he answered. The amusement was now apparent. 'She's dead.'

I stared at him as he picked his way across the dusty stone floor towards the doorway.

'It's to be hoped you'll do somewhat better as a healer than the late Davie Beaton, Mrs Beauchamp,' he said. He turned and paused at the door, regarding me sardonically. The sunbeam held him as though in a spotlight.

'Ye could hardly do worse,' he said, and vanished into the dark.

Next day, having spent some time in the herb garden, I returned to investigate Beaton's domain. I wandered up and down the narrow little room, looking at everything. Likely most of it was rubbish, but there might be a few useful things to be salvaged. I pulled out one of the tiny drawers in the apothecary's chest, letting loose a gust of camphor. Well, *that* was useful, right enough. I pushed the drawer in again and rubbed my dusty fingers on my skirt. Perhaps I should wait until Mrs Fitz's merry maids had had a chance to clean the place before I continued my investigations.

I peered out into the corridor. Deserted. No noises, either. But I was not naive enough to assume that no one was nearby. Whether by order or by tact – they were fairly subtle about it – I was being watched. When I went to the garden, someone went with me. When I climbed the stair to my room I would see someone casually glance up from the foot to see which way I turned. And as we had ridden in, I hadn't failed to note the armed guards sheltering under the overhang from the rain. No, I definitely wasn't going to be allowed simply to walk out of here, let alone be provided with transport and means to leave.

I sighed. At least I was alone for the moment. And solitude was something I very much wanted, at least for a little.

I had tried repeatedly to think about everything that had happened to me since I stepped through the standing stone.

But things moved so rapidly around this place that I had hardly had a moment to myself when I wasn't asleep.

Apparently I had one now, though. I pulled the dusty chest away from the wall and sat down, leaning back against the stones. They were very solid. I reached back and rested my palms against them, thinking about the stone circle, trying to recall every tiny detail of what had happened.

The screaming stones were the last thing I could truly say I remembered. And even that I had doubts about. The screaming had kept up, all the time. It was possible, I thought, that the noise came not from the stones themselves but from . . . whatever . . . I had stepped into. Were the stones a door of some kind? And into what did they open? There simply were no words for whatever it was. A crack through time, I supposed, because clearly I had been *then*, and I was *now*, and the stones were the only connection.

And the sounds. They had been overwhelming, but looking back from a short distance, I thought they were very similar to the sounds of battle. The field hospital at which I was stationed had been shelled three times. Even knowing that the flimsy walls of our temporary structures would not protect us, still doctors, nurses and orderlies had all dashed inside at the first alarm, huddling together for courage. Courage is in very short supply when there are mortar shells screaming overhead and bombs going off next door. And the kind of terror I had felt then was the closest thing to what I had felt in the stone.

I now realized that I did recall some things about the actual trip through the stone. Very minor things. I remembered a sensation of physical struggle, as though I were caught in a current of some kind. Yes, I had deliberately fought against it, whatever it was. There were images in the current, too, I thought. Not pictures, exactly, more like incomplete thoughts. Some were terrifying and I had fought away from them as I . . . well, as I 'passed'. Had I fought towards others? I had some consciousness of fighting towards a surface of some kind. Had I actually *chosen* to come to this particular time because it offered some sort of haven from that whirling maelstrom?

I shook my head. I could find no answers by thinking about it. Nothing was clear except the fact that I would have to go back to the standing stones.

'Mistress?' A soft Scottish voice from the doorway made me look up. Two girls, perhaps sixteen or seventeen, hung back shyly in the corridor. They were roughly dressed, barefoot, with homespun scarves covering their hair. The one who had spoken carried a brush and several folded cloths, while her companion held a steaming pail. Mrs Fitz's lasses, here to clean the surgery.

'We'll no be disturbin' ye, mistress?' one asked anxiously.

'No, no,' I assured them. 'I was about to leave anyway.'

'You've missed dinner,' the other informed me. 'But Mrs Fitz said to tell ye as there's food for ye in the kitchens whenever ye like to go there.'

I glanced out of the window at the end of the corridor. The sun was, in fact, a little past the zenith, and I became conscious of increasing hunger pangs. I smiled at the girls. 'I might just do that. Thank you.'

I brought dinner to the fields again, fearing that Jamie might get nothing to eat until supper otherwise. Seated on the grass, watching him eat, I asked him why he had been living in the wild, raiding cattle and thieving into the Lowlands. I had seen enough by now both of the folk who came and went from the nearby village and of the castle dwellers, to be able to tell that Jamie was both higher born and much better educated than most. It seemed likely that he came from a fairly wealthy family, judging from the brief description he had given me of their farm estate. Why was he so far from home?

'I'm an outlaw,' he said, as though surprised that I didn't know. 'The English have a price of ten pounds sterling on my head. Not quite so much as a highwayman,' he said deprecatingly, 'but a bit more than a pickpocket.'

'Just for obstruction?' I said in disbelief. Ten pounds sterling here was half the yearly income of a small farm; I couldn't imagine a single escaped prisoner was worth that much to the English government.

140

'Och, no. Murder.' I choked on a mouthful of oatcake. Jamie pounded me helpfully on the back until I could speak again.

Eyes watering, I asked, 'Wh-who did you k-kill?'

He shrugged. 'Well, it's a bit odd. I didna actually kill the man whose murder I'm outlawed for. Mind ye, I've done for a few other redcoats along the way, so I suppose it's not unjust.'

He paused and shifted his shoulders, as though rubbing against some invisible wall. I had noticed him do it before, when I had doctored him and seen the marks on his back.

'It was at Fort William. I could hardly move for a day or two, after I'd been flogged the second time, and then I had fever from the wounds. Once I could stand again, though, some . . . friends made shift to get me out of the camp, by means I'd best not go into. Anyhow, there was some stramash as we left, and an English sergeant was shot – by coincidence, it was the man that gave me the first flogging. I'd not ha' shot him, though; I had nothing personal against him, and I was too weak to do more than hang on to the pony, in any case.' The wide mouth tightened and thinned. 'Though had it been Captain Randall, I expect I'd ha' made the effort.' He eased his shoulders again, stretching the rough linen shirt taut across his back, and shrugged.

'There it is, though. That's one reason I do not go far from the castle alone. This far into the Highlands, there's little chance of running into an English patrol, but they do cross from the Lowlands quite often. And then there's the Watch, though they'll not come near the castle, either. Callum's not much need of their services, having his own men to hand.' He smiled, running a hand through his bright copper hair till it stood on end like hedgehog quills.

'I'm no precisely inconspicuous, ye ken. I doubt there's informers in the castle itself, but there might be a few here and there about the countryside as would be glad enough to earn a few pence by letting the English know where I was, did they know I was a wanted man.' He smiled at me. 'Ye'll have gathered the name's not MacTavish?'

'Does the laird know?'

141

'That I'm an outlaw? Oh, aye, Callum knows. Most people through this part of the Highlands likely know that; what happened at Fort William caused quite a bit of stir at the time, and news travels fast here. What they won't know is that Jamie MacTavish is the man that's wanted; provided nobody that knows me by my own name sees me.' His hair was still sticking up absurdly. I had a sudden impulse to smooth it for him, but resisted.

'Why do you wear your hair cropped?' I asked suddenly, then blushed. 'I'm sorry, it's none of my business. I only wondered, since most of the other men I've seen here wear it long . . .'

He flattened the spikes, looking a bit self-conscious.

'I used to wear mine long as well. It's short now because the monks had to shave the back of my head and it's had but a few months to grow again.' He bent forward at the waist, inviting me to inspect the back of his head.

'See there, across the back?' I could certainly feel it, and see it as well when I spread the thick hair aside; a six-inch weal of freshly healed scar tissue, still pink and slightly raised. I pressed gently along its length. Cleanly healed, and a nice neat job by whoever had stitched it; a wound like that must have gaped and bled considerably.

'Do you have headaches?' I asked professionally. He sat up, smoothing the hair down over the wound. He nodded.

'Sometimes, though none so bad as it was. I was blind for a month or so after it happened, and my head ached like fury all the time. The headache started to go away when my sight came back.' He blinked several times, as though testing his vision.

'Fades a bit sometimes,' he explained, 'if I'm verra tired. Things get blurry round the edges.'

'It's a wonder it didn't kill you,' I said. 'You must have a good thick skull on you.'

'That I have. Solid bone, according to my sister.' We both laughed.

'How did it happen?' I asked. He frowned, and a look of uncertainty came over his face.

'Weel, there's just the question,' he answered slowly. 'I

142

dinna remember anything about it. I was down near the coast with a few lads at the cattle-lifting Laggan. Last I knew, I was pushing my way uphill through a wee thicket; I remember pricking my hand on a hollybush and thinking the blood drops looked just like the berries. And the next thing I remember is waking in France, in the Abbey of Sainte Anne de Beaupré, with my head throbbing like a drum and someone I couldn't see giving me something cool to drink.'

He rubbed the back of his head as though it ached yet.

'Sometimes I think I remember little bits of things – a lamp over my head, swinging back and forth, a sort of sweet oily taste on my lips, people saying things to me – but I do not know if any of it's real. I know the monks gave me opium, and I dreamed nearly all the time.' He pressed his fingers flat over closed eyelids.

'There was one dream I had over and over. Tree roots growing inside my head, big gnarled things, growing and swelling, pushing out through my eyes, thrusting down my throat to choke me. It went on and on, with the roots twisting and curling and getting bigger all the time. Finally they'd get big enough to burst my skull and I'd wake hearing the sound of the bones popping apart.' He grimaced. 'Sort of a juicy, cracking noise, like gunshots under water.'

'Ugh!'

A shadow fell suddenly over us and a stout boot shot out and nudged Jamie in the ribs.

'Idle young bastard,' the newcomer said without heat, 'stuffin' yerself while the horses run wild. And when's that filly goin' to be broke, hey, lad?'

'None the sooner for my starving myself, Alick,' Jamie replied. 'Meanwhile, have a bit; there's plenty.' He reached a chunk of cheese up to a hand knotted with arthritis. The fingers, permanently curled in a half grip, slowly closed on the cheese as their owner sank down on the grass.

With unexpectedly courtly manners, Jamie introduced the visitor; Alick McMahon MacKenzie, Master of Horse of Castle Leoch. I raised my estimate of Callum's wealth by a few notches. In the Highlands, where the lack of roads made the little Highland ponies only slightly better than a man's feet for transport, ordinary horses were much more a measure of riches than a practical addition to the livestock of an estate.

A squat figure in leather breeks and rough shirt, the Master of Horse had an air of authority sufficient, I thought, to quell the most recalcitrant stallion. An 'eye like Mars, to threaten or command', the quotation sprang at once to mind. A single eye it was, the other being covered with a black cloth patch. As if to make up for the loss, his eyebrows sprouted profusely from a central point, sporting long grey hairs like insects' antennae that waved threateningly from the basic brown tufts.

After an initial nod of acknowledgement, auld Alick (for so Jamie referred to him, no doubt to distinguish him from the young Alick who had been my guide) ignored me, dividing his attention instead between the food and the three young horses switching their tails in the meadow below. I rather lost interest during a long discussion involving the parentage of several no doubt distinguished horses not among those present, details of breeding records of the entire stable for several years, and a number of incomprehensible points of equine conformation, dealing with hocks, withers, shoulders and other items of anatomy. Since the only points I noticed on a horse were nose, tail and ears, the subtleties were lost on me.

I leaned back on my elbows and basked in the warming spring sun. There was a curious peace in this day, a sense of things working quietly in their proper courses, nothing minding the upsets and turmoils of human concerns. Perhaps it was the peace that one always finds outdoors, far enough away from buildings and clatter. Maybe it was the result of gardening, that quiet sense of pleasure in touching growing things, the satisfaction of helping them thrive. Perhaps just the relief of finally having found work to do, rather than rattling around the castle feeling out of place, conspicuous as an inkblot on parchment.

In spite of the fact that I took no part in the horsey conversation, I didn't feel out of place here at all. Old Alick

144

acted as though I were merely a part of the landscape, and while Jamie cast an occasional glance my way, he, too, gradually ignored me as their conversation shifted into the sliding rhythms of Gaelic, a sure sign of a Scot's emotional involvement in his subject matter. Since I gathered no sense from the talk, it was as soothing as listening to bees humming in the heather blossoms. Oddly contented and drowsy, I pushed away all thoughts of Callum's suspicions, my own predicament and other disturbing ideas. 'Sufficient unto the day,' I thought sleepily, picking up the biblical quotation from some recess of memory.

It may have been the chill from a passing cloud, or the changed tone of the men's conversation that woke me some time later. The talk had switched back to English, and the tone was serious, no longer the meandering chat of the horse-obsessed.

'It's no but a week till the Gathering, laddie,' Alick was saying. 'Have ye made up your mind what you'll do then?'

There was a long sigh from Jamie. 'No, Alick, that I havena. Sometimes I think one way, sometimes the other. Granted that it's good here, working wi' the beasts and with you.' There was a smile somewhere in the young man's voice, which disappeared as he went on. 'And Callum's promised me to . . . well, you'll not know about that. But kiss the iron and change my name to MacKenzie, and forswear all I'm born to? Nay, I canna make up my mind to it.'

'Stubborn as your da, ye are,' remarked Alick, though the words held a tone of grudging approval. 'You've the look of him about ye sometimes, for all you're tall and fair as your mother's folk.'

'Knew him, did ye?' Jamie sounded interested.

'Oh, a bit. And heard more. I've been here at Leoch since before your parents wed, ye ken. And to hear Dougal and Callum speak of Black Brian, ye'd think he was the De'il himself, if not worse. And your ma the Virgin Mary, swept awa' to the Bad Place by him.'

Jamie laughed. 'And I'm like him, am I?'

'Ye are and all that, laddie. Aye, I see why it'd stick in

your craw to be Callum's man, weel enough. But there's considerations the other way, no? If it comes to fighting for the Stuarts, say, and Dougal has his way. Come out on the right side in *that* fight, laddie, and you'll ha' your land back and more besides, whatever Callum does.'

Jamie replied with what I had come to think of as a 'Scottish noise', that indeterminate sound made low in the throat that can be interpreted to mean almost anything. This particular noise seemed to indicate some doubt as to the likelihood of such a desirable outcome.

'Aye,' he said, 'and if Dougal doesna get his way, then what? Or if the fight goes against the house of Stuart?'

Alick made a guttural sound of his own. 'Then you stay here, laddie. Be Master of Horse in my place; I'll not last so much longer, and there's no better hand I've seen wi' a horse.'

Jamie's modest grunt indicated appreciation of the compliment.

The older man went on, disregarding such interruptions. 'The MacKenzies are kin to ye, too; it's not a matter of forswearing your blood. And there's other considerations, too' – his voice took on a teasing note – 'like Mistress Laoghaire, perhaps?'

He got another noise in response, this one indicating embarrassment and dismissal.

'See now, lad, a young lad doesna let himself be beaten for the sake of a lass he cares nothin' for. And ye know her father will no let her wed outside the clan.'

'She was verra young, Alick, and I felt sorry for her,' said Jamie defensively. 'There's nothin' more to it than that.' This time it was Alick who made the Scottish noise, a guttural snort full of derisory disbelief.

'Tell that one to the gable end, laddie, it's no more brains than to believe ye. Weel, even if it's no Laoghaire – and ye could do a deal worse, mark me – ye'd be a better prospect for marriage did ye ha' a bit of money and a future; as ye would if ye're next Master. Ye could take yer choice of the lasses – if one doesna choose *you* first!' Alick snorted with the half-choked mirth of a man who seldom laughs. 'Flies round a honeypot would be nothin' to it, lad! Penniless and nameless as ye are now, the lasses still sigh after ye – I've seen 'em!' More snorting. 'Even this Sassenach wench can no keep away from ye, and her a new widow!'

Wishing to prevent what promised to be a series of increasingly distasteful personal remarks, I decided it was time to be officially awake. Stretching and yawning, I sat up, ostentatiously rubbing my eyes to avoid looking at either of the speakers.

'Mmmm. I seem to have fallen asleep,' I said, blinking prettily at them. Jamie, rather red around the ears, was taking an exaggerated interest in packing up the remains of the picnic. Auld Alick stared down at me, apparently taking notice of me for the first time.

'Interested in horses, are ye, lass?' he demanded. I could hardly say no, under the circumstances. Agreeing that horses were most interesting, I was treated to a detailed discourse on the filly in the paddock, now standing drowsily at rest, tail twitching for the occasional fly.

'Ye're welcome to come and watch any time, lass,' Alick concluded, 'so long as ye dinna get so close ye distract the horses. They need to work, ye ken.' This was plainly intended as a dismissal, but I stood my ground, remembering my original purpose in coming here.

'Yes, I'll be careful next time,' I promised. 'But before I go back to the castle, I wanted to check Jamie's shoulder and take the dressings off.'

Alick nodded slowly, but to my surprise, it was Jamie who refused my attentions, turning away to go back to the paddock.

'Ah, it'll wait awhile, lass,' he said, looking away. 'There's much to be done yet today; perhaps later, after supper, hey?' This seemed very odd; he hadn't been in any hurry to return to work earlier. But I could hardly force him to submit to my ministrations if he didn't want to. Shrugging, I agreed to meet him after supper, and turned uphill to go back to the castle.

As I made my way back up the hill I considered the shape of the scar on Jamie's head. It wasn't a straight line, as might be made by an English broadsword. The wound was curved, as though made by a blade with a definite bend. A blade like a Lochaber axe? But so far as I knew, the murderous axes had been – no, were, I corrected myself – carried only by clansmen.

It was only as I walked away that it occurred to me. For a young man on the run, with unknown enemies, Jamie had been remarkably confiding to a stranger.

Leaving the picnic basket in the kitchens, I returned to the late Beaton's surgery, now dustless and pristine after the visitation by Mrs Fitz's energetic assistants. Even the dozens of glass vials in the cupboard gleamed in the dim light from the window.

The cupboard seemed a good place to start, with an inventory of the herbs and medicaments already on hand. I had spent a few moments the previous night, before sleep overcame me, thumbing through the blue leather-bound book I had taken from the surgery. This proved to be *The Physician's Guide and Handbook*, a listing of recipes for the treatment of assorted symptoms and diseases, the ingredients for which were apparently displayed before me.

The book was divided into several sections: 'Centauries, Vomitories and Electuaries', 'Troches and Lodochs', 'Assorted Plasters and Their Virtus', 'Decoctions and Theriacs', and a quite extensive section ominously headed with the single word 'Purges'.

Reading through a few of the recipes, the reason for the late Davie Beaton's lack of success with his patients became apparent. 'For headache,' read one entry, 'take ye one ball of horse dunge, this to be carefully dried, pounded to powder, and the whole drunk, stirred into hot ale.' 'For convulsions in children, five leeches to be applied behind the ear.' And a few pages later, 'Decoctions made of the roots of celandine, turmeric and juice of 200 slaters cannot but be of great service in a case of jaundice.' I closed the book, marvelling at the large number of the late doctor's patients who, according to his meticulous log, had not only survived the treatment meted out to them but actually recovered from their original ailments.

There was a large brown glass jar in the front containing several suspicious-looking balls, and in view of Beaton's recipes, I had a good idea what they might be. Turning the jar around, I triumphantly read the hand-lettered label: DUNGE OF HORSES. Reflecting that such a substance likely didn't improve much with keeping, I gingerly set the jar aside without opening it.

Subsequent investigation proved PURLES OVIS to be a latinate version of a similar substance, this time from sheep. MOUSE-EAR also proved to be animal in nature, rather than herbal; I pushed aside the vial of tiny pinkish dried ears with a small shudder.

I had been wondering about the 'slaters', spelt variously as 'slatters', 'sclaters' and 'slatears', which seemed to be an important ingredient in a number of medicines, so I was pleased to see a clear cork-stoppered vial with this name on the label. The vial was about half full of what appeared to be small grey pills. These were no more than a quarter of an inch in diameter, and so perfectly round that I marvelled at Beaton's dispensing skill. I brought the vial up close to my face, wondering at its lightness. Then I saw the fine striations across each 'pill' and the tiny legs, folded into the central crease. I hastily set the vial down, wiping my hand on my apron, and made another entry in the mental list I had been compiling. For 'slaters', read 'woodlice'.

There were a number of more or less harmless substances in Beaton's jars, as well as several containing dried herbs or extractions that might actually be helpful. I found some of the aromatic vinegar that Mrs Fitz had used to treat Jamie MacTavish's injuries. Also angelica, wormwood, rosemary and something labelled STINKING ARAG. I opened this one cautiously, but it proved to be nothing more than the tender tips of fir branches, and a pleasant balsamic fragrance floated out of the unsealed bottle. I left the bottle open and set it on the table to perfume the air in the dark little room as I went on with my inventory.

I discarded jars of dried snails; OIL OF EARTHWORMS –

149

which appeared to be exactly that; VINUM MILLEPEDATUM –
millipedes, these crushed to pieces and soaked in wine;
POWDER OF EGYPTIANE MUMMIE – an indeterminate-
looking dust, whose origin I thought more likely a silty
streambank than a pharaoh's tomb; PIGEONS BLOOD, ant
eggs, a number of dried toads painstakingly packed in moss,
and HUMAN SKULL, POWDERED. Whose? I wondered.

It took most of the afternoon to finish my inspections
of the cupboard and multi-drawered cabinet. When I had
finished, there was a great heap of discarded bottles, boxes
and flasks set outside the door of the surgery for disposal,
and a much smaller collection of possibly useful items
stowed back into the cupboard.

I had considered a large packet of cobwebs for some
time, hesitating between the piles. Both the *Guide* and my
own dim memories of folk medicine held that spider's web
was efficacious in dressing wounds. While my own inclination was to consider such usage unhygienic in the
extreme, my experience with bandages by the roadside had
shown me the desirability of having something with adhesive
as well as absorbent properties for dressings. At last I set
the cobwebs back in the cupboard, resolving to see whether
there might be a way of sterilizing them. Not boiling, I
thought. Maybe steam would cleanse them without destroying the stickiness?

I rubbed my hands against my apron, considering. I had
inventoried almost everything now – except the wooden
chest against the wall. I flung back the lid and recoiled at
once from the stench that gusted out.

The chest was the repository of the surgical side of
Beaton's practice. Within were a number of sinister-looking
saws, knives, chisels and other tools looking more suited to
building construction than to use on delicate human tissues.
The stench apparently derived from the fact that Davie
Beaton had seen no particular benefit to cleaning his instruments between uses. I grimaced in distaste at the sight of
the dark stains on some of the blades, and slammed shut
the lid.

I dragged the chest towards the door, intending to tell

Mrs Fitz that the instruments, once safely boiled, should be given to the castle carpenter, if there were such a personage.

A stir behind alerted me, in time to avoid crashing into the person who had just come in. I turned to see two young men, one supporting the other, who was hopping on one foot. The lame foot was bound up in an untidy bundle of rags, stained with fresh blood.

I glanced around, then gestured at the chest, for lack of anything else. 'Sit down,' I said. Apparently the new physician of Castle Leoch was now in practice.

8

An Evening's Entertainment

I lay on my bed feeling altogether exhausted. Oddly enough, I had quite enjoyed the rummage through the memorabilia of the last Beaton, and treating a few patients, with however meagre a resource, had made me feel truly solid and useful once more. I still missed Frank terribly, and worried about when and how I was to get back to the stone circle, but feeling flesh and bone beneath my fingers, taking pulses, inspecting tongues and eyeballs, all the familiar routine, had done much to settle the feeling of hollow panic that had been with me since my fall through the rock. However strange my circumstances and however out of place I might be, it was somehow very comforting to realize that these were truly other people. Warm-fleshed and hairy, with hearts that could be felt beating and lungs that breathed audibly. Bad-smelling, louse-ridden and filthy, some of them, but that was nothing new to me. Certainly no worse than conditions in a field hospital, and the injuries were so far reassuringly minor. It was immensely satisfying to be able once again to relieve a pain, reset a joint, repair damage. To take responsibility for the welfare of others made me feel less victimized by the whims of whatever impossible fate had brought me here, and I was grateful to Callum for suggesting it.

Callum MacKenzie. Now there was a strange man. A cultured man, courteous to a fault, and thoughtful as well, with a reserve that all but hid the steely core within. The steel was much more evident in his brother Dougal. A warrior born, that one. And yet, to see them together, it was clear which was the stronger. Callum was a chieftain, twisted legs and all.

Toulouse-Lautrec syndrome. I had never seen a case

152

before, but I had heard it described. Named for its most famous sufferer (who did not yet exist, I reminded myself), it was a degenerative disease of bone and connective tissue. Victims often appeared normal, if sickly, until their early teens, when the long bones of the legs, under the stress of bearing a body upright, began to crumble and collapse upon themselves.

The pasty skin, with its premature wrinkling, was another outward effect of the poor circulation that characterized the disease. Likewise the dryness and pronounced callousing of fingers and toes that I had already noticed. As the legs twisted and bowed, the spine was put under stress and often twisted as well, causing immense discomfort to the victim. I mentally read back the textbook description to myself, idly smoothing out the tangles of my hair with my fingers. Low white-cell count, increased susceptibility to infection, liable to early arthritis. Because of the poor circulation and the degeneration of connective tissue, victims were invariably sterile, and often impotent as well.

I stopped suddenly, thinking of Hamish. *My son*, Callum had said, proudly introducing the boy. Mmm, I thought to myself. Perhaps not impotent then. Or perhaps so. But rather fortunate for Letitia that so many of the MacKenzie males resembled each other to such a marked degree.

I was disturbed in these interesting ruminations by a sudden knock on the door. One of the ubiquitous small boys stood without, bearing an invitation from Callum himself. There was to be singing in the hall, he said, and Himself would be honoured by my presence, if I cared to come down.

I was curious to see Callum again, in light of my recent speculations. So with a quick glance in the looking glass and a futile smoothing of my hair, I shut the door behind me and followed my escort through the cold and winding corridors.

The hall looked different at night, quite festive with pine torches crackling all along the walls, popping with an occasional blue flare of turpentine. A large fire burned on the hearth, sustained by two huge, slow-burning logs.

153

The tables and benches were pushed back slightly to allow for a clear space near the hearth; apparently that was to be the centre of entertainment, for Callum's large carved chair was placed to one side. Callum himself was seated in it, a warm rug laid across his legs and a small table with decanter and goblets within easy reach.

Seeing me hesitating in the archway he beckoned me to his side with a friendly gesture, waving me on to a nearby bench.

'I'm pleased you've come down, Mistress Claire,' he said, pleasantly informal. 'Gwyllyn will be glad of a new ear for his songs, though we're always willing to listen.' The MacKenzie chieftain looked rather tired, I thought; the wide shoulders slumped a bit and the premature lines on his face were deeply cut.

I murmured something inconsequential and looked around the hall. People were beginning to drift in, and sometimes out, standing in small groups to chat, gradually taking seats on the benches ranged against the walls.

'I beg your pardon?' I turned, having missed Callum's words in the growing noise, to find him offering me the decanter, a lovely bell-shaped thing of pale green crystal. The liquid within, seen through the glass, seemed green as the sea-depths, but once poured out it proved to be a beautiful pale-rose colour, with the most delicious bouquet. The taste was fully up to the promise, and I closed my eyes in bliss, letting the wine fumes tickle the back of my palate before reluctantly allowing each sip of nectar to trickle down my throat.

'Good, isn't it?' The deep voice held a note of amusement, and I opened my eyes to find Callum smiling at me in approval.

I opened my mouth to reply, and found that the smooth delicacy of the taste was deceptive; the wine was strong enough to cause a mild paralysis of the vocal cords.

'Won – wonderful,' I managed to get out.

Callum nodded. 'Aye, that it is. Rhenish, ye know. You're not familiar with it?' I shook my head as he tipped the decanter over my goblet, filling the bowl with a pool of glowing rose. He held his own goblet by the stem, turning it before his face so that the firelight lit the contents with dashes of vermilion.

'You know good wine, though,' Callum said, tilting the glass to enjoy the rich scent himself. 'But that's natural, I suppose, with your family French. Or half French, I should say,' he corrected himself with a quick smile. 'What part of France do your folk come from?'

I hesitated a moment, then thought: Stick to the truth, so far as you can; and answered, 'It's an old connection, and not a close one, but such relatives as I may have there come from the north, near Compiègne.' I was mildly startled to realize that at this point, my relatives *were* in fact near Compiègne. Stick to the truth, indeed.

'Ah. Never been there yourself, though?'

I tilted the glass, shaking my head as I did so. I closed my eyes and breathed deeply, inhaling the wine's perfume.

'No,' I said, eyes still closed. 'I haven't met any of my relatives there, either.' I opened my eyes to find him watching me closely. 'I told you that.'

He nodded, not at all perturbed. 'So ye did.' His eyes were a beautiful soft grey, thickly lashed with black. A very attractive man, Callum MacKenzie, at least down to the waist. My gaze flickered past him to the group nearest the fire, where I could see his wife, Letitia, part of a group of several ladies, all engaged in animated conversation with Dougal MacKenzie. Also a most attractive man, and a whole one.

I pulled my attention back to Callum and found him gazing abstractedly at one of the wall hangings.

'And as I also told you before,' I said abruptly, bringing him out of his momentary inattention, 'I'd like to be on my way to France as soon as possible.'

'So ye did,' he said again pleasantly, and picked up the decanter with a questioning lift of the brow. I held my goblet steady, gesturing at the halfway point to indicate that I wanted only a little, but he filled the delicate hollow nearly to the rim once more.

'Well, as *I* told *you*, Mistress Beauchamp,' he said, eyes fixed on the rising wine, 'I think ye must be content to bide here a bit, until suitable arrangements can be made for your transport. No need for haste, after all. It's only the spring of the year, and months before the autumn storms make the crossing chancy.' He raised eyes and decanter together, and fixed me with a shrewd look.

'But if ye'd care to give me the names of your kin in France, I might manage to send word ahead – so they'll be fettled against your coming, eh?'

Bluff called, I had little choice but to mutter something of the yes-well-perhaps-later variety, and excuse myself hastily on the pretext of visiting the necessary facilities before the singing should start. Game and set to Callum, but not yet match.

My pretext had not been entirely fictitious, and it took me some time, wandering about the darkened halls of the castle, to find the place I was seeking. Groping my way back, wine glass still in hand, I found the lighted archway to the hall, but realized on entering that I had reached the lower entrance, and was now at the opposite end of the hall from Callum. Under the circumstances this suited me quite well, and I strolled unobtrusively into the long room, taking pains to merge with small groups of people as I worked my way along the wall towards one of the benches.

Casting a look at the upper end of the hall, I saw a slender man who must be Gwyllyn the bard, judging from the small harp he carried. At Callum's gesture, a servant hastened up to bring the bard a stool, on which he seated himself and proceeded to tune the harp, plucking lightly at the strings, ear close to the instrument. Callum poured another glass of wine from his own decanter, and with another wave dispatched it via the servant in the bard's direction.

'Oh, he called for his pipe, and he called for his bowl, and he called for his fiddlers threeee,' I sang irreverently under my breath, eliciting an odd look from the girl Laoghaire. She was seated under a tapestry showing a hunter with six elongated and cross-eyed dogs, in erratic pursuit of a single hare.

'Bit of overkill, don't you think?' I said breezily, waving a hand at it and plumping myself down beside her on the bench.

'Oh! er, aye,' she answered cautiously, edging away slightly. I tried to engage her in friendly conversation but she answered mostly in monosyllables, blushing and starting when I spoke to her, and I soon gave it up, my attention drawn by the scene at the end of the room.

Harp tuned to his satisfaction, Gwyllyn had brought out from his coat three wooden flutes of varying sizes, which he laid on a small table, ready to hand.

Suddenly I noticed that Laoghaire was not sharing my interest in the bard and his instruments. She had stiffened slightly and was peering over my shoulder towards the lower archway, simultaneously leaning back into the shadows under the tapestry to avoid detection.

Following the direction of her gaze I spotted the tall, red-haired figure of Jamie MacTavish, just entering the hall.

'Ah! The gallant hero! Fancy him, do you?' I asked the girl at my side. She shook her head frantically, but the brilliant blush staining her cheeks was answer enough.

'Well, we'll see what we can do, shall we?' I said, feeling expansive and magnanimous. I stood up and waved cheerily to attract his attention.

Catching my signal, the young man made his way through the crowd, smiling. I didn't know what might have passed between them in the courtyard, but I thought his manner in greeting the girl was warm, if still formal. His bow to me was slightly more relaxed; after the forced intimacy of our relations to date, he could hardly treat me as a stranger.

A few tentative notes from the upper end of the hall signalled an imminent beginning to the entertainment, and we hastily took our places, Jamie seating himself between Laoghaire and myself.

Gwyllyn was an insignificant-looking man, light-boned and mousy-haired, but you didn't see him once he began to sing. He only served as a focus, a place for the eyes to rest while the ears enjoyed themselves. He began with a simple song, something in Gaelic with a strong rhyming

157

chime to the lines, accompanied by the merest touch of his harp strings, so that each plucked string seemed by its vibration to carry the echo of the words from one line to the next. The voice was also deceptively simple. You thought at first there was nothing much to it – pleasant, but without much strength. And then you found that the sound went straight through you, and each syllable was crystal clear, whether you understood it or not, echoing poignantly inside your head.

The song was received with a warm surge of applause, and the singer launched at once into another, this time in Welsh, I thought. It sounded like a very tuneful sort of gargling to me, but those around me seemed to follow well enough; doubtless they had heard it before.

During a brief pause for retuning, I asked Jamie in a low voice, 'Has Gwyllyn been at the castle long?' Then, remembering, I said, 'Oh, but you wouldn't know, would you? I'd forgotten you were so new here yourself.'

'I've been here before,' he answered, turning his attention to me. 'Spent a year at Leoch when I was sixteen or so, and Gwyllyn was here then. Callum's fond of his music, ye see. He pays Gwyllyn well to stay. Has to; the Welshman would be welcome at any laird's hearth where he chose to roost.'

'I remember when you were here, before.' It was Laoghaire, still blushing pinkly but determined to join the conversation. Jamie turned his head to include her, smiling slightly.

'Do ye, then? You canna have been more than seven or eight yourself. I'd not think I was much to see then, so as to be remembered.' Turning politely to me, he said, 'Do ye have the Welsh, then?'

'Well, I do remember, though,' Laoghaire said, pursuing it. 'You were, er, ah ... I mean ... do ye not remember me, from then?' Her hands fiddled nervously with the folds of her skirt. She bit her nails, I saw.

Jamie's attention seemed distracted by a group of people across the room, arguing in Gaelic about something.

'Ah?' he said, vaguely. 'No, I dinna think so. Still,' he

said with a smile, pulling his attention suddenly back to her, 'I wouldna be likely to. A young burke of sixteen's too taken up wi' his own grand self to pay much heed to what he thinks are naught but a rabble of snot-nosed bairns.'

I gathered he had meant this remark to be deprecatory to himself, rather than his listener, but the effect was not what he might have hoped. I thought perhaps a brief pause to let Laoghaire recover her self-possession was in order, and broke in hastily with, 'No, I don't know any Welsh at all. Do you have any idea what it is he was saying?'

'Oh, aye.' And Jamie launched into what appeared to be a verbatim recitation of the song, translated into English. It was an old ballad, apparently, about a young man who loved a young woman (what else?), but feeling unworthy of her because he was poor, went off to make his fortune at sea. The young man was shipwrecked, met sea serpents who menaced him and mermaids who entranced him, had adventures, found treasure, and came home at last only to find his young woman wed to his best friend, who, if somewhat poorer, also apparently had better sense.

'And which would you do?' I asked, teasing a bit. 'Would you be the young man who wouldn't marry without money, or would you take the girl and let the money go hang?' This question seemed to interest Laoghaire as well, who cocked her head to hear the answer, meanwhile pretending great attention to an air on the flute that Gwyllyn had begun.

'Me?' Jamie seemed entertained by the question. 'Well, as I've no money to start with, and precious little chance of ever getting any, I suppose I'd count myself lucky to find a lass would wed me without.' He shook his head, grinning. 'I've no stomach for sea serpents.'

He opened his mouth to say something further but was silenced by Laoghaire, who laid a hand timidly on his arm, then blushing, snatched it back as though he were red hot.

'Sshh,' she said. 'I mean . . . he's going to tell stories. Do ye not want to hear?'

'Oh, aye.' Jamie sat forward a bit in anticipation, then realizing that he blocked my view, insisted that I sit on the other side of him, displacing Laoghaire down the bench. I could see the girl was not best pleased at this arrangement, and I tried to protest that I was all right as I was, but he was firm about it.

'No, you'll see and hear better there. And then, if he speaks in the Gaelic, I can whisper in your ear what he says.'

Each part of the bard's performance had been greeted with warm applause, though people chatted quietly while he played, making a deep hum below the high, sweet strains of harp or flute. But now a sort of expectant hush descended on the hall. Gwyllyn's speaking voice was as clear as his singing, each word pitched to reach the end of the high, draughty hall without strain.

'It was a time, two hundred years ago . . .' He spoke in English, and I felt a sudden sense of *déjà vu*. It was exactly the way our guide on Loch Ness had spoken, telling legends of the Great Glen.

It was not a story of ghosts or heroes, though, but a tale of the Wee Folk he told.

'There was a clan of the Wee Folk as lived near Dundreggan,' he began. 'And the hill there is named for the dragon that dwelt there, that Fionn slew and buried where he fell, so the dun is named as it is. And after the passing of Fionn and the Feinn, the Wee Folk that came to dwell in the dun came to want mothers of men to be wet nurses to their own fairy bairns, for a man has something that a fairy has not, and the Wee Folk thought that it might pass through the mother's milk to their own small ones.

'Now, Ewan MacDonald of Dundreggan was out in the dark, tending his beasts, on the night when his wife bore her firstborn son. A gust of the night wind passed by him, and in the breath of the wind he heard his wife's sighing. She sighed as she sighed before the child was born, and hearing her there, Ewan MacDonald turned and flung his knife into the wind in the name of the Trinity. And his wife dropped safe to the ground beside him.'

The story was received with a sort of collective 'ah' at the conclusion, and was quickly followed by tales of the cleverness and ingenuity of the Wee Folk, and others about their interactions with the world of men. Some were in Gaelic and some in English, used apparently according to which language best fitted the rhythm of the words, for all of them had a beauty to the speaking, beyond the content of the tale itself. True to his promise, Jamie translated the Gaelic for me in an undertone, so quickly and easily that I thought he must have heard these stories many times before.

There was one I noticed particularly, about the man out late at night upon a fairy hill, who heard the sound of a woman singing 'sad and plaintive' from the very rocks of the hill. He listened more closely and heard the words:

'I am the wife of the Laird of Balnain
The Folk have stolen me over again.'

So the listener hurried to the house of Balnain and found there the owner gone and his wife and baby son missing. The man hastily sought out a priest and brought him back to the fairy knoll. The priest blessed the rocks of the dun and sprinkled them with holy water. Suddenly the night grew darker and there was a loud noise as of thunder. Then the moon came out from behind a cloud and shone upon the woman, the wife of Balnain, who lay exhausted on the grass with her child in her arms. The woman was tired, as though she had travelled far, but could not tell where she had been, nor how she had come there.

Others in the hall had stories to tell, and Gwyllyn rested on his stool to sip wine as one gave place to another by the fireside, telling stories that held the hall rapt.

Some of these I hardly heard, I was rapt myself, but by my own thoughts, which were tumbling about, forming patterns under the influence of wine, music and fairy legends.

'It was a time, two hundred years ago . . .'

It's always two hundred years in Highland stories, said the Reverend Mr Wakefield's voice in memory. *The same thing as 'Once upon a time', you know.*

And women trapped in the rocks of fairy duns, travelling

161

far and arriving exhausted, who knew not where they had been, nor how they had come there.

I could feel the hair rising on my forearms, as though with cold, and rubbed them uneasily. Two hundred years. From 1946 to 1743; yes, near enough. And women who travelled through the rocks. Was it always women? I wondered suddenly.

Something else occurred to me. The women came back. Holy water, spell or knife, *they came back*. So perhaps, just perhaps, it was possible. I must get back to the standing stones on Craigh na Dun. I felt a rising excitement that made me feel a trifle sick, and I reached for the wine goblet to calm myself.

'Be careful!' As my groping fingers fumbled the edge of the nearly full crystal goblet which I had carelessly set on the bench beside me, Jamie's long arm shot across my lap, narrowly saving the goblet from disaster. He lifted the glass, holding the stem delicately between two large fingers, and passed it gently back and forth under his nose. He handed it back to me, eyebrows lifted.

'Rhenish,' I explained helpfully.

'Aye, I know,' he said, still looking quizzical. 'Callum's, is it?'

'Why, yes. Would you like to try some? It's very good.' I held out the glass, a trifle unsteadily. After a moment's hesitation he accepted the glass and tried a small sip.

'Aye, it's good,' he said, handing the goblet back. 'It's also double strength. Callum takes it at night because his legs pain him. How much of it have you had?' he asked, eyeing me narrowly.

'Two, no, three glasses,' I said, with some dignity. 'Are you implying that I'm intoxicated?'

'No,' he said, brows still raised, 'I'm impressed that you're not. Most folk that drink wi' Callum are under the table after the second glass.' He reached out and took the goblet from me again.

'Still,' he added firmly, 'I think you'd best drink no more of it, or ye won't get back up the stairs.' He tilted the glass and deliberately drained it himself, then handed the empty goblet to Laoghaire without looking at her.

'Take that back, will ye, lass,' he said casually. 'It's grown late; I believe I'll see Mistress Beauchamp to her chamber.' And putting a hand under my elbow, he steered me towards the archway, leaving the girl staring after us with an expression that made me relieved that looks in fact cannot kill.

Jamie followed me up to my chamber and, somewhat to my surprise, came in after me. The surprise vanished when he shut the door and immediately shed his shirt. I had forgotten the dressing, which I had been meaning to remove for the last two days.

'I'll be glad to get this off,' he said, rubbing at the rayon and linen harness arrangement under his arm. 'It's been chafing me for days.'

'I'm surprised you didn't take it off yourself, then,' I said, reaching up to untie the knots.

'I was afraid to, after the scolding ye gave me when you put the first one on,' he said, grinning impudently down at me. 'Thought I'd get my bum smacked if I touched it.'

'You'll get it smacked now if you don't sit down and keep still,' I answered, mock-stern. I put both hands on his good shoulder and, a little unsteadily, pulled him down on to the bedroom stool.

I slipped the harness off and carefully probed the shoulder joint. It was still slightly swollen, with some bruising, but thankfully I could find no evidence of torn muscles.

'If you were so anxious to get rid of it, why didn't you let me take it off for you this afternoon?' His behaviour at the paddock had puzzled me then, and did so still more, now that I could see the patches of reddened skin where the rough edges of the linen bandages had rubbed him nearly raw. I lifted the wound dressings cautiously, but all was well beneath.

He glanced sidelong at me, then looked down a bit sheepishly. 'Well, it's – ah, it's only that I didna want to take my shirt off before Alick.'

'Modest, are you?' I asked dryly, making him raise his

arm to test the extension of the joint. He winced slightly at the movement, but smiled at the remark.

'If I were, I should hardly be sittin' half naked in your chamber, should I? No, it's the marks on my back.' Seeing my raised eyebrows he went on to explain, 'Alick knows who I am – I mean, he's heard I was flogged, but he's not seen it. And to know something like that is no the same as seein' it wi' your own eyes.' He felt the sore shoulder tentatively, eyes turned away. He frowned at the floor. 'It's – maybe you'll not know what I mean. But when you know a man's suffered some harm, it's only one of the things you know about him, and it doesna make much difference to how ye see him. Alick knows I've been flogged, like he knows I've red hair, and it doesna matter to how he treats me.' He looked up then, searching for some sign of understanding from me.

'But when you see it yourself, it's like –' he hesitated, looking for words – 'it's a bit . . . personal, maybe, is what I mean. I think . . . if he were to see the scars, he couldna see *me* any more without thinking of my back. And I'd be able to see him thinking of it, and that would make me remember it, and – ' He broke off, shrugging.

'Well. That's a poor job of explaining, no? I daresay I'm too tender-minded about it, in any case. After all, I canna see it for myself; perhaps it's not as bad as I think.' I had seen wounded men making their way on crutches down the street, and people passing them with averted eyes, and I thought it was not at all a bad job of explanation.

'You don't mind my seeing your back?'

'No, I don't.' He sounded mildly surprised, and paused a moment to think about it. 'I suppose . . . it's that ye seem to have a knack for letting me know you're sorry for it, without makin' me feel pitiful about it.'

He sat patiently, not moving as I circled behind him and inspected his back. I didn't know how bad he thought it was, but it was bad enough. Even by candlelight and having seen it once before, I was appalled. Before, I had seen only the one shoulder. The scars covered his entire back from shoulders to waist. While many had faded to little more than thin white lines, the worst formed thick silver wedges, cutting across the smooth muscles. I thought with some regret that it must have been quite a beautiful back at one time. His skin was fair and fresh, and the lines of bone and muscle were still solid and graceful, the shoulders flat and square-set and the backbone a smooth, straight groove cut deep between the rounded columns of muscle that rose on either side of it.

Jamie was right too. Looking at this wanton damage I could not avoid a mental picture of the process that had caused it. I tried not to imagine the muscular arms raised, spread-eagled and tied, ropes cutting into wrists, the coppery head pressed hard against the post in agony, but the marks brought such images all too readily to mind. Had he screamed when it was done? I pushed the thought hastily away. I had heard the stories that trickled out of postwar Germany, of course, of atrocities much worse than this, but he *was* right; hearing is not at all the same as seeing.

Involuntarily I reached out as though I might heal him with a touch and erase the marks with my fingers. He sighed deeply but didn't move as I traced the deep scars, one by one, as though to show him the extent of the damage he couldn't see. I rested my hands at last lightly on his shoulders in silence, groping for words.

He placed his own hand over mine and squeezed lightly in acknowledgement of the things I couldn't find to say.

'There's worse has happened to others, lass,' he said quietly. Then he let go and the spell was broken.

'It feels as though it's healing well,' he said, trying to look sideways at his wounded shoulder. 'It doesna pain me much.'

'That's good,' I said, clearing my throat of some obstruction that seemed to have lodged there. 'It *is* healing well; it's scabbed over nicely, and there's no drainage at all. Just keep it clean, and don't use the arm more than you must for another two or three days.' I patted the undamaged shoulder, signifying dismissal. He put his shirt back on without assistance, tucking the long tails down into the kilt.

There was an awkward moment as he paused by the door,

seeking something to say in farewell. Finally, he invited me to come and see a newborn foal at the stables when I had time. I promised that I would, and we said goodnight, both speaking together. We laughed and nodded absurdly to each other as I shut the door. I went at once to bed and fell asleep in a winy haze, to dream unsettling dreams that I would not recall come morning.

Next day, after a long morning of treating new patients, rummaging the stillroom for useful herbs to replenish the medical supplies cupboard, and – with some ceremony – recording the details in Davie Beaton's black ledger, I left my narrow closet in search of air and exercise.

There was no one about for the moment, and I took the opportunity to explore the upper floors of the castle, poking into empty chambers and winding staircases, mapping the castle in my mind. It was a most irregular floor plan, to say the least. Bits and pieces had been added here and there over the years until it was difficult to say whether there ever *had* been a plan originally. In this hall, for example, there was an alcove built into the wall by the stairs, apparently serving no purpose but to fill in a blank space too small for a complete room.

The alcove was partly shielded from view by a hanging curtain of striped linen; I would have passed by without stopping, had a sudden flash of white from within not attracted my attention. I stopped just short of the opening and peered inside to see what it was. It was the sleeve of Jamie's shirt, passing around a girl's back, drawing her close for a kiss. She sat on his lap, and her yellow hair caught the sunlight coming through a slit, reflecting light like the surface of a trout stream on a bright morning.

I paused, uncertain what to do. I had no desire to spy on them, but was afraid the sound of my footsteps on the corridor stones would draw their attention. While I hesitated, Jamie broke from the embrace and looked up. His eyes met mine, and his face twitched from alarm to recognition. With a raised eyebrow and a faintly ironic shrug, he settled the girl more firmly on his knee and bent to his work. I shrugged back and tiptoed away. Not my business. I had little doubt, however, that both Callum and the girl's father would consider this 'consorting' highly improper. The next beating might well be on his own account, if they weren't more careful in choosing a meeting place. Finding him at supper that night with Alick, I sat down opposite at the long table. Jamie greeted me pleasantly enough, but with a watchful expression in his eyes. Auld Alick gave me his usual 'Mmphm'. Women, as he had explained to me at the paddock, have no natural appreciation of horses, and are therefore difficult to talk to.

'How's the horse-breaking coming along?' I asked, to interrupt the industrious chewing on the other side of the table.

'Well enough,' answered Jamie cautiously.

I peered at him across a platter of boiled kale. 'Your mouth looks a bit swollen, Jamie. Get thumped by a horse, did you?' I asked wickedly.

'Aye,' he answered, narrowing his eyes. 'Swung its head when I wasna looking.' He spoke placidly, but I felt a large foot come down on top of mine under the table. It rested lightly at the moment, but the threat was explicit.

'Too bad; those fillies can be dangerous,' I said innocently.

The foot pressed down hard as Alick said, 'Filly? Ye're no workin' fillies now, are ye, lad?' I used my other foot as a lever; that failing, I used it to kick his ankle sharply. Jamie jerked suddenly.

'What's wrong wi' ye?' Alick demanded.

'Bit my tongue,' muttered Jamie, glaring at me over the hand he had clapped to his mouth.

'Clumsy young dolt. No more than I'd expect from an idjit as canna even keep clear of a horse when . . .' Alick went on for several minutes, accusing his assistant at length of clumsiness, idleness, stupidity and general ineptitude. Jamie, possibly the least clumsy person I had ever seen in my life, kept his head down and ate stolidly through the diatribe, though his cheeks flushed hotly. I kept my eyes demurely on my plate for the rest of the meal.

Refusing a second helping of salt beef, Jamie left the table abruptly, putting an end to Alick's tirade. The old horsemaster and I munched silently for a few minutes. Wiping his plate with the last bit of bread, the old man pushed it into his mouth and leaned back, surveying me sardonically with his one blue eye.

'Ye shouldna devil the lad, ye ken,' he said conversationally. 'If her father or Callum comes to know about it, young Jamie could get summat more than a blackened eye.'

'Like a wife?' I said, looking him squarely in the eye. He nodded slowly.

'Could be. And that's not the wife he should have.'

'No?' I was a bit surprised at this, after overhearing Alick's remarks in the paddock.

'Nay, he needs a woman, not a girl. And Laoghaire will be a girl when she's fifty.' The grim old mouth twisted in something like a smile. 'Ye may think I've lived in a stable all my life, but I had a wife as was a woman, and I ken the difference verra weel.' The blue eye flashed as he made to get up. 'So do you, lass.'

I reached out a hand impulsively to stop him. 'How did you know – ' I began. Auld Alick snorted derisively.

'I may ha' but one eye, lass; it doesna mean I'm blind.' He creaked off, snorting as he went. I found the stairs and went up to my room, contemplating what, if anything, the old horsemaster had meant by his final remark.

9

The Gathering

My life seemed to be assuming some shape, if not yet a formal routine. Rising at dawn with the rest of the castle inhabitants, I breakfasted in the great hall, then, if Mrs Fitz had no patients for me to see, I went to work in the small walled garden. Other women worked there at times, with an attending phalanx of lads in varying sizes, who came and went, hauling rubbish, tools and loads of manure. I generally worked through the day there, sometimes going to the kitchens to help prepare a newly picked crop for eating or preserving, unless a medical emergency called me back to the Skulkery, as I called the late Beaton's closet of horrors.

Once in a while I would take up Alick's invitation and visit the stables or paddock, enjoying the sight of the horses and ponies shedding their shaggy winter coats in clumps, growing strong and glossy with spring grass.

Some evenings I would go to bed immediately after supper, exhausted by the day's work. Other times, when I could keep my eyes open, I would join the gathering in the Great Hall to listen to the evening's entertainment of stories, song or the music of harp or pipes. I could listen to Gwyllyn the Welsh bard for hours, enthralled in spite of my total ignorance of what he was saying, most times.

As the castle inhabitants grew accustomed to my presence, and I to theirs, some of the women began to make shy overtures of friendship and to include me in their conversations. With an eye towards the prospects of escape, I encouraged such overtures. If I could convince them that I was harmless, if strange, they might relax the constant polite vigilance to which I had been subject since my arrival, giving me a chance to bolt. The urge simply to flee came over me frequently, especially when I thought of Frank, and how he must be seeking me, but I had so far controlled it, knowing I wouldn't get far. They were plainly very curious about me, but I replied to all their tentative questions with variations of the story I had told Callum, and after a bit they accepted that as all they were likely to know. Having found out that I knew something of medicine and healing, though, they grew still more interested in me and began to ask questions about the ailments of their children, husbands and beasts, in most cases making little distinction between the latter two in level of importance.

Besides the normal questions and gossip there was considerable talk of the coming Gathering that I had heard Auld Alick mention at the paddock. I concluded that this was an occasion of some importance, and grew more convinced by the extent of the preparations for it. A constant stream of foodstuffs poured into the great kitchens, and more than twenty skinned carcasses hung in the slaughter shed, behind a screen of fragrant smoke that kept the flies away. Hogsheads of ale were delivered and carted down to the castle cellars, and bags of fine flour were brought from the mill for baking. The enormous pantry shelves were nearly filled now with pastries, cordials, hams and assorted-delicacies.

'How many people customarily come to a Gathering?' I asked Magdalen, one of the girls with whom I had become friendly.

She wrinkled a snub freckled nose in thought. 'I dinna ken for sure. The last great Gathering at Leoch was over twenty year past, and then there were oh, maybe ten score of men come then – when old Jacob died, ye ken, and Callum was made laird. Might be more this year; a good many will bring their wives and bairns along.'

Visitors were already beginning to arrive at the castle, though I had heard that the official parts of the Gathering, the oath-taking, the tinchel and the games, would not take place for several days. The more illustrious of Callum's tacksmen and tenants were housed in the castle proper, while the poorer men-at-arms and cottars set up camp on a fallow field below the stream that fed the castle's loch.

170

Roving gypsies and sellers of small goods had set up a sort of impromptu fair near the bridge. The inhabitants of both castle and nearby village had begun to visit the spot in the evenings, when the day's work was done, to buy tools and bits of finery, watch the jugglers and catch up on the latest gossip.

I kept a close eye on the comings and goings, and made a point of paying frequent visits to stable and paddock. There were ponies in plenty now, those of the visitors being accommodated in the castle stables. Among the confusion and disturbance of the Gathering, I thought, I should have no difficulty in finding my chance to escape.

It was on a herb-picking expedition by the paddock that I first met Geillis Duncan. Finding a small patch of wood sorrel beneath the roots of an alder, I was hunting for more. I worked my way around the paddock, stooping or dropping on hands and knees to gather the fragile stalks.

'Those are good for helping the monthlies,' said a voice from behind me. I straightened up from the patch I had been bending over, thumping my head smartly on a branch of the pine they were growing under.

As my vision cleared I could see that the peals of laughter were coming from a tall young woman, perhaps a few years older than myself, fair of hair and skin, with the loveliest green eyes I had ever seen.

'I am sorry to be laughing at you,' she said, dimpling as she stepped down into the hollow where I stood. 'I could not help it.'

'I imagine I looked funny,' I said rather ungraciously, rubbing the sore spot on top of my head.

'And did you know that these' – she stooped and came up with a handful of tiny blue flowers with heart-shaped leaves – 'will *start* bleeding?'

'No,' I said, startled. 'Why would anyone want to start bleeding?'

She looked at me with an expression of exasperated patience. 'To get rid of a child ye don't want, I mean. It

171

brings on your flux, but only if ye use it early. Too late, and it can kill you as well as the child.'

'You seem to know a lot about it,' I remarked, still stung by having appeared stupid.

'A bit. The girls in the village come to me now and again for such things, and sometimes the married women too. They say I'm a witch,' she said, widening her brilliant eyes in feigned astonishment. She grinned. 'But my husband's the procurator fiscal for the district, so they don't say it too loud.

'Now the young lad ye brought with ye,' she went on, nodding in approval, 'there's one that's had a few love-philtres bought on his behalf. Is he yours?'

'Mine? Who? You mean, er, Jamie?' I was startled.

The young woman looked amused. She sat down on a log, twirling a lock of fair hair idly around her index finger.

'Och, aye. There's quite a few would settle for a fellow wi' eyes and hair like that, no matter the price on his head or whether he's any money. Their fathers may think differently, o'course.

'Now, me,' she went on, looking off into the distance, 'I'm a practical sort. I married a man with a fair house, a bit o' money put away and a good position. As for hair, he hasn't any, and as for eyes, I never noticed, but he doesna trouble me much.' She held out the basket she carried for my inspection. It was partly filled with familiar leafy stalks.

'Comfrey,' she said. 'My husband suffers from a chill on the stomach now and again. Farts like an ox.'

I thought it best to stop this line of conversation before things got out of hand. 'I haven't introduced myself,' I said, extending a hand to help her up from the log. 'My name is Claire. Claire Beauchamp.'

The hand that took mine was slender, with long tapering white fingers, though I noticed the tips were stained, probably with the juices of the plants and roots resting alongside the comfrey in her basket.

'I know who ye are,' she said. 'The village has been humming with talk of ye, since ye came to the castle. My name is Geillis, Geilie Duncan.' She peered into my basket.

'If it's wood sorrel you're looking for, I can show you where they grow best.'

I accepted her offer, and we wandered for some time through the small corries near the paddock, poking under bushes and crawling around the rim of the sparkling tarns, where the tiny plants grew in profusion. Geillis was very knowledgeable about the local plants and their medicinal uses, though she suggested a few usages I thought questionable, to say the least. I thought it very unlikely, for instance, that roseroot would be effective in making warts grow on a rival's nose, and I strongly doubted whether wood betony was useful in transforming toads into pigeons. She made these explanations with a mischievous glance that suggested she was testing my own knowledge, or perhaps the local suspicion of witchcraft.

Despite the occasional teasing I found her a pleasant companion, with a ready wit and a cheerful, if cynical, outlook on life. She appeared to know everything there was to know about everyone in village, countryside and castle, and our explorations were punctuated by rests during which she entertained me with complaints about her husband's stomach trouble, and amusing if somewhat malicious gossip.

'They say young Hamish is not his father's son,' she said at one point, referring to Callum's only child, the red-haired lad of eight or so whom I had seen at dinner in the hall.

I was not particularly startled by this bit of gossip, having formed my own conclusions on the matter. I was only surprised that there was but one child of questionable parentage, surmising that Letitia had been either lucky, or smart enough to seek out someone like Geilie in time. Unwisely, I said as much to Geilie.

She flung back her long fair hair and laughed. 'No, not me. The fair Letitia does not need any help in such matters, believe me. If people are seeking a witch in this neighbourhood, they'd do better to look in the castle than the village.'

Anxious to change the subject to something safer, I seized on the first thing that came to mind.

'If young Hamish isn't Callum's son, whose is he supposed to be?' I asked, scrambling over a heap of boulders.

'Why, the lad's, of course.' She turned to face me, small mouth mocking and green eyes bright with mischief. 'Young Jamie.'

Returning to the paddock alone, I met Magdalen, hair coming loose under her kerchief and wide-eyed with worry.

'Oh, there ye are,' she said, heaving a sigh of relief. 'We were going back to the castle, when I missed ye.'

'It was kind of you to come back for me,' I said. 'I know the way, though.'

She shook her head. 'You should take care, my dearie, walking alone in the woods, wi' all the tinkers and folk coming for the Gathering. Callum's given orders – ' She stopped abruptly, hand over her mouth.

'That I'm to be watched?' I suggested gently. She nodded reluctantly, clearly afraid I would be offended. I shrugged and tried to smile reassuringly at her.

'Well, that's natural, I suppose,' I said. 'After all, he's no one's word but my own for who I am or how I came here.' Curiosity overcame my better judgement. 'Who does he think I am?' I asked. But the girl shook her head.

'You're English,' was all she said.

I didn't return to my herb-gathering next day. Not because I was ordered to remain in the castle, but because there was a sudden outbreak of food poisoning among the castle inhabitants that demanded my attention as physician. Having done what I could for the sufferers, I set out to track the trouble to its source.

This proved to be a tainted beef carcass from the salting shed. I was in the shed next day, giving the chief smoker a piece of my mind regarding proper methods of meat preserving, when the door swung open behind me, sending a thick wave of choking smoke over me.

I turned, eyes watering, to see Dougal MacKenzie looming through the clouds of juniper smoke.

'Supervising the butchering as well as the physicking, are ye now, mistress?' he asked mockingly. 'Soon ye'll have the whole castle under your thumb, and Mrs Fitz will be seeking employment elsewhere.'

174

'I have no desire to have anything to do with your filthy castle,' I snapped, wiping my streaming eyes and coming away with charcoal streaks on my handkerchief. 'All I want is to get out of here, as fast as possible.'

He inclined his head courteously, still grinning. 'Well, I might be in a position to gratify that wish, mistress,' he said. 'At least temporarily.'

I dropped the handkerchief and stared at him. 'What do you mean?'

He coughed and waved a hand at the smoke, now drifting in his direction. He drew me outside the shed and turned in the direction of the stables.

'You were saying yesterday to Callum that ye needed betony and some odd bits of herbs?'

'Yes, to make up some medicines for the people with food poisoning. What of it?' I demanded, still suspicious.

He shrugged good-naturedly. 'Only that I'm going down to the village, to the tanner's shed. The fiscal's wife is something of a herb-woman, and has stocks to hand. Doubtless she has the simples that you're needing. And if it please ye, lady, you're welcome to ride one of the ponies down wi' me to the village.'

'The fiscal's wife? Mrs Duncan?' I immediately felt happier. The prospect of escaping the castle altogether, even if only for a short time, was irresistible.

I mopped my face hurriedly and tucked the soiled kerchief in my belt.

'Let's go,' I said.

I enjoyed the short ride downhill to the village of Cranesmuir, even though the day was dark and overcast. Dougal himself was in high spirits, and chatted and joked pleasantly as we went along.

We stopped first at the tanner's, then went on up the High Street to the Duncans' house. This was an imposing half-timbered manor of three storeys, the lower two equipped with elegant leaded-glass windows; diamond-shaped panes in watery tones of purple and green.

Geilie greeted us with delight, pleased to have company on such a dreary day.

'How splendid!' she exclaimed. 'I've been wanting an excuse to go through the stillroom and sort out some things. Anne!'

A short, middle-aged serving woman with a face like a winter apple popped out of a door I hadn't noticed, concealed as it was in the bend of the chimney.

'Take Mistress Claire to the stillroom,' Geilie ordered, 'and then go and fetch us a bucket of spring water. From the spring, mind, not the well in the square!' She turned to Dougal. 'I've the tonic put by that I promised your brother. If you'll come out to the kitchen with me for a moment?'

I followed the serving woman's pumpkin-shaped rear up a set of narrow wooden stairs, emerging unexpectedly into a long, airy loft. Unlike the rest of the house, this room was furnished with casement windows, shut now against the damp, but still providing a great deal more light than had been available in the fashionably gloomy parlour downstairs.

It was clear that Geilie knew her business as a herbalist. The room was equipped with long drying frames netted with gauze, hooks above the small fireplace for heat-drying, and open shelves along the walls, drilled with holes to allow for air circulation. The air was thick with the delicious, spicy scent of herbs. A surprisingly modern long counter ran along one side of the room, displaying a remarkable assortment of mortars, pestles, mixing bowls and spoons, all immaculately clean.

It was some time before Geilie appeared, flushed from climbing the stairs, but smiling in anticipation of a long afternoon of herb-pounding and gossip.

It began to rain lightly, drops spattering the long casements, but a small fire was burning on the stillroom hearth, and it was very cosy. I enjoyed Geilie's company immensely; she had a wry-tongued, cynical viewpoint that was a refreshing contrast to the sweet, shy clanswomen at the castle, and clearly she had been well educated, for a woman in a small village.

She also knew every scandal that had occurred either in village or castle in the last ten years, and she told me endless amusing stories. Oddly enough, she asked me few questions about myself. I thought perhaps that was not her way; she would find out what she wanted to know about me from other people.

For some time I had been conscious of noises coming from the street, but had attributed them to the traffic of villagers coming from Sunday Mass; the chapel was located at the end of the street by the well, and the High Street ran from chapel to square, spreading from there into a fan of tiny lanes and walks.

In fact I had amused myself on the ride to the tanner's by imagining an aerial view of the village as a representation of a skeletal forearm and hand; the High Street was the radius, along which lay the shops and businesses and the residences of the more well-to-do. St Margaret's Lane was the ulna, a narrower street running parallel with the High, tenanted by smithy, tannery and the less genteel artisans and businesses. The village square (which, like all village squares I had ever seen was not square at all, but roughly oblong) formed the carpals and metacarpals of the hand, while the several lanes of cottages made up the phalangeal joints of the fingers.

The Duncans' house stood on the square, as behooved the residence of the procurator fiscal. This was a matter of convenience as well as status; the square could be used for those judicial matters which, by reason of public interest or legal necessity, overflowed the narrow confines of Arthur Duncan's study. And it was, as Dougal explained, convenient to the pillory, a homely wooden contraption that stood on a small stone plinth in the centre of the square, adjacent to the wooden stake used – with thrifty economy of purpose – as whipping post, maypole, flagstaff and horse tether, depending on requirements.

The noise outside was now much louder, and altogether more disorderly than seemed appropriate to people coming soberly home from chapel to their dinners. Geillis put aside the jars with an exclamation of impatience and threw open the window to see what caused the uproar.

Joining her at the window, I could see a crowd of folk dressed in chapel-going garb of gowns, coat and bonnet, led by the stocky figure of Father Bain, the priest who served both village and castle. He had in his custody a youth, perhaps twelve years old, whose ragged trews and smelly shirt proclaimed him a tanner's lad. The priest had the boy gripped by the nape of the neck, a hold made somewhat difficult to maintain by the fact that the lad was slightly taller than his minatory captor. The crowd followed the pair at a small distance, rumbling with disapproving comment like a passing thunder cloud in the wake of a lightning bolt.

As we watched from the upper window Father Bain and boy disappeared beneath us, into the house. The crowd remained outside, muttering and jostling. A few of the bolder souls chinned themselves on the window ledges, attempting to peer within.

Geilie shut the window with a slam, making a break in the anticipatory rumble below.

'Stealing, most like,' she said laconically, returning to the herb table. 'Usually is, wi' the tanner's lads.'

'What will happen to him?' I asked curiously. She shrugged, crumbling dried rosemary between her fingers into the mortar.

'Depends on whether Arthur's dyspeptic this morning, I should say. If he's made a good breakfast, the lad might get off with a whipping. But happen he's costive or flatulent' – she made a moue of distaste – 'the boy'll lose an ear or a hand, most like.'

I was horrified, but hesitant to interfere directly in the matter. I was an outsider, and an Englishwoman to boot, and while I thought I would be treated with some respect as an inhabitant of the castle, I had seen many of the villagers surreptitiously make the sign against evil as I passed. My intercession might easily make things worse for the boy.

178

'Can't *you* do anything?' I asked Geilie. 'Speak to your husband, I mean; ask him to be, er, lenient?'

Geilie looked up from her work, surprised. Clearly the thought of interfering in her husband's affairs had never crossed her mind.

'Why should you care what happens to him?' she asked, but curiously, not with any hostile meaning.

'Of course I care!' I said. 'He's only a lad; whatever he did, he doesn't deserve to be mutilated for life!'

She raised pale brows; plainly this argument was unconvincing. Still, she shrugged and handed me the mortar and pestle.

'Anything to oblige a friend,' she said, rolling her eyes. She scanned her shelves and selected a bottle of greenish stuff, labelled, in fine cursive script, EXTRACT OF PEPPERMINT.

'I'll go and dose Arthur, and whilst I'm about it, I'll see if aught can be done for the lad. It may be too late, mind,' she warned. 'And if that poxy priest's got a hand in, he'll want the stiffest sentence he can get. Still, I'll try. You keep after the pounding; rosemary takes for ever.'

I took up the pestle as she left, and pounded and ground automatically, paying little heed to the results. The shut window blocked the sound both of the rain and the crowd below; the two blended in a soft, pattering susurration of menace. Like any schoolchild I had read Dickens. And earlier authors, as well, with their descriptions of the pitiless justice of these times, meted out to all ill-doers, regardless of age or circumstance. But to read, from a cosy distance of one or two hundred years, accounts of child hangings and judicial mutilation, was a far different thing than to sit quietly pounding herbs a few feet above such an occurrence.

Could I bring myself to interfere directly, if the sentence went against the boy? I moved to the window, carrying the mortar with me, and peered out. The crowd had increased as other folk, attracted by the gathering, wandered down the High Street to investigate. Newcomers leaned close as the standees excitedly relayed the details, then merged into

179

the body of the crowd, more faces turned expectantly to the door of the house.

Looking down on the assembly, standing patiently in the drizzle awaiting a verdict, I suddenly had a vivid understanding of something. Like so many, I had heard, appalled, the reports that trickled out of postwar Germany; the stories of deportations and mass murder, of concentration camps and burnings. And like so many others had done, and would do, for years to come, I had asked myself, 'How could the German people have let it happen? They must have known, must have seen the trucks, the coming and going, the fences and smoke. How could they stand by and do nothing?' Well, now I knew.

The stakes were not even life or death in this case. And Callum's patronage would likely prevent any physical attack on me. But my hands grew clammy around the bowl as I thought of myself stepping out, alone and powerless, to confront that mob of solid and virtuous citizens, avid for the excitement of punishment and blood to alleviate the tedium of existence.

People are gregarious by necessity. Since the days of the first cave dwellers, humans – weak and helpless save for cunning – have survived by joining together in groups; knowing, as so many other edible creatures have found, that there is protection in numbers. And that knowledge, bred in the bone, is what lies behind mob rule. Because to step outside the group, let alone to stand against it, was for uncounted thousands of years death to the creature who dared it. To stand against a crowd would take something more than ordinary courage; something that went beyond human instinct. And I feared I did not have it and, fearing, was ashamed.

It seemed for ever before the door opened and Geilie stepped in, looking cool and unperturbed as usual, a small stick of charcoal in her hand.

'We'll need to filter it after it's boiled,' she remarked, as though going on with our previous conversation. 'I think we'll run it through charcoal in muslin; that's best.'

'Geilie,' I said impatiently. 'Don't try me. What about the tanner's boy?'

'Oh, that.' She lifted a shoulder dismissively but a mischievous smile lurked about the corners of her lips. She dropped the facade then, and laughed.

'You should have seen me,' she said, giggling. 'I was awfully good, an' I say it myself. All wifely solicitude and womanly kindness, with a small dab o' maternal pity mixed in. "Oh, Arthur," ' she dramatized, ' "had our own union been blessed" – not much chance, if I've aught to say about it,' she said, dropping the soulful mask for a moment with a tilt of her head towards the herb shelves – ' "why, how would ye feel, my darling, should your own son be taken so? Nae doubt it was but hunger made the lad take to thievery. Oh, Arthur, can ye no find it in your heart to be merciful – and you the soul of justice?" ' She dropped on to a stool, laughing and pounding her fist lightly against her leg. 'What a pity there's no place for acting here!'

The sound of the crowd outside had changed, and I moved to the window to see what was happening, ignoring Geilie's self-congratulations.

The throng parted and the tanner's lad came out, walking slowly between priest and judge. Arthur Duncan was swollen with benevolence, bowing and nodding to the more eminent members of the assembly. Father Bain, on the other hand, resembled a sullen potato more than anything else, brown face lumpy with resentment.

The little procession proceeded to the centre of the square, where the village lockman, one John MacRae, stepped out of the crowd to meet them. This personage was dressed as befitted his office in the sober elegance of dark breeches and coat and grey velvet hat (removed for the nonce and tenderly sheltered from the rain beneath the tail of his coat). He was not, as I had at first assumed, the village gaoler, though in a pinch he did perform such office. His duties were primarily those of constable, customs inspector and, when needed, executioner; his title came from the wooden 'lock' or scoop that hung from his belt, with which he was entitled to take a percentage of each bag of grain sold in the Thursday market: the remuneration of his office.

I had found all this out from the lockman himself. He had been to the castle only a few days before to see whether I could treat a persistent felon on his thumb. I had lanced it with a sterile needle and dressed it with plantain ointment, finding MacRae a shy and soft-spoken man with a pleasant smile.

There was no trace of a smile now, though; MacRae's face was suitably stern. Reasonable, I thought; no one wants to see a grinning executioner.

The miscreant was brought to stand on the plinth in the centre of the square. The lad looked pale and frightened but did not move as Arthur Duncan, procurator fiscal for the parish of Cranesmuir, drew his plumpness up into an approximation of dignity and prepared to pronounce sentence.

'The ninny had already confessed by the time I came in,' said a voice by my ear. Geilie peered interestedly over my shoulder. 'I couldna get him freed entirely. I got him off as light as could be, though; only an hour in the pillory and one ear nailed.'

'One ear nailed! Nailed to *what?*'

'Why, the pillory, o' course.' She shot me a curious look, but turned back to the window to watch the execution of this light sentence obtained by her merciful intercession.

The crush of bodies around the pillory was so great that little of the miscreant could be seen, but the crowd drew back a bit to allow the lockman free movement for the ear-nailing. The lad, white-faced and small in the jaws of the pillory,· had both eyes tight shut and kept them that way, shuddering with fear. He uttered a high, thin scream when the nail was driven in, audible through the closed windows, and I shuddered a bit myself.

We turned away, as did most of the spectators in the square, but I could not help rising to glance out from time to time. A few idlers passing by paused to jeer at the victim and throw balls of mud, and now and then a more sober citizen was to be seen, seizing a moment to attend to the

182

moral improvement of the delinquent by means of a few well-chosen words of reproval and advice.

It was still an hour to the late spring sunset, and we were drinking tea in the parlour when a pounding at the door announced the arrival of a visitor. The day was so dark from the rain that one could hardly tell the level of the sun. The Duncans' house, however, boasted a clock, a magnificent contrivance of walnut panels, brass pendulums and a face decorated with choiring cherubim, and this instrument pointed to half-past six.

The scullery maid opened the door to the parlour and unceremoniously announced, 'In here.' Jamie MacTavish ducked automatically as he came through the door, bright hair darkened by the rain to the colour of ancient bronze. He wore an elderly and disreputable coat against the wet, and carried a riding cloak of heavy green velvet folded under one arm.

He nodded in acknowledgement as I rose and introduced him to Geilie.

'Mistress Duncan, Mrs Beauchamp.' He waved a hand towards the window. 'I see ye've had a wee bit doing this afternoon.'

'Is he still there?' I asked, peering out. The boy was only a dark shape seen through the distortion of the wavering drawing-room panes. 'He must be soaked through.'

'He is.' Jamie spread the cloak and held it for me. 'So you'd be as well, Callum thought. I'd business in the village, so he sent along the cloak with me for ye. You're to ride back wi' me.'

'That was kind of him.' I spoke absently, for my mind was still on the tanner's lad.

'How long must he stay there?' I asked Geilie. 'The lad in the pillory,' I added impatiently, seeing her blank look.

'Oh, him,' she said, frowning slightly at the introduction of such an unimportant topic. 'An hour, I told you. The lockman should ha' freed him from the pillory by now.'

'He has,' Jamie assured her. 'I saw him as I was crossing the green. It's only the lad's not got up courage to tear the griss from his lug yet.'

My mouth dropped open. 'You mean the nail won't be taken out of his ear? He's to *tear* himself loose?'

'Oh, aye.' Jamie was cheerfully offhand. 'He's still a bit nervous, but I imagine he'll set his mind to it soon. It's wet out, and growing dark as well. We must leave ourselves, or we'll get naught but scraps to our supper.' He bowed to Geilie and turned to go.

'Wait a bit,' she said to me. 'Since you've a big, strong lad like yon to see ye home, I've a chest of dried herbs and other simples as I've promised to Mrs FitzGibbons up at the castle. Perhaps Mr MacTavish would be so kind?'

Jamie assenting, she had a manservant fetch down the chest from her workroom, handing over the enormous wrought-iron key for the purpose. While the servant was gone she busied herself for a moment at a small writing desk in the corner. By the time the chest, a sizable wooden box with brass bands, was brought in, she had finished her note. She hastily sanded it, folded and sealed it with a blob of wax from the candle, and pressed it into my hand.

'There,' she said. 'That's the bill for it. Will ye give it to Dougal for me? It's him that handles the payments and such. Dinna give it to anyone else, or I'll not be paid for weeks.'

'Yes, of course.' She embraced me warmly, and with admonitions about avoiding the chill, saw us to the door.

I stood sheltering beneath the eave of the house as Jamie tied the box to his horse's saddle. The rain was coming down harder now, and the eaves ran with a ragged sheet of water.

I eyed the broad back and muscular forearms as he lifted the heavy box with little apparent effort. Then I glanced at the plinth, where the tanner's boy, in spite of encouragement from the re-gathered crowd, was still firmly pinioned. Granted this was not a lovely young girl with moonbeam hair, but Jamie's earlier actions in Callum's hall of justice made me think that he might not be unsympathetic to the youngster's plight.

'Er, Mr MacTavish?' I began hesitantly. There was no response. The comely face did not change expression; the wide mouth stayed relaxed, the blue eyes focused on the strap he was fastening.

'Ah, Jamie?' I tried again, a little louder, and he looked up at once. So it really wasn't MacTavish. I wondered what it was.

'Aye?' he said.

'You're, er, quite sizable, aren't you?' I said. A half smile curved his lips and he nodded, clearly wondering what I was up to.

'Big enough for most things,' he answered.

I was encouraged, and moved casually closer so as not to be overheard by any stragglers from the square.

'And tolerably strong in the fingers?' I asked.

He flexed one hand and the smile widened. 'Aye, that's so. Happen you've a few chestnuts you want cracked?' He looked down at me with a shrewd and merry glint.

I glanced briefly past him to the knot of onlookers in the square.

'More like one to be pulled from the fire, I think.' I looked up to meet that questioning blue gaze. 'Could you do it?'

He stood looking down at me for a moment, still smiling, then shrugged. 'Aye, if the shank's long enough to grip. Can ye draw the crowd away, though? Interference wouldna be looked on kindly, and me a stranger.'

I had not anticipated the possibility that my request might put him in any danger, and I hesitated, but he seemed game to try, danger notwithstanding.

'Well, if we both went over for a closer look, and then I were to faint at the sight, do you think – ?'

'You being so unused to blood and all?' One brow lifted sardonically and he grinned. 'Aye, that'll do. If ye can make shift to fall off the plinth, still better.'

I had in fact felt a bit squeamish about looking, but it was not so daunting a sight as I had feared. The ear was pinned firmly through the upper flange, close to the edge, and a full two inches of the nail's square, headless shank was free above the pinioned appendage. There was almost no blood, and it was clear from the boy's face that while he

185

was both frightened and uncomfortable he was in no great pain. I began to think that Geilie perhaps had been right in considering this a fairly lenient sentence, given the overall state of current Scottish jurisprudence, though this didn't alter by one whit my opinion as to the barbarity of it.

Jamie edged casually through the fringe of lookers-on. He shook his head reprovingly at the boy.

'Na then, lad,' he said, clicking his tongue. 'Got yourself in a rare swivet, have ye no?' He rested one large, firm hand on the wooden edge of the pillory, under pretext of looking more closely at the ear. 'Och, laddie,' he said, disparaging, 'yon's no job to be making heavy weather of. A wee snatch o' the head and it's over. Here, shall I help ye?' He reached out as though to grasp the lad by the hair and wrench his head free. The boy yelped in fear.

Recognizing my cue, I stepped back, taking care to tread heavily on the toes of the woman behind me, who yipped in anguish as my heel crushed her metatarsals.

'I beg your pardon,' I gasped. 'I'm . . . so dizzy! Please . . .' I turned away from the pillory and took two or three steps, staggering artfully and clutching at the sleeves of those nearby. The edge of the plinth was only six inches away; I took a firm hold on a slightly built girl I had marked out for the purpose and pitched headfirst over the edge, taking her with me.

We rolled on the wet grass in a tangle of skirts and squeals. Letting go of her blouse at last, I relaxed into a dramatically spread-eagled heap, rain pattering down on my upturned face.

I was in truth a trifle winded by the impact – the girl had fallen on top of me – and I fought for breath, listening to the babble of concerned voices gathered around me. Speculations, suggestions and shocked interjections rained on me, thicker than the drops of water from the sky, but it was a pair of familiar arms that raised me to a sitting position and a pair of gravely concerned blue eyes that I saw when I opened my own. A faint flicker of the eyelids told me that the mission had been accomplished, and in fact I could see the tanner's lad, napkin clutched to his ear, making off at speed in the direction of his loft, unnoticed by the crowd that had turned to attend to this new sensation.

The villagers, so lately calling for the lad's blood, were kindness itself to me. I was tenderly gathered up and carried back to the Duncans' house, where I was plied with brandy, tea, warm blankets and sympathy. I was only allowed to depart at last by Jamie's stating bluntly that we must go, then lifting me bodily off the couch and heading for the door, disregarding the expostulations of my hosts.

Mounted once more in front of him, my own pony led by the rein, I tried to thank him for his help.

'No trouble, lass,' he said, dismissing my thanks.

'But it was a risk to you,' I said, persisting. 'I didn't realize you'd be in danger when I asked you.'

'Ah,' he said noncommittally. And a moment later, with a hint of amusement, 'Ye wouldna expect me to be less bold than a wee Sassenach lassie, now would ye?'

He urged the animals into a trot as the shadows of dusk gathered by the roadside. We did not speak much on the rest of the journey home. And when we reached the castle he left me at the gate with no more than a softly mocking, 'Good e'en, Mistress Sassenach.' But I felt as though a friendship had been begun that ran a bit deeper than shared gossip over the herb-gathering.

10

The Oath-Taking

There was a terrific stir over the next two days, with comings and goings and preparations of every sort. My medical practice dropped off sharply; the food-poisoning victims were well again, and everyone else seemed to be much too busy to fall sick. Aside from a slight rash of splinters-in-fingers among the boys hauling in wood for the fires, and a similar outbreak of scalds and burns among the busy kitchen-maids, there were no accidents either.

I was excited myself. Tonight was the night. Mrs Fitz had told me that all the fighting men of Leoch would be in the hall tonight, to make their oaths of allegiance to Callum. With a ceremony of this importance going on inside, no one would be watching the stables.

During my hours helping in the kitchens and garden I had managed to stow away sufficient food to see me provided for several days, I thought. I had no water flask, but had contrived a substitute using one of the heavier glass jugs from the surgery. I had stout boots and a warm cloak, courtesy of Callum. I would have a decent pony; on my afternoon visit to the stables I had marked out the one I meant to take. I had no money, but my patients had given me a handful of small trinkets, ribbons and bits of carving or jewellery. If necessary I might be able to use these to trade for anything else I needed.

My heart hammered at the thought of imminent escape. It was going to be a risky journey; social custom aside, there were excellent reasons why ladies didn't travel alone in the Highlands – roads were few and the passage physically dangerous in many regards, including wild beasts, wild weather and wild clansmen. Add to that, that I had only a vague idea of the direction to take, was ignorant of the mountain routes and spoke no Gaelic, and I could scarcely ignore the fact that I might well be leaping from the frying pan into the fire.

Overriding all fears, though, was the thought of Frank. I had to get back, whatever the risk. I had no idea what would happen when I reached the stone circle again, but that ancient monument held the only hope of reaching him. I closed my eyes and envisioned Frank's arms around me once more, to give me courage.

I felt badly about abusing Callum's hospitality and the friendship of the castle inhabitants by leaving without a word or a note of farewell, but after all, what could I possibly say? I had pondered the problem for some time, but finally decided just to leave. For one thing I had no writing paper, and was not willing to take the risk of visiting Callum's quarters in search of any.

An hour past first dark I approached the stable cautiously, ears alert for any signs of human presence, but it seemed that everyone was up in the hall, readying themselves for the ceremony. The door stuck, but gave with a slight push, its leather hinges letting it swing silently inwards.

The air inside was warm and alive with the faint stirrings of resting animals. It was also black as the inside of an undertaker's hat, as Uncle Lamb used to say. Such few windows as there were for ventilation were narrow slits, too small to admit the faint starlight outside. Hands outstretched, I walked slowly into the main part of the stable, feet shuffling in the straw.

I groped carefully in front of me, looking for the edge of a stall to guide me. My hands found only empty air, but my shins met a solid obstruction resting on the floor, and I pitched headlong with a startled cry that rang in the rafters of the old stone building.

The obstruction rolled over with a startled oath and grasped me hard by the arms. I found myself held against the length of a sizable male body, with someone's breath tickling my ear.

'Who are you?' I gasped, jerking backwards. 'And what

are you doing here?' Hearing my voice, the unseen assailant relaxed his grip.

'I might ask the same of you, Sassenach,' said the deep voice of Jamie MacTavish, and I relaxed a little in relief. There was a stirring in the straw, and he sat up.

'Though I suppose I could guess,' he added dryly. 'How far d'ye think you'd get, lassie, on a dark night and a strange beast, wi' half the MacKenzie clan after ye by morning?'

I was ruffled, in more ways than one.

'They wouldn't be after me. They're all up at the hall, and if one in five of them is sober enough to stand by morning, let alone ride, I'll be *most* surprised.'

He laughed, and standing up, reached down a hand to help me to my feet. He brushed the straw from the back of my skirt with somewhat more force than I thought strictly necessary.

'Well, that's verra sound reasoning on your part, Sassenach,' he said, sounding mildly surprised that I was capable of reason. 'Or would be,' he added, 'did Callum not have guards posted all round the castle and scattered through the woods. He'd hardly leave the castle unprotected, and all the fighting men of Leoch inside it. Granted that stone doesna burn so well as wood . . .'

I gathered he was referring to the infamous Glencoe Massacre, when one John Campbell, on government orders, had put thirty-eight members of the MacDonald clan to the sword and burned the houses above them. I calculated rapidly. That would have been only fifty-some years before; recent enough to justify any defensive precautions on Callum's part.

'In any case, ye could scarcely have chosen a worse night to try to escape,' MacTavish went on. He seemed entirely unconcerned with the fact that I *had* meant to escape, only with the reasons why it wouldn't work, which struck me as a little odd. 'Besides the guards, and the fact that every good horseman for miles around is here, the way to the castle will be filled wi' folk coming from the countryside for the tinchel and the games.'

'The tinchel? That's the hunt, isn't it?'

'Yes. It's usually stags, maybe a boar this time; one of the stable lads told Auld Alick there's a large one in the east wood.' He put a large hand in the centre of my back and turned me towards the faint oblong of the open door.

'Come along,' he said. 'I'll take ye back up to the castle.'

I pulled away from him. 'Don't bother,' I said ungraciously. 'I can find my own way.'

He took my elbow with considerable firmness. 'I daresay ye can. But you'll not want to meet any of Callum's guards alone.'

'And why not?' I snapped. 'I'm not doing anything wrong; there's no law against walking outside the castle, is there?'

'No. I doubt they'd mean to do ye harm,' he said, peering thoughtfully into the shadows. 'But it's far from unusual for a man to take a flask along to keep him company when he stands guard. And the drink may be a boon companion, but it's no a verra good adviser as to suitable behaviour, when a small sweet lass comes on ye alone in the dark.'

'I came on *you* in the dark, alone,' I reminded him with some boldness. 'And I'm neither particularly small, nor very sweet – at least at present.'

'Aye, well, I was asleep, not drunk,' he responded briefly. 'And questions of your temper aside, you're a good bit smaller than most of Callum's guards.'

I put that aside as an unproductive line of argument, and tried another tack. 'And why *were* you asleep in the stable?' I asked. 'Haven't you a bed somewhere?' We were in the outer reaches of the kitchen gardens by now and I could see his face in the faint light. He was intent, checking the stone arches carefully as we went, but he glanced sharply aside at this.

'Aye,' he said. He continued to stride forward, still gripping me by the elbow, but went on after a moment, 'I thought I'd be better out of the way.'

'Because you don't mean to swear allegiance to Callum MacKenzie?' I guessed. 'And you don't want to stand any racket about it?'

He glanced at me, amused at my words. 'Something like that,' he admitted.

191

One of the side gates had been left welcomingly ajar and a lantern perched atop the stone ledge next to it shed a yellow glow on the path. We had almost reached this beacon when a hand suddenly descended on my mouth from behind and I was jerked abruptly off my feet.

I struggled and bit, but my captor was heavily gloved and, as Jamie had said, a good deal larger than I.

Jamie himself seemed to be having minor difficulties, judging from the sound of it. The grunting and muffled cursing ceased abruptly with a thud and a rich Gaelic expletive.

The struggle in the dark stopped, and there was an unfamiliar laugh.

'God's eyes, if it's no the young lad; Callum's nephew. Come late to the oath-taking, are ye not, lad? And who's that wi' ye?'

'It's a lassie,' replied the man holding me. 'And a sweet juicy one, too, by the heft of her.' The hand left my mouth and administered a hearty squeeze elsewhere. I squeaked in indignation, reached over my shoulder, got hold of his nose and yanked. The man set me down with a quick oath of his own, less formal than those about to be taken within the hall. I stepped back from the blast of whisky fumes, feeling a sudden surge of appreciation for Jamie's presence. Perhaps his accompanying me had been prudent after all.

He appeared to be thinking otherwise as he made a vain attempt to remove the clinging grip of the two men-at-arms who had attached themselves to him. There was nothing hostile about their actions, but there was a considerable amount of firmness. They began to move purposefully towards the open gate, their captive in tow.

'Nay, let me go and change first, man,' he protested. 'I'm no decent to be going into the oath-taking like this.'

His attempt at graceful escape was foiled by the sudden appearance of Rupert, fatly resplendent in ruffled shirt and gold-laced coat, who popped out of the narrow gate like a cork from a bottle.

'Dinna worry yourself about that, laddie,' he said, surveying Jamie with a gleaming eye. 'We'll outfit ye proper –

inside.' He jerked his head towards the gate and Jamie disappeared within, under compulsion. A meaty hand gripped my own elbow and I followed willy-nilly.

Rupert appeared to be in very high spirits, as did the other men I saw inside the castle. There were perhaps sixty or seventy men, all dressed in their best, festooned with dirks, swords, pistols and sporrans, milling about in the courtyard nearest the entrance to the Great Hall. Rupert gestured to a door set in the wall and the men hustled Jamie into a small lighted room. It was one apparently used for storage; odds and ends of all kinds littered the tables and shelves with which it was furnished.

Rupert surveyed Jamie critically, with an eye to the oatstraws in his hair and the stains on his shirt. I saw his glance flicker to the oatstraws in my own hair, and a cynical grin split his face.

'No wonder ye're late, laddie,' he said, digging Jamie in the ribs. 'Dinna blame ye a bit.

'Willy!' he called to one of the men outside. 'We need some clothes here. Something suitable for the laird's nephew. See to it, man, and hurry!'

Jamie looked around, thin-lipped, at the men surrounding him. Six clansmen, all in tearing high spirits at the prospect of the oath-taking and brimming over with a fierce MacKenzie pride. The spirits had plainly been assisted by an ample intake from the tub of ale I had seen in the yard. Jamie's eyes lighted on me, his expression still grim. This was *my* doing, his face seemed to say.

He could, of course, announce that he did not mean to swear his oath to Callum, and head back to his warm bed in the stables. If he wanted a serious beating or his throat cut, that is. He raised an eyebrow at me, shrugged, and submitted with a fair show of grace to Willy, who rushed up with a pile of snowy linen in his arms and a hairbrush in one hand. The pile was topped by a flat blue bonnet of velvet, adorned with a metal badge that held a sprig of holly. I picked up the bonnet to examine it as Jamie fought his way into the clean shirt and brushed his hair with suppressed savagery.

The badge was round and the engraving surprisingly fine. It showed five volcanos in the centre, spouting most realistic flames. And on the border was a motto, *Luceo Non Uro.*

'I shine, not burn,' I translated aloud.

'Aye, lassie; the MacKenzie motto,' said Willy, nodding approvingly at me. He snatched the bonnet from my hands and pushed it into Jamie's before dashing off in search of further clothing.

'Er . . . I'm sorry,' I said in a low voice, taking advantage of Willy's absence to move closer. 'I didn't mean – '

Jamie, who had been viewing the badge on the bonnet with disfavour, glanced down at me, and the grim line of his mouth relaxed.

'Ah, dinna worry yourself on my account, Sassenach. It would ha' come to it sooner or later.' He twisted the badge loose from the bonnet and smiled sourly at it, weighing it speculatively in his hand.

'D'ye ken my own motto, lass?' he asked. 'My clan's, I mean?'

'No,' I answered, startled. 'What is it?'

He flipped the badge once in the air, caught it and dropped it neatly into his sporran. He looked rather bleakly towards the open archway, where the MacKenzie clansmen were massing in untidy lines.

'*Je suis prest,*' he replied in surprisingly good French. He glanced back, to see Rupert and another large MacKenzie I didn't know, faces flushed with high spirits and spirits of another kind, advancing with solid purpose. Rupert held a huge length of MacKenzie tartan.

Without preliminaries the other man reached for the buckle of Jamie's kilt.

'Best leave, Sassenach,' Jamie advised briefly. 'It's no place for women.'

'So I see,' I responded dryly, and was rewarded with a wry smile as his hips were swathed in the new kilt and the old one yanked deftly away beneath it, modesty preserved. Rupert and friend took him firmly by the arms and hustled him towards the archway.

I turned without delay and made my way back towards

the stair to the minstrels' gallery, carefully avoiding the eye of any clansman I passed. Once around the corner I paused, shrinking back against the wall to avoid notice. I waited for a moment, until the corridor was temporarily deserted, then nipped inside the gallery door and pulled it quickly to behind me before anyone else could come round the corner and see where I had gone. The stairs were dimly lit by the glow from above, and I had no trouble keeping my footing on the worn flags. I climbed towards the noise and light, thinking of that last brief exchange.

'*Je suis prest.*' *I am ready.* I hoped he was.

The gallery was lit by pine torches, brilliant flares that rose straight up in their sockets, outlined in black by the soot their predecessors had left on the walls. Several faces turned, blinking, to look at me as I came out of the hangings at the back of the gallery; from the looks of it, all the women of the castle were up here. I recognized the girl Laoghaire, Magdalen and some of the other women I had met in the kitchens and, of course, the stout form of Mrs FitzGibbons, in a position of honour near the balustrade.

Seeing me, she beckoned in a friendly manner, and the women squeezed against each other to let me pass. When I reached the front I could see the whole hall spread out beneath.

The walls were decked with myrtle and holly branches, and the fragrance of the evergreens rose up into the gallery, mingled with the smoke of fires and the harsh reek of men. There were dozens of them, coming, going, standing talking in small groups scattered throughout the hall, and all clad in some version of the clan tartan, be it only a plaid or a tartan bonnet worn above ordinary working shirt and tattered breeches. The actual patterns varied wildly, but the colours were mostly the same – greens and blues.

Most of them were completely dressed as Jamie now was, kilt, plaid, bonnet and – in most cases – badges. I caught a glimpse of him standing near the wall, still looking grim. Rupert had disappeared into the throng, but two more burly MacKenzies flanked Jamie, obviously guards.

The confusion in the hall was gradually becoming organized as the castle residents pushed and led the newcomers into place at the lower end.

Tonight was plainly special; the young lad who played the pipes at Hall had been augmented by two other pipers, one a man whose bearing and ivory-mounted pipes proclaimed him a master piper. This man nodded to the other two, and soon the hall was filled with the fierce drone of pipe music. Much smaller than the great Northern pipes used in battle, these smaller versions made a most effective racket.

The chanters laid a trill above the drones that made the blood itch. The women stirred around me, and I thought of a line from 'Maggie Lauder':

> Oh, they call me Rab the Ranter,
> And the lassies all go daft,
> When I blow up my chanter.

If not daft, the women around me were fully appreciative, and there were many murmurs of admiration as they hung over the rail, pointing out one man or another striding about the hall decked in his finery. One girl spotted Jamie, and with a muffled exclamation, beckoned her friends to see. There was considerable whispering and murmuring over his appearance.

Some of it was admiration for his fine looks, but more was speculation about his presence at the oath-taking. I noticed that Laoghaire, in particular, glowed like a candle as she watched him, and I remembered what Alick had said in the paddock – *Ye know her father will no let her wed outside the clan*. And Callum's nephew, was he? The lad might be quite a catch, at that. Bar the minor matter of outlawry, of course.

The pipe music rose to a fervent pitch and then abruptly ceased. In the dead silence of the hall, Callum MacKenzie stepped out from the upper archway and strode purposefully to a small platform that had been erected at the head of the room. If he made no effort to hide his disability, he did not flaunt it now either. He was splendid in an azure-blue coat, heavily laced with gold, buttoned with silver, and with rose silk cuffs that turned back almost to the elbow. A tartan kilt in fine wool hung past his knees, covering most of his legs and the checked stockings on them. His bonnet was blue, but the silver badge held plumes, not holly. The entire hall held its breath as he took centre stage. Whatever else he was, Callum MacKenzie was a showman.

He turned to face the assembled clansmen, raised his arms and greeted them with a ringing shout.

'*Tulach Ard!*'

'*Tulach Ard!*' the clansmen gave back in a roar. The woman next to me shivered.

There was a short speech next, given in Gaelic. This was greeted with periodic roars of approval, and then the oath-taking proper commenced.

Dougal MacKenzie was the first man to advance to Callum's platform. The small rostrum gave Callum enough height that the brothers met face to face. Dougal was richly dressed, but in plain chestnut velvet with no gold lace, so as not to distract attention from Callum's magnificence.

Dougal drew his dirk with a flourish and sank to one knee, holding the dirk upright by the blade. His voice was less powerful than Callum's, but loud enough so that every word rang through the hall.

'I swear by the cross of our Lord Jesus Christ, and by the holy iron that I hold, to give ye my fealty and pledge ye my loyalty to the name of the Clan MacKenzie. If ever my hand shall be raised against ye in rebellion, I ask that this holy iron shall pierce my heart.'

He lowered the dirk, kissed it at the juncture of haft and tang, and thrust it home in its sheath. Still kneeling, he offered both hands clasped to Callum, who took them between his own and lifted them to his lips in acceptance of the oath so offered. Then he raised Dougal to his feet.

Turning, Callum picked up a silver quaich from its place on the tartan-covered table behind him. He lifted the heavy eared cup with both hands, drank from it, and offered it to Dougal. Dougal took a healthy swallow and handed back the cup. Then, with a final bow to the laird of Leoch, he stepped to one side to make room for the next man in line.

This same process was repeated over and over, from vow to ceremonial drink. Viewing the number of men in the line, I was impressed anew at Callum's capacity. I was trying to work out how many pints of spirit he would have consumed by the end of the evening, given one swallow per oath-taker, when I saw Jamie approach the head of the line.

Dougal, his own oath completed, had taken up station to Callum's rear. He saw Jamie before Callum, who was occupied with another man, and I saw his sudden start of surprise. He stepped close to his brother and muttered something. Callum kept his eyes fixed on the man before him, but I saw him stiffen slightly. He was surprised too and, I thought, not altogether pleased.

The level of feeling in the hall, high to start with, had risen through the ceremony. If Jamie were to refuse his oath at this point, I thought he could easily be torn to shreds by the overwrought clansmen around him. I wiped my palms surreptitiously against my skirt, feeling guilty at having brought him into such a precarious situation.

He seemed composed. Hot as the hall was, he wasn't sweating. He waited patiently in line, showing no signs of realizing that he was surrounded by a hundred men, armed to the teeth, who would be quick to resent any insult offered to Himself and the clan. *Je suis prest*, indeed. Or perhaps he had decided after all to take Alick's advice?

My nails were digging into my palms by the time it came to his turn.

He went gracefully to one knee and bowed deeply before Callum. But instead of drawing his knife for the oath, he rose to his feet and looked Callum in the face. Fully erect, he stood head and shoulders over most of the men in the hall, and he topped Callum on his rostrum by several inches. I glanced at the girl Laoghaire. She had gone pale when he rose to his feet, and I saw that she also had her fists clenched tight.

Every eye in the hall was on him, but he spoke as though

to Callum alone. His voice was as deep as Callum's, and every word was clearly audible.

'Callum MacKenzie, I come to you as kinsman and as ally. I give ye no vow, for my oath is pledged to the name that I bear.' There was a low, ominous growl from the crowd, but he ignored it and went on. 'But I give ye freely the things that I have: my help and my goodwill, wherever ye should find need of them. I give ye my obedience, as kinsman and as laird, and I hold myself bound by your word, so long as my feet rest on the lands of Clan MacKenzie.'

He stopped speaking and stood tall and erect, hands relaxed at his sides. Ball now in Callum's court, I thought. One word from him, one sign, and they'd be scrubbing the young man's blood off the flags come morning.

Callum stood unmoving for a moment, then smiled and held out his hands. After an instant's hesitation, Jamie placed his own hands lightly on Callum's palms.

'We are honoured by your offer of friendship and good-will,' said Callum clearly. 'We accept your obedience and hold you in good faith as an ally of the Clan MacKenzie.'

There was a lessening of the tension over the hall and almost an audible sigh of relief in the gallery as Callum drank from the quaich and offered it to Jamie. The young man accepted it with a smile. Instead of the customary ceremonial sip, however, he carefully raised the nearly full vessel, tilted it and drank. And kept on drinking. There was a gasp of mingled respect and amusement from the spectators as the powerful throat muscles kept moving. Surely he'd have to breathe soon, I thought, but no. He drained the heavy cup to the last drop, lowered it with an explosive gasp for air, and handed it back to Callum.

'The honour is mine,' he said, a little hoarsely, 'to be allied with a clan whose taste in whisky is so fine.'

There was an uproar at this, and he made his way towards the archway, much impeded by congratulatory handshakes and thumps on the back as he passed. Apparently Callum MacKenzie was not the only member of the family with a knack for good theatre.

The heat in the gallery was stifling and the rising smoke

was making my head ache before the oath-taking finally came to an end, with what I assumed were a few stirring words by Callum. Unaffected by six shared quaiches of spirit, the strong voice still reverberated off the stones of the hall. At least his legs wouldn't pain him tonight, I thought, in spite of all the standing.

There was a massive shout from the floor below, an outbreak of skirling pipes, and the solemn scene dissolved into a heaving surge of riotous yelling. An even louder shout greeted the tubs of ale and whisky that now appeared on trestles, accompanied by platters of steaming bannocks and smoked beef. Mrs Fitz, who must have organized this part of the proceedings, leaned precariously across the balustrade, keeping a sharp eye on the behaviour of the stewards, mostly lads too young to swear a formal oath.

'And where's the chickens got to, then?' she muttered under her breath, surveying the incoming platters. 'Or the spatchcocked eels, either? Drat that Mungo Grant, I'll skin him if he's burnt the eels!' Making up her mind, she turned and began to squeeze towards the back of the gallery, plainly unwilling to leave administration of something so critical as the feasting in the untried hands of Mungo Grant.

Seizing the opportunity, I pushed along behind her, taking advantage of the sizable wake she left through the crowd. Others, clearly thankful for a reason to leave, joined me in the exodus.

Mrs Fitz, turning at the bottom, saw the flock of women above and scowled ferociously.

'You wee lassies clear off to your rooms right sharp,' she commanded. 'If you'll not stay up there safe out o' sight, ye'd best scamper awa' to your own places. But no lingering in the corridors nor peeping round the corners. There's not a man in the place who's not half in his cups already, and they'll be far gone in an hour. 'Tis no place for lasses tonight.'

Pushing the door ajar, she peered cautiously into the corridor. The coast apparently clear, she shooed the women out of the door, one at a time, sending them hurriedly on their way to their sleeping quarters on the upper floors.

'Do you need any help?' I asked as I came even with her. 'In the kitchens, I mean?'

She shook her head but smiled at the offer. 'Nay, there's no need, lass. Get along wi' ye now, you're no safer than the rest.' And a kindly shove in the small of the back sent me hurtling out into the dim passage.

I was inclined to take her advice, after the encounter with the guard outside. The men in the hall were rioting, dancing and drinking, with no thought of restraint or control. No place for a woman, I agreed.

Finding my way back to my room was another matter altogether. I was in an unfamiliar part of the castle, and while I knew the next floor had a short stairway that connected it to the corridor leading to my room, I couldn't find anything resembling stairs.

I came around a corner, and smack into a group of clansmen. These were men I didn't know, come from the outlying clan lands and unused to the genteel manners of a castle. Or so I deduced from the fact that one man, apparently in search of the latrines, gave it up and chose to relieve himself in a corner of the hallway as I came upon them.

I whirled at once, intending to go back the way I had come, stairs or no stairs. Several hands reached to stop me, though, and I found myself pressed against the wall of the corridor, surrounded by bearded Highlanders with whisky on their breath and rape on their minds.

Seeing no point in preliminaries, the man in front of me grabbed me by the waist and plunged his other hand into my bodice. He leaned close, rubbing his bearded cheek against my ear. 'And how about a sweet kiss, now, for the brave lads of the Clan MacKenzie? *Tulach Ard!*'

'*Erin go bragh,*' I said rudely, and pushed with all my strength. Unsteady with drink, he staggered backwards into one of his companions. I dodged to the side and fled, kicking off my clumsy shoes as I ran.

Another shape loomed in front of me, and I hesitated. There seemed to be only one in front of me, though, and at least ten behind me, catching up fast despite their cargo of drink. I raced forward, intending to dodge around him. He stepped sharply in front of me, though, and I came to a halt, so fast that I had to put my hands on his chest to avoid crashing into him. It was Dougal MacKenzie.

'What in hell – ?' he began, then saw the men after me. He pulled me behind him and barked something at my pursuers in Gaelic. They protested in the same language, but after a short exchange like the snarling of wolves they gave it up and went off in search of better entertainment.

'Thank you,' I said, a little dazed. 'Thank you. I'll . . . I'll go. I shouldn't be down here.' Dougal glanced down at me and took my arm, pulling me around to face him. He was dishevelled and clearly had been joining in the roistering in the hall.

'True enough, lass,' he said. 'Ye shouldna be here. Since ye are, weel, you'll have to pay the penalty for that,' he murmured, eyes gleaming in the half dark. And without warning he pulled me hard against him and kissed me. Kissed me hard enough to bruise my lips and force them apart. His tongue flicked against mine, the taste of whisky sharp in my mouth. His hands gripped me firmly by the bottom and pressed me against him, making me feel the rigid hardness under his kilt through my layers of skirts and petticoats.

He released me as suddenly as he had seized me, and nodded and gestured down the hall, breathing a little unsteadily. A lock of russet hair hung loose over his forehead and he brushed it back with one hand.

'Get ye gone, lassie,' he said. 'Before ye pay a greater price.'

I went, barefoot.

Given the carryings-on of the night before, I had expected most inhabitants of the castle to lie late the next morning, possibly staggering down for a restorative mug of ale when the sun was high – assuming that it chose to come out at all, of course. But the Highland Scots of Clan MacKenzie were a tougher bunch than I had reckoned with, for the castle was a buzzing hive long before dawn, with rowdy

202

voices calling up and down the corridors and a great clanking of armoury and thudding of boots as men prepared for the tinchel.

It was cold and foggy, but Rupert, whom I met in the courtyard on my way to the hall, assured me that this was the best sort of weather in which to hunt boar.

'The beasts ha' such a thick coat, the cold's no hindrance to them,' he explained, sharpening a spearpoint with enthusiasm against a foot-driven grindstone, 'and they feel safe wi' the mist so heavy all round them – canna see the men coming towards them, ye ken.'

I forbore to point out that this meant the hunting men would not be able to see the boar they were approaching, either, until they were upon it.

As the sun began to streak the mist with blood and gold the hunting party assembled in the forecourt, spangled with damp and bright-eyed with anticipation. I was glad to see that the women were not expected to participate, but contented themselves with offering bannocks and draughts of ale to the departing heroes. Seeing the large number of men who set out for the east wood, armed to the teeth with boar spears, axes, bows, quivers and daggers, I felt a bit sorry for the boar.

This attitude was revised to one of awed respect an hour later when I was hastily summoned to the forest's edge to dress the wounds of a man who had, as I surmised, stumbled over the beast unawares in the fog.

'Bloody Christ!' I said, examining a gaping, jagged wound that ran from knee to ankle. 'An *animal* did this? What's it got, stainless steel teeth?'

'Eh?' The victim was white with shock and too shaken to answer me, but one of the fellows who had assisted him from the wood gave me a curious look.

'Never mind,' I said, and yanked tight the compression bandage I had wound about the injured calf. 'Take him up to the castle and we'll have Mrs Fitz give him hot broth and blankets. That'll have to be stitched, and I've no tools for it here.'

The rhythmic shouts of the same beaters still echoed in

the mists of the hillside. Suddenly there was a piercing scream that rose high above fog and tree, and a startled pheasant broke from its hiding place nearby with a frightening rattle of wings.

'Dear God in heaven, what now?' Seizing an armful of bandages I abandoned my patient to his caretakers and headed into the forest at a dead run.

The fog was thicker under the branches and I could see no more than a few feet ahead, but the sound of excited shouting and thrashing underbush guided me in the right direction.

It brushed past me from behind. Intent on the shouting, I didn't hear it, and I didn't see it until it had passed, a dark mass moving at incredible speed, the absurdly tiny cloven hooves almost silent on the sodden leaves.

I was so stunned by the suddenness of the apparition that it didn't occur to me at first to be frightened. I simply stared into the mist where the bristling black thing had vanished. Then, raising my hand to brush back the ringlets that were curling damply around my face. I saw the blotched red streak across it. Looking down, I found a matching streak on my skirt. The beast was wounded. Had the scream come from the boar, perhaps?

I thought not; I knew the sound of mortal wounding. And the pig was moving well under its own power when it had passed me. I took a deep breath and went on into the wall of mist in search of a wounded man.

I found him at the bottom of a small slope, surrounded by kilted men. They had spread their plaids over him to keep him warm, but the cloth covering his legs was ominously dark with wetness. A wide scrape of black mud showed where he had tumbled down the length of the slope, and a scrabble of muddied leaves and churned earth, where he had met the boar. I sank to my knees beside the man, pulled back the cloth and set to work.

I had scarcely begun when the shouts of the men around us made me turn to see the nightmare shape appear, once more soundless, out of the trees.

This time I had time to see the dagger hilt protruding

from the beast's side, perhaps the work of the man on the ground before me. And the wicked yellow ivory, stained red as the mad little eyes.

The men around me, as stunned as I was, began to stir and reach for weapons. Faster than the rest, a tall man seized a boar spear from the hands of a companion who stood frozen, and stepped out into the clearing.

It was Dougal MacKenzie. He walked almost casually, carrying the spear low, braced in both hands, as though about to lift a spadeful of earth. He was intent on the beast, speaking to it in an undertone, murmuring in Gaelic as though to coax it from the shelter of the tree it stood beside.

The first charge was sudden as an explosion. The beast shot past, so closely that the muted hunting tartan flapped in the breeze of its passing. It spun at once and came back, a blur of muscular rage. Dougal leapt aside like a bullfighter, jabbing at it with his spear. Back, forth and again. It was less a rampage than a dance, both adversaries rooted in strength, but so nimble they seemed to float above the ground.

The whole thing lasted only a minute or so, though it seemed much longer. It ended when Dougal, whirling aside from the slashing tusks, raised the point of the short, stout spear and drove it straight down between the beast's sloping shoulders. There was the thunk of the spear and a shrill squealing noise that made the hairs stand up along my forearms. The small, piggy eyes cast to and fro, veering wildly in search of nemesis, and the dainty hooves sank deep in mud as the boar staggered and lurched. The squealing went on, rising to an inhuman pitch as the heavy body toppled to one side, driving the protruding dagger hilt-deep in the hairy flesh. The delicate hooves spurned the ground, churning up thick clods of damp earth.

The squeal stopped abruptly. There was silence for a moment and then a thoroughly piggish grunt, and the bulk was still.

Dougal had not waited to make sure of the kill, but had circled the twitching animal and made his way back to the injured man. He sank to his knees and put an arm behind the victim's shoulders, taking the place of the man who had been supporting him. A fine spray of blood had spattered the high cheekbones, and drying droplets matted his hair on one side.

'Now then, Geordie,' he said, rough voice suddenly gentle. 'Now then. I've got him, man. It's all right.'

'Dougal? Is't you, man?' The wounded man turned his head in Dougal's direction, struggling to open his eyes.

I was surprised, listening as I rapidly checked the man's pulse and vital signs. Dougal the fierce, Dougal the ruthless, was speaking to the man in a low voice, repeating words of comfort, hugging the man hard against him, stroking the tumbled hair.

I sat back on my heels and reached again towards the pile of cloths on the ground beside me. There was a deep wound, running at least eight inches from the groin down the thigh, from which the blood was gushing in a steady flow. It wasn't spurting, though; the femoral artery wasn't cut, which meant there was a good chance of stopping it.

What couldn't be stopped was the ooze from the man's belly, where the ripping tushes had laid open skin, muscles and gut alike. There were no large vessels severed there, but the intestine was punctured; I could see it plainly through the jagged rent in the man's skin. This sort of abdominal wound was frequently fatal, even with a modern operating room, sutures and penicillin readily to hand. The contents of the ruptured gut, spilling out into the body cavity, simply contaminated the whole area and made infection a deadly certainty. And here, with nothing but cloves of garlic and yarrow flowers to treat it with . . .

My gaze met Dougal's as he also looked down at the hideous wound. His lips moved, mouthing soundlessly over the man's head the words, 'Can he live?'

I shook my head mutely. He paused for a moment, holding Geordie, then reached forward and deliberately untied the emergency tourniquet I had placed around the man's thigh. He looked at me, challenging me to protest, but I made no move save a small nod. I could stanch the bleeding and allow the man to be transported by litter back to the castle. Back to the castle, there to linger in increasing agony as the belly wound festered, until the corruption spread far enough finally to kill him, wallowing perhaps for days in long-drawn-out pain. A better death, perhaps, was what Dougal was giving him – to die cleanly under the sky, his heart's blood staining the same leaves as the blood of the beast that killed him. I crawled over the damp leaves to Geordie's head, and took half his weight on my own arm.

'It will be better soon,' I said, and my voice was steady, as it always was, as it had been trained to be. 'The pain will be better soon.'

'Aye. It's better . . . now. I canna feel my leg any more . . . nor my hands . . . Dougal . . . are ye there? Are ye there, man?' The numb hands were blindly flailing before the man's face. Dougal grasped them firmly between his own and leaned close, murmuring in the man's ear.

Geordie's back arched suddenly and his heels dug deeply into the muddy ground, his body in violent protest at what his mind had begun already to accept. He gasped deeply from time to time, starving for oxygen.

The forest was very quiet. No birds sang in the mist, and the men who waited patiently hunkered in the shadow of the trees were silent as the trees themselves. Dougal and I leaned close together over the struggling body, murmuring and comforting, sharing the messy, heartrending and necessary task of helping a man to die.

The trip up the hill to the castle was silent. I walked beside the dead man, borne on a makeshift litter of pine boughs. Behind us, borne in precisely similar fashion, came the body of his foe. Dougal walked ahead, alone.

As we entered the gate to the main courtyard I caught sight of the tubby little figure of Father Bain, the village priest, hurrying belatedly to the aid of his fallen parishioner.

Dougal paused, reaching out to stay me as I turned towards the stair leading to the surgery. The bearers with Geordie's plaid-shrouded body on its litter passed on, heading towards the chapel, leaving us together in the deserted corridor. Dougal held me by the wrist, looking me over intently.

'You've seen men die before,' he said flatly. 'By violence.' Not a question, almost an accusation.

'Many of them,' I said, just as flatly. And pulling myself free, I left him standing there and went to tend my living patient.

The death of Geordie, hideous as it was, put only a momentary damper on the celebrations. A lavish funeral Mass was said over him that afternoon in the castle chapel, and the games began the next morning.

I saw little of them, being occupied in patching up the participants. All I could say for sure of authentic Highland games is that they were played for keeps. I bound up some fumble-foot who had managed to slash himself trying to dance between swords, I set the broken leg of a hapless victim who'd got in the way of a carelessly thrown hammer, and I doled out castor oil and peppermint syrup to countless children who had over-indulged in sweeties. By late afternoon I was near exhaustion.

I climbed up on the surgery table in order to reach the tiny window for some air. The shouts and laughter and music from the field where the games were held had ceased. Good. No more new patients, then, at least not until tomorrow. What had Rupert said they were going to do next? Archery? Hmm. I checked the supply of bandages, and wearily closed the surgery door behind me.

Leaving the castle, I trailed downhill towards the stables. I could do with some good nonhuman, nonspeaking, nonbleeding company. I also had in mind that I might find Jamie, whatever his last name was, and try again to apologize for involving him in the oath-taking. True, he had brought it off well, but clearly he would not have been there at all if he'd been left to his own devices. As to the gossip Rupert might now be spreading about our supposed amorous dalliance, I preferred not to think.

As to my own predicament, I preferred not to think about that, either, but I would have to, sooner or later. Having so completely failed to escape at the beginning of the Gathering, I wondered whether the chances might be better at the end. True, most of the mounts would be leaving, along with the visitors. But there would be a number of castle ponies still available. And with luck, the disappearance of one would be put down to random thievery; there were plenty of villainous-looking scoundrels hanging about the fairground and the games. And in the confusion of leaving, it might be some time before anyone discovered that I was gone.

I scuffed along the paddock wall, pondering escape routes. The difficulty was that I had only the vaguest idea where I was, with reference to where I wanted to go. And since I was now known to virtually every MacKenzie between Leoch and the Lowlands, thanks to my doctoring at the games, I would not be able to ask directions.

I wondered suddenly whether Jamie had told Callum or Dougal of my abortive attempt to escape on the night of the oath-taking. Neither of them had mentioned it to me, so perhaps not.

I pushed open the stable door, and my heart skipped a beat to see both Jamie and Dougal seated side by side on a pile of hay. They looked almost as startled at my appearance as I was at theirs, but gallantly rose and invited me to sit down.

'That's all right,' I said, backing towards the door. 'I didn't mean to intrude on your conversation.'

'Nay, lass,' said Dougal, 'what I've just been saying to young Jamie here concerns you too.'

I cast a quick look at Jamie, who responded with a trace of a headshake. So he hadn't told Dougal about my attempted escape.

I sat down, a bit wary of Dougal. I remembered that little scene in the corridor on the night of the oath-taking, though he had not referred to it since by word or gesture.

'I'm leaving in two days' time,' he said abruptly. 'And I'm taking the two of you with me.'

'Taking us where?' I asked, startled. My heart began to beat faster.

'Through the MacKenzie lands. Callum doesna travel, so visiting the tenants and tacksmen that canna come to the

Gathering – that's left to me. And to take care of the bits of business here and there . . .' He waved a hand, dismissing these as trivial.

'But why me? Why us, I mean?' I demanded.

He considered for a moment before answering. 'Why, Jamie's a handy lad wi' the horses. And as to you, lass, Callum thought it wise I should take ye along as far as Fort William. The commander there might be able to . . . assist ye in finding your family in France.' Or to assist *you*, I thought, in determining who I really am. And how much else are you not telling me? Dougal stared down at me, obviously wondering how I would take this news.

'All right,' I said tranquilly. 'That sounds a good idea.' Outwardly tranquil, inwardly I was rejoicing. What luck! Now I wouldn't have to try again the chancy business of an escape from the castle. Once on the road, and with a pony already under me, I thought I might easily steal away. And then make my way alone, to Craigh na Dun. To the circle of standing stones. And with luck, back home.

PART THREE

On the Road

11

Conversations with a Lawyer

We rode out of the gates of Castle Leoch two days later, just before dawn. In twos and threes and fours, to the sound of shouted farewells, the ponies stepped their way carefully over the stone bridge. I glanced behind from time to time, until the bulk of the castle disappeared at last behind a curtain of shimmering mist. The thought that I would never again see that grim pile of stone or its inhabitants gave me an odd feeling of regret.

The noise of the ponies' hooves seemed muffled in the mist. Voices carried strangely through the damp air, so that calls from one end of the long string were sometimes heard easily at the other, while the sounds of nearby conversations were lost in broken murmurs. It was like riding through a vapour peopled by ghosts. Disembodied voices floated in the air, speaking far away, then remarkably near at hand.

My place fell in the middle of the party, flanked on the one side by a man-at-arms whose name I did not know, and on the other by Ned Gowan, the little scribe I had seen at work in Callum's hall. He was something more than a scribe, I found, as we fell into conversation on the road.

Ned Gowan was a lawyer. Born, bred and educated in Edinburgh, he looked the part thoroughly. A small, elderly man of neat, precise habits, he wore a coat of fine broadcloth, fine woollen hose, a linen shirt whose stock bore the merest suggestion of lace, and breeches of a fabric that was a nicely judged compromise between the rigours of travel and the status of his calling. A small pair of gold-rimmed half-spectacles, a neat hair-ribbon and a tricorne of black beaver completed the picture. He was so perfectly the quintessential man of law that I couldn't look at him without smiling.

He rode alongside me on a quiet mare whose saddle was burdened with two enormous bags of worn leather. He explained that one held the tools of his trade: inkhorn, quills and papers.

'And what's the other for?' I asked, eyeing it. While the first bag was plump with its contents, the second seemed nearly empty.

'Oh, that's for Himself's rents,' the lawyer replied, patting the limp bag.

'He must be expecting rather a lot, then,' I suggested. Mr Gowan shrugged good-naturedly.

'Not so much as all that, m'dear. But the most of it will be in doits and pence and other small coins. And such, unfortunately, take up more room than the larger denominations of currency.' He smiled, a quick curve of thin, dry lips. 'At that, a weighty mass of copper and silver is still easier of transport than the bulk of MacKenzie's income.'

He turned to direct a piercing look over his shoulder at the carts that accompanied the party.

'Bags of grain and suchlike have at least the benefit of lack of motion. Fowl, if suitably trussed and caged, I have nae argument with. Nor with goats, though they prove some inconvenience in terms of their omnivorous habits; one ate a handkerchief of mine last year, though I admit the fault was mine in allowin' the fabric to protrude injudiciously from my coat pocket.' The thin lips set in a determined line. 'I have given explicit directions this year, though. We shall *not* accept live pigs.'

The necessity of protecting Mr Gowan's saddlebags and the carts explained the presence of the twenty or so men who made up the rest of the rent-collecting party, I supposed. All were armed and mounted, and there were a number of garrons bearing what I assumed were supplies for the sustenance of the party. Mrs Fitz, among her farewells and exhortations, had told me that accommodations would be primitive or nonexistent, with many nights spent encamped along the road.

I was quite curious to know what had led a man of Mr Gowan's obvious qualifications to take up a post in the

214

remote Scottish Highlands, far from the amenities of civilized life to which he must be accustomed.

'Well, as to that,' he said, in answer to my questions, 'as a young man, I had a small practice in Edinburgh. With lace curtains in the window, and a shiny brass plate by the door, with my name inscribed upon it. But I grew rather tired of making wills and registering instruments of sasine, and seeing the same faces in the street day after day. So I left,' he said simply.

He had purchased a horse and some supplies and set off, with no idea where he was going, or what to do once he got there.

'Ye see, I must confess,' he said, dabbing his nose primly with a monogrammed handkerchief, 'to something of a taste for . . . adventure. However, neither my stature nor my family background had fitted me for the life of highwayman or seafarer, which were the most adventurous occupations I could envision at the time. As an alternative I determined that my best path lay upwards, into the Highlands. I thought that in time I might perhaps induce some clan chieftain to, well, to allow me to serve him in some way.'

And in the course of his travels he had in fact encountered such a chieftain.

'Jacob MacKenzie,' he said, with a fond, reminiscent smile. 'And a wicked, red auld rascal he was.' Mr Gowan nodded towards the front of the line, where Jamie MacTavish's bright hair blazed in the mist. 'His grandson's verra like him, ye ken. We met first at the point of a pistol, Jacob and I, as he was robbing me. I yielded my horse and my bags with good grace, having little other choice. But I believe he was a bit taken aback when I insisted upon accompanying him, on foot if necessary.'

'Jacob MacKenzie. That would be Callum and Dougal's father?' I asked.

The elderly lawyer nodded. 'Aye. Of course, he was not laird then. That happened a few years later . . . with a very small bit of assistance from me,' he added modestly. 'Things were less . . . civilized then,' he said nostalgically.

215

'Oh, were they?' I said politely. 'And Callum, er, inherited you, so to speak?'

'Something of the kind,' Mr Gowan said. 'There was a wee bit o' confusion when Jacob died, d'ye see. Callum was heir, to be sure, but he . . .' The lawyer paused, looking ahead and behind to see that no one was close enough to listen. The man-at-arms had ridden forward, though, to catch up with some of his mates, and a good four lengths separated us from the cart behind.

'Callum was a whole man to the age of eighteen or so,' he resumed his story, 'and gave promise to be a fine leader. He took Letitia to wife as part of an alliance with the Camerons – I drew up the marriage contract,' he added, as a footnote, 'but soon after the marriage he had a bad fall, during a raid. Broke the long bone of his thigh, and it mended poorly.'

I nodded. It would have, of course.

'And then,' Mr Gowan went on with a sigh, 'he rose from his bed too soon, and took a tumble down the stairs that broke the other leg. He lay in his bed close on a year, but it soon became clear that the damage was permanent. And that was when Jacob died, unfortunately.'

The little man paused to marshal his thoughts. He glanced ahead again, as though looking for someone. Failing to find them, he settled back into the saddle.

'That was about the time there was all the fuss about his sister's marriage too,' he said. 'And Dougal . . . well, I'm afraid Dougal did not acquit himself so verra weel over that affair. Otherwise, d'ye see, Dougal might have been made laird at the time, but 'twas felt he'd not the judgement for it yet.' He shook his head. 'Oh, there was a great stramash about it all. There were cousins and uncles and tacksmen, and a great Gathering to decide the matter.'

'But they did choose Callum, after all?' I said. I marvelled once again at the force of personality of Callum MacKenzie. And, casting an eye at the withered little man who rode at my side, I rather thought Callum had also had some luck in choosing his allies.

'They did, but only because the brothers stood firm

216

together. There was nae doubt, ye see, of Callum's courage, nor yet of his mind, but only of his body. 'Twas clear he'd never be able to lead his men into battle again. But there was Dougal, sound and whole, if a bit reckless and hotheaded. And he stood behind his brother's chair and vowed to follow Callum's word and be his legs and his sword-arm in the field. So a suggestion was made that Callum be allowed to become laird, as he should in the ordinary way, and Dougal be made war chieftain, to lead the Leoch branch in time of battle. It was a situation not without precedent,' he added primly.

The modesty with which he had said 'A suggestion was made . . .' left no doubt as to just whose suggestion it had been.

'And whose man are you?' I asked. 'Callum's or Dougal's?'

'My interests must lie with the MacKenzie clan as a whole,' Mr Gowan said circumspectly. 'But as a matter of form, I have sworn my oath to Callum.'

A matter of form, my foot, I thought. I had seen that oath-taking, though I did not recall the small lawyer specifically among so many men. No man could have been present at that ceremony and remained unmoved, not even a born lawyer. And the little man on the bay mare, dry as his bones might be, and steeped to the marrow in the law, had by his own testimony the soul of a romantic.

'He must find you a great help,' I said diplomatically.

'Oh, I do a bit from time to time,' he said, 'in a small way. As I do for others. Should ye find yourself in need of advice, m'dear,' he said, beaming genially, 'do feel free to call upon me. My discretion may be relied upon, I do assure you.' He bowed quaintly from his saddle.

'To the same extent as your loyalty to Callum MacKenzie?' I said, arching my brows. The small brown eyes met mine full on, and I saw both the cleverness and the humour that lurked in their faded depths.

'Ah, weel,' he said, without apology. 'Worth a try.'

'I suppose so,' I said, more amused than angered. 'But I assure *you*, Mr Gowan, that I have no need of your discretion, at least at present.' It's catching, I thought, hearing myself. I sound just like him.

'I am an English lady,' I added firmly, 'and nothing more. Callum is wasting his time – and yours – in trying to extract secrets from me that don't exist.' Or that do exist, but are untellable, I thought. Mr Gowan's discretion might be limitless, but not his belief.

'He didn't send you along just to coerce me into damaging revelations, did he?' I demanded, suddenly struck by the thought.

'Oh, no.' Mr Gowan gave a short laugh at the idea. 'No, indeed, m'dear. I fulfil an essential function, in managing the records and receipts for Dougal and performing such small legal requirements that the clansmen in the more distant areas may have. And I am afraid that even at my advanced age I have not entirely outgrown the urge to seek adventure. Things are much more settled now than they used to be' – he heaved a sigh that might have been one of regret – 'but there is always the possibility of robbery along the road.'

He patted the second bag on his saddle. 'This bag is not entirely empty, ye ken.' He turned back the flap long enough for me to see the gleaming grips of a pair of scroll-butted pistols, snugly set in twin loops that kept them within easy reach.

He surveyed me with a glance that took in every detail of my costume and appearance.

'Ye should really be armed yourself, m'dear,' he said in a tone of mild reproof. 'Though I suppose Dougal thought it would not be suitable . . . still. I'll speak to him about it,' he promised.

We passed the rest of the day in pleasant conversation, wandering among his reminiscences of the dear departed days when men were men and the pernicious weed of civilization was less rampant upon the bonny wild face of the Highlands.

At nightfall we made camp in a clearing beside the road. I had a blanket, rolled and tied behind my saddle, and with this I prepared to spend my first night of freedom from the castle. As I left the fire and made my way to a spot behind the trees, though, I was conscious of the glances that followed me. Even in the open air, it seemed, freedom had definite limits.

We reached the first stopping place near noon of the second day. It was no more than a cluster of three or four huts, set off the road at the foot of a small glen. A stool was brought out from one of the cottages for Dougal's use, and a plank laid across two others to serve as a writing surface for Mr Gowan.

He withdrew an enormous square of starched linen from the tailpocket of his coat and laid it neatly over a stump, temporarily withdrawn from its usual function as chopping block. He seated himself upon this and began to lay out inkhorn, ledgers and receipt-book, as composed in his manner as though he were still behind his lace curtains in Edinburgh.

One by one the men from the nearby cot-houses appeared, to conduct their annual business with the laird's representative. This was a leisurely affair and conducted with a good deal less formality than the goings-on in the hall of Castle Leoch. Each man came, fresh from field or byre, and drawing up a vacant stool sat alongside Dougal in apparent equality, explaining, complaining or merely chatting.

Some were accompanied by a sturdy son or two, bearing bags of grain or wool. At the conclusion of each conversation the indefatigable Ned Gowan would write out a receipt for the payment of the year's rent, recording the transaction neatly in his ledger, and flick a finger to one of the drovers, who would obligingly heave the payment on to a cart. Less frequently a small heap of coins would disappear into the depths of his leather bag with a faint chinking sound. Meanwhile the men-at-arms lounged beneath the trees or disappeared up the wooded bank – to hunt, I supposed.

Variations of this scene were repeated over the next few days. Now and then I would be invited into a cottage for a cup of milk, and all of the women would crowd into the small single room to talk with me. Sometimes a cluster of rude huts would be large enough to support a pot-house or even an inn, which became Dougal's headquarters for the day.

Once in a while the rents would include a garron, a sheep or other livestock. These were generally traded to someone in the neighbourhood for something more portable, or if Jamie declared a pony fit for inclusion in the castle stables, it would be added to our string.

I wondered about Jamie's presence in the party. While the young man clearly knew ponies well, so did most of the men, including Dougal himself. Considering also that ponies were both a rare sort of payment and usually nothing special in the way of breeding, I wondered why it had been thought necessary to bring an expert along. It was a week after we had set out, in a village with an unpronounceable name, that I found out the real reason why Dougal had wanted Jamie.

The village, though small, was large enough to boast a pot-house with two or three tables and several rickety stools. Here Dougal held his hearings and collected his rents. And after a rather indigestible dinner of stale oatcake and hard cheese he held court, buying ale for the tenants and cottars who had lingered after their transactions, and a few villagers who drifted in to gawk at the strangers and hear such news as we carried.

I sat quietly on a settle in the corner, sipping sour ale and enjoying the respite from horseback. I was paying little attention to Dougal's talk, which shifted back and forth between Gaelic and English, ranging from bits of gossip and farming talk to what sounded like vulgar jokes and meandering stories.

I was wondering idly how, exactly, I might best part company with the Scots of Castle Leoch without becoming equally entangled with the English army garrison. Lost in my own thoughts, I had not noticed that Dougal had been speaking for some time alone, as though making a speech of some kind. His hearers were following him intently, with occasional brief interjections and exclamations. Coming

220

gradually back to an awareness of my surroundings, I realized that he was skilfully rousing his audience to a high pitch of excitement about *something*.

I glanced around. Fat Rupert and the little lawyer, Ned Gowan, sat against the wall behind Dougal, tankards of ale forgotten on the bench beside them as they listened intently. Jamie, frowning into his own tankard, leaned forward with his elbows on the table. Whatever Dougal was saying, he didn't seem to care for it.

With no warning, Dougal stood, seized Jamie's collar and pulled. Old, and shabbily made to begin with, the shirt tore cleanly down the seams. Taken completely by surprise, Jamie froze. His eyes narrowed, and I saw his jaw set tightly, but he didn't move as Dougal spread aside the ripped flaps of cloth to display his back to the onlookers.

There was a general gasp at sight of the scarred back, then a buzz of excited indignation. I opened my mouth, then caught the word 'Sassenach', spoken with no kindly intonation, and shut it again.

Jamie, with a face like stone, stood and stepped back from the small crowd clustering around him. He carefully peeled off the remnants of his shirt, wadding the cloth into a ball. An elderly little woman, who reached the level of his elbow, was shaking her head and patting his back gingerly, making what I assumed were comforting remarks in Gaelic. If so, they were clearly not having the hoped-for effect.

He replied tersely to a few questions from the men present. The two or three young girls who had come in to fetch their families' supper ale were clustered together against the far wall, whispering intently to each other, with frequent big-eyed glances across the room.

With a look at Dougal that should by rights have turned the older man to stone, Jamie tossed the ruins of his shirt into a corner of the hearth and left the room in three long strides, shaking off the sympathetic murmurs of the crowd.

Deprived of spectacle, their attentions turned back to Dougal. I didn't understand most of the comment, though the bits I caught seemed to be highly anti-English in nature. I was torn between wanting to follow Jamie outside and staying inconspicuously where I was. I doubted that he wanted any company, though, so I shrank back into my corner and kept my head down, studying my blurry, pale reflection in the surface of my tankard.

The clink of metal made me look up. One of the men, a sturdy-looking cottar in leather trews, had tossed a few coins on the table in front of Dougal, and seemed to be making a short speech of his own. He stood back, thumbs braced in his belt, as though daring the rest to something. After an uncertain pause one or two bold souls followed suit, and then a few more, digging copper doits and pence out of purse and sporran. Dougal thanked them heartily, waving a hand at the landlord for another round of ale. I noticed that the lawyer Ned Gowan was tidily stowing the new contributions in a separate pouch from that used for the MacKenzie rents bound for Callum's coffers, and I realized what the purpose of Dougal's little performance must be.

Rebellions, like most other business propositions, require capital. The raising and provisioning of an army takes gold, as does the maintenance of its leaders. And from the little I remembered of Bonnie Prince Charlie, the Young Pretender to the throne, most of his support had come from France, but a small part of the finances behind his unsuccessful rising had come from the shallow, threadbare pockets of the people he proposed to rule. So Callum, or Dougal, or both, were Jacobites; supporters of the Young Pretender against the lawful occupant of the throne, George II.

Finally, the last of the cottars and tenants drifted away to their suppers, and Dougal stood up and stretched, looking moderately satisfied, like a cat that has dined at least on milk if not cream. He weighed the smaller pouch and tossed it back to Ned Gowan for safekeeping.

'Aye, well enough,' he remarked. 'Canna expect a great deal from such a small place. But manage enough of the same and it will be a respectable sum.'

' "Respectable" is not quite the word I'd use,' I said, rising stiffly from my lurking place.

Dougal turned as though noticing me for the first time.

222

'No?' he said, mouth curling in amusement. 'Why not? Have ye an objection to loyal subjects contributing their mite in support of their sovereign?'

'None,' I said, meeting his stare. 'No matter which sovereign it is. It's your collection methods I don't care for.'

Dougal studied me carefully, as though my features might tell him something. 'No matter which sovereign it is?' he repeated softly. 'I thought ye had no Gaelic.'

'I haven't,' I said shortly. 'But I've the sense I was born with, and two ears in good working order. And whatever "King George's health" may be in Gaelic, I doubt very much that it sounds like "Bragh Stuart".'

He tossed back his head and laughed. 'That it doesna,' he agreed. 'I'd tell ye the proper Gaelic for your liege lord and ruler, but it isna a word suitable for the lips of a lady, Sassenach or no.'

Stooping, he plucked the balled-up shirt out of the ashes of the hearth and shook the worst of the soot off it.

'Since ye dinna care for my methods, perhaps ye'd wish to remedy them,' he suggested, thrusting the ruined shirt into my hands. 'Get a needle from the lady of the house and mend it.'

'Mend it yourself!' I shoved it back into his arms and turned to leave.

'Suit yourself,' Dougal said pleasantly from behind me. 'Jamie can mend his own shirt, then, if you're not disposed to help.'

I stopped, then turned reluctantly, hand out.

'All right,' I began, but was interrupted by a large hand that snaked over my shoulder and snatched the shirt from Dougal's grasp. Dividing an opaque glance evenly between us, Jamie tucked the shirt under his arm and left the room as silently as he had entered it.

We found accommodation for the night at a cottage. Or I should say I did. The men slept outside, disposed in various haystacks and patches of bracken. In deference to my sex or my status as semi-captive, I was provided with a pallet on the floor inside, near the hearth.

While my pallet seemed vastly preferable to the one bedstead in which the entire family of six was sleeping, I rather envied the men their open-air sleeping arrangements. The fire was not put out, only damped for the night, and the air in the cottage was stifling with warmth and the scents and sounds of the tossing, turning, groaning, snoring, sweating, farting inhabitants.

After some time I gave up any thought of sleeping in that smothered atmosphere. I rose and stole quietly outside, taking a blanket with me. The air outside was so fresh by contrast with the congestion in the cottage that I leaned against the stone wall, gulping in enormous lungfuls of the delicious cool stuff.

There was a guard, sitting in quiet watchfulness under a tree by the path, but he merely glanced at me. Apparently deciding that I was not going far in my shift, he went back to whittling at a small object in his hands. The moon was bright, and the blade of the tiny *skein dhu* flickered in the leafy shadows.

I walked around the cottage and a little way up the hill behind it, careful to watch for slumbering forms in the grass. I found a pleasant private spot between two large boulders and made a comfortable nest for myself from heaped grass and the blanket. Stretched at length on the ground, I watched the full moon on its slow voyage across the sky.

Just so had I watched the moon rise from the window of Castle Leoch on my first night as Callum's unwilling guest. A month, then, since my calamitous passage through the circle of standing stones. At least I now thought I knew why the stones had been placed there.

Likely of no particular importance in themselves, they were markers. Just as a signpost warns of rockfalls near a cliff edge, the standing stones were meant to mark a spot of danger. A spot where . . . what? Where the crust of time was thin? Where a gate of some sort stood ajar? Not that the makers of the circles would have known what it was they were marking. To them, the spot would have been one of terrible mystery and powerful magic; a spot where people disappeared without warning. Or appeared, perhaps, out of thin air.

That was a thought. What would have happened, I wondered, had anyone been present on the hill of Craigh na Dun when I made my abrupt appearance? I supposed it might depend on the time one entered. Here, had a cottar encountered me under such circumstances, I would doubtless have been thought a witch or a fairy. More likely a fairy, popping into existence on that particular hill, with its reputation.

And that might well be where its reputation came from, I thought. If people through the years had suddenly disappeared, or just as suddenly appeared from nowhere at a certain spot, it might with good reason acquire a name for enchantment.

I poked a foot out from under the blanket and waggled my long toes in the moonlight. Most unfairylike, I decided critically. At five foot six, I was quite a tall woman for these times; as tall as many men. Since I could hardly pass as one of the Wee Folk, then, I would likely have been thought a witch or an evil spirit of some kind. From the little I knew of current methods for dealing with such manifestations, I could only be grateful that no one in fact had seen me appear.

I wondered idly what would happen if it worked the other way. What if someone disappeared from this time, and popped up in my own? That, after all, was precisely what I was intending to do, if there were any possible way of managing it. How would a modern-day Scot like Mrs Buchanan, the postmistress, react if someone like Murtagh, for instance, were suddenly to spring from the earth beneath her feet?

The most likely reaction, I thought, would be to run, to summon the police, or perhaps to do nothing at all, beyond telling one's friends and neighbours about the most extraordinary thing that happened the other day...

As for the visitor? Well, he might manage to fit into the new time without arousing excessive attention, if he was cautious and lucky. After all, I was managing to pass with some success as a normal resident of this time and place, though my appearance and language had certainly aroused plenty of suspicion.

What if a displaced person were *too* different, though, or went about loudly proclaiming what had happened to him? If the exit were in primitive times, likely a conspicuous stranger would simply have been killed on the spot without further inquiry. And in more enlightened times they would most likely be considered mad and tidied away into an institution somewhere, if they didn't quieten down.

This sort of thing could have been going on as long as the earth itself, I reflected. Even when it happened in front of witnesses there would be no clues at all; nothing to tell what had happened, because the only person who knew would be gone. And as for the disappeared, they'd be likely to keep their mouths shut at the other end.

Deep in my thoughts, I hadn't noticed the faint murmur of voices or the stirrings of footsteps through the grass, and I was quite startled to hear a voice speak only a few yards away.

'Devil take ye, Dougal MacKenzie,' it said. 'Kinsman or no, I dinna owe ye that.' The voice was pitched low, but tight with anger.

'Do ye no?' said another voice, faintly amused. 'I seem to recall a certain oath, giving your obedience. "So long as my feet rest on the lands of Clan MacKenzie", I believe was the way of it.' There was a soft thud, as of a foot stamping earth. 'And MacKenzie land it is, laddie.'

'I gave my word to Callum, not to you.' So it was young Jamie MacTavish, and precisely three guesses as to what he was upset about.

'One and the same, man, and ye ken it well.' There was the sound of a light slap, as of a hand against a cheek. 'Your obedience is to the chieftain of the clan, and outside of Leoch I am Callum's head and arms and hands as well as his legs.'

'And never saw I a better case of the right hand not knowin' what the left is up to,' came the quick rejoinder. Despite the bitterness of the tone, there was a lurking wit

226

that enjoyed this clash of wills. 'What d'ye think the right is going to say about the left collecting gold for the Stuarts?'

There was a brief pause before Dougal replied, 'MacKenzies and MacBeolains and MacVinichs; they're free men all. None can force them to give against their will, and none can stop them, either. And who knows? It may happen that Callum will give more for Prince Charlie than all o' them put together, in the end.'

'It may,' the deeper voice agreed. 'It may rain straight up tomorrow instead of down, as well. That doesna mean I'll stand waiting at the stairhead wi' my wee bucket turned upside down.'

'No? You've more to gain from a Stuart throne than I have, laddie. And naught from the English, save a noose. If ye dinna care for your own silly neck – '

'My neck is my own concern,' Jamie interrupted savagely. 'And so is my back.'

'Not while ye travel with me, sweet lad,' said his uncle's mocking voice. 'If ye wish to hear what Horrocks may tell ye, you'll do as you're told, yourself. And wise to do it, at that; a fine hand ye may be wi' a needle, but you've no but the one clean shirt.'

There was a shifting as of someone rising from his seat on a rock, and the soft passage of footsteps through the grass. Only one set of footsteps, though, I thought. I sat up as quietly as I could and peered cautiously around the edge of one of the boulders that hid me.

Jamie was still there, sitting hunched on a rock a few feet away, elbows braced on his knees, chin sunk on his locked hands. His back was mostly to me. I was easing backwards, not wishing to intrude on his solitude, when he suddenly spoke.

'I know you're there,' he said. 'Come out, if ye like.' From his tone it was a matter of complete indifference to him. I rose and started to come out, then realized I had been lying in my shift. Reflecting that he had enough to worry about without needing to blush for me as well, I tactfully wrapped myself in the blanket before emerging.

I sat down near him and leaned back against a rock,

watching him a little diffidently. Beyond a brief nod of acknowledgement he ignored me, completely occupied with thoughts of no very pleasant form, to judge from the dark frown on his face. One foot tapped restlessly against the rock he sat on, and he twisted his fingers together, clenching then spreading them with a force that made several knuckles pop with soft crackling sounds.

It was the popping knuckles that reminded me of Captain Manson. The supply officer for the field hospital where I had worked, Captain Manson suffered shortages, missed deliveries and the endless idiocies of the army bureaucracy as his own personal slings and arrows. Normally a mild and pleasant-spoken man, when the frustrations became too great he would retire briefly into his private office and punch the wall behind the door with all the force he could muster. Visitors in the outer reception area would watch in fascination as the flimsy wallboard quivered under the force of the blows. A few moments later Captain Manson would re-emerge, bruised of knuckle but once more calm of spirit, to deal with the current crisis. By the time he was transferred to another unit the wall behind his door was pocked with dozens of fist-sized holes.

Watching the young man on the rock trying to disjoint his own fingers, I was forcibly reminded of the captain facing some insoluble problem of supply.

'You need to hit something,' I said.

'Eh?' He looked up in surprise, apparently having forgotten I was there.

'Hit something,' I advised. 'You'll feel better for it.'

His mouth quirked as though about to say something, but instead he rose from his rock, headed decisively for a sturdy-looking young tree, and dealt it a solid blow. Apparently finding this some palliative to his feelings, he smashed the quivering trunk several times more, causing a shower of leaves and twigs to rain down upon his head.

Sucking a grazed knuckle, he came back a moment later.

'Thank ye,' he said with a wry smile. 'Perhaps I'll sleep tonight after all.'

'Did you hurt your hand?' I rose to examine it but he

shook his head, rubbing the knuckles gently with the palm of the other hand.

'Nay, it's nothing.'

We stood a moment in awkward silence. I didn't want to refer to the scene I had overhead, or to the earlier events of the evening. I broke the silence finally by saying, 'I didn't know you were a lefty.'

'A lefty? Oh, cack-handed, ye mean. Aye, always have been. The schoolmaster used to tie that one to my belt behind my back, to make me write wi' the other.'

'Can you? Write with the other, I mean?'

He nodded, reapplying the injured hand to his mouth. 'Aye. Makes my head ache to do it, though.'

'Do you fight left-handed too?' I asked, wanting to distract him. 'With a sword, I mean?' He was wearing no arms at the moment except his dirk and *skein dhu*, but during the day he customarily wore both swords and pistols, as did most of the men in the party.

'No, I use a sword well enough in either hand. A left-handed swordsman's at a disadvantage, ye ken, wi' a broadsword, for ye fight wi' your left side turned to the enemy, and your heart's on that side, d'ye see?'

Too filled with nervous energy to keep still, he had begun to stride about the grassy clearing, making illustrative gestures with an imaginary sword. 'It makes little difference wi' a claymore,' he said. He extended both arms straight out, hands together, and swept them in a flat, graceful arc through the air. 'Ye use both hands, usually,' he explained.

'Or if you're close enough to use only one, it doesna matter much which, for you come down from above and cleave the man through the shoulder. Not the head,' he added instructively, 'for the blade may slip off easy. Catch him clean in the notch, though' – he chopped the edge of his hand at the juncture of neck and shoulder – 'and he's dead. And if it's not a clean cut, still the man will no fight again that day – or ever, likely,' he added.

His left hand dropped to his belt and he drew the dirk in a motion like water pouring from a glass.

'Now, to fight wi' sword and dirk together,' he said, 'if

ye have no targe to shelter your dirk hand, then you favour
the right side, wi' the broadsword in that hand, and come
up from underneath wi' the dirk if ye fight in close. But if
the dirk hand is well shielded, ye can come from either
side, and twist your body about' – he ducked and weaved,
illustrating – 'to keep the enemy's blade away, and use the
dirk only if ye lose the sword or the use of the sword arm.'

He dropped low and brought the blade up in a swift,
murderous jab that stopped an inch short of my breast. I
stepped back involuntarily, and at once he stood upright,
sheathing the dirk with an apologetic smile.

'I'm sorry. I'm showin' off. I didna mean to startle ye.'

'You're awfully good,' I said, with sincerity. 'Who taught
you to fight? I'd think you'd need another left-handed fighter to show you.'

'Aye, it was a left-handed fighter. The best I've ever
seen.' He smiled briefly, without humour. 'Dougal
MacKenzie.'

Most of the leaves had fallen from his head by now; only
a few clung to his shoulders, and I reached out to brush
them away. The seams of his shirt had been mended neatly,
I saw, if without artistry. Even a rip through the fabric had
been catch-stitched together.

'He'll do it again?' I said abruptly, unable to stop myself.

He paused before answering, but there was no pretence
of not understanding what I meant.

'Oh, aye,' he said at last, nodding. 'It gets him what he
wants, ye see.'

'And you'll let him do it? Let him use you that way?'

He looked past me, down the hill towards the cottage.
His face was smooth and blank as a wall.

'For now.'

We continued on our rounds, moving no more than a few
miles a day, often stopping for Dougal to conduct business
at a track crossing or a cottage, where several tenants would
gather with their bags of grain and bits of carefully hoarded
money. All was recorded in ledgers by the quick-moving

pen of Ned Gowan, and such receipts as were needed dispensed from his scrap-bag of parchment and papers.

And when we reached a hamlet or village large enough to boast a pot-house or tavern, Dougal would once more do his turn, standing drinks, telling stories, making speeches; and finally, if he judged the prospects good enough, he would force Jamie to his feet to show his scars. And a few more coins would be added to the second bag, the purse bound for Rome and the court of King James the Pretender.

I tried to judge such scenes as they developed, and step outside before the climax, public crucifixion never having been much to my taste. While the initial reaction to the sight of Jamie's back was horrified pity, followed by bursts of invective against the English army and King George, often there was a slight flavour of contempt that even I could pick up. On one occasion I heard a man remark softly to a friend in English, 'An awfu' sight, man, is it no? Christ, I'd die in my blood before I let a whey-faced Sassenach to use me so.'

Angry and miserable to start with, Jamie grew more wretched each day. He would shrug back into his shirt as soon as possible, avoiding questions and commiseration, and seek an excuse to leave the gathering, avoiding everyone until we took horse the following morning.

The breaking point came a few days later, in a small village called Tunnaig. This time Dougal was still exhorting the crowd, a hand on Jamie's bare shoulder, when one of the onlookers, a young lout with long, dirty brown hair, made some personal remark to Jamie. I couldn't tell what was said, but the effect was instantaneous. Jamie wrenched out of Dougal's grasp and hit the lad in the stomach, knocking him flat.

I was slowly learning to put a few words of Gaelic together, though I could in no way be said to understand the language yet. However, I had noticed that I often could tell what was being said from the attitude of the speaker, whether I understood the words or not.

'Get up and say that again' *looks* the same said in any schoolyard, pub or alley in the world.

So do 'Right you are, mate' and 'Get him, lads!'

Jamie disappeared under an avalanche of grimy work clothes as the rents table went over with a crash beneath the weight of brown-hair and two of his friends. Innocent bystanders pressed back against the walls of the pot-house and prepared to enjoy the spectacle. I sidled closer to Ned and Murtagh, eyeing the heaving mass of limbs uneasily. A lonely flash of red hair showed occasionally in the twisting sea of arms and legs.

'Shouldn't you help him?' I murmured to Murtagh out of the corner of my mouth. He looked surprised at the idea.

'No, why?'

'He'll call for help if he needs it,' said Ned Gowan, tranquilly watching from my other side.

'Whatever you say.' I subsided doubtfully.

I wasn't at all sure Jamie would be able to call for help if he needed it; at the moment he was being throttled by a stout lad in green. My personal opinion was that Dougal would soon be short one prime exhibit, but he didn't seem concerned. In fact, none of the watchers appeared at all bothered by the mayhem taking place on the floor at our feet. A few bets were being taken, but the overall air was one of quiet enjoyment of the entertainment.

I was glad to notice that Rupert drifted casually across the path of a couple of men who seemed to be contemplating joining the action. As they took a step towards the fray he bumbled absentmindedly into their way, hand lightly resting on his dirk. They fell back, deciding to leave well enough alone.

The general feeling appeared to be that three to one was reasonable odds. Given that the one was quite large, an accomplished fighter and obviously in the grip of a berserk fury, that might be true.

The contest seemed to be evening out with the abrupt retirement of the stout party in green, dripping blood as the result of a well-placed elbow to the nose.

It went on for several minutes, but the conclusion became

more and more obvious, as a second fighter fell by the wayside and rolled under a table, moaning and clutching his groin. Jamie and his original antagonist were still hammering each other earnestly in the middle of the floor, but the Jamie-backers amongst the spectators were already collecting their winnings. A forearm across the windpipe, accompanied by a vicious kidney punch, decided brown-hair that discretion was the better part of valour.

I added a mental translation of 'That's enough, I give up' to my growing Gaelic/English word list.

Jamie rose slowly off the body of his last opponent to the cheers of the crowd. Nodding breathlessly in acknowledgement, he staggered to one of the few benches still in place and flopped down, streaming sweat and blood, to accept a tankard of ale from the ale-wife. Gulping it down, he set the empty tankard on the bench and leaned forward, gasping for breath, elbows on his knees and the scars on his back defiantly displayed.

For once he was in no hurry to resume his shirt; in spite of the chill in the ale-house he remained half naked, only putting on his shirt to go outside when it was time to seek our lodging for the night. He left to a chorus of respectful goodnights, looking more relaxed than he had in days, in spite of the pain from scrapes, cuts and bruises.

'One scraped shin, one cut eyebrow, one split lip, one bloody nose, *six* smashed knuckles, one sprained thumb and two loosened teeth. Plus more assorted contusions than I care to count.' I completed my inventory with a sigh. 'How do you feel?' We were alone, in the small shed behind the inn where I had taken him to administer first aid.

'Fine,' he said, grinning. He started to stand up, but froze halfway, grimacing. 'Aye, well. Perhaps the ribs hurt a bit.'

'Of course they hurt. You're black and blue – again. Why do you do such things? What in God's name do you think you're made of? Iron?' I demanded irritably.

He grinned ruefully and touched his swollen nose.

'No, I wish I were.'

I sighed again and prodded him gently around the middle.

'I don't think they're cracked; it's only bruises. I'll strap them, though, in case. Stand up straight, roll up your shirt, and hold your arms out from your sides.' I began to tear strips from an old shawl I'd got from the ale-wife. Muttering under my breath about sticking plaster and other amenities of civilized life, I improvised a strap dressing, pulling it tight and fastening it with the ring-brooch off his plaid.

'I can't breathe,' he complained.

'If you breathe, it will hurt. Don't move. Where did you learn to fight like that? Dougal again?'

'No.' He winced away from the vinegar I was applying to the cut eyebrow. 'My father taught me.'

'Really? What was your father, the local boxing champion?'

'What's boxing? No, he was a farmer. Bred horses too.' Jamie sucked in his breath as I continued the vinegar application on his barked shin.

'When I was nine or ten, he said he thought I was going to be big as my mother's folk, so I'd have to learn to fight.' He was breathing more easily now, and held out a hand to let me rub marigold ointment into the knuckles.

'He said, "If you're sizable, half the men ye meet will fear ye, and the other half will want to try ye. Knock one down," he said, "and the rest will let ye be. But learn to do it fast and clean, or you'll be fightin' all your life." So he'd take me to the stable and knock me into the straw until I learned to hit back. Ow! That stings.'

'Fingernail gouges are nasty wounds,' I said, swabbing busily at his neck. 'Especially if the gouger doesn't wash regularly. And I doubt that greasy-haired lad bathes once a year. "Fast and clean" isn't quite how I'd describe what you did tonight, but it *was* impressive. Your father would be proud of you.'

I spoke with some sarcasm, and was surprised to see a shadow pass across his face.

'My father's dead,' he said flatly.

'I'm sorry.' I finished the swabbing, then said softly, 'But I meant it. He *would* be proud of you.'

He didn't answer, but gave me a half smile in reply. He

suddenly seemed very young, and I wondered just how old he was. I was about to ask when a raspy cough from behind announced a visitor to the shed.

It was the stringy little man named Murtagh. He eyed Jamie's strapped-up ribs with some amusement, and lobbed a small wash-leather bag through the air. Jamie put up a large hand and caught it easily, with a small clinking sound.

'And what's this?' he asked.

Murtagh raised one sketchy brow. 'Your share o' the wagers, what else?'

Jamie shook his head and made to toss the bag back.

'I didna wager anything.'

Murtagh raised a hand to stop him. 'You did the work. You're a verra popular fellow at the moment, at least wi' those that backed ye.'

'But not with Dougal, I don't suppose,' I interjected.

Murtagh was one of those men who always looked a bit startled to find that women had voices, but he nodded politely enough.

'Aye, that's true. Still, I dinna see as that should trouble ye,' he said to Jamie.

'No?' A glance passed between the two men, with a message I didn't understand. Jamie blew his breath out softly through his teeth, nodding slowly to himself.

'When?' he asked.

'A week. Ten days, perhaps. Near a place called Lag Cruime. You'll know it?'

Jamie nodded again, looking more content than I had seen him in some time. 'I know it.'

I looked from one face to the other, both closed and secretive. So Murtagh had found out something. Something to do with the mysterious 'Horrocks' I had overheard Dougal speaking of to Jamie, perhaps? I shrugged. Whatever the cause, it appeared that Jamie's days as an exhibition were over.

'I suppose Dougal can always tap-dance instead,' I said.

'Eh?' The secretive looks changed to looks of startlement.

'Never mind. Sleep well.' I picked up my box of medical supplies and went to find my own rest.

12

The Garrison Commander

We were drawing nearer to Fort William, and I began to ponder seriously what my plan of action should be, once we had arrived there.

It depended, I thought, upon what the garrison commander was likely to do. If he believed that I was a gentlewoman in distress, I might just find a way to persuade him to escort me back to Inverness. From there, surely I could find a way to slip off on my own and reach Craigh na Dun.

But he might be suspicious of me, turning up in the company of the MacKenzies. Still, I was patently not a Scot myself; surely he would not be inclined to think me a spy of some sort? That was evidently what Callum and Dougal thought – that I was an English spy.

Which made me wonder what I was meant to be spying on? Well, unpatriotic activities, I supposed; of which, collecting money for the support of Prince Charles Edward Stuart, Young Pretender to the throne, was definitely one.

But in that case, why had Dougal allowed me to see him do it? He could easily enough have sent me out of earshot before that part of the proceedings. Of course, the proceedings had all been held in Gaelic, I argued with myself.

Perhaps that was the point, though. I remembered the odd gleam in his eyes and his question, 'I thought ye had no Gaelic?' Perhaps it was a test, to see whether I really was ignorant of the language. For an English spy scarcely would have been sent into the Highlands, unable to speak with more than half the people there.

But no, the conversation I had overheard between Jamie and Dougal would seem to indicate that Dougal was indeed a Jacobite, though Callum apparently was not – yet.

My head was beginning to buzz with all these suppositions, and I was glad to see that we were approaching a fairly large village. Likely that meant a good inn, as well, and a decent supper.

The inn was in fact commodious, by the standards I had grown accustomed to. If the bed was apparently designed for midgets – and flea-bitten ones at that – at least it was in a chamber to itself. In several of the smaller villages I had slept on a settle in the larger room of a two-roomed house, surrounded by snoring and the humped shadows of plaid-wrapped shapes.

Customarily I fell asleep immediately, whatever the sleeping conditions, worn out by a day in the saddle and an evening of Dougal's politicizing. The first evening in an inn, though, I had remained awake for a good half hour, fascinated by the remarkable variety of noises the male respiratory apparatus could produce. An entire dormitory full of student nurses couldn't come close.

It occurred to me, listening to the chorus, that men in a hospital ward seldom really snore. Breathe heavily, yes. They gasp, groan occasionally, and sometimes sob or cry out in sleep. But there was no comparison to this healthy racket. Perhaps it was that sick or injured men could not sleep deeply enough to relax into that sort of din.

If my observations were sound, then my companions were plainly in the most robust health. They certainly looked it, limbs casually asprawl, faces slack and glowing in the firelight. The complete abandon of their sleep on hard boards was the satisfying of an appetite as hearty as the one they had brought to supper. Obscurely comforted by the cacophony, I had pulled my travelling cloak around my shoulders and went to sleep myself.

By comparison, I found myself now rather lonely here in the solitary splendour of my tiny, smelly attic. Despite having removed the bedclothes and beaten the mattress to discourage unwelcome cohabitants, I had some difficulty in sleeping, so silent and dark did the chamber seem after I had blown out the candle.

There were a few faint echoes from the common room below, and a brief flurry of noise and movement, but this

237

served only to emphasize my own isolation. It was the first time I had felt so completely alone since my arrival at the castle, and I was not at all sure I liked it.

I was hovering uneasily on the verge of sleep when my ears picked up an ominous creaking of floorboards in the hall outside. The step was slow and halting, as though the intruder hesitated in his path, picking the soundest-appearing of the boards for each next step. I sat bolt upright, groping for the candle and flint box by the bed.

My hand, blindly searching, struck the flint box and knocked it to the floor with a soft thump. I froze, and the steps outside did likewise.

There was a soft scratching at the door, as of someone groping for the latch. I knew the door was unbolted; though it was fitted with brackets for a bolt, I had searched unavailingly for the bolt itself before retiring. I grabbed the candlestick, yanked the stub of the candle out, and slid out of bed as quietly as I could, clutching the heavy pottery.

The door squeaked slightly on its hinges as it gave. The room's only window was tightly shuttered against both elements and light; nonetheless I could just make out the dim outline of the door as it opened. The outline grew, then to my surprise, it shrank and disappeared as the door shut again. Everything was quiet once more.

I stayed pressed against the wall for what seemed like ages, holding my breath and trying to hear through the noise of my pounding heart. At last I inched towards the door, edging carefully around the room next to the wall, thinking the floorboards must surely be more solid here. I eased my foot down at each step, gradually trusting my weight to it, then pausing and groping with bare toes for the seam between two boards before setting the other foot as solidly as I could judge.

Once the door was reached, I paused, ear pressed to the thin panels, hands braced on the frame, on guard against a sudden bursting inwards. I thought perhaps I heard slight sounds, but wasn't sure. Was it only the sounds of the activity down below, or was it the stifled breathing of someone on the other side of the panel?

The constant flow of adrenalin was making me slightly sick. Tiring at last of this nonsense, I took a firm grip of my candlestick, yanked open the door and rushed into the hallway.

I say 'rushed'; in actuality I took two steps, trod heavily on something soft, and fell headlong into the passageway, skinning my knuckles and banging my head quite painfully on something solid.

I sat up, clutching my brow with both hands, completely uncaring that I might be assassinated at any moment.

The person I had stepped on was swearing in a rather breathless manner. Through the haze of pain I was dimly aware that he (I assumed from the size and the smell of sweat that my visitor was male) had risen and was groping for the fastening of the shutters in the wall above us.

A sudden inrush of fresh air made me wince and shut my eyes. When I opened them there was enough light from the night sky for me to see the intruder.

'What are *you* doing here?' I asked accusingly.

At the same time Jamie asked, in a similarly accusatory tone, 'How much do ye weigh, Sassenach?'

Still a bit addled, I actually replied 'Nine stone' before thinking to ask 'Why?'

'Ye nearly crushed my liver,' he answered, gingerly prodding the affected area. 'Not to mention frightening the hell out of me.' He reached a hand down and hauled me to my feet. 'Are ye all right?'

'No, I bumped my head.' Rubbing the spot, I looked dazedly around the bare hallway. 'What did I bang it on?' I demanded.

'*My* head,' he said – rather grumpily, I thought.

'Serves you right,' I said nastily. 'What were you doing, sneaking about outside my door?'

He gave me a testy look.

'I wasna "sneaking about", for God's sake. I was sleeping – or trying to.' He rubbed what appeared to be a knot forming on his temple.

'Sleeping? *Here?*' I looked up and down the cold, bare,

filthy hallway with exaggerated amazement. 'You do pick the oddest places; first stables, now this.'

'It may interest ye to know that there's a small party of English dragoons stepped in to the taproom below,' he informed me coldly. 'They're a bit gone in drink, and disporting themselves a bit reckless with two women from the town. Since there's but the two lasses, and five men, some of the soldiers seemed a bit inclined to venture upwards in search of . . . ah, partners. I didna think you'd care overmuch for such attentions.' He flipped his plaid back over his shoulder and turned in the direction of the stairway.

'If I was mistaken in that impression, then I apologize. I'd no intention of disturbin' your rest. Good e'en to ye.'

'Wait a minute.' He stopped but did not turn back, forcing me to walk around him. He looked down at me, polite but distant.

'Thank you,' I said. 'It was very kind of you. I'm sorry I stepped on you.'

He smiled then, his face changing from a forbidding mask to its usual expression of good humour.

'No harm done, Sassenach,' he said. 'As soon as the headache goes away and the cracked rib heals, I'll be good as new.'

He turned back and pushed open the door of my room, which had swung shut in the wake of my hasty exit, owing to the fact that the builder had apparently constructed the inn without benefit of a plumb line. There wasn't a right angle in the place.

'Go back to bed, then,' he suggested. 'I'll be here.'

I looked at the hall floor. Besides its essential hardness and coldness, the boards were blotched with expectorations, spills and forms of filth I didn't wish even to contemplate. The builder's mark in the door lintel had said 1732, and that was plainly the last time the boards had been cleaned.

'You can't sleep out here,' I said. 'Come in; at least the floor in the room isn't quite this bad.'

Jamie froze, hand on the door frame.

'Sleep in your room with ye?' He sounded truly shocked. 'I couldna do that! Your reputation would be ruined!'

He really meant it. I started to laugh, but converted it into a tactful coughing fit. Given the exigencies of Highland travel, the crowded state of the lodgings and the crudity or complete lack of sanitary facilities, I was on terms of such physical intimacy with these men, Jamie included, that I found the idea of such prudery hilarious.

'You've slept in the same room with me before,' I pointed out when I had recovered a bit. 'You and twenty other men.'

He sputtered a bit. 'That isna at all the same thing! I mean, it was a quite public room, and . . .' He paused as an awful thought struck him. 'You didna think I meant that you were suggesting anything improper?' he asked anxiously. 'I assure ye, I – '

'No, no. Not at all.' I made haste to reassure him that I had taken no offence.

Seeing that he could not be persuaded, I insisted that at the least he must take the blankets from my bed to lie upon. He agreed to this reluctantly, and only upon my repeated assurances that I would not use them myself in any case, but intended to sleep as usual in the cover of my thick travelling cloak.

I tried to thank him again, as I paused by the makeshift pallet before returning to my fetid sanctuary, but he waved away my appreciation with a gracious hand.

'It isna entirely disinterested kindness on my part, ye ken,' he observed. 'I'd as soon avoid notice myself.'

I had forgotten that he had his own reasons for keeping away from English soldiery. It did not escape me, however, that this could have been much better accomplished, not to say more comfortably, by his sleeping in the warm and airy stables, rather than on the floor before my door.

'But if anyone *does* come up here,' I protested, 'they'll find you then.'

He reached a long arm out to grasp the swinging shutter and pulled it to. The hall was plunged in blackness, and Jamie appeared as no more than a shapeless bulk.

'They canna see my face,' he pointed out. 'And in the condition they're in, my name would be of no interest to them, either, even were I to give them the right one, which I dinna mean to do.'

'That's true,' I said doubtfully. 'Won't they wonder, though, what you're doing up here in the dark?' I could see nothing of his face, but the tone of his voice told me he was smiling.

'Not at all, Sassenach. They'll just think I'm waiting my turn.'

I laughed and went in then. I curled myself on the bed and went to sleep, marvelling at the mind that could make such ribald jokes even as it recoiled at the thought of sleeping in the same room as me.

When I awoke, Jamie was gone. Going down to breakfast I met Dougal at the foot of the stairs, waiting for me.

'Eat up quickly, lass,' he said. 'You and I are riding to Brockton.'

He declined to tell me anything further, but he seemed a bit uneasy, I thought. I ate quickly, and we soon found ourselves trotting through the misty early morning. Birds were busy in the shrubbery, and the air gave promise of a warm June day to come.

'Who are we going to see?' I asked. 'You may as well tell me, since if I don't know I'll be surprised, and if I do I'm intelligent enough to act surprised, anyway.'

Dougal cocked an eye at me, considering, but decided that my argument was sound.

'The garrison commander from Fort William,' he said.

I felt a minor shock. I wasn't quite ready for this. I had thought we had three days yet until we reached the fort.

'But we're nowhere near Fort William!' I exclaimed.

'Mmmphm.'

Apparently this garrison commander was an energetic sort. Not content to stay at home minding his garrison, he was out inspecting the countryside with a party of dragoons. The soldiers who had come to our inn the night before were part of this group, and had told Dougal that the commander was presently in residence at Brockton.

This presented a problem, and I was silent for the rest

of the ride, contemplating it. I had counted on being able to extract myself from Dougal's company at Fort William. Would the garrison commander have sufficient men with him to wrest me away from Dougal and his men by force, if necessary?

We reached Brockton at mid-morning. I could see why the commander had chosen it as his temporary headquarters. The village was large enough to boast a tavern with attached stable. Here we stopped, turning our ponies over to the attention of a small boy, who had barely succeeded in reaching the stable door by the time we were inside and Dougal was ordering refreshment from the alewife.

I was left below, contemplating a plate of rather stale-looking oatcakes, while Dougal mounted the stair to the commander's sanctum. It felt a bit strange to see him go. There were three or four English soldiers in the taproom, who eyed me speculatively, chatting to each other in low voices. After six weeks among the Scots of Clan MacKenzie, the presence of English dragoons made me unaccountably nervous. I told myself I was being silly. After all, they were my own countrymen, out of time or not.

Still, I found myself missing the congenial company of Mr Gowan and the pleasant familiarity of Jamie whatever-his-name-was. I was feeling rather sorry that I had had no chance to bid farewell to anyone before leaving that morning, when I heard Dougal's voice calling from the stair behind me. He was standing at the top, beckoning me upwards.

He looked somewhat more grim than usual, I thought, as he stood aside without speaking and gestured me into the room. The garrison commander stood by the open window, his slim, straight figure silhouetted by the light. He gave a short laugh when he saw me.

'Yes, I thought so. It had to be you, from MacKenzie's description.' The door closed behind me – Dougal had left me with Captain Jonathan Randall of His Majesty's Eighth Dragoons.

He was dressed this time in a clean red-and-fawn uni-

243

form, with a lace-trimmed stock and a neatly curled and powdered wig. But the face was the same – Frank's face. My breath caught in my throat. This time, though, I noticed the small lines of ruthlessness around his mouth and the touch of arrogance in the set of his shoulders. Still, he smiled affably enough and invited me to sit down.

The room was plainly furnished, with no more than a desk and chair, a long deal table and a few stools. Captain Randall motioned to a young corporal who stood to attention near the door, and a mug of ale was clumsily poured and set before me.

The Captain waved the corporal back and poured his own ale, then sank gracefully on to a stool across the table from me.

'All right,' he said pleasantly. 'Who don't you tell me who you are, and how you come to find yourself here?'

Having little choice at this point, I told him the same story I had given Callum, omitting only the less tactful references to his own behaviour, which he knew about in any case. I had no idea how much Dougal had told him, and didn't wish to risk being tripped up.

The Captain appeared polite but sceptical throughout my recital. He took less trouble to hide it than Callum had, I reflected. He rocked back on his stool, considering.

'Oxfordshire, you say? There are no Beauchamps in Oxfordshire that I know of.'

'How would you know?' I snapped. 'You're from Sussex yourself.'

His eyes popped open in surprise. I could have bitten my tongue.

'And may I ask just how you know *that*?' he asked.

'Er, your voice. Yes, it's your accent,' I said hastily. 'Clearly Sussex.'

The graceful dark brows nearly touched the curls of his wig.

'Neither my tutors nor my parents would be much obliged to hear that my speech so clearly reflects my birthplace, madam,' he said dryly. 'They having gone to considerable trouble and expense to remedy it. But, being the expert at local speech patterns that you are' – he turned to the man standing against the wall – 'no doubt you can also identify my corporal's place of origin. Corporal Hawkins, would you oblige me by reciting something? Anything at all will do,' he added, seeing the confusion on the man's face. 'Some popular verse, perhaps?'

The corporal, a young man with a stupid, beefy face and broad shoulders, glanced wildly about the room seeking inspiration, then drew himself up to attention and intoned,

> 'Buxom Meg, she washed my clothes,
> And took them all away.
> I waited thus in sore distress,
> And then I made her pay.'

'Er, that will do, Corporal, thank you.' Randall made a dismissive motion, and the corporal subsided against the wall, sweating freely.

'Well?' Randall turned to me, questioning.

'Er, Cheshire,' I guessed.

'Close. Lancashire.' He eyed me narrowly. Putting his hands together behind his back, he strolled over to the window and peered out. Checking to see whether Dougal had brought any men with him? I wondered.

Suddenly he whirled back to me with an abrupt *'Parlez-vouz français?'*

'Très bien,' I promptly replied. 'What of it?'

Head to one side, he looked me over carefully.

'Damn me if I think you're French,' he said, as though to himself. 'Could be, I suppose, but I've yet to meet a Frenchie could tell a Cockney from a Cornishman.'

His neatly manicured fingers tapped the wood of the tabletop. 'What was your maiden name, Mrs Beauchamp?'

'Look, Captain,' I said, smiling as charmingly as I could, 'entertaining as it is to play Twenty Questions with you, I should really like to conclude these preliminaries and arrange for the continuation of my journey. I've already been delayed for some time, and – '

'You do not help your case by adopting this frivolous

attitude, madam,' he interrupted, narrowing his eyes. I had seen Frank do that when displeased about something, and I felt a little weak in the knees. I put my hands on my thighs to brace myself.

'I have no case to help,' I said, as boldly as I could. 'I'm making no claims on you, the garrison or, for that matter, on the MacKenzies. All I want is to be allowed to resume my journey in peace. And I see no reason why you ought to have any objection to that.'

He glared at me, lips pressed tight together in irritation. 'Oh, you don't? Well, consider my position for a moment, madam, and perhaps my objections will become clearer. Six weeks ago I was, with my men, in hot pursuit of a band of unidentified Scottish bandits who had absconded with a small herd of cattle when – '

'Oh, so that's what they were doing!' I exclaimed. 'I wondered,' I added lamely.

Captain Randall breathed heavily, then decided against whatever he had been going to say, in favour of continuing his story.

'In the midst of this lawful pursuit,' he went on, in measured tones, 'I encounter a half-dressed Englishwoman – in a place where no Englishwoman should be, even with a proper escort – who resists my inquiries, assaults my person – '

'You assaulted mine first!' I said hotly.

'Whose accomplice renders me unconscious by a cowardly attack, and who then flees the area, plainly with some assistance. My men and I searched that area most thoroughly, and I assure you, madam, there was no trace of your murdered servant, your plundered baggage, your discarded gown nor the merest sign that there is the slightest truth to your story!'

'Oh?' I said a little weakly.

'Yes. Furthermore, there have been no reports of bandits in that area within the last four months. And *now*, madam, you turn up in company with the war chieftain of the MacKenzie of Leoch, who tells me that his brother is convinced you are a spy, presumably working for *me*!'

'Well, I'm not, am I?' I said reasonably. 'You know that, at least.'

'Yes, I know that,' he said with exaggerated patience. 'What I don't know is who the devil you are! But I mean to find out, madam, have no doubts as to that. I am the commander of the Fort William garrison. As such, I am empowered to take certain steps in order to secure the safety of this area against traitors, spies and any other persons whose behaviour I consider suspicious. And those steps, madam, I am fully prepared to take.'

'And just what might those steps be?' I inquired. I honestly wanted to know, though I suppose the tone of my question must have sounded rather baiting.

He stood up, looked down at me consideringly for a moment, then walked around the table, extended his hand, and drew me to my feet.

'Corporal Hawkins,' he said, still staring at me, 'I shall require your assistance for a moment.'

The youth by the wall looked profoundly uneasy, but sidled over to us.

'Stand behind the lady, please, Corporal,' Randall said, sounding bored. 'And take her firmly by both elbows.'

He drew back his arm and hit me in the pit of the stomach.

I made no noise, because I had no breath. I sat on the floor, doubled over, struggling to draw air into my lungs. I was shocked far beyond the actual pain of the blow, which was beginning to make itself felt, along with a wave of giddy sickness. In a fairly eventful life, no one had ever purposely struck me before.

The Captain squatted down in front of me. His wig was slightly awry, but aside from that and a certain brightness to his eyes he showed no change from his normal controlled elegance.

'I trust you are not with child, madam,' he said in a conversational tone, 'because if you are, you won't be for long.'

I was beginning to make a rather odd wheezing noise as the first wisps of oxygen found their way painfully into my

247

throat. I rolled on to my hands and knees and groped feebly for the edge of the table. The corporal, after a nervous glance at the Captain, reached down to help me up.

Waves of blackness seemed to ripple over the room. I sank on to the stool and closed my eyes.

'Look at me.' The voice was as light and calm as though he were about to offer me tea. I opened my eyes and looked up at him through a slight fog. His hands were braced on his exquisitely tailored hips.

'Have you anything to say to me now, madam?' he demanded.

'Your wig is crooked,' I said, and closed my eyes again.

13

A Marriage is Announced

I sat at a table in the taproom, gazing into a cup of milk and fighting off waves of nausea.

Dougal had taken one look at my face as I came downstairs, supported by the beefy young corporal, and strode purposefully past me, up the stairs to Randall's room. The floors and doors of the inn were stout and well constructed, but I could still hear the sound of raised voices upstairs.

I raised the cup of milk but my hands were still shaking too badly to drink it.

I was gradually recovering from the physical effects of the blow, but not from the shock of it. I *knew* the man was not my husband, but the resemblance was so strong and my habits so ingrained that I had been half inclined to trust him, and had spoken to him as I would have to Frank, expecting civility if not active sympathy. To have those feelings abruptly turned inside out by his vicious attack was what was making me ill now.

Ill, and frightened as well. I had seen his eyes as he crouched next to me on the floor. Something had moved in their depths, just for a moment. It was gone in a flash, but I did not want ever to see it again.

The sound of a door opening above brought me out of my reverie. The thud of heavy footsteps was succeeded by the rapid appearance of Dougal, followed closely by Captain Randall. So closely indeed that the Captain appeared to be in pursuit of the Scot, and was brought up short when Dougal, catching sight of me, halted suddenly at the foot of the stairs.

With a glare over his shoulder at Captain Randall, Dougal came swiftly over to where I was seated, tossed a small coin on the table in payment and jerked me to my feet without a word. He was hustling me out the door before I had time to do more than register the extraordinary look of speculative acquisitiveness on the face of the redcoat officer.

We were mounted and moving before I had even tucked the voluminous skirts around my legs, and the material billowed around me like a settling parachute. Dougal was silent, but the ponies seemed to pick up his sense of urgency; we were all but galloping along the track.

Near a crossing of tracks marked with a Pictish cross, Dougal abruptly reined to a halt. Dismounting, he seized the bridles of both ponies and tied them loosely to a sapling. He helped me down, them abruptly disappeared into the bushes, beckoning me to follow.

I followed the swing of his kilt up the hillside, ducking as the branches he pushed out of the way snapped back across the path over my head. The hillside was overgrown with birch and scrubby pine. I could hear titmice in the copse to the left, and a flock of finches calling out to each other as they fed, further on. The grass was the fresh green of early summer, clumps of sturdy growth shooting out of the rocks and furring the ground under the birches. Nothing grew under the pines, of course; the needles lay inches thick, affording protection for the small crawling things that hid there from sunlight and predators.

The sharp scents made my throat ache. I had been up such hillsides before, and smelled these same scents. But then the pine and grass scent had been diluted with the smell of petrol fumes from the road below and the voices of day trippers replaced those of the birds. Last time I walked such a path, the ground was littered with sandwich wrappers and cigarette butts instead of primula and angelica. Sandwich wrappers seemed a reasonable enough price to pay, I supposed, for such blessings of civilization as penicillin and telephones, but just for the moment I was willing to settle for the plants. I badly needed a little peace, and I felt it here.

Dougal turned suddenly aside just below the crest of the hill and disappeared into a thick growth of broom. Shoving my way in after him with some difficulty, I found him seated

250

on the flat stone edging of a small pool. A weathered block of stone stood askew behind him, with a dim and vaguely human figure etched in the stained surface. It must be a saint's pool, I realized. Tattered remnants of fabric flapped from the branches of a rowan tree that overhung the water; pledges from visitors who petitioned the saint, for health or a safe journey, perhaps.

Dougal greeted my appearance with a nod. He crossed himself, bent his head and scooped up a double handful of water. The water had an odd dark colour, and a worse smell – likely a sulphur spring, I thought. The day was hot and I was thirsty, though, so I followed Dougal's example. The water was faintly bitter, but cold and not unpalatable. I drank some, then splashed my face. The road had been dusty.

I looked up, face dripping, to find him watching me with a very odd expression. Something between curiosity and calculation, I thought.

'Bit of a climb for a drink, isn't it?' I asked lightly. There were water bottles on the ponies. And I doubted that Dougal meant to petition the patron of the spring for our safe journey. He struck me as a believer in more worldly methods.

'How well d'ye know the Captain?' he asked abruptly.

'Less well than you,' I snapped back. 'I've met him once before today, and that by accident. We didn't get on.'

Surprisingly, the stern face lightened a bit.

'Well,' he admitted, 'I canna say as I care for the man much myself.' He drummed his fingers on the stone coping, considering something. 'He's well thought of by some, though,' he said, eyeing me. 'A brave soldier and a bonny fighter, by what I hear.'

I raised my eyebrows. 'Not being an English general, I am not impressed.' He laughed, showing startlingly white teeth. The sound disturbed three rooks in the tree overhead, who flapped off, full of hoarse complaint.

'Are ye a spy for the English or the French?' he asked with another bewildering change of subject. At least he was being direct, for a change.

'Certainly not,' I said crossly. 'I'm plain Claire Beauchamp, and nothing more.' I soaked my handkerchief in the water and used it to wipe my neck. Small refreshing trickles ran down my back under the grey serge of my travelling gown. I pressed the wet cloth to my bosom and squeezed, producing a similar effect.

Dougal was silent for several minutes, watching me intently as I conducted my haphazard ablutions.

'You've seen Jamie's back,' he said suddenly.

'I could hardly help doing so,' I said a little coldly. I had given up wondering what he was up to with these disconnected questions. Presumably he would tell me when he was ready.

'You mean did I know Randall did it, then? Or did you know that yourself?'

'Aye, *I* kent it well enough,' he answered, calmly appraising me, 'but I wasna aware that *you* did.'

I shrugged, implying that what I knew and what I didn't were hardly his concern.

'I was there, ye ken,' he said, casually.

'Where?'

'At Fort William. I had a bit of business there, with the garrison. The clerk there knew Jamie was some kin to me, and sent me word when they arrested him. So I went along to see could aught be done for him.'

'Apparently you weren't very successful,' I said, with an edge.

Dougal shrugged. 'Unfortunately not. Had it been the regular sergeant in charge, I might ha' saved Jamie at least the second go-round, but as it was, Randall was new in command. He didna know me, and was indisposed to listen much to what I said. I thought at the time, it was only he meant to make an example of Jamie, to show everyone at the start that there'd be no softness from him.' He tapped the sword he wore at his belt. 'It's a sound enough principle, when you're in command of men. Earn their respect before ye do aught else. And if you canna do that, earn their fear.'

I remembered the expression on the face of Randall's

corporal, and thought I knew which route the Captain had taken.

Dougal's deep-set eyes were on my face, interested.

'You knew it was Randall. Did Jamie tell ye about it?'

'A bit,' I said cautiously.

'He must think well of ye,' he said musingly. 'He doesna generally speak of it to anyone.'

'I can't imagine why not,' I said, provoked. I still held my breath each time we came to a new pot-house, until it was clear that the company had settled for an evening of drinking and gossip by the fire. Dougal smiled sardonically, clearly knowing what was in my mind.

'Well, it wasna necessary to tell me, was it? Since I kent it already.' He swished a hand idly through the strange dark water, stirring up brimstone fumes.

'I'd not know how it goes in Oxfordshire,' he said with a sarcastic emphasis that made me squirm slightly, 'but hereabouts, ladies are generally not exposed to such sights as floggings. Have ye ever seen one?'

'No, nor do I much want to,' I responded sharply. 'I can imagine what it would take to make marks like the ones on Jamie's back, though.'

Dougal shook his head, flipping water out of the pool at a curious tit that ventured close.

'Now, there you're wrong, lass, and you'll pardon my saying so. Imagination is all verra well, but it isna equal to the sight of a man having his back laid open. A verra nasty thing – it's meant to break a man, and most often it succeeds.'

'Not with Jamie.' I spoke rather more sharply than I had intended. Jamie was my patient, and to some extent my friend as well. I had no wish to discuss his personal history with Dougal, though I would, if pressed, admit to a certain morbid curiosity. I had never met anyone more open and at the same time more mysterious than the tall young Mac-Tavish.

Dougal laughed shortly and wiped his wet hand through his hair, pasting back the strands that had escaped during our flight – for so I thought of it – from Randall.

'Weel, Jamie's as stubborn as the rest of his family – like rocks, the lot of them, and he's the worst.' But there was a definite tone of respect in his voice, grudging though it was.

'Jamie told ye he was flogged for escape?'

'Yes.'

'Aye, he went over the wall of the camp just after dark, same day as the dragoons brought him in. That was a fairly frequent occurrence there, the prisoners' accommodations not bein' as secure as might be wished, so the English ran patrols near the walls every night. The garrison clerk told me Jamie put up a good fight, from the look of him when he came back, but it was six against one, and the six all wi' muskets, so it didna last long. Jamie spent the night in chains, and went to the whipping post first thing in the morning.' He paused, checking me for signs of faintness or nausea, I supposed.

'Floggings were done right after assembly, so as to start everyone off in the proper frame of mind for the day. There were three to be flogged that day, and Jamie was the last of them.'

'You actually *saw* it?'

'Oh, aye. And I'll tell ye, lass, watchin' men bein' flogged is not pleasant. I've had the good fortune never to experience it, but I expect bein' flogged is not verra pleasant, either. Watching it happen to someone else while waitin' for it yourself is probably least pleasant of all.'

'I don't doubt it,' I murmured.

Dougal nodded. 'Jamie looked grim enough, but he didna turn a hair, even listening to the screams and the other noises – did ye know ye can *hear* the flesh being torn?'

'Ugh!'

'So I thought myself, lass,' he said, grimacing in memory of it. 'To say nothing of the blood and bruises. Ech!' He spat, carefully avoiding the pool and its coping. 'Turned my stomach to see, and I'm no a squeamish man by any means.'

Dougal went on with his ghastly story.

'Come Jamie's turn, he walks up – some men have to be dragged, but not him – and holds out his hands so the corporal can unlock the manacles he's wearing. The corporal goes to pull his arm, like, to haul him into place, but Jamie shakes him off and steps back a pace. I was half expectin' him to make a dash for it, but instead he just pulls off his shirt. It's torn here and there and filthy as a clout, but he folds it up careful like it was his Sunday best, and lays it on the ground. Then he walks over to the post steady as a soldier and puts his hands up to be bound.'

Dougal shook his head, marvelling. The sunlight filtering through the rowan leaves dappled him with lacy shadows, so he looked like a man seen through a doily. I smiled at the thought, and he nodded approvingly at me, thinking my response due to his story.

'Aye, lass, courage like that is uncommon rare. Boldness in battle is nothing out of the way for a Scotsman, ye ken, but to face down fear in cold blood is rare in any man. He was but nineteen at the time,' Dougal added as an afterthought.

'Must have been rather gruesome to watch,' I said ironically. 'I wonder you weren't sick.'

Dougal saw the irony, and let it lie. 'I nearly was, lass,' he said, lifting his dark brows. 'The first lash drew blood, and the lad's back was half red and half blue within a minute. He didna scream, though, or beg for mercy, or twist round to try and save himself. He just set his forehead hard against the post and stood there. He flinched when the lash hit, of course, but nothin' more. I doubt I could do that,' he admitted, 'nor are there many that could. He fainted half through it, and they roused him wi' water from a jug and finished it.'

'Very nasty indeed,' I observed. 'Why are you telling me about it?'

'I havena finished telling ye about it.' Dougal pulled the dirk from his belt and began to clean his fingernails with the point. He was a fastidious man, in spite of the difficulties of keeping clean on the road.

'Jamie was slumped in the ropes; I dinna think he'd fainted, he was just too wambly to stand for the moment. But just then Captain Randall came down into the yard. I don't know why he'd not been there to begin with; had business that delayed him, perhaps. Anyway, Jamie saw him coming, and had the presence o' mind left to close his eyes and let his head flop, like as if he were unconscious.'

Dougal knitted his brows, concentrating fiercely on a recalcitrant hangnail.

'The Captain was fair put out that they'd flogged Jamie already; seems that was a pleasure he'd meant to have for himself. Still, not much to be done about it at the moment. But then he thought to make inquiries about how Jamie came to escape in the first place.'

He held up the dirk, examining it for nicks, then began to sharpen the edge against the stone he sat on. 'Had several soldiers shaking in their boots before he was done – the man's a way wi' words, I'll say that for him.'

'That he has,' I said dryly.

The dirk scraped rhythmically against the stone. Every so often, a faint spark leapt from the metal as it struck a rough patch in the rock.

'Weel, in the course of this inquiry, it came out that Jamie'd had the heel of a loaf and a bit of cheese with him when they caught him – taken it along when he went over the wall. Whereupon the Captain thinks for a moment, then smiles a smile I should hate to see on my grandmother's face. He declares that theft bein' a serious offence, the penalty should be commensurate, and sentences Jamie on the spot to another hundred lashes.'

I flinched in spite of myself. 'That would kill him!'

Dougal nodded. 'Aye, that's what the garrison doctor said. He said as he'd permit no such thing; in good conscience, the prisoner must be allowed a week to heal before receiving the second flogging.'

'Well, how humanitarian of him,' I said. 'Good conscience, my Aunt Fanny! And what did Captain Randall think of this?'

'He was none too pleased at first, but he reconciled himself. Once he did, the sergeant, who knew a real faint when he saw one, had Jamie untied. The lad staggered a bit, but he kept to his feet, and a few of the men there cheered, which didna go ower a treat wi' the Captain. He wasna best pleased when the sergeant picked up Jamie's shirt and handed it back to the lad, either, though it was quite a popular move with the men.'

Dougal twisted the blade back and forth, examining it critically. Then he laid it across his knee and gave me a direct look.

'Ye know, lass, it's fairly easy to be brave, sittin' in a warm pot-house ower a glass of ale. 'Tis not so easy, squatting in a cold field, wi' musket balls going past your head and heather ticklin' your arse. And it's still less easy when you're standing face to face wi' your enemy, wi' your own blood running down your legs.'

'I wouldn't suppose so,' I said. I did feel a little faint, in spite of everything. I plunged both hands into the water, letting the dark liquid chill my wrists.

'I did go back to see Randall, later in the week,' Dougal said defensively, as though he felt some need to justify the action. 'We talked a good bit, and I even offered him compensation – '

'Oh, I *am* impressed,' I murmured, but desisted in the face of his glare. 'No, I mean it. It was kind of you. I gather Randall declined your offer, though?'

'Aye, he did. And I still dinna ken why, for I've not found English officers on the whole to be ower-scrupulous when it comes to their purses, and clothes such as the Captain's come a bit dear.'

'Perhaps he has – other sources of income,' I suggested.

'He does, for a fact,' Dougal confirmed, but with a sharp glance at me.

'Still . . .' he hesitated, then proceeded more slowly.

'I went back, then, to be there for Jamie when he came up again, though there wasna much I could do for him at that point, poor lad.'

The second time, Jamie had been the only prisoner up for flogging. The guards had removed his shirt before bringing him out, just after sunrise on a cold October morning.

'I could see the lad was dead scairt,' said Dougal, 'though he was walking by himself and wouldna let the guard touch him. I could see him shaking, as much wi' the cold as wi'' nerves, and the gooseflesh thick on his arms and chest, but the sweat was standing on his face as well.'

A few minutes later, Randall came out, the whip tucked under his arm, the lead plummets at the tips of the lashes clicking softly together as he walked. He had surveyed Jamie coolly, then motioned to the sergeant to turn the prisoner around to show his back.

Dougal grimaced. 'A pitiful sight, it was, too – still raw, no more than half healed.'

Randall then turned to the sergeant and said, 'A pretty job, Sergeant Wilkes. I must see if I can do as well.' With considerable punctilio, he then called for the garrison doctor and had him certify officially that Jamie was fit enough to be flogged.

'You've seen a cat play wi' a wee mousie?' Dougal asked. ''Twas like that. Randall strolled around the lad, making one kind of remark and another, none of them what ye'd call pleasant. And Jamie stood there like an oak tree, sayin' nothing and keeping his eyes fixed on the post, not lookin' at Randall at all. I could see the lad was hugging his elbows to try to stop the shivering, and ye could tell Randall saw it too.

'His mouth tightened up and he says, "I thought this was the young man who only a week past was shouting that he wasn't afraid to die. Surely a man who's not afraid to die isn't afraid of a few lashes?" and he gives Jamie a poke in the belly wi' the handle of the whip.

'Jamie met Randall's eye straight on then, and said, "No, but I'm afraid I'll freeze stiff before ye're done talking." '

Dougal sighed. 'Well. It was a braw speech, but damn reckless for a' that. Now, scourging a man is never a pretty business, but there's ways to make it worse than it might be.' He shook his head. 'Verra ugly.'

He frowned, choosing his words slowly.

'Randall's face was – intent, I suppose ye'd say – and sort o' lighted up, like when a man is lookin' at a lass he's soft on, if ye know what I mean. 'Twas as though he were doin' somethin' much worse to Jamie than just skinning him alive. The blood was running down the lad's legs by the fifteenth stroke, and the tears running down his face wi' the sweat.'

I swayed a little, and put out a hand to the stone coping.

'Well,' he said abruptly, catching sight of my expression, 'I'll say no more except that he lived through it. When the corporal untied his hands, Jamie nearly fell, but the corporal and sergeant each caught him by an arm and kind o' steadied him till he could keep his feet. He was shakin' worse than ever from shock and cold, but his head was up and his eyes blazin' – I could see it from twenty feet away. He keeps his eyes fixed on Randall while they help him off – it's like watching Randall is the only thing keeping him on his feet. Randall's face was almost as white as Jamie's, and his eyes were locked wi' the lad's – as though either of them would fall if he took his eyes away.' Dougal's own eyes were fixed, still seeing the eerie scene.

Everything was quiet in the small glade except for the faint rush of wind through the leaves of the rowan tree. I closed my eyes and listened to it for some time.

'Why?' I asked finally, eyes still closed. 'Why did you tell me that?'

Dougal was watching me intently when I opened my eyes. I dipped a hand in the spring again, and applied the cool water to my temples.

'I thought it might serve as what ye may call a character illustration,' he said.

'Of Randall?' I uttered a short, mirthless laugh. 'I don't need any further evidence as to his character, thank you.'

'Of Randall,' he agreed, 'and Jamie too.'

I looked at him, suddenly ill at ease.

'Ye see, I have *orders*' – he emphasized the word sarcastically – 'from the good Captain.'

'Orders to do what?' I asked, the agitated feeling increasing.

'To produce the person of an English subject, one Claire Beauchamp by name, at Fort William on Monday, the eighteenth of June. For questioning.'

I must have looked truly alarming, for he jumped to his feet and came over to me.

259

'Put your head between your knees, lass,' he instructed, pushing on the back of my neck, ''till the faintness passes off.'

'I know what to do,' I said irritably, doing it nonetheless. I closed my eyes, feeling the ebbing blood begin the throb in my temples again. The clammy sensation around my face and ears began to disappear, though my hands were still icy. I concentrated on breathing properly, counting *in*-one-two-three-four, *out*-one-two-three-four, *in*-one-two-three-four . . .

At length I sat up, feeling more or less in possession of all my faculties. Dougal had resumed his seat on the stone coping and was waiting patiently, watching to be sure that I didn't fall backwards into the spring.

'There's a way out of it,' he said abruptly. 'The only one I can see.'

'Lead me to it,' I said with an unconvincing attempt at a smile.

'Verra well, then.' He sat forward, leaning towards me to explain. 'Randall's the right to take ye for questioning because you're a subject of the English Crown. Well, then, we must change that.'

I stared at him, uncomprehending. 'What do you mean? You're a subject of the Crown as well, aren't you? How could you change such a thing?'

'Scots law and English law are similar,' he said, frowning, 'but no the same. And an English officer canna compel the person of a Scot, unless he's firm evidence of a crime committed, or grounds for serious suspicions. Even with suspicion, he could no remove a Scottish subject from clan lands without the permission of the laird concerned.'

'You've been talking to Ned Gowan,' I said, beginning to feel a little dizzy again.

He nodded. 'Aye, I have. I thought it might come to this, ye ken. And what he told me is what I thought myself; the only way I can legally refuse to give ye to Randall is to change ye from an Englishwoman into a Scot.'

'Into a Scot?' I said, the dazed feeling quickly being replaced by a horrible suspicion.

This was confirmed by his next words.

'Aye,' he said, nodding at my expression. 'Ye must marry a Scot. Young Jamie.'

'I couldn't do that!'

'Weel.' He frowned, considering. 'I suppose ye could take Rupert, instead. He's a widower, and he's the lease of a small farm. Still, he's a good bit older, and – '

'I don't want to marry Rupert, either! That's the ... the most absurd ...' Words failed me. Springing to my feet in agitation, I paced around the small clearing, old leaves crunching under my feet.

'Jamie's a goodly lad,' Dougal argued, still sitting on the coping. 'He's not much in the way of property just now, true, but he's a kind-hearted lad. He'd not be cruel to ye. And he's a bonny fighter, with verra good reason to hate Randall. Nay, marry him, and he'll fight to his last breath to protect ye.'

'But ... but I *can't* marry anyone!' I burst out.

Dougal's eyes were suddenly sharp. 'Why not, lass? Do ye have a husband living still?'

'No. It's just ... it's ridiculous! Such things don't happen!'

Dougal had relaxed when I said 'no'. Now he glanced up at the sun and rose to go.

'Best get moving, lass. There are things we'll have to attend to.'

He took my arm, still muttering to himself. I wrenched it away.

'I will not marry anyone,' I said firmly.

He seemed undisturbed by this, merely raising his brows.

'You *want* me to take you to Randall?'

'No!' Something occurred to me. 'So at least you believe me when I say I'm not an English spy?'

'I do *now*.' He spoke with some emphasis.

'Why now and not before?'

He nodded at the spring, and at the worn figure etched in the rock. It must be hundreds of years old, much older even than the giant rowan tree that shaded the spring.

'St Ninian's spring. Ye drank the water before I asked ye.'

I was thoroughly bewildered by this time.

'What does that have to do with it?'

He looked surprised, then his mouth twisted in a smile. 'Ye didna know? They call it the liar's spring, as well. The water smells o' the fumes of hell. Anyone who drinks the water and then tells untruth will ha' the gizzard burnt out of him.'

'I see.' I spoke between my teeth. 'Well, my gizzard is quite intact. So you can believe me when I say I'm not a spy, English *or* French. And you can believe something else, Dougal MacKenzie. I'm not marrying anyone!'

He wasn't listening. In fact, he had already pushed his way through the bushes that screened the spring. Only a quivering branch marked his passage. Seething, I followed him.

I remonstrated at some length further on the ride back. Dougal advised me finally to save my breath to cool my parritch with, and after that we rode in silence.

Reaching the inn, I flung my reins to the ground and stamped upstairs to the refuge of my room.

The whole idea was not only outrageous but unthinkable. I paced around and around the narrow room, feeling increasingly like a rat in a trap. Why in hell hadn't I had the nerve to steal away from the Scots earlier, whatever the risk?

I sat down on the bed and tried to think calmly. Considered strictly from Dougal's point of view, no doubt the idea had merit. If he refused point-blank to hand me over to Randall, with no excuse, the Captain might easily try to take me by force. And whether he believed me or not, Dougal might understandably not want to engage in a skirmish with a lot of English dragoons for my sake.

And, viewed in cold blood, the idea had some merit from my side as well. If I were married to a Scot I would presumably no longer be watched and guarded. It would be that much easier to get away when the time came. And if it were Jamie – well, he liked me, clearly. And he knew the

Highlands like the back of his hand. He would perhaps take me to Craigh na Dun, or at least in the general direction. Yes, possibly marriage was the best way to gain my goal.

That was the cold-blooded way to look at it. My blood, however, was anything but cold. I was hot with fury and agitation, and could not keep still, pacing and fuming, looking for a way out. Any way. After an hour of this, my face was flushed and my head throbbing. I went to the window, sticking my head out into the cooling breeze.

There was a peremptory rap on the door behind me. Dougal entered as I pulled my head in. He bore a sheaf of stiff paper like a salver and was followed by Rupert and the immaculate Ned Gowan, bringing up the rear like royal equerries.

'Please do come in,' I said courteously.

Ignoring me as usual, Dougal removed a water jug from its resting place on the table and fanned the sheets of paper out ceremoniously on the rough oak surface.

'All done,' he said, with the pride of one who has shepherded a difficult project to a successful conclusion. 'Ned's drawn up the papers; nothing like a lawyer – so long as he's on your side, eh, Ned?'

The men all laughed, evidently in good humour.

'Not really difficult, ye ken,' Ned said modestly. 'It's but a simple contract.' He riffled the pages with a proprietary forefinger, then paused, wrinkling his brow at a sudden thought.

'You've no property in France, have ye?' he asked, peering worriedly at me over the half-spectacles he wore for close work. I shook my head and he relaxed, shuffling the papers back into a pile and tapping the edges neatly together.

'That's that, then. You'll only need to sign here at the foot, and Dougal and Rupert to witness.'

The lawyer set down the inkpot he had brought in, and whipping a clean quill from his pocket, presented it ceremoniously to me.

'And just what is this?' I asked. This was in the nature of a rhetorical question, for the top page of the bundle said

263

CONTRACT OF MARRIAGE in a clear hand, the letters two inches high and starkly black across the page.

Dougal suppressed a sigh of impatience at my recalcitrance.

'Ye ken quite weel what it is,' he said shortly. 'And unless you've had another bright thought for keeping yourself out of Randall's hands, you'll sign it and have done with it. Time's short.'

Bright thoughts were in particularly short supply at the moment, despite the hour I had spent hammering away at the problem. It really began to seem that this incredible alternative was the best I could do, struggle as I might.

'But I don't *want* to marry!' I said stubbornly. It occurred to me as well that mine was not the only point of view involved. I remembered the girl with blonde hair I had seen kissing Jamie in the alcove at the castle.

'And maybe Jamie doesn't want to marry me!' I said. 'What about that?' Dougal dismissed this as unimportant.

'Jamie's a soldier; he'll do as he's told. So will you,' he said pointedly, 'unless, of course, ye'd prefer an English prison.'

I glared at him, breathing heavily. I had been in a stir ever since our abrupt removal from Brockton, and my level of agitation had now increased substantially, confronted with the choice in black and white, as it were.

'I want to talk to him,' I said abruptly. Dougal's eyebrows shot up.

'Jamie? Why?'

'*Why?* Because you're forcing me to marry him, and so far as I can see, you haven't even told him!'

Plainly this was an irrelevancy as far as Dougal was concerned, but he eventually gave in and, accompanied by his minions, went to fetch Jamie from the taproom.

Jamie appeared shortly, looking understandably bewildered.

'Did you know that Dougal wants us to marry?' I demanded bluntly.

His expression cleared. 'Oh, aye. I knew that.'

'But surely,' I said, 'a young man like yourself; I mean,

264

isn't there anyone else you're, ah, interested in?' He looked blank for a moment, then understanding dawned.

'Oh, am I promised? Nay, I'm no much of a prospect for a girl.' He hurried on as though feeling this might sound insulting. 'I mean, I've no property to speak of, and nothing more than a soldier's pay to live on.'

He rubbed his chin, eyeing me dubiously. 'Then there's the minor difficulty that I've a price on my head. No father much wants his daughter married to a man as may be arrested and hanged any time. Did ye think of that?'

I flapped my hand, dismissing the matter of outlawry as a minor consideration compared to the whole monstrous idea. I had one last try.

'Does it bother you that I'm not a virgin?' He hesitated a moment before answering.

'Well, no,' he said slowly, 'so long as it doesna bother you that I am.' He grinned at my drop-jawed expression, and backed towards the door.

'Reckon one of us should know what they're doing,' he said. The door closed softly behind him; clearly the courtship was over.

The papers duly signed, I made my way cautiously down the inn's steep stairs and into the taproom.

'Whisky,' I said to the rumpled old creature who presided there. He glared rheumily, but a nod from Dougal made him oblige with a jug and rough-blown glass. The latter was thick and greenish, a bit smeared, with a chip out of the rim, but it had a hole in the top, and that was all that mattered at the moment.

Once the searing effect of swallowing the stuff had passed, it did induce a certain spurious calmness. I felt detached, noticing details of my surroundings with a peculiar intensity: the curve of the handle on a copper-bottomed dipper that hung on the wall next to me, a green-bellied fly struggling on the edges of a sticky puddle on the table. With a certain amount of fellow feeling, I nudged it out of danger with the edge of my glass.

I gradually became aware of raised voices behind the

closed door on the far side of the room, where Dougal had gone, presumably to finalise arrangements with the other contracting party. I was pleased to hear that, judging from the sound of it, my intended bridegroom was cutting up rough, despite his apparent lack of objection earlier. Perhaps he hadn't wanted to offend me.

'Stick to it, lad,' I murmured, and took another gulp.

Some time later I was dimly conscious of a hand prying my fingers open in order to remove the greenish glass. Another hand was steadyingly under my elbow.

'Christ, she's drunk as an auld besom in a bothy,' said a voice in my ear. The voice rasped unpleasantly, I thought, as though its owner had been eating sandpaper. I giggled softly at the thought.

'Quiet yerself, woman!' said the unpleasant rasping voice. It grew fainter as the owner turned to talk to someone else. 'Drunk as a laird and screechin' like a parrot – what do ye expect – '

Another voice interrupted the first, but I couldn't tell what it said; the words were blurred and indistinguishable. It was a pleasanter sound, though, deep and somehow reassuring. It came nearer, and I could make out a few words. I made an effort to focus, but my attention had begun to wander again.

The fly had found its way back to the puddle and was floundering in the middle, hopelessly mired. The light from the window fell on it, glittering like sparks on the straining green belly. My gaze fixed on the tiny green spot, which seemed to pulsate as the fly twitched and struggled.

'Brother . . . you haven't a chance,' I said, and the spark went out.

14

A Marriage Takes Place

There was a low, beamed ceiling over me when I woke, and a thick quilt tucked tidily under my chin. I seemed to be clad only in my shift. I started to sit up to look for my clothes, but thought better of it halfway up. I eased myself very carefully back down, closed my eyes and held on to my head to prevent it from rolling off the pillow and bouncing on the floor.

I woke again, some time later, when the door of the room opened. I cracked one eye cautiously. A wavering outline resolved itself into the dour figure of Murtagh, staring disapprovingly down at me from the foot of the bed. I closed the eye. I heard a muffled Scottish noise, presumably indicating appalled disgust, but when I looked again he was gone.

I was just sinking thankfully back into unconsciousness when the door opened again, this time to reveal a middle-aged woman I took to be the gudewife of the establishment, carrying a ewer and basin. She bustled cheerily into the room and banged the shutters open with a crash that reverberated through my head like a tank collision. Advancing on the bed like a Panzer division, she ripped the quilt from my feeble grasp and tossed it aside, leaving me quaking and exposed.

'Come along then, my dearie,' she said. 'We mun' get ye ready now.' She put a hefty forearm behind my shoulders and levered me into a sitting position. I clutched my head with one hand, my stomach with the other.

'Ready?' I said, through a mouth filled with decayed moss.

The woman began briskly washing my face. 'Och, aye,' she said. 'Ye dinna want to miss yer own wedding, now, do ye?'

'Yes,' I said, but was ignored as she unceremoniously stripped off my shift and stood me in the middle of the floor for further intimate attentions.

A bit later I sat on the bed, fully dressed, feeling dazed and belligerent, but thanks to a glass of port supplied by the landlady, at least functional. I sipped carefully at a second glass as the woman tugged a comb through the thickets of my hair.

I jumped and shuddered, spilling the port, as the door crashed open once more. One damn thing after another, I thought balefully. This time it was a double visitation, Murtagh and Ned Gowan, wearing similar looks of disapprobation. I exchanged glares with Ned while Murtagh came into the room and walked slowly around the bed, surveying me from every angle. He returned to Ned and muttered something in a tone too low for me to hear. With a final glance of despair in my direction, he pulled the door shut behind them.

At last my hair was dressed to the woman's satisfaction, swept back and pulled high in a knot at the crown, curls picked loose to tumble to the back, and ringlets in front of my ears. It felt as though my scalp were going to pop off from the tension of the strained-back hair, but the effect in the looking glass the woman provided was undeniably becoming. I began to feel slightly more human, and even brought myself to thank her for her efforts. She left me the looking glass, and departed, remarking that it was so lucky to be married in summer, wasn't it, as I'd have plenty of flowers for my hair.

'We who are about to die,' I said to my reflection, sketching a salute in the glass. I collapsed on the bed, plastered a wet cloth over my face and went back to sleep.

I was having a rather nice dream, something to do with grassy fields and wild flowers, when I became aware that what I had thought a playful breeze tugging at my sleeves was a pair of none-too-gentle hands. I sat up with a jerk, blindly flailing.

When I got my eyes open, I saw that my small chamber now resembled a tube station, with faces wall to wall: Ned

Gowan, Murtagh, the innkeeper, the innkeeper's wife, and a lanky young man who turned out to be the innkeeper's son, with his arms full of assorted flowers, which accounted for the scents in my dream. There was also a young woman armed with a round wicker basket, who smiled amiably at me, displaying the lack of several rather important teeth.

This person, it developed, was the village sempstress, recruited to repair the deficiencies of my wardrobe by adjusting the fit of a dress, obtained on short notice from some local connection of the innkeeper's. Ned was carrying the dress in question, hanging from one hand like a dead animal. Smoothed out on the bed, it proved to be a low-necked gown of heavy cream-coloured satin, with a separate bodice that fastened with dozens of tiny cloth-covered buttons, each embroidered with a gold fleur-de-lys. The neckline and the belled sleeves were heavily ruched with lace. The innkeeper was half buried in the petticoats he carried, his bristling whiskers barely visible over the foamy layers.

I looked at the port-wine stain on my grey serge skirt and vanity won out. If I were in fact to be married, I didn't want to do it looking like the village drudge.

After a short spell of frenetic activity, with me standing like a dressmaker's dummy and everyone else racing about fetching, carrying, criticizing and tripping over each other, the final product was ready, complete to white roses pinned in my hair and a heart pounding madly away beneath the lacy bodice. The fit was not quite perfect, and the gown smelled rather strongly of its previous owner, but the satin was weighty and swished rather fascinatingly about my feet, over the layers of petticoats. I felt quite regal, and not a little lovely.

'You can't make me do this, you know,' I hissed threateningly at Murtagh's back as I followed him downstairs, but he and I both knew my words were empty bravado. If I had ever had the strength of character to defy Dougal and take my chances with the English, it had drained away with the whisky.

Dougal, Ned and the rest were in the taproom at the foot of the stair, drinking and exchanging pleasantries with a few villagers who seemed to have nothing better to do with their afternoon than hang about getting sloshed.

Dougal caught sight of me slowly descending, and abruptly stopped talking. The others fell silent as well, and I floated down in a most gratifying cloud of reverent admiration. Dougal's deep-set eyes covered me slowly from head to foot and returned to my face with a completely ungrudging nod of acknowledgement.

What with one thing and another it was some time since a man had looked at me that way, and I nodded quite graciously back.

After the first silence, the rest of those in the taproom became vocal in their admiration, and even Murtagh allowed himself a small smile, nodding in satisfaction at the results of his efforts. *And who appointed* you *fashion editor?* I thought disagreeably. Still, I had to admit that he was responsible for my not marrying in grey serge.

Marrying. Oh, God. Buoyed temporarily by port wine and cream lace, I had momentarily managed to ignore the significance of the occasion. I gripped the banister as fresh realization hit like a blow in the stomach. I *had* a husband. I had Frank. I couldn't marry another man!

Looking over the throng, though, I noticed one glaring omission. My groom was nowhere in sight. Heartened by the thought that he might have succeeded in escaping out of a window and be miles away by now, I accepted a parting cup of wine from the innkeeper before following Dougal outside.

Ned and Rupert went to fetch the ponies. Murtagh had disappeared somewhere, perhaps to search for traces of Jamie.

Dougal held me by one arm; ostensibly to support me lest I stumble in my satin slippers, in reality to prevent any last-minute breaks for freedom.

It was a 'warm' Scottish day, meaning that the mist wasn't quite heavy enough to qualify as a drizzle, but not far off, either. Suddenly the inn door opened and the sun came out, in the person of James. If I was a radiant bride, the groom was positively resplendent. My mouth fell open and stayed that way.

A Highlander in full regalia is an impressive sight – any Highlander, no matter how old, ill-favoured or crabbed in appearance. A tall, straight-bodied and by no means ill-favoured young Highlander at close range is breathtaking.

The thick red hair had been brushed to a smooth gleam that swept the collar of a fine lawn shirt with tucked front, belled sleeves and lace-trimmed wrist frills that matched the cascade of the starched jabot at the throat, decorated with a ruby stickpin.

His tartan was a brilliant crimson, blue and black that blazed among the more sedate MacKenzies in their green and white. The flaming wool, fastened by a circular silver brooch, fell from his right shoulder in a graceful drape, caught by a silver-studded sword belt before continuing its sweep past neat calves clothed in woollen hose and stopping just short of the silver-buckled black leather shoes. Sword, dirk and sporran completed the ensemble.

Well over six feet tall, broad in proportion and striking of feature, he was a far cry from the grubby horse-handler I was accustomed to – and he knew it. Making a leg in courtly fashion, he swept me a bow of impeccable grace, murmuring 'Your servant, ma'am,' eyes glinting with mischief.

'Oh,' I said faintly.

I had seldom seen the taciturn Dougal at a loss for words before. Thick brows knotted over a suffused face, he seemed in his way as taken aback by this apparition as I was.

'Are ye mad, man?' he hissed at last. 'What if someone's to see ye!'

Jamie cocked a sardonic eyebrow at the older man. 'Why, Uncle,' he said. 'Insults? And on my wedding day too. You wouldna have me shame my wife now, would ye? Besides,' he added with a malicious gleam, 'I hardly think it would be legal, did I not marry in my own name. And you do want it legal, now, don't you?'

With an apparent effort Dougal recovered his self-possession. 'If ye're quite finished, Jamie, we'll get on wi' it,' he said.

But Jamie was not quite finished, it seemed. Ignoring Dougal's fuming, he drew a short string of white beads from his sporran. He stepped forward and fastened the necklace around my neck. Looking down, I could see it was a string of small baroque pearls, those irregularly shaped productions of freshwater mussels, interspersed with tiny pierced-work gold roundels. Smaller pearls dangled from the gold beads.

'They're only Scottish pearls,' he said apologetically, 'but they look bonny on you.' His fingers lingered a moment on my neck.

'Those were your mother's pearls!' said Dougal, glowering at the necklace.

'Aye,' said Jamie calmly, 'and now they're my wife's. Shall we go?'

Wherever we were going, it was some distance from the village. We made a rather morose wedding party, the bridal pair encircled by the others like convicts being escorted towards some distant prison. The only conversation was a muted apology from Jamie for being late, explaining that there had been some difficulty in finding a clean shirt and coat large enough to fit him.

'I think this one belongs to the local laird's son,' he said, flipping the lacy jabot. 'Bit of a dandy, it looks like.'

We dismounted and left the ponies at the foot of a small hill. A footpath led upwards through the heather.

'Ye've made the arrangements?' I heard Dougal say in an undertone to Rupert as they tethered the beasts.

'Och, aye.' There was a flash of teeth in the black beard. He patted his sporran, which clinked musically, giving me some idea of the nature of the arrangements for a marriage made in haste.

Through the drizzle and mist I saw the chapel jutting out of the heather. With a sense of complete disbelief I saw the round-shouldered roof and the odd little many-paned windows which I had last seen on the bright sunny morning of my marriage to Frank Randall.

'No!' I exclaimed. 'Not here! I can't!'

'Hst, now, hst. Dinna worry, lass, dinna worry. It will be all right.' Dougal put a large paw on my shoulder, making soothing Scottish noises as if I were a skittish pony. ''Tis natural to be a bit nervous,' he said, to all of us. A firm hand in the small of my back urged me on up the path. My slippers sank moistly in the damp layer of fallen leaves.

Jamie and Dougal walked close on either side of me, preventing escape. Their looming tartan presences were unnerving, and I felt a mounting sense of hysteria. Two hundred years ahead, more or less, I had been married in this chapel, charmed then by its ancient picturesqueness. The chapel now was creaking with newness, not yet settled into charm, and I was about to marry a twenty-three-year-old Scottish Catholic virgin with a price on his head, whose –

I turned to Jamie in sudden panic. 'I can't marry you! I don't even know your last name!'

He looked down at me and cocked a ruddy eyebrow. 'Oh. It's Fraser. James Alexander Malcolm MacKenzie Fraser.' He pronounced it formally, each name slow and distinct.

Completely flustered, I said, 'Claire Elizabeth Beauchamp,' and stuck out my hand idiotically. Apparently taking this as a plea for support, he took the hand and tucked it firmly into the crook of his elbow. Thus inescapably pinioned, I squelched up the path to my wedding.

Last time – next time? – I had been married in a white linen suit with alligator pumps. Frank had worn grey Harris tweed. I caught myself thinking wildly of Uncle Lamb, who had witnessed the wedding.

'Pity to waste the surroundings with this modern stuff,' he had said, casually patting Frank's tweed sleeve. 'It's a genuine eighteenth-century Scottish chapel, you know. You ought to have got yourselves up appropriately, kilts and dirks and long gowns and such.' Looking up at the formidable sight of my intended bridegroom, I had a sudden unhinged vision of Uncle Lamb nodding approvingly. 'Much better,' he said, in my imagination. 'Just the thing.'

Rupert and Murtagh were waiting for us in the chapel, keeping guard over a captive cleric, a spindly young priest with a red nose and a justifiably terrified expression. Rupert was idly slicing a willow twig with a large knife, and while he had laid aside his horn-handled pistols on entering the church, they remained in easy reach on the rim of the baptismal font.

The other men also disarmed, as was suitable in the house of God, leaving an impressively bristling pile of lethality in the back pew. Only Jamie kept his dagger and sword, presumably as a ceremonial part of his dress.

We knelt before the wooden altar, Murtagh and Dougal took their places as witnesses, and the ceremony began.

The form of the Catholic marriage service has not changed appreciably in several hundred years, and the words linking me with the red-headed young stranger at my side were much the same as those that had consecrated my wedding to Frank. I felt like a cold, hollow shell. The young priest's stammering words echoed somewhere in the empty pit of my stomach.

I stood automatically when it came time for the vows, watching in a sort of numbed fascination as my chilly fingers disappeared into my bridegroom's substantial grasp. His fingers were as cold as my own, and it occurred to me for the first time that despite his outwardly cool demeanour he might be as nervous as I was.

I had so far avoided looking at him, but now glanced up to find him staring down at me. His face was white and carefully expressionless; he looked as he had when I dressed the wound in his shoulder. I tried to smile at him, but the corners of my mouth wobbled precariously. The pressure of his fingers on mine increased. I had the impression that we were holding each other up; if either of us let go or looked away, we would both fall down. Oddly, the feeling was mildly reassuring. Whatever we were in for, at least there were two of us.

'I take thee, Claire, to be my wife . . .' His voice didn't

shake, but his hand did. I tightened my grip. Our stiff fingers clenched together like boards in a vice. '. . . to love, honour and protect . . . for better and for worse . . .' The words came from far away. The blood was draining from my head. The boned bodice was infernally tight, and though I felt cold, sweat ran down my sides beneath the satin. I hoped I wouldn't faint.

There was a small stained-glass window set high in the wall at the side of the sanctuary, a crude rendering of John the Baptist in his sheepskin. Green and blue shadows flowed over my sleeve, and I wished fervently for a drink.

My turn. I stuttered slightly, to my fury. 'I t-take thee, James . . .' I stiffened my spine. Jamie had got through his half creditably enough; I could try to do as well. '. . . to have and to hold, from this day forth . . .' My voice came stronger now.

'Till death do us part.' The words rang out in the quiet chapel with a startling finality. Everything was still, as though in suspended animation. Then the priest asked for the ring.

There was a sudden stir of agitation and I caught a glimpse of Murtagh's stricken face. I barely registered the fact that someone had forgotten to provide for the ring when Jamie released my hand long enough to twist a ring from his own finger.

I still wore Frank's ring on my left hand. The fingers of my right looked frozen, pallid and stiff in a pool of blue light, as the large metal circlet passed over the third finger. It hung loose on the digit and would have slid off, had Jamie not folded my fingers around it and enclosed my fist once more in his own.

More mumbling from the priest, and Jamie bent to kiss me. It was clear that he intended only a brief and ceremonial touching of lips, but his mouth was soft and warm and I moved instinctively towards him. I was vaguely conscious of noises, Scottish whoops of enthusiasm and encouragement from the spectators, but really noticed nothing beyond the enfolding warm solidness. Sanctuary.

We drew apart, both a little steadier, and smiled ner-

275

vously. I saw Dougal draw Jamie's dirk from its sheath and wondered why. Still looking at me, Jamie held out his right hand, palm up. I gasped as the point of the dirk scored across his wrist, leaving a dark line of welling blood. There was not time to jerk away before my own hand was seized and I felt the burning slice of the blade. Swiftly Dougal pressed my wrist to Jamie's and bound the two together with a strip of white linen.

I must have swayed a bit, because Jamie gripped my elbow with his free left hand.

'Bear up, lass,' he urged softly. 'It's not long now. Say the words after me.' It was a short bit of Gaelic, two or three sentences. The words meant nothing to me, but I obediently repeated them after Jamie, stumbling on the slippery vowels. The linen was untied, the wounds blotted clean, and we were married.

There was a general air of relief and exhilaration on the way back down the footpath. It might have been any merry wedding party, albeit a small one, and one composed entirely of men, save the bride.

We were nearly at the bottom when lack of food, the remnants of a hangover and the general stresses of the day caught up with me. I came to lying on damp leaves, my head in my new husband's lap. He put down the wet cloth with which he had been wiping my face.

'That bad, was it?' He grinned down at me but his eyes held an uncertain expression that rather touched me, in spite of everything. I smiled shakily back.

'It's not you,' I assured him. 'It's just . . . I don't think I've had anything at all to eat since breakfast yesterday – and rather a lot to drink, I'm afraid.'

His mouth twitched. 'So I heard. Well, that I can remedy. I've not a lot to offer a wife, as I said, but I do promise to keep ye fed.' He smiled and shyly pushed a stray curl off my face with a forefinger.

I started to sit up and grimaced at a slight burning in one wrist. I had forgotten that last bit of the ceremony. The cut had come open, no doubt as a result of the fall I had taken.

I took the cloth from Jamie and wrapped it awkwardly around the wrist.

'I thought it might have been that that made ye faint,' he said, watching. 'I should have thought to warn ye about it; I didna realize you weren't expecting it until I saw your face.'

'What was it, exactly?' I asked, trying to tuck in the ends of the cloth.

'It's a bit pagan, but it's customary hereabouts to have a blood vow, along with the regular marriage service. Some priests won't have it, but I don't suppose this one was likely to object to anything. He looked almost as scared as I felt,' he said, smiling.

'A blood vow? What do the words mean?'

Jamie took my right hand and gently tucked in the last end of the makeshift bandage.

'It rhymes, more or less, when ye say it in English. It says:

"Ye are Blood of my Blood, and Bone of my Bone.
I give ye my Body, that we Two might be One.
I give ye my Spirit, till our Life shall be Done." '

He shrugged. 'About the same as the regular vows, just a bit more . . . ah, primitive.'

I gazed down at my bound wrist. 'Yes, you could say that.'

I glanced about; we were alone on the path, under an aspen tree. The round dead leaves lay on the ground, gleaming in the wet like rusted coins. It was very quiet, save for the occasional splat of water droplets falling from the trees.

'Where are the others? Did they go back to the inn?'

Jamie grimaced. 'No. I made them go away so I could tend ye, but they'll be waitin' for us just over there.' He gestured with his chin, in the countryman's manner. 'They're no going to trust us alone till everything's official.'

'Isn't it?' I said blankly. 'We're married, aren't we?'

He seemed embarrassed, turning away and elaborately brushing dead leaves from his kilt.

'Mmmphm. Aye, we're married, right enough. But it's no legally binding, ye know, until it's been consummated.' A slow, fierce blush burned its way up from the lacy jabot. 'Mmmphm,' I said. 'Let's go and find something to eat.'

15

Revelations of the Bridal Chamber

At the inn, food was readily available in the form of a modest wedding feast, including wine, fresh bread and roast beef.

Dougal took me by the arm as I started for the stairs to freshen myself before eating.

'I want this marriage consummated, wi' no uncertainty whatsoever,' Dougal instructed me firmly in an undertone. 'There's to be no question of it bein' a legal union and no way open for annulment, or we're all riskin' our necks.'

'Seems to me you're doing that anyway,' I remarked crossly. 'Mine, especially.'

Dougal patted me firmly on the rump.

'Dinna ye worry about that; ye just do your part.' He looked me over critically, as though judging my capacity to perform my role adequately.

'I kent Jamie's father. If the lad's much like him, ye'll have no trouble at all. Ah, Jamie lad!' He hurried across the room to where Jamie had come in from stabling the ponies. From the look on Jamie's face, he was getting his orders as well.

How in the name of God did this happen? I asked myself some time later. Six weeks ago I had been innocently collecting wild flowers on a Scottish hill, to take home to my husband. I was now shut in the room of a rural inn, awaiting a completely different husband, whom I scarcely knew, with firm orders to consummate a forced marriage, at risk of my life and liberty.

And what about my *old* husband? My stomach knotted with grief and fear. What would Frank be thinking now? What would he be feeling? I had been gone for more than

279

a month; he would have been searching for me, calling out the police as his concern turned to fear, turning the Scottish countryside upside down. Not far enough, though; it would never occur to him to look inside a fairies' hill, even were such a thing possible.

I sat on the bed, stiff and terrified in my borrowed finery. There was a faint noise as the heavy door of the room swung open, then shut.

Jamie leaned against the door, watching me. The air of embarrassment between us deepened. It was Jamie who broke the silence finally.

'You dinna need to be afraid of me,' he said softly. 'I wasna going to jump on ye.' I laughed in spite of myself.

'Well, I didn't think you would.' In fact, I didn't think he would touch me, until and unless I invited him to; the fact remained that I was going to have to invite him to do considerably more than that, and soon.

I eyed him dubiously. I supposed it would be harder if I found him unattractive; in fact, the opposite was true. Still, I had not slept with any man but Frank in over eight years. Not only that, this young man, by his own acknowledgement, was completely inexperienced. I had never deflowered anyone before. Even dismissing my objections to the whole arrangement, and considering matters from a completely practical standpoint, how on earth were we to start? At this rate we would still be here, staring at each other, three or four days hence.

I cleared my throat and patted the bed beside me.

'Ah, would you like to sit down?'

'Aye.' He came across the room, moving like a big cat. Instead of sitting beside me, though, he pulled up a stool and sat down facing me. Somewhat tentatively he reached out and took my hands between his own. They were large, blunt-fingered and very warm, the backs lightly furred with reddish hairs. I felt a slight shock at the touch, and thought of an Old Testament passage – 'For Jacob's skin was smooth, while his brother Esau was an hairy man.' Frank's hands were long and slender, nearly hairless and aristocratic-looking. I had always loved watching them as he lectured.

'Tell me about your husband,' said Jamie, as though he had been reading my mind. I almost jerked my hands away in shock.

'What?'

'Look ye, lass. We have three or four days together here. While I dinna pretend to know all there is to know, I've lived a good bit of my life on a farm, and unless people are verra different from other animals, it isna going to take that long to do what we have to do. We have a bit of time to talk, and get over being scairt of each other.' This blunt appraisal of our situation relaxed me a little bit.

'Are you scared of me?' He didn't look it. Perhaps he was nervous, though. Even though he was no timid sixteen-year-old lad, this *was* the first time. He looked into my eyes and smiled.

'Aye. More scairt than you, I expect. That's why I'm holdin' your hands; to keep my own from shaking.' I didn't believe this, but squeezed his hands tightly in appreciation.

'It's a good idea. It feels a little easier to talk while we're touching. Why did you ask about my husband, though?' I wondered a bit wildly if he wanted me to tell him about my sex life with Frank, so as to know what I expected of him.

'Well, I knew ye must be thinking of him. Ye could hardly not, under the circumstances. I do not want ye ever to feel as though ye canna talk of him to me. Even though I'm your husband now – that feels verra strange to say – it isna right that ye should forget him, or even try to. If ye loved him, he must ha' been a good man.'

'Yes, he . . . was.' My voice trembled, and Jamie stroked the backs of my hands with his thumbs.

'Then I shall do my best to honour his spirit by serving his wife.' He raised my hands and kissed each one formally.

I cleared my throat. 'That was a very gallant speech, Jamie.'

He grinned suddenly. 'Aye. I made it up while Dougal was making toasts downstairs.'

I took a deep breath. 'I have questions,' I said.

He looked down, hiding a smile. 'I'd suppose ye do,' he agreed. 'I imagine you're entitled to a bit of curiosity, under the circumstances. What is it ye want to know?' He looked up suddenly, blue eyes bright with mischief in the lamplight. 'Why I'm a virgin yet?'

'Er, I should say that that was more or less your own business,' I murmured. It seemed to be getting rather warm suddenly, and I pulled one hand free to grope for my handkerchief. As I did so I felt something hard in the pocket of my gown.

'Oh, I forgot! I still have your ring.' I drew it out and gave it back to him. It was a heavy gold circlet, set with a cabochon ruby. Instead of replacing it on his finger, he opened his sporran to put it inside.

'It was my father's wedding ring,' he explained. 'I dinna wear it customarily, but I . . . well, I wished to do ye honour today by looking as well as I might.' He flushed slightly at this admission, and busied himself with refastening the sporran.

'You did do me great honour,' I said, smiling in spite of myself. Adding a ruby ring to the blazing splendour of his costume was coals to Newcastle, but I was touched by the anxious thought behind it.

'I'll get one that fits ye, so soon as I may,' he promised.

'It's not important,' I said, feeling slightly uncomfortable. I meant, after all, to be gone soon.

'Er, I have one main question,' I said, calling the meeting to order. 'If you don't mind telling me. Why did you agree to marry me?'

'Ah.' He let go of my hands and sat back a bit. He paused for a moment before answering, smoothing the woollen cloth over his thighs. I could see the long line of muscle taut under the drape of the heavy fabric.

'Well, I would ha' missed talking to ye, for one thing,' he said, smiling.

'No, I mean it,' I insisted. 'Why?'

He sobered then. 'Before I tell ye, Claire, there's one thing I'd ask of you,' he said slowly.

'What's that?'

'Honesty.'

I must have flinched uncomfortably, for he leaned forward earnestly, hands on his knees.

'I know there are things ye'd not wish to tell me, Claire. Perhaps things that ye *can't* tell me.'

You don't know just how right you are, I thought.

'I'll not press you, ever, or insist on knowin' things that are your own concern,' he said seriously. He looked down at his hands, now pressed together, palm to palm.

'There are things that I canna tell *you,* at least not yet. And I'll ask nothing of ye that ye canna give me. But what I would ask of ye – when you do tell me something, let it be the truth. And I'll promise the same. We have nothing now between us, save – respect, perhaps. And I think that respect has maybe room for secrets, but not for lies. Do ye agree?' He spread his hands out, palms up, inviting me. I could see the dark line of the blood vow across his wrist. I placed my own hands lightly on his palms.

'Yes, I agree. I'll give you honesty.' His fingers closed tightly about mine.

'And I shall give ye the same. Now' – he drew a deep breath – 'you asked why I wed ye.'

'I *am* just the slightest bit curious,' I said.

He smiled, the wide mouth taking up the humour that lurked in his eyes. 'Well, I canna say I blame ye. I had several reasons. And in fact, there's one – maybe two – that I canna tell ye yet, though I will in time. The main reason, though, is the same reason you wed me, I imagine; to keep ye safe from the hands of Black Jack Randall.'

I shuddered a bit at the memory of the Captain, and Jamie's hands tightened on mine.

'You *are* safe,' he said firmly. 'You have my name and my family, my clan, and if necessary, the protection of my body as well. The man willna lay hands on ye again, while I live.'

'Thank you,' I said. Looking at the strong, young, determined face, with its broad cheekbones and solid jaw, I felt for the first time that this preposterous scheme of Dougal's might actually have been a reasonable suggestion.

The protection of my body. The phrase struck with particular impact, looking at him – the resolute set of the wide shoulders and the memory of his graceful ferocity, 'showing off' at swordplay in the moonlight. He meant it; and young as he was, he knew what he meant, and bore the scars to prove it. He was no older than many of the pilots and infantrymen I had nursed, and he knew as well as they the price of commitment. It was no romantic pledge he had made me, but the blunt promise to guard my safety at the cost of his own. I hoped only that I could offer him something in return.

'That's *most* gallant of you,' I said, with absolute sincerity. 'But was it worth, well, worth marriage?'

'It was,' he said, nodding. He smiled again, a little grimly this time. 'I've good reason to know the man, ye ken. I wouldna see a dog given into his keeping if I could prevent it, let alone a helpless woman.'

'How flattering,' I remarked wryly, and he laughed. He stood up and went to the table near the window. Someone – perhaps the landlady – had supplied a bouquet of wild flowers, set in water in a whisky cup. Behind this stood two wine glasses and a bottle.

Jamie poured out two glasses and came back, handing me one as he resumed his seat.

'Not quite so good as Callum's private stock,' he said with a smile, 'but none so bad, either.' He raised his glass briefly. 'To Mrs Fraser,' he said softly, and I felt a thump of panic again. I quelled it firmly and raised my own glass.

'To honesty,' I said, and we both drank.

'Well, that's one reason,' I said, lowering my glass. 'Are there others you can tell me?'

He studied his wine glass with some care. 'Perhaps it's just that I want to bed you.' He looked up abruptly. 'Did ye think of that?'

If he meant to disconcert me, he was succeeding nicely, but I resolved not to show it.

'Well, do you?' I said boldly.

'If I'm bein' honest, yes, I do.' The blue eyes were steady over the rim of the glass.

284

'You wouldn't necessarily have had to marry me for that,' I objected.

He appeared honestly scandalized. 'You do not think I would take ye without offering you marriage?'

'Many men would,' I said, amused at his innocence.

He sputtered a bit, at a momentary loss. Then regaining his composure, he said with formal dignity, 'Perhaps I am pretentious in saying so, but I would like to think that I am not "many men", and that I dinna necessarily place my behaviour at the lowest common denominator.'

Rather touched by this speech I assured him that I had so far found his behaviour both gallant and gentlemanly, and apologized for any doubt I might inadvertently have cast on his motives.

On this precariously diplomatic note we paused while he refilled our empty glasses.

We sipped in silence for a time, both feeling a bit shy after the frankness of that last exchange. So, apparently there *was* something I could offer him. I couldn't, in fairness, say the thought had not entered my mind, even before the absurd situation in which we found ourselves arose. He was a very engaging young man. And there had been that moment, right after my arrival at the castle, when he had held me on his lap, and –

I tilted my wine glass back and drained the contents. I patted the bed beside me again.

'Sit down here with me,' I said. 'And' – I cast about for some neutral topic of conversation to ease us over the awkwardness of close proximity – 'and tell me about your family. Where did you grow up?'

The bed sank noticeably under his weight, and I braced myself not to roll against him. He sat closely enough that the sleeve of his shirt brushed my arm. I let my hand lie open on my thigh, relaxed. He took it naturally as he sat, and we leaned against the wall, neither of us looking down, but as conscious of the link as though we had been welded together.

'Well, now, where shall I start?' He put his rather large

feet up on the stool and crossed them at the ankles. With some amusement I recognized the Highlander settling back for a leisurely dissection of that tangle of family and clan relationships which forms the background of almost any event of significance in the Scottish Highlands. Frank and I had spent one evening in the village pub, enthralled by the conversation between two old codgers, in which the responsibility for the recent destruction of an ancient barn was traced back through the intricacies of a local feud dating, so far as I could tell, from about 1790. With the sort of minor shock to which I was becoming accustomed, I realized that that particular feud, whose origins I had thought shrouded in the mists of time, had not yet begun. Suppressing the mental turmoil this realization caused, I forced my attention to what Jamie was saying.

'My father was a Fraser, of course; a younger half-brother to the present Master of Lovat. My mother was a MacKenzie, though. Ye'll know that Dougal and Callum are my uncles?' I nodded. The resemblance was clear enough, despite the difference in colouring. The broad cheekbones and long, straight, knife-edged nose were plainly a MacKenzie inheritance.

'Aye, well, my mother was their sister, and there were two more sisters, besides. My Auntie Janet is dead, like my mother, but my Auntie Jocasta married a cousin of Rupert's, and lives up near the edge of Loch Eilean Mhor. Auntie Janet had six children, four boys and two girls, Auntie Jocasta had three, all girls, Dougal's got the four girls, Callum has little Hamish only, and my parents had me and my sister, who's named for my Auntie Janet, but we called her Jenny always.'

'Rupert's a MacKenzie, too?' I asked, already struggling to keep everyone straight.

'Aye. He's – ' Jamie paused a moment considering. 'He's Dougal's, Callum's and Jocasta's first cousin, which makes him my second cousin. Rupert's father and my grandfather Jacob were brothers, along with – '

'Wait a minute. Don't let's go back any farther than we have to, or I shall be getting hopelessly muddled. We haven't even got to the Frasers yet, and I've already lost track of your cousins.'

He rubbed his chin, calculating. 'Hmm. Well, on the Fraser side it's a bit more complicated, because my grandfather Simon married three times, so my father had two sets of half-brothers and half-sisters. Let's leave it for now that I've six Fraser uncles and three aunts still living, and we'll leave out all the cousins from that lot.'

'Yes, let's.' I leaned forward and poured another glass of wine for each of us.

The clan territories of MacKenzie and Fraser, it turned out, adjoined each other for some distance along their inner borders, running side by side from the western seacoast past the lower end of Loch Ness. This shared border, as borders tend to be, was an unmapped and most uncertain line, shifting to and fro in accordance with time, custom and alliance. Along this border, at the southern end of the Fraser clan lands, lay the small estate of Broch Tuarach, the property of Brian Fraser, Jamie's father.

'It's a fairly rich bit of ground, and there's decent fishing and a good patch of forest for hunting. It maybe supports sixty tenants, and the small village – Broch Mordha, it's called. Then there's the farmhouse, of course – that's modern,' he said, with some pride, 'and the old broch that we use now for the beasts and the grain.

'Dougal and Callum were not at all pleased to have their sister marrying a Fraser, and they insisted that she not be a tenant on Fraser land, but live on her own land. So, Lallybroch – that's what the folk that live there call it – was deeded to my father, but there was a clause in the deed stating that the land was to pass to my mother, Ellen's, issue only. If she died without children, the land would go back to Lord Lovat after my father's death, whether Father had children by another wife or no. But he didn't remarry, and I am my mother's son. So Lallybroch's mine, for what that's worth.'

'I thought you were telling me yesterday that you didn't have any property.' I sipped the wine, finding it rather good;

it seemed to be getting better, the more I drank of it. I thought perhaps I had better stop soon.

Jamie wagged his head from side to side. 'Well, it belongs to me, right enough. The thing is, though, it doesna do me much good at present, as I can't go there.' He looked apologetic. 'There's the minor matter of the price on my head, ye see.'

After his escape from Fort William he had been taken to Dougal's house, Beannachd (means 'Blessed', he explained), to recover from his wounds and the consequent fever. From there he had gone to France, where he had spent two years fighting with the French army, around the Spanish border.

'You spent two years in the French army and stayed a virgin?' I blurted out incredulously. I had had a number of Frenchmen in my care, and I doubted very much that the Gallic attitude towards women had changed appreciably in two hundred years.

One corner of Jamie's mouth twitched and he looked down at me sideways.

'If ye had seen the harlots that service the French army, Sassenach, ye'd wonder I've the nerve even to touch a woman, let alone bed one.'

I choked, spluttering wine and coughing until he was obliged to pound me on the back. I subsided, breathless and red-faced, and urged him to go on with his story.

He had returned to Scotland a year or so ago, and spent six months alone or with a gang of 'broken men' – men without clans – living hand to mouth in the forest, or raiding cattle from the Lowlands.

'And then, someone hit me in the head wi' an axe or something o' the sort,' he said, shrugging. 'And I've to take Dougal's word for what happened during the next two months, as I wasna taking much notice of things myself.'

Dougal had been on a nearby estate at the time of the attack. Summoned by Jamie's friends, he had somehow managed to transport his nephew to France.

'Why France?' I asked. 'Surely it was taking a frightful risk to move you so far.'

'More of a risk to leave me where I was. There were English patrols all over the district – we'd been fairly active thereabouts, ye see, me and the lads – and I suppose Dougal didna want them to find me lying senseless in some cottar's hut.'

'Or in his own house?' I said a little cynically.

'I imagine he'd ha' taken me there, but for two things,' Jamie replied. 'For one, he'd an English visitor at the time. For a second, he thought from the look of me I was going to die in any case, so he sent me to the abbey.'

The Abbey of Ste Anne de Beaupré, on the French coast, was the domain, it seemed, of the erstwhile Alexander Fraser, now abbot of that sanctuary of learning and worship. One of Jamie's six Fraser uncles.

'He and Dougal do not get on, particularly,' Jamie explained, 'but Dougal could see there was little to be done for me here, while if there was aught to help me, it might be found there.'

And it was. Assisted by the monks' medical knowledge and his own strong constitution, Jamie had survived and gradually mended, under the care of the holy brothers of St Benedict.

'Once I was well again, I came back,' he explained. 'Dougal and his men met me at the coast, and we were headed for the MacKenzie lands when we, er, met with you.'

'Captain Randall said you were stealing cattle,' I said.

He smiled, undisturbed by the accusation. 'Well, Dougal isna the man to overlook an opportunity of turning a bit of a profit,' he observed. 'We came on a nice bunch of beasts, grazing in a field, and no one about. So . . .' He shrugged with a fatalistic acceptance of the inevitability of life.

Apparently I had come upon the end of the confrontation between Dougal's men and Randall's dragoons. Spotting the English bearing down on them, Dougal had sent half his men around a thicket, driving the cattle before them, while the rest of the Scots had hidden among the saplings, ready to ambush the English as they came by.

'Worked verra well too,' Jamie said in approval. 'We

popped out at them and rode straight through them, yelling. They took after us, of course, and we led them a canty chase uphill and through burns and over rocks and such; and all the while the rest of Dougal's men were making off wi' the kine. We lost the lobsterbacks, then, and denned up at the cottage where I first saw ye.'

'I see,' I said. 'Why did you come back to Scotland in the first place, though? I should have thought you'd be much safer in France.'

He opened his mouth to reply, then reconsidered, sipping wine. Apparently I was getting near the edge of his own area of secrecy.

'Well, that's a long story, Sassenach,' he said, avoiding the issue. 'I'll tell it ye later, but for now, what about you? Will ye tell me about your own family? If ye feel ye can, of course,' he added hastily.

I thought for a moment, but there really seemed little risk in telling him about my parents and Uncle Lamb. There was, after all, some advantage to Uncle Lamb's choice of profession. A scholar of antiquities made as much – or as little – sense in the eighteenth century as in the twentieth.

So I told him, omitting only such minor details as automobiles and aeroplanes, and of course the war. As I talked he listened intently, asking questions now and then, expressing sympathy at my parents' death and interest in Uncle Lamb and his discoveries.

'And then I met Frank,' I finished up. I paused, not sure how much more I could say without getting into dangerous territory. Luckily Jamie saved me.

'And ye'd as soon not talk about him right now,' he said understandingly. I nodded, wordless, my vision blurring a little. Jamie let go of the hand he had been holding and putting an arm around me, pulled my head gently down on his shoulder.

'It's all right,' he said, softly stroking my hair. 'Are ye tired, lass? Shall I leave ye to your sleep?'

I was tempted for a moment to say yes, but I felt that that would be both unfair and cowardly. I cleared my throat and sat up, shaking my head.

'No,' I said, taking a deep breath. He smelled faintly of soap and wine. 'I'm all right. Tell me – tell me what games you used to play, when you were a boy.'

The room was furnished with a thick twelve-hour candle, rings of dark wax marking the hours. We talked through three of the rings, only letting go of each other's hands to pour wine or get up to visit the privy stool behind the curtain in the corner. Returning from one of these trips, Jamie yawned and stretched.

'It is awfully late,' I said, getting up too. 'Maybe we should go to bed.'

'All right,' he said, rubbing the back of his neck. 'To bed? Or to sleep?' He cocked a quizzical eyebrow and the corner of his mouth twitched.

In truth I had been feeling so comfortable with him that I had almost forgotten why we were there. At his words I suddenly felt a hollow panic. 'Well – ' I said faintly.

'Either way, you're no intending to sleep in your gown, are ye?' he asked in his usual practical manner.

'Well, no, I suppose not.' In fact, during the rush of events I had not even thought about a sleeping garment – which I did not possess, in any case. I had been sleeping in my chemise or nothing, depending on the weather.

Jamie had nothing but the clothes he wore; he was plainly going to sleep in his shirt or naked, a state of affairs which was likely to bring matters rapidly to a head.

'Well, then, come here and I'll help ye wi' the laces and such.'

His hands did in fact tremble briefly as he began to undress me. He lost some of his self-consciousness, though, in the struggle with the dozens of tiny buttons that attached the bodice.

'Ha!' he said in triumph as the last one came loose, and we laughed together.

'Now let me do you,' I said, deciding that there was no point in further delay. I reached up and unfastened his shirt, sliding my hands inside and across his shoulders. I brought my palms slowly down across his chest, feeling the springy hair and the soft indentations around his nipples. He stood still, hardly breathing, as I knelt down to unbuckle the studded belt around his hips.

If it must be some time, it may as well be now, I thought, and deliberately ran my hands up the length of his thighs, hard and lean under his kilt. Though by this time I knew perfectly well what most Scotsmen wore beneath their kilts – nothing – it was still something of a shock to find only Jamie.

He lifted me to my feet then, and bent his head to kiss me. It went on a long while, and his hands roamed downwards, finding the fastening of my petticoats. They fell to the floor in a billow of starched flounces, leaving me in my chemise.

'Where did you learn to kiss like that?' I said, a little breathless. He grinned and pulled me close again.

'I said I was a virgin, not a monk,' he said, kissing me again. 'If I find I need guidance, I'll ask.'

He pressed me firmly to him and I could feel that he was more than ready to get on with the business at hand. With some surprise I realized that I was ready too. In fact, whether it was the result of the late hour, the wine, his own attractiveness or simple deprivation, I wanted him quite badly.

I pulled his shirt loose at the waist and ran my hands up over his chest, circling his nipples with my thumbs. They grew hard in a second, and he crushed me suddenly against his chest.

'Oof!' I said, struggling for breath. He let go, apologizing.

'No, don't worry; kiss me again.' He did, this time slipping the straps of the chemise down over my shoulders. He drew back slightly, cupping my breasts and rubbing my nipples as I had done his. I fumbled with the buckle that held his kilt; his fingers guided mine and the clasp sprang free.

Suddenly he lifted me in his arms and sat down on the bed, holding me on his lap. He spoke a little hoarsely.

'Tell me if I'm too rough, or tell me to stop altogether,

if ye wish. Any time until we are joined; I dinna think I can stop after that.'

In answer I put my hands behind his neck and pulled him down on top of me. I guided him to the slippery cleft between my legs.

'Holy God,' said James Fraser, who never took the name of his Lord in vain.

'Don't stop now,' I said.

Lying together afterwards, it seemed natural for him to cradle my head on his chest. We fitted well together, and most of our original constraint was gone, lost in shared excitement and the novelty of exploring each other. 'Was it like you thought it would be?' I asked curiously. He chuckled, making a deep rumble under my ear.

'Almost; I had thought – nay, never mind.'

'No, tell me. What did you think?'

'I'm no goin' to tell ye; ye'll laugh at me.'

'I promise not to laugh. Tell me.' He caressed my hair, smoothing the curls back from my ear.

'Oh, all right. I didna realize that ye did it face to face. I thought ye must do it the back way, like; like horses, ye know.'

It was a struggle to keep my promise, but I didn't laugh.

'I know that sounds silly,' he said, defensively. 'It's just . . . well, ye know how you get ideas in your head when you're young, and then somehow they just stick there?'

'You've never seen *people* make love?' I was surprised at this, having seen the cot-houses where the whole family shared a single room. Granted that Jamie's family were not cottars, still it must be the rare Scottish child who had never waked to find his elders coupling nearby.

'Of course I have, but generally under the bedclothes, ye know. I couldna tell anything except the man was on top. *That* much I knew.'

'Mm. I noticed.'

'Did I squash you?' he asked a little anxiously.

'Not much. Really, though, is that what you thought?' I

293

didn't laugh, but couldn't help grinning broadly. He turned slightly pink around the ears.

'Aye. I saw a man take a woman plain, once, out in the open. But that . . . well, it was a rape, was what it was, and he took her from the back. It made some impression on me, and as I say, it's just the idea stuck.'

He continued to hold me, using his horse-gentling techniques again. These gradually changed, though, to a more determined exploration.

'I want to ask ye something,' he said, running a hand down the length of my back.

'What's that?'

'Did ye like it?' he said a little shyly.

'Yes, I did,' I said quite honestly.

'Oh, I thought ye did, though Murtagh told me that women generally do not care for it, so I should finish as soon as I could.'

'What would Murtagh know about it?' I said indignantly. 'The slower the better, as far as most women are concerned.' Jamie chuckled again.

'Well, you'd know better than Murtagh. I had considerable good advice offered me on the subject last night, from Murtagh and Rupert and Ned. A good bit of it sounded verra unlikely to me, though, so I thought I'd best use my own judgement.'

'It hasn't led you wrong yet,' I said, curling one of his chest hairs around my finger. 'What other sage bits of advice did they give you?' His skin was a ruddy gold in the candlelight; to my amusement it grew still redder in embarrassment.

'I could no repeat most of it. As I said, I think it's likely wrong, anyway. I've seen a good many kinds of animals mate with each other, and most seem to manage it without any advice at all. I would suppose people could do the same.'

I was privately entertained by the notion of someone picking up pointers on sexual technique from barnyard and forest, rather than locker rooms and dirty magazines.

'What kinds of animals have you seen mating?'

'Oh, all kinds. Our farm was near the forest, ye see, and I spent a good deal of time there, hunting, or seeking cows as had got out and suchlike. I've seen horses and cows, of course, chickens, doves, dogs, cats, deer, squirrels, rabbits, wild boar, oh, and once even a pair of snakes.'

'Snakes!?'

'Aye. Did ye know that snakes have two cocks? – male snakes, I mean.'

'No, I didn't. Are you sure about that?'

'Aye, and both of 'em forked, like this.' He spread his second and third fingers apart in illustration.

'That sounds terribly uncomfortable for the female snake,' I said, giggling.

'Well, she appeared to be enjoying herself,' said Jamie. 'Near as I could tell; snakes havena got much expression on their faces.'

I buried my face in his chest, snorting with mirth. His pleasant musky smell mingled with the harsh scent of linen.

'Take off your shirt,' I said, sitting up and pulling at the hem of the garment.

'Why?' he asked, but sat up and obliged. I knelt in front of him, admiring his naked body.

'Because I want to look at you,' I said. He was beautifully made, with long graceful bones and flat muscles that flowed smoothly from the curves of chest and shoulder to the slight concavities of belly and thigh. He raised his eyebrows.

'Well then, fair's fair. Take off yours, then.' He reached out and helped me squirm out of the wrinkled chemise, pushing it down over my hips. Once it was off, he held me by the waist, studying me with intense interest. I grew almost embarrassed as he looked me over.

'Haven't you ever seen a naked woman before?' I asked.

'Aye, but not one so close.' His face broke into a broad grin. 'And not one that's mine.' He stroked my hips with both hands. 'You have good wide hips; ye'd be a good breeder, I expect.'

'What!?' I drew away indignantly but he pulled me back and collapsed on the bed with me on top of him. He held

295

me until I stopped struggling, then raised me enough to meet his lips again.

'I know once is enough to make it legal, but . . .' He paused shyly.

'You want to do it again?'

'Would ye mind verra much?'

I didn't laugh this time either, but I felt my ribs creak under the strain.

'No,' I said gravely. 'I wouldn't mind.'

'Are you hungry?' I asked softly, some time later.

'Famished.' He bent his head to bite my breast softly, then looked up with a grin. 'But I need food too.' He rolled to the edge of the bed. 'There's cold beef and bread in the kitchen, I expect, and likely wine as well. I'll go and bring us some supper.'

'No, don't you get up. I'll fetch it.' I jumped off the bed and headed for the door, pulling on shawl and shift against the chill of the corridor.

'Wait, Claire!' Jamie called. 'Ye'd better let me – ' but I had already opened the door.

My appearance at the door was greeted by a raucous cheer from some fifteen men, lounging around the fireplace in the main room below, drinking, eating and tossing dice. I stood nonplussed on the balcony for a moment, fifteen leering faces flickering out of the firelit shadows at me.

'Hey, lass!' shouted Rupert, one of the loungers. 'Ye're still able t' walk! Isn't Jamie doin' his duty by ye, then?'

This sally was greeted with gales of laughter and a number of even cruder remarks regarding Jamie's prowess.

'If ye've worn Jamie out a'ready, I'll be happy t' take his place!' offered a short dark-haired youth.

'Nay, nay, 'e's no good, lass, take me!' shouted another.

'She'll ha' none o' ye, lads!' yelled Murtagh, uproariously drunk. 'After Jamie, she'll need somethin' like this to satisfy 'er!' He waved a huge meat bone overhead, causing the room to rock with laughter.

I whirled back into the room, slammed the door and

stood with my back to it, glaring at Jamie, who lay naked on the bed, shaking with laughter.

'I tried to warn ye,' he said, gasping. 'You should see your face!'

'Just what,' I hissed, 'are all those men doing out there?'

Jamie slid gracefully off our wedding couch and began rummaging on his knees through the pile of discarded clothing on the floor. 'Witnesses,' he said briefly. 'Dougal is no takin' any chances of this marriage bein' annulled.' He straightened with his kilt in his hands, grinning at me as he wrapped it around his loins. 'I'm afraid your reputation's compromised beyond repair, Sassenach.'

He turned shirtless for the door. 'Don't go out there!' I said in sudden panic. He turned to smile reassuringly, hand on the latch. 'Dinna worry, lass. If they're witnesses, they may as well have somethin' to see. Besides, I'm no intendin' to starve for the next three days for fear of a wee bit o' chaff.'

He stepped out of the room to a chorus of bawdy applause, leaving the door slightly ajar. I could hear his progress towards the kitchen, marked by shouted congratulations and ribald questions and advice.

'How was yer first time, Jamie? Did ye bleed?' shouted Rupert's easily recognized gravel-pit voice.

'Nay, but ye will, ye auld bugger, if ye dinna clapper yer face,' came Jamie's spiked tones in broad Scots reply. Howls of delight greeted this sally, and the raillery continued, following Jamie down the hall to the kitchen and back up the stairs.

I pulled open the door a crack to admit Jamie, face red as the fire below and hands piled high with food and drink. He sidled in, followed by a final burst of hilarity from below. I choked it off with a decisive slam of the door, and shot the bolt to.

'I brought enough so we'll no need to go out again for a bit,' Jamie said, laying out dishes on the table, carefully not looking at me. 'Will ye have a bite?'

I reached past him for the bottle of wine. 'Not just yet. What I need is a drink.'

There was a powerful urgency in him that roused me to response despite his awkwardness. Not wanting to lecture nor yet to highlight my own experience, I let him do what he would, only offering an occasional suggestion, such as that he might carry his weight on his elbows and not on my chest.

As yet too hungry and too clumsy for tenderness, still he made love with a sort of unflagging joy that made me think that male virginity might be a highly underrated commodity. He exhibited a concern for my safety, though, that I found at once endearing and irritating.

At some time in our third encounter, I arched tightly against him and cried out. He drew back at once, startled and apologetic.

'I'm sorry,' he said. 'I didna mean to hurt ye.'

'You didn't.' I stretched languorously, feeling dreamily wonderful.

'Are you sure?' he said, inspecting me for damage. Suddenly it dawned on me that a few of the finer points had likely been left out of his hasty education at the hands of Murtagh and Rupert.

'Does it happen every time?' he asked, fascinated, once I had enlightened him. I felt rather like the Wife of Bath, or a Japanese geisha. I had never envisioned myself as an instructress in the arts of love, but I had to admit to myself that the role held certain attractions.

'No, not every time,' I said, amused. 'Only if the man is a good lover.'

'Oh.' His ears turned faintly pink. I was slightly alarmed to see the look of frank interest being replaced with one of growing determination.

'Will you tell me what I should do next time?' he asked.

'You don't need to do anything special,' I assured him. 'Just go slowly and pay attention. Why wait, though? You're still ready.'

He was surprised. 'You don't need to wait? I canna do it again right away after – '

'Well, women are different.'

'Aye, I noticed,' he muttered.

He circled my wrist with thumb and index finger. 'It's just ... you're so small; I'm afraid I'm going to hurt you.'

'You are not going to hurt me,' I said impatiently. 'And if you did, I wouldn't mind.' Seeing puzzled incomprehension on his face, I decided to show him what I meant.

'What are you doing?' he asked, shocked.

'Just what it looks like. Hold still.' After a few seconds, I began to use my teeth, pressing progressively harder until he drew in his breath with a sharp hiss. I stopped.

'Did I hurt you?' I asked.

'Yes. A little.' He sounded half strangled.

'Do you want me to stop?'

'No!'

I went on, being deliberately rough, until he suddenly convulsed, with a groan that sounded as though I had torn his heart out by the roots. He lay back, quivering and breathing heavily. He muttered something in Gaelic, eyes closed.

'What did you say?'

'I said,' he answered, opening his eyes, 'I thought my heart was going to burst.'

I grinned, pleased with myself. 'Oh, Murtagh and company didn't tell you about that, either?'

'Aye, they did. That was one of the things I didn't believe.'

I laughed. 'In that case, maybe you'd better not tell me what else they told you. Do you see what I meant, though, about not minding if you're rough?'

'Aye.' He drew a deep breath and blew it out softly. 'If I did that to you, would it feel the same?'

'Well, you know,' I said, slowly, 'I don't really know.' I had been doing my best to keep thoughts of Frank at bay, feeling that there should really be no more than two people in a marriage bed, regardless of how they got there. Jamie was very different from Frank, both in body and mind, but there are in fact only a limited number of ways in which two bodies can meet, and we had not yet established that territory of intimacy in which the act of love takes on infinite

299

variety. The echoes of the flesh were unavoidable, but there were a few territories still unexplored.

Jamie's brows were tilted in an expression of mocking threat. 'Oh, so there's something you don't know? Well, we'll find out then, won't we? As soon as I've the strength for it.' He closed his eyes again. 'Next week, some time.'

I woke in the hours before dawn, shivering and rigid with terror. I could not recall the dream that woke me, but the abrupt plunge into reality was equally frightening. It had been possible to forget my situation for a time the night before, lost in the pleasures of newfound intimacy. Now I was alone, next to a sleeping stranger with whom my life was inextricably linked, adrift in a place filled with unseen threat.

I must have made some sound of distress, for there was a sudden upheaval of bedclothes as the stranger in my bed vaulted to the floor with the heart-stopping suddenness of a pheasant rising underfoot. He came to rest in a crouch near the door of the chamber, barely visible in the pre-dawn light.

Pausing to listen carefully at the door, he made a rapid inspection of the room, gliding soundlessly from door to window to bed. The angle of his arm told me that he held a weapon of some sort, though I could not see what it was in the darkness. Sitting down next to me, satisfied that all was secure, he slid the knife or whatever it was back into its hiding place above the headboard.

'Are you all right?' he whispered. His fingers brushed my wet cheek.

'Yes. I'm sorry to wake you. I had a nightmare. What on earth – ' I started to ask what it was that had made him spring so abruptly to the alert.

A large warm hand ran down my bare arm, interrupting my question. 'No wonder; you're frozen.' The hand urged me under the pile of quilts and into the warm space recently vacated. 'My fault,' he murmured. 'I've taken all the quilts. I'm afraid I'm no accustomed yet to share a bed.' He wrapped the quilts comfortably around us and lay back

300

beside me. A moment later he reached again to touch my face.

'Is it me?' he asked quietly. 'Can ye not bear me?'

I gave a short hicupping laugh, not quite a sob. 'No, it isn't you.' I reached out in the dark, groping for a hand to press reassuringly. My fingers met a tangle of quilts and warm flesh, but at last I found the hand I had been seeking. We lay side by side, looking up at the low beamed ceiling.

'What if I said I couldn't bear you?' I asked suddenly. 'What on earth could you do?' The bed creaked as he shrugged.

'Tell Dougal you wanted an annulment on the grounds of nonconsummation, I suppose.'

This time I laughed outright. 'Nonconsummation! With all those witnesses?'

The room was growing light enough to see the smile on the face turned towards me. 'Aye well, witnesses or no, it's only you and me that can say for sure, isn't it? And I'd rather be embarrassed than wed to someone that hated me.'

I turned towards him. 'I don't hate you.'

'I don't hate you, either. And there's many good marriages have started wi' less than that.' Gently he turned me away from him and fitted himself to my back so we lay nestled together. His hand cupped my breast, not in invitation or demand but because it seemed to belong there.

'Don't be afraid,' he whispered into my hair. 'There's the two of us now.' I felt warm, soothed and safe for the first time in many days. It was only as I drifted into sleep under the first rays of daylight that I remembered the knife above my head, and wondered again, what threat would make a man sleep armed and watchful in his bridal chamber?

16

One Fine Day

The hard-won intimacy of the night seemed to have evaporated with the dew, and there was considerable restraint between us in the morning. After a mostly silent breakfast taken in our room, we climbed the small hillock behind the inn, exchanging rather strained politenesses from time to time.

At the crest I settled on a log to rest, while Jamie sat on the ground, back against a pine sapling, a few feet away. Some bird was active in the bush behind me, a finch, I supposed, or possibly a thrush. I listened to its dilatory rustlings, watched the small fluffy clouds float by, and pondered the etiquette of the situation.

The silence was becoming really too heavy to bear, when Jamie suddenly said, 'I hope – ' then stopped and blushed. Though I rather felt it should be me blushing, I was glad that at least one of us was able to do it.

'What?' I said as encouragingly as possible.

He shook his head, still pink. 'It doesna matter.'

'Go ahead.' I reached out a foot and nudged his leg with a tentative toe. 'Honesty, remember?' It was unfair, but I really couldn't stand any more nervous throat-clearing and eye-twitching.

His clasped hands tightened around his knees and he rocked back a bit, but fixed his gaze directly on me.

'I was going to say,' he said softly, 'that I hoped the man who had the honour to lie first wi' you was as generous as you were with me.' He smiled, a little shyly. 'But on second thought, that didna sound quite right. What I meant . . . well, all I wanted was to say thank you.'

'Generosity had nothing to do with it!' I snapped, looking down and brushing energetically at a nonexistent spot on

302

my dress. A large boot pushed into my downcast field of vision and nudged my ankle.

'Honesty, is it?' he echoed, and I looked up to meet a derisively raised pair of eyebrows above a wide grin.

'Well,' I said defensively, 'not after the first time, anyway.' He laughed, and I discovered to my horror that I was not beyond blushing after all.

A cool shadow fell over my heated face and a large pair of hands took firm hold of mine and pulled me to my feet. Jamie took my place on the log and patted his knee invitingly.

'Sit,' he said.

I reluctantly obliged, keeping my face turned away. He settled me comfortably against his chest and wrapped his arms about my waist. I felt the steady thump of his heart against my back.

'Now then,' he said. 'If we canna talk easy yet without touching, we'll touch for a bit. Tell me when you're accustomed to me again.' He leaned back so that we were in the shade of a pine, and held me close without speaking, just breathing slowly, so that I felt the rise and fall of his chest and the stir of his breath in my hair.

'All right,' I said after a moment.

'Good.' He loosened his grip and turned me to face him. At close range I could see the bristle of auburn stubble on cheek and chin. I brushed my fingers across it; it was like the plush on an old-fashioned sofa, stiff and soft at the same time.

'I'm sorry,' he said, 'I couldna shave this morning. Dougal gave me a razor before the wedding yesterday, but he took it back – in case I cut my throat after the wedding night, I expect.' He grinned down at me and I smiled back.

The reference to Dougal reminded me of our conversation of the night before.

'I wondered . . .' I said. 'Last night, you said Dougal and his men met you at the coast when you came back from France. Why did you come back with him, instead of going to your own home, or the Fraser lands? I mean, the way Dougal's treated you . . .' I trailed off, hesitant.

303

'Oh,' he said, shifting his legs to bear my weight more evenly. I could almost hear him thinking to himself. He made up his mind quite quickly.

'Well, it's something ye should know, I suppose.' He frowned to himself. 'I told ye why I'm outlawed. Well, for a time after – after I left Fort William, I didna care much . . . about anything. My father died about that time, and my sister . . .' He paused again, and I sensed some kind of struggle going on inside him. I twisted around to look at him. The normally cheerful face was shadowed with some strong emotion.

'Dougal told me,' he said slowly, 'Dougal told me that – that my sister was wi' child. By Randall.'

'Oh, dear.'

He glanced sideways at me, then away. His eyes were bright as sapphires and he blinked hastily once or twice.

'I . . . I couldna bring myself to go back,' he said, low-voiced. 'To see her again, after what happened. And too' – he sighed, then set his lips firmly – 'Dougal told me that she . . . that after the child was born, she . . . well, of course, she couldna help it; she was alone – damn it, I *left* her alone! He said she had taken up wi' another English soldier, someone from the garrison, he didna know which one.'

He swallowed heavily, then went on more firmly. 'I sent back what money I could, of course, but I could not . . . well, I couldna bring myself to write to her. What could I say?' He shrugged helplessly.

'Anyway, after a time I grew tired of soldiering in France. And I heard through my Uncle Alick that he'd had word of an English deserter, named Horrocks. The man had left the army and taken service wi' Francis MacLean o' Dunweary. He was in his cups one day and let out that he'd been stationed wi' the garrison at Fort William when I escaped. And he'd seen the man who shot the sergeant that day.'

'So he could prove that it wasn't you!' This sounded good news, and I said so. Jamie nodded.

'Well, yes. Though the word of a deserter would likely not count for much. Still, it's a start. At least I'd know myself who it was. And while I . . . well, I dinna see how I can go back to Lallybroch; still it would be as well if I could walk the soil of Scotland without the risk of being hanged.'

'Yes, that seems a good idea,' I said dryly. 'But where do the MacKenzies come into it?'

There followed a certain amount of complicated analysis of family relationships and clan alliances, but when the smoke cleared away it appeared that Francis MacLean was some connection with the MacKenzie side, and had sent word of Horrocks to Callum, who had sent Dougal to make contact with Jamie.

'Which is how he came to be nearby when I was wounded,' Jamie finished up. He paused, squinting into the sun. 'I wondered, afterwards, ye know, whether perhaps he'd done it.'

'Hit you with an axe? Your own uncle? Why on earth!?'

He frowned as though weighing how much to tell me, then shrugged.

'I dinna ken how much ye know about the Clan MacKenzie,' he said, 'though I imagine ye canna have ridden wi' old Ned Gowan for days without hearin' something of it. He canna keep off the subject for long.'

He nodded at my answering smile. 'Well, you've seen Callum for yourself. Anyone can see that he'll not make old bones. And wee Hamish is barely eight; he'll no be able to lead a clan for ten years yet. So what happens if Callum dies before Hamish is ready?' He looked at me, prompting.

'Well, Dougal would be laird, I suppose,' I said slowly, 'at least until Hamish is old enough.'

'Aye, that's true.' Jamie nodded. 'But Dougal's not the man Callum is, and there are those in the clan that wouldna follow him so gladly – if there were an alternative.'

'I see,' I said slowly, 'and you are the alternative.'

I looked him over carefully, and had to admit that there was a certain amount of possibility there. He was old Jacob's grandson; a MacKenzie by blood, if only on his mother's side. A big, comely, well-made lad, plainly intelligent, and with the family knack for managing people. He had fought in France and proved his ability to lead men in battle; an

305

important consideration. Even the price on his head might not be an insurmountable obstacle – if he were laird.

The English had enough trouble in the Highlands, between the constant small rebellions, the Lowland raids and the warring clans, not to risk a major uprising by accusing a chieftain of a major clan of murder – which would seem no murder at all to the clansmen.

To hang an unimportant Fraser clansman was one thing; to storm Castle Leoch and drag out the laird to face English justice was something else again.

'Do you mean to be laird, if Callum dies?' It was one way out of his difficulties, after all, though I suspected it was a way hedged with its own considerable obstacles.

He smiled briefly at the thought. 'No. Even if I felt myself entitled to it – which I don't – it would split the clan, Dougal's men against those that might follow me. I havena the taste for power at the cost of other men's blood. But Dougal and Callum couldna be sure of that, could they? So they might think it safer just to kill me than to take the risk.'

My brow was furrowed, thinking it all out. 'But surely you could tell Dougal and Callum that you don't intend . . . oh.' I looked up at him with considerable respect. 'But you did. At the oath-taking.'

I had thought already how well he had handled a dangerous situation there; now I saw just *how* dangerous it had been. The clansmen had certainly wanted him to take his oath; just as certainly Callum had not. To swear such an oath was to declare himself a member of the Clan MacKenzie, and as such a potential candidate for chieftain of the Leoch sept. He risked open violence or death for refusal; he risked the same – more privately – for compliance.

Seeing the danger, he had taken the prudent course of staying away from the ceremony. And when I, by my botched escape attempt, had led him straight back to the edge of the abyss, he had set a sure and certain foot on a tightrope, and walked it to the other side. *Je suis prest*, indeed.

He nodded, seeing the thoughts cross my face.

'Aye. If I had sworn my oath that night, chances are I wouldna have seen the dawn.'

I felt a little shaky at the thought, as well as at the knowledge that I had unwittingly exposed him to such danger. The knife over his bed suddenly seemed nothing more than a sensible precaution. I wondered how many nights he had slept armed at Leoch, expecting death to come visiting.

'I always sleep armed, Sassenach,' he said, though I had not spoken. 'Except for the monastery, last night is the first time in months I've not slept wi' my dirk in my fist.' He grinned, plainly remembering what *had* been in his fist instead.

'How the bloody hell did you know what I was thinking?' I demanded, ignoring the grin. He shook his head good-naturedly.

'You'd make a verra poor spy, Sassenach. Everything ye think shows on your face, plain as day. You looked at my dirk and then ye blushed.' He studied me appraisingly, bright head on one side. 'I asked ye for honesty last night, but it wasna really necessary; it isna in you to lie.'

'Just as well, since I'm apparently so bad at it,' I observed with some asperity. 'Am I to take it that at least *you* don't think I'm a spy, then?'

He didn't answer. He was looking over my shoulder towards the inn, body suddenly tense as a bowspring. I was startled for a moment, but then heard the sounds that had attracted his attention. The thud of hooves and jangle of harness; a large group of mounted men was coming down the track towards the inn.

Moving cautiously, Jamie crouched behind the screen of bushes at a spot commanding a view of the road. I tucked my skirts up and crawled after him as silently as I could.

The road hooked sharply past a rocky outcrop, then curved more gently down to the hollow where the inn lay. The morning breeze carried the sounds of the approaching group in our direction, but it was a minute or two before the first mount poked its nose into sight.

It was a group of some twenty or thirty men, mostly

wearing leather trews and tartan-clad, but in a variety of colours and patterns. All, without exception, were well-armed. Each mount bore at least one musket strapped to the saddle, and there was an abundance of pistols, dirks and swords on view, plus whatever further armament might be concealed in the capacious saddlebags of the four pack ponies. Six of the men also led extra mounts, unburdened and saddleless.

Despite their warlike accoutrements the men seemed relaxed; they were chatting and laughing in small groups as they rode, though here and there a head raised, watchful of the surroundings. I fought back the urge to duck as one man's gaze passed over the spot where we lay hidden; it seemed as though that searching look must surely discover some random movement or the gleam of the sun off Jamie's hair.

Glancing up at this thought, I discovered that it had occurred to him as well; he had pulled a fold of his plaid up over his head and shoulders so that the dull hunting pattern made him effectively part of the shrubbery. As the last of the men wound down into the innyard Jamie dropped the plaid and motioned back towards the path up the hill.

'Do you know who they are?' I panted as I followed him up into the heather.

'Oh, aye.' Jamie took the steep path like a mountain goat, with no loss of breath or composure. Glancing back, he noticed my laboured progress and stopped, reaching down a hand to help me.

'It's the Watch,' he said, nodding back in the direction of the inn. 'We're safe enough, but I thought we'd as soon be a bit further away.'

I had heard of the famous Black Watch, that informal police force which kept order in the Highlands, and heard also that there were other Watches. I was seized by a sudden irrational terror.

'They're not looking for you, are they?'

Startled, he looked back as though expecting to see men scrambling up the hill in pursuit, but there was no one and

308

he looked back at me with a relieved smile and put an arm about my waist to help me along.

'Nay, I doubt it. Ten pound sterling is not enough to make me worth the hunting by a pack like that. And if they kent I was at the inn they wouldna have come as they did, traipsing up to the door all of a piece.' He shook his head decisively. 'No, were they hunting anyone, they'd send men to guard the back and the windows before coming in the front door. They've but stopped there for refreshment, likely.'

We continued to climb, past the spot where the rude path petered out in clumps of gorse and heather. We were among foothills here, and the rocks rose higher than Jamie's head, reminding me uncomfortably of the standing stones of Craigh na Dun.

We emerged then on to the top of a small dun, and the hills sloped away in a breathtaking fall of rocks and green on all sides. Most places in the Highlands gave me a feeling of being surrounded by trees or rocks or mountains, but here under a solitary pine we were exposed to the fresh draughts of the wind and the rays of the sun, which had come out as though in celebration of our unorthodox marriage.

I experienced a heady sense of freedom at being out from under Dougal's influence and the claustrophobic company of so many men. I was tempted to urge Jamie to run away and to take me with him, but common sense prevailed. We had little money, and no food beyond the bit of lunch that he carried in his sporran. We would certainly be pursued if we did not return to the inn by sundown. And while Jamie could plainly climb rocks all day without breaking a sweat or getting out of breath, I was in no such training. Noticing my red face, he led me to a rock and sat beside me, contentedly gazing out over the hills while he waited for me to regain my breath. We were certainly safe here.

Thinking of the Watch, I laid a hand impulsively on Jamie's arm.

'I'm awfully glad you're not worth very much,' I said.

He regarded me for a moment, rubbing his nose, which was beginning to redden.

'Well, I might take that several ways, Sassenach, but under the circumstances,' he said, 'thank you.'

'I should thank *you*,' I said, 'for marrying me. I must say that I'd rather be here than in Fort William.'

'I thank ye for the compliment, lady,' he said, with a slight bow. 'So would I. And while we're busy thanking each other,' he added, 'I should thank you for marrying *me*, as well.'

'Er, well . . .' I blushed once more.

'Not only for that, Sassenach,' he said, his grin widening. 'Though certainly for that as well. But I imagine you've also saved my life for me, at least so far as the MacKenzies are concerned.'

'Whatever do you mean?'

'Being half MacKenzie is one thing,' he explained. 'Being half MacKenzie wi' an English wife is quite another. There isna much chance of a Sassenach wench ever becoming lady of Leoch, whatever the clansmen might think of me alone. That's why Dougal picked me to wed ye to, ye ken.'

He lifted one brow, reddish-gold in the morning sun. 'I hope ye wouldna have preferred Rupert, after all?'

'No, I wouldn't,' I said with emphasis.

He laughed and got up, brushing pine needles from his kilt.

'Well, my mother told me I'd be some lassie's choice one fine day.' He reached down a hand and helped me up.

'I told her,' he continued, 'that I thought it was the man's part to choose.'

'And what did she say to that?' I asked.

'She rolled her eyes and said, "You'll find out, my fine wee cockerel, you'll find out".' He laughed. 'And so I have.'

He looked upwards, to where the sun was now seeping through the pine needles in lemon threads.

'And it is a fine day, at that. Come along, Sassenach. I'll take ye fishin'.'

We went further up into the hills. This time Jamie turned to the north, and over a jumble of stone and through a crevice, into the head of a tiny glen, rock-walled and leafy, filled with the gurgling of water from the burn that spilled from a dozen wee falls among the rocks and plunged roistering down the length of the glen into a series of rills and pools below.

We dangled our feet in the water, moving from shade to sun and back to shade as we grew too warm, talking of this and that and not much of anything, both aware of each other's smallest movements, both content to wait until chance should bring us to that moment when a glance should linger, and a touch should signal more.

Above one dark speckled pool, Jamie showed me how to tickle trout. Crouched to avoid the low-growing branches overhead, he duck-walked along an overhanging ledge, arms outstretched for balance. Halfway along, he turned carefully on the rock and stretched out his hand, urging me to follow.

I had my skirts tucked up already, for walking through rough country, and managed well enough. We stretched full length on the cool rock, head to head, peering down into the water, willow branches brushing our backs.

'All it is,' he said, 'is to pick a good spot, and then wait.' He dipped one hand below the surface, smoothly, no splashing, and let it lie on the sandy bottom, just outside the line of shadow made by the rocky overhang. The long fingers curled delicately towards the palm, distorted by the water so that they seemed to wave gently to and fro in unison, like the leaves of a water plant, though I saw from the still muscling of his forearm that he was not moving his hand at all. The column of his arm bent abruptly at the surface, seeming as disjointed as it had been when I had met him, just six weeks – my God, only six weeks? – before.

Met six weeks, married one day. Bound by vows and by blood. And by friendship as well. When the time came to leave, I hoped that I would not hurt him too badly. I found myself glad for the moment I need not think about it; we were far from Craigh na Dun, and not a chance in the world of escape from Dougal for the present.

'There he is.' Jamie's voice was low, hardly more than a breath; he had told me that trout have sensitive ears.

From my angle of view the trout was little more than a stirring of the speckled sand. Deep in the rock shadow there was no telltale gleam of scales. Speckles moved on speckles, shifted by the fanning of transparent fins, invisible but for their motion. The minnows that had gathered to pluck curiously at the hairs on Jamie's wrist fled away into the brightness of the pool.

One finger bent slowly, so slowly it was hard to see the movement. I could tell it moved only by its changing position relative to the other fingers. Another finger, slowly bent. And after a long, long moment, another.

I scarcely dared breathe and my heart beat against the cold rock with a rhythm faster than the breathing of the fish. Sluggishly the fingers bent back, lying open, one by one, and the slow hypnotic wave began again, one finger, one finger, one finger more, the movement a smooth ripple like the edge of a fish's fin.

As though drawn by the slow-motion beckoning the trout's nose pressed outwards, a delicate gasping of mouth and gills, busy in the rhythm of breathing, pink lining show- ing, not showing, showing, not showing, as the opercula beat like a heart.

The chewing mouth groped and bit water. Most of the body was clear of the rock now, hanging weightless in the water, still in the shadow. I could see one eye, twitching to and fro in a blank, directionless stare.

An inch more would bring the flapping gill-covers right over the treacherous beckoning fingers. I found that I was gripping the rock with both hands, pressing my cheek hard against it as though I could make myself still more incon- spicuous.

There was a sudden explosion of motion. Everything happened so fast I couldn't see what actually *did* take place. There was a heavy splatter of water that sluiced across the rock an inch from my face, a flurry of tartan as Jamie rolled across the rock above me and a heavy splat as the fish's body sailed through the air and struck the leaf-strewn bank.

Jamie surged off the ledge and into the shallows of the side pool, splashing across to retrieve his prize before the stunned fish could succeed in flapping its way back to the sanctuary of the water. Seizing it by the tail, he slapped it expertly against a rock, killing it at once, then waded back to show it to me.

'A good size,' he said proudly, holding out a solid fourteen-incher. 'Do nicely for breakfast.' He grinned up at me, wet to the thighs, hair hanging in his face, shirt splotched with water and dead leaves. 'I told you I'd not let ye go hungry.'

He wrapped the trout in layers of dock leaves and cool mud. Then he rinsed his fingers in the cold water of the burn and, clambering up on to the rock, handed me the neatly wrapped parcel.

'An odd wedding present, maybe' – he nodded at the trout – 'but not without precedent, as Ned Gowan might say.'

'There are precedents for giving a new wife a fish?' I asked, entertained.

He stripped off his stockings to dry and laid them on the rock to lie in the sun. His long bare toes wiggled in enjoyment of the warmth.

'It's an old love song, from the Isles. D'ye want to hear it?'

'Yes, of course. Er, in English, if you can,' I added.

'Oh, aye. I've no voice for music, but I'll give you the words.' And fingering the hair back out of his eyes, he recited,

'Thou daughter of the King of bright-lit mansions
On the night that our wedding is on us,
If living man I be in Duntulm,
I will go bounding to thee with gifts.
Thou wilt get a hundred badgers, dwellers in banks,
A hundred brown otters, natives of streams,
A hundred silver trout, rising from their pools . . .'

And on through a remarkable list of the flora and fauna of the Isles. I had time, watching him declaim, to reflect on the oddity of sitting on a rock in a Scottish pool, listening to love songs, with a large dead fish in my lap. And the greater oddity that I was enjoying myself very much indeed.

When he finished I applauded, keeping hold of the trout by gripping it between my knees.

'Oh, I like that one! Especially the "I will go bounding to thee with gifts". He sounds a most enthusiastic lover.'

Eyes closed against the sun, Jamie laughed. 'I suppose I could add a line for myself – "I will leap into pools for thy sake".'

We both laughed, and then were quiet for a time, basking in the warm sun of the early summer. It was very peaceful there, with no sound but the rushing of water beyond our still pool. Jamie's breathing had calmed. I was very conscious of the slow rise and fall of his breast and the slow beat of the pulse in his neck. He had a small triangular scar, just there at the base of his throat.

I could feel the shyness and constraint beginning to creep back. I reached out a hand and grasped his tightly, hoping that the touch would re-establish the ease between us as it had before. He slid an arm about my shoulders but it only made me aware of the hard lines of his body beneath the thin shirt. I pulled away, under the pretext of plucking a bunch of yellow-flowered St John's wort that grew by the rock.

'Good for headache,' I explained, tucking them into my belt.

'It troubles you,' he said, tilting his head to look at me intently. 'Not headache, I don't mean. Frank. You're thinking of him, and so it troubles you when I touch you, because ye canna hold us both in your mind. Is that it?'

'You're very perceptive,' I said, surprised. He smiled, but made no move to touch me again.

'No great task to puzzle that out, lass. I knew when we married that you couldna help but have him often in your mind, did ye want to or no.'

I didn't, at the moment, but he was right; I couldn't help it.

'Am I much like him?' he asked suddenly.

'No.'

314

In fact it would be difficult to imagine a greater contrast. Frank was slender, lithe and dark, where Jamie was large, powerful and fair as a ruddy sunbeam. While both men had the compact grace of athletes, Frank's was the build of a tennis player, Jamie's the body of a warrior, shaped – and battered – by the abrasion of sheer physical adversity. Frank stood a scant four inches above my own five foot six. Face to face with Jamie, my nose fitted comfortably into the small hollow at the centre of his chest, and his chin could rest easily on top of my head.

Nor was the physical the only dimension where the two men varied. There was nearly fifteen years' difference in their ages, for one thing, which likely accounted for some of the difference between Frank's urbane reserve and Jamie's frank openness. As a lover Frank was polished, sophisticated, considerate and skilled. Lacking experience or the pretence of it, Jamie simply gave me all of himself, without reservation. And the depth of my response to that unsettled me completely.

Jamie was watching my struggle, not without sympathy.

'Well, then, it would seem I have two choices in the matter,' he said. 'I can let you brood about it, or . . .'

He leaned down and gently fitted his mouth over mine. I had kissed my share of men, particularly during the war years, when flirtation and instant romance were the light-minded companions of death and uncertainty. Jamie, though, was something different. His extreme gentleness was in no way tentative; rather it was a promise of power known and held in leash; a challenge and a provocation the more remarkable for its lack of demand. I am yours, it said. And if you will have me, then . . .

I would, and my mouth opened beneath his, whole-heartedly accepting both promise and challenge without consulting me. After a long moment he lifted his head and smiled down at me.

'Or, I can try to distract ye from your thoughts,' he finished.

He pressed my head against his shoulder, stroking my hair and smoothing the leaping curls around my ears.

'I do not know if it will help,' he said quietly, 'but I will tell you this: it is a gift and a wonder to me, to know that I can please you – that your body can rouse to mine. I hadna thought of such a thing – beforehand.'

I drew a long breath before replying. 'Yes,' I said. 'It helps. I think.'

We were silent again for what seemed a long time. At last Jamie drew away and looked down at me, smiling.

'I told ye I've neither money nor property, Sassenach?'

I nodded, wondering what he intended.

'I should have warned ye before that we'd likely end up sleeping in haystacks, wi' naught but heather ale and drammach for food.'

'I don't mind,' I said.

He nodded towards an opening in the trees, not taking his eyes off me.

'I havena got a haystack about me, but there's a fair patch of fresh bracken yonder. If ye'd care to practise, just to get the way of it . . . ?'

A little later I stroked his back, damp with exertion and the juice of crushed ferns.

'If you say "thank you" once more, I will slap you,' I said.

Instead I was answered with a gentle snore. An overhanging frond brushed his cheek, and an inquisitive insect crawled across his hand, making the long fingers twitch in his sleep.

I brushed it away and leaned back on one elbow, watching him. His lashes were long, seen thus with his eyes closed, and thick. Oddly coloured, though; dark auburn at the tips, they were very light, almost blond at the roots.

The firm line of his mouth had relaxed in sleep. While it kept a faintly humorous curl at the corner, his lower lip now eased into a fuller curve that seemed both sensual and innocent.

'Damn,' I said softly to myself.

I had been fighting it for some time. Even before this ridiculous marriage I had been more than conscious of his

316

attraction. It had happened before, as it doubtless happens to almost everyone. A sudden sensitivity to the presence, the appearance, of a particular man – or woman, I suppose. The urge to follow him with my eyes, to arrange small 'inadvertent' meetings, to watch him unawares as he went about his work, an exquisite sensitivity to the small details of his body – the shoulder-blades beneath the cloth of his shirt, the lumpy bones of his wrists, the soft place underneath his jaw, where the first prickles of his beard began to show.

Infatuation. It was common, among the nurses and the doctors, the nurses and the patients, among any gathering of people thrown for long periods into one another's company.

Some acted on it, and brief, intense affairs were frequent. If they were lucky the affair flamed out within a few months and nothing resulted from it. If they were not . . . well. Pregnancy, divorce, here and there the odd case of venereal disease. Dangerous thing, infatuation.

I had felt it, several times, but had had the good sense not to act on it. And as it always does, after a time the attraction had lessened, and the man lost his golden aura and resumed his usual place in my life, with no harm done to him, to me, or to Frank.

And now. Now I had been forced to act on it. And God only knew what harm might be done by that action. But there was no turning back from this point.

He lay at ease, sprawled on his stomach. The sun glinted off his red mane and lit the tiny soft hairs that crested his spine, running down to the reddish-gold fuzz that dusted his buttocks and thighs, and deepened into the thicket of soft auburn curls that showed briefly between his spread legs.

I sat up, admiring the long legs, with the smooth line of muscling that indented the thigh from hip to knee, and another that ran from knee to long, elegant foot. The bottoms of his feet were smooth and pink, slightly calloused from going barefoot.

My fingers ached, wanting to trace the line of his small, neat ear and the blunt angle of his jaw. Well, I thought, the

317

action *had* been taken, and it was far past the time for restraint. Nothing I did now could make matters worse, for either of us. I reached out and gently touched him.

He slept very lightly. With a suddenness that made me jump, he flipped over, bracing himself on his elbows as though to leap to his feet. Seeing me, he relaxed, smiling.

'Madam, you have me at a disadvantage.'

He made a very creditable courtly bow, for a man stretched at full length in a patch of ferns, wearing nothing but a few dappled splotches of sunlight, and I laughed. The smile stayed on his face but it altered as he looked at me, naked in the ferns. His voice was suddenly husky.

'In fact, madam, you have me at your mercy.'

'Have I, then?' I said softly.

He didn't move as I reached out once more and drew my hand slowly down his cheek and neck, over the gleaming slope of his shoulder and down. He didn't move, but he closed his eyes.

'Dear Holy Lord,' he said.

He drew his breath in sharply.

'Don't worry,' I said. 'It doesn't *have* to be rough.'

'Thank God for small mercies.'

'Keep still.'

His fingers dug deeply into the crumbling earth, but he obeyed.

'Please,' he said after a time. Glancing up, I could see that his eyes were open now.

'No,' I said, enjoying myself. He closed his eyes again.

'You'll pay for this,' he said a short time later. A fine dew of sweat shone on the straight bridge of his nose.

'Really?' I said. 'What are you going to do?'

The tendons stood out in his forearms as he pressed his palms against the earth, and he spoke with an effort, as though his teeth were clenched.

'I don't know, but ... by Christ and St Agnes ... I will ... th-think of s-something! God! Please!'

'All right,' I said, releasing him.

And I uttered a small shriek as he rolled on to me, pinning me against the bracken.

'Your turn,' he said with considerable satisfaction.

We returned to the inn at sunset, pausing at the top of the hill to be sure that the mounts of the Watch were no longer hobbled outside. The inn looked welcoming, light already shining through the small windows.

'Dougal's not back yet, either,' I observed as we came down the hill. The large black gelding he customarily rode was not in the inn's small paddock. Several other beasts were missing as well; Ned Gowan's for one.

'No, he shouldna come back for another day at least – maybe two.' Jamie offered me his arm and we descended the hill slowly, careful of the many rocks that poked through the short grass.

'Where on earth has he gone?' Caught in the rush of recent events, I had not thought to question his absence – or even to notice it.

Jamie handed me over the stile at the back of the inn.

'To do his business wi' the cottars nearby. He's got but a day or two before he's supposed to produce you at the fort, ye ken.' He squeezed my arm reassuringly. 'Captain Randall willna be best pleased when Dougal tells him he's not to have ye, and Dougal would as soon not linger in the area afterwards.'

'Sensible of him,' I observed. 'Also kind of him to leave us here to, er . . . get acquainted with each other.'

Jamie snorted. 'Not kindness. That was one of the conditions I set for takin' ye. I said I'd wed if I must, but damned if I'd consummate my marriage under a bush, wi' twenty clansmen lookin' on and offering advice.'

I stopped, staring at him. So that was what the shouting had been about.

'*One* of the conditions?' I said slowly. 'And what were the others?'

It was growing too dark to see his face clearly, but I thought he seemed embarrassed.

'Only two others,' he said finally.

'Which were?'

'Well,' he said, kicking a pebble diffidently out of the

319

way. 'I said ye must wed me proper, in kirk, before a priest. Not just by contract. As for the other – he must find ye a suitable gown to be wed in.' He looked away, avoiding my gaze, and his voice was so soft I could scarcely hear him.

'I – I knew ye didna wish to wed. I wanted to make it . . . as pleasant as might be for you. I thought ye might feel a bit less . . . well, I wanted ye to have a decent dress, is all.'

I opened my mouth to say something, but he turned away towards the inn.

'Come along, Sassenach,' he said gruffly. 'I'm hungry.'

The price of food was company, as was obvious from the moment of our appearance at the door of the inn's main room. We were greeted by raucous cheers, and hurriedly pushed into seats at the table, where a hearty supper was already in progress.

Having been somewhat prepared this time, I didn't mind the rough jests and crude remarks at our expense. For once I was pleased to be modestly self-effacing, scrunching back into the corner and leaving Jamie to deal with the rough teasing and bawdy speculations about what we had been doing all day.

'Sleeping,' said Jamie, in answer to one question of this sort. 'Didna catch a wink last night.' The roars of laughter that greeted this were topped by louder ones as he added in confidential tones, 'She snores, ye ken.'

I obligingly cuffed his ear, and he gathered me to him and kissed me soundly, to general applause.

After supper there was dancing, to the accompaniment of the landlord's fiddle. I had never been much of a dancer, being rather prone to trip over my own feet in times of stress. I scarcely expected that I would do better, attired in long skirts and clumsy footgear. Once I had shed the shoes, though, I was surprised to find that I danced with no difficulty and great enjoyment.

Women being in short supply, the innkeeper's wife and I tucked up our skirts and danced jigs and reels and strathspeys without ceasing, until I had to stop and lean against the settle, red-faced and gasping for breath.

The men were absolutely indefatigable, whirling about like tartan tops, by themselves or with each other. Finally they stood back against the wall, watching, cheering and clapping, as Jamie took both my hands and led me through something fast and frantic that left me hair-tangled and breathless.

Ending up by forethought near the stair, we swirled to a close with his arm about my waist. Here we paused and he made a short speech, mixed in Gaelic and English, which was received with further applause, particularly when he reached into his sporran and tossed a small wash-leather bag to the landlord, instructing that worthy to serve whisky so long as it lasted. I recognized it as his share of the wagers from his fight at Tunnaig. Likely all the money he had in the world; I thought it could not have been better spent.

We had made it up to the balcony, followed by a hail of indelicate good wishes, when a voice louder than the others called Jamie's name.

Turning, I saw Rupert's broad face, redder than usual above its bush of black beard, grinning up from below.

'No good, Rupert,' called Jamie. 'She's mine.'

'Wasted on ye, lad,' said Rupert, mopping his face with his sleeve. 'She'll ha' ye on the floor in an hour. No stayin' power, these young lads,' he called to me. 'Ye want a man who doesna waste his time sleepin', lass, let me know. In the meantime . . .' He flung something upwards.

A fat little bag clanked to the floor at my feet.

'A wedding present,' he called. 'Courtesy of the men of the Shimi mac Ailean Watch.'

'Eh?' Jamie stooped to pick it up.

'*Some* of us didna spend our day idlin' about the grassy banks, lad,' he said reprovingly, rolling his eyes lewdly at me. 'That money was hard earned.'

'Oh, aye,' said Jamie, grinning. 'Dice or cards?'

'Both.' A raffish grin split the black beard. 'Skint 'em to the bone, lad. To the bone.'

Jamie opened his mouth but Rupert held up a broad, calloused palm.

'Nay, lad, nay need o' thanks. Just give her a good one for me, eh?'

I pressed my fingers to my lips and blew him a kiss. Slapping a hand to his face as though struck, he staggered back with an exclamation and reeled off into the next room, weaving as though drunk, which he wasn't.

After all the hilarity below, our room seemed a haven of peace and quiet. Jamie, still laughing quietly to himself, sprawled out on the bed to recover his breath.

I loosened my bodice, which was uncomfortably tight, and sat down to comb the tangles out of my dance-disordered hair.

'You've the loveliest hair,' said Jamie, watching me.

'What? *This?*' I raised a hand self-consciously to my locks, which as usual could be politely described as higgledy-piggledy.

He laughed. 'Well, I like the other too,' he said, deliberately straight-faced, 'but yes, I meant that.'

'But it's so . . . curly,' I said, blushing a little.

'Aye, of course.' He looked surprised. 'I heard one of Dougal's girls say to a friend at the castle that it would take three hours with the hot tongs to make hers look like that. She said she'd like to scratch your eyes out for looking like that and not lifting a hand to do so.' He sat up and tugged gently at one curl, stretching it down so that, uncurled, it reached nearly to my breast. 'My sister Jenny's hair is curly, too, but not so much as yours.'

'Is your sister's hair red, like yours?' I asked, trying to envision what the mysterious Jenny might look like. She seemed to be often in Jamie's mind.

He shook his head, still twisting curls in and out between his fingers. 'No. Jenny's hair is black. Black as night. I'm red like my mother, and Jenny takes after Father. Brian Dubh, they called him, "Black Brian", for his hair and his beard.'

'I've heard that Captain Randall is called "Black Jack",' I ventured. Jamie laughed humourlessly.

'Oh, aye. But that's with reference to the colour of his

soul, not his hair.' His gaze sharpened as he looked down at me.

'You're not worrying about him, are ye, lass? Ye shouldna do so.' His hands left my hair and tightened possessively on my shoulders.

'I meant it, ye know,' he said softly. 'I will protect you. From him, or anyone else. To the last drop of my blood, *mo duinne*.'

'*Mo duinne?*' I asked, a little disturbed by the intensity of this speech. I didn't want to be responsible for *any* of his blood being spilt, last drop or first.

'It means "my brown one".' He raised a lock of hair to his lips and smiled, with a look in his eyes that started all the drops of my own blood chasing each other through my veins. '*Mo duinne*,' he repeated, softly. 'I have been longing to say that to you.'

'Rather a dull colour, brown, I've always thought,' I said practically, trying to delay things a bit. I kept having the feeling of being whirled along much faster than I intended.

Jamie shook his head, still smiling.

'No, I'd not say that, Sassenach. Not dull at all.' He lifted the mass of my hair with both hands and fanned it out. 'It's like the water in a burn, where it ruffles over the stones. Dark in the wavy spots, with bits of silver on the surface where the sun catches it.'

Nervous and a little breathless, I pulled away in order to pick up the comb I had dropped on the floor. I came up to find Jamie eyeing me steadily.

'I said I wouldna ask for anything you did not wish to tell me,' he said, 'and I won't, but I draw my own conclusions. Callum thought perhaps you were an English spy, though he couldna imagine in that case why you'd no Gaelic. Dougal thinks you're likely a French spy, maybe looking for support for King James. But in that case, *he* canna imagine why you were alone.'

'And what about you?' I asked, pulling hard at a stubborn tangle. 'What do you think I am?'

He tilted his head appraisingly, looking me over carefully.

'To look at, you could be French. You've that fine-boned

look through the face that some of the Angevin ladies have. Frenchwomen are usually sallow-faced, though, and you have skin like an opal.' He traced a finger slowly across the curve of my collarbone, and I felt the skin glow beneath his touch.

The finger moved to my face, drawing from temple to cheek, smoothing the hair back behind my ear. I remained immobile under his scrutiny, trying not to move as his hand passed behind my neck, thumb gently stroking my earlobe.

'Golden eyes; I've seen a pair like that once before – on a leopard.' He shook his head. 'Nay, lass. Ye could be French, but you're not.'

'How do you know?'

'I've talked with you a good deal; and listened to you besides. Dougal thinks you're French because you speak French well – verra well.'

'Thank you,' I said sarcastically. 'And the fact that I speak French well proves I'm not French?'

He smiled and tightened his grip on my neck. '*Tu parles très bien* – but not quite as well as I do,' he added, dropping back into English. He released me suddenly. 'I spent a year in France, after I left the castle, and two more later on with the army. I know a native speaker of French when I hear one. And French is not your mother tongue.' He shook his head slowly.

'Spanish? Perhaps, but why? Spain's no interests in the Highlands. German? Surely not.' He shrugged. 'Whoever you are, the English would want to find out. They canna afford to have unknown quantities at large, with the clans restless and Prince Charlie perhaps waiting to set sail from France. And their methods of finding out are not very gentle. I've reason to know.'

'And how do you know I'm not an *English* spy, then? Dougal thought I was, you said so.'

'It's possible, though your spoken English is more than a little odd too. If you were, though, why would you choose to wed me, rather than go back to your own folk? That was another reason for Dougal's makin' ye wed me – to see would ye bolt last night, when it came to the point.'

'And I didn't bolt. So what does that prove?'

He laughed and lay back down on the bed, an arm over his eyes to shield them from the lamp.

'Damned if I know, Sassenach. *Damned* if I know. There isna any reasonable explanation I can think of for you. You might be one of the Wee Folk, for all I know' – he peeked sideways from under his arm – 'no, I suppose not. You're too big.'

'Aren't you afraid I might kill you in your sleep some night, if you don't know who I am?'

He didn't answer but took his arm away from his eyes, and his smile widened. His eyes must be from the Fraser side, I thought. Not deep-set like the MacKenzies', they were set at an odd angle, so that the high cheekbones made them look almost slanted.

Without troubling to lift his head he opened the front of his shirt and spread the cloth aside, laying his chest bare to the waist. He drew the dirk from its sheath and tossed it towards me. It thunked on the boards at my feet.

He put his arm back over his eyes and stretched his head back, showing the place where the dark stubble of his sprouting beard stopped abruptly, just below the jaw.

'Straight up, just under the breastbone,' he advised. 'Quick and neat, though it takes a bit of strength. The throat-cutting's easier, but it's verra messy.'

I bent to pick up the dirk.

'Serve you right if I did,' I remarked. 'Cocky bastard.'

The grin visible beneath the crook of his arm widened still further.

'Sassenach?'

I stopped, dirk still in my hand.

'What?'

'I'll die a happy man.'

17

We Meet a Beggar

We slept fairly late the next morning, and the sun was high as we left the inn, heading south this time. Most of the horses were gone from the paddock, and none of the men from our party seemed to be about. I wondered aloud where they had gone.

Jamie grinned. 'I canna say for sure, but I could guess. The Watch went *that* way yesterday' – he pointed west – 'so I should say Rupert and the others have gone *that* way.' Pointing east.

'Cattle,' he explained, seeing that I still didn't understand. 'The estate-holders and tacksmen pay the Watch to keep an eye out, and get back their cattle, if they're stolen in a raid. But if the Watch is riding west towards Lag Cruime, any herds to the east are helpless – for a bit, anyway. Rupert's one of the best cattle-lifters I've ever seen. Beasts will follow him anywhere, wi' scarcely a bleat amongst them. And since there's no more entertainment to be had here, most likely he's got restless.'

Jamie himself seemed rather restless, and set a good pace. There was a deer trail through the heather, and the going was fairly easy, so I kept up with no difficulty. After a bit we came out on to a stretch of moorland where we could walk side by side.

'What about Horrocks?' I asked suddenly. Hearing him mention the town of Lag Cruime, I had remembered the English deserter and his possible news. 'You were supposed to meet him in Lag Cruime, weren't you?'

He nodded. 'Aye. But I canna go there now, wi' both Randall and the Watch headed that way. Too dangerous.'

'Could someone go for you? Or do you trust anyone enough?'

He glanced at me and smiled. 'Well, there's you. Since ye didna kill me last night after all, I suppose I may trust you. But I'm afraid you couldna go to Lag Cruime alone. No, if necessary, Murtagh will go for me. But I may be able to arrange something else – we'll see.'

'You trust Murtagh?' I asked curiously. I had no very friendly feelings towards the scruffy little man, since he was more or less responsible for my present predicament, having kidnapped me in the first place. Still, there was clearly a friendship of some kind between him and Jamie.

'Oh, aye.' He glanced at me, surprised. 'Murtagh's known me all my life. When I decided to come over from France I sent word to him, asking him to meet me at the coast.' He smiled wryly. 'I didna ken, ye see, whether it was Dougal who tried to kill me earlier. And I did not quite like the idea of meeting several MacKenzies alone, just in case. Didna want to end up washing about in the surf, if that's what they had in mind.'

'I see. So Dougal isn't the only one who believes in witnesses.'

He nodded. 'Very handy things, witnesses.'

On the other side of the moorland was a stretch of twisted rocks, pitted and gouged by the advance and retreat of glaciers long gone. Rainwater filled the deeper pits, and thistle and ox-eye daisy and meadowsweet surrounded these tarns with thick growth, the flowers reflected in the still water.

Sterile and fishless, these pools dotted the landscape and formed traps for unwary travellers, who might easily stumble into one in the darkness and be forced to spend a wet and uncomfortable night on the moor. We sat down beside one pool to eat our morning meal of bread and cheese.

This tarn at least had birds; swallows dipped low over the water to drink, and plovers and curlews poked long bills into the muddy earth at its edges, digging for insects.

I tossed crumbs of bread on to the mud for the birds. A curlew eyed one suspiciously, but while it was still making up its mind, a quick pipit zoomed in under its bill and made off with the treat. The curlew ruffled its feathers and went back to its industrious digging.

Jamie called my attention to a plover, calling and dragging a seemingly broken wing near us.

'She's a nest somewhere near,' I said.

'Over there.' He had to point it out several times before I finally spotted it; a shallow depression, quite out in the open, but with its four spotted eggs so close in appearance to the leaf-speckled bank that when I blinked I lost sight of the nest again.

Picking up a stick, Jamie gently poked the nest, pushing one egg out of place. The mother plover, excited, ran up almost in front of him. He sat on his heels, quite motionless, letting the bird dart back and forth, squalling. There was a flash of movement and he held the bird in his hand, suddenly still.

He spoke to the bird in Gaelic, a quiet, hissing sort of speech, as he stroked the soft brown plumage with one finger. The bird crouched in his hand, completely motionless, even the reflections frozen in its round black eyes.

He set it gently on the ground, but the bird did not move away until he said a few more words and waved his hand slowly back and forth behind it. It gave a short jerk and darted away into the weeds. He watched it go, and, quite unconscious, crossed himself.

'Why did you do that?' I asked, curious.

'What?' He was momentarily startled; I think he had forgotten I was there.

'You crossed yourself when the bird flew off; I wondered why.'

He shrugged, mildly embarrassed.

'Ah, well. It's an old tale, is all. Why plovers cry as they do, and run keening about their nests like that.' He motioned to the far side of the tarn, where another plover was doing exactly that. He watched the bird for a few moments, abstracted.

'Plovers have the souls of young mothers dead in childbirth,' he said. He glanced aside at me shyly. 'The story goes that they cry and run about their nests because they canna believe the young are safe hatched; they're mourning always for the lost one – or looking for a child left behind.' He squatted by the nest and nudged the egg with his stick, turning it bit by bit until the pointed end faced in, like the others. He stayed squatting, even after the egg had been replaced, balancing the stick across his thighs, staring out over the still waters of the tarn.

'It's only habit, I suppose,' he said. 'I did it first when I was much younger, when I first heard that story. I didna really believe they have souls, of course, even then, but, ye ken, just as a bit of respect . . .' He looked up at me and smiled suddenly. 'Done it so often now, I'd not even notice. There's quite a few plovers in Scotland, ye ken.' He rose and tossed the stick aside. 'Let's go on, now; there's a place I want to show you, near the top of the hill yonder.' He took my elbow to help me out of the declivity, and we set off up the slope.

I had heard what he said to the plover he released. Though I had only a few words of Gaelic, I had heard the old salutation often enough to be familiar with it. 'God go with ye, Mother,' he had said.

A young mother, dead in childbirth. And a child left behind. I touched his arm and he looked down at me.

'How old were you?' I asked.

He gave me a half-smile. 'Eight,' he answered. 'Weaned, at least.'

He spoke no more, but led me uphill. We were in sloping foothills now, thick with heather. Just beyond, the country-side changed abruptly, with huge heaps of granite rearing up from the earth, surrounded by clusters of pine and birch. We came over the crest of the hill and left the plovers crying by the tarns behind us.

The sun was growing hot, and after an hour of shoving through thick foliage – even with Jamie doing most of the shoving – I was ready for a rest.

We found a shady spot at the foot of one of the granite outcrops. The spot reminded me a bit of the place where I had first met Murtagh – and parted company with Captain

329

Randall. Still, it was pleasant here. Jamie told me that we were alone, because of the constant birdsong all around. If anyone came near, most birds would stop singing.

'Always hide in a forest, Sassenach,' he advised me. 'If ye dinna move too much yourself, the birds will tell you in plenty of time if anyone's near.'

Looking back from pointing out a squawking raven in the tree overhead, his eyes caught mine. And we sat as though frozen, within hand's reach but not touching, barely breathing. After a time the bird grew bored with us and left. It was Jamie who looked away first, with an almost imperceptible shiver, as though he were cold.

The heads of shaggy-cap mushrooms poked whitely through the mould beneath the ferns. Jamie's blunt forefinger flipped one off its stem, and traced the spokes of the basidium as he marshalled his next words. When he spoke carefully, as now, he all but lost the slight Scots accent that usually marked his speech.

'I do not wish to . . . that is . . . I do not mean to imply . . .' He looked up suddenly and smiled, with a helpless gesture. 'I dinna want to insult you by sounding as though I think you've a vast experience of men, is all. But it would be foolish to pretend that ye don't know more than I do about such matters. What I meant to ask is, is this . . . usual? What it is between us, when I touch you, when you . . . lie with me? Is it always so between a man and a woman?'

In spite of his difficulties I knew exactly what he meant. His gaze was direct, holding my eyes as he waited for my answer. I wanted to look away, but couldn't.

'There's often something like it,' I said, and had to stop and clear my throat. 'But no. No, it isn't – usual. I have no idea why, but no. This is . . . different.'

He relaxed a bit, as though I had confirmed something about which he had been anxious.

'I thought perhaps not. I've not lain with a woman before, but I've . . . ah, had my hands on a few.' He smiled shyly and shook his head. 'It wasna the same. I mean, I've held women in my arms before, and kissed them, and . . . well.' He waved his hand, dismissing the *and*. 'It was verra pleasant indeed. Made my heart pound and my breath come short, and all that. But it wasna at all as it is when I take you in my arms and kiss you.' His eyes, I thought, were the colour of lakes and skies, and as fathomless as either.

He reached out and touched my lower lip, barely brushing the edge. 'It starts out the same, but then, after a moment,' he said, speaking softly, 'suddenly it's as though I've a living flame in my arms.' His touch grew firmer, outlining my lips and caressing the line of my jaw. 'And I want only to throw myself into it and be consumed.'

I thought of telling him that his own touch seared my skin and filled my veins with fire. But I was already alight and glowing like a brand. I closed my eyes and felt the kindling touch move to cheek and temple, ear and neck, and shuddered as his hands dropped to my waist and drew me close.

Jamie seemed to have a definite idea where we were going. At length he stopped at the foot of a huge rock, some twenty feet high, warty with lumps and jagged cracks. Ragwort and eglantine had taken root in the cracks, and waved in precarious yellow and pink flags against the stone. He took my hand and nodded at the rock face before us.

'D'ye see the steps, there, Sassenach? Think ye can manage it?' There were, in fact, faintly marked protuberances in the stone, rising at an angle across the face of the rock. Some were bona fide ledges and others merely a foothold for lichens. I couldn't tell whether they were natural, or perhaps had known some assistance in their forming, but I thought it might just be possible to climb them, even in a full-length skirt and tight bodice.

With some slippages and scares, and with Jamie pushing helpfully from the rear on occasion, I made it to the top of the rock and paused to look around. The view was spectacular. The dark bulk of a mountain rose to the east, while far below to the south the foothills ran out into a vast, barren moorland. The top of the rock sloped inwards from all sides, forming a shallow dish. In the centre of the dish was a blackened circle, with the sooty remnants of charred sticks. We were not the first visitors, then.

'You knew this place?' Jamie stood to one side a little, observing me and taking pleasure in my raptness. He shrugged, deprecating.

'Oh, aye. I know most places through this part of the Highlands. Come here, there's a spot ye can sit, and see down to where the track comes past the hill.' The inn also was visible from here, reduced from dolls-house to child's building block by the distance. A few tethered ponies were clustered under the trees by the road, small blobs of brown and black from here.

No trees grew on the top of the rock, and the sun was hot on my back. We sat side by side, legs dangling over the edge, and companionably shared one of the bottles of ale that Jamie had thoughtfully lifted from the well in the inn-yard as we left.

Smaller plants, the ones that could gain a foothold in the precarious cracks and root themselves in meagre soil, sprouted here and there, raising their faces bravely to the hot summer sun. There was a small clump of daisies shelter-ing in the lee of an outcrop near my hand, and I reached to pluck one.

There was a faint whir, and the daisy leaped off its stem and landed on my knee. I stared stupidly, my mind unable to make sense of this bizarre behaviour. Jamie, a good deal faster than I in his apprehensions, had flung himself flat on the rock.

'Get *down!*' he hissed. A large hand fastened on my elbow and jerked me flat beside him. As I hit the spongy moss I saw the shaft of an arrow, still quivering above my face, where it had struck home in the cleft of the outcrop.

I froze, afraid even to look around, and tried to press myself still flatter against the ground. Jamie was motionless at my side, so still that he might have been a stone himself. Even the birds and insects seemed to have paused in their song, and the air hung breathless and waiting. Suddenly Jamie began to laugh.

He sat up, and grasping the arrow by the shaft, twisted

it carefully out of the rock. It was fletched with the split tail-feathers of a woodpecker, I saw, and banded with blue thread, wrapped in a line half an inch wide below the quills.

Laying the arrow aside, Jamie cupped his hands around his mouth and gave a remarkably good imitation of the call of a great spotted woodpecker. He lowered his hands and waited. In a moment the call was answered from the grove below, and a broad smile spread across his face.

'A friend of yours?' I guessed. He nodded, eyes intent on the narrow path up the rock face.

'Hugh Munro, unless someone else has taken to making arrows in his style.'

We waited a moment longer, but no one appeared on the path below.

'Ah,' said Jamie softly, and whirled around just in time to confront a head, rising slowly above the edge of the rock behind us.

The head burst into a jack-o'-lantern grin, snaggle-toothed and jolly, beaming with pleasure at surprising us. The head itself was roughly pumpkin-shaped, the impression enhanced by the orange-brown, leathery skin that covered not only the face but the round, bald crown of the head as well. Few pumpkins, however, could boast such a luxuriant growth of beard, nor such a pair of bright blue eyes. Stubby hands with filthy nails planted themselves beneath the beard and swiftly hoisted the remainder of the jack-o'-lantern up into view.

The body rather matched the head, having a distinct look of the Halloween goblin about it. The shoulders were very broad, but hunched and slanted, one being considerably higher than the other. One leg, too, seemed somewhat shorter than its fellow, giving the man a rather hopping, hitching sort of gait.

Munro, if this were indeed Jamie's friend, was clad in what appeared to be multiple layers of rags, the faded colours of berry-dyed fabric peeking out through rents in a shapeless garment that might once have been a woman's smock.

He carried no sporran at his belt – which was in any case

no more than a frayed length of rope from which two furry carcasses swung, head down. Instead he had a fat leather wallet slung across his chest, of surprisingly good quality, considering the rest of the outfit. A collection of small metal oddments dangled from the strap of the wallet: religious medals, military decorations, what looked to be old uniform buttons, worn coins pierced and sewn on, and three or four small rectangular bits of metal, dull grey and with cryptic marks incised in their surfaces.

Jamie rose as the creature hopped nimbly over the intervening protrusions of rock, and the two men embraced warmly, thumping each other hard on the back in the odd fashion of manly greeting.

'And how goes it then, with the house of Munro?' inquired Jamie, standing back at length and surveying his old companion.

Munro ducked his head and made an odd gobbling noise, grinning. Then, raising his eyebrows, he nodded in my direction and waved his stubby hands in a strangely graceful interrogatory gesture.

'My wife,' said Jamie, reddening slightly with a mixture of shyness and pride at the new introduction. 'Married but the two days.'

Munro smiled more broadly still at this information, and executed a remarkably complex and graceful bow, involving the rapid touching of head, heart and lips and ending up in a near-horizontal position on the ground at my feet. Having executed this striking manoeuvre he sprang to his feet with the grace of an acrobat and thumped Jamie again, this time in apparent congratulation.

Munro then began an extraordinary ballet of the hands, motioning to himself, away down towards the forest, at me and back to himself, with such an array of gestures and wavings that I could hardly follow his flying hands. I had seen deaf-and-dumb talk before, but never executed so swiftly and gracefully.

'Is that so, then?' Jamie exclaimed. It was his turn to buffet the other man in congratulation. No wonder men got impervious to superficial pain, I thought. It came from this habit of hammering each other incessantly.

'He's married as well,' Jamie explained, turning to me. 'Six months since, to a widow – oh, all right, to a *fat* widow,' he amended, in response to an emphatic gesture from Munro, 'with six children, down in the village of Dubhlairn.'

'How nice,' I said politely. 'It looks as though they'll eat well, at least.' I motioned to the rabbits hanging from his belt.

Munro at once unfastened one of the corpses and handed it to me, with such an expression of beaming goodwill that I felt obliged to accept it, smiling back and hoping privately that it didn't harbour fleas.

'A wedding gift,' said Jamie. 'And most welcome, Munro. Ye must allow us to return the favour.' With which, he extracted one of the bottles of ale from its mossy bed and handed it across.

The courtesies attended to in this manner, we all sat down again to a companionable sharing of the third bottle. Jamie and Munro carried on an exchange of news, gossip and conversation which seemed no less free for the fact that only one of them spoke.

I took little part in the conversation, being unable to read Munro's hand-signs, though Jamie did his best to include me by translation and reference.

At one point Jamie jabbed a thumb at the rectangular bits of lead that adorned Munro's strap.

'Gone official, have ye?' he asked. 'Or is that just for when the game is scarce?' Munro bobbed his head and nodded like a jack-in-the-box.

'What are they?' I asked curiously.

'Gaberlunzie tokens.'

'Oh, to be sure,' I said. 'Pardon my asking.'

'A gaberlunzie is a beggar, Sassenach,' Jamie explained. 'And the token is a licence to beg, good within the borders of the parish, and only on the one day a week when begging's allowed. Each parish has its own, so the beggars from one parish canna take overmuch advantage of the charity of the next.'

'A system with a certain amount of elasticity, I see,' I said, eyeing Munro's stock of four lead seals.

'Ah, well, Munro's a special case, d'ye see. He was captured by the Turks at sea. Spent a good many years rowing up and down in a galley, and a few more as a slave in Algiers. That's where he lost his tongue.'

'They . . . cut it out?' I felt a bit faint.

Jamie seemed undisturbed by the thought, but then he had apparently known Munro for some time.

'Oh, aye. And broke his leg for him, as well. The back, too, Munro? No,' he amended, at a series of signs from Munro, 'the back was an accident, something that happened jumping off a wall in Alexandria. The feet, though; that was the Turks' doing.'

I didn't really want to know, but both Munro and Jamie seemed dying to tell me. 'All right,' I said, resigned. 'What happened to his feet?'

With something approaching pride, Munro stripped off his battered sandals and hose, exposing broad, splayed feet on which the skin was thickened and roughened, white shiny patches alternating with angry red areas.

'Boiling oil,' said Jamie. 'It's how they force captive Christians to convert to the Mussulman religion.'

'It looks a very effective means of persuasion,' I said. 'So that's why several parishes will give him leave to beg? To make up for his trials on behalf of Christendom.'

'Aye, exactly.' Jamie was evidently pleased with my swift appreciation of the situation. Munro also expressed his admiration with another deep salaam, followed by a very expressive if indelicate sequence of hand movements which I gathered were meant to be praising my physical appearance as well.

'Thank ye, man. Aye, she'll do me proud, I reckon.' Jamie, seeing my uplifted brows, tactfully turned Munro so that his back was to me and the flying fingers hidden. 'Now, tell me what's doing in the clachans?'

The two men drew closer together, continuing their lopsided conversation with an increased intensity. Since Jamie's part seemed to be limited mainly to grunts and exclamations of interest, I could glean little of the content, and busied myself instead with a survey of the strange little rock plants sprouting from the surfaces of our perch.

I had collected a pocketful of eyebright and self-heal by the time they finished talking and Hugh Munro rose to go. With a final bow to me and a thump on the back for Jamie, he shuffled to the edge of the rock and disappeared as quickly as one of the rabbits he poached might vanish into its hole.

'What fascinating friends you have,' I said.

'Oh, aye. Nice fellow, Hugh. I hunted wi' him and some others, last year. He's on his own, now that he's an official beggar, but his work keeps him moving about the parishes; he'll know everything that goes on within the neighbourhood.'

'Including the whereabouts of Horrocks?' I guessed.

Jamie nodded. 'Aye. And he'll carry a message for me, to change the meeting place.'

'Which foxes Dougal rather neatly,' I observed. 'If he had any ideas about holding you to ransom over Horrocks.'

He nodded, and a smile creased one corner of his mouth. 'Aye, there's that about it.'

It was near supper-time again when we reached the inn. This time, though, Dougal's big black gelding and its five companions were standing in the innyard, contentedly munching hay.

Dougal himself was inside, washing the road dust from his throat with sour ale. He nodded to me and swung round to greet his nephew. Instead of speaking, though, he just stood there, head on one side, eyeing Jamie quizzically.

'Ah, that's it,' he said finally, in the satisfied tones of a man who has solved a difficult puzzle. 'Now I know what ye mind me of, lad.' He turned to me.

'Ever seen a stag near the end of the rutting season, lass?' he said confidentially. 'The poor beasts dinna sleep nor eat for several weeks, because they canna spare the time, between fightin' off the other stags and serving the does. By the end o' the season they're naught but skin and bones.

337

Their eyes are deep-sunk in their heads, and the only part o' them that doesna shake wi' palsy is their – '

The last of this was lost in a chorus of laughter as Jamie pulled me up the stairs. We did not come down to supper.

Much later, on the edge of sleep, I felt Jamie's arm around my waist and his breath warm against my neck.

'Does it ever stop? The wanting you?' His hand came around to caress my breast. 'Even when I've just left ye, I want you so much my chest feels tight and my fingers ache with wanting to touch ye again.'

He cupped my face in the dark, thumbs stroking the arcs of my eyebrows. 'When I hold ye between my two hands and feel you quiver like that, waitin' for me to take you . . . Lord, I want to pleasure you till you cry out under me and open yourself to me. And when I take my own pleasure from you, I feel as though I've given ye my soul along with my cock.'

He rolled above me and I opened my legs, wincing slightly as he entered me. He laughed softly. 'Aye, I'm a bit sore, too. Do ye want me to stop?' I wrapped my legs around his hips in answer and pulled him closer.

'*Would* you stop?' I asked.

'No. I can't.'

We laughed together, and rocked slowly, lips and fingers exploring in the dark.

'I see why the Church says it is a sacrament,' Jamie said dreamily.

'This?' I said, startled. 'Why?'

'Or at least holy,' he said. 'I feel like God himself when I'm in you.'

I laughed so loud he nearly came out. He stopped and gripped my shoulders to steady me.

'What's so funny?'

'It's hard to imagine God doing this.'

Jamie resumed his movements. 'Well, if God made man in his own image, I should imagine he's got a cock.' He started to laugh as well, losing his rhythm again. 'Though ye dinna remind me much of the Blessed Virgin, Sassenach.'

We shook in each other's arms, laughing until we came uncoupled and rolled apart.

Recovering, Jamie slapped my hip. 'Get on your knees, Sassenach.'

'Why?'

'If you'll not let me be spiritual about it, you'll have to put up wi' my baser nature. I'm going to be a beast.' He bit my neck. 'Do ye want me to be a horse, a bear, or a dog?'

'A hedgehog.'

'A hedgehog? And just how does a hedgehog make love?' he demanded.

No, I thought. I won't. I will *not*. But I did. '*Very* carefully,' I replied, giggling helplessly. So now we know just how old *that* one is, I thought.

Jamie collapsed in a ball, wheezing with laughter. At last he rolled over and got to his knees, groping for the flint box on the table. He glowed like red amber against the room's darkness as the wick caught and the light swelled behind him.

He flopped back on the foot of the bed, grinning down at me, where I still shook on the pillow with spasms of giggles. He rubbed the back of his hand across his face and assumed a mock-stern expression.

'All right, woman. I see the time has come when I shall have to exert my authority as your husband.'

'Oh, you will?'

'Aye.' He dived forward, grabbing my thighs and spreading them. I squeaked and tried to wriggle upwards.

'No, don't do that!'

'Why not?' He lay full length between my legs, squinting up at me. He kept a firm hold on my thighs, preventing my struggles to close them.

'Tell me, Sassenach. Why don't ye want me to do that?' He rubbed his cheek against the inside of one thigh, ferocious young beard rasping the tender skin. 'Be honest. Why not?' He rasped the other side, making me kick and squirm wildly to get away, to no avail.

I turned my face into the pillow, which felt cool against

my flushed cheek. 'Well, if you must know,' I muttered, 'I don't think – well, I'm afraid that it doesn't – I mean, the smell . . .' My voice faded off into an embarrassed silence. There was a sudden movement between my legs, as Jamie heaved himself up. He put his arms around my hips, laid his cheek on my thigh, and laughed until the tears ran down his cheeks.

'Jesus God, Sassenach,' he said at last, snorting with mirth, 'don't ye know what's the first thing you do when you're getting acquainted with a new horse?'

'No,' I said, completely baffled.

He raised one arm, displaying a soft tuft of cinnamon-coloured hair. 'You rub your oxter over the beast's nose a few times, to give him your scent and get him accustomed to you, so he won't be nervous of ye.' He raised himself on his elbows, peering up over the slope of belly and breast.

'That's what you should have done wi' me, Sassenach. You should ha' rubbed my face between your legs first thing. Then I wouldn't have been skittish.'

'Skittish!'

He lowered his face and rubbed it deliberately back and forth, snorting and blowing in imitation of a nuzzling horse. I writhed and kicked him in the ribs, with exactly as much effect as kicking a brick wall. Finally he pressed my thighs flat again and looked up.

'Now,' he said, in a tone that brooked no opposition, 'lie still.'

I felt exposed, invaded, helpless – and as though I were about to disintegrate. Jamie's breath was alternately warm and cool on my skin.

'Please,' I said, not knowing whether I meant 'please stop' or 'please go on'. It didn't matter, he didn't mean to stop.

Consciousness fragmented into a number of small separate sensations: the roughness of the linen pillow, nubbled with embroidered flowers; the oily reek of the lamp, mingled with the fainter scent of roast beef and ale and the still fainter wisps of freshness from the wilting flowers in the cup; the cool timber of the wall against my left foot, the firm hands on my hips. The sensations swirled and coalesced behind my closed eyelids into a glowing sun that swelled and shrank and finally exploded with a soundless *pop* that left me in a warm and pulsing darkness.

Dimly, from a long way away, I heard Jamie sit up.

'Well, that's a bit better,' said a voice, gasping between words. 'Takes a bit of effort to make *you* properly submissive, doesn't it?' The bed creaked with a shifting of weight and I felt my knees being nudged further apart.

'Not as dead as you look, I hope?' said the voice, coming nearer. I arched upwards with an inarticulate sound as exquisitely sensitive tissues were firmly parted in a fresh assault.

'Jesus Christ,' I said. There was a faint chuckle near my ear.

'I only said I *felt* like God, Sassenach,' he murmured. 'I never said I *was*.'

And later, as the rising sun began to dim the glow of the lamp, I roused from a drifting sleep to hear Jamie murmur once more, 'Does it ever stop, Claire? The wanting?'

My head fell back on to his shoulder. 'I don't know, Jamie. I really don't.'

18

Raiders in the Rocks

'What did Captain Randall say?' I asked.

With Dougal on one side and Jamie on the other there was barely room for the three ponies to ride abreast down the narrow track. Here and there, one or both of my companions would have to drop back or spur up, in order to avoid becoming entangled in the overgrowth that threatened to reclaim the crude track.

Dougal glanced at me, then back at the track in order to guide his pony around a large rock. A wicked grin spread slowly across his features.

'He wasna best pleased about it,' he said circumspectly. 'Though I am not sure I should tell ye what he actually *said*; there's likely limits even to *your* tolerance for bad language, Mistress Fraser.'

I overlooked his sardonic use of my new title, as well as the implied insult, though I saw Jamie stiffen in his saddle.

'I, er, don't suppose he means to take any steps about it?' I asked. Despite Jamie's assurances I had visions of scarlet-coated dragoons bursting out of the bushes, slaughtering the Scots and dragging me away to Randall's lair for questioning. I had an uneasy feeling that Randall's ideas of interrogation might be creative, to say the least.

'Shouldn't think so,' Dougal answered casually. 'He's more to worry about than one stray Sassenach wench, no matter how pretty.' He raised an eyebrow and half bowed towards me, as though the compliment were meant in apology. 'He's also better sense than to rile Callum by kidnapping his niece,' he said more matter of factly.

Niece. I felt a small shiver run down my spine in spite of the warm weather. Niece to MacKenzie of Leoch. Not to mention to his war chieftain, riding so nonchalantly

342

beside me. And on the other side I was now presumably linked with Lord Lovat, chief of Clan Fraser, with the abbot of a powerful French abbey, and with who knew how many other assorted Frasers. No, perhaps John Randall *wouldn't* think it worthwhile to pursue me. And that, after all, had been the point of this ridiculous arrangement.

I stole a glance at Jamie, riding ahead now. His back was straight as an alder sapling and his hair shone under the sun like a helmet of burnished metal.

Dougal followed my glance.

'Could have been worse, no?' he said with an ironic lift of his brow.

Two nights later we were encamped on a stretch of moorland, near one of those strange outcroppings of glacier-pocked stone. It had been a long day's travel, with only a hasty meal eaten in the saddle, and everyone was pleased to stop for a cooked supper. I had tried early on to assist with the cooking, but my help had been more or less politely rejected by the taciturn clansman whose job it apparently was.

One of the men had killed a deer that morning, and a portion of the fresh meat, cooked with onions and whatever else he could find, had made a delicious meal. Bursting with food and contentment, we all sprawled around the fire, listening to stories and songs. Surprisingly enough, little Murtagh, who seldom opened his mouth to speak, had a beautiful, clear tenor voice. While it was difficult to persuade him to sing, the results were worth it.

I nestled close to Jamie, trying to find a comfortable spot to sit on the hard granite. We had camped at the edge of the rocky outcrop, where a broad shelf of greenish granite gave us a natural hearth, and the towering jumble of rocks behind made a place to hide the ponies. When I asked why we did not sleep more comfortably on the springy grass of the moor, Ned Gowan had informed me that we were now near the southern border of the MacKenzie lands. And thus near the territory of both Grants and Chisholms.

'Dougal's scouts say there's no sign of anyone nearabouts,' he had said, standing on a large boulder to peer into the sunset himself, 'but ye can never tell. Better safe than sorry, ye ken.'

When Murtagh called it quits, Rupert began to tell stories. While he lacked Gwyllyn's elegant way with words, he had an inexhaustible fund of stories, about fairies, ghosts, the *tannasg* or evil spirits, and other inhabitants of the Highlands such as the waterhorse. These beings, I was given to understand, inhabited almost all bodies of water, being especially common at fords and crossings, though many lived in the depths of the lochs.

'There's a spot at the eastern end of Loch Garve, ye ken,' he said, rolling his eyes around the gathering to be sure everyone was listening, 'that never freezes. It's always black water there, even when the rest o' the loch is frozen solid, for that's the waterhorse's chimney.'

The waterhorse of Loch Garve, like so many of his kind, had stolen a young girl who came to the loch to draw water, and carried her away to live in the depths of the loch and be his wife. Woe betide any maiden, or any man, for that matter, who met a fine horse by the water's side and thought to ride upon him, for a rider once mounted could not dismount, and the horse would step into the water, turn into a fish and swim to his home with the hapless rider still stuck fast to his back.

'Now, a waterhorse beneath the waves has but fish's teeth,' said Rupert, wiggling his palm like an undulating fish, 'and feeds on snails and waterweeds and cold, wet things. His blood runs cold as the water, and he's no need of fire, d'ye ken, but a human woman's a wee bit warmer than that.' Here he winked at me and leered outrageously, to the enjoyment of the listeners.

'So the waterhorse's wife was sad and cold and hungry in her new home beneath the waves, not caring owermuch for snails and waterweed for her supper. So, the waterhorse being a kindly sort, takes himself to the bank of the loch near the house of a man with the reputation of a builder. And when the man came down to the river and saw the fine golden horse with his silver bridle, shining in the sun, he couldna resist seizing the bridle and mounting.

'Sure enough, the waterhorse carries him straight into the water, and down through the depths to his own cold, fishy home. And there he tells the builder if he would be free, he must build a fine hearth, and a chimney as well, that the waterhorse's wife might have a fire to warm her hands and fry her fish.'

I had been resting my head on Jamie's shoulder, feeling pleasantly drowsy and looking forward to bed, even if that were only a blanket spread over granite. Suddenly I felt his body tense. He put a hand on my neck, warning me to keep still. I looked around the campsite and could see nothing amiss, but I caught the air of tension running from man to man as though transmitted by wireless.

Looking in Rupert's direction I saw him nod fractionally as he caught Dougal's eye, though he went on with the story imperturbably.

'So the builder, havin' little choice, did as he was bid. And so the waterhorse kept his word, and returned the man to the bank near his home. And the waterhorse's wife was warm, then, and happy, and full of the fish she fried for her supper. And the water never freezes over the east end of Loch Garve because the heat from the waterhorse's chimney melts the ice.'

Rupert was seated on a rock, his right side towards me. As he spoke he bent down as though casually to scratch his leg. Without the slightest hitch in his movements he grasped the knife that lay on the ground near his foot and transferred it smoothly to his lap, where it lay hidden in the folds of his kilt.

I wriggled closer and pulled Jamie's head down as though overcome by amorousness. 'What is it?' I whispered in his ear.

He seized my earlobe between his teeth and whispered back. 'The ponies are restless. Someone's near.'

One man got up and strolled to the edge of the rock to relieve himself. When he returned he sat down in a new spot, next to one of the drovers. Another man rose and peered into the cook-pot, helping himself to a morsel of venison. All around the campsite there was a subtle shifting and moving, while Rupert kept on talking.

Watching carefully, with Jamie's arm tight around me, I finally realized that the men were moving closer to wherever their weapons had been placed. All of them slept with their dirks, but generally left swords, pistols and the round leather shields called targes in small, neat heaps near the edge of the campsite. Jamie's own pair of pistols lay on the ground with his sword, just a few feet away.

I could see the firelight dancing on the damascened blade. While his pistols were no more than the customary anti-quated 'dags' worn by most of the men, both broadsword and claymore were something special. He had showed them to me with pride at one of our stops, turning the gleaming blades over lovingly in his hands.

The claymore was wrapped inside my blanket roll; I could see the enormous T-shaped hilt, the grip roughened for battle by careful sanding. I had lifted it, and nearly dropped it. It weighed close to fifteen pounds, Jamie told me.

If the claymore was sombre and lethal-looking, the broad-sword was beautiful. Two thirds the weight of the larger weapon, it was a deadly, gleaming thing with Islamic tracery snaking its way up the blue steel blade to the spiralled basket hilt, enamelled in reds and blues. I had seen Jamie use it in playful practice, first right-handed with one of the men-at-arms, later left-handed with Dougal. He was a glory to watch under those conditions, swift and sure, with a grace made the more impressive by his size. But my mouth grew dry at the thought of seeing that skill used in earnest.

He bent towards me, planting a tender kiss under the edge of my jaw and taking the opportunity to turn me slightly so that I faced one of the jumbled piles of rock.

'Soon, I think,' he murmured, kissing me industriously. 'D'ye see the small opening in the rock?' I did; a space less than three feet high, formed by two large slabs fallen together.

He clasped my face and nuzzled me lovingly. 'When I say go, get into it and stay there. Have ye the dirk?'

He had insisted I keep the dirk he had tossed to me that night at the inn, despite my own insistence that I had neither the skill nor the inclination to use it. And when it came to insisting, Dougal had been right; Jamie *was* stubborn.

Consequently, the dirk was in one of the deep pockets of my gown. After a day of uncomfortable awareness of its weight against my thigh, I had grown almost oblivious to it. He ran a hand playfully down my leg, checking to make certain of its presence.

He lifted his head then, like a cat scenting the breeze. Looking up, I could see him glance at Murtagh, then down at me. The little man gave no outward sign, but rose and stretched himself thoroughly. When he sat down again he was several feet nearer to me.

A pony whickered nervously behind us. As though it had been a signal they came screaming over the rocks. Not English, as I had feared, nor bandits. Highlanders, shrieking like banshees. Grants, I supposed. Or Chisholms.

On hands and knees I made for the rocks. I banged my head and scraped my knees, but managed to wedge myself into the small crevice. Heart hammering, I fumbled for the dirk in my pocket, almost jabbing myself in the process. I had no idea what to do with the long, wicked knife, but felt slightly better for having it. There was a moonstone set in the hilt and it was comforting to feel the small bulge against my palm.

The fighting was so confused that at first I had no idea what was going on. The small clearing was filled with yelling bodies heaving to and fro, rolling on the ground and running back and forth. My sanctuary was luckily to one side of the main combat, so I was in no danger for the moment. Glancing around, I saw a small, crouching figure close by, pressed against my rock in the shadow. I took a firmer grip on my dirk, but realized almost at once that it was Murtagh.

So that was the purpose of Jamie's glance. Murtagh had been ordered to guard me. I couldn't see Jamie himself anywhere. Most of the fighting was taking place in the rocks and shadows near the carts.

Of course, that must be the object of the raid; the carts

and the ponies. The attackers were an organized band, well armed and decently fed, from the little I could see of them in the light of the dying fire. If these were Grants, then perhaps they were seeking either booty or revenge for the cattle Rupert and friends had pilfered a few days before. Confronted with the results of that impromptu raid, Dougal had been mildly annoyed – not with the fact of the raid, but only concerned that the cattle would slow our progress. He had managed to dispose of them almost at once, though, at a small market in one of the villages.

It was soon clear that the attackers were not much concerned with inflicting harm on our party; only with getting to the ponies and carts. One or two succeeded. I crouched low as a barebacked pony leaped the fire and disappeared into the darkness of the moor, a caterwauling man clinging to its mane.

Two or three more raced away on foot, clutching bags of Callum's grain, pursued by furious MacKenzies shouting Gaelic imprecations. From the sound of it, the raid was dying down. Then a large group of men staggered out into the firelight and the action picked up again.

This seemed to be serious fighting, an impression borne out by the flashing of blades and the fact that the participants were grunting a good deal, but not yelling. At length I got it sorted out. Jamie and Dougal were at the centre of it, fighting back to back. Each of them held his broadsword in the left hand, dirk in the right, and both of them were putting the arms to good use, so far as I could see.

They were surrounded by four men – or five; I lost count in the shadows – armed with short swords, though one man had a broadsword hung on his belt and at least two more carried undrawn pistols.

It must be Dougal, or Jamie, or both, that they wanted. Alive, for preference. For ransom, I supposed. Thus the deliberate use of whingers, which might merely wound, rather than the more lethal broadsword or pistols.

Dougal and Jamie suffered from no such scruples, and were attending to business with considerable grim efficiency. Back to back, they formed a complete circle of threat, each man covering the other's weaker side. When Dougal drove his dirk hand upwards with considerable force, I thought that 'weaker' might not be precisely the term.

The whole roiling, grunting, cursing mess was staggering towards me. I pressed myself back as far as I could, but the crevice was barely two feet deep. I caught a stir of movement from the corner of my eye. Murtagh had decided to take a more active part in affairs.

I could scarcely pull my horrified gaze away from Jamie, but saw the little clansman draw his pistol, so far unfired, in a leisurely manner. He checked the firing mechanism carefully, rubbed the weapon on his sleeve, braced it on his forearm and waited.

And waited. I was shivering with fear for Jamie, who had given up finesse and was slashing savagely from side to side, beating back the two men who now faced him with sheer bloody-mindedness. Why in hell didn't the man fire? I thought furiously. And then I realized why not. Both Jamie and Dougal were in the line of fire. I seemed to recall that snaphance pistols sometimes lacked a bit in the way of accuracy.

This supposition was borne out in the next minute, as an unexpected lunge by one of Dougal's opponents caught him at the wrist. The blade ripped up the length of his forearm and he sank to one knee. Feeling his uncle fall, Jamie pulled back his own blade and took two quick steps backwards. This put his back near a rock face, Dougal crouched to one side within reach of the protection of his blade. It also brought the attackers side on to my hiding place and Murtagh's pistol.

Close at hand, the report of the pistol was startlingly loud. It took the attackers by surprise, particularly the one who was hit. The man stood still for a moment, shook his head in a confused way, then very slowly sat down, fell limply backwards and rolled down a slight decline into the dying embers of the fire.

Taking advantage of the surprise, Jamie knocked the sword from the hand of one attacker. Dougal was on his feet again, and Jamie moved to the side to give him room for swordplay. One of the fighters had abandoned the fray and run down the hill to drag his wounded companion out of the hot ashes. Still, that left three of the raiders, and Dougal wounded. I could see dark drops splashing against the rock face as he wielded the sword.

They were close enough now that I could see Jamie's face, calm and intent, absorbed with the exultancy of battle. Suddenly Dougal shouted something to him. Jamie tore his eyes from his opponent's face for a split second and looked down. Glancing back just in time to avoid being skewered, he ducked to one side and *threw* his sword.

His opponent gazed in considerable surprise at the sword sticking in his leg. He touched the blade in some bemusement, then grasped it and pulled. From the ease with which it came out, I assumed the wound was not deep. The man still seemed slightly bewildered, and glanced up as though to ask the purpose of this unorthodox behaviour.

He uttered a scream, dropped the sword and ran, limping heavily. Startled by the noise, the other two attackers looked over, turned, and likewise fled, pursued by Jamie, moving like an avalanche. He had succeeded in yanking the huge claymore out of the blanket roll and was swinging it in a murderous, two-handed arc. Backing him up came Murtagh, shouting something highly uncomplimentary in Gaelic and brandishing both sword and reloaded pistol.

Things mopped up quite quickly after that, and it was only a quarter of an hour or so before the MacKenzie party had reassembled and assessed its damages.

These had been slight; two ponies had been taken, and three bags of grain, but the drovers, who slept with their loads, had prevented further depredations on the carts, while the men-at-arms had succeeded in driving off the would-be horse thieves. The major loss seemed to be one of the men.

I thought when he was missed at first that he must have been wounded or killed in the scrimmage, but a thorough search of the area failed to turn him up.

'Kidnapped,' said Dougal grimly. 'Blast, he'll cost me a month's income in ransom.'

'Could ha' been worse, Dougal,' said Jamie, mopping his face on his sleeve. 'Think what Callum would say if they'd taken *you*!'

'If they'd taken *you*, lad, I'd ha' let them keep ye, and ye could change your name to Grant,' Dougal retorted, but the mood of the party lightened substantially.

I unearthed the small box of medical supplies I had packed, and lined up the injured in order of severity. Nothing really bad, I was pleased to see. The wound on Dougal's arm was likely the worst.

Ned Gowan was bright-eyed and fizzing with vitality, apparently so intoxicated with the thrill of the fight as hardly to notice the tooth that had been knocked out by an ill-aimed dagger hilt. He had, however, retained sufficient presence of mind to keep it carefully under his tongue.

'Just on the off-chance, d'ye see,' he explained, spitting it into the palm of his hand. The root was not broken and the socket still bled slightly, so I took the chance and pressed the tooth firmly back into place. The little man went quite white but didn't utter a sound. He gratefully swished his mouth with whisky for disinfectant purposes, though, and thriftily swallowed it.

I had bound Dougal's wound at once with a pressure bandage, and was glad to see that the bleeding had all but stopped by the time I unwrapped it. It was a clean slash, but a deep one. A tiny rim of yellow fat showed at the edge of the gaping cut, which went at least an inch deep into the muscle. No major vessels severed, thank goodness, but it would have to be stitched.

The only needle available turned out to be a sturdy thing like a slender awl, used by the drovers to mend harness. I eyed it dubiously, but Dougal merely held out his arm and looked away.

'I dinna mind blood in general,' he explained, 'but I've some objection to seein' my own.' He sat on a rock as I worked, teeth clenched hard enough to make his jaw muscles quiver. The night was turning cold, but sweat stood out on the high forehead in beads. At one point he asked me politely to stop for a moment, turned aside and was neatly sick behind a rock, then turned back and braced his arm on his knee again.

By good luck one pot-house owner had chosen to remit his rent this quarter in the form of a small keg of whisky, and it came in quite handily. I used it to disinfect some of the open wounds, and then let my patients self-medicate as they liked. I even accepted a cupful myself at the conclusion of the doctoring. I drained it with pleasure and dropped thankfully on to my blanket. The moon was sinking, and I was shivering, half with reaction and half with cold. It was a wonderful feeling to have Jamie lie down and firmly gather me in next to his large, warm body.

'Will they come back, do you think?' I asked, but he shook his head.

'Nay, it was Malcolm Grant and his two boys – it was the oldest I stuck in the leg. They'll be home in their own beds by now,' he replied. He stroked my hair and said in softer tones, 'Ye did a braw bit o' work tonight, lass. I was proud of ye.'

I rolled over and put my arms about his neck.

'Not as proud as I was. You were wonderful, Jamie. I've never seen anything like that.'

He snorted deprecatingly, but I thought he was pleased nonetheless.

'Only a raid, Sassenach. I've been doin' that since I was fourteen. It's only in fun, ye see; it's different when you're up against someone who really means to kill ye.'

'Fun,' I said a little faintly. 'Yes, quite.'

In the morning everyone behaved as usual, if moving a little more stiffly from the effects of fighting and sleeping on rocks. Everyone was in a cheerful humour, even those with minor wounds.

The general humour was improved still further when Dougal announced that we would travel only as far as the clump of woods we could see from the edge of our rocky platform. There we could water and graze the ponies, and rest a bit ourselves. I wondered whether this change of plan would affect Jamie's rendezvous with the mysterious Horrocks, but he seemed undisturbed at the announcement.

The day was overcast but not drizzling, and the air was warm. Once the new camp was made, the animals taken care of and the wounded all rechecked, everyone was left to his own devices, to sleep in the grass, to hunt or fish, or merely to stretch legs after several days in the saddle.

I was sitting under a tree talking to Jamie and Ned Gowan when one of the men-at-arms came up and flipped something into Jamie's lap. It was the dirk with the moonstone hilt.

'Yours, lad?' he asked. 'Found it in the rocks this morning.'

'I must have dropped it, in all the excitement,' I said. 'Just as well; I've no idea what to do with it. I'd likely have stabbed myself if I'd tried to use it.'

Ned eyed Jamie censoriously over his half-spectacles.

'Ye gave her a knife and didn't teach her to use it?'

'There wasna time, under the circumstances,' Jamie defended himself. 'But Ned's right, Sassenach. Ye should learn how to handle arms. There's no tellin' what may happen on the road, as ye saw last night.'

So I was marched out into the centre of a clearing and the lessons began. Seeing the activity, several of the MacKenzie men came by to investigate and stayed to offer advice. In no time I had half a dozen instructors, all arguing the fine points of technique. After a good deal of amiable discussion they agreed that Rupert was likely the best among them at dirks, and he took over the lesson.

He found a reasonably flat spot, free of rocks and pine cones, in which to demonstrate the art of dagger-wielding.

'Look, lass,' he said. He held the dagger balanced on his middle finger, resting an inch or so below the blade. 'The balance point, that's where ye want to hold it, so it fits comfortable in yer hand.' I tried it with my dagger. When I had it comfortably fitted he showed me the difference between an overhand strike and an underhanded stab.

'Generally, ye want to use the underhand; overhand is

only good when ye're comin' down on someone wi' a considerable force from above.' He eyed me speculatively, then shook his head.

'Nay, you're tall for a woman, but even if ye could reach as high as the neck ye wouldna have the force to penetrate, unless he's sittin'. Best stick to underhand.' He pulled up his shirt, revealing a substantial furry paunch already glistening with sweat.

'Now, here,' he said, pointing to the centre, just under the breastbone, 'is the spot to aim for, if ye're killin' face to face. Aim straight up and in, as hard as ye can. That'll go into the heart, and it kills wi'in a minute or two. The only problem is to avoid the breastbone; it goes down lower than ye think, and if ye get yer knife stuck in that soft bit on the tip it will hardly harm yer victim at all, but ye'll be wi'out a knife, and he'll ha' you. Murtagh! Ye ha' a skinny back; come 'ere and we'll show the lass how to stick from the back.' Spinning a reluctant Murtagh around, he yanked up the grubby shirt to show a knobbly spine and prominent ribs. He poked a blunt forefinger under the lower rib on the right, making Murtagh squeak in surprise.

'This is the spot on the back – either side. See, wi' all the ribs and such, 'tis verra difficult to hit anythin' vital when ye stab in the back. *If* ye can slip the knife between the ribs, that's one thing, but that's harder to do than ye might think. But here, under the last rib, ye stab upwards into the kidney. Get him straight up, and he'll drop like a stone.'

Rupert then set me to try stabbing in various positions and postures. As he grew winded all the men took it in turns to act as victim, obviously finding my efforts hilarious. They obligingly lay on the grass or turned their backs so I could ambush them, or leaped at me from behind, or pretended to choke me so I could try to stab them in the belly.

The spectators urged me on with cries of encouragement, and Rupert instructed me firmly not to pull back at the last moment.

'Thrust as though ye meant it, lass,' he said. 'Ye canna pull back if it's in earnest. And if any o' these laggards canna get themselves out of the way in time they deserve what they get.'

I was timid and extremely clumsy at first, but Rupert was a good teacher, very patient and good about demonstrating moves, over and over. He rolled his eyes in mock lewdness when he moved behind me and put his arm about my waist, but he was quite businesslike about taking hold of my wrist to show me the way of ripping an enemy across the eyes.

Dougal sat under a tree minding his wounded arm and making sardonic comments on the training as it progressed. It was he, though, who suggested the dummy.

'Give her something she can sink her dirk into,' he said when I had begun to show some facility at lunging and jabbing. 'It's a shock, the first time.'

'So it is,' Jamie agreed. 'Rest a bit, Sassenach, while I manage something.'

He went off to the carts with two of the men-at-arms and I could see them standing heads together, gesticulating and pulling bits of things from the loads. Thoroughly winded, I collapsed under the tree next to Dougal.

He nodded, a slight smile on his face. Like most of the men he had not bothered to shave while travelling, and a heavy growth of dark beard framed his mouth, accentuating the full lower lip.

'How is it, then?' he asked, not meaning my skill with small arms.

'Well enough,' I answered warily, not meaning knives either. Dougal's gaze flicked towards Jamie, busy with something by the carts.

'Marriage seems to suit the lad,' he observed.

'Rather healthy for him – under the circumstances,' I agreed, somewhat coldly. His lips curved at my tone.

'And you, lass, as well. A good arrangement for everyone, it seems.'

'Particularly for you and your brother. And speaking of him, just what do you think Callum's going to say when he hears about it?'

The smile widened. 'Callum? Ah, well. I should think

he'd be only too pleased to welcome such a niece to the family.'

The dummy was ready, and I went back into training. It proved to be a large bag of wool, about the size of a man's torso, with a piece of tanned bull hide wrapped around it, secured with rope. This I was to practise stabbing, first as it was tied to a tree at man-height, later as it was thrown or rolled past me.

What Jamie hadn't mentioned was that they had inserted several flat pieces of wood between the wool sack and the hide; to simulate bones, as he later explained.

The first few stabs were uneventful, though it took several tries to get through the bull hide. It was tougher than it looked. So is the skin on a man's belly, I was informed. On the next try I attempted a direct overhand strike, and hit one of the wood pieces.

I thought for a moment that my arm had suddenly fallen off. The shock of impact reverberated all the way to my shoulder, and the dirk dropped from my nerveless fingers. Everything below the elbow was numb, but an ominous tingling warned me that it wouldn't be for long.

'Jesus H. Roosevelt Christ,' I said. I stood gripping my elbow and listening to the general hilarity. Finally Jamie took me by the shoulder and massaged some feeling back into the arm, pressing the tendon at the back of the elbow and digging his thumb into the hollow at the base of my wrist.

'All right,' I said through my teeth, gingerly flexing my tingling right hand. 'What do you do when you hit a bone and lose your knife? *Is* there a standard operating procedure for that?'

'Oh, aye,' said Rupert, grinning. 'Draw your pistol wi' the left hand and shoot the bastard dead.' This resulted in more howls of laughter, which I ignored.

'All right,' I said, more or less calmly. I gestured at the long scroll-butted pistol Jamie wore on his left hip. 'Are you going to show me how to load and shoot that, then?'

'I am not.' He was firm.

I bristled a bit at this. 'Why not?'

'Because you're a woman, Sassenach.'

I felt my face flush at this. 'Oh?' I said sarcastically. 'You think women aren't bright enough to understand the workings of a gun?'

He looked levelly at me, mouth twisting a bit as he thought over various replies.

'I've a mind to let ye try it,' he said at last. 'It would serve ye right.'

Rupert clicked his tongue in annoyance at us both. 'Dinna be daft, Jamie. As for you, lass' – turning to me – 'it's not that women are stupid, though sure enough some o' 'em are; it's that they're small.'

'Eh?' I gaped stupidly at him for a moment. Jamie snorted and drew the pistol from its loop. Seen up close, it was enormous; a full eighteen inches of silvered weapon measured from stock to muzzle.

'Look,' he said, holding it in front of me. 'Ye hold it here, ye brace it on your forearm, and ye sight along here. And when ye pull the trigger it kicks like a stallion. I'm near a foot taller than you, four stone heavier, and I know what I'm doin'. It gives *me* a wicked bruise when I fire it; it might knock *you* flat on your back, if it didna catch ye in the face.' He twirled the pistol and slid it back into its loop.

'I'd let ye see for yourself,' he said, raising one eyebrow, 'but I like ye better wi' all of your teeth. You've a nice smile, Sassenach, even if ye *are* a bit feisty.'

Slightly chastened by this episode I accepted without argument the men's judgement that even the lighter small-sword was too heavy for me to wield efficiently. The tiny sock dagger was deemed acceptable, and I was provided with one of those, a wicked-looking, needle-sharp piece of black iron about three inches long, with a short hilt. I practised drawing it from its place of concealment over and over while the men watched critically, until I could sweep up my skirt, grab the knife from its place and come up in the proper crouch all in one smooth move, ending up with the knife held underhand, ready to slash across an adversary's throat.

Finally I was passed as a novice knife-wielder, and allowed

to sit down to dinner, amid general congratulations – with one exception. Murtagh shook his head dubiously.

'I still say the only good weapon for a woman is poison.'

'Perhaps,' replied Dougal, 'but it has its deficiencies in face-to-face combat.'

19

The Waterhorse

We camped the next night on the banks above Loch Ness.
It gave me an odd feeling to see the place again; so little
had changed. Or would change, I should say. The birches
and alders were the deeper green of summer, and the
flowers had changed from the fragile pinks and whites of
May blossom and woodruff to the warmer golds and yellows
of gorse and broom. The sky was a deeper blue, but the
surface of the loch was the same: a flat blue-black that
caught the reflections from the bank above and held them
trapped, colours muted under smoked glass.

There were even a few boats visible, far up the loch –
though when one drew near I saw it was a coracle, a rough
half-shell of tanned leather on a frame, not the sleek
wooden shape I was used to.

The loch had its own scent; a tangy mix of raspberry
canes, sun-warmed stone and the smell of cold dark water.
Above all there was that same feeling of lurking strangeness
about the place. The men as well as the ponies seemed to
feel it, and the air of the camp was subdued.

Having found a comfortable place for my bedroll, I
wandered down to the edge of the loch to wash my face
and hands before supper.

The bank sloped sharply down until it broke in a jumble
of large rock slabs that formed a sort of irregular jetty. It
was very peaceful under the bank, out of sight and sound
of the camp, and I sat down beneath a birch tree to enjoy
a moment's privacy. Since my hasty marriage to Jamie I was
no longer followed every moment; that much had been
accomplished.

I was idly plucking the leaves from a low-hanging branch
and tossing them out into the loch when I noticed the tiny

waves against the rocks growing stronger, as though pushed by an oncoming wind.

A great flat head broke the surface not ten feet away. I could see the water purling away from keeled scales that ran in a crest down the sinuous neck. The water was agitated for some considerable distance, and I caught a glimpse here and there of dark and massive movement beneath the surface of the loch, though the head itself stayed relatively still.

I stood quite still myself. Oddly enough I was not really afraid. I felt some faint kinship with it, a creature further from its own time than I, the flat eyes old as its ancient Eocene seas, eyes grown dim in the murky depths of its shrunken refuge. And there was a sense of familiarity mingled with its unreality. The sleek skin was a smooth deep blue, with a vivid slash of green shining with brilliant iridescence beneath the jaw. And the strange, pupil-less eyes were a deep and glowing amber. So very beautiful.

And so very different from the smaller, mud-coloured replica I remembered, adorning a diorama in the British Museum. But the shape was unmistakable. The colours of living things begin to fade with the last breath, and the soft, springy skin and supple muscle rot within weeks. But the bones sometimes remain, faithful echoes of the shape, to bear some last faint witness to the glory of what was.

Valved nostrils opened suddenly with a startling hiss of breath; a moment of suspended motion, and the creature sank again, a churning roil of waters the only testimony to its passage.

I had risen to my feet when it appeared. And unconsciously I must have moved closer in order to watch it, for I had found myself standing on one of the rock slabs that jutted out into the water, watching the dying waves fall back into the smoothness of the loch.

I stood there for a moment, looking out across the fathomless loch. 'Goodbye,' I said at last to the empty water. I shook myself and turned back to the bank.

A man was standing at the top of the slope. I was startled at first, then recognized him as one of the drovers from our party. His name was Peter, I recalled, and the bucket in his hand gave the reason for his presence. I was about to ask him whether he had seen the beast, but the expression on his face as I drew near was more than sufficient answer. His face was paler than the daisies at his feet, and tiny droplets of sweat trickled down into his beard. His eyes showed white all around like those of a terrified horse, and his hand shook so that the bucket bumped against his leg.

'It's all right,' I said as I came up to him. 'It's gone.'

Instead of finding this statement reassuring, it seemed occasion for fresh alarm. He dropped the bucket, fell to his knees before me and crossed himself.

'Ha-have mercy, lady,' he stammered. To my extreme embarrassment he then flung himself flat on his face and clutched at the hem of my dress.

'Don't be ridiculous,' I said with some asperity. 'Get up.' I prodded him gently with my toe, but he only quivered and stayed pressed to the ground like a flattened fungus. 'Get up,' I repeated. 'Stupid man, it's only a . . .' I paused, trying to think. Telling him its Latin name was unlikely to help.

'It's only a wee monster,' I said at last, and grabbing his hand tugged him to his feet. I had to fill the bucket, as (not unreasonably) he would not go near the water's edge again. He followed me back to the camp, keeping a careful distance, and scuttled off at once to tend to his animals, casting apprehensive glances over his shoulder at me as he went.

As he seemed undisposed to mention the creature to anyone else, I thought perhaps I should keep quiet as well. While Dougal, Jamie and Ned were educated men the rest were largely illiterate Highlanders from the remote crags and glens of the MacKenzie lands. They were courageous fighters and dauntless warriors, but they were also as superstitious as any primitive tribesmen from Africa or the Middle East.

So I ate my supper quietly and went to bed, conscious all the time of the wary gaze of the drover Peter.

20

Deserted Glades

Next day we turned again to the north. We were drawing closer to the rendezvous with Horrocks, and Jamie seemed abstracted from time to time, perhaps considering what importance the English deserter's news might have.

I had not seen Hugh Munro again, but I had wakened in darkness the night before to find Jamie gone from the blanket beside me. I tried to stay awake, waiting for him to return, but fell asleep as the moon began to sink. In the morning he was sound asleep beside me, and on my blanket rested a small parcel, done up in a sheet of thin paper, fastened with the tail feather of a woodpecker thrust through the sheet. Unfolding it carefully I found a large chunk of rough amber. One face of the chunk had been smoothed off and polished, and in this window could be seen the delicate dark form of a tiny dragonfly, suspended in eternal flight.

I smoothed out the wrapping. A message was incised on the grimy white surface, written in small and surprisingly elegant lettering.

'What does it say?' I asked Jamie, squinting at the odd letters and marks. 'I think it's in Gaelic.'

He raised up on one elbow, examining the paper.

'Not Gaelic. Latin. Munro was a schoolmaster once, before the Turks took him. It's a bit from Catullus,' he said.

> '. . . da mi basia mille, diende centum,
> dein mille altera, dein secunda centum . . .'

A faint blush pinkened his earlobes as he translated:

362

'Then let amorous kisses dwell
On our lips, begin and tell
A Thousand, and a Hundred, score
An Hundred, and a Thousand more.'

'Well, that's a bit more high-class than your usual valentine,' I observed, amused.

'What?' Jamie looked startled.

'Never mind,' I said hastily. 'Did Munro find Horrocks for you?'

'Oh, aye. It's arranged. I'll meet him in a small place I know in the hills, a mile or two above Lag Cruime. In four days' time, if nothing goes wrong meanwhile.'

The mention of things going wrong made me a bit nervous.

'Do you think it's safe? I mean, do you trust Horrocks?'

He sat up, rubbing the remnants of sleep from his eyes and blinking.

'An English deserter? God, no. I imagine he'd sell me to Randall as soon as he'd spit, except that he canna very well go to the English himself. They hang deserters. No, I dinna trust him. That's why I came wi' Dougal on this journey, instead of seeking out Horrocks alone. If the man's up to anything, at least I'll have company.'

'Oh.' I wasn't sure that Dougal's presence was all that reassuring, given the apparent state of affairs between Jamie and his two scheming uncles.

'Well, if you think so,' I said doubtfully. 'I don't suppose Dougal would take the opportunity to shoot you, at least.'

'He did shoot me,' Jamie said cheerfully, buttoning his shirt. 'You should know, ye dressed the wound.'

I dropped the comb I had been using.

'Dougal! I thought the English shot you!'

'Well, the English shot *at* me,' he corrected. 'And I shouldna say it was Dougal shot me; in fact, it was probably Rupert – he's the best marksman among Dougal's men. No, when we were running from the English I realized we were near the edge of the Fraser lands, and I thought I'd take my chances there. So I spurred up and cut to the left, around Dougal and the rest. There was a good deal of shooting goin' on, mind ye, but the ball that hit me came from behind. Dougal and Rupert were back of me then. And the English were all in front – in fact, when I fell off the pony I rolled down the hill and ended almost in their laps.' He bent over the bucket of water I had brought, splashing cold handfuls over his face. He shook his head to clear his eyes, then blinked at me, grinning, glistening drops clinging to his thick lashes and brows.

'Come to that, Dougal had a sore fight to get me back. I was lyin' on the ground, not fit for much, and he was standing over me, pulling on my belt with one hand to get me up and his sword in the other, going hand-to-hand with a dragoon who thought he had a certain cure for my ills. Dougal killed the man and got me on his own pony.' He shook his head. 'Everything was a bit dim to me then; all I could think of was how hard it must be on the animal, tryin' to make it up a hill like that with four hundred pounds on his back.'

I sat back, a little stunned.

'But . . . if he'd wanted to, Dougal could have killed you then.'

Jamie shook his head, taking out the straight razor he had borrowed from Dougal. He moved the bucket slightly, so the surface formed a reflecting pool, and pulling his face into the tortuous grimace men use when they shave, began to scrape his cheeks.

'No, not in front of the men. Besides, Dougal and Callum didna necessarily want me dead – especially not Dougal.'

'But – ' My head was beginning to whirl again, as it seemed to do whenever I encountered the complexities of Scottish family life.

Jamie's words were a little muffled as he stuck out his chin, tilting his head to reach the bit of stubble beneath his jaw.

'It's Lallybroch,' he explained, feeling with his free hand for stray whiskers. 'Besides being a rich bit of ground, the estate sits at a mountain pass, d'ye see. The only good pass into the hills for ten miles in either direction. Come to another Rising, it would be a valuable bit of land to control. And if I were to die before wedding, chances are the land would go back to the Frasers.'

He grinned, stroking his neck. 'No, I'm a pretty problem to the brothers MacKenzie. On the one hand, if I'm a threat to young Hamish's chieftainship, they want me safely dead. On the other, if I'm not, they want me – and my property – securely on their side if it comes to war – not wi' the Frasers. That's why they're willing to help me wi' Horrocks, ye see. I canna do much wi' Lallybroch while I'm outlawed, even though the land's still mine.'

I rolled up the blankets, shaking my head in bewilderment over the intricate – and dangerous – circumstances through which Jamie seemed to move so nonchalantly. And it struck me suddenly that not only Jamie was involved now. I looked up.

'You said that if you died before wedding, the land would go back to the Frasers,' I said. 'But you're married now. So who – '

'That's right,' he said, nodding at me with a lopsided grin. The morning sun lit his hair with flames of gold and copper. 'If I'm killed now, Sassenach, Lallybroch is yours.'

It was a beautiful sunny morning, once the mist had risen. Birds were busy in the heather and the track was wide here, for a change, and softly dusty under the ponies' hooves.

Jamie rode up close beside me as we crested a small hill. He nodded to the right.

'See that wee glade down below there?'

'Yes.' It was a small green patchwork of pines, birch and aspen, set back some distance from the road.

'There's a spring with a pool there, under the trees, and smooth grass. A very bonny place.'

I looked at him quizzically.

'A little early for dinner, isn't it?'

'That's not precisely what I had in mind.' Jamie, I had found out by accident a few days previously, had never mastered the art of winking one eye. Instead, he blinked solemnly, like a large red owl.

'And just what *did* you have in mind?' I inquired. My suspicious look met an innocent, childlike gaze of blue.

'I was just wondering what you'd look like ... on the grass ... under the trees ... by the water ... with your skirts up around your ears.'

'Er – ' I said.

'I'll tell Dougal we're going to fetch water.' He spurred up ahead, returning in a moment with the water bottles from the other ponies. I heard Rupert shout something after us in Gaelic as we rode down the hill, but couldn't make out the words.

I reached the glade first. Sliding down, I relaxed on the grass and shut my eyes against the glare of the sun. Jamie reined up beside me a moment later and swung down from the saddle. He slapped the pony and sent it away, reins dangling, to graze with mine, before dropping to his knees on the grass. I reached up and pulled him down to me.

It was a warm day, redolent with grass and flower scents. Jamie himself smelled like a fresh-plucked grass blade, sharp and sweet.

'We'll have to be quick,' I said, 'they'll be wondering why it's taking so long to get water.'

'They won't wonder,' he said, undoing my laces with a practised ease. 'They know.'

'What do you mean?'

'Did ye no hear what Rupert said as we left?'

'I heard him, but I couldn't tell what he said.' My Gaelic was improving to the point where I could understand the more common words, but conversation was still far beyond me.

'Good. It wasna fit for your ears.' Having freed my breasts he buried his face in them, sucking and biting gently until I could stand it no more and slid down beneath him, tucking my skirts up out of the way. Feeling absurdly self-conscious, I had been shy about letting him make love to me near the camp, and the woods were too thick to safely move very far from the campsite. Both of us were feeling the mild and pleasant strain of abstinence, and now, safely removed from curious eyes and ears, we came together with an impact that made my lips and fingers tingle with a rush of blood.

We were both nearing the end when Jamie froze abruptly. Opening my eyes I saw his face dark against the sun, wearing a perfectly indescribable expression. There was something black pressed against his head. My eyes at last adjusting to the glare, I saw it was a musket barrel.

'Get up, you rutting bastard.' The barrel moved sharply, jarring against Jamie's temple. Very slowly he rose to his feet. A drop of blood began to well from the graze, dark against his white face.

There were two of them; redcoat deserters from the look of their ragtag remnants of uniform. Both were armed with musket and pistol, and looked very much amused by what chance had delivered into their hands. Jamie stood with his hands raised, the barrel of a musket pressed against his chest, face carefully expressionless.

'You might ha' let 'im finish, 'Arry,' said one of the men. He grinned broadly, with a fine display of rotting teeth. 'Stoppin' in the middle like that's bad for a man's 'ealth.'

His fellow prodded Jamie in the chest with the musket.

' 'Is 'ealth's no concern o' mine. An' it won't be any concern to 'im for much longer. I've a mind to take a piece o' that' – he nodded briefly in my direction – 'but I don't care to come second to any man, let alone a Scottish whoreson like this.'

Rotten-teeth laughed. 'I bain't so bloody particular. Kill 'im, then, and get on wi' it.'

Harry, a short, stout man with a squint, considered a moment, eyeing me speculatively. I still sat on the ground, knees drawn up and skirts pressed firmly around my ankles. I had made some effort to close my bodice, but a good deal was still exposed. Finally the short man laughed and beckoned to his companion.

'No, let 'im watch. Come ower 'ere, Arnold, and 'old your musket on 'im.' Arnold obeyed, still grinning widely. Harry set his musket down on the ground and dropped his pistol belt beside it in preparation.

Pressing my skirts down, I became aware of a hard object

367

in the right-hand pocket. The dagger Jamie had given me. Could I bring myself to use it? Yes, I decided, looking at Harry's pimpled, leering face, I definitely could.

I would have to wait till the last possible second, though, and I had my doubts as to whether Jamie could control himself that long. I could see the urge to kill marked strong on his features; soon consideration of the consequences would no longer be enough to hold him back.

I didn't dare let too much show on my face, but narrowed my eyes and glared at him as hard as I could, willing him not to move. The cords stood out in his neck and his face was suffused with dark blood, but I saw an infinitesimal nod in acknowledgement of my message.

I struggled as Harry pressed me to the ground and tried to pull up my skirts, more in order to get my hand on the dagger hilt than in actual resistance. He slapped me hard across the face, ordering me to be still. My cheek burned and my eyes watered, but the dagger was now in my hand, concealed under the folds of my skirt.

I lay back, breathing heavily, and concentrated on my objective, trying to erase everything else from my mind. It would have to be in the back; the quarters were too close to try for the throat.

The filthy fingers were digging into my thighs now, wrenching them apart. In my mind I could see Rupert's blunt finger stabbing at Murtagh's ribs, and hear his voice: 'Here, lass, up under the lowest ribs, close to the backbone. Stab hard, upwards into the kidney, and he'll drop like a stone.'

It was almost time; Harry's foul breath was disgustingly warm on my face, and he was fumbling between my bared legs, intent on his goal.

'Take a good look, laddie-buck, and see how it's done,' he panted, 'I'll 'ave your slut moaning for more before – '

I whipped my left arm around his neck to hold him close; holding the knife hand high, I plunged it in as hard as I could. The shock of impact reverberated up my arm, and I nearly lost my hold on the dagger. Harry yelped and squirmed, twisting to get away. Unable to see, I had aimed too high, and the knife had skittered off a rib.

I couldn't let go now. Luckily, my legs were free of the entangling skirts. I wrapped them tightly around Harry's sweating hips, holding him down for the precious seconds I needed for another try. I stabbed again, with a desperate strength, and this time found the spot.

Rupert had been right. Harry bucked in a hideous parody of the act of love, then collapsed without a sound in a limp heap on top of me, blood jetting in diminishing spurts from the wound in his back.

Arnold's attention had been distracted for an instant by the spectacle on the ground, and an instant was more than long enough for the maddened Scotsman he held at bay. By the time I had gathered my wits sufficiently to attempt to wriggle out from under the defunct Harry, Arnold had joined his companion in death, throat neatly cut from ear to ear by the small knife that Jamie carried in his stocking.

Jamie knelt beside me, pulling me out from under the corpse. We were both shaking with nerves and shock, and we clung together without speaking for minutes. Still without speaking, he picked me up and carried me away from the two bodies, to a grassy space behind a screen of aspen.

He lowered me to the ground and sat down awkwardly beside me, collapsing as though his knees had suddenly given way. I felt a chilly isolation, as though the winter wind blew through my bones, and reached for him. He raised his head from his knees, face haggard, and stared at me as though he had never seen me before. When I put my hands on his shoulders he pulled me hard against his chest with a sound midway between a groan and a sob.

We took each other then, in a savage, urgent silence, thrusting fiercely and finishing within moments, driven by a compulsion I didn't understand, but knew we must obey, or be lost to each other for ever. It was not an act of love, but one of necessity, as though we knew that left alone, neither of us could stand. Our only strength lay in fusion, drowning the memories of death and near-rape in the flooding of the senses.

We clung together on the grass then, dishevelled, bloodstained and shivering in the sunshine. Jamie muttered something, his voice so low that I caught only the word 'sorry'.

'Not your fault,' I muttered, stroking his hair. 'It's all right, we're both all right.' I felt dreamlike, as though nothing whatever was real around me, and I dimly recognized the symptoms of delayed shock.

'Not that,' he said. 'Not that. It *was* my fault... So foolish to come here without taking proper heed. And to let you be... I didna mean that, though. I meant... I'm sorry for using ye as I did just now. To take you like that, so soon after... like some sort of animal. I'm sorry, Claire... I don't know what... I couldna help it, but... Lord, you're so cold, *mo duinne*, your hands are ice. Come then, let me warm ye.'

Shock, too, I thought fuzzily. Funny how it takes some people in talk. Others just shake quietly. Like me. I pressed his mouth against my shoulder to quiet him.

'It's all right,' I said, over and over. 'It's all right.'

Suddenly a shadow fell across us, making us both jump. Dougal stood glowering down at us, arms folded. He courteously averted his eyes while I hastily did up my laces, frowning instead at Jamie.

'Now look ye, lad, takin' your pleasure wi' your wife is all verra weel, but when it comes to leavin' us all waiting for more than an hour, and being so taen up wi' each other that ye dinna even hear me comin' – that kind o' behaviour will get ye in trouble one day, laddie. Why, someone could come up behind ye and clap a pistol to your head before ye knew – '

He stopped in his tirade to stare incredulously at me, rolling on the grass in hysterics. Jamie, red as a beetroot, led Dougal to the other side of the aspen screen, explaining in a subdued voice. I continued to whoop and giggle uncontrollably, finally stuffing a handkerchief in my mouth to muffle the noise. The sudden release of emotions, coupled with Dougal's words, had evoked a picture of Jamie's face, caught in the act as it were, that I found totally hilarious in my unhinged state. I laughed and moaned until my sides ached. Finally I sat up, wiping my eyes on my kerchief, to see Dougal and Jamie standing over me, wearing identical expressions of disapproval. Jamie hoisted me to my feet and led me, still hiccupping and snorting occasionally, to where the rest of the men were waiting with the mounts.

Except for a lingering tendency to laugh hysterically over nothing, I seemed to suffer no ill effects from our encounter with the deserters, though I became very cautious about leaving the campsite. Dougal assured me that bandits were not, in fact, that common on the Highland ways, only because there were not many travellers worth robbing, but I found myself starting nervously at sounds in the wood, and hastening back from routine chores like fetching wood and water, eager for the sight and sound of the MacKenzie men. I also found new reassurance in the sound of their snoring around me at night, and lost whatever self-consciousness I might have had about the discreet writhings that took place under our blankets.

I was still somewhat fearful of being alone when, a few days later, the time for the meeting with Horrocks arrived.

'Stay here?' I said in disbelief. 'No! I'm going with you.'

'You can't,' said Jamie patiently, once more. 'The bulk of the men will go on to Lag Cruime wi' Ned, to collect the rents as expected. Dougal and a few of the others are coming wi' me to the meeting, in case of any treachery by Horrocks. You can't be seen in the open near Lag Cruime, though; Randall's men may be about, and I wouldna put it past him to take ye by force. And as for the meeting wi' Horrocks, I've no idea what may happen. No, there's a small copse near the bend of the road – it's thick and grassy, and there's water nearby. You'll be comfortable there until I come back for ye.'

'No,' I said stubbornly. 'I'm coming with you.' Some sense of pride made me unwilling to tell him that I was frightened of being away from him. But I was willing to tell him that I was frightened *for* him.

'You said yourself you don't know what will happen with Horrocks,' I argued. 'I don't want to stay here alone, worrying all day.'

He sighed impatiently but didn't argue further. When we reached the copse, though, he leaned over and seized my pony's bridle, forcing me off the road into the grass. He slid off his mount, tying both sets of reins to a bush. Ignoring my vociferous objections, he disappeared into the trees. Stubbornly I refused to dismount. He couldn't *make* me stay, I thought.

He came down at last to the road. The others had gone on before, but Jamie, mindful of our last experience with deserted glades, wouldn't leave until he had thoroughly searched the copse, quartering methodically through the trees and swishing the tall grass with a stick. Coming back, he untied the animals and swung up into his saddle.

'It's safe,' he said. 'Ride up well into the thicket, Claire, and hide yourself and the pony. I'll be back for ye as soon as our business is done. I canna tell how long, but surely by sunset.'

'No! I'm coming with you.' I couldn't stand the thought of stewing in a forest, not knowing what was happening. I would far rather be in active danger than be left for anxious hours, waiting and wondering. And alone.

Jamie curbed his impatience to be gone. He reached over and grasped my shoulder.

'Did ye no promise to obey me?' he asked, shaking me gently.

'Yes, but – ' But only because I had to, I was going to say, but he was already urging my pony's head around towards the thicket.

'It's verra dangerous, and I'll not have ye there, Claire. I shall be busy, and if it comes to it, I can't fight and protect you at the same time.' Seeing my mutinous look, he dropped his hand to the saddlebag and began rummaging.

'What are you looking for?'

'Rope. If ye willna do as I say, I shall tie ye to a tree until I come back.'

'You wouldn't!'

'Aye, I would!' Plainly he meant it. I gave in with bad grace, and reluctantly reined in my mount. Jamie leaned to kiss me glancingly on the cheek, already turning to go.

'Take care, Sassenach. You've your dirk? Good. I shall come back as soon as I can. Oh, one more thing.'

'What's that?' I said sullenly.

'If you leave that copse before I come for ye, I'll tan your bare arse wi' my sword belt. Ye wouldna enjoy walking all the way to Leoch. Remember,' he said, pinching my cheek gently, 'I dinna make idle threats.' He didn't, either. I rode slowly towards the grove, looking back to watch him racing away, bent low over the saddle, one with the pony, the ends of his plaid flying behind.

It was cool under the trees; the pony and I both exhaled with relief as we entered the shade. It was one of those rare hot days in Scotland when the sun blazed out of a bleached muslin sky and the early haze is burnt away by eight o'clock. The copse was loud with birds; a gang of titmice was foraging in the birch clump to the left, and I could hear what I thought was a willow warbler in the near distance.

I had always been an enthusiastic amateur birdwatcher. If I were marooned here till it suited my overbearing, domineering, pig-headed jackass of a husband to finish risking his stupid neck, I'd use the time to see what I could spot.

I hobbled the pony and turned him loose to graze in the lush grass at the edge of the copse, knowing he wouldn't go far. The grass ceased abruptly a few feet from the trees, smothered by encroaching heather.

It was a glade in mixed conifers and birch, perfect for birdwatching. I wandered through it, still mentally fuming at Jamie, but growing gradually calmer as I listened for the distinctive *tsee* of a spotted flycatcher and the harsh chatter of the mistle thrush.

The glade ended quite suddenly on the far side, on the edge of a small precipice. I thrust my way through birch saplings and the sound of birdsong was drowned in rushing water. I stood on the lip of a small burn, a steep rocky ravine with waterfalls bounding down the jagged walls to splash in the brown and silver pools below. I sat down on the edge of the bank and let my feet dangle over the water, enjoying the sun on my face.

A crow shot past overhead, closely pursued by a pair of

gulls. The bulky black body zigzagged through the air, trying to avoid the dive-bombers. I smiled, watching the furious parents chivying the crow to and fro, and wondered whether crows, left to their own devices, really did fly in a straight line. That one, if it kept to a straight path, would head straight for . . .

I stopped dead.

I had been so intent on arguing with Jamie that it had not until this minute dawned on me that the situation I had been vainly trying to bring about for two months had finally occurred. I was alone. And I knew where I was. Looking across the burn, my eyes were dazzled by the morning sun blazing through the rowan trees on the far bank. So that was east. My heart began to beat faster. If we were as close as I thought to Fort William, then if I followed this small stream, I would eventually reach the Great Glen. And the Great Glen, whatever dangers it held in terms of wild beasts, outlaws and potential starvation, also provided a direct connection between Fort William and Inverness. And near Inverness was the hill I had dreamed of for weeks – Craigh na Dun.

I clenched my fists, feeling the nails dig into my palms. It was the hell of a risk. It could take weeks to make that journey on foot. And I had no shelter other than the cloak I wore, and no food whatever. I would have to depend on what I could find, steal or beg. And run the risks attendant on stealing or begging; any cottars in the Glen were unlikely to receive me with less caution than had Callum MacKenzie.

I started back into the copse, but changed my mind. I dared not take the road. This close to Fort William and the several small settlements that surrounded it, there was too much risk of meeting someone. And I could not take a pony down the precipitous course of the burn. In fact, I had some doubt that it could be managed on foot; the rock walls were sheer in some spots, plunging directly into the foaming water of the stream, with no real footing save the tops of scattered rocks sticking out of the rushing water.

I hesitated, but I could feel desperation well up from the

pit of my stomach. I might never have such an opportunity again. More than that, I might never again have the strength to take such an opportunity. I couldn't hide from myself my growing attachment to Jamie; to wait longer was to risk a greater pain from leaving – or to risk never leaving.

My stomach gave a sudden lurch as I thought of Jamie. God, how could I do it? Leave him without a word of explanation or apology? Disappear without a trace, after what he had done for me?

With that thought I finally decided to leave the pony. At least he would think I had not left him willingly; he might believe I had been killed by wild beasts – I touched the dagger in my pocket – or possibly kidnapped by outlaws. And finding no trace of me, eventually he would forget me, and wed again. Perhaps the lovely young Laoghaire, back at Leoch.

Absurdly enough I found that the thought of Jamie sharing Laoghaire's bed upset me as much as the thought of leaving him. I cursed myself for idiocy, but I couldn't help imagining her sweet round face, flushed with ardent longing, and his big hands burying themselves in that moonbeam hair . . .

I unclenched my teeth and resolutely wiped the tears off my cheeks. I hadn't time or energy for senseless reflections. I must go, and now, while I could. I knew that I would never be able to forget Jamie, but for now I must put him out of my mind, or I wouldn't be able to concentrate on the job at hand, which was tricky enough.

Cautiously I picked my way down the steep bank to the edge of the water. The noise of the rushing stream drowned out the birds in the copse above. The going was rough, but there was at least room to walk by the water's edge here. The bank was muddy, and strewn with rocks, but passable. Further down I saw that I would have to step out actually into the water and make my way precariously from rock to rock, balancing above the flood, until the bank widened enough to go ashore again.

I picked my way painfully along, estimating how much time I might have. Jamie had said only that they would return before sundown. It was three or four miles to Lag Cruime, but I had no way of knowing what the track was like, nor how long the business with Horrocks might take – if he were there. But he would be, I argued with myself. Hugh Munro had said so, and outlandish as that grotesque figure had been, Jamie plainly considered him a reliable source of information.

My foot slipped off the first rock in the stream, plunging me into icy water to the knee and soaking my skirt. I withdrew to the bank, tucked my skirts as high as I could and removed and pocketed both shoes and stockings, and set my foot again on the rock.

I found that by gripping with my toes I could manage to step from rock to rock without slipping. The bunches of my tucked-up skirt made it difficult to see where I was going to step next, though, and more than once I found myself sliding into the water. My legs were chilled, and as my feet grew numb it got harder to maintain my grip.

Luckily the bank widened again and I stepped gratefully ashore into warm, sticky mud. Short periods of more or less comfortable squelching alternated with much longer periods of precarious rock-hopping through the freezing rapids, and I found to my relief that I was much too busy to think very much about Jamie.

After a time I had the routine worked out. Step, grip, pause, look around, locate next step. Step, grip, pause, and so on. I must have become over-confident, or perhaps only tired, because I got careless and undershot my goal. My foot skidded helplessly down the near side of the slime-coated rock. I waved my arms wildly, trying to move back to the rock I had been on, but my balance had shifted too far. Skirts, petticoats, dagger and all, I plunged into the water.

And kept on plunging. While the stream overall was only a foot or two deep, there were intermittent deep pools where the scouring water had scooped out deep depressions in the bed. The rock on which I'd lost my footing was perched on the edge of one such pool, and when I hit the water I sank like a rock myself.

376

I was so stunned by the shock of the icy water rushing into my nose and mouth that I didn't cry out. Silvery bubbles shot out of the bodice of my dress and rushed past my face towards the surface. The fabric soaked through almost at once and the freezing grip of the water paralysed my breathing.

I began almost at once to fight my way up to the surface, but the weight of my garments pulled me down. I yanked frantically at the laces of my bodice, but there was no hope of getting everything off before I drowned. I made a number of savage and uncharitable silent observations about dressmakers, women's fashions and the stupidity of long skirts, while kicking frenziedly to keep the entangling folds away from my legs.

The water was crystal clear. My fingers brushed the rock wall, sliding through the dark slick streamers of weed and algae. Slippery as waterweed, that's what Jamie said about my . . .

The thought jarred me out of my panic. Suddenly I realized that I shouldn't be exhausting myself trying to kick to the surface. The pool couldn't be more than eight or nine feet deep; what I needed to do was relax, float down to the bottom, brace my feet and spring upwards. With luck that would get my head clear for a breath, and even if I went down again I could continue bouncing off the bottom until I worked my way close enough to the edge to get a decent grip on a rock.

The descent was agonizingly slow. As I was no longer fighting upwards, my skirts rose round me in billows, floating in front of my face. I batted them away; I must keep my face clear. My lungs were bursting and there were dark spots behind my eyes by the time my feet touched the smooth bottom of the pool. I let my knees bend slightly, pressing my skirts around me, then shoved upwards with all my might.

It worked, just barely. My face broke the surface at the top of my leap, and I had just time for the briefest of life-saving gulps before the water closed over me again. But it was enough. I knew I could do it again. I pressed my arms down to my sides to streamline myself and make the descent more rapid. Once more, Beauchamp, I thought. Bend your knees, brace yourself, jump!

I shot up, arms extended upwards. I had seen a flash of green overhead when I broke water last; there must be a tree overhanging the water. Perhaps I could get hold of a branch.

As my face broke water something seized my outstretched hand. Something hard, warm and reassuringly solid. Another hand.

Coughing and spluttering, I groped blindly with my free hand, too glad of rescue to regret the interruption of my escape attempt. Glad at least until, wiping the hair out of my eyes, I looked up into the beefy, anxious Lancashire face of young Corporal Hawkins.

21

Un Mauvais Quart d'heure after Another

I delicately removed a strand of still-damp waterweed from my sleeve and placed it squarely in the centre of the dispatch. Then, seeing the inkstand handy, I picked up the weed and dipped it in, using the result to paint interesting patterns on the official-looking document. Getting fully into the spirit of the thing, I finished off my masterpiece with a rude word, carefully sprinkled it with sand and blotted it with another dispatch before propping it up against the bank of pigeon-holes.

I stepped back to admire the effect, then looked around for any other diversions that might take my mind off the impending advent of Captain Randall.

Not bad for the private office of a captain, I thought, eyeing the paintings on the wall, the silver desk fittings and the thick rug. I moved back on to the rug in order to drip more effectively. The ride to Fort William had dried my outer garments fairly well, but the underlying layers of petticoat were still wringing wet.

I opened a small cupboard behind the desk and discovered the Captain's spare wig, neatly bestowed on one of a pair of wrought-iron stands, with a matched silverbacked set of looking glass, military brushes and tortoiseshell comb laid out in orderly ranks before it. Carrying the wig stand over to the desk I gently sifted the remaining contents of the sander over it before replacing it in the cupboard.

I was seated behind the desk, comb in hand, studying my reflection in the looking glass, when the Captain came in. He gave me a glance that took in my dishevelled appearance, the rifled cupboard and the disfigured dispatch.

Without blinking he drew up a chair and sat down across from me, lounging casually with one booted foot resting on the opposite knee. A riding crop dangled from one fine, aristocratic hand. I watched the braided tip, black and scarlet, as it swung slowly back and forth over the carpet.

'The idea has its attractions,' he said, watching my eyes follow the sweep of the whip. 'But I could probably think of something better, given a few moments to collect myself.'

'I daresay you could,' I said, fingering a thick sheaf of hair out of my eyes. 'But you aren't allowed to flog women, are you?'

'Only under certain circumstances,' he said politely. 'Which your situation doesn't meet – yet. That's rather public, though. I had thought we might get better acquainted in private, first.' He reached to the sideboard behind him for a decanter.

We sipped the claret in silence, eyeing each other over the wine.

'I had forgotten to offer you felicitations on your marriage,' he said suddenly. 'Forgive my lack of manners.'

'Think nothing of it,' I said graciously. 'I'm sure my husband's family will be most obliged to you for offering me hospitality.'

'Oh, I rather doubt it,' he said with an engaging smile. 'But then, I didn't think I'd tell them you were here.'

'What makes you think they don't know?' I asked, beginning to feel rather hollow despite my earlier resolve to brazen it out. I cast a quick glance at the window, but it was on the wrong side of the building. The sun wasn't visible, but the light looked yellow; perhaps mid-afternoon? How long before Jamie found my abandoned pony? And how long after that before he followed my trail into the stream – and promptly lost it? Disappearing without a trace had its drawbacks. In fact, unless Randall decided to send word of my whereabouts to Dougal, there was no way on earth the Scots could know where I had gone.

'If they knew,' the Captain said, arching one elegantly shaped brow, 'they would presumably be calling on me already. Considering the sorts of names Dougal MacKenzie applied to me on the occasion of our last meeting, I scarcely think he feels me a suitable chaperon for a kinswoman. And the Clan MacKenzie seems to think you're of such value that they'd rather adopt you as one of their own than see you fall into my hands. I can hardly imagine they would allow you to languish in durance vile here.'

He looked mc over disapprovingly, taking in every detail of my waterlogged costume, unkempt hair and generally dishevelled appearance.

'Damned if I know what they want you for,' he observed. 'Or, if you're so valuable to them, why the devil they let you wander about the countryside by yourself. I thought even barbarians took better care of their womenfolk than that.' A sudden gleam came into his eyes. 'Or have you perhaps decided to part company with them?' He sat back, intrigued by this new speculation.

'The wedding night was more of a trial than you antici- pated?' he inquired. 'I must confess I was somewhat put out to hear that you preferred the alternative of bedding one of those hairy, half-naked savages to further discussions with me. That argues a high devotion to duty, madam, and I must congratulate whomever employs you on their ability to inspire it. But' – he leaned still further back in his chair, balancing the claret glass on his knee – 'I am afraid I still must insist on the name of your employer. If you have indeed parted company with the MacKenzies, the most likely supposition is that you're a French agent. But whose?'

He stared at me intently, like a snake hoping to fascinate a bird. By now I had had enough claret to fill part of the hollow space inside me, though, and I stared back.

'Oh,' I said, elaborately polite, 'I'm included in this con- versation, am I? I thought you were doing quite well by yourself. Pray continue.'

The graceful line of his mouth tightened a bit and the deep crease at the corner grew deeper, but he didn't say anything. Setting his glass aside, he rose, and taking off his wig went to the cupboard, where he placed it on the empty stand. I saw him pause for a moment as he saw the grains of sand adorning his other wig, but his expression didn't change noticeably.

Unwigged, his hair was dark, thick, fine-textured and shiny. It was also disturbingly familiar-looking, though it was shoulder length and tied back with a blue silk ribbon. He removed this, plucked the comb from the desk and tidied the hair flattened by the wig, then retied the ribbon with some care. I helpfully held up the looking glass so that he could judge the final effect. He took it from me in a marked manner and restored it to its place, shutting the cupboard door with what was almost a slam.

I couldn't tell whether this delay was in hopes of unnerving me – in which case, it was working – or merely because he couldn't decide what to do next.

The tension was slightly relieved by the entrance of a servant bearing a tray of tea things. Still silent, Randall poured out and offered me a cup. We sipped some more.

'Don't tell me,' I said finally. 'Let me guess. It's a new form of persuasion you've invented – torture by bladder. You ply me with drinkables until I promise to tell you anything in exchange for five minutes with a chamber pot.'

He was so taken by surprise that he actually laughed. It quite transformed his face, and I had no difficulty seeing why there were so many scented envelopes with feminine handwriting in the bottom left-hand drawer of his desk. Having let the facade crack, he didn't stifle the laugh but let it go. Finished, he stared at me again, a half smile lingering on his mouth.

'Whatever else you may be, madam, at least you're a diversion,' he remarked. He yanked at a bellpull hanging by the door, and when the servant reappeared, instructed him to convey me to the necessary facilities.

'But take care not to lose her on the way, Thompson,' he added, opening the door for me with a sardonic bow.

I leaned weakly against the door of the privy to which I was shown. Being out of his presence was a relief, but a short-lived one. I had had ample opportunity to judge Randall's true character, both from the stories I had heard and from personal experience. But there were those damnable flashes of Frank that kept showing through the gleaming, ruthless exterior. It had been a mistake to make him laugh, I thought.

I sat down, ignoring the stench in my concentration on the problem at hand. Escape seemed unlikely. The vigilant Thompson aside, Randall's office was in a building located near the centre of the compound. And while the fort itself was no more than a stone stockade, the walls were ten feet high and the double gates well guarded.

I thought of feigning illness and remaining in my refuge, but dismissed it – and not only because of the unpleasantness of the surroundings. The unpalatable truth was that there was little point in delaying tactics, unless I had something to delay for, and I didn't. No one knew where I was, and Randall didn't mean to tell anyone. I was his, for as long as he cared to amuse himself with me. Once again I regretted making him laugh. A sadist with a sense of humour was particularly dangerous.

Thinking frantically in search of something useful I might know about the Captain, I latched on to a name. Half heard and carelessly remembered, I hoped I had it right. It was a pitifully small card to play, but the only one I had. I drew a deep breath, hastily let it out again, and stepped out of my sanctuary.

Back in the office I stirred my tea carefully and blew on it. Having drawn out the ceremony as long as I could, I was forced to look at Randall. He was sitting back in his favourite pose, cup elegantly suspended in midair, the better to look at me over.

'Well?' I said. 'You needn't worry about spoiling my appetite, since I haven't got one. What do you mean to do about me?'

He smiled and took a careful sip of tea before replying. 'Nothing.'

'Really?' I lifted my brows in surprise. 'Invention failed you, has it?'

'I shouldn't care to think so,' he said, polite as usual. His eyes travelled over me once more, far from polite.

'No,' he said, his gaze lingering on the edge of my bodice

where the tucked kerchief left the upper swell of my breasts visible, 'much as I would like to give you a badly needed lesson in manners, I am afraid the pleasure must be postponed indefinitely. I'm sending you to Edinburgh with the next posting of dispatches. And I shouldn't care to have you arrive damaged in any visible way; my superiors might consider it careless of me.'

'Edinburgh?' I couldn't hide my surprise.

'Yes. You've heard of the Tolbooth, I imagine?'

I had. One of the most noisome and notorious prisons of the period, it was famous for filth, crime, disease and darkness. A good)many of the prisoners held there died before they could be brought to trial. I swallowed hard, forcing down the bitter bile that had risen at the back of my throat, mingling with the swallow of tea.

Randall sipped his own tea, pleased with himself.

'You should feel quite cosy there. After all, you seem to prefer a certain dank squalor in your surroundings.' He cast a condemning glance at the soggy hem of my petticoat, sagging below my gown. 'Should be quite homelike, after Castle Leoch.'

I rather doubted that the cuisine at the Tolbooth was as good as that to be had at Callum's board. And general questions of amenities aside, I couldn't – *could not* – allow him to send me to Edinburgh. Once immured in the Tolbooth, I would never get back to the stone circle.

The time to play my card had arrived. Now or never. I raised my own cup.

'Just as you like,' I said calmly. 'What do you suppose the Duke of Sandringham will have to say about it?'

He upset the teacup on his doeskin lap and made several very gratifying noises.

'*Tsk*,' I said reprovingly.

He subsided, glaring. The teacup lay on its side, its brown contents soaking into the small leaf-patterned rug at his feet, but he made no move towards the bellpull. A small muscle jumped in the side of his neck.

I had already found the pile of starched handkerchiefs in

the upper left-hand drawer of the desk, alongside an enamelled snuffbox. I pulled one out and handed it to him.

'I do hope it doesn't stain,' I said sweetly.

'No,' he said, ignoring the handkerchief. He eyed me
closely. 'No, it isn't possible.'

'Why not?' I asked, affecting nonchalance, wondering
what wasn't possible.

'I would have been told. And if *you* were working for
Sandringham, why the devil would you act in such a damned
ridiculous manner?'

'Perhaps the Duke is testing your loyalty,' I suggested at
random, preparing to leap to my feet if necessary. His fists
were bunched at his sides and the discarded riding crop
was within much too easy a reach on the desk nearby.

He snorted in response to this suggestion.

'*You* may be testing my gullibility. Or my tolerance to
irritation. Both, madam, are extremely low.' His eyes narrowed speculatively and I braced myself for a quick dash.

He lunged, and I flung myself to one side. Getting hold
of the teapot, I threw it at him. He dodged, and it hit the
door with a satisfying crash. The servant, who must have
been lingering just outside, poked a startled head in.

Breathing heavily, the Captain motioned him impatiently
into the room.

'Hold her,' he ordered brusquely, crossing towards the
desk. I began to breathe deeply, both in hopes of calming
myself and in anticipation of not being able to do it in a
moment.

Instead of hitting me, though, he merely pulled out the
lower right-hand drawer, which I had not had time to investigate, and pulled out a long strand of thin rope.

'What kind of gentleman keeps rope in his desk drawers?'
I inquired indignantly.

'A prepared one, madam,' he murmured, tying my wrists
securely behind me.

'Go,' he said impatiently to the servant, jerking his head
towards the door. 'And don't come back, no matter what
you hear.'

This sounded distinctly ominous, and my forebodings

385

were abundantly justified as he reached into the drawer once more.

There is something unnerving about a knife. Otherwise brave men will shrink from a naked blade. I shrank myself, until my bound hands collided with the whitewashed wall. The wicked gleaming point lowered and pressed against my breast.

'Now,' he said pleasantly, 'you are going to tell me everything you know about the Duke of Sandringham.' The blade pressed a little harder, making a dent in the fabric of my gown. 'Take as long as you like about it, my dear. I am in no hurry whatsoever.' There was a small *pop!* as the point punctured the fabric. I felt it, cold as fear, a tiny spot directly over my heart.

Randall slowly drew the knife in a semicircle under one breast. The serge came free and fell away with a flutter of white chemise, and my breast sprang out. Randall seemed to have been holding his breath; he exhaled slowly now, his eyes fixed on mine.

I sidled away from him, but there was very little room to manoeuvre. I ended up pressed against the desk, bound hands gripping the edge. If he came close enough, I thought, I might be able to rock backwards on my hands and kick the knife out of his hand. I doubted that he meant to kill me; certainly not until he had found out just what I knew about his relations with the Duke. Somehow that conclusion was of relatively little comfort.

He smiled, with that unnerving resemblance to Frank's smile; that lovely smile which I had seen charm students and melt the stoniest college administrator. Possibly under other circumstances, I would have found this man charming, but just at present . . . no.

He moved in fast, thrusting a knee between my thighs and pushing my shoulders back. Unable to keep my balance, I fell heavily backwards on the desk, crying out as I landed painfully on my bound wrists. He pressed himself between my legs, scrabbling with one hand to raise my skirts while the other fastened on my bared breast, rolling and pinching. I kicked frantically but my skirts got in the way. He grasped my foot and ran a hand up my leg, pushing damp petticoats, skirt and chemise out of the way, tossing them up above my waist. His hand dropped to his breeches.

Shades of Harry the deserter, I thought furiously. What in God's name is the British army coming to? Glorious traditions, my Aunt Fanny.

In the midst of an English garrison, screaming was unlikely to attract any helpful attention, but I filled my lungs and had a try, more as a token protest than anything else. I had expected a slap or shake in return, to shut me up. Instead, unexpectedly, he appeared to like it.

'Go ahead and scream, sweeting,' he murmured, busy with his flies. 'I'll enjoy it much more if you scream.'

I looked him straight in the eye and snapped 'Get stuffed!' with perfect clarity and terrible inaptness.

A lock of dark hair came loose and fell across his forehead in rakish disarray. He looked so like his six-times-great-grandson that I was seized by a horrible impulse to open my legs and respond to him. He twisted my breast savagely and the impulse disappeared at once.

I was furiously angry, disgusted, humiliated and revolted, but curiously not very frightened. I felt a heavy flopping movement against my leg and suddenly realized why. He wasn't going to enjoy it *unless* I screamed – and possibly not then.

'Oh, like that, is it?' I said, and was rewarded at once with a sharp slap across the face. I shut my mouth grimly and turned my head away lest I be tempted into any more injudicious remarks. I realized that rape or not, I was in considerable danger from his unstable temper. Looking away from the sight of Randall, I caught a sudden flicker of movement at the window.

'I'll thank ye,' said a cool, level voice, 'to take your hands off my wife.' Randall froze with a hand still on my breast. Jamie was crouched in the window frame, a large, brass-handled pistol braced across one forearm.

Randall stood frozen for a second, as though unable to believe his ears. As his head turned slowly towards the window his right hand, shielded from Jamie's view, left my breast, sliding stealthily towards the knife which he had laid on the desk next to my head.

'*What* did you say?' he said incredulously. As his hand fastened on the knife he turned far enough to see who had spoken. He stopped again for a moment, staring, then began to laugh.

'Lord help us, it's the young Scottish wildcat! I thought I'd dealt with you once and for all! Back healed after all, did it? And this is *your* wife, you say? Quite a tasty little wench, she is, quite like your sister.'

Still shielded by his partly turned body, Randall's knife-hand swivelled; the blade was now pointed at my throat. I could see Jamie over his shoulder, braced in the window like a cat about to spring. The pistol barrel didn't waver, nor did he change expression. The only clue to his emotions was the dusky red creeping up his throat; his collar was unbuttoned and the small scar on his neck flamed crimson.

Almost casually Randall slowly raised the knife into view, point almost touching my throat. He half turned towards Jamie.

'Perhaps you'd better toss that pistol over here – unless you're weary of married life. If you'd prefer to be a widower, of course . . .' Their eyes locked tight as a lover's embrace, neither man moved for a long minute. Finally Jamie's body relaxed its springlike tension. He let out his breath in a long sigh of resignation and tossed the pistol into the room. It hit the floor with a clunk and slid almost to Randall's feet.

Randall bent and scooped up the gun in a quicksilver motion. As soon as the knife left my throat I tried to sit up, but he placed a hand on my chest and shoved me flat again. He held me down with one hand, using the other to aim the pistol at Jamie. The discarded knife lay somewhere on the floor near my feet, I thought. Now, if only I had prehensile toes . . . The dirk in my pocket was as unreachable as if it were on Mars.

The smile had not left Randall's features since Jamie's appearance. Now it broadened, enough to show the pointed dogteeth.

'Well, that's a bit better.' The pressing hand left my chest to return to the swelling flies of his breeches. 'I was engaged when you arrived, my dear fellow. You'll forgive me if I get on with what I was doing before I attend to you.'

The red colour had spread completely over Jamie's face but he stood motionless with the gun pointed at his middle. As Randall finished his manœuvres Jamie launched himself at the open mouth of the pistol. I tried to scream, to stop him, but my mouth was dry with terror. Randall's knuckles whitened as he squeezed the trigger.

The hammer clicked on an empty chamber, and Jamie's fist drove into Randall's stomach. There was a dull crunching sound as his other fist splintered the officer's nose and a fine spray of blood spattered my skirt. Randall's eyes rolled up in his head and he dropped to the floor like a stone.

Jamie was behind me, pulling me up, sawing at the rope around my wrists.

'You bluffed your way in here with an *empty* gun?' I croaked hysterically.

'If it were loaded I would ha' just shot him in the first place, wouldn't I?' Jamie hissed.

Feet were coming down the corridor towards the office. The rope came free and Jamie yanked me to the window. It was an eight-foot drop to the ground, but the footsteps were almost to the door. We jumped together.

I landed with a bone-shaking jar and rolled in a tumble of skirts and petticoats. Jamie jerked me to my feet and pressed me against the wall of the building. Feet were passing the corner of the building; six soldiers came into view but didn't look in our direction.

As soon as they were safely past, Jamie took my hand and motioned towards the other corner. We sidled along the building, stopping short of the corner. I could see where we were now. About twenty feet away steps led up to a platform that ran along the inside of the fort's outer wall. He nodded towards it; this was our objective.

He brought his head close to mine and whispered, 'When ye hear an explosion, run like hell and get up that stair. I'll be behind ye.'

I nodded understanding. My heart was hammering; glancing down, I saw that one breast was still exposed. Not much to be done about it just at present. I rucked up my skirts, ready to run.

There was an almighty roar from the other side of the building, like a mortar explosion. Jamie gave me a shove and I was off, running as fast as I could go. I jumped for the steps and scrambled up, hearing Jamie close behind.

Turning at the top, I had a bird's-eye view of the fort. Black smoke was billowing up from a small building near the far wall, and men were running towards it from every direction.

Jamie popped up beside me. 'This way.' He ran crouching along the platform, and I followed. We stopped near the flag staff set in the wall. The ensign flapped heavily above us, halyard beating a rhythmic tattoo against the pole. Jamie was peering over the wall, looking for something.

I looked back over the camp. The men were clustering at the small building, milling and shouting. Off to one side I spotted a small wooden platform, set three or four feet high, with steps leading up. A heavy wooden post rose out of the centre, cross-beamed, with rope manacles dangling from the arms of the cross.

Suddenly Jamie gave a whistle; looking over the wall, I saw Rupert, mounted and leading Jamie's pony. He looked up at the sound of the whistle and manœuvred the ponies close to the wall below us.

Jamie was cutting the halyard from the flagpole. The heavy red and blue folds of the flag drooped and slid down, landing with a swishing thud next to me. Twisting a rope end rapidly around the foot of the pole, Jamie tossed the rest down the outside of the wall.

'Come on!' he said. 'Hold tight with both hands, brace your feet against the wall! Go!' I went, bracing my feet and paying out rope; the thin cordage slipped and burned in my hands. I dropped next to the ponies and hurried to mount. Jamie vaulted into the saddle behind me a moment later and we took off at a gallop, the rest of our men soon joining us.

We slowed our pace a mile or two from the camp, when it became apparent that we had lost any pursuers. After a short conference Dougal decided that we had better head north towards safety.

It was mid-afternoon by then; we set off at a steady pace, our pony with its double load lagging slightly behind the others. My pony, I supposed, was still happily eating grass in the copse, waiting to be led home by whoever was lucky enough to find it.

'How did you find me?' I asked. I was beginning to shake in reaction, and folded my arms around myself to still the quivering. My clothes had dried by this time, but I felt a chill that went bone deep.

'I thought better of leaving ye alone, and sent a man back to stay wi' ye. He didna see ye leave, but he saw the English soldiers cross the ford, and you wi' them.' Jamie's voice was cold. I couldn't blame him, I supposed. My teeth were beginning to chatter.

'I'm s-surprised that you didn't just think I was an English spy and l-leave me there.'

'Dougal wanted to. But the man who saw ye with the soldiers said you were struggling. I had to go and see, at least.' He glanced down at me, not changing expression.

'You're lucky, Sassenach, that I saw what I did in that room. At least Dougal must admit that you're not in league wi' the English.'

'D-Dougal, eh? And what about you? Wh-what do *you* think?' I demanded.

He did not reply but only snorted briefly. He did at last take pity on me to the extent of jerking off his plaid and flinging it over my shoulders, but he would not put his arm around me nor touch me more than strictly necessary. He rode in grim silence, handling the reins with an angry jerkiness quite unlike his usual smooth grace.

Upset and unsettled myself, I was in no frame of mind to put up with moods.

'Well, what is it, then? What's the matter?' I asked impatiently. 'Don't sulk, for heaven's sake!' I spoke more sharply than I intended, and felt him stiffen still further.

391

Suddenly he turned the pony's head aside and reined up at the side of the track. Before I knew what was happening he had dismounted and jerked me from the saddle as well. I landed awkwardly, staggering to keep my balance as my feet hit the ground.

Dougal and the others paused, seeing us stop. Jamie made a short, sharp gesture, sending them on, and Dougal waved in acknowledgement. 'Don't take too long,' he called, and they set off again.

Jamie waited until they were out of earshot. Then he yanked me around to face him. He was clearly furious, on the verge of explosion. I felt my own wrath rising; what right did he have to treat me like this?

'Sulking!' he said. 'Sulking, is it? I'm using all the self-control I've got to keep from shakin' ye till your teeth rattle, and you tell me not to sulk!'

'What in the name of God is the matter with you?' I asked angrily. I tried to shake off his grip but his fingers dug into my upper arms like the teeth of a trap.

'What's the matter wi' me? I'll tell ye what the matter is, since ye want to know!' he said through clenched teeth. 'I'm tired of having to prove over and over that you're no English spy. I'm tired of having to watch ye every minute, for fear of what foolishness you'll try next. And I'm *verra* tired of people trying to make me watch while they rape you! I dinna enjoy it a bit!'

'And you think *I* enjoy it?' I yelled. 'Are you trying to make out it's *my* fault?!' At this he did shake me slightly.

'It *is* your fault! Did ye stay put where I ordered ye to stay this mornin', this would never have happened! But no, ye won't listen to me, I'm no but your husband, why mind *me*? You take it into your mind to do as ye damn please, and next I ken, I find ye flat on your back wi' your skirts up, an' the worst scum in the land between your legs, on the point of takin' ye before my eyes!' His Scots accent, usually slight, was growing broader by the second, sure sign that he was upset, had I needed any further indication.

We were almost nose to nose by this time, shouting into

392

each other's face. Jamie was flushed with fury and I felt the blood rising in my own face.

'It's your own fault, for ignoring me and suspecting me all the time! I told you the truth about who I am! And I told you there was no danger in my going with you, but would you listen to *me*? No! I'm only a woman, why should you pay any attention to what I say? Women are only fit to do as they're told, and follow orders, and sit meekly around with their hands folded, waiting for the *men* to come back and tell them what to do!'

He shook me again, unable to control himself.

'And if ye'd done that, we wouldna be on the run, with a hundred redcoats on our tail! God, woman, I dinna know whether to strangle ye or throw ye on the ground and hammer ye senseless, but by Jesus I want to do *something* to you.'

At this I made a determined effort to kick him in the balls. He dodged, and jammed his own knee between my legs, effectively preventing any further attempts.

'Try that again and I'll slap you till your ears ring,' he growled.

'You're a brute and a fool,' I panted, struggling to escape his grip on my shoulders. 'Do you think I went out and got captured by the English on purpose?'

'I do think ye did it on purpose, to get back at me for what happened in the glade!'

My mouth fell open.

'In the glade? With the English deserters?'

'Aye! Ye think I should ha' been able to protect ye there, an' you're right. But I couldna do it; you had to do it yourself, and now you're tryin' to make me pay for it by deliberately putting yourself, *my* wife, in the hands of a man that's shed my blood!'

'*Your* wife! *Your* wife! You don't care a thing about me! I'm just your property; it only matters to you because you think I belong to you, and you can't stand to have someone else take something that belongs to you!'

'Ye *do* belong to me,' he roared, digging his fingers into

my shoulders like spikes. 'And you *are* my wife, whether ye like it or no.'

'I don't like it! I don't like it a bit! But that doesn't matter either, does it? As long as I'm there to warm your bed you don't care what I think or how I feel! That's all a wife is to you – something to stick your cock into when you feel the urge!'

At this his face went dead white and he began to shake me in earnest. My head jerked violently and my teeth clacked together, making me bite my tongue painfully.

'Let go of me!' I shouted. 'Let go, you' – I deliberately used the words of Harry the deserter, trying to hurt him – 'you rutting bastard!' He did let go, and fell back a pace, eyes blazing.

'Ye foul-tongued bitch! Ye'll no speak to me that way!'

'I'll speak any way I want to! You can't tell me what to do!'

'Seems I can't! Ye'll do as ye wish, no matter who ye hurt by it, won't ye? Ye selfish, wilful – '

'It's your bloody pride that's hurt!' I shouted. 'I saved us both from those deserters in the glade, and you can't stand it, can you? You just stood there! If I hadn't had a knife we'd both be dead by now!'

Until I spoke the words I had had no idea that I had been angry with him for failing to protect me from the English deserters. In a more rational mood the thought would never have entered my mind. It wasn't his fault, I would have said. It was just luck that I had the knife, I would have said. But now I realized that fair or not, rational or not, I *did* somehow feel that it was his responsibility to protect me, and that he had failed me. Perhaps because *he* so clearly felt that way.

He stood glaring at me, panting with emotion. When he spoke again his voice was low and ragged with passion.

'You saw that post in the yard of the fort?' I nodded shortly.

'Well, I was tied to that post, tied like an animal, and whipped till my blood ran! I'll carry the scars from it till I die. If I'd not been lucky as the devil this afternoon that's the least as would have happened to me. Likely they'd have flogged me, then hanged me.' He swallowed hard, and went on.

'I knew that, and I didna hesitate for one second to go into that place after you, even thinking that Dougal might be right! Do ye know where I got the gun I used?' I shook my head numbly, my own anger beginning to fade. 'I killed a guard near the wall. He fired at me; that's why it was empty. He missed and I killed him wi' my dirk; left it sticking in his wishbone when I heard you cry out. I would have killed a dozen men to get to you, Claire.' His voice cracked.

'And when ye screamed, I went to you, armed wi' nothing but an empty gun and my two hands.' Jamie was speaking a little more calmly now, but his eyes were still wild with pain and rage. I was silent. Unsettled by the horror of my encounter with Randall, I had not at all appreciated the desperate courage it had taken for him to come into the fort after me.

He turned away suddenly, shoulders slumping.

'You're right,' he said quietly. 'Aye, you're quite right.' Suddenly the rage was gone from his voice, replaced by a tone I had never heard in him before, even in the extremities of physical pain.

'My pride is hurt. And my pride is about all I've got left to me.' He leaned his forearms against a rough-barked pine and let his head drop on to them, exhausted. His voice was so low I could barely hear him.

'You're tearin' my guts out, Claire.'

Something very similar was happening to my own. Tentatively I came up behind him. He didn't move, even when I slipped my arms around his waist. I rested my cheek on his bowed back. His shirt was damp, sweated through with the intensity of his passion, and he was trembling.

'I'm sorry,' I said simply. 'Please forgive me.' He turned then, to hold me tightly. I felt his trembling ease bit by bit.

'Forgiven, lass,' he murmured at last into my hair. Releasing me, he looked down at me, sober and formal.

'I'm sorry too,' he said. 'I'll ask your pardon for what I

said; I was sore, and I said more nor I meant. Will ye forgive
me too?' After his last speech I hardly felt that there was
anything for me to forgive, but I nodded and pressed his
hands.

'Forgiven.'

In an easier silence we mounted again. The path was
straight for a long way here, and far ahead I could see a
small cloud of dust that must be Dougal and the other men.

Jamie was back with me again; he held me with one arm
as we rode, and I felt safer. But there was still a vague
sense of injury and constraint; things were not yet healed
between us. We had forgiven each other, but our words still
hung in memory, not to be forgotten.

22

Reckonings

We reached a village inn well after dark. Dougal closed his eyes briefly in pain as he paid the innkeeper; it would take quite a bit of extra silver to ensure his silence as to our presence.

The silver, however, also ensured a hearty supper with plenty of ale. Despite the food, supper was a grim affair, eaten mostly in silence. Sitting there in my ruined gown, modestly covered by Jamie's extra shirt, I was plainly in disgrace. Except for Jamie the men behaved as though I were completely invisible, and even Jamie did no more than shove bread and meat in my direction from time to time. It was a relief at last to go up to our chamber, small and cramped though it was.

I sank on the bed with a sigh, disregarding the state of the bedclothes.

'I'm done in. It's been a long day.'

'Aye, it has that.' Jamie unfastened his collar and cuffs and unbuckled his sword belt, but made no move to undress further. He pulled the strap from the scabbard and doubled it, flexing the leather meditatively.

'Come to bed, Jamie. What are you waiting for?'

He came to stand by the bed, swinging the leather belt gently back and forth.

'Well, lass, I'm afraid we've a matter still to settle between us before we sleep tonight.' I felt a sudden stab of apprehension.

'What is it?'

He didn't answer at once. Deliberately not sitting down on the bed by me, he pulled up a stool and sat facing me instead.

'Do ye realize, Claire,' he said quietly, 'that all of us came close to bein' killed this afternoon?'

I looked down at the quilt, shamefaced. 'Yes, I know. My fault. I'm sorry.'

'Aye, so ye realize,' he said. 'Do ye know that if a man among us had done such a thing, to put the rest in danger, he would ha' likely had his ears cropped, or been flogged, if not killed outright?' I blanched at this.

'No, I didn't know.'

'Well, I know as you're not yet familiar wi' our ways, and it's some excuse. Still, I did tell ye to stay hid, and had ye done so it would never have happened. Now the English will be lookin' high and low for us; we shall have to lie hid during the days and travel at night now.'

He paused. 'And as for Captain Randall . . . aye, that's something else again.'

'He'll be looking for you especially, you mean, now that he knows you're here?' He nodded absently, looking off into the fire.

'Aye. He . . . it's personal with him, ye know?'

'I'm so sorry, Jamie,' I said. Jamie dismissed this with a wave of the hand.

'Eh, if it were only me ye'd hurt by it, I wouldna say more about it. Though since we're talkin'' – he shot me a sharp glance – 'I'll tell ye that it near killed me to see that animal with his hands on you.' He looked off into the fire, grim-faced, as though reliving the afternoon's events.

I thought of telling him about Randall's . . . difficulties, but was afraid it would do more harm than good. I desperately wanted to hold Jamie and beg him to forgive me, but I didn't dare to touch him. After a long moment of silence he sighed and stood up, slapping the belt lightly against his thigh.

'Well, then,' he said. 'Best get on wi' it. You've done considerable damage by crossing my orders, and I'm going to punish ye for it, Claire. Ye'll recall what I told ye when I left ye this morning?' I recalled all right, and I hastily flung myself across the bed so my back was pressed to the wall.

'What do you mean?'

'Ye know quite well what I mean,' he said firmly. 'Kneel down by the bed and lift your skirts, lass.'

'I'll do no such thing!' I took a good hold on the bedpost with both hands and wormed my way further into the corner.

Jamie watched me through narrowed eyes for a moment, debating what to do next. It occurred to me that there was nothing whatever to stop him doing anything he liked to me; he outweighed me by a good four stone. He at last decided on talk rather than action, though, and carefully laid the strap aside before crawling over the bedclothes to sit beside me.

'Now, Claire – ' he began.

'I've said I'm sorry!' I burst out. 'And I am. I'll never do such a thing again!'

'Well, that's the point,' he said slowly. 'Ye might. And it's because ye dinna take things as serious as they are. Ye come from a place where things are easier, I think. 'Tis not a matter of life or death where ye come from, to disobey orders or take matters into your own hands. At worst ye might cause someone discomfort or be a bit of a nuisance, but it isna likely to get someone killed.' I watched his fingers pleating the brownish tartan of his kilt as he arranged his thoughts.

'It's the hard truth that a light action can have verra serious consequences in places and times like these – especially for a man like me.' He patted my shoulder, seeing that I was close to tears.

'I know ye would never endanger me or anyone else on purpose. But ye might easily do so without meanin' it, like ye did today, because ye do not really believe me yet when I tell ye that some things are dangerous. You're accustomed to think for yourself, and I know' – he glanced sideways at me – 'that you're not accustomed to lettin' a man tell ye what to do. But you must learn to do so, for all our sakes.'

'All right,' I said slowly. 'I understand. You're right, of course. All right; I'll follow your orders, even if I don't agree with them.'

'Good.' He stood up and picked up the belt. 'Now then, get off the bed and we'll get it over with.'

My mouth dropped open in outrage. 'What?! I *said* I'd follow your orders!'

He sighed, exasperated, then sat down again on the bed. He looked at me levelly.

'Now, listen. Ye understand me, ye say, and I believe it. But there's a difference between understandin' something with your mind and really knowing it, deep down.' I nodded reluctantly.

'All right. Now, I will have to punish you, and for two reasons: first, so that ye *will* know.' He smiled suddenly. 'I can tell ye from my own experience that a good hiding makes ye consider things in a more serious light.' I took a tighter hold on the bedpost.

'The other reason,' he went on, 'is because of the other men. Ye'll have noticed how they were tonight?' I had; it had been so uncomfortable at supper that I was glad to escape to the room.

'There's such a thing as justice, Claire. You've done wrong to them all, and you'll have to suffer for it.' He took a deep breath. 'I'm your husband; it's my duty to attend to it, and I mean to do it.'

I had strong objections to this proposal on several levels. Whatever the justice of the situation – and I had to admit that at least some of it lay on his side – my sense of *amour-propre* was deeply offended at the thought of being beaten, by whoever and for whatever reason.

I felt deeply betrayed that the man I depended on as friend, protector and lover intended to do such a thing to me. And my sense of self-preservation was quietly terrified at the thought of submitting myself to the mercies of someone who handled a fifteen-pound claymore as though it were a flywhisk.

'I will not allow you to beat me,' I said firmly, keeping a tight hold on the bedpost.

'Oh, you won't?' He raised coppery brows. 'Well, I'll tell ye, lass, I doubt you've much to say about it. You're my wife, like it or not. Did I want to break your arm or feed ye naught but bread and water or lock ye in a cupboard for days – and don't think ye don't tempt me, either – I could do that, let alone warm your bum for you.'

'I'll scream!'

'Likely. If not before, certainly during. I expect they'll hear ye at the next farm; you've got good lungs.' He grinned odiously and came across the bed after me.

He pried my fingers loose with some difficulty and pulled firmly, hauling me to the side of the bed. I kicked him in the shins but did no damage, not having shoes on. Grunting slightly, he managed to turn me face down on the bed, twisting my arm to hold me there.

'I mean to do it, Claire! Now if you'll cooperate wi' me, we'll call the account square with a dozen strokes.'

'And if not?' I quavered. He picked up the strap and slapped it against his leg with a nasty thwapping sound.

'Then I shall put a knee in your back and beat you till my arm tires, and I warn ye, you'll tire of it long before I do.'

I bounced off the bed and whirled to face him, fists clenched.

'You barbarian! You . . . you sadist!' I hissed furiously. 'You're doing this for your own pleasure! I'll never forgive you for this!' Jamie paused, twisting the belt.

He replied levelly, 'I dinna know what's a sadist. And if I forgive you for this afternoon, I reckon you'll forgive me too, as soon as ye can sit down again.

'As for my pleasure . . .' His lip twitched. 'I said I would have to punish you. I did *not* say I wasna going to enjoy it.' He crooked a finger at me.

'Come here.'

I was reluctant to leave the sanctuary of the room next morning, and fiddled about, tying and untying ribbons and brushing my hair. I had not spoken to Jamie since the night before, but he noticed my hesitation and urged me to come out with him to breakfast.

'You dinna need to fear meetin' the others, Claire. They'll chaff ye a bit, likely, but it won't be bad. Chin up.'

He chucked me under the chin and I bit his hand, sharply but not deep.

'Ooh!' He snatched his fingers back. 'Be careful, lass; you don't know where they've been.' He left me, chuckling, and went in to breakfast.

He might well be in a good mood, I thought bitterly. If it were revenge he'd wanted the night before, he'd had it.

It had been a most unpleasant night. My reluctant acquiescence had lasted precisely as far as the first searing crack of leather on flesh. This was followed by a short, violent struggle which left Jamie with a bloody nose, three lovely gouges down one cheek and a deeply bitten wrist. Not surprisingly, it left me half smothered in the greasy quilts with a knee in my back, being beaten within an inch of my life.

Jamie, damn his black Scottish soul, turned out to be right. The men were restrained in their greetings but friendly enough; the hostility and contempt of the night before had vanished.

As I was dishing eggs at the sideboard, Dougal came up and slipped a fatherly arm around my shoulders. His beard tickled my ear as he spoke in a confidential rumble.

'I hope Jamie wasna too harsh wi' ye last night, lass. It sounded as though ye were bein' murdert, at least.'

I flushed hotly and turned away so he wouldn't see it. After Jamie's obnoxious remarks I had resolved to keep my mouth firmly shut through the whole ordeal. However, when it came to the event I would have challenged the Sphinx itself to keep a shut mouth while on the receiving end of a strap wielded by Jamie Fraser.

Dougal turned to call to Jamie, seated at the table eating bread and cheese. 'Hey now, Jamie, it wasna necessary to half kill the lass. A gentle reminder would ha' sufficed.' He patted me firmly on the posterior in illustration, making me wince. I glowered at him.

'A blistered bum never did anyone no permanent harm,' said Murtagh through a mouthful of bread.

'No, indeed,' said Ned, grinning. 'Come have a seat, lassie.'

'I'll stand, thank you,' I said with dignity, making them all roar with laughter. Jamie was careful not to meet my eyes as he studiously cut up a bit of cheese.

There was a bit more good-natured chaff during the day, and each of the men made some excuse to pat my rump in mock sympathy. On the whole, though, it was bearable, and I grudgingly began to consider that Jamie might have been right, though I still wanted to strangle him.

Since sitting down was completely out of the question I busied myself during the morning with small chores such as hemming and button-sewing, which could be done at the window sill, with the excuse of needing the light to sew by. After dinner, which I ate standing, we all went to our rooms to rest. Dougal had decided that we would wait till full dark to set out for the next stop on our journey. Jamie followed me to our room, but I shut the door firmly in his face. Let him sleep on the floor again.

He had been fairly tactful last night, buckling his belt back on and leaving the room without speaking immediately after he'd finished. He had come back an hour later, after I'd put out the light and gone to bed, but had had sense enough not to try to come into bed with me. After peering into the darkness where I lay unmoving, he had sighed deeply, wrapped himself in his plaid and gone to sleep on the floor near the door.

Too angry, upset and physically uncomfortable to sleep, I had lain awake most of the night, alternately thinking over what Jamie had said with wanting to get up and kick him in some sensitive spot.

Were I being objective, which I was in no mood to be, I might admit that he was right when he said that I didn't take things with the proper seriousness. He was wrong, though, when he said it was because things were less precarious in my own place — wherever that was. In fact, I thought, it was more likely the opposite was true.

This time was in many ways still unreal to me; something from a play or a fancy-dress pageant. Compared to the sights of mechanized mass warfare I had come from, the small pitched battles I had seen — a few men armed with swords and muskets – seemed picturesque rather than threatening to me.

I was having trouble with the scale of things. A man killed by a musket was just as dead as one killed by a mortar. It was just that the mortar killed impersonally, destroying dozens of men, while the musket was fired by one man who could see the eyes of the one he killed. That made it murder, it seemed to me, not war. How many men to make a war? Enough, perhaps, so they didn't really have to see each other? And yet this plainly was war – or serious business at least – to Dougal, Jamie, Rupert and Ned. Even little rat-faced Murtagh had a reason for violence beyond his natural inclinations.

And what about those reasons? One king rather than another? Hanovers and Stuarts? To me these were still no more than names on a chart on the schoolroom wall. What were they, compared with an unthinkable evil like Hitler's Reich? It made a difference to those who lived under the kings, I supposed, though the differences might seem trivial to me. Still, when had the right to live as one wished ever been considered trivial? Was a struggle to choose one's own destiny less worthwhile than the necessity to stop a great evil? I shifted irritably, gingerly rubbing my sore bottom. I glared at Jamie, curled into a ball by the door. He was breathing evenly, but lightly; perhaps he couldn't sleep either. I hoped not.

I had been inclined at first to take this whole remarkable misadventure as melodrama; such things just did not happen in real life. I had had many shocks since I stepped through the rock, but the worst to date had been this afternoon.

Jack Randall, so like and so horribly unlike Frank. His touch on my breasts had suddenly forged a link between my old life and this one, bringing my separate realities together with a bang like a thunderclap. And then there was Jamie: his face, stark with. fear in the window of Randall's room, contorted with rage at the trackside, tight with pain at my insults.

Jamie. Jamie was real, all right, more real than anything

had ever been to me, even Frank and my life in 1946. Jamie, tender lover and perfidious blackguard.

Perhaps that was part of the problem. Jamie filled my senses so completely that his surroundings seemed almost irrelevant. But I could no longer afford to ignore them. My recklessness had almost killed him this afternoon, and my stomach turned over at the thought of losing him. I sat up suddenly, intending to go and wake him to tell him to come to bed with me. As my weight fell full on the results of his handiwork, I just as suddenly changed my mind and flounced angrily back on to my stomach.

A night spent thus torn between fits of rage and philosophy had left me worn out. I slept all afternoon, and stumbled blearily down for a light supper when Rupert roused me just before dark.

Dougal, no doubt writhing at the expense, had procured another pony for me. A sound beast, if inelegantly built, with a kindly eye and a short, bristly mane; at once I named it Thistle.

I had not reckoned on the effects of a long horseback ride following a severe beating. I eyed Thistle's hard saddle dubiously, suddenly realizing what I was in for. A thick cloak plopped across the saddle, and Murtagh's shiny black rat-eye winked conspiratorially at me from the opposite side. I determined that I would at least suffer in dignified silence, and grimly set my jaw as I hoisted myself into the saddle.

There seemed to be an unspoken conspiracy of gallantry among the men; they took turns stopping at frequent intervals to relieve themselves, allowing me to dismount for a few minutes and surreptitiously rub my aching fundament. Now and again one would suggest stopping for a drink, which necessitated my stopping as well, since Thistle carried the water bottles.

We jolted along for a couple of hours in this manner, but the pain grew steadily worse, keeping me shifting in the saddle incessantly. Finally I decided to hell with dignified suffering, I simply must get off for a while.

'Whoa!' I said to Thistle, and swung down. I pretended

to examine her front left foot as the other ponies came to a milling stop around us.

'I'm afraid she's had a stone in her shoe,' I lied. 'I've got it out, but I'd better walk her a bit; don't want her to go lame.'

'No, we can't have that,' said Dougal. 'All right, walk for a bit, then, but someone must stay wi' ye. 'Tis a quiet enough path, but I canna have ye walkin' alone.' Jamie immediately swung down.

'I'll walk with her,' he said quietly.

'Good. Dinna tarry too long; we must be at the inn before dawn. The sign of the Red Boar; landlord's a friend.' With a wave he gathered the others and they set off at a brisk trot, leaving us in the dust.

Several hours of torture by saddle had not improved my temper. Let him walk with me. I was damned if I'd speak to him, the sadistic, violent brute.

He didn't look particularly brutish in the light of the half moon rising, but I hardened my heart and limped along, carefully not looking at him.

My abused muscles at first protested the unaccustomed exercise, but after half an hour or so I began to move more easily.

'You'll feel much better by tomorrow,' Jamie observed casually. 'Though you won't sit easy till the next day.'

'And what makes you such an expert?' I flared at him. 'Do you beat people all that frequently?'

'Well, no,' he said, undisturbed by my attitude. 'This is the first time I've tried it. I've considerable experience on the other end, though.'

'You?' I gaped at him. The thought of anyone taking a strap to this towering mass of muscle and sinew was completely untenable.

He laughed at my expression. 'When I was a bit smaller, Sassenach. I've had my backside leathered more times than I could count, between the ages of eight and thirteen. That's when I got taller than my father, and it got unhandy for him to bend me over a gate.'

'Your father beat you?'

'Aye, mostly. The schoolmaster, too, of course, and Dougal or one of the other uncles now and then, depending on where I was and what I'd been doing.'

I was growing interested, in spite of my determination to ignore him.

'What *did* you do?'

He laughed again, a quiet but infectious sound in the still night air.

'Well, I canna remember everything. I will say I generally deserved it. I don't think my da ever beat me unfairly, at least.' He paced without speaking for a minute, thinking.

'Mm. Let's see, there was once for stoning the chickens, and once for riding the cows and getting them too excited for milking, and then for eating all the jam out of the cakes and leaving the cakes behind. Ah, and letting the ponies out of the stable by leaving the door unlatched, and setting the thatch of the dovecote on fire – that was an accident, I didna do it on purpose – and losing my schoolbooks – I did do that on purpose – and . . .' He broke off, shrugging, as I laughed despite myself.

'The usual sorts of things. Most often, though, it was for opening my mouth when I should ha' kept it closed.'

He snorted at some memory. 'Once my sister Jenny broke a pitcher; I made her angry, teasing, and she lost her temper and threw it at me. When my da came in and demanded to know who'd done it, she was too scared to speak up, and she just looked at me, with her eyes all wide and frightened – she's got blue eyes, like mine, but prettier, wi' black lashes all around.' Jamie shrugged again. 'Anyway, I told my father I'd done it.'

'That was very noble of you,' I said sarcastically. 'Your sister must have been grateful.'

'Aye, well, she might have been. Only my father'd been on the other side of the open door all along, and he'd seen what really happened. So she got whipped for losing her temper and breaking the pitcher, and I got whipped twice; once for teasing her and again for lying.'

'That's not fair!' I said indignantly.

'My father wasna always gentle, but he was usually fair,' Jamie said imperturbably. 'He said the truth is the truth, and people should take responsibility for their own actions, which is right.' He shot me a sidelong glance.

'But he said it was goodhearted of me to take the blame, so while he'd have to punish me, I could take my choice between being thrashed or going to bed without my supper.' He laughed ruefully, shaking his head. 'Father knew me pretty well. I took the thrashing with no questions.'

'You're nothing but a walking appetite, Jamie,' I said.

'Aye,' he agreed without rancour, 'always have been. You too, glutton,' he said to his mount. 'Wait a bit, till we stop for a rest.' He twitched the rein, pulling his mount's questing nose from the tempting tufts of grass along the way.

'Aye, Father was fair,' he went on, 'and considerate about it, though I certainly didna appreciate that at the time. He wouldn't make me wait for a beating; if I did something wrong I got punished at once – or as soon as he found out about it. He always made sure I knew what I was about to get walloped for, and if I wanted to argue my side of it, I could.'

Oh, so that's what you're up to, I thought. You disarming schemer. I doubted he could charm me out of my set intention of disembowelling him at the first opportunity, but he was welcome to try.

'Did you ever win an argument?' I asked.

'No. It was generally a straightforward-enough case, with the accused convicted out of his own mouth. But sometimes I got the sentence reduced a bit.' He rubbed his nose.

'Once I told him I thought beating your son was a most uncivilized method of getting your own way. He said I'd about as much sense as the post I was standing next to, if as much. He said respect for your elders was one of the cornerstones of civilized behaviour, and until I learned that I'd better get used to looking at my toes while one of my barbaric elders thrashed my arse off.'

This time I laughed along with him. It was peaceful on the track, with that sort of absolute quiet that comes when you are miles from other people. The sort of quiet so hard to come by in my own more crowded time, when machines spread the influence of man, so that a single person could make as much noise as a crowd. The only sounds here were the stirrings of plants, the occasional *skreek* of a nightbird and the soft thudding steps of the ponies.

I was walking a little easier now as my cramped muscles began to stretch freely with the exercise. My prickly feelings began to relax a little too, listening to Jamie's stories, all humorous and self-deprecating.

'I didna like being beaten at all, of course, but if I had a choice I'd rather my da than the schoolmaster. We'd mostly get it across the palm of the hand with a tawse, in the schoolhouse, instead of on the backside. Father said if he whipped me on the hand I'd not be able to do any work, whereas if he whipped my arse I'd at least not be tempted to sit down and be idle.

'We had a different schoolmaster each year, usually; they didna last long – usually turned farmer or moved on to richer parts. Schoolmasters are paid so little, they're always skinny and starving. Had a fat one once, and I could never believe he was a real schoolmaster; he looked like a parson in disguise.' I thought of plump little Father Bain and smiled in agreement.

'One I remember especially, because he'd make ye stand out in the front of the schoolroom with your hand out, and then he'd lecture ye at great length about your faults before he started, and again in between strokes. I'd stand there wi' my hand out, smarting, just praying he'd stop yammering and get on with the job before I lost all my courage and started crying.'

'I imagine that's what he wanted you to do,' I said, feeling some sympathy in spite of myself.

'Oh, aye,' he replied matter of factly. 'It took some time for me to realize that, though. And once I did, as usual I couldna keep my mouth shut.' He sighed.

'What happened?' I had all but forgotten to be furious by this time.

'Well, he had me up one day – I got it a lot because I couldna write properly with my right hand, kept doing it

409

with my left. He'd smacked me three times – takin' nearly five minutes to do it, the bastard – and he was goin' on at me for being a stupid, idle, stubborn young lout before givin' me the next. My hand burned something fierce, because it was the second time that day, and I was scared because I knew I'd get an awful thrashing when I got home – that was the rule; if I got a beating at school, I'd get another directly I came home, for my father thought schooling important – anyway, I lost my temper.' His left hand curled involuntarily around the rein, as though protecting the sensitive palm.

He paused and glanced at me. 'I seldom lose my temper, Sassenach, and generally regret it when I do.' And that, I thought, was likely to be as close to an apology as I'd get.

'Did you regret it that time?'

'Well, I doubled up my fists and glared up at him – he was a tall, scrawny fellow, maybe twenty, I suppose, though he looked quite old to me – and I said "I'm not afraid o' you, and ye can't make me cry, no matter how hard you hit me!" ' He drew a deep breath and blew it out slowly. 'I suppose it was a bit of a mistake in judgement to tell him that while he was still holding the strap.'

'Don't tell me,' I said. 'He tried to prove you were wrong?'

'Oh, aye, he tried,' Jamie nodded, head dark against the cloud-lit sky. His voice held a certain grim satisfaction on the 'tried'.

'He didn't succeed, then?'

The shaggy head shook back and forth. 'No. At least he couldna make me cry. He surely made me regret not keeping quiet, though.'

He paused for a moment, turning his face towards me. The cloud cover had parted for a moment and the light touched the edges of jaw and cheek, making him look gilded, like a Renaissance archangel.

'When Dougal was describing my character to ye, before we wed, did he by chance mention that I'm sometimes a bit stubborn?' The slanted eyes glinted, much more Lucifer than Michael.

I laughed. 'That's putting it mildly. As I recall, what he

said is that all the Frasers are stubborn as rocks, and you're the worst of the lot. Actually,' I said a little dryly, 'I'd noticed something of the kind myself.'

He smiled as he reined his pony around a deep puddle, leading mine by the bearing rein after him.

'Mmph, well, I'll no just say Dougal's wrong,' he said, once the hazard had been negotiated. 'But if I'm stubborn, I come by it honest. My father was just the same, and we'd get in wrangles from time to time that we couldna get out of without the application of force, usually wi' me bent over the gate.

'– Hey now! Hush! *Stad, mo dubh!*' He put out a hand to grab my pony's rein as the beast reared and snorted. His own, less spooked, only jerked and tossed its head nervously.

'What is it?' I could see nothing despite the patches of moonlight that mottled track and field. There was a pine grove up ahead, and the animals seemed disinclined to go any nearer to it.

'I don't know. Stay here and keep quiet. Mount your pony and hold mine. If I call to ye, drop the bearing rein and run for it.' Jamie's voice was low and casual, calming me as well as the ponies. With a muttered '*Sguir!*' to the pony and a slap on the neck to urge it closer to me, he faded into the heather, hand on his dirk.

I strained eyes and ears to discern whatever it was still troubling the animals; they shifted and stamped, ears and tails twitching in agitation. The clouds by now had shredded and flown on the night wind, leaving only scattered trails across the face of a brilliant half moon. In spite of the brightness I could see nothing on the track ahead, or in the menacing grove.

It seemed a late hour and an unprofitable lurking place for highwaymen, scarce as these were anywhere in the Highlands; there were too few travellers to make an ambush worthwhile.

The grove was dark, but not still. The pines roared softly to themselves, millions of needles scouring in the wind. Very ancient trees, pines, and eerie in the gloom. Gymnosperms, cone-bearers, winged-seed scatterers, older and sterner by far than the soft-leaved, frail-limbed birch and aspens. A suitable home for Rupert's ghosts and evil spirits.

Only you, I thought crossly to myself, could work yourself up into being afraid of a lot of trees. Where was Jamie, though?

The hand gripping my thigh made me squeak like a startled bat; a natural consequence of trying to scream with your heart in your mouth. With the unreasonable fury of the irrationally afraid, I struck out at him, kicking him in the chest.

'Don't sneak up on me like that!'

'Hush,' he said, 'come with me.' Tugging me unceremoniously from the saddle he swung me down and hastily tethered the mounts, who whickered uneasily after us as he led me into the tall grass.

'What is it?' I hissed, stumbling blindly over roots and rocks.

'Quiet. Don't speak. Look down and watch my feet. Step where I step, and stop when I touch you.'

Slowly and more or less silently we made our way into the edges of the pine grove. It was dark under the trees, with only crumbs of light falling through to the needle litter underfoot. Even Jamie couldn't walk absolutely silently on that, but the rustle of dry needles was lost in that of the green ones overhead.

There was a rift in the litter, a mass of stone rising from the forest floor. Here Jamie put me in front of him, guiding my hands and feet to climb the sloping crumble of the mound. At the top there was enough room to lie belly-flat, side by side. Jamie put his mouth next to my ear, barely breathing. 'Thirty feet ahead, to the right. In the clearing. See them?'

Once I saw them, I could hear as well. Wolves, a small pack, eight or ten animals, perhaps. No howling, not these. The kill lay in the shadow, a blob of dark with an upthrust leg, stick-thin and vibrating under the impact of teeth yanking at the carcass. There was only the occasional soft growl and yip as a cub was batted away from an adult's morsel, and the contented sounds of feeding, crunching and the crack of a bone.

As my eyes grew more accustomed to the moon-flecked scene I could pick out several shaggy forms stretched under the trees, glutted and peaceful. Bits of grey fur shone here and there, as those still at the carcass pushed and rooted for tender bits overlooked by the earlier diners.

A broad, yellow-eyed head thrust suddenly up into a blotch of light, ears pricked. The wolf made a soft, urgent noise, something between a whine and a growl, and there was a sudden stillness under the trees.

The saffron eyes seemed fixed on my own. There was no fear in the animal's posture, nor curiosity, only a wary acknowledgement. Jamie's hand on my back warned me not to move, though I felt no desire to run. I could have stayed locked in the wolf's eyes for hours, I think, but she – I was sure it was a female, though I didn't know how I knew – flicked her ears once, as though dismissing me, and bent once more to her meal.

We watched them for a few minutes, peaceful in the scattered light. At last Jamie signalled that it was time to go, with a touch on my arm.

He kept the hand on my arm to support me as we made our way back through the trees to the road. It was the first time I had willingly allowed him to touch me since he had beaten me. Still charmed by the sight of the wolves we did not speak much, but began to feel comfortable with each other again.

As I walked, considering the stories he had told me, I couldn't help but admire the job he had done. Without one word of direct explanation or apology he had given me the message he intended. I gave you justice, it said, as I was taught it. And I gave you mercy, too, so far as I could. While I could not spare you pain and humiliation, I make you a gift of my own pains and humiliations, that yours might be easier to bear.

'Did you mind a lot?' I said abruptly. 'Being beaten, I mean. Did you get over it easily?'

He squeezed my hand lightly before letting it go.

413

'Mostly I forgot it as soon as it was over. Except for the last time; that took a while.'

'Why?'

'Ah, well. I was sixteen, for one thing, and a man grown . . . I thought. For another, it hurt like hell.'

'You don't have to tell me about it if you don't want to,' I said, sensing his hesitation. 'Is it a painful story?'

'Not nearly as painful as the beating,' he said, laughing. 'No, I don't mind tellin' ye. It's a long story, is all.'

'It's a long way to the inn yet.'

'So it is. Well, then. You recall I told ye I spent a year at Castle Leoch when I was sixteen? It was an agreement between Callum and my father – so I'd be familiar wi' my mother's clan. I fostered wi' Dougal for two years, and then went to the castle for a year, to learn manners, and Latin and such.'

'Oh. I wondered how you'd come to be there.'

'Aye, that was the way of it. I was big for my age, or tall at least; a good swordsman even then, and a better horseman than most.'

'Modest, too,' I said.

'Not very. Cocky as hell, and even faster with my tongue than I am now.'

'The mind boggles,' I said, amused.

'Well it might, Sassenach. I found I could make people laugh wi' my remarks, and I made them more frequent, without carin' much what I said, or to whom. I was cruel sometimes, not meanin' it, just not able to resist it if I thought of something clever to say.'

He looked up at the sky to gauge the time. Blacker still, now that the moon had gone down. I recognized Cassiopeia floating above the hills, and was strangely comforted by the familiar sight.

'So, one day I went too far. Said the wrong thing to the wrong person and came up for judgement before Callum at Hall.' He chuckled to himself.

'I got verra bold, though, and I stood up and said if I had to be beaten, I'd take it wi' fists. I was tryin' to be verra calm and grown-up about it all, though my heart was going like a blacksmith's hammer, and I felt a bit sick when I looked at Angus's hands; they looked like stones, and big ones at that. There were a few laughs from the folk gathered in the hall; I wasna so tall then as I am now, and I weighed less than half as much. Wee Angus could ha' torn my head off with one blow.

'Anyway, Callum and Dougal both frowned at me, though I thought they were really a bit pleased I'd had the nerve to ask it. Then Callum said no, if I was goin' to behave like a child, I'd be punished like one. He gave a nod, and before I could move, Angus bent me across his knee, turned up the edge of my kilt and blistered me with his strap in front of the entire Hall.'

'Oh, Jamie!'

'Mmmphm. You'll have noticed Angus is verra professional about his work? To this day I could tell ye exactly where each stroke landed.' He shuddered reminiscently.

He reached out and broke a clump of pine needles from the nearest tree, spreading them like a fan between thumb and fingers. The scent of turpentine was suddenly sharper.

'Then I was plunked down on a stool next to Callum, and bid to sit there till Hall was ended.' He hunched his shoulders protectively. 'That was the worst hour I ever spent. My face was on fire and so was my arse, and I couldna look anywhere but at my feet, but the worst of it was that I had to piss something awful. I almost died; I'd ha' burst before I wet myself in front of everyone on top of it all, but it was a near thing. I sweated right through my shirt.'

I suppressed my urge to laugh. 'Couldn't you have told Callum what was the matter?' I asked.

'He knew perfectly well what was the matter; so did everyone else in the hall, the way I was squirming on that stool. People were making wagers as to whether I'd last or not.' He shrugged.

'Callum would have let me go, if I'd asked. But – well, I got stubborn about it.' He grinned a bit sheepishly, teeth white in a dark face. 'Thought I'd rather die than ask, and nearly did. When at last Callum said I could go I made it out of the hall, but only as far as the nearest door. Threw myself behind the wall and spurted streams; I thought I'd never stop.

'So' – he spread his hands deprecatingly, dropping the clump of pine needles – 'now you know the worst thing that ever happened to me.'

I couldn't help it; I laughed until I had to sit down at the side of the track. Jamie waited patiently for a minute, then sank down on his knees beside me.

'What are you laughing for?' he demanded. 'It wasna funny at all.' But he was smiling himself.

I shook my head, still laughing. 'No, it isn't. It's an awful story. It's just . . . I can see you sitting there, being stubborn about it, with your jaw clenched and steam coming out of your ears.'

Jamie snorted, but laughed a little too. 'Aye. It's no verra easy to be sixteen, is it?'

'So you did help that girl Laoghaire because you felt sorry for her,' I said when I had recovered my composure. 'You knew what it was like.'

He was surprised. 'Aye, I said so. It's a lot easier to get punched in the face at three-and-twenty than to have your bum strapped in public at sixteen. Bruised pride hurts worse than anything, and it bruises easy then.'

'Mmm.' I nodded agreement. 'I thought – ' I said, then stopped in embarrassment.

'Ye thought what? Oh, about me and Laoghaire, ye mean,' he said, divining my thought. 'You and Alick and everyone else, including Laoghaire. I'd have done the same if she'd been plain.' He nudged me in the ribs. 'Though I dinna expect you'll believe that.'

'Well, I did see you together that day in the alcove,' I defended myself, 'and *somebody* certainly taught you how to kiss.'

Jamie shuffled his feet in the dust, embarrassed. He ducked his head shyly. 'Well now, Sassenach, I'm no better than most men. Sometimes I try, but I dinna always manage. Ye know that bit in St Paul, where he says 'tis better to marry than burn? Well, I was burnin' quite badly there.'

I laughed again, feeling light-hearted as a sixteen-year-old myself. 'So you married me,' I teased, 'to avoid the occasion of sin?'

'Aye. That's what marriage is good for, it makes a sacrament out of things ye'd otherwise have to confess.'

I collapsed again.

'Oh, Jamie, I do love you!'

This time it was his turn to laugh. He doubled over, then sat down at the trackside, fizzing with mirth. He slowly fell over backwards and lay in the long grass, wheezing and choking.

'What on earth is the matter with you?' I demanded, staring at him. At long last he sat up, wiping his streaming eyes. He shook his head, gasping.

'Murtagh was right about women. Sassenach, I risked my life for ye, committing theft, arson, assault and murder into the bargain. In return for which ye call me names, insult my manhood, kick me in the bollocks and claw my face. Then I beat you half to death and tell ye all the most humiliating things have ever happened to me, and you say ye love me.' He laid his head on his knees and laughed some more. Finally he rose and held out a hand to me, wiping his eyes with the other.

'You're no verra sensible, Sassenach, but I like ye fine. Let's go.'

It was getting late – or early, depending on your viewpoint, and it was necessary to ride if we were to make the inn by dawn. I was enough recovered by this time to bear sitting, though the effects were still noticeable.

We rode in a companionable silence for some way. Left to my own thoughts, I considered for the first time at leisure what would happen if and when I ever managed to find my way back to the circle of standing stones. Married to him by coercion and dependent on him from necessity, I had undeniably grown very fond of Jamie.

More to the point, perhaps, were his feelings about me. Linked at first by circumstance, then by friendship, and finally by a startlingly deep bodily passion, still he had never

417

made even a casual statement to me about his feelings. And yet.

He had risked his life for me. That much he might do for the sake of his marriage vow; he would, he said, protect me to the last drop of his blood, and I believed he meant it.

I was more touched by the events of the last twenty-four hours, when he had suddenly admitted me to his emotions and his personal life, warts and all. If he felt as much for me as I thought perhaps he did, what would he feel if I suddenly disappeared? The remnants of physical discomfort receded as I grappled with these uncomfortable thoughts.

We were within three miles of the inn when Jamie suddenly broke the silence.

'I havena told you how my father died,' he said abruptly.

'Dougal said he had a stroke – an apoplexy, I mean,' I said, startled. I supposed that Jamie, alone with his thoughts as well, had found them dwelling on his father as a result of our earlier conversation, but I could not imagine what led him to this particular subject.

'That's right. But it . . . he . . .' He paused, considering his words, then shrugged, abandoning carefulness. He drew a deep breath and let it out. 'You should know about it. It's to do with . . . things.' The track here was wide enough to ride easily abreast, provided only that we kept a sharp eye out for protruding rocks.

'It was at the fort,' Jamie said, picking his way around a bad patch, 'where we were yesterday. Where Randall and his men took me from Lallybroch. Where they flogged me. Two days after the first time, Randall summoned me to his office – two soldiers came for me and took me from the cells up to his room – the same where I found you; it's how I knew where to go.

'Just outside, we met my father in the courtyard. He'd found out where they'd taken me, and come to see if he could get me out some way – or at least to see for himself that I was all right.'

Jamie kicked a heel gently into his mount's ribs, urging it on with a soft click of his tongue. There was no trace of daylight yet, but the look of the night had changed. Dawn could be no more than an hour away.

'I hadna realized until I saw him just how alone I'd felt there – or how scairt. The soldiers would not give us any time alone together, but at least they let me greet him.' He swallowed and went on.

'I told him I was sorry – about Jenny, I meant, and the whole sorry mess. He told me to hush, though, and hugged me tight to him. He asked me was I hurt badly – he knew about the flogging – and I said I'd be all right. The soldiers said I must go then, so he squeezed my arms tight and told me to remember to pray. He said he would stand by me no matter what happened, and I must just keep my head up and try not to worry myself. He kissed my cheek and the soldiers took me away. That was the last time I ever saw him.'

His voice was steady, but a little thick. My own throat felt tight and I would have touched him if I could, but the way narrowed through a small glen and I was forced to fall back behind him for a moment. By the time I came along-side again he had composed himself.

'So,' he said, taking a deep breath, 'I went in to see Captain Randall. He sent the soldiers out, so we were alone, and offered me a stool. He said my father had offered security for my bond, to have me released, but that my charge was a serious one, and I could not be bonded without a written clearance signed by the Duke of Argyll, whose boundaries we were under. I reckoned that was where my father was headed, then, to see Argyll.

'In the meantime, Randall went on, there was the matter of this second flogging I was sentenced to.' He stopped a minute, as though uncertain how to go on.

'He . . . was strange in his manner, I thought. Verra cor-dial, but with something under it I didna understand. He kept watching me, as though he expected me to do some-thing, though I was just sitting still.

'He half apologized to me, saying he was sorry that our relations had been so difficult to the present, and that he wished the circumstances had been different, and so on.'

Jamie shook his head. 'I couldna imagine what he was talking about; two days earlier, he'd been having me beat near to death. When he finally got down to it, though, he was blunt enough.'

'What did he want, then?' I asked. Jamie glanced at me, then away. The dark hid his features, but I thought he seemed embarrassed.

'Me,' he said baldly.

I started so violently that my pony tossed its head and whickered reproachfully. Jamie shrugged again.

'He was quite plain about it. If I would . . . ah, make him free of my body, he'd cancel the second flogging. If I would not – then I'd wish I'd never been born, he said.'

I felt quite sick.

'I was already wishing something of the sort,' he said with a glint of humour. 'My belly felt as though I'd swallowed broken glass, and if I hadna been sitting, my knees would have knocked together.'

'But what . . .' My voice was hoarse, and I cleared my throat and started over. 'But what did you do?'

He sighed. 'Well, I'll no lie to ye, Sassenach. I considered it. The first stripes were still so raw on my back I could scarce bear a shirt, and I felt giddy whenever I stood up. The thought of going through that again – being bound and helpless, waiting for the next lash . . .' He shuddered involuntarily.

'I'd no real idea,' he said wryly, 'but I rather thought being buggered would be at least a bit less painful. Men have died under the lash sometimes, Sassenach, and from the look on his face I thought he meant me to be one of them, were that my choice.' He sighed again.

'But . . . well, I could still feel my father's kiss on my cheek, and thought of what he'd say, and . . . well, I couldna do it, that's all. I did not stop to think what my death might mean to my father.' He snorted as though finding something faintly amusing. 'Then, too, I thought, the man's already raped my sister – damned if he'll have me too.'

I didn't find this amusing. I was seeing Jack Randall in

a new and revolting light. Jamie rubbed the back of his neck, then dropped his hand to the pommel.

'So, I took what little courage I had left by then, and said no. I said it loud, too, and added whatever filthy names I could think of to call him, all at the top of my lungs.'

He grimaced. 'I was afraid I'd change my mind if I thought about it; I wanted to make sure there was no chance of going back. Though I dinna suppose,' he added thoughtfully, 'that there's any really tactful way to refuse an offer like that.'

'No,' I agreed dryly. 'I don't suppose he'd have been pleased, no matter what you said.'

'He wasn't. He backhanded me across the mouth to shut me up. I fell down – I was still a bit weak – and he stood over me, just staring down at me. I'd better sense than to try to get up, so I just lay there until he called the soldiers to take me back to my cell.' He shook his head. 'He didna change expression at all; just said as I left, "I'll see you on Friday" as though we had an appointment to discuss business or somesuch.'

The soldiers had not returned Jamie to the cell he had shared with three other prisoners. Instead he was put into a small room by himself, to await Friday's reckoning with no distractions save the daily visit of the garrison's physician, who came to dress his back.

'He wasna much of a doctor,' Jamie said, 'but he was kindly enough. The second day he came, along wi' the goose grease and charcoal, he brought me a small Bible that belonged to a prisoner who'd died. Said he understood I was a papist, and whether I found the word of God any comfort or not, at least I could compare my troubles with Job's.' He laughed.

'Oddly enough, it *was* some comfort. Our Lord had to put up wi' being scourged too; and I could reflect that at least I wasna going to be hauled out and crucified afterwards. On the other hand,' he said judiciously, 'Our Lord wasna forced to listen to indecent proposals from Pontius Pilate, either.'

Jamie had kept the small Bible. He rummaged in his

saddlebag and handed it across now for me to look at. It was a worn, leather-covered volume, about five inches long, printed on paper so flimsy the print showed through from one side of each page to the other. On the flyleaf was written ALEXANDER WILLIAM RODERICK MACGREGOR, 1733. The ink was faded and blurred, and the covers warped as though the book had been wet on more than one occasion.

I turned the little book over curiously. Small as it was, it must have cost something in effort to keep it by him through the travels and adventures of the last four years.

'I've never seen you read it.' I handed it back.

'No, that's not why I keep it,' he said. He tucked it away, stroking the edge of the worn cover with a thumb as he did so. He patted the saddlebag absently.

'There's a debt owing to Alick MacGregor; I mean to repay it sometime.

'Anyway,' he continued, returning to his story, 'Friday came at last, and I don't know whether I was glad or sorry to see it. The waiting and the fear were almost worse than I thought the pain would be. When it came, though . . .' he made that odd half-shrugging gesture of his, easing the shirt across his back. 'Well, you've seen the marks. You know what it was like.'

'Only because Dougal told me. He said he was there.'

Jamie nodded. 'Aye, he was there. And my father as well, though I didna know it at the time. I'd no mind for anything much beyond my own problems then.'

'Oh,' I said slowly, 'and your father – '

'Mmm. That's when it happened. Some of the men there told me after that they thought I was dead, halfway through, and I reckon my father thought so too.' He hesitated, and his voice was thick when he resumed. 'When I fell, Dougal told me, my father made a small sound and put his hand to his head. Then he dropped like a rock. And did not get up again.'

The birds were moving in the heather, trilling and calling from the still-dark leaves of the trees. Jamie's head was bowed, face still invisible.

'I did not know he was dead,' he said softly. 'They didna

tell me until a month later – when they thought I was strong enough to bear it. So I did not bury him, as his son should have done. And I have never seen his grave – because I am afraid to go home.'

'Jamie,' I said. 'Oh, Jamie, dear.'

After what seemed a long silence I said, 'But you don't – you *can't* – feel responsible. Jamie, there was nothing you could have done; or done differently.'

'No?' he said. 'No, maybe not; though I wonder would it still have happened, had I chosen the other way. But to know that does not much help the way I feel – and I feel as though I had done him to death with my own hands.'

'Jamie – ' I said again, and stopped, helpless. He rode silently for a bit, then straightened up and squared his shoulders once more.

'I've not told anyone about it,' he said abruptly. 'But I thought that now ye should know – about Randall, I mean. You've a right to know what it is that lies between him and me.'

What it is that lies between him and me. The life of a good man, the honour of a girl, and an indecent lust that found its vent in blood and fear. And, I supposed with a lurch of the stomach, that there was now one more item weighing the scales. Me. For the first time I began to realize what Jamie had felt, crouching in the window of Randall's room with an empty gun in his hand. And I began to forgive him for what he had done to me.

As though reading my mind he said, not looking at me, 'Do you know . . . I mean, can ye understand, maybe, why I thought it needful to beat you?'

I waited a moment before answering. I understood, all right, but that was not quite all there was to it.

'I understand,' I said. 'And so far as that goes, I forgive you. What I can't forgive,' I said, my voice rising slightly in spite of myself, 'is that you enjoyed it!'

He bent forward in the saddle, clasping the pommel, and laughed for a long time. He revelled in the release of tension before finally tossing his head back and turning to me. The sky was noticeably lighter now, and I could see his face, lined with exhaustion, strain and mirth. The scratches down his cheek were black in the dim light.

'Enjoyed it! Sassenach,' he said, gasping, 'you don't know just how much I enjoyed it. You were so . . . God, you looked lovely. I was so angry, and you fought me so fierce. I hated to hurt you, but I wanted to do it at the same time . . . Jesus,' he said, breaking off and wiping his nose, 'yes. Yes, I did enjoy it.

'Though, come to that,' he said, 'you might give me some credit for exercising restraint.'

I was getting rather angry again. I could feel my cheeks flushing hotly against the cool dawn air.

'Restraint, was it? I was under the impression that what you were exercising was your good left arm. You almost crippled me, you arrogant Scottish bastard!'

'Did I want to cripple ye, Sassenach, you'd know it,' he answered dryly. 'I meant afterwards. I slept on the floor, if ye recall.'

I eyed him narrowly, breathing through my nose. 'Oh, so that was restraint, was it?'

'Well, I didna think it right to roger you in that state, however fierce I wanted to. And I did want to,' he added, laughing again. 'Terrible strain on my natural instincts.'

'Roger me?' I said, diverted by the expression.

'I would hardly call it "lovemaking" under the circumstances, would you?'

'Whatever you might call it,' I said evenly, 'it's a good thing you didn't try it or you'd now be missing a few valued bits of your anatomy.'

'That thought occurred to me.'

'And if you think you deserve applause for nobly refraining from committing rape on top of assault – ' I choked on my choler.

We rode a half mile or so in silence. Then he heaved a sigh. 'I can see I should not have started this conversation. What I was tryin' to do was to work up to asking ye would you allow me to share your bed again, once we get to the inn.' He paused shyly. 'It's a bit cold on the floor.'

I rode for a good five minutes before answering. When

I had decided what to say I reined in, turning across the road so as to force Jamie to stop as well. The village was in sight, rooftops just visible in the dawning light.

I urged my pony parallel with the other, so that I was no more than a foot away from Jamie. I looked him in the eye for a minute before speaking.

'Will you do me the honour of sharing my bed, O lord and master?' I asked politely.

Obviously suspecting something, he considered a moment, then nodded, just as formally. 'I will. Thank you.' He was raising the reins to go when I stopped him.

'There's just one more thing, master,' I said, still polite.

'Aye?'

I whipped my hand from the deep pocket in my skirt and the dawn light struck sparks from the blade of the dagger pressed against his chest.

'If,' I said through my teeth, 'you ever raise a hand to me again, James Fraser, I'll cut out your heart and fry it for breakfast!'

There was a long silence, broken only by the shiftings and creakings of ponies and harness. Then he held out his hand, palm up.

'Give it to me.' When I hesitated he said impatiently, 'I'm no going to use it on ye. Give it to me!'

He held the dirk by the blade, upright so that the rising sun caught the moonstone in the hilt and made it glow. Holding the dagger like a crucifix, he recited something in Gaelic. I recognized it from the oath-taking ceremony in Callum's hall, but he followed it with the English translation for my benefit.

'I swear on the Cross of my Lord Jesus, and by the holy iron which I hold, that I give ye my fealty and pledge ye my loyalty. If ever my hand is raised against you in rebellion or in anger, then I ask that this holy iron may pierce my heart.' He kissed the dirk at the juncture of haft and tang, and handed it back to me.

'I don't made idle threats, Sassenach,' he said, raising one brow, 'and I don't take frivolous vows. Now, can we go to bed?'

23

Return to Leoch

Dougal was waiting for us at the sign of the Red Boar, impatiently pacing to and fro outside.

'Made it, did ye?' he asked, watching with approval as I dismounted without assistance, staggering only slightly. 'Gallant lass – ten miles without a whimper. Get up to your bed then; ye've earned it. Jamie and I will stable the horses.' He patted me, very gently, on the rump in dismissal. I was only too glad to follow his suggestion, and was asleep almost before my head touched the pillow.

I didn't stir when Jamie crawled in beside me, but woke suddenly in the late afternoon, convinced that there was something important I had forgotten.

'Horrocks!' I exclaimed suddenly, sitting bolt upright in bed.

'Hah?' Jamie, startled out of a sound sleep, shot sideways out of bed, ending on the floor in a crouch, hand on the dirk he had left on top of his piled clothes. 'What?' he demanded, staring wildly around the room. 'What is it?'

I stifled a giggle at the sight of him, crouched naked on the floor, red hair standing on end like quills.

'You look like a fretful porpentine,' I said.

'Whatever that might be.' He gave me a dirty look and rose to his feet, replacing the dirk on the stool that held his clothes.

'You couldna wait till I woke to tell me that?' he inquired. 'You thought it would make more impression if ye woke me out of a sound sleep by shouting in my ear?'

'Horrocks,' I explained. 'I remembered all at once that I'd forgotten to ask you about him. Did you find him?'

He sat down on the bed and sank his head in his hands.

He rubbed his face vigorously, as though to restore circulation.

'Oh, aye,' he said through the muffling fingers. 'Aye, I found him.'

I could tell from the tone of his voice that the deserter's information had not been good.

'Would he not tell you anything after all?' I asked sympathetically. That had always been a possibility, though Jamie had gone prepared to part with not only his own money, and some provided by Dougal and Callum, but even his father's ring if necessary.

Jamie lay back on the bed beside me, staring up at the ceiling.

'No,' he said. 'No, he told me all right. And at a reasonable price.'

I rolled up on to an elbow in order to look down at his face.

'Well, then?' I demanded. 'Who *did* shoot the sergeant?'

He looked up at me and smiled a trifle grimly.

'Randall,' he said, and shut his eyes.

'Randall?' I said blankly. 'But why?'

'I don't know,' he said, eyes still shut. 'I could guess, perhaps, but it doesna much matter. Damn-all chance of proving it.'

I had to agree that this was true. I sank back on the bed beside him and stared up at the black beams of the low ceiling.

'What can you do then?' I asked. 'Go to France? Or perhaps' – a bright thought occurred to me – 'perhaps to America? You could likely do well in the New World.'

'Across the ocean?' A brief shudder ran through him. 'No. No, I couldna do that.'

'Well, what then?' I demanded, turning my head to look at him. He opened one eye enough to give me a jaundiced look.

'I'd thought for a start that I might get another hour's sleep,' he said, 'but apparently not.' Resigned, he pulled himself up in bed, leaning against the wall, and I noticed a

427

suspicious red spot on the quilt near his knee. I kept a wary eye on it as he talked.

'You're right,' he agreed, 'we could go to France.' I started, having momentarily forgotten that whatever he decided to do, I was now included in the decision.

'But there isna that much for me there,' he said, idly scratching his thigh. 'Only soldiering, and that's no life for you. Or to Rome, to join King James's court. That might be managed; I've some Fraser uncles and cousins with a foot in that camp, who would help me. I've no great taste for politics, and less for princes, but aye, it's a possibility. I'd rather try first to clear myself in Scotland, though. If I did, at the worst I might end up as a small cottar in the Fraser lands; at best I might be able to go back to Lally-broch.' His face clouded, and I knew he was thinking of his sister. 'For myself,' he said softly, 'I wouldna go, but it isn't only me any more.'

He looked down at me and smiled, his hand gently smoothing my hair. 'I forget sometimes that there's you now, Sassenach,' he said.

I felt extraordinarily uncomfortable. I felt like a traitor, in fact. Here he was, making plans that would affect his entire life, taking my comfort and safety into account, when I had been doing my best to abandon him completely, dragging him into substantial danger in the process. I had meant none of it, but the fact remained. Even now I was thinking that I should try to talk him out of going to France, as that would carry me farther away from my own goal: the stone circle.

'Is there any way to stay in Scotland, though?' I asked, looking away from him. I thought the red spot on the quilt had moved, but I wasn't sure. I fixed my eyes on it, staring hard.

Jamie's hand travelled under my hair and began idly to fondle my neck.

'Aye,' he said thoughtfully. 'There may be. That's why Dougal waited up for me; he's had some news.'

'Really? What sort?' I turned my head to look up at him again; the movement brought my ear within reach of his fingers, and he began to stroke lightly around it, making me want to arch my neck and purr like a cat. I repressed the impulse, though, in favour of finding out what he meant to do.

'A messenger from Callum,' he said. 'He didna think to find us here, but he passed Dougal on the way by accident. Dougal's to return at once to Leoch, and leave Ned Gowan to manage the rest of the rents. Dougal's suggested we should go with him.'

'Back to Leoch?' It wasn't France, but it wasn't a lot better. 'Why?'

'There's a visitor expected shortly, an English noble that's had dealings wi' Callum before. He's a powerful man, and it might be he could be persuaded to do something for me. I've not been tried or condemned on the charge of murder. He might be able to have it dismissed, or arrange to have me pardoned.' He grinned wryly. 'It goes a bit against the grain to be pardoned for something I've not done, but it's better than being hanged.'

'Yes, that's true.' The spot *was* moving. I squinted, trying to focus on it. 'Which English noble is it?'

'The Duke of Sandringham.'

I jerked upright with an exclamation.

'What is it, Sassenach?' Jamie asked, alarmed.

I pointed a trembling finger at the red spot, which was now proceeding up his leg at a slow but determined pace.

'What's that?!' I said.

He glanced at it, and casually flicked it off with a fingernail.

'Oh, that? It's only a bedbug, Sassenach. Nothing to – '

He was interrupted by my abrupt exit. At the word bedbug, I had shot out from under the covers and stood pressed against the wall, as far away as possible from the teeming nest of vermin I now envisioned as our bed.

Jamie eyed me appreciatively.

'Fretful porpentine, was it?' he asked. He tilted his head, examining me inquisitively. 'Mmm,' he said, running a hand over his head to smooth down his own hair. 'Fretful, at least. You're a fuzzy wee thing when ye awake, to be sure.'

He rolled over towards me, reaching out a hand.

'Come here, my wee thistle. We'll not leave before sunset. If we're not going to sleep . . .'

In the end we did sleep a bit more, peacefully entangled on the floor, atop a hard but bugless bed composed of my cloak and Jamie's kilt.

It was a good thing that we had slept while we had the chance. Anxious to reach Castle Leoch before the Duke of Sandringham, Dougal kept to a fast pace and a gruelling schedule. Travelling without the carts we made much better time, despite bad tracks. Dougal pushed us, though, stopping only for the briefest of rests.

By the time we rode once more through the gates of Leoch we were nearly as bedraggled as the first time we had arrived there, and certainly as tired.

I slid off my pony in the courtyard, then had to catch the stirrup to keep from falling. Jamie held my elbow, then realizing that I couldn't stand, swung me up into his arms. He carried me through the archway, leaving the mounts to the grooms and stable boys.

'Are ye hungry, Sassenach?' he asked, pausing in the corridor. The kitchens lay in one direction, the stairs to the bedchambers in the other. I groaned, struggling to keep my eyes open. I *was* hungry, but knew I would end up face down in the soup if I tried to eat before sleeping.

There was a stir to one side and I groggily opened my eyes to see the massive form of Mrs FitzGibbons looming disbelievingly alongside.

'Why, what's the matter wi' the poor child?' she demanded of Jamie. 'Has she had an accident o' some sort?'

'No, it's only she's married me,' he said, 'though if ye care to call it an accident, ye may.' He moved to one side, to push through what proved to be an increasing throng of kitchen-maids, grooms, cooks, gardeners, men-at-arms and assorted castle inhabitants, all inquisitively drawn to the scene by Mrs Fitz's loud questions.

Making up his mind, Jamie pressed to the right, towards the stairs, giving disjointed explanations to the hail of questions from every side. Blinking owlishly against his chest, I could do no more than nod to the surrounding welcomers, though most of the faces seemed friendly as well as curious.

As we came around a corner of the hallway I saw one face that seemed a good deal friendlier than the rest. It was the girl Laoghaire, face shining and radiant as she heard Jamie's voice. Her eyes grew wide and the rosebud mouth dropped unbecomingly open, though, as she saw what he carried.

There was no time for her to ask questions, though, before the stir and bustle around us halted abruptly. Jamie stopped too. Raising my head I saw Callum, whose startled face was now on a level with mine.

'What – ' he began.

'They're married,' said Mrs Fitz, beaming. 'How sweet! You can give them your blessing, sir, while I get a room ready.' She turned and made off for the stairs, leaving a substantial gap in the crowd, through which I could see the now pasty-white face of the girl Laoghaire.

Callum and Jamie were both talking together, questions and explanations colliding in midair. I was beginning to wake up, though it would have been overstating matters to say I was entirely myself.

'Well,' Callum was saying, not altogether approvingly, 'if you're married, you're married. I'll have to talk to Dougal and Ned Gowan – there'll be legal matters to attend to. There are a few things you're entitled to when ye wed, by the terms of your mother's dower contract.'

I felt Jamie straighten slightly.

'Since ye mention it,' he said casually, 'I believe that's true. And one of the things I'm entitled to is a share of the quarterly rents from the MacKenzie lands. Dougal's brought back what he's collected so far; perhaps you'll tell him to leave aside my share when he does the reckoning? Now, if ye'll excuse me, Uncle, my wife is tired.' And hoisting me into a more solid position, he turned to the stairs.

I staggered across the room, still wobbly-legged, and collapsed gratefully on the huge tester bed our newly married status apparently entitled us to. It was soft, inviting, and – thanks to the ever-vigilant Mrs Fitz – clean. I wondered whether it were worth the effort to get up and wash my face before succumbing to the urge to sleep.

I had just about decided that I might get up for Gabriel's Trump, but not much else, when I saw that Jamie, who had not only washed face and hands but combed his hair to boot, was headed towards the door.

'Aren't you going to sleep?' I called. I thought he must be at least as tired as I, if less saddle sore.

'In a bit, Sassenach. I've a small errand to do first.' He went out, leaving me staring at the oaken door with a very unpleasant sensation in the pit of my stomach. I was remembering the look of gay anticipation on Laoghaire's face as she came round the corner, hearing Jamie's voice, and the look of angry shock that replaced it when she saw me cradled in his arms. I remembered the momentary tightening of his joints as he saw her, and wished most fervently that I had been able to see his face at that moment. I thought it likely he had gone now, unrested but washed and combed, to find the girl and break the news of his marriage. Had I seen his face I would at least have some idea what he meant to say to her.

Absorbed in the events of the last month, I had forgotten the girl entirely – and what she might mean to Jamie, or he to her. Granted, I had thought of her when the question of our abrupt marriage first occurred, and Jamie then had given no sign that she constituted an impediment so far as he was concerned.

But, of course, if her father would not allow her to marry an outlaw – and if Jamie needed a wife, in order to collect his share of the MacKenzie rents . . . well, one wife would do as well as another, in that case, and doubtless he would take what he could get. I thought I knew Jamie well enough now to see that practicality with him went deep – as it must, with a man who had spent the last few years of his life on the run. He would not, I thought, be swayed in his decisions by sentiment or the attraction of rose-leaf cheeks and hair like liquid gold. But that didn't mean that neither sentiment nor attraction existed.

There was, after all, the little scene I had witnessed in the alcove, Jamie holding the girl on his knee and kissing her ardently. (*I've held women in my arms before*, his voice came back to me, *and they've made my heart pound and my breath come short . . .*) I found that my hands were clenched, making bunched ridges in the green and yellow quilt. I released it and wiped my hands over my skirt, realizing in the process just how filthy they were, grimed with the dirt of two days of holding reins, with no respite in between for washing.

I rose and went to the basin, forgetting my tiredness. I found, a bit to my surprise, that I strongly disliked the memory of Jamie kissing Laoghaire. I remembered what he had said about that, too – *'Tis better to marry than burn, and I was burning badly then*. I burned a bit myself, flushing strongly as I remembered the effect of Jamie's kisses on my own lips. Burning, indeed.

I splashed water on my face, spluttering, trying to dissipate the feeling. I had no claim on Jamie's affections, I reminded myself firmly. I had married him from necessity. And he had married me for his own reasons, one of them being the frankly stated desire to alter his virginal state.

Another reason apparently being that he needed a wife in order to collect his income, and could not induce a girl of his own kind to marry him. A reason much less flattering than the first, if no more lofty.

Quite awake by now, I slowly changed from my stained travelling garments into a fresh shift, provided, as were the basin and ewer, by Mrs Fitz's minions. How she had managed to make accommodation for two newlyweds in the time between Jamie's abrupt announcement to Callum and the time we had mounted the stairs was one of the mysteries of the ages. Mrs Fitz, I reflected, would have done quite well in charge of the Savoy Hotel or the Ritz.

Such reflections made me suddenly more lonely for my own world than I had been in many days. *What am I doing here?* I asked myself for the thousandth time. Here, in this strange place, unreachable distances from everything familiar, from home and husband and friends, adrift and alone among what amounted to savages?

Husband. The thought brought me up short with a fresh jolt of panic. *Which* husband? The events following my one halfway-successful attempt to escape had happened with such swiftness that I had not had a moment alone to dwell upon my failure – or its consequences.

These consequences were rapidly becoming obvious. Accepting marriage to Jamie only from necessity, I had thought the expedient justified because it would assist me to regain the stone circle and – perhaps – find my way home to Frank. So far from doing that, I had landed right back where I had started this incredible adventure, but with the additional complication of a new husband – of whom I was undeniably very fond. I had begun to feel safe and even intermittently happy during the last weeks with Jamie. But now I realized that the happiness was probably an illusion, even if the safety were not.

I had no doubt that he would abide by what he conceived to be his responsibilities, and continue to protect me from any harm that threatened. But here, returned from the dreamlike isolation of our days among the wild hills and rough tracks, the filthy inns and fragrant forests, he must surely feel the pull of his old associations, as I felt mine. We had grown very close in the two weeks of our marriage, but I had felt that closeness crack under the strains of the last few days, and thought it might now shatter completely among the practical realities of life at Castle Leoch.

I leaned my head against the stone of the window casement, looking out across the courtyard. Alick MacKenzie and two of his stable lads were visible at the far side, rubbing down the ponies we had ridden in. The beasts, fed and watered adequately for the first time in two days, exuded contentment as willing hands curried the glossy sides and cleansed the dirt from hock and fetlock with twists of straw. A stable boy led away my fat little Thistle, who followed him happily towards the well-earned rest of her stable.

And with her, I thought, went my hopes of any imminent

escape and return to my own place. Oh, Frank. I closed my eyes, letting a tear slide down the side of my nose. I opened my eyes wide on the courtyard then, blinked and shut them tight, trying frantically to recall Frank's features. Just for a moment, when I closed my eyes, I had seen not my beloved husband but his ancestor, Black Jack Randall, full lips curved in a mocking smile. And shying mentally from that image, my mind had summoned at once a picture of Jamie, face set in fear and anger as I had seen him in the window of Randall's private office. Try as I might, I could not bring back Frank's remembered image with any certainty.

I felt suddenly quite cold with panic, and clasped my hands about my elbows. And what if I had succeeded in escaping and finding my way back to the circle of stone? What then? Jamie would, I hoped, soon find solace – with Laoghaire, perhaps. I had worried before about his reaction to finding me gone. But aside from that hasty moment of regret on the edge of the burn, it had not before occurred to me to wonder how I would feel to part with him. If I meant to leave, as I did, I was doing neither of us a favour by allowing the bond between us to strengthen any further. I should not allow him to fall in love with me.

If he meant to do any such thing, I thought, remembering once more Laoghaire and the conversation with Callum. If he had married me so cold-bloodedly as it seemed, perhaps his emotions were safer than mine.

Between fatigue, hunger, disappointment and uncertainty, I had by this time succeeded in reducing myself to such a state of confused misery that I could neither sleep nor sit still. Instead I roamed unhappily about the room, picking up objects and putting them down at random.

The draught from the opening door upset the delicate equilibrium of the comb I had been balancing on its end, heralding Jamie's return. He looked faintly flushed and oddly excited.

'Oh, you're awake,' he said, obviously surprised and disconcerted to find me so.

'Yes,' I said unkindly, 'were you hoping I'd be asleep so you could go back to her?'

His brows drew together for a moment, then raised in inquiry. 'Her? To Laoghaire, ye mean?'

Hearing her name spoken in that casual Highland lilt – 'L'heer' – suddenly made me irrationally angry.

'Oh, so you *have* been with her!' I snapped.

Jamie looked puzzled and wary, and slightly annoyed. 'Aye,' he said. 'I met her by the stair as I went out. Are ye well, Sassenach? Ye look a bit fashed, all in all.' He eyed me appraisingly. I picked up the looking glass and found that my hair was standing out in a bushy mane round my head and there were dark circles under my eyes. I put it down again with a thump.

'No, I'm perfectly all right,' I said, with an effort at controlling myself. 'And how is Laoghaire?' I asked, assuming casualness.

'Oh, quite bonny,' he said. He leaned back against the door, arms crossed, watching me speculatively. 'A bit surprised to hear we were married, I reckon.'

'Bonny,' I said, and took a deep breath. I looked up to find him grinning at me.

'You'd not worry yourself over the lassie, would ye now, Sassenach?' he asked shrewdly. 'She's naught to you – or me,' he added.

'Oh, no? She wouldn't – or couldn't – marry you. You had to have someone, so you took me when the chance offered. I don't blame you for that' – not much I didn't – 'but I –'

He crossed the room in two steps and took me by the hands, interrupting me. He put a finger under my chin and forced my gaze up.

'Claire,' he said evenly, 'I shall tell ye in my own time why I've wed ye – or I won't. I asked honesty of you, and I've given ye the same. And I give it to you now. The girl has no claim on me beyond that of courtesy.' He squeezed my chin lightly. 'But that claim she has, and I'll honour it.' He released my chin and chucked me softly under it. 'D'ye hear me, Sassenach?'

'Oh, I hear!' I jerked free, rubbing my chin resentfully.

'And I'm sure you'll be very courteous to her. But next time draw the drapes of the alcove – I don't want to see it.'

The coppery brows shot up, and his face reddened slightly.

'Are ye suggesting I've played ye false?' he said unbelievingly. 'We've been back to the castle less than an hour, I'm covered wi' the sweat and dust of two days in the saddle, and so tired my knees wobble, and yet ye think I've gone straight out to seduce a maid of sixteen?' He shook his head, looking stunned. 'I canna tell whether ye mean to compliment my virility, Sassenach, or insult my morals, but I dinna care much for either suggestion. Murtagh told me women were unreasonable, but Jesus God!' He ran a large hand through his hair, making the short ends stick up wildly.

'Of course I don't mean I think you've been seducing her,' I said, struggling to inject an air of calmness into my tone. 'All I mean . . .' It occurred to me that Frank had handled this kind of thing much more gracefully than I was managing to do, and yet I had been angry then too. Likely there was no good way to suggest such a possibility to one's mate.

'I simply mean that . . . that I realize that you married me for your own reasons – and those reasons are your own business,' I added hastily, 'and that I have no claim at all on you. You're at perfect liberty to behave as you wish. If you . . . if there's an attraction elsewhere . . . I mean . . . I won't stand in your way,' I finished lamely. The blood was hot in my cheeks and I could feel my ears burning.

Looking up, I found that Jamie's ears were burning as well, visibly, and so was the rest of him from the neck up. Even his eyes, bloodshot from lack of sleep, seemed to be flaming slightly.

'No claim on me!' he exclaimed. 'And what d'ye think a wedding vow is, lassie? Just words in a church?' He brought his big fist down on the chest with a crash that shook the porcelain ewer. 'No claim,' he muttered, as though to himself. 'At liberty to behave as I wish. And you'll not stand in my way?!'

He bent to pull off his boots, then picked them up and

threw them, one after the other, as hard as he could at the wall. I winced as each one thudded off the stones and bounced to the floor. He yanked off his plaid and tossed it heedlessly behind him. Then he started towards me, glaring.

'So you've no claim on me, Sassenach? You'll free me to take my pleasure where I like, is that it? Well, is it?' he demanded.

'Er, well, yes,' I said, taking a step backwards despite myself. 'That's what I meant.' He grabbed my arms, and I found the combustion had spread to his hands as well. His calloused palms were so hot on my skin that I jerked involuntarily.

'Well, if you've no claim on me, Sassenach,' he said, 'I've one on you! Come here.' He took my face in his hands and set his mouth on mine. There was nothing either gentle or undemanding about that kiss, and I fought against it, trying to pull back from him.

He bent and scooped me up with an arm under my knees, ignoring my attempts to get down. I hadn't realized just how bloody strong he really was.

'Let go of me!' I said. 'What do you think you're doing?'

'Well, I should ha' thought that was reasonably clear, Sassenach,' he said through his teeth. He lowered his head, the clear gaze piercing me like a hot iron. 'Though if ye want telling,' he said, 'I mean to take ye to bed. Now. And keep ye there until you've learned just what claim I have on you.' And he kissed me again, deliberately hard, cutting off my protest.

'I don't want to sleep with you!' I said, when at last he freed my mouth.

'I dinna intend to sleep, Sassenach,' he replied evenly. 'Not just yet.' He reached the bed and set me carefully on the quilt.

'You know bloody well what I mean!' I rolled, meaning to escape from the other side, but was stopped by a solid grip on my shoulder that flipped me back to face him. 'I don't want to make love with you, either!'

Blue eyes blazed down at me from close range, and my breath came thick in my throat.

'I didna ask your preference in the matter, Sassenach,' he answered, voice dangerously low. 'You are my wife, as I've told ye often enough. If ye didna wish to wed me, still ye chose to. And if ye didna happen to notice at the time, your part of the proceedings included the word "obey". You're my wife, and if I want ye, woman, then I'll have you, and be damned to ye!' His voice rose throughout, until he was near shouting.

I rose to my knees, fists balled at my sides, and shouted back at him. The contained misery of the last hour had reached explosion point and I let him have it, point-blank.

'I *will* be damned if I'll have *you*, you bullying swine! You think you can order me to your bed? Use me like a whore when you feel like it? Well, you can't, you fucking bastard! Do that, and you're no better than your precious Captain Randall!'

He glared at me for a moment, then stood abruptly aside. 'Leave, then,' he said, jerking his head towards the door. 'If that's what ye think of me, go! I'll not hinder ye.'

I hesitated for a moment, watching him. His jaw was clenched with anger and he was looming over me like the Colossus of Rhodes. His temper this time was under tight rein, though he was as angry now as he had been after extricating me from Fort William. But he meant it. If I chose to leave, he wouldn't stop me.

I lifted my chin, my own jaw clenched as tightly as his. 'No,' I said. 'No. I don't run away from things. And I'm not afraid of you.'

His gaze fastened on my throat, where my pulse was going at a frantic rate.

'Aye, I see,' he said. He stared down at me and his face gradually relaxed into a look of grudging acquiescence. He sat down gingerly on the bed, keeping a good distance between us, and I sat back warily. He breathed deeply several times before speaking, his face fading a bit towards its natural ruddy bronze.

'I don't run either, Sassenach,' he said gruffly. 'Now, then. What does "fucking" mean?'

My surprise must have shown plainly, for he said irritably,

439

'If ye must call me names, that's one thing. But I dinna care to be called things I can't answer. I know it's a damn filthy word, from the way ye said it, but what does it mean?'

Taken off guard, I laughed a little shakily. 'It . . . it means . . . what you were about to do to me.'

One brow lifted, and he looked sourly amused. 'Oh, swiving? Then I was right; it is a damn filthy word. And what's a sadist? Ye called me that the other day.'

I suppressed the urge to laugh. 'It's, er, it's a person who . . . who, er, gets sexual pleasure from hurting someone.' My face was crimsoning, but I couldn't stop the corners of my mouth from turning up slightly.

Jamie snorted briefly. 'Well, ye dinna flatter me owermuch,' he said, 'but I canna fault your observations.' He took a deep breath and leaned back, unclenching his hands. He stretched his fingers deliberately, then laid his hands flat on his knees and looked directly at me.

'What is it, then? Why are ye doing this? The girl? I've told ye the plain truth there. But it's not a matter for proof. It's a question of whether ye believe me or no. Do ye believe me?'

'Yes, I believe you,' I admitted grudgingly. 'But that's not it. Or not all of it,' I added, in an attempt at honesty. 'It's . . . I think it's finding that you married me for the money you'd get.' I looked down, tracing the pattern of the quilt with my finger. 'I know I've no right to complain – I married you for selfish reasons, too, but' – I bit my lip and swallowed to steady my voice – 'but I have a small bit of pride too, you know.'

I stole a glance at him and found him staring at me with an expression of complete dumbfoundedness.

'Money?' he said blankly.

'Yes, money!' I blazed, angered at his pretence of ignorance. 'When we came back, you couldn't wait to tell Callum you were married and collect your share of the MacKenzie rents!'

He stared at me for a moment longer, mouth opening gradually as though to say something. Instead he began to shake his head slowly back and forth, and then began to laugh. He threw his head back and roarcd, in fact, then sank his head between his hands, still laughing hysterically. I flung myself back on the pillows in indignation. Funny, was it?

Still shaking his head and wheezing intermittently, he stood up and set hands to the buckle of his belt. I flinched involuntarily as he did so, and he saw it.

Face still flushed with a mixture of anger and laughter, he looked down at me in total exasperation. 'No,' he said dryly, 'I dinna mean to beat you. I gave ye my word I'd not do so again – though I didna think I'd regret it quite so soon.' He laid the belt aside, groping in the sporran attached to it.

'My share of the MacKenzie rents comes to about twenty pounds a quarter, Sassenach,' he said, digging through the oddments inside the pouch. 'And that's Scots, not sterling. About the price of half a cow.'

'That's . . . that's all?' I said stupidly. 'But – '

'That's all,' he confirmed. 'And all I ever will have from the MacKenzies. Ye'll have noticed Dougal's a thrifty man, and Callum's twice as tightfisted wi' his coin. But even the princely sum of twenty pounds a quarter is hardly worth marrying to get, I should think,' he added sarcastically, eyeing me.

'I wouldna have asked for it straight away, at that,' he added, bringing out a small paper-wrapped parcel, 'but there was something I wanted to buy with some of it. That's where my errand took me; meeting Laoghaire was an accident.'

'And what did you want to buy so much?' I asked suspiciously.

He sighed and hesitated for a moment, then tossed the small package lightly into my lap.

'A wedding ring, Sassenach,' he said. 'I got it from Ewen the armourer; he makes such things in his own time.'

'Oh,' I said in a small voice.

'Go ahead,' he said, a moment later. 'Open it. It's yours.'

The outlines of the little package blurred under my fin-

441

gers. I blinked and sniffed, but made no move to open it. 'I'm sorry,' I said.

'Well, so ye should be, Sassenach,' he said, but his voice was no longer angry. Reaching, he took the package from my lap and tore away the wrapping, revealing a wide silver band, decorated in the Highland interlace style, a small and delicate Jacobean thistle bloom carved in the centre of each link.

So much I saw, and then my eyes blurred again.

I found a handkerchief thrust into my hand, and did my best to stanch the flow with it. 'It's . . . beautiful,' I said, clearing my throat and dabbling at my eyes.

'Will ye wear it, Claire?' His voice was gentle now, and his use of my name, mostly reserved for occasions of formality or tenderness, nearly made me break down again.

'You needna do so,' he said, looking at me seriously over his cupped palm. 'The marriage contract between us is satisfied – it's legal. You're protected, safe from anything much save a warrant, and even from that, so long as you're at Leoch. If ye wish, we may live apart – if that's what ye were trying to say wi' all yon rubbish about Laoghaire. You need have little more to do wi' me, if that's your honest choice.' He sat motionless, waiting, holding the tiny circlet near his heart.

So he was giving me the choice I had started out to give him. Forced on me by circumstance, he would force himself on me no longer, if I chose to reject him. And there was the alternative, of course: to accept the ring, and all that went with it.

The sun was setting. The last rays of light shone through a blue glass flagon that stood on the table, streaking the wall with a shaft of brilliant lapis. I felt as fragile and as brilliant as the glass, as though I would shatter with a touch, and fall in glittering fragments to the floor. If I had meant to spare either Jamie's emotions or my own, it seemed I was very much too late.

I couldn't speak, but held out my right hand to him, fingers trembling. The ring slipped cool and bright over my knuckle and rested snug at the base of my finger – a good fit.

Jamie held my hand a moment, looking at it, then suddenly pressed my knuckles hard against his mouth. He raised his head and I saw his face for an instant, fierce and urgent, before he pulled me roughly on to his lap.

He held me hard against him then, without speaking, and I could feel the pulsebeat in his throat, hammering like my own. His hands went to my shoulders and he held me slightly away, so that I was looking upwards into his face. His hands were large and very warm, and I felt slightly dizzy.

'I want ye, Claire,' he said, sounding choked. He paused a moment, as though unsure what to say next. 'I want ye so much – I can scarcely breathe. Will – ' He swallowed, then cleared his throat. 'Will ye have me?'

By now I had found my voice. It squeaked and wobbled, but it worked.

'Yes,' I said. 'Yes, I'll have you.'

'I think . . .' he began, then stopped. He fumbled loose the buckle of his kilt, but then looked up at me, bunching his hands at his sides. He spoke with difficulty, controlling something so powerful that his hands shook with the effort. 'I'll not . . . I can't . . . Claire, I canna be gentle about it.'

I had time only to nod once, in acknowledgement or permission, before he bore me back before him, his weight pinning me to the bed.

We did not pause to undress further. I could smell the road dust in his shirt and taste the sun and sweat of travel on his skin. He held me, arms outstretched, wrists pinioned. One hand brushed the wall, and I felt the tiny scrape of one wedding ring chiming against the stone. One ring for each hand, one silver, one gold. And the thin metal suddenly heavy as the bonds of matrimony, as though the rings were tiny shackles, fastening me spread-eagled to the bed, stretched for ever between two poles, held in bondage like Prometheus on his lonely rock, divided love the vulture that tore at my heart.

He spread my thighs with his knee and sheathed himself to the root in a single thrust that made me gasp. He made a sound that was almost a groan, and gripped me tighter.

'You're mine, *mo duinne*,' he said softly, pressing himself into my depths. 'Mine alone, now and for ever. Mine, whether ye will it or no.' I pulled against his grip and sucked in my breath with a faint 'ah' as he pressed even deeper.

'Aye, I mean to use ye hard, my Sassenach,' he whispered. 'I want to own you, to possess you, body and soul.' I struggled slightly and he pressed me down, hammering me, a solid, inexorable pounding that reached my womb with each stroke. 'I mean to make ye call me "Master", Sassenach.' His soft voice was a threat of revenge for the agonies of the last minutes. 'I mean to make you mine.'

I quivered and moaned then, my flesh clutching in spasms at the invading, battering presence. The movement went on, disregarding, on and on for minutes, striking me over and over with an impact on the edge between pleasure and pain. I felt dissolved, as though I existed only at the point of the assault, being forced to the edge of some total surrender.

'No!' I gasped. 'Stop, please, you're hurting me!' Beads of sweat ran down his face and dropped on the pillow and on my breasts. Our flesh met now with the smack of a blow that was fast crossing the edge into pain. My thighs were bruising with the repeated impact, and my wrists felt as though they would break, but his grip was inexorable.

'Aye, beg me for mercy, Sassenach. Ye shallna have it, though; not yet.' His breath came hot and fast but he showed no signs of tiring. My entire body convulsed, legs rising to wrap around him, seeking to contain the sensation.

I could feel the jolt of each stroke deep in my belly, and cringed from it, even as my hips rose traitorously to welcome it. He felt my response and redoubled his assault, pressing now on my shoulders to keep me pinned under him.

There was no beginning and no end to my response, only a continuous shudder that rose to a peak with each thrust. The hammering was a question, repeated over and over in my flesh, demanding my answer. He pushed my legs flat again, and bore me down past pain and into pure sensation, over the edge of surrender.

'Yes!' I cried. 'Oh God, Jamie, yes!' He gripped my hair

and forced my head back to meet his eyes, glowing with furious triumph.

'Aye, Sassenach,' he muttered, answering my movements rather than my words. 'Ride ye I will!' His hands dropped to my breasts, squeezing and stroking, then slid down my sides. His whole weight rested on me now as he cupped and raised me for still greater penetration. I screamed then and he stopped my mouth with his, not a kiss, but another attack, forcing my mouth open, bruising my lips and rasping my face with bearded stubble. He thrust harder and faster, as though he would force my soul as he forced my body. In body or soul, somewhere he struck a spark, and an answering fury of passion and need sprang from the ashes of surrender. I arched upwards to meet him, blow for blow. I bit his lip and tasted blood.

I felt his teeth then on my neck and dug my nails into his back. I raked him from nape to buttocks, spurring him to rear and scream in his turn. We savaged each other in desperate need, biting and clawing, trying to draw blood, trying each to pull the other into ourselves, tearing each other's flesh in the consuming desire to be one. My cry mingled with his, and we lost ourselves finally in each other in that last moment of dissolution and completion.

I returned only slowly to myself, lying half on Jamie's breast, sweated bodies still glued together, thigh to thigh. He breathed heavily, eyes closed. I could hear his heart under my ear, beating with the preternaturally slow and powerful rhythm that follows climax.

He felt me wake and drew me close, as though to preserve a moment longer the union we had reached in those last seconds of our perilous joining. I curled beside him, putting my arms around him.

He opened his eyes then and sighed, the long mouth curling in a faint smile as his glance met mine. I raised my brows in silent question.

'Oh, aye, Sassenach,' he answered a bit ruefully. 'I am your master . . . and you're mine. Seems I canna possess your soul without losing my own.' He turned me on my

445

side and curled his body around me. The room was cooling in the evening breeze from the window, and he reached to draw a quilt over us. *You're too quick by half, lad*, I thought drowsily to myself. *Frank never did find that out.* I fell asleep with his arms locked hard around me and his breathing warm in my ear.

I was lame and sore in every muscle when I woke next morning. I shuffled to the privy closet, then to the wash basin to strip and wash. My innards felt like churned butter. It felt as though I had been beaten with a blunt object, I reflected, then thought that that was very near the truth. The blunt object in question was visible as I came back to bed, looking now relatively harmless. Its possessor woke as I sat down next to him, and examined me with something that looked very much like male smugness.

'Looks as though it was a hard ride, Sassenach,' he said, lightly touching a blue bruise on my inner thigh. 'A bit saddle-sore, are ye?'

I narrowed my eyes and traced a deep bite-mark on his shoulder with my finger.

'You look a bit ragged around the edges yourself, my lad.'

'Ah, weel,' he said in broad Scots, 'if ye bed wi' a vixen, ye must expect to get bit.' He reached up and grasped me behind the neck, pulling me down to him. 'Come here to me, vixen. Bite me some more.'

'Oh, no you don't,' I said, pulling back. 'I can't possibly; I'm too sore.'

James Fraser was not a man to take no for an answer.

'I'll be verra gentle,' he wheedled, dragging me inexorably under the quilt. And he was gentle, as only big men can be, cradling me like a quail's egg, paying me court with a humble patience that I recognized as reparation – and a gentle insistence that I knew was a·continuation of the lesson so brutally begun the night before. Gentle he would be, denied he would not.

He shook in my arms at his own finish, shuddering with

446

the effort not to move, not to hurt me by thrusting, letting the moment shatter him as it would.

Afterwards, still joined, he traced the fading bruises his fingers had left on my shoulders by the track above Fort William.

'I'm sorry for those, *mo duinne*,' he said, gently kissing each one. 'I was in a rare temper when I did it, but it's no excuse. It's shameful to hurt a woman, in a rage or no. I'll not do it again.'

I laughed ironically. 'You're apologizing for *those*? What about the rest? I'm a mass of bruises, from head to toe!'

'Och?' He drew back to look me over judiciously. 'Well now, these I've apologized for' – touching my shoulder – '*those*' – slapping my rear lightly – 'ye deserved, and I'll not say I'm sorry for it, because I'm not.

'As for these,' he said, stroking my thigh, 'I'll not apologize for that, either. Ye paid me full measure already.' He rubbed his shoulder, grimacing. 'Ye drew blood in at least two places, Sassenach, and my back stings like holy hell.'

'Well, bed with a vixen . . .' I said, grinning. 'You won't get an apology for that.' He laughed in response and pulled me on top of him.

'I didna say I wanted an apology, did I? If I recall aright, what I said was "Bite me again".'

PART FOUR

A Whiff of Brimstone

24

By the Pricking of my Thumbs

The hubbub occasioned by our sudden arrival and the announcement of our marriage was overshadowed almost at once by an event of greater importance.

We were sitting at supper in the Great Hall that day, accepting the toasts and good wishes being offered in our honour.

'*Buidheachas, mo caraid.*' Jamie bowed gracefully to the latest toaster, and sat down amid the increasingly sporadic applause. The wooden bench shook under his weight, and he closed his eyes briefly.

'Getting a bit much for you?' I whispered. He had borne the brunt of the toasting, matching each cup drained on our behalf, while I had so far escaped with no more than token sips, accompanied by bright smiles at the incomprehensible Gaelic toasts.

He opened his eyes and looked down at me, smiling himself.

'Am I drunk, do ye mean? Nay, I could drink this stuff all night.'

'You practically have,' I said, peering at the array of empty wine bottles and stone ale-jars lined up on the board in front of us. 'It's getting rather late.' The candles on Callum's table burned low in their holders and the guttered wax glowed gold, the light marking the MacKenzie brothers with odd patches of shadow and glinting flesh as they leaned together, talking in low voices. They could have joined the company of carved gnomic heads that edged the huge fireplace, and I wondered how many of those caricatured figures had in fact been drawn from the patronizing features of earlier MacKenzie lairds – perhaps by a carver with a sense of humour ... or a strong family connection.

Jamie stretched slightly in his seat, grimacing in mild discomfort.

'On the other hand,' he said, 'my bladder's going to burst in another moment or two. I'll be back shortly.' He put his hands on the bench and hopped nimbly up and over it, disappearing through the lower archway.

I turned my attention to my other side, where Geillis Duncan sat, demurely sipping at a silver cup of ale. Her husband Arthur sat at the next table with Callum, as befitted the procurator fiscal of the district, but Geilie had insisted on sitting next to me, saying that she had no wish to be wearied by hearing man-talk all through supper.

Arthur's deep-set eyes were half closed, blue-pouched and sunk with wine and fatigue. He leaned heavily on his forearms, face slack, ignoring the conversation of the MacKenzies next to him. While the light threw the sharp-cut features of the laird and his brother into a high relief, it merely made Arthur Duncan look fat and ill.

'Your husband isn't looking very well,' I observed. 'Has his stomach trouble grown worse?' The symptoms were rather puzzling; not like ulcer, I thought, nor cancer – not with that much flesh still on his bones – perhaps just chronic gastritis, as Geilie insisted.

She cast the briefest of glances at her spouse before turning back to me with a shrug.

'Oh, he's well enough,' she said. 'No worse, at any rate. But what about *your* husband?'

'Er, what about him?' I replied cautiously.

She dug me familiarly in the ribs with a rather sharp elbow, and I realized that there were a fair number of bottles at her end of the table as well.

'Well, what d'ye think? Does he look as nice out of his sark as he does in it?'

'Um . . .' I groped for an answer as she craned her neck towards the entryway.

'And you claiming you didna care a bit for him! Clever-boots. Half the girls in the castle would like to tear your hair out by the roots – I'd be careful what I ate, if I were you.'

'What I eat?' I looked down in bafflement at the wooden platter before me, empty but for a smear of grease and a forlorn boiled onion.

'Poison,' she hissed dramatically in my ear, along with a considerable wafting of brandy fumes.

'Nonsense,' I said rather coldly, drawing away from her. 'No one would want to poison me simply because I . . . well, because . . .' I was floundering a bit, and it occurred to me that I might have had a few sips more than I had realized.

'Now, really, Geilie. This marriage . . . I didn't plan it, you know. I didn't *want* it!' No lie there. 'It was merely a . . . sort of . . . necessary business arrangement,' I said, hoping the candlelight hid my blushes.

'Ha,' she said cynically. 'I ken the look of a lass that's been well bedded.' She glanced towards the archway where Jamie had disappeared. 'And damned if I think those are midge bites on the laddie's neck, either.' She raised one silver brow at me. 'If it was a business arrangement I'd say ye got your money's worth.'

She leaned close again.

'Is it true?' she whispered. 'About the thumbs?'

'Thumbs? Geilie, what in God's name are you babbling about?'

She looked down her small, straight nose at me, frowning in concentration. The beautiful green eyes were slightly unfocused, and I hoped she wouldn't fall over.

'Surely ye know that? Everyone knows! A man's thumbs tell ye the size of his cock. Great toes, too, of course,' she added judiciously, 'but those are harder to judge, usually, what wi' the shoon and all. Yon wee fox cub' – she nodded towards the archway, where Jamie had just reappeared – 'he could cup a good-sized marrow in those hands of his. Or a good-sized arse, hm?' she added, nudging me once more.

'Geillis Duncan, will . . . you . . . shut . . . up!' I hissed, face flaming. 'Someone will hear you!'

'Oh, no one who – ' she began, but stopped, staring. Jamie had passed right by our table as though he didn't see

453

us. His face was pale and his lips set firmly, as though bent on some unpleasant duty.

'Whatever ails him?' Geilie asked. 'He looks like Arthur after he's eaten raw apples.'

'I don't know.' I pushed back the bench, hesitating. He was heading for Callum's table. Should I follow him? Plainly something had happened.

Geilie, peering back down the room, suddenly tugged at my sleeve, pointing in the direction from which Jamie had appeared.

A man stood just within the archway . . . a messenger. Someone else from the Duke? After all the rush to get back to Leoch, we had been greeted with a message to the effect that the Duke had been delayed, and would not arrive for several weeks more. Perhaps he had had second thoughts, or was cancelling his journey altogether? Whatever the message, he had passed it on to Jamie, who was even now bending to whisper it in Callum's ear.

No, not Callum. Dougal. The red head bent low between the two dark ones, the broad handsome features of the three faces taking on an unearthly similarity in the light of the dying candles. And as I watched, I realized that the similarity was due not so much to the inheritance of bone and sinew that they shared, but to the expression of shocked grief that they now held in common.

Geilie's hand was digging into the flesh of my forearm.

'Bad news,' she said unnecessarily.

'Twenty-four years,' I said softly. 'It seems a long time to be married.'

'Aye, it does,' Jamie agreed. A warm wind stirred the branches of the tree above us, lifting the hair from my shoulders to tickle my face. 'Longer than I've been alive.'

I glanced at him leaning on the paddock wall, all lanky grace and strong bones. I tended to forget how young he really was; he seemed so self-assured and capable.

'Still,' he said, flicking a straw into the churned mud of the paddock, 'I doubt Dougal spent more than three years of that with her. He was generally here, ye ken, at the

454

castle – or here and there about the lands, doing Callum's business for him.'

Dougal's wife, Maura, had died at their estate of Beannachd. A sudden fever. Dougal himself had left at dawn, in company with Ned Gowan and the messenger who had brought the news the night before, to arrange the funeral and dispose of his wife's property.

'Not a close marriage, then?' I asked curiously.

Jamie shrugged.

'As close as most, I should reckon. She had the children and the running of the house to keep her busy; I doubt she missed him greatly, though she seemed glad enough to see him when he came home.'

'That's right, you lived with them for a time, didn't you?' I was quiet, thinking. I wondered whether this was Jamie's idea of marriage; separate lives, joining only infrequently for the breeding of children. Yet, from the little he had said, his own parents' marriage had been a close and loving one.

With that uncanny trick of reading my thoughts, he said, 'It was different wi' my own folk, ye ken. Dougal's was an arranged marriage, like Callum's, and a matter more of lands and business than the wanting of each other. But my parents – well, they wed for love, against the wishes of both families, and so we were . . . not cut off, exactly; but more by ourselves at Lallybroch. My parents didna go often to visit relatives or do business outside, and so I think they turned more to each other than husband and wife usually do.'

He laid a hand low on my back and urged me closer to him. He bent his head and brushed his lips across the top of my ear.

'It was an arrangement between us,' he said softly. 'Still, I would hope . . . perhaps one day – ' he broke off awkwardly, with a crooked smile and a gesture of dismissal.

Not wanting to encourage him in that direction, I smiled back as neutrally as I could and turned towards the paddock. I could feel him there beside me, not quite touching, big hands gripping the wall. I gripped it myself, to keep from taking his hand. I wanted more than anything to turn to him, offer him comfort, assure him with body and words that what lay between us *was* more than a business arrangement. It was the truth of it that stopped me.

What it is between us, he had said. *When I lie with you, when you touch me.* No, it wasn't usual at all. It wasn't a simple infatuation, either, as I had first thought. Nothing could be less simple.

The fact remained that I was bound, by vows and loyalty and law, to another man. And by love as well.

I could not, could *not* tell Jamie what I felt for him. To do that and then to leave, as I must, would be the height of cruelty. Neither could I lie to him.

'Claire.' He had turned to me, was looking down at me; I could feel it. I didn't speak, but raised my face to him as he bent to kiss me. I couldn't lie to him that way either, and didn't. After all, I thought dimly, I had promised him honesty.

We were interrupted by a loud 'Ahem!' from behind the paddock wall. Jamie, startled, whirled towards the sound, instinctively thrusting me behind him. Then he stopped and grinned, seeing Auld Alick standing there in his filthy trews, viewing us sardonically with his one bright blue eye.

The old man held a wicked-looking pair of gelding shears, which he raised in ironic salute.

'I was goin' to use these on Mahomet,' he remarked. 'Perhaps they could be put to better use here, eh?' He snicked the thick blades invitingly. 'It'd keep your mind on your work and off your cock, laddie.'

'Don't even jest about it, man,' said Jamie, grinning. 'Wanting me, were ye?'

Alick waggled an eyebrow like a woolly caterpillar.

'No, what gives ye to think that? I thought I'd like to try gelding a blooded two-year-old all by mysel', for the joy of it.' He wheezed briefly at his own wit, then waved the shears towards the castle.

'Off wi' ye, lassie. Ye can have him back at supper – for what good he'll be to ye by then.'

Apparently not trusting the nature of this last remark, Jamie reached out a long arm and neatly snagged the shears.

'I'll feel safer if *I've* got these,' he said, cocking an eyebrow at the old man. 'Go along, Sassenach. When I've finished doing all of Alick's work for him I'll come and find ye.'

He leaned down to kiss my cheek, and whispered in my ear, 'The stables. When the sun's mid-sky.'

The stables of Castle Leoch were better built than many of the cottages I had seen on our journey with Dougal: stone floored and stone walled, the only openings the narrow windows at one end, the door at the other, and the narrow slits under the thick thatched roof, intended for the convenience of the owls who kept down the mice in the hay. They let in plenty of air, though, and enough light that the stables were pleasantly dim rather than gloomy.

Up in the hayloft, just under the roof, the light was even better, striping the piled hay with yellow bars and lighting the drifting dust motes like showers of gold dust. The air came in through the chinks in warm draughts, scented with stock and horseradish and garlic from the gardens outside, and the pleasant animal smell of the horses and ponies wafted up from below. Jamie and I had taken to meeting there on quiet afternoons.

Jamie stirred under my hand and sat up, the movement bringing his head from the shadow into a blaze of sunlight like the lighting of a candle.

'What is it?' I asked sleepily, turning my head in the direction he was looking.

'Wee Hamish,' he said softly, peering over the edge of the loft into the stable. 'Wants his pony, I expect.'

I rolled awkwardly on to my stomach beside him, dragging the folds of my shift over me for modesty's sake; a silly thought, as no one below could see more than the top of my head.

Callum's son Hamish was walking slowly down the aisle of the stable between the stalls. He seemed to hesitate near some stalls, though he ignored the curious heads of chestnut

457

and sorrel poking out to inspect him. Clearly he was looking for something, and it wasn't his fat brown pony, placidly munching straw in its stall near the stable door.

'Holy God, he's going for Donas!' Jamie seized his kilt and wrapped it hurriedly about himself before swinging down from the edge of the loft. Not bothering with the ladder, he hung by his hands and then dropped to the floor. He landed lightly on the straw-scattered stones, but with enough of a thud to make Hamish whirl around with a startled gasp.

The small freckled face relaxed somewhat as he realized who it was, but the blue eyes stayed wary.

'Needing a bit of help, coz?' Jamie inquired pleasantly. He moved towards the stalls and leaned against one of the uprights, managing to insert himself between Hamish and the stall the boy had been heading for.

Hamish hesitated, but then drew himself up, small chin thrust out.

'I'm going to ride Donas,' he said, in a tone that tried for determination, but fell somewhat short.

Donas – his name meant 'demon' and was in no way meant as flattery – was in a stall to himself at the far end of the stable, safely separated by an empty stall from the nearest neighbouring animals. A huge, evil-tempered sorrel stallion, he was rideable by no one, and only Alick and Jamie dared go near him. There was an irritable squeal from the shadows of his stall, and an enormous coppery head shot suddenly out, huge yellow teeth clacking together as the horse made a vain attempt to bite the bare shoulder so temptingly displayed.

Jamie stayed motionless, knowing that the stallion couldn't reach him. Hamish jumped back with a squeak, clearly scared speechless by the sudden appearance of that monstrous shimmering head with its rolling, bloodshot eyes and flaring nostrils.

'I dinna think so,' observed Jamie mildly. He reached down and took his small cousin by the shoulder, steering him away from the horse, who kicked his stall in protest.

Hamish shuddered in concert with the boards of the stall as the lethal hooves crashed against the wood.

Jamie turned the boy around to face him and stood looking down at him, hands on his kilted hips.

'Now then,' he said firmly. 'What's this all about? Why are ye wanting aught to do wi' Donas?'

Hamish's jaw was set stubbornly, but Jamie's face was both encouraging and adamant. He punched the boy gently on the shoulder, getting a tiny smile in response.

'Come on, laddie,' Jamie said softly. 'Ye know I willna tell anyone. Have ye done something foolish?'

A faint flush came up on the boy's fair skin.

'No. At least . . . no. Well, maybe a bit foolish.'

After a bit more encouragement the story came out, reluctantly at first, then in a tumbling flood of confession.

He had been out on his pony, riding with some of the other boys the day before. Several of the older lads had started competing, to see who could jump his horse over a higher obstacle. Jealously admiring them, Hamish found his better judgement finally overcome by bravado, and he had tried to force his fat little pony over a stone wall. Lacking both ability and interest, the pony had come to a dead stop at the wall, tossing young Hamish over his head, over the wall, and ignominiously into a nettle patch on the other side. Stung both by nettles and by the hoots of his comrades, Hamish was determined to come out today on 'a proper horse', as he put it.

'They wouldna laugh if I came out on Donas,' he said, envisioning the scene with grim relish.

'No, they wouldna laugh,' Jamie agreed. 'They'd be too busy picking up the pieces.'

He eyed his cousin, shaking his head slowly. 'I'll tell ye, lad. It takes courage and sense to make a good rider. You've the courage, but the sense is a wee bit lacking, yet.' He put a consoling arm round Hamish's shoulders, drawing him down towards the end of the stable.

'Come along, man. Help me fork the hay, and we'll get ye acquainted wi' Cobhar. You're right; ye should have a better mount if you're ready, but it isna necessary to kill yourself to prove it.'

Glancing up into the loft as he passed, he raised his eyebrows and shrugged helplessly. I smiled and waved down at him, telling him to go ahead, it was all right. I watched them as Jamie took an apple from the basket of windfalls kept near the door. Fetching a pitchfork from the corner, he led Hamish back to one of the centre stalls.

'Here, coz,' he said, pausing. He whistled softly through his teeth and a wide-browed bay pony put its head out, blowing through its nostrils. The dark eyes were large and kind and the ears had a slight forward cock that gave the horse an expression of friendly alertness.

'Now then, Cobhar, *ciamar a tha thu?*' Jamie patted the big pony's sleek neck firmly and scratched the cocked ears.

'Come on up,' he said, motioning to his small cousin. 'That's it, next to me. Near enough he can smell ye. Horses like to smell ye.'

'*I* know.' Hamish's high voice was scornful, but he reached out and patted. He stood his ground as the big head sniffed interestedly around his ear, whuffling in his hair.

'Give me an apple,' he said to Jamie, who obliged. The soft velvet lips plucked the fruit delicately out of Hamish's palm and flicked it back between the huge molars, where it vanished with a juicy crunch. Jamie watched approvingly.

'Aye. You'll get on fine. Go on and make friends, then, while I finish feeding the others, then ye can take him out to ride.'

'By myself?' Hamish asked eagerly. Cobhar, whose name meant Foam, was good-tempered, but big nonetheless, and a far cry from the brown pony.

'Twice round the paddock wi' me watchin' ye, and if ye dinna fall off or jerk his mouth, ye can take him by yourself. No jumping him till I say, though.' The long back bent, gleaming in the warm dusk of the stable, as Jamie caught up a forkful of hay from the pile in one corner and carried it to a stall.

He straightened and smiled at his cousin. 'Give me one

of those, will ye?' He leaned the fork against a stall and bit into the proffered fruit. The two stood companionably eating, leaning side by side against the stable wall. When he finished, Jamie handed the core to a nuzzling sorrel and fetched his fork again. Hamish followed him down the aisle, chewing slowly.

'I've heard my father was a good rider,' Hamish offered tentatively, after a moment's silence. 'Before – before he couldn't any more.'

Jamie shot a swift glance at his cousin, but pitched some hay into the sorrel's stall before speaking. When he did, he answered the thought rather than the words.

'I never saw him ride, but I'll tell ye, lad, I hope never to need as much courage as Callum has.'

I saw Hamish's gaze rest curiously on Jamie's scarred back, but he said nothing. After a second apple, his thoughts appeared to have shifted to another topic.

'Rupert said ye had to get married,' he remarked through a mouthful of apple.

'I *wanted* to get married,' Jamie said firmly, replacing the pitchfork against the wall.

'Oh. Well . . . good,' Hamish said uncertainly, as though disconcerted by this novel idea. 'I only wondered . . . do ye mind?'

'Mind what?' Seeing that this conversation might take a while, Jamie sat down on the pile of hay, and Hamish joined him.

'Do ye mind being married?' he said, staring at his cousin. 'Getting into bed every night with a lady, I mean.'

'No,' said Jamie. 'No, in fact it's verra pleasant.'

Hamish looked doubtful.

'I dinna think I should like it much. But then all the girls I know are skinny as sticks, and they smell o' barley water. The lady Claire – your lady, I mean,' he added hastily, as though wishing to avoid confusion, 'she's, er, she looks as though she'd be nicer to sleep with. Soft, I mean.'

Jamie nodded. 'Aye, that's true. Smells all right, too,' he offered. Even in the dim light I could see a small muscle twitching near the corner of his mouth, and knew he didn't dare look up in the direction of the loft.

There was a long pause.

'How d'ye know?' Hamish said.

'Know what?'

'Which is the right lady to get married to,' the boy said impatiently.

'Oh.' Jamie rocked back and settled himself against the stone wall, hands behind his head.

'I asked my own da that, once,' he said. 'He said ye just ken. And if ye dinna ken, then she's no the right lassie.'

'Mmmphm.' This seemed a less than satisfactory explanation, to judge from the expression on the small freckle-spattered face. Hamish sat back, consciously aping Jamie's posture. Small as he was, his sturdy frame gave promise of someday matching his cousin's. The set of the square shoulders and the tilt of the solid, graceful skull were nearly identical.

'John – ' he started, wrinkling his sandy brows in thought, 'John says – '

'John the stable lad, John the cook-boy, or John Cameron?' Jamie asked.

'The stable lad.' Hamish waved a hand, pushing away the distraction. 'He said, er, about getting married . . .'

'Mmm?' Jamie made an encouraging noise, keeping his face tactfully turned away. Rolling his eyes upwards, his glance met mine as I peered over the edge. I grinned down at him, causing him to bite his lip to keep from grinning back.

Hamish drew a deep breath and let it out in a rush, propelling his words like a burst of birdshot. 'He-said-ye-must-serve-a-lass-like-a-stallion-does-a-mare-and-I-didna-believe-him-but-is-it-true?'

I bit my finger hard to keep from laughing out loud. Not so fortunately placed, Jamie dug his fingers into the fleshy part of his leg, turning as red in the face as Hamish. They looked like two tomatoes, set side by side for judging at a vegetable show.

'Er, aye . . . weel, in a way . . .' he said, sounding strangled. Then he got a grip on himself.

'Yes,' he said firmly, 'yes, ye do.'

Hamish cast a half-horrified glance into the nearby stall, where a bay stallion was relaxing, a foot or so of reproductive equipment protruding from its sheath. He glanced doubtfully down into his lap then, and I stuffed a handful of fabric into my mouth as far as it would go.

'There's some difference, ye ken,' Jamie went on. The rich colour was beginning to fade from his face, though there was still an ominous quiver around his mouth. 'For one thing, it's . . . more gentle.'

'Ye dinna bite them on the neck, then?' Hamish had the serious, intent expression of one taking careful notes. 'To make them keep still?'

'Er . . . no. Not customarily, anyway.' Exercising his not inconsiderable willpower, Jamie faced up manfully to the responsibilities of enlightenment.

'There's another difference, as well,' he said, carefully not looking upwards. 'Ye may do it face to face, instead of from the back. As the lady prefers.'

'The lady?' Hamish seemed dubious about this. 'I think *I'd* rather do it from the back. I dinna think I'd like to have anyone lookin' at me while I did something like that. Is it hard,' he inquired, 'is it hard to keep from laughing?'

I was still thinking about Jamie and Hamish when I came to bed that night. I turned down the thick quilts, smiling to myself. There was a cool draught from the window, and I looked forward to crawling under the quilts and nestling against Jamie's warmth. Impervious to cold, he seemed to carry a small furnace within himself, and his skin was always warm; sometimes almost hot, as though he burned more fiercely in answer to my own cool touch.

I was still a stranger and an outsider, but no longer a guest at the castle. While the married women seemed somewhat friendlier, now that I was one of them, the younger girls seemed strongly to resent the fact that I had removed an eligible young bachelor from circulation. In fact, noting the number of cold glances and behind-the-hand remarks, I rather wondered just how many of the castle maidens had found their way into a secluded alcove with Jamie MacTavish during his short residency.

MacTavish no longer, of course. Most of the castle inhabitants had always known who he was, and whether I were an English spy or not I now knew of necessity as well. So he became Fraser publicly, and so did I. It was as Mistress Fraser that I was welcomed into the room above the kitchens where the married women did their sewing and rocked their babies, exchanging bits of mother-lore and eyeing my own waistline with frank appraisal.

Because of my earlier difficulties in conceiving I had not considered the possibility of pregnancy when I agreed to marry Jamie, and I waited in some apprehension until my monthly occurred on time. My feelings now were entirely of relief, with none of the sadness that usually accompanied it. My life was more than complicated enough at the moment without introducing a baby into it. I thought that Jamie perhaps felt a small twinge of regret, though he also professed himself relieved. Fatherhood was a luxury that a man in his position could ill afford.

The door opened and he came in, still rubbing his head with a linen towel, water droplets from his wet hair darkening his shirt.

'Where have you been?' I asked in astonishment. Luxurious as Leoch might be in contrast to the residences of village and farm, it didn't boast any bathing facilities beyond a copper tub that Callum used to soak his aching legs, and a slightly larger one used by such ladies as thought the labour involved in filling it worth the privacy. All other washing was done either in bits, using basin and ewer, or outside in the loch or in a small, stone-floored chamber off the garden, where the young women were accustomed to stand naked and let their friends throw buckets of water over them.

'In the loch,' he answered, hanging the damp towel neatly over the window sill. '*Someone*,' he said grimly, 'left the stall door ajar, and the stable door as well, and Cobhar had a wee swim in the twilight.'

'Oh, so that's why you weren't at supper. But ponies don't like to swim, do they?' I asked.

He shook his head, running his fingers through his hair to dry it.

'No, they don't. But they're just like folk, ye ken; all different. And Cobhar is fond of the young water plants. He was down nibbling by the water's edge when a pack of dogs from the village came along and chased him into the loch. I had to run them off and then go in after him. Wait till I get my hands on wee Hamish,' he said, with grim intent. 'I'll teach him to leave gates ajar.'

'Are you going to tell Callum about it?' I asked, feeling a qualm of sympathy for the culprit.

Jamie shook his head, groping in his sporran. He drew out a bannock and a chunk of cheese, apparently filched from the kitchens on his way up to the chamber.

'No,' he said. 'Callum's fair strict wi' the lad. If he heard he'd been so careless he'd not let him ride for a month – not that he could, after the thrashing he'd get. Lord, I'm starving.' He bit ferociously into the bannock, scattering crumbs.

'Don't get into bed with that,' I said, sliding under the quilts myself. 'What are you planning to do to Hamish, then?'

He swallowed the remainder of the bannock and smiled at me. 'Dinna worry. I'm going to row him out on the loch just before supper tomorrow and toss him in. By the time he makes it to shore and dries off, supper will be over.' He finished the cheese in three bites and unashamedly licked his fingers. 'Let *him* go to bed wet and hungry and see how he likes it,' he concluded darkly.

He stripped rapidly and crawled in next to me, shivering. Though his extremities were chilled from his swim in the icy loch his body was still blissfully warm.

'Mm, you're nice to croodle wi',' he murmured, doing what I assumed was croodling. 'You smell different; been digging plants today?'

'No,' I said, surprised. 'I thought it was you – the smell, I mean.' It was a tangy, herbal smell, not unpleasant but unfamiliar.

'*I* smell like fish,' he observed, sniffing the back of his hand. 'And wet horse. No –' he leaned closer, inhaling. 'No, it isna you, either. But it's close by.'

He slid out of bed and turned back the quilts, searching. We found it under my pillow.

'What on earth . . . ?' I picked it up and promptly dropped it. 'Ouch! It has thorns!'

It was a small bundle of plants, plucked up roughly by the roots, and bound together with a twist of multicoloured threads. The plants were wilted, but a pungent smell still rose from the drooping leaves. There was one flower in the bouquet, a crushed stone bramble, whose thorny stem had pricked my thumb.

I sucked the offended digit, turning the bundle over more cautiously with my other hand. Jamie stood still, staring down at it for a moment. Then he suddenly picked it up, and crossing to the open window flung it out into the night. Returning to the bed, he energetically brushed the crumbs of earth from the plants' roots into the palm of his hand and threw them out after the bundle. He closed the window with a slam and came back, dusting his palms.

'It's gone,' he said unnecessarily. He climbed back into bed. 'Come back to bed, Sassenach.'

'What was it?' I asked, climbing in beside him.

'A joke, probably,' he said. 'A nasty one, but only a joke.' He raised himself on one elbow and blew out the candle. 'Come here, *mo duinne*,' he said. 'I'm cold.'

Despite the unsettling ill wish I slept well, secure in the dual protection of a bolted door and Jamie's arms. Towards dawn I dreamed of grassy meadows filled with butterflies. Yellow, brown, white and orange, they swirled around me like autumn leaves, lighting on my head and shoulders, sliding down my body like rain, the tiny feet tickling on my skin and the velvet wings beating like faint echoes of my own heart.

I floated gently to the surface of reality and found that the butterfly feet on my shoulder were the flaming tendrils of Jamie's soft red thatch, and the butterfly wings on my skin were his fingers.

'Mmm,' I said, some time later. 'Well, that's all very well for me, but what about you?'

'About three quarters of a minute, if you keep on in that fashion,' he said, putting my hand away with a grin. 'But I'd rather take my time over it – I'm a slow and canny man by nature, d'ye see. Might I ask the favour of your company for this evening, mistress?'

'You might,' I said. I put my arms behind my head and fixed him with a half-lidded look of challenge. 'If you mean to tell me that you're so decrepit you can't manage more than once in a day any more.'

He regarded me narrowly from his seat on the edge of the bed. There was a sudden flash of white as he lunged, and I found myself pressed deep into the featherbed.

'Aye, well,' he said into the tangles of my hair, 'you'll no say I didna warn ye.'

Two and a half minutes later he groaned and opened his eyes. He scrubbed his face and head vigorously with both hands, making the shorter ends stick up like quills. Then, with a muffled Gaelic oath, he slid reluctantly out from under the quilts and began to dress, shivering in the chilly morning air.

'I don't suppose,' I asked hopefully, 'that you could tell Alick you're sick, and come back to bed?'

He laughed and bent to kiss me before groping under the bed for his stockings. 'Would that I could, Sassenach. I doubt much short of pox, plague or grievous bodily harm would answer as an excuse, though. If I weren't bleeding, Auld Alick would be up here in a trice, dragging me off my deathbed to help wi' the worming.'

I eyed his graceful long calves as he pulled a stocking up neatly and folded the top. ' "Grievous bodily harm", eh? I might manage something along those lines,' I said darkly.

He grunted as he reached across for the other stocking. 'Well, watch where ye toss your elf-darts, Sassenach.' He tried a lewd wink, but wound up squinting at me instead. 'Aim too high, and I'll be no good to *you*, either.'

I arched one eyebrow and snuggled back under the quilts. 'Not to worry. Nothing above the knee, I promise.'

He patted one of my rounder bulges and left for the stables, singing rather loudly the air from 'Up among the Heather' The refrain floated back from the stairwell:

'Sittin' wi' a wee girl, holdin' on my knee –
When a bumblebee stung me, weel above the kneeeee –
Up among the heather, at the head o' Bendikee!'

He was right, I decided; he *didn't* have any ear for music.

I relapsed temporarily into a state of satisfied somnolence, but roused myself shortly to go down for breakfast. Most of the castle inhabitants had eaten and gone to their work already; those still in the hall greeted me pleasantly enough. There were no sidelong looks, no expressions of veiled hostility, of someone wondering how well their nasty little trick had worked. But I watched the faces nonetheless.

The morning was spent alone in the garden and fields with my basket and digging stick. I was running short of some of the most popular herbs. Generally the village people went to Geillis Duncan for help, but there had been several patients from the village turning up of late in my dispensary, and the traffic in nostrums had been heavy. Maybe her husband's illness was keeping her too busy to care for her regular customers.

I spent the latter part of the afternoon in my dispensary. There were few patients to be seen; only a case of persistent eczema, a dislocated thumb, and a kitchen boy who had spilled a pot of hot soup down one leg. Having dispensed ointment of quince, and reset and bound the thumb, I settled down to the task of pounding some juniper berries in one of the late Beaton's smaller mortars.

It was tedious work, but well suited to this sort of lazy afternoon. The weather was fair and I could see blue shadows lengthening under the trees to the west when I stood on my table to peer out.

Inside, the glass bottles gleamed in orderly ranks, neat stacks of bandages and compresses in the cupboards next to them. The apothecary's cabinet had been thoroughly cleaned and disinfected, and now held stores of dried leaves, roots and fungi, neatly packed in gauze bags. I took a deep breath of the sharp, spicy odours of my sanctum and let it out in a sigh of contentment.

Then I stopped pounding and set the pestle down. I *was* contented, I realized with a shock. Despite the myriad uncertainties of life here, despite the unpleasantness of the ill wish, despite the small, constant ache of missing Frank, I was in fact not unhappy. Quite the contrary.

I felt immediately ashamed and disloyal. How *could* I bring myself to be happy, when Frank must be demented with worry? Assuming that time was in fact continuing without me – and I couldn't see why it wouldn't – I must have gone missing for upwards of four months, and August was almost over. I imagined him searching the Scottish countryside, calling the police, waiting for some sign, some word of me. By now he must nearly have given up hope and be waiting, instead, for word that my body had been found.

I set down the mortar and paced up and down the length of my narrow room, rubbing my hands on my apron in a spasm of guilty sorrow and regret. I should have got away sooner. I should have tried harder to return. But I had, I reminded myself. I had tried repeatedly. And look what had happened.

Yes, look. I was married to a Scottish outlaw, the both of us hunted by a sadistic captain of dragoons and living with a lot of barbarians, who would as soon kill Jamie as look at him if they thought him a threat to their precious clan succession. And the worst of it all was that I was happy.

I sat down, staring helplessly at the array of jars and bottles. I had been living day to day since our return to Leoch, deliberately suppressing the memories of my earlier life. Deep down I knew that I must soon make some kind of decision, but I had delayed, putting off the necessity from day to day and hour to hour, burying my uncertainties in the pleasures of Jamie's company – and his arms.

There was a sudden bumping and cursing out in the corridor, and I rose hastily and went to the door just in time to see Jamie himself stumble in, supported by the bowed form of Auld Alick on one side and the earnest but spindly efforts of one of the stable lads on the other. He sank on to my stool, left foot outstretched, and grimaced unpleasantly at it. The grimace seemed to be more of annoyance than pain, so I knelt to examine the offending append-age with relatively little concern.

'Mild strain,' I said, after a cursory inspection. 'What did you do?'

'Fell off,' Jamie said succinctly.

'Off the wall?' I asked, teasing. He glowered.

'No. Off Donas.'

'You were *riding* that thing?' I asked incredulously. 'In that case, you're lucky to get off with a strained ankle.' I fetched a length of bandage and began to wrap the joint.

'Weel, it wasna sae bad as a' that,' said Alick judiciously. 'In fact, lad 'ye were doin' quite weel wi' him for a bit.'

'I know I was,' snapped Jamie, gritting his teeth as I pulled the bandage tight. 'A wasp stung him.'

The bushy brows lifted. 'Oh, that was it? Beast acted like he'd been struck wi' an elf-dart,' he confided to me. 'Went straight up in the air on all fours and came down again, then went stark, staring mad – all over the pen like a bumblebee in a jar. Yon wee laddie stuck on too,' he said, nodding at Jamie, who invented a new unpleasant expression in response, 'until the big yellow fiend went ower the wall.'

'Over the wall? Where is he now?' I asked, standing up and dusting my hands.

'Halfway back to hell, I expect,' said Jamie, putting his foot down and trying his weight gingerly on it. 'And wel-come to stay there.' Wincing, he sat back.

'I doubt the De'il's got much use for a half-broke stal-lion,' observed Alick. 'Bein' able to turn himself into a horse when needed.'

'Perhaps that's who Donas really is,' I suggested, amused.

'I wouldna doubt it,' said Jamie, still smarting but beginning to recover his usual good humour. 'The De'il's customarily a black stallion, though, is he no?'

'Oh, aye,' said Alick. 'A great black stallion, that travels as fast as the thought between a man and a maid.'

He grinned genially at Jamie and rose to go.

'And speakin' of that,' he said, with a wink at me, 'I'll no expect ye in the stables tomorrow. Keep to your bed, laddie, and, er . . . rest.'

'Why is it,' I demanded, looking after the crusty old horsemaster, 'that everyone seems to assume we've no more on our minds than to get into bed with each other?'

Jamie tried his weight on the foot again, bracing himself on the counter.

'For one thing we've not been married long,' he observed. 'For another – ' He looked up and grinned, shaking his head. 'I've told ye before, Sassenach. Everything ye think shows on your face.'

'Bloody hell,' I said.

Aside from a quick trip to the dispensary to check for emergencies, I spent the next morning ministering to the rather demanding needs of my solitary patient.

'You are supposed to be resting,' I said reprovingly at one point.

'I am. Well, my ankle is resting, at least. See?'

A long, unstockinged shin thrust up into the air and a bony, slender foot waggled back and forth. It stopped abruptly in mid-waggle with a muffled 'ouch' from its owner. He lowered it and tenderly massaged the still-puffy ankle.

'That'll teach you,' I said, swinging my own legs out from under the quilts. 'Come along now. You've been frowsting in bed quite long enough. You need fresh air.'

He sat up, hair falling over his face.

'I thought ye said it was rest I needed.'

'You can rest in the fresh air. Get up. I'm making up the bed.'

Amid complaints about my general unfeelingness and lack of consideration for a gravely injured man, he got dressed and sat long enough for me to bind up the weak ankle before his natural exuberance asserted itself.

'It's a bit saft out,' he said, with a glance through the casement; the mild drizzle had just decided to buckle down to it and become a major downpour. 'Let's go up to the roof.'

'The roof? Oh, to be sure. I couldn't think of a better prescription for a strained ankle than climbing six flights of stairs.'

'Five. Besides, I've a stick.' He produced the stick in question, an aged hawthorn club, from behind the door with a triumphant flourish.

'Wherever did you get that?' I inquired, examining it. At closer range it was even more battered, a three-foot length of chipped wood, age-hardened as a diamond.

'Alick lent it me. He uses it on the garrons; raps them twixt the eyes wi' it to make them pay attention.'

'Sounds very effective,' I said, eyeing the scuffed wood. 'I must try it some time. On you.'

We emerged at last in a small sheltered spot, just under the overhang of the slate roof. A low parapet guarded the edge of this small lookout.

'Oh, it's beautiful!' Despite the gusty rain, the view from the roof was magnificent; we could see the broad silver sweep of the loch and the towering crags beyond, thrusting into the solid grey of the sky like ridged black fists.

Jamie leaned on the parapet, taking the weight from his injured foot.

'Aye, it is. I used to come up here sometimes, when I was at the castle before.'

He pointed across the loch, dimpling under the beat of the rain.

'D'ye see the notch there, between those two *craigs*?'

'In the mountains? Yes.'

'That's the way to Lallybroch. When I'd feel lonely for my home, sometimes I'd come up here and look that way. I'd imagine flying like a corbie across that pass, and the look of the country on the other side of the mountain, and all the way to Lallybroch.'

I touched him gently on the arm.

'Do you want to go back, Jamie?'

He turned his head and smiled down at me.

'Well, I've been thinking of it. I don't know if I want to, precisely, but I think we must. I canna say what we'll find there, Sassenach. But . . . aye. I'm wed now. You're lady of Broch Tuarach. Outlaw or no, I need to go back, even if just long enough to set things straight.'

I felt a thrill, compounded of relief and apprehension, at the thought of leaving Leoch and its assorted intrigues.

'When will we go?'

He frowned, drumming his fingers on the parapet. The stone was dark and slick with rain.

'Well, I think we must wait for the Duke to come. It's possible that he might see his way to doing Callum a favour by taking up my case. If he cannot get me cleared he might be able to arrange a pardon. There'd be a good deal less danger in going back to Lallybroch then, ye see.'

'Well, yes, but . . .' He glanced sharply at me as I hesitated.

'What is it, Sassenach?'

I took a deep breath. 'Jamie . . . if I tell you something will you promise not to ask me how I know?'

He took me by both arms, looking down into my face. The rain misted his hair and small droplets ran down the sides of his face. He smiled at me.

'I told you that I wouldna ask for anything that ye dinna wish to tell me. Yes, I promise.'

'Let's sit down. You shouldn't be standing on that foot so long.'

We made our way to the wall where the overhanging slates of the roof sheltered a small dry patch of pavement, and settled ourselves comfortably, backs against the wall.

'All right, Sassenach. What is it?' Jamie asked.

'The Duke of Sandringham,' I said. I bit my lip. 'Jamie, don't trust him. I don't know everything about him myself, but I do know – there's something about him. Something wrong.'

'You know about that?' He looked surprised.

Now it was my turn to stare.

'You mean *you* know about him already? Have you met him?' I was relieved. Perhaps the mysterious links between Sandringham and the Jacobite cause were much better known than Frank and the minister had thought.

'Oh, aye. He was here, visiting, when I was sixteen. When I . . . left.'

'Why did you leave?' I was curious, remembering suddenly what Geillis Duncan had said when first I'd met her in the wood. The odd rumour that Jamie was the real father of Callum's son Hamish. I knew myself that he wasn't, couldn't have been – but I was quite possibly the only person in the castle who *did* know. A suspicion of that sort could easily have led to Dougal's earlier attempt on Jamie's life – if in fact that's what the axe attack had been.

'It wasn't because of . . . the lady Letitia, was it?' I asked with some hesitation.

'Letitia?' His startled astonishment was plain, and something inside me that I hadn't known was clenched suddenly relaxed. I hadn't *really* thought there was anything to Geilie's supposition, but still . . .

'What on earth makes ye mention Letitia?' Jamie asked curiously. 'I lived at the castle for a year, and had speech of her maybe once that I remember, when she called me to her chamber and gave me the raw side of her tongue for leading a game of shinty through her rose garden.'

I told him what Geilie had said, and he laughed, breath misting in the cool, rainy air.

'God,' he said, 'as though I'd have the nerve!'

'You don't think Callum suspected any such thing, do you?' I asked.

He shook his head decidedly.

'No I don't, Sassenach. If he had any inkling of such a thing, I wouldna have lived to be seventeen, let alone achieve the ripe old age of three-and-twenty.'

This more or less confirmed my own impression of Callum, but I was relieved nonetheless. Jamie's expression had grown thoughtful, blue eyes suddenly remote.

'Come to think on it, though, I don't know that Callum

does know why I left the castle so sudden, then. And if Geillis Duncan is goin' about the place spreading such rumours – that woman's a troublemaker, Sassenach; a gossip and a scold, if not the witch folk say she is – well, I'd best see that he finds out, then.'

He glanced up at the sheet of water pouring from the eaves.

'Perhaps we'd best go down, Sassenach. It's getting a wee bit damp out.'

We took a different way down, crossing the roof to an outer stairway that led down to the kitchen garden, where I wanted to pull a bit of borage, if the downpour would let me. We sheltered under the wall of the castle, one of the jutting window ledges diverting the rain above.

'What do ye do wi' borage, Sassenach?' Jamie asked with interest, looking out at the straggly vines and plants beaten to the earth by the rain.

'When it's green, nothing. First you dry it, and then – '

I was interrupted by a terrific noise of barking and shouting, coming from outside the garden wall. I raced through the downpour towards the wall, followed more slowly by Jamie, limping.

Father Bain, the village priest, was running up the path, puddles exploding under his feet, pursued by a yelping pack of dogs. Hampered by his voluminous soutane, the priest tripped and fell, water and mud flying in spatters all around him. In a moment, the dogs were upon him, growling and snapping.

A blur of tartan vaulted over the wall next to me, and Jamie was among them, laying about with his stick and shouting in Gaelic, adding his voice to the general racket. If the shouts and curses had little effect, the stick had more. There were sharp yelps as the club struck hairy flesh, and gradually the pack retreated, finally turning and running off in the direction of the village.

Jamie wiped the hair out of his eyes, panting.

'Bad as wolves,' he said. 'I've told Callum about that pack already; they're the ones that chased Cobhar into the loch two days ago. Best he has them shot before they kill someone.' He looked down at me as I knelt next to the fallen priest, inspecting. The rain dripped from the ends of my hair and I could feel my shawl growing sodden.

'They haven't yet,' I said. 'Bar a few toothmarks, he's basically all right.'

Father Bain's soutane was ripped down one side, showing an expanse of hairless white thigh with an ugly gash and several puncture marks beginning to ooze blood. The priest, pasty-white with shock, was struggling to his feet; plainly he wasn't too badly injured.

'If you'll come to the surgery with me, Father, I'll cleanse those cuts for you,' I offered, suppressing a smile at the spectacle the fat little priest presented, soutane flapping and argyle hose revealed.

At the best of times Father Bain's face resembled a clenched fist. This similarity was made more pronounced at the moment by the red mottling that streaked his jowls and emphasized the vertical creases between cheeks and mouth. He glared at me as though I had suggested that he commit some public indecency.

Apparently I had, for his next words were 'What, a man o' God to expose his pairsonal parts to the handling of a wumman? Weel, I'll tell ye, madam, I've no notion what sorts of immorality are practised in the circles you're accustomed to move in, but I'll have ye to ken that such'll no be tolerated here – not sae long as I've the cure of the souls in this parish!' With that he turned and stumped off, limping rather badly and trying unsuccessfully to hold up the torn side of his robe.

'Suit yourself,' I called after him. 'If you don't let me cleanse it, it will fester!'

The priest did not respond but hunched his round shoulders and hitched his way up the garden stair a step at a time.

'That man doesn't care overmuch for women, does he?' I remarked to Jamie.

'Considering his occupation, I imagine that's as well,' he replied. 'Let's go and eat.'

476

After dinner I sent my patient back to bed to rest – alone, this time, in spite of his protestations – and went down to the surgery. The heavy rain seemed to have made business slack; people tended to stay safely inside rather than running over their feet with ploughshares or falling off roofs.

I passed the time pleasantly enough, bringing the records in Davie Beaton's book up to date. Just as I finished, though, a visitor darkened my door.

He literally darkened it, his bulk filling it from side to side. Squinting in the semi-darkness, I made out the form of Auld Alick, swathed in an extraordinary get-up of coats, shawls and odd bits of horse-blanket.

He advanced with a slowness that reminded me of Callum's first visit to the surgery with me, and gave me a clue to his problem.

'Rheumatism, is it?' I asked with sympathy as he subsided stiffly into my single chair with a stifled groan.

'Aye. The damp settles in my bones,' he said. 'Aught to be done about it?' He laid his huge, gnarled hands on the table, letting the fingers relax. The hands opened slowly, like night-blooming flowers, to show the calloused palms within. I picked up one of the knotted appendages and turned it gently to and fro, stretching the fingers and massaging the horny palm. The seamed old face above the hand contorted for a moment as I did it, but then relaxed as the first twinges passed.

'Like wood,' I said. 'A good slug of whisky and a deep massage is the best I can recommend. Birchleaf tea will do only so much.'

He laughed, shawls slipping off his shoulder.

'Whisky, eh? I had my doubts, lassie, but I see ye've the makings of a fine physician.'

I reached into the back of my medicine cupboard and pulled out the anonymous brown bottle that held my supply from the Leoch distillery. I plunked it on the table before him with a horn cup.

'Drink up,' I said, 'then get stripped off as far as you think decent and lie on the table. I'll make up the fire so it will be warm enough.'

The blue eye surveyed the bottle with appreciation, and a crooked hand reached slowly for the neck.

'Best have a nip yourself, lassie,' he advised. 'It'll be a big job.'

He groaned, with a cross between pain and contentment, as I leaned hard on his left shoulder to loosen it, then lifted from underneath and rotated the whole quarter of his body.

'My wife used to iron my back for me,' he remarked, 'for the lumbago. But this is even better. Ye've a good strong pair of hands, lassie. Make a good stable lad, ye would.'

'I'll assume that's a compliment,' I said dryly, pouring more of the heated oil-and-tallow mixture into my palm and spreading it over the broad white expanse of his back. There was a sharp line of demarcation between the weathered, mottled brown skin of his arms, where the rolled-up sleeves of his shirt would stop, and the milk-white skin of his shoulders and back.

'Well, you were a fine, fair laddie at one time,' I remarked. 'The skin of your back's as white as mine.'

A deep chuckle shook the flesh under my hands.

'Never know now, would ye? Aye, Ellen MacKenzie once saw me wi' my sark off, birthin' a foal, and told me it looked like the good Lord had put the wrong head to my body – should have had a bag of milk pudding on my shoulders, instead of a face from the altarpiece.'

I gathered he was referring to the rood screen in the chapel, which featured a number of extremely unattractive demons engaged in torturing sinners.

'Ellen MacKenzie sounds as though she were rather free with her opinions,' I observed. I was more than slightly curious about Jamie's mother. From the small things he said now and then I had some picture of his father Brian, but I knew nothing about her, other than that she had died young, in childbed.

'Oh, she had a tongue on her, did Ellen, and a mind of her own to go wi' it.' Untying the garters of his trews, I tucked them up out of the way and began operations on the muscular calves of his legs. 'But enough sweetness with it that no one minded much, other than her brothers. And she wasna one to pay much heed to Callum or Dougal.'

'Mm. So I heard. Eloped, didn't she?' I dug my thumbs into the tendons behind his knee and he let out a sound that would have been a squeak in anyone less dignified.

'Oh, aye. Ellen was the eldest o' the five MacKenzie bairns – a year or two older than Callum, and the apple of auld Jacob's eye. That's why she'd gone so long unwed; wouldna ha' aught to do wi' John Munro or Malcolm Grant, or any of the others she might have gone to, and her father wouldna force her against her will.'

When old Jacob died, he told me, Callum had less patience with his sister's foibles. Struggling desperately to consolidate his shaky hold on the clan, he had sought an alliance with Munro to the north, or Grant to the south. Both clans had young chieftains who would make useful brothers-in-law. Young Jocasta, only fifteen, had obligingly accepted the suit of John Munro, and gone north. Ellen, on the verge of spinsterhood at twenty-two, had been a good deal less cooperative.

'I take it Malcolm Grant's suit was rather firmly rejected, judging from his attack on our camp in June,' I observed.

Auld Alick laughed, the laugh turning to a satisfied groan as I pressed deeper.

'Aye. I never heard exactly what she said to him, but I expect it stung. It was at the big Gathering, ye ken, that they met. Out in the rose garden they went, in the evening, and everyone waiting to see would she tak' him or no. And it grew dark, and they still waiting. And darker still, and the lanterns all lit, and the singing begun, and no sign yet of Ellen or Malcolm Grant.'

'Goodness. It must have been quite a conversation.' I poured another dollop of the liniment between his shoulder blades, and he grunted with the warm pleasure of it.

'So it seemed. But time went on, and they didna come back, and Callum began to fear as Grant had eloped wi' her; taken her by force, ye see. And it seemed as that must be the way of it, for they found the rose garden empty. And when he sent down to the stables for me, sure enough – I told him Grant's men had come for the mounts, and the whole boiling of 'em was gone awa' without a word of farewell.'

Furious, eighteen-year-old Dougal had mounted at once and set out on the track of Malcolm Grant, not waiting either for company nor for conference with Callum.

'When Callum heard as Dougal had gone after Grant, he sent me and some others helter-skelter after him, Callum being well acquent wi' Dougal's temper and not wishing to have his new brother-in-law slain in the road before the banns were called. For he reckoned as how Malcolm Grant, not being able to talk Ellen into wedding him, must ha' taken her away in order to have his way wi' her and force her into marriage that way.'

Alick paused meditatively. 'All Dougal could see was the insult, of course. But I dinna think Callum was that upset about it, to tell the truth, insult or no. It would ha' solved his problem – and Grant would likely have had to take Ellen wi'out her dower and pay reparation to Callum as well.'

He snorted cynically. 'Callum is no the man to let an opportunity pass by him. He's quick, and he's ruthless, is Callum.' The single ice-blue eye swivelled back to regard me over one humped shoulder. 'Ye'd be wise to bear that in mind, lassie.'

'I'm not likely to forget it,' I assured him with some grimness. I remembered Jamie's story of his punishment at Callum's order, and wondered how much of that had been in revenge for Ellen's rebellion.

Still, Callum had had no chance to seize the opportunity of marrying his sister to the chieftain of Clan Grant. Towards dawn, Dougal had found Malcolm Grant camped along the main way with his followers, asleep under a gorse bush, wrapped in his plaid.

And when Alick and the others had come pelting along the road some time later they had been stopped in their tracks by the sight of Dougal MacKenzie and Malcolm Grant, both stripped to the waist and scarred with the marks of battle, swaying and staggering up and down the trackway, still exchanging random blows whenever they got within reach of each other. Grant's retainers were perched along the verge like a row of owls, heads turning one way and then the other, as the waning fight meandered up and down in the dripping dawn.

'They were both of them puffing like blown horses, and the steam rising off their bodies in the chill. Grant's nose was swelled to twice its size and Dougal could scarce see out o' either eye, and both wi' their blood dripping down and dried ower their breasts.'

Upon the appearance of Callum's men, Grant's tacksmen had all sprung to their feet, hands upon their swords, and the meeting would likely have resulted in serious bloodshed had some sharp-eyed lad among the MacKenzies not noted the rather important fact that Ellen MacKenzie was nowhere to be seen among the Grants.

'Weel, after they'd poured water on Malcolm Grant and brought him to his senses, he managed to tell them what Dougal wouldna pause to hear – that Ellen had spent but a quarter hour wi' him in the rose garden. He wouldna say what had passed between them, but whatever it was he'd been so offended as to wish to take his leave at once, without showing his face in the hall. And he'd left her there, and seen her no more, nor did he wish ever to hear the name of Ellen MacKenzie spoken in his presence again. And wi' that he mounted his beast – a bit unsteady, still – and rode awa'. And been no friend since, to anyone of the Clan MacKenzie.'

I listened, fascinated. 'And where *was* Ellen all this time?'

Auld Alick laughed, with the sound of a stable-door hinge creaking.

'Ower the hills and far away. But they didna find it out for some time yet. We turned about and pelted home again, to find Ellen still missing and Callum standing white-faced in the courtyard, leanin' on Angus Mhor.'

There followed more confusion still, for with all the guests, the rooms of the castle were full, as were all the lofts and cubbyholes, the kitchens and closets. It seemed hopeless to tell which of all the folk in the castle might also be missing, but Callum called all of the servants and went doggedly down the lists of the invited, asking who had been seen the evening before, and where, and when. And finally he found a kitchen-maid who recalled seeing a man in a back passage, just before the supper was served.

She had noticed him only because he was so handsome; tall and sturdy, she said, with hair like a black silkie's and eyes like a cat. She had watched him down the passage, admiring him, and seen him meet someone at the outer door – a woman dressed in black from head to toe, and shrouded in a hooded cloak.

'What's a silkie?' I asked.

Alick's eye slanted towards me, crinkling at the corners.

'Ye call them seals in English. For quite a bit after that, even after they knew the truth of it, folk in the village would tell the tale to each other that Ellen MacKenzie was taken to the sea, to live among the seals. Did ye know that the silkies put aside their skins when they come ashore, and walk like men? And if ye find a silkie's skin and hide it, he – or she – ' he added, fairly, 'canna go into the sea again, but must stay with ye on the land. It's thought good to take a seal-wife that way, for they're very good cooks, and most devoted mothers.

'Still,' he said judiciously, 'Callum wasna inclined to believe his sister'd gone off wi' a seal, and said so. So he called the guests down, one by one, and asked them all who knew a man of that description. And at long last they worked it out that his name was Brian, but no one knew his clan or his surname; he'd been at the Games, but there they only called him Brian Dubh.'

So there the matter seemed to rest for a time, for the searchers had no idea in which direction to look. Still, even the best of hunters must stop at a cottage now and then, to ask for a handful of salt or a pannikin of milk. And eventually word of the pair reached Leoch, for Ellen MacKenzie was a maid of no ordinary appearance.

'Hair like fire,' Alick said dreamily, enjoying the warmth of the oil on his back. 'And eyes like Callum's – grey, and fringed wi' black lashes – verra pretty, but the kind would go through ye like a bolt. A tall woman; even taller than you. And sae fair it would hurt the eyes to see her.

'I heard tell later as they'd met at the Gathering, taken one look and decided on the spot as there could be none other for either one o' them. So they laid their plans and they stole awa', under the noses of Callum MacKenzie and three hundred guests.'

He laughed suddenly, remembering. 'Dougal finally found them, living in a cot-house on the edge of the Fraser lands. They'd decided the only way to manage was to hide until Ellen was wi' child, and big enough that there'd be no question whose it was. Then Callum would have to give his blessing to the marriage, like it or no – and he didn't.'

Alick grinned. 'Whiles ye were on the road, did ye chance to see a scar Dougal carries, running down his breast?'

I had; a thin white line that crossed his heart and ran from shoulder to ribs.

'Did Brian do that?' I asked.

'No, Ellen,' he replied, grinning at my expression 'To stop him cutting Brian's throat, which he was about to do. I wouldna mention it to Dougal, if I were you.'

'No, I don't suppose I will.'

Luckily, the plan had worked, and Ellen was five months gone with child by the time that Dougal found them.

'There was the great to-do about it all, and a lot of verra nasty letters exchanged between Leoch and Lallybroch, but they settled it in the end, and Ellen and Brian took up house at Lallybroch the week before the child was born. They were married in the dooryard,' he added, as an afterthought, 'so he could carry her over the threshold for the first time as a wife. He said after as he nearly ruptured himself, lifting her.'

'You talk as though you knew them well,' I said. Finishing my ministrations, I wiped the slippery ointment off my hands with a towel.

'Oh, a bit,' Alick said, drowsy with warmth. The lid drooped over his single eye, and the lines of his old face had relaxed from the expression of mild discomfort that normally made him look so fierce.

'I kent Ellen weel, of course. Then Brian I met years later, when he brought the lad to stay – we got on. A good man wi' a horse.' His voice trailed off, and the lid fell shut.

I drew a blanket up over the old man's prostrate form and tiptoed away, leaving him dreaming by the fire.

Leaving Alick asleep I had gone up to our chamber, only to find Jamie in the same condition. There are a limited number of activities suitable for indoor amusement on a dark, rainy day, and assuming that I didn't wish either to rouse Jamie or to join him in oblivion, that seemed to leave reading or needlework. Given the worse-than-mediocre state of my abilities in the latter direction, I had decided to borrow a book from Callum's library.

In accordance with the peculiar architectural principles governing the construction of Leoch – based on a general abhorrence of straight lines – the stair leading to Callum's suite had two right-angled bends in it, each marked by a small landing. An attendant usually stood on the second landing, ready to run errands or lend assistance to the laird, but he wasn't at his station today. I could hear the rumble of voices from above; perhaps the attendant was with Callum. I paused outside the door, uncertain whether to interrupt.

'I've always known ye to be a fool, Dougal, but I didna think ye *quite* such an idiot.' Accustomed to the company of tutors since youth, and unused to venturing out as his brother did among fighting men and common people, Callum normally spoke without the broad Scots that marked Dougal's speech. The cultured accent had slipped a bit now, though, and the two voices were nearly indistinguishable, both thickened by anger. 'I might have expected such behaviour from ye when ye were in your twenties, but for God's sake, man, you're five-and-forty!'

'Well, it isna a matter *you'd* know owermuch about, now, is it?' Dougal's voice held an ugly sneer.

'No,' came Callum's cutting tones in response. 'And while I've seldom found cause to thank the Lord, perhaps he's done better by me than I've thought. I've heard it said often enough that a man's brain stops workin' when his cock's standin', and now I think maybe I believe it.' There was a loud scrape as chairlegs were pushed back across the stone flooring. 'If the brothers MacKenzie have but one cock and one brain between the two of them, then I'm glad of my half of the bargain!'

I decided that a third participant in this particular conversation would be decidedly unwelcome, and stepped softly back from the door, turning to go down the stair.

The sound of rustling skirts from the first landing made me stop in my tracks. I didn't wish to be discovered eavesdropping outside the laird's study, and turned back towards the door. The landing here was wide, and a tapestry covered one wall almost from floor to ceiling. My feet would show, but it couldn't be helped.

Lurking like a rat behind the arras, I heard the steps from below slow as they approached the door, and stop at the far side of the landing as the unseen visitor realized, as I had, the private nature of the brothers' conversation.

'No,' Callum was saying, calmer now, 'No, of course not. The woman's a witch, or next thing to it.'

'Aye, but – ' Dougal's response was cut short by his brother's impatient tones.

'I've said I'll attend to it, man. Don't worry yourself over it, little brother; I'll see she's done rightly by.' A note of grudging affection had crept into Callum's voice.

'I'll tell ye, man. I've written the Duke as he may have leave to hunt the lands above Erlick – he's keen to have a shot at the stags there. I mean to send Jamie along wi' him; may be as he still has some feeling for the lad – '

Dougal interrupted with something in Gaelic, evidently a coarse remark, for Callum laughed and said, 'Nay, I reckon Jamie's big enough to have a care for himself. But if the Duke's a mind to intercede for him with His Majesty, it's the lad's best chance for a pardon. If ye will, I'll tell His Grace you'll go as well. You can aid Jamie as ye may, and you'll be out of the way while I settle matters here.'

There was a muffled thump from the far side of the landing, and I risked peeping out. It was the girl Laoghaire, pale as the plastered wall behind her. She was holding a tray with a decanter; a pewter cup had fallen from the tray to the carpeted floor, making the sound I had heard.

'What's that?' Callum's voice, suddenly sharp, spoke from inside the study. Laoghaire dropped the tray on the table next to the door, almost upsetting the decanter in her haste, and turning, fled precipitately.

I could hear Dougal's footsteps approaching the door, and knew I would never make it down the stairs without discovery. I barely had time to wriggle out of my hiding place and pick up the fallen cup before the door opened.

'Oh, it's you.' Dougal sounded mildly surprised. 'Is that the stuff Mrs Fitz sent for Callum's raw throat?'

'Yes,' I said glibly. 'She says she hopes he'll be better presently.'

'I'll do.' Moving more slowly, Callum came into view in the open door. He smiled at me. 'Thank Mrs Fitz for me. And my thanks to you, my dear, for bringing it. Will ye sit a moment while I drink it?'

The conversation I had overheard had effectually made me forget my original purpose, but I now remembered my intention of borrowing a book. Dougal excused himself, and I followed Callum slowly into his library, where he offered me the run of his shelves.

Callum's colour was still high, the quarrel with his brother still fresh in his mind, but he answered my questions about the books with a good approximation of his usual poise. Only the brightness of his eyes and a certain tenseness of posture betrayed his thoughts.

I found one or two herbals that looked interesting and put them aside while I browsed a novel.

Callum crossed to the birds' cage, no doubt intending to soothe himself in his customary way by watching the beautiful little self-absorbed creatures hop about amongst the branches, each a world unto itself.

The sound of shouts from outside attracted my attention. From this high point the fields behind the castle were visible, all the way to the loch. A small group of riders was sweeping around the end of the loch, shouting with exhilaration, as the rain pelted them on.

As they drew nearer I could see that they weren't men after all, but boys, mostly teenagers, but with a younger lad here and there pressing hard to stay up with the older youths. I wondered if Hamish were with them, and quickly found the telltale spot of bright hair – gleaming despite the rain – above Cobhar's back in the middle of the pack.

The gang came charging towards the castle, headed for one of the innumerable stone walls that separated one field from another. One, two, three, four, the older boys on their mounts popped over the wall with the careless ease born of experience.

It was doubtless my imagination that made the bay seem to hang back a moment, for Cobhar followed the other horses with apparent eagerness. He charged the fence, set himself, braced and leaped.

He seemed to do it just as the others had, and yet something happened. Perhaps a hesitation by his rider, a too-hard pulling on the reins, or a not-quite-firm seat. For the front hooves struck the wall just a few inches too low, and horse, rider and all somersaulted over the wall in the most spectacular parabola of doom I had ever seen.

'Oh!'

Drawn by my exclamation, Callum turned his head to the window in time to see Cobhar land heavily on his side, the small figure of Hamish pinned beneath. Crippled as he was, Callum moved with speed. He was by my side, leaning out of the window, before the pony had even begun to struggle to his feet.

The wind and rain beat in, soaking the velvet of Callum's coat. Peering anxiously over his shoulder I saw a cluster of lads, pushing and shoving each other in their eagerness to help. It seemed a long time before the crowd parted and we saw the small, sturdy figure stumble out of the press, clutching his stomach. He shook his head to the many offers of help and staggered purposefully to the wall, where he leaned over and vomited profusely. Then he slid down the wall and sat in the wet grass, legs sprawled, face upturned to the rain. When I saw him stick out his tongue to catch the falling drops, I laid a hand on Callum's shoulder.

'He's all right,' I said. 'Only had the wind knocked out of him.'

Callum closed his eyes and let his breath out, body sagging suddenly with the release of tension. I watched him with sympathy.

'You care for him as though he were your own, don't you?' I asked.

The grey eyes blazed suddenly into mine with the most extraordinary expression of alarm. For an instant there was no sound in the study but the ticking of the gilt clock on the shelf. Then a drop of water rolled down Callum's nose, to hang glimmering from the tip. I reached involuntarily to blot it with my handkerchief, and the tension in his face broke.

'Yes,' he said simply.

In the end I told Jamie only about Callum's plan to send him hunting with the Duke. I was convinced by now that his feelings for Laoghaire were only those of a chivalrous friendship, but I didn't know what he might do if he knew that his uncle had seduced the girl and got her with child. Apparently Callum didn't mean to procure the services of Geilie Duncan in the emergency; I wondered if the girl would be wed to Dougal, or if Callum would find her another husband before the child began to show. In any case, if Jamie and Dougal were going to be shut up together in a hunting lodge for days on end, I thought it might be as well if the shade of Laoghaire were not one of the party.

'Hm,' he said thoughtfully. 'Worth a try. Ye get verra friendly wi' each other, hunting all day and coming back to drink whisky by the fire.' He finished fastening my gown up the back and bent to kiss my shoulder briefly.

'I'd be sorry to leave ye, Sassenach, but it might be best.'

'Don't mind for me,' I said. I hadn't realized before that his departure would necessarily leave me alone at the castle, and the thought made me more than slightly nervous. Still, I was resolved to manage, if it might help him.

'Are you ready for supper?' I asked. His hand lingered on my waist, and I turned towards him.

'Mmm,' he said a moment later. 'I'd be willing to go hungry.'

'Well, *I* wouldn't,' I said. 'You'll just have to wait.'

I glanced down the supper table and across the room. By now I knew most of the faces, some intimately. And a motley crew they were, I reflected. Frank would have been fascinated by the gathering – so many different facial types.

Thinking about Frank was rather like touching a sore tooth; my inclination was to shy away. But the time was coming when I would be able to delay no longer, and I forced my mind back, carefully drawing him in my mind, tracing the long, smooth arcs of his brows with my thoughts as I had once traced them with my fingers. No matter that my fingers tingled suddenly with the memory of rougher, thicker brows and the deep blue of the eyes beneath them.

I hastily turned towards another face as an antidote to such disturbing thoughts. It happened to be Murtagh's. Well, at least he looked like neither of the men who haunted my thoughts.

Short, slightly built but sinewy as a gibbon, with long arms that reinforced the simian resemblance, he had a low brow and narrow jaw that for some reason made me think of cave dwellers and pictures of Early Man shown in some of Frank's texts. Not a Neanderthal, though. A Pict. That was it. There was something very durable about the small clansman that reminded me of the weathered, patterned stones, ancient even now, that stood their implacable guard over cross tracks and burial grounds.

Amused at the idea, I looked over the other diners with an eye to spotting ethnic types. That man near the hearth, for example, John Cameron, his name was, was a Norman if I'd ever seen one – not that I had – high cheekbones and a high, narrow brow, long upper lip, and the dark skin of a Gaul.

The odd fair Saxon here and there ... ah, Laoghaire, the perfect exemplar. Pale-skinned, blue-eyed and just the tiniest bit plump ... I repressed the uncharitable observation. She carefully avoided looking at either me or Jamie, chattering animatedly with her friends at one of the lower tables.

I looked in the opposite direction, towards the next table, where Dougal MacKenzie sat, apart from Callum for once. A bloody Viking, that one. With his impressive height and those broad, flat cheekbones, I could easily imagine him in command of a dragon ship, deepsunk eyes gleaming with avarice and lust as he peered through the fog at some rocky coastal village.

A large hand, wrist lightly haired with copper, reached past me to take a small loaf of oat-bread from the tray. Another Norseman, Jamie. He reminded me of Mrs Baird's legends of the race of giants who once walked Scotland and laid their long bones in the earth of the north.

The conversation was general, as it usually was, small groups buzzing between mouthfuls. But my ears suddenly caught a familiar name, spoken at a nearby table. Sandringham. I thought the voice was Murtagh's, and turned around to see. He was seated next to Ned Gowan, munching industriously.

'Sandringham? Ah, old Willie the arse-bandit,' said Ned meditatively.

'What?' said one of the younger men-at-arms, choking on his ale.

'Our revered Duke has something of a taste for boys, or so I understand,' Ned explained.

'Mmm,' agreed Rupert, his mouth full. Swallowing, he added, 'Had a wee bit of a taste for young Jamie here, last time he visited these parts, if I remember rightly. That were when, Dougal? Thirty-eight? Thirty-nine?'

'Thirty-six,' Dougal answered from the next table. He narrowed his eyes at his nephew. 'Ye were rather a pretty lad at sixteen, Jamie.'

Jamie nodded, chewing. 'Aye. Fast, too.'

When the laughter had died down, Dougal began to tease Jamie.

'I didna ken ye were a favourite, Jamie lad. There's several about the Duke as ha' traded a sore arse for lands and offices.'

'Ye'll notice I havena got either one,' responded Jamie with a grin, to further roars of laughter.

'What? Never even got close?' said Rupert, chewing noisily.

'A good bit closer than I would have liked, truth be known.'

'Ah, but how close would ye ha' liked it, hey, lad?' The shout came from further down the table, from a tall, brown-bearded man I didn't recognize, and was greeted with more laughter and ribald remarks. Jamie smiled tranquilly and reached for another loaf, undisturbed by the teasing.

'Is that why ye left the castle so sudden and went back to your father?' asked Rupert.

'Aye.'

'Why, ye should ha' told me ye were having trouble that way, Jamie lad,' said Dougal with mock concern. Jamie made a low Scottish noise in his throat.

'And if I'd told ye about it, you old rogue, ye would have slipped a bit of poppy juice in my ale some evening, and left me in His Grace's bed as a wee gift.'

The table roared, and Jamie dodged as Dougal hurled an onion at him.

Rupert squinted across at Jamie. 'Seems to me, lad, I saw ye, soon before ye left, goin' into the Duke's chambers near nightfall. Ye're sure ye're not holdin' back on us?' Jamie grabbed another onion and threw it at him. It missed and rolled away into the rushes.

'Nay,' Jamie said, laughing. 'I'm a maiden still – that way, at least. But if ye must know all about it before you can sleep, Rupert, I'll tell ye, and welcome.'

Amid shouts of 'Tell! Tell!' he deliberately poured a mug of ale and sat back in the classic storyteller's posture. I could see Callum at the head table, head cocked forward to hear, as attentive as the ostlers and fighting-men at our table.

'Well,' he began, 'it's true enough what Ned says. His Grace had something of an eye for me, though being the innocent I was at sixteen – ' Here he was interrupted by a number of cynical remarks, and raised his voice to go on.

'Bein', as I say, innocent of such carryings on, I'd no idea what he meant, though it seemed a bit strange to me, the way His Grace was always wanting to pat me like a wee dog and was so interested in what I might ha' in my sporran.' ('Or under it!' shouted a drunken voice.)

'I thought it stranger still,' he went on, 'when he found me washing myself at the river and wanted to wash my back for me. When he finished my back and went on wi' the rest, I began to get a wee bit nervous, and when he put his hand under my kilts, I began to get the general idea. I may have been an innocent, but no a complete fool, ye ken.

'I got out of that particular situation by diving into the water, kilts and all, and swimming across to the other side; His Grace being not of a mind to risk his costly clothes in the mud and water. Anyway, after that I was verra wary of being alone with him. He caught me once or twice in the garden or the courtyard, but there was room to get away, wi' no more harm than him kissing my ear. The only other bad time was when he came on me alone in the stables.'

'In *my* stables?' Auld Alick looked aghast. He half rose to his feet and called across the room to the head table, 'Callum, ye'll see that man stays oot o' my sheds! I'll not have him frightening my horses, duke or no! Or troubling the boys, neither!' he added as an obvious afterthought.

Jamie went on with his story, unperturbed by the interruption. Dougal's two teenaged daughters were listening raptly, mouths slightly agape.

'I was in a horse's stall, ye ken, and there wasna room to manoeuvre much. I was bendin' over' (more ribald remarks) 'bendin' over the manger, I say, muckin' up husks from the bottom, when I hear a sound behind me, and before I can straighten up, my kilts are tossed up round my waist, and there's something hard pressed against my arse.'

He waved a hand to still the tumult before going on. 'Weel, I didna care much for the thought of being buggered in a stall, but I didna see much way out at that point, either. I was just gritting my teeth and hoping it wouldn't hurt too much, when the horse – it was that big black gelding, Ned, the one ye got at Brocklebury – you know, the one Callum sold to Breadalbane – anyway, the horse took an objection to the noise His Grace was making. Now, most horses like ye to talk to them, and so did that one, but he had a peculiar aversion to verra high voices; I couldna take him in the yard when there were small bairns about, because he'd get nervous at their squeaks, and start pawing and stamping.

'His Grace, ye might recall, has a rather high-pitched voice, and it was a bit higher than usual on this occasion, him bein' a trifle excited. Weel, as I say, the horse didna care for it – nor did I, I must say – and he starts stamping, and snorting, and swings his body round and squashes His Grace flat against the side of the stall. As soon as the Duke let go of me, I jumped into the manger and eased away round the other side of the horse, leavin' His Grace to get out as best he might.'

Jamie paused for breath and a sip of ale. He had the attention of the whole room by this time, faces turned towards him, gleaming in the light of the torches. Here and there might have been discerned a frown at these revelations concerning a most puissant sprig of the aristocracy, but the overriding reaction was an untrammelled delight in the scandal. I gathered that the Duke was not a particularly popular personage at Castle Leoch.

'Havin' been so close, as ye might say, His Grace made up his mind as he'd have me, come what might. So next day he tells Himself that his body servant's fallen ill, and can he borrow me to help him wash and dress.' Callum covered his face in mock dismay, to the amusement of the crowd. Jamie nodded to Rupert.

'That's why ye saw me go to His Grace's room in the evening. Under orders, ye might say.'

'You could have told me, Jamie. I'd not have made you go,' Callum called, with a look of reproach.

Jamie shrugged and grinned. 'I was prevented by my natural modesty, Uncle. Besides, I knew ye were trying to deal with the man; I thought it might impair your negotiations a bit if you were forced to tell His Grace to keep his hands off your nephew's bum.'

'Very thoughtful of you, Jamie,' said Callum dryly. 'So you sacrificed yourself for my interests, did you?'

Jamie raised his mug in a mock toast. 'Your interests are always foremost in my mind, Uncle,' he said, and I thought that in spite of the teasing tone there was a sharp undercurrent of truth to this, one that Callum perceived as well as I.

Jamie drained the mug and set it down. 'But, no,' he said, wiping his mouth, 'in this case, I didna feel that family duty required quite that much of me. I went to the Duke's rooms, because you told me to, but that was all.'

'And ye came out again wi' yer arse-hole unstretched?' Rupert sounded sceptical.

Jamie grinned. 'Aye, I did. Ye see, directly I heard about it, I went to Mrs Fitz and told her I was in desperate need of a dose of syrup of figs. When she gave it to me I saw where she put the bottle, and I came back quite a bit later, and drank the whole lot.'

The room rocked with laughter, including Mrs Fitz, who turned so red in the face I thought she might have a seizure. She rose ceremoniously from her place, waddled round the table and cuffed Jamie good-naturedly on the ear.

'So that's what became of my good physick, ye young wretch!' Hands on her hips, she wagged her head, making the green ear-bobbles wink like dragonflies. 'The best lot I ever made too!'

'Oh, it was most effective,' he assured her, laughing up at the massive dame.

'I should think so! When I think what that much physick must have done to your innards, lad, I hope it was worth it to ye. Ye canna have been much good to yourself for days after.'

He shook his head, still laughing.

'I wasn't, but then, I wasna much good for what His Grace had in mind, either. He did not seem to mind at all when I begged leave to remove myself from his presence. But I knew I couldna do it twice, so as soon as the cramps eased up, I got a horse from the stables and lit out.'

Dougal beckoned for a new jug of ale, which he passed down the board hand-to-hand to Jamie.

'Aye, your father sent word he thought perhaps you'd learned enough of castle life for the present,' he said, smiling ruefully. 'I thought there was a tone to his letter I did not quite understand at the time.'

'Weel, I hope ye've laid up a new batch of fig syrup, Mrs Fitz,' Rupert interrupted, poking her familiarly in the ribs. 'His Grace is likely to be here in a day or two. Or are ye counting on your new wife to guard ye this time, Jamie?' He leered at me. 'From all accounts, ye may need to guard *her*. I hear the Duke's servant does not share His Grace's preferences, though he's every bit as active.'

Jamie pushed back the bench and rose from the table, handing me out. He put an arm around my shoulders and smiled back at Rupert.

'Well, then, I suppose the two of us will just have to fight it out back to back.'

Rupert's eyes flew open in horrified dismay.

'Back to back!?' he exclaimed. 'I knew we'd forgot to tell ye something before your wedding, lad! No wonder you've not got her with child yet!'

Jamie's hand tightened on my shoulder, turning me towards the archway, and we made our escape, pelted by a hail of laughter and bawdy advice.

In the dark hall outside, Jamie leaned against the stones, doubled over. Unable to stand, I sank to the ground at his feet and giggled helplessly.

'You didn't tell him, did you?' Jamie gasped at last.

I shook my head. 'No, of course not.' Still wheezing, I groped for his hand and he hauled me upright. I collapsed against his chest.

'Let me see if I've got it right, now.' He cupped my face between his hands and pressed his forehead to mine, face so close that his eyes blurred into one large blue orb and his breath was warm on my chin.

'Face to face. Is that it?' The fizz of laughter was dying down in my blood, replaced by something else just as potent.

I touched my tongue against his lips, while my hands busied themselves lower down.

'Faces are not the essential parts. But you're learning.'

Next day I was in my surgery, listening patiently to an elderly lady from the village, some relation to the soup cook, who was rather garrulously detailing her daughter-in-law's bout with stomach pains which theoretically had something to do with her own current complaint of quinsy, though I couldn't at the moment see the connection. A shadow fell across the doorway, interrupting the old lady's catalogue of symptoms.

I looked up, startled, to see Jamie rush in, followed by Auld Alick, both men looking worried and excited. Jamie unceremoniously removed the makeshift tongue depressor I was holding and pulled me to my feet, clasping both hands between his own.

'What – ' I began, but was interrupted by Alick peering over Jamie's shoulder at my hands, which Jamie was displaying to him.

'Aye, that's verra weel, but the arms, man? Has she the arm for it?'

'Look,' Jamie grasped one of my hands and stretched my arm out straight, measuring it along one of his.

'Weel,' said Alick, examining it doubtfully, 'could do. Aye, it could.'

'Would you care to tell me what you think you're doing?' I inquired, but before I could finish I was being hustled down the stairs between the two men, leaving my aged patient to gape after us in perplexity.

A few moments later I was dubiously eyeing the large, shiny, brown hindquarters of a horse, located some six inches from my face. The problem had been made clear on the way to the stables, Jamie explaining and Auld Alick chiming in with remarks, imprecations and interjections.

Losgann, customarily a good foaler, and a prize member of Callum's stable, was having trouble. This much I could see for myself; the mare lay on her side and periodically the shining flanks heaved and the enormous body seemed to shiver. Down on hands and knees at the rear of the horse, I could see the lips of the vagina gape slightly with each contraction, but nothing further happened; no sight of tiny hoof or delicate wet nose appeared at the opening. The foal, a late one, was evidently presenting side-on or backwards. Alick thought side-on, Jamie thought backwards, and they paused to argue about it for a moment, until I impatiently called the meeting to order to ask what they expected me to do about it, in either case.

Jamie looked at me as though I were a bit simple. 'Turn the foal, of course,' he said patiently. 'Bring the forelegs round so it can get out.'

'Oh, is *that* all?' I looked at the horse. Losgann, whose elegant name actually meant Frog, was delicately boned for a horse, but bloody big for all that.

'Er, reach inside, you mean?' I glanced covertly at my hand. It probably would fit – the opening was big enough – but what then?

Both men's hands were clearly too big for the job. And Roderick, the stable lad who was usually pressed into service in such delicate situations, was, of course, immobilized with a splint and sling of my devising on his right arm – he had broken it two days before. Willy, the other stable lad, had gone to fetch Roderick nonetheless, to give advice and moral encouragement. At this juncture he arrived, clad in nothing but a pair of ragged breeches, thin chest glimmering whitely in the dim stable.

'It's hard work,' he said dubiously, apprized of the situation and the suggestion that I substitute for him. 'Tricky, ye ken. There's a knack to it, but it takes a bit of strength as well.'

'Nay worry,' said Jamie confidently. 'Claire's stronger by far than you, ye poor weed. If you'll tell her what to feel for and what to do, she'll have it round in no time.'

I appreciated the vote of confidence but was in no way so sanguine myself. Telling myself firmly that this was no worse than assisting at abdominal surgery, I retired to a stall to change my gown for breeches and a rough smock of sacking, and lathered my hand and arm up to the shoulder with greasy tallow soap.

'Well, over the top,' I muttered under my breath, and slid my hand inside.

There was very little room to manoeuvre, and at first I couldn't tell what I was feeling. I closed my eyes to concentrate better, though, and groped cautiously. There were smooth expanses and bumpy bits. The smooth parts would be body and the bumps legs or head. It was legs I wanted – forelegs, to be specific. Gradually I became accustomed to the feel of things, and the necessity for keeping quite still when a contraction came on; the amazingly powerful muscles of the uterus clamped down on my hand and arm like a vice, grinding my own bones very painfully until the constriction eased and I could resume my groping.

At last, my fumbling fingers encountered something I was sure of.

'I've got my fingers in its nose!' I cried triumphantly. 'I've found the head!'

'Good lass, good! Dinna let go!' Alick crouched anxiously alongside, patting the mare reassuringly as another contraction set in. I gritted my teeth and leaned my forehead against the shining rump as my wrist was crushed by the force. It eased, though, and I kept my grip. Feeling cautiously upwards, I found the curve of the eyesocket and brow, and the small ridge of the folded ear. Waiting through one more contraction, I followed the curve of the neck down to the shoulder.

'It's got its head turned back on its shoulder,' I reported. 'The head's pointing the right way, at least.'

'Good.' Jamie, at the horse's head, ran his hand soothingly down the sweating chestnut neck. 'Likely the legs will be folded under the chest. See can you get a hand on one knee.'

So it went on, feeling, fumbling, up to my shoulder in the warm darkness of the horse, feeling the awful force of the birth pangs and their grateful easing, struggling blindly to reach my goal. I felt rather as though I were giving birth myself, and bloody hard work it was, too.

At last I had my hand on a hoof; I could feel the rounded surface, and the sharp edge of the yet-unused curve. Following the anxious, often contradictory instructions of my guides as best I could, I alternately pulled and pushed, easing the unwieldy mass of the foal around, bringing one foot forward, pushing another back, sweating and groaning along with the mare.

And then suddenly everything worked. A contraction eased, and all at once, everything slid smoothly into place. I waited, not moving, for the next contraction. It came, and a small wet nose popped suddenly out, pushing my hand out with it. The tiny nostrils flared briefly, as though interested in this new sensation, then the nose vanished.

'Next one will do it!' Alick was almost dancing in ecstasy, his rheumatic form capering up and down in the hay. 'Come on, Losgann. Come on, my sweet wee froggie!'

As though in answer there was a convulsive grunt from the mare. Her hindquarters flexed sharply and the foal slid smoothly on to the clean straw in a slither of knobbly legs and big ears.

I sat back on the straw, grinning idiotically. I was covered with soap and slime and blood, exhausted and aching, and smelt strongly of the less pleasant aspects of horse. I was euphoric.

I sat watching as Willy and the one-handed Roderick tended the new arrival, wiping him down with wisps of straw. And cheered with the rest when Losgann turned and licked him, butting him gently and nosing him to stand at last on his huge, wobbly feet.

'A damn good job, lassie! *Damn* good!' Alick was exuberant, pumping my unslimed hand in congratulation. Suddenly realizing that I was swaying on my perch, and much less than presentable, he turned and barked at one of the lads to bring some water. Then he circled behind me and set his horny old hands on my shoulders. With an amazingly deft and gentle touch, he pressed and stroked, easing the strain in my shoulders, relaxing the knots in my neck.

'There, lassie,' he said at last. 'Hard work, no?' He smiled down at me, then beamed adoringly at the new colt.

'Bonny laddie,' he crooned. 'Who's a sweet lad, then?'

Jamie helped me to clean up and change. My fingers were too stiff to manage the buttons of my bodice, and I knew my entire arm would be blue with bruising by morning, but I felt thoroughly peaceful and contented.

The rain seemed to have lasted for ever, so that when a day finally dawned bright and fair, I squinted in the daylight like a newly emerged mole.

'Your skin is so fine I can see the blood moving beneath it,' Jamie said, tracing the path of a sunbeam across my bare stomach. 'I could follow the veins from your hand to your heart.' He drew his finger gently up my wrist to the bend of the elbow, up the inner side of my upper arm and across the slope below my collarbone.

'That's the subclavian vein,' I remarked, looking down my nose at the path of his tracking finger.

'Is it? Oh, aye, because it's below your clavicle. Tell me some more.' The finger moved slowly downwards. 'I like to hear the Latin names for things; I never dreamed it would be so pleasant to make love to a physician.'

'That,' I said primly, 'is an areola, and you know it, because I told you last week.'

'So ye did,' he murmured. 'And there's another one, fancy that.' The bright head dipped to let his tongue replace the finger, then travelled lower.

'Umbilicus,' I said with a short gasp.

'Um,' he said, muffled lips stretching in a smile against my transparent skin. 'And what's this, then?'

'You tell me,' I said, clutching his head. But he was incapable of speech.

Later I lounged in my surgery chair, basking dreamily in memories of awaking in a bed of sunbeams, sheets tumbled in blinding shoals of white like the sands of a beach. One hand rested on my breast, and I toyed idly with the nipple, enjoying the feel of it rising against my palm beneath the thin calico of my bodice.

'Enjoying yourself?'

The sarcastic voice from the door brought me upright so quickly that I bumped my head on a shelf.

'Oh,' I said, rather grumpily. 'Geilie. Who else? What are you doing here?'

She glided into the surgery, moving as though on wheels. I knew she had feet; I'd seen them. What I couldn't figure out was where she put them when she walked.

'I came to bring Mrs Fitz some saffron from Spain; she was wanting it against the Duke's coming.'

'More spices?' I said, beginning to recover my good humour. 'If the man eats half the things she's fixing for him, they'll need to roll him home.'

'They could do that now. He's a wee round ball of a fellow, I've heard.' Dismissing the Duke and his physique, she asked whether I'd like to join her for an expedition to the nearby foothills.

'I'm needing a bit of moss,' she explained. She waved her long, boneless hands gracefully to and fro. 'Makes a wonderful lotion for the hands, boiled in milk with a bit of sheep's wool.'

I cast a look up at my slit window, where the dust motes were going mad in the golden light. A faint scent of ripe fruit and fresh-cut hay floated on the breeze.

'Why not?'

Waiting as I gathered my baskets and bottles together, Geilie strolled about my surgery, picking things up and putting them down at random. She stopped at a small table and picked up the object that lay there, frowning.

'What's this?'

I stopped what I was doing and came to stand beside her. She was holding a small bundle of dried plants tied with three twisted threads: black, white and red.

'Jamie says it's an ill wish.'

'He's right. Where did ye come to get it?'

I told her about the finding of the small bundle in my bed.

'I went and found it under the window next day, where Jamie threw it. I meant to bring it round to your house and ask if you knew anything about it, but I forgot.'

501

She stood tapping a fingernail thoughtfully against her front teeth, shaking her head.

'No, I canna say that I do. But there might be a way of finding out who left it for ye.'

'Really?'

'Aye. Come to my house in the morning tomorrow, and I'll tell ye then.'

Refusing to say more, she whirled about in a swirl of green cloak, leaving me to follow as I would.

She led me well up into the foothills, galloping where there was road enough to do so, walking when there wasn't. An hour's ride from the village she stopped near a small brook overhung by willows.

We forded the brook and wandered into the foothills, gathering such late summer plants as still lingered, together with the ripening berries of early autumn and the thick yellow shelf fungus that sprouted from the trunks of trees in the small shady glens.

Geilie's figure disappeared into the bracken above me as I paused to scrape a bit of aspen bark into my basket. The globules of dried sap on the papery bark looked like frozen drops of blood, the deep crimson refulgent with trapped sunlight.

A sound startled me and I looked up the hill, in the direction it seemed to come from.

I heard the sound again; a high-pitched, mewling cry. It seemed to come from a rocky notch near the crest of the hill. I set my basket down and began to climb.

'Geilie!' I shouted. 'Come over here! Someone's left a baby!'

The sound of scrabbling and muttered imprecations preceded her as she fought her way through the entangling bushes on the slope. Her fair face was flushed and cross and she had twigs in her hair.

'What in God's name – ' she began, and then darted forward. 'Christ's blood! Put it down!' She hastily snatched the baby from my arms, then laid it back where I had found it, in a small depression in the rock. The smooth, bowl-shaped hollow was less than a yard across. At one side of the hollow was a shallow wooden bowl half full of fresh milk, and at the baby's feet was a small bouquet of wild flowers tied with a bit of red twine.

'But it's sick!' I protested, stooping towards the child again. 'Who would leave a sick child up here by itself?'

The baby was plainly very ill; the small pinched face was greenish, with dark hollows under the eyes, and the little fists waved weakly under the blanket. The child had hung slack in my arms when I picked it up; I wondered that it had had the strength to cry.

'Its parents,' Geilie said briefly, restraining me with a hand on my arm. 'Leave it. Let's get out of here.'

'Its parents?' I said indignantly. 'But – '

'It's a changeling,' she said impatiently. 'Leave it and come. Now!'

Dragging me with her, she dodged back into the undergrowth. Protesting, I followed her down the slope until we arrived, breathless and red faced, at the bottom, where I forced her to stop.

'What is this?' I demanded. 'We can't just abandon a sick child, out in the open like that. And what do you mean, it's a changeling?'

'A changeling,' she said impatiently. 'Surely you know what a changeling is? When the fairies steal a human child away they leave one of their own in its place. You know it's a changeling because it cries and fusses all the time and doesn't thrive or grow.'

'Of course I know what it is,' I said. 'But you don't believe that nonsense, do you?'

She shot me a sudden strange look, full of wary suspicion. Then the lines of her face relaxed into their normal expression of half-amused cynicism.

'No, I don't,' she admitted. 'But the folk here do.' She glanced nervously up the slope, but no further sound came from the rocky notch. 'The family will be somewhere near about. Let's go.'

Reluctantly I allowed her to tow me away in the direction of the village.

'Why did they put it up there?' I asked, sitting on a rock

to remove my stockings before wading across a small stream. 'Do they hope the Wee Folk will come and cure it?' I was still bothered about the child; it seemed desperately ill. I didn't know what was wrong with it, but perhaps I could help.

Maybe I could leave Geilie in the village, then come back for the child. It would have to be soon, though; I glanced up at the eastern sky, where soft grey rain clouds were swiftly darkening into purple dusk. A pink glow still showed to the west, but there could be no more than half an hour's light left.

Geilie looped the twisted withy handle of her basket over her neck, picked up her skirt and stepped into the stream, shivering at the cold water.

'No,' she said. 'Or rather, yes. That's one of the fairies' hills, and it's dangerous to sleep there. If ye leave a changeling out overnight in such a place, the Folk will come and take it back, and leave the human child they've stolen in its place.'

'But they won't, because it isn't a changeling,' I said, sucking in my breath at the touch of the melted snow water. 'It's only a sick child. It might very well not survive a night in the open!'

'It won't,' she said briefly. 'It will be dead by morning. And I hope to God no one saw us near it.'

I stopped abruptly in the midst of putting on my shoes.

'Dead! Geilie, I'm going back for it. I can't leave it there.' I turned and started back across the stream.

She caught me from behind and pushed me flat on my face into the shallow water. Floundering and gasping, I managed to rise to my knees, sloshing water in all directions. Geilie stood calf-deep in the stream, skirts soaked, glaring down at me.

'You bloody pig-headed English ass!' she shouted at me. 'There's nothing ye can do! Do ye hear me? Nothing! That child's as good as dead! I'll not stand here and let ye risk your own life and mine for some crackbrained notion of yours!' Snorting and grumbling under her breath, she reached down and got me under the arms with both hands, lugging me to my feet.

'Claire,' she said urgently, shaking me by the arms. 'Listen to me. If ye go near that child and it dies – and it will, believe me, I've seen them like that – then the family will blame you for it. Do ye see the danger of it? Don't ye know what they say about you in the village?'

I stood shivering in the cold breeze of sunset, torn between her obvious panic for my safety and the thought of a helpless child slowly dying alone in the dark, with wild flowers at its feet.

'No,' I said, shaking the wet hair out of my face. 'Geilie, no, I can't. I'll be careful, I promise, but I have to go.' I pulled myself out of her grasp and turned towards the far bank, stumbling and splashing in the uncertain shadows of the streambed.

There was a muffled cry of exasperation from behind me, then a frenzied sploshing in the opposite direction Well, at least she wouldn't hamper me further.

It was growing dark fast, and I pushed through the bushes and weeds as quickly as I could. I wasn't sure I could find the right hill if it grew dark before I reached it; there were several nearby, all about the same height. And fairies or not, the thought of wandering about alone out here in the dark was not one I cared for. The question of how I was going to make it back to the castle with a sick baby was something I would deal with when the time came.

I found the hill, finally, by spotting the stand of young trees I remembered at the base. It was nearly full dark by this time, a moonless night, and I stumbled and fell frequently. The trees stood huddled together, talking quietly in the evening breeze with clicks and creaks and rustling sighs.

Bloody place *is* haunted, I thought, listening to the leafy conversation overhead as I threaded my way through the slender trunks. I wouldn't be surprised to meet a ghost behind the next tree.

I *was* surprised, though. Actually, I was scared out of my

505

wits when the shadowy figure slid out and grabbed me. I let out a piercing shriek and struck at it.

'Jesus Christ,' I said, 'what are you doing here?' I crumpled for a moment against Jamie's chest, relieved to see him in spite of the fright he had given me.

He took me by the arm and turned to lead me out of the wood.

'Came for you,' he said, low voiced. 'I was coming to meet you because night was coming on; I met Geillis Duncan and she told me where you were.'

'But the baby – ' I began, turning back towards the hill.

'The child's dead,' he said briefly, tugging me back. 'I went up there first, to see.'

I followed him then without demur, distressed over the child's death but relieved that I would not, after all, have to face the climb to the fairies' crest or the long journey back alone. Oppressed by the dark and the whispering trees, I didn't speak until we had crossed the brook again. Still damp from the previous immersion, I didn't bother removing my stockings but sloshed across regardless. Jamie, still dry, stayed that way by leaping from the bank to a central boulder that stood above the current, then vaulting to my bank like a long-jumper.

'Have ye any idea how dangerous it is to be out alone at night like that, Sassenach?' he inquired. He didn't seem angry, just curious.

'No . . . I mean yes. I'm sorry if I worried you. But I *couldn't* leave a child out there, I just couldn't.'

'Aye, I know.' He hugged me briefly. 'You've a kind heart, Sassenach. But you've no idea what you're dealing with here.'

'Fairies, hm?' I was tired, and disturbed over the incident, but covered it with flippancy. 'I'm not afraid of superstitions.' A thought struck me. 'Do *you* believe in fairies and changelings, and all that?'

He hesitated for a moment before answering.

'No. No, I dinna believe in such things, though damned if I'd care to sleep all night on a fairies' hill, for a' that. But I'm an educated man, Sassenach. I had a German tutor, a good one, who taught me Latin and Greek and such, and later when I went to France at eighteen – well, I studied history and philosophy and I saw that there was a good deal more to the world than the glens and the moors, and the waterhorses in the lochs. But these people . . .' He waved an arm, taking in the darkness behind us.

'They've ne'er been more than a day's walk from the place they were born, except for a great thing like a clan Gathering, and that might happen twice in a lifetime. They live among the glens and the lochs, and they hear no more of the world than what Father Bain tells them in chapel of a Sunday. That and the old stories.'

He held aside an alder branch and I stooped under it. We were on the track Geilie and I had followed earlier, and I was heartened by this fresh evidence that he could find his way, even in the dark. Away from the fairies' hill he spoke in his normal voice, only pausing occasionally to brush away some tangling growth from his path.

'Those tales are naught but entertainment in Gwyllyn's hands, when ye sit in the hall drinking Rhenish wine.' He preceded me down the path and his voice floated back to me, soft and emphatic in the cool night air.

'Out here, though, and even in the village – nay, that's something else. Folk live by them. I suppose there's some truth behind some of them.'

I thought of the amber eyes of the waterhorse, and wondered which others were true.

'And others . . . well,' his voice grew softer, and I had to strain to hear him. 'For the parents of that child, maybe it will ease them a bit to believe it is the changeling who died, and think of their own child, healthy and well, living for ever with the fairies.'

We reached the ponies then, and within an hour the lights of Castle Leoch shone through the darkness to welcome us. I had never thought I would consider that bleak edifice an outpost of advanced civilization, but just now the lights seemed those of a beacon of enlightenment.

It was not until we drew closer that I realized the

507

impression of light was due to the string of lanterns blazing along the parapet of the bridge.

'Something's happened,' I said, turning to Jamie. And seeing him for the first time in the light, I realized that he was not wearing his usual worn shirt and grubby kilt. His snowy linen shone in the lantern light, and his best – his only – velvet coat lay across his saddle.

'Aye,' he nodded. 'That's why I came to get you. The Duke's arrived at last.'

The Duke was something of a surprise. I don't know quite what I had been expecting, but it wasn't the bluff, hearty, red-faced sportsman I met in Leoch's hall. He had a pleasantly blunt, weather-beaten face, with light blue eyes that always squinted slightly, as though looking into the sun after the flight of a pheasant.

I wondered for a moment whether that earlier bit of theatrics regarding the Duke might have been overstated. Looking around the hall, though, I noticed that every boy under eighteen wore a slightly wary expression, keeping his eyes fixed on the Duke as he laughed and talked animatedly with Callum and Dougal. Not merely theatrics, then; they had been warned.

When I was presented to the Duke I had some difficulty in keeping a straight face. He was a big man, fit and solid, the sort you so often see booming out their opinions in pubs, bearing down the opposition by dint of loudness and repetition. I had been warned, of course, by Jamie's story, but the physical impression was so overwhelming that when the Duke bowed low over my hand and said, 'But how charming to find a countrywoman in this remote spot, mistress,' in a voice like an overwrought mouse, I had to bite the inside of my cheek to keep from disgracing myself in public.

Worn out from travel, the Duke and his party retired early to bed. The next night, though, there was music and conversation after supper, and Jamie and I joined Callum, Dougal and the Duke. Sandringham grew expansive over Callum's Rhenish wine and talked volubly, expounding equally upon the horrors of travel in the Highlands and the beauties of the countryside. We listened politely, and I tried not to catch Jamie's eye as the Duke squeaked out the story of his travails.

'Broke an axletree outside of Stirling, and we were becalmed three days – *in* the pouring rain, mind you – before my footman could find a blacksmith to come and repair the blasted thing. And not half a day later, we bounced into the most tremendous pothole I've ever seen and broke the dam' thing again! And then one horse threw a shoe, and we had to unload the coach and walk beside it – *in* the mud – leading the lame nag. And *then* . . .' As the tale went on, from misfortune to misfortune, I felt an increasing urge to giggle, and attempted to drown it with more wine – possibly an error in judgement.

'But the game, MacKenzie, the game!' the Duke exclaimed at one point, rolling his eyes in ecstasy. 'I could scarce believe it. No wonder you set such a table.' He gently patted his large, solid stomach. 'I swear I'd give my eyeteeth for a try at a stag like the one we saw two days ago; splendid beast, simply splendid. Leapt out of the brush right in front of the coach, m'dear,' he confided to me. 'Startled the horses so we near as a toucher went off the road *again*!'

Callum raised the bell-shaped decanter, with an inquiring cock of one dark brow. As he poured to the proffered glasses he said, 'Well, perhaps we might arrange a hunt for ye, Your Grace. My nephew's a bonny huntsman.' He glanced sharply from under his brows at Jamie; there was a scarcely perceptible nod in response.

Callum sat back, replacing the decanter, and said casually, 'Aye, that'll do well, then. Perhaps early next week. You'll see plenty of pheasant, and the stag hunting will be fine.' He turned to Dougal, lounging in a padded chair to one side. 'My brother might go along; if you have it in mind to travel northwards, he can show ye the lands we were discussing earlier.'

'Capital, capital!' The Duke was delighted. He patted Jamie on the leg; I saw the muscles tighten, but Jamie didn't move. He smiled tranquilly, and the Duke let his hand linger just a moment too long. Then His Grace caught my eye on him and smiled jovially at me, his expression saying 'Worth a try, eh?' Despite myself, I smiled back. Much to my surprise, I quite liked the man.

In the excitement of the Duke's arrival I had forgotten Geilie's offer to help me discover the sender of the ill wish. And after the unpleasant scene with the changeling child on the fairies' hill I wasn't sure that I wanted to try anything she might suggest.

Still, curiosity overcame suspicion, and when Callum asked Jamie to ride down and escort the Duncans to the castle for the Duke's banquet two days later, I went with him.

Thus it was that Thursday found me and Jamie in the Duncans' parlour, being entertained with a sort of awkard friendliness by the fiscal, while his wife finished her dressing upstairs. Largely recovered from the effects of his last gastric attack, Arthur still did not look terribly healthy. Like many fat men who lose weight abruptly, the weight had gone from his face rather than his stomach. His paunch still swelled the green silk of his waistcoat, while the skin on his face drooped in flabby folds.

'Perhaps I could slip upstairs and help Geilie with her hair or something,' I suggested. 'I've brought her a new ribbon.' Foreseeing the possible need of an excuse for talking to Geilie alone, I had brought a small package with me. Producing it as an excuse, I was through the door and up the stairs before Arthur could protest.

She was ready for me.

'Come on,' she said, 'we'll go up to my private room for this. We'll have to hurry, but it won't take too long.'

I followed Geilie up the narrow, twisting stair. The steps were irregular heights; some of the risers were so high I had to lift my skirts to avoid tripping on the way up. I concluded that eighteenth-century carpenters either had faulty methods of measuring or rich senses of humour.

Geilie's private sanctum was at the top of the house, in one of the remote attics above the servants' quarters. It was guarded by a locked door, opened by a truly formidable key which Geilie produced from her apron pocket; it was at least six inches long, with a broad fretwork head ornamented with a vine-and-flower pattern. It must have weighed nearly a pound; held by the barrel, it would have made a good weapon. Both lock and hinges were well oiled, and the thick door swung inwards silently.

The attic room was small, lit by the gabled dormers that cut across the front of the house. Shelves lined every inch of wall space, holding jars, bottles, flasks, vials and beakers. Bunches of drying herbs, carefully tied with threads of different colours, hung neatly in rows from the rafters, brushing my hair with a fragrant dust as we passed beneath.

This was nothing like the clean, businesslike order of the herb room downstairs, though. It was crowded, almost cluttered, and dark in spite of the dormer windows.

One shelf held books, mostly old and crumbling, the spines unmarked. I ran a curious finger over the row of leather bindings. Most were calf, but there were two or three bound in something different; something soft but unpleasantly oily to the touch. And one that to all appearances was bound in fish skin. I pulled a volume out and opened it gingerly. It was handwritten in a mixture of archaic French, and even more obsolete Latin, but I could make out the title: *L'Grimoire d'le Comte St Germain.*

I closed the book and set it back on the shelf, feeling a slight shock. A grimoire. A handbook of magic. I could feel Geilie's gaze boring into my back, and turned to meet a mixture of mischief and wary speculation. What would I do, now that I knew?

'So it isn't a rumour, then, is it?' I said, smiling. 'You really are a witch.' I wondered just how far it went, and whether she believed it herself, or whether these were merely the trappings of an elaborate make-believe that she used to alleviate the boredom of marriage to Arthur. I also wondered just what sort of magic she practised – or thought she practised.

'Oh, white,' she said, grinning. 'Definitely white magic.'

I thought ruefully that Jamie must be right about my face – *everyone* seemed to be able to tell what I was thinking.

'Well, that's good,' I said. 'I'm really not much of a one for dancing round bonfires at midnight and riding brooms, let alone kissing the Devil's arse.'

Geilie tossed back her hair and laughed delightedly.

'Ye don't kiss anyone's much, that I can see,' she said. 'Nor do I. Though if I had a sweet fiery devil like yours in my bed, I'll not say I might not come to it in time.'

'That reminds me – ' I began, but she had already turned away and was about her preparations, murmuring to herself.

Checking first to see that the door was securely locked behind us, Geilie crossed the room and rummaged in a chest built into a window seat. She pulled out a large, shallow pan and a tall white candle stuck in a pottery holder. A further foray produced a worn quilt, which she spread on the floor as protection against dust and splinters.

'What exactly is it you're planning to do, Geilie?' I asked, examining the preparations suspiciously. Offhand, I couldn't see much sinister intent in a pan, a candle and a quilt, but then I was a novice magician, to say the least.

'Summoning,' she said, tugging the corners of the quilt around so that the sides lay straight with the boards of the floor.

'Summoning whom?' I asked. Or what.

She stood and brushed her hair back. Baby-fine and slippery, it was coming down from its fastenings. Muttering, she yanked the pins from her hair and let it fall down in a straight, shiny curtain, the colour of heavy cream.

'Oh, ghosts, spirits, visions. Anything ye might have need of,' she said. 'It starts the same in any case, but the herbs and the words are different for each thing. What we want now is a vision – to see who it is who's ill wished ye. Then we can turn the ill wish back upon them.'

'Er, well . . .' I really had no wish to be vindictive, but I *was* curious – both to see what summoning was like and to know who had left me the ill wish.

Setting the pan in the middle of the quilt, she poured water into it from a jug, explaining, 'You can use any vessel big enough to make a good reflection, though the grimoire says to use a silver *bassin*. Even a pond or a puddle of water outside will do for some kinds of summoning, though it must be secluded. Ye need peace and quiet to do this.'

She passed rapidly from window to window, drawing the heavy black curtains until virtually all the light in the room was extinguished. I could barely see Geilie's slender form flitting through the gloom, until she lit the candle. The wavering flame lit her face as she carried it back to the quilt, throwing wedge-shaped shadows under the nose and chiselled jaw.

She set the candle next to the pan of water, on the side away from me. She added water to the pan very carefully, so that the water bulged slightly above the rim, kept from spilling by its surface tension. Leaning over, I could see that the surface of the water provided an excellent reflection, far better than that obtainable in any of the castle's looking glasses. As though mind reading again, Geilie explained that in addition to its use in summoning spirits, the reflecting pan was an excellent accessory for dressing the hair.

'Don't bump into it, or you'll get soaked,' she advised. Something about the practical tone of the remark, so prosaic in the midst of these supernatural preparations, reminded me of someone. Looking up at the slender, pallid figure I couldn't think at first of whom she reminded me. But of course. While no one could be less like that dowdy figure athwart the teapot in the Reverend Mr Wakefield's kitchen, the tone of voice had been that of Mrs Graham, exactly.

Perhaps it was an attitude they shared, a pragmatism that regarded the occult as merely a collection of phenomena like the weather. Something to be approached with cautious respect, of course – much as one would take care in using a sharp kitchen knife – but certainly nothing to avoid or fear.

Or it might have been the smell of lavender water. Geilie's loose, flowing gowns smelled always of the plants she used: marigold, camomile, bay leaf, dill, mint, marjoram. Today, though, it was lavender that drifted from the folds of the white dress. The same scent that permeated Mrs

Graham's practical blue cotton and wafted from the corrugations of her bony chest.

If Geilie's chest was likewise underlaid by such skeletal supports, there was no hint of it visible, in spite of her robe's low neckline. It was the first time I had seen Geilie Duncan *en déshabille;* customarily she wore the severe and voluminous gowns, buttoned high at the neck, that were suitable to the wife of a fiscal. The swelling opulence now revealed was a surprise, a creamy abundance almost the same shade as the dress she wore, and gave me some idea why a man like Arthur Duncan might have married a penniless girl of no family.

Geilie selected three of the jars from the shelf, pouring a small quantity from each into the bowl of a tiny metal brazier. She lit the layer of charcoal underneath from the candle flame, and blew on the dawning flame to encourage it. A fragrant smoke began to rise as the spark took hold.

The air in the attic was so still that the greyish smoke rose straight up without diffusing, forming a column that echoed the shape of the tall white candle. Geilie sat between the two columns like a priestess in her temple, legs folded gracefully under her.

'Well then, that will do nicely, I think.' Briskly dusting crumbs of rosemary from her fingers, Geilie surveyed the scene with satisfaction. The black drapes, with their mystic symbols, shut out all intrusive beams of sunlight and left the candle as the only source of direct illumination. The flame was reflected and diffused through the pan of still water, which seemed to glow as though it, too, were a source rather than a reflection of light.

'What now?' I inquired.

The large green eyes glowed like the water, alight with anticipation. She waved her hands across the surface of the water, then folded them between her legs.

'Just sit quiet for a moment,' she said. 'Listen to your heartbeat. Do you hear it? Breathe easy, slow and deep.' In spite of the liveliness of her expression her voice was calm and slow, a distinct contrast to her usual sprightly conversation.

I obediently did as she instructed, feeling my heart slow as my breathing steadied to an even rhythm. I recognized the scent of rosemary in the smoke, but I wasn't sure of the other two herbs; foxglove, perhaps, or cinquefoil? I had thought the purple flowers were those of nightshade, but surely that couldn't be. Whatever they were, the slowness of my breathing did not seem to be attributable only to the power of Geilie's suggestion. I felt as though a weight were pressing against my breastbone, slowing my breathing without my having to will it.

Geilie herself sat perfectly still, watching me with unblinking eyes. She nodded, once, and I looked down obediently into the still surface of the water.

She began to talk, in an even, conversational way that reminded me again of Mrs Graham, calling down the sun in the circle of stones.

The words were not English, and yet not quite *not* English, either. It was a strange tongue, but one I felt that I should know, as though the words were spoken just below the level of my hearing.

I felt my hands begin to go numb, and wanted to move them from their folded position in my lap, but they wouldn't move. Her even voice went on, soft and persuading. Now I *knew* that I understood what was being said, but still could not summon the words to the surface of my mind.

I realized dimly that I was either being hypnotized or under the influence of some drug, and my mind took a last foothold on the edge of conscious thought, resisting the pull of the sweet-scented smoke. I could see my reflection in the water, pupils shrunk to pinpoints, irises wide as a sun-blind owl's. The word opium drifted through my fading thoughts.

'Who are you?' I couldn't tell which of us had asked the question, but I felt my own throat move as I answered, 'Claire.'

'Who sent you here?'

'I came.'

'Why did you come?'

'I can't tell.'

'Why can't you tell?'

'Because no one would believe me.'

The voice in my head grew still more soothing, friendly, beguiling.

'I will believe you. Believe me. Who are you?'

'Claire.'

A sudden loud noise broke the spell. Geilie started and her knee bumped the basin, startling the reflection back into the water.

'Geillis? My dear?' A voice called through the door, tentative yet commanding. 'We must be going, my dear. The horses are ready, and you're not yet gowned.'

Muttering something rude under her breath, Geilie rose and flung open the window, so that the fresh air rushed into my face, making me blink and dispelling some of the fog in my head.

She stood looking down at me speculatively, then stooped to help me up.

'Come along, then,' she said. 'Come over a bit queer, have you? Sometimes it takes folk that way. You'd best lie down on my bed while I dress.'

I lay flat on the coverlet in her bedroom below, eyes closed, listening to the small rustling noises Geilie made in her privy closet, wondering what the hell *that* had been all about. Nothing to do with the ill wish or its sender, clearly. Only with my identity. With sharpness returning gradually to my wits, it occurred to me to wonder whether Geilie perhaps was a spy for Callum. Placed as she was, she heard the business and the secrets of the whole district. And who, other than Callum, would be so interested in my origins?

What would have happened, I wondered, had Arthur not interrupted the summoning? Would I have heard, somewhere in the scented fog, the standard hypnotist's injunction, 'When you wake, you will remember nothing'? But I did remember, and I wondered.

In the event, however, there was no chance to ask Geilie about it. The bedroom door flew open and Arthur Duncan came in. Crossing to the door of the privy closet, he knocked once, hastily, and went in.

There was a small startled scream from within, and then dead silence.

Arthur Duncan reappeared in the door, eyes wide and staring-blind, face so white that I thought perhaps he was suffering an attack of some sort. I leaped to my feet and hurried towards him as he leaned heavily against the door jamb.

Before I reached him, though, he pushed himself away from the door and went out of the room, staggering slightly, brushing past me as though he didn't see me.

I knocked on the door myself.

'Geilie! Are you all right?'

There was a moment's silence, then a perfectly composed voice said, 'Aye, of course. I'll be out in a moment.'

When we at length descended the stairs we found Arthur, apparently somewhat recovered, sipping brandy with Jamie. He seemed a bit abstracted, as though he were thinking of something, but greeted his wife with a mild compliment on her appearance, before sending the groom for the horses.

The banquet was just beginning as we arrived, and the fiscal and his wife were shown to their places of honour at the head table. Jamie and I, somewhat lower in status, took our places at a table with Ned Gowan and Rupert.

Mrs Fitz had excelled herself, and beamed in gratification at the compliments heaped upon the food, the drink and other preparations.

It was in fact delicious. I had never tasted roast pheasant stuffed with honeyed chestnuts, and was helping myself to a third slice when Ned Gowan watching in some amusement at my appetite, asked whether I had yet tried the suckling pig.

My reply was interrupted by a stir at the far end of the hall. Callum had risen from his table and was headed towards me, accompanied by Auld Alick.

'I see there is no end to your talents, Mistress Fraser,' Callum remarked, bowing slightly. A broad smile marked the arresting features.

'From dressing wounds and healing the sick to delivering foals. We shall be calling upon you to raise the dead before long, I suppose.' There was a general chuckle at this, though I noticed one or two men glancing nervously in the direction of Father Bain, in attendance this evening, who was methodically stuffing himself with roast mutton in the corner.

'In any case,' Callum continued, reaching into his coat pocket, 'you must allow me to present you with a small token of my gratitude.' He handed me a small wooden box, lid carved with the MacKenzie badge. I hadn't realized just how valuable a horse Losgann was, and mentally thanked whatever benign spirits presided over such events that nothing had gone wrong.

'Nonsense,' I said, trying to give it back. 'I didn't do anything out of the way. It was only luck that I have small hands.'

'Nevertheless.' Callum was firm. 'If you prefer, consider it a small wedding gift, but I wish you to have it.'

At a nod from Jamie I reluctantly accepted the box and opened it. It contained a beautiful rosary of jet, each bead intricately carved, and the crucifix inlaid with silver.

'It's lovely,' I said sincerely. And it was, though I had no notion what I might do with it. Though nominally a Catholic I had been raised by Uncle Lamb, the completest of agnostics, and had only the vaguest idea of the significance of a rosary. Nonetheless I thanked Callum warmly, and gave the rosary to Jamie to keep for me in his sporran.

I curtsied to Callum, gratified to find that I was mastering the art of doing so without falling on my face. He opened his mouth to take a gracious leave, but was interrupted by a sudden crash that came from behind me. Turning, I could see nothing but backs and heads, as people leaped from their benches to gather round whatever had caused the uproar. Callum made his way with some difficulty around the table, clearing aside the crowd with an impatient wave of the hand. As people stepped respectfully out of his way I could see the rotund form of Arthur Duncan on the floor, limbs flailing convulsively, batting away the helpful hands of would-be assistants. His wife pushed her way through the muttering throng, dropped to the floor beside him and made a vain attempt to cradle his head in her lap. The

518

stricken man dug his heels into the floor and arched his back, making gargling, choking noises.

Glancing up, Geilie's green eyes anxiously scanned the crowd as though looking for someone. Assuming that I was the one she was looking for, I took the path of least resistance, dodging under the table and crawling across on hands and knees.

Reaching Geilie's side, I grabbed her husband's face between my hands and tried to pry his jaws open. I thought, from the sounds he was making, that he had perhaps choked on a piece of meat, which might still be lodged in his windpipe.

His jaws were clamped and rigid, though, lips blue and flecked with a foamy spittle that didn't seem consistent with choking. Choking he surely was, though; the plump chest heaved vainly, fighting for breath.

'Quickly, turn him on his side,' I said. Several hands reached out at once to help, and the heavy body was deftly turned, broad black-serge back towards me. I drove the heel of my hand hard between the shoulder-blades, smacking him repeatedly with a dull thumping noise. The massive back quivered slightly with the blows, but there was no answering jerk as of an obstruction suddenly released.

I gripped a meaty shoulder and pulled him on to his back once more. Geilie bent close over the staring face, calling his name, massaging his mottled throat. The eyes were rolled back now, and the drumming heels began to slacken their beat. The hands, clawed in agony, suddenly flung wide, smacking an anxiously crouching onlooker in the face.

The sputtering noises abruptly ceased, and the stout body went limp, lying inert as a sack of barley on the stone flags. I felt frantically for a pulse in one slack wrist, noticing with half an eye that Geilie was doing the same, pulling up the slack chin and pressing her fingertips hard into the flesh under the angle of the jaw in search of the carotid artery.

Both searches were futile. Arthur Duncan's heart, already taxed by the necessity of pumping blood through that massive frame for so many years, had given up the struggle.

I tried all the resuscitative techniques at my disposal,

useless though I knew them now to be: arm-flapping, chest-massage, even mouth-to-mouth breathing, distasteful as that was, but with the expected result. Arthur Duncan was dead as a doornail.

I straightened wearily and stood back as Father Bain, with a nasty glare at me, dropped to his knees by the fiscal's side and began hastily to administer the final rites. My back and arms ached, and my face felt oddly numb. The hubbub around me seemed strangely remote, as though a curtain separated me from the crowded hall. I closed my eyes and rubbed a hand across my tingling lips, trying to erase the taste of death.

Despite the death of the fiscal and the subsequent formalities of obsequies and burial, the Duke's stag hunt was delayed by no more than a week.

The realization of Jamie's imminent departure was deeply depressing; I suddenly realized just how much I looked forward to seeing him at supper after the day's work, how my heart would leap when I saw him unexpectedly at odd moments during the day, and how much I depended on his company and his solid, reassuring presence amid the complexities of life in the castle. And, to be perfectly honest, how much I liked the smooth, warm strength of him in bed each night, and waking to his tousled, smiling kisses in the mornings. The prospect of his absence was bleak.

He held me closely, my head snuggled under his chin.

'I'll miss you, Jamie,' I said softly.

He hugged me tighter and gave a rueful chuckle.

'So will I, Sassenach. I hadna expected it, to tell the truth – but it will hurt me to leave ye.' He stroked my back gently, fingers tracing the bumps of the vertebrae.

'Jamie . . . you'll be careful?'

I could feel the deep rumble of amusement in his chest as he answered.

'Of the Duke or the horse?' He was, much to my apprehension, intending to ride Donas at the stag hunting. I had visions of the huge sorrel beast plunging over a cliff out of sheer wrong-headedness, or trampling Jamie under those lethal hooves.

'Both,' I said dryly. 'If the horse throws you and you break a leg, you'll be at the Duke's mercy.'

'True. Dougal will be there, though.'

I snorted. 'He'll break the other leg.'

He laughed and bent his head to kiss me.

'I'll be careful, *mo duinne*. Will ye give me the same promise?'

'Yes,' I said, meaning it. 'Do you mean whoever left the ill wish?'

The momentary amusement was gone now.

'Perhaps. I dinna think you're in any danger, or I wouldna leave ye. But still . . . oh, and stay away from Geillis Duncan.'

'What? Why?' I drew back a little to look up at him. It was a dark night and his face was invisible, but his tone was altogether serious.

'The woman's known as a witch, and the stories about her – well, they've got a deal worse since her husband died. I dinna want ye anywhere near her, Sassenach.'

'Do you honestly think she's a witch?' I demanded. His strong hands cupped my bottom and scooped me in close to him. I put my arms around him, enjoying the feel of his smooth, solid torso.

'No,' he said finally. 'But it isna what *I* think that could be a danger to ye. Will ye promise?'

'All right.' In truth, I had little reluctance to give the promise; since the incidents of the changeling and the summoning, I had not felt much desire to visit Geilie. I put my mouth on Jamie's nipple, flicking it lightly with my tongue. He made a small sound deep in his throat and pulled me nearer.

'Open your legs,' he whispered. 'I mean to be sure you'll remember me while I'm gone.'

Some time later I woke feeling cold. Groping sleepily for the quilt, I couldn't find it. Suddenly it came up over me of its own accord. Surprised, I raised up on one elbow to look.

521

'I'm sorry,' Jamie said. 'I didna mean to wake ye, lass.'

'What are you doing? Why are you awake?' I squinted over my shoulder at him. It was still dark, but my eyes were so accustomed that I could see the faintly sheepish expression on his face. He was wide awake, sitting on a stool by the side of the bed, his plaid flung around him for warmth.

'It's only . . . well, I dreamed you were lost, and I couldna find ye. It woke me, and . . . I wanted to look at ye, is all. To fix ye in my mind, to remember while I'm gone. I turned back the quilt; I'm sorry you were chilled.'

'It's all right.' The night was cold and very quiet, as though we were the only two souls in the world. 'Come into bed. You must be chilled, too.'

He slid in next to me and curled himself against my back. His hands stroked me from neck to shoulder, waist to hip, tracing the lines of my back, the curves of my body.

'*Mo duinne,*' he said softly. 'But now I should say *mo airgeadach.* My silver one. Your hair is silver-gilt and your skin is white velvet. *Calman geal.* White dove.'

I pressed my hips back against him, inviting, and settled against him with a sigh as his solid hardness filled me. He held me against his chest and moved with me, slowly, deeply. I gasped a little and he slackened his hold.

'I'm sorry,' he murmured. 'I didna mean to hurt ye. But I do want to be in you, to stay in you, so deep. I want to leave the feel of me deep inside ye with my seed. I want to hold ye so and stay wi' you till dawn, and leave you sleeping and go, with the shape of you warm in my hands.'

I pressed firmly back against him.

'You won't hurt me.'

After Jamie's departure I moped about the castle. I saw patients in the surgery, I occupied myself as much as I could in the garden, and I tried to distract myself by browsing in Callum's library, but still time hung heavy on my hands.

I had been alone nearly two weeks when I met the girl Laoghaire in the corridor outside the kitchens. I had watched her covertly now and then, since the day when I had seen her on the landing outside Callum's study. She seemed blooming enough, but there was an air of tenseness about her that was easily discernible. She seemed distracted and moody – and little wonder, poor girl, I thought kindly.

Today, though, she looked somewhat excited.

'Mistress Fraser!' she said. 'I've a message for you.' The widow Duncan, she said, had sent word that she was ill, and requested me to come and tend her.

I hesitated, remembering Jamie's injunctions, but the twin forces of compassion and boredom were sufficient to set me on the road to the village within the hour, my medicine box strapped behind me on the saddle.

The Duncans' house when I arrived had an air of neglected abandon, a sense of disorder that extended through the house itself. There was no answer to my knock, and when I pushed the door open I found the entry hall and parlour scattered with books and dirty glasses, mats askew and dust thick on the furniture. My calls produced no maidservant, and the kitchen proved to be as empty and disordered as the rest of the house.

Increasingly anxious, I went upstairs. The bedroom in front also was vacant, but I heard a faint shuffling noise from the stillroom across the landing.

Pushing open the door, I saw Geilie sitting in a comfortable chair, feet propped on the counter. She had been drinking; there was a glass and decanter on the counter, and the room smelled strongly of brandy.

She was startled to see me, but struggled to her feet, smiling. Her eyes were slightly out of focus, I thought, but she certainly seemed well enough.

'What's the matter?' I asked. 'Aren't you ill?'

She goggled at me in amazement. 'Ill? Me? No. The servants have all left, and there's no food in the house, but there's plenty of brandy. Will ye have a drop?' She turned back towards the decanter. I grabbed her sleeve.

'You didn't send for me?'

'No.' She stared at me, wide-eyed.

'Then why – ' My question was interrupted by a noise from outside. A far-off, rumbling, muttering sort of noise.

I had heard it before, from this room, and my palms had grown sweaty then at the thought of confronting the mob that made it.

I wiped my hands on the skirts of my dress. The rumbling was nearer, and there was neither need nor time for questions.

25

Thou Shalt not Suffer a Witch to Live

The drab-clad shoulders ahead of me parted on darkness. My elbow struck wood with a bone-numbing thump as I was shoved roughly over a threshold of some sort, and I fell headlong into a black stench, alive and wriggling with unseen forms. I shrieked and thrashed, trying to free myself from entanglement with innumerable scrabbling tiny feet and an attack by something larger, which squealed and struck me a hard blow on the thigh.

I succeeded in rolling away, though only a foot or two before I hit an earthen wall that sent a shower of dirt cascading down on my head. I huddled as close to it as I could get, trying to suppress my own gasping breath so that I could hear whatever was trapped in this reeking pit with me. Whatever it was, it was large and breathing hoarsely, but not growling. A pig, perhaps?

'Who's there?' came a voice from the Stygian black, sounding scared but defiantly loud. 'Claire, is it you?'

'Geilie!' I gasped and groped towards her, meeting her hands likewise searching. We clasped each other tightly, rocking slightly back and forth in the gloom.

'Is there anything else in here besides us?' I asked, glancing cautiously around. Even with my eyes now accustomed to the dark, there was precious little to be seen. There were faint streaks of light coming from somewhere above, but the tenebrous shadows were shoulder-high here below; I could barely make out Geilie's face, level with my own and only a few inches away.

She laughed, a little shakily. 'Several mice, I think, and other vermin. And a smell that would knock a ferret over.'

'I noticed the smell. Where in God's name are we?'

'The thieves' hole. Stand back!'

There was a grating sound from overhead and a sudden shaft of light. I pressed myself against the wall, barely in time to avoid a shower of mud and filth that cascaded through a small opening in the roof of our prison. A single soft plop followed the deluge. Geilie bent and picked up something from the floor. The opening above remained, and I could see that what she held was a small loaf, stale and smeared with assorted muck. She wiped it gingerly with a fold of her skirt.

'Dinner,' she said. 'Hungry, are you?'

The hole above remained open, and empty, save for the occasional missile flung by a passerby. The drizzle came in, and a searching wind. It was cold, damp, and thoroughly miserable. Suitable, I supposed, for the malefactors it was meant to house. Thieves, vagrants, blasphemers, adulterers . . . and suspected witches.

Geilie and I huddled together for warmth against one wall, not speaking much. There was little to say, and precious little either of us could do for ourselves, beyond possess our souls in patience.

The hole above grew gradually darker as the night came on, until it faded into the black all around.

'How long do you think they mean to keep us here?'

Geilie shifted, stretching her legs so that the small oblong of morning light from above shone on the striped linen of her skirt. Originally a fresh pink and white, it was now considerably the worse for wear.

'Not too long,' she said. 'They'll be waiting for the ecclesiastical examiners. Arthur had letters last month, arranging for it. The second week of October, it was. They should be here any time.'

She rubbed her hands together to warm them, then put them on her knees in the little square of sunlight.

'Tell me about the examiners,' I said. 'What will happen, exactly?'

'I canna say, exactly. I've ne'er seen a witch trial, though I've heard of them, of course.' She paused a moment, considering. 'They'll not be expecting a witch trial, since they were coming to try some land disputes. So they'll not have a witch-pricker, at least.'

'A what?'

'Witches canna feel pain,' Geilie explained. 'Nor do they bleed when they're pricked.' The witch-pricker, equipped with a variety of pins, lancets and other pointed implements, was charged with testing for this condition. I vaguely recalled something of this from Frank's books, but had thought it a practice common to the seventeenth century, not this one. On the other hand, I thought wryly, Cranesmuir was not precisely a hotbed of civilization.

'In that case, it's too bad there won't be one,' I said, though recoiling slightly at the thought of being stabbed repeatedly. 'We could pass that test with no difficulty. Or I could,' I added caustically. 'I imagine they'd get ice water, not blood, when they tried it on you.'

'I'd not be too sure,' she said reflectively, overlooking the insult. 'I've heard of witch-prickers with special pins – made to collapse when they're pressed against the skin, so it looks as though they go in, though they don't.'

'But why? Why try to prove someone a witch on purpose?'

The sun was on the decline now, but the afternoon light was enough to suffuse our hutch with a dim glow. The elegant oval of Geilie's face showed only pity for my innocence.

'Ye still dinna understand, do ye?' she said. 'They mean to kill us. And it doesna matter much what the charge is, or what the evidence shows. We'll burn, all the same.'

The night before I had been too shocked from the mob's attack and the misery of our surroundings to do more than huddle with Geilie and wait for the dawn. Now what remained of my spirit was beginning to awake.

'Why, Geilie?' I asked, feeling rather breathless. 'Do you know?' The atmosphere in the hole was thick with the stench of rot, filth and damp soil, and I felt as though the impenetrable earthen walls were about to cave in upon me like the sides of an ill-dug grave.

I felt rather than saw her shrug; the shaft of light from above had moved with the sun, and now struck the walls of our prison, leaving us in cold dark below.

'If it's much comfort to ye,' she said dryly, 'I misdoubt ye were meant to be taken. It's a matter between me and Callum – you had the ill luck to be with me when the townsfolk came. Had ye been wi' Callum you'd likely have been safe enough, Sassenach or no.'

The term 'Sassenach', spoken in its usual derogatory sense, suddenly struck me with a sense of desperate longing for the man who called me so in affection. I wrapped my arms around my body, hugging myself to contain the lonely panic that threatened to envelop me.

'Why did you come to my house?' Geilie asked curiously.

'I thought you had sent for me. One of the girls at the castle brought me a message – from you, she said.'

'Ah,' she said thoughtfully. 'Laoghaire, was it?'

I sat down and rested my back against the earth wall, despite my revulsion for the muddy, stinking surface. Feeling my movement, Geilie shifted closer. Friends or enemies, we were each other's only source of warmth in the hole; we huddled together perforce.

'How did you know it was Laoghaire?' I asked, shivering.

''Twas her that left the ill wish in your bed,' Geilie replied. 'I told ye at the first there were those minded your taking the red-haired laddie. I suppose she thought if ye were gone, she'd have a chance at him again.'

I was struck dumb at this, and it took a moment to find my voice.

'But she couldn't!'

Geilie's laugh was hoarsened by cold and thirst, but still held that edge of silver.

'Anyone seein' the way the lad looks at ye would know that. But I dinna suppose she's seen enough o' the world to ken such things. Let her lie wi' a man once or twice, and she'll know, but not now.'

'That's not what I meant!' I burst out. 'It isn't Jamie she wants; the girl's with child by Dougal MacKenzie.'

'What?!' She was genuinely shocked for a moment, and her fingers bit into the flesh of my arm. 'How d'ye come to think that?'

I told her of seeing Laoghaire on the stair outside Callum's study, and the conclusions I had come to.

Geilie snorted.

'Pah! She heard Callum and Dougal talking about me; that's what made her blench – she'd think Callum had heard she'd been to me for the ill wish. He'd have her whipped to bleeding for that; he doesna allow any truck wi' such arts.'

'*You* gave her the ill wish?' I was staggered.

Geilie drew herself sharply away at this.

'I didn't *give* it to her, no. I sold it to her.'

I stared, trying to meet her eyes through the gathering darkness.

'There's a difference?'

'Of course there is.' She spoke impatiently. 'It was a matter of business, that was all. And I don't give away my customers' secrets. Besides, she didna tell me who it was meant for. And you'll remember that I did try to warn ye.'

'Thanks,' I said with some sarcasm. 'But . . .' My brain was churning, trying to rearrange my ideas in the light of this new information. 'But if she put the ill wish in my bed, then it was Jamie she wanted. That *would* explain her sending me to your house. But what about Dougal?'

Geilie hesitated for a moment, then seemed to come to some decision.

'The girl's no more wi' child by Dougal MacKenzie than you are.'

'How can you be so sure?'

She groped for my hand in the darkness. Finding it, she drew it close and placed it squarely on the swelling bulge beneath her gown.

'Because I am,' she said simply.

'Not Laoghaire then,' I said. 'You.'

'Me.' She spoke quite simply, without any of her usual affectation. 'What was it Callum said – "I'll see that she's done rightly by"? Well, I suppose this is his idea of a suitable disposal of the problem.'

I was silent for a long time, mulling things over.

'Geilie,' I said at last, 'that stomach trouble of your husband's . . .'

She sighed. 'White arsenic,' she said. 'I thought it would finish him before the child began to show too much, but he hung on longer than I thought possible.'

I remembered the look of mingled horror and realization on Arthur Duncan's face as he burst out of his wife's closet on the last day of his life.

'I see,' I said. 'He didn't know you were with child until he saw you half dressed, the day of the Duke's banquet. And when he found out . . . I suppose he had good reason to know it wasn't his?'

There was a faint laugh from the far corner.

'The bromide I put in his tea came dear, but it was worth every farthing.'

I shuddered slightly, hunched against the wall.

'But that's why you had to risk killing him in public, at the banquet. He would have denounced you as an adulteress – and a poisoner. Or do you think he realized about the arsenic?'

'Oh, Arthur knew,' she said. 'He wouldna admit it, to be sure – not even to himself. But he knew. We'd sit across the board from each other at supper, and I'd ask, "Will ye have a bit more o' the brose, my dear?" or "A sup of ale, my own?" And him watching me, with those eyes like poached eggs, and he'd say no, he didna feel himself with an appetite just then. And he'd push his plate back, and later I'd hear him in the kitchen, secret-like, gobbling his food standing by the hutch, thinking himself safe, because he ate no food that came from my hand.'

Her voice was light and amused as though she had been recounting some bit of juicy gossip. I shuddered again, drawing away from the thing that shared the darkness with me.

'He didna guess it was in the tonic he took. He'd take no medicine I made; ordered a patent tonic from London – cost the earth too.' Her voice was resentful at the extravagance. 'The stuff had arsenic in it to start; he didna notice any difference in the taste when I added a bit more.'

I had always heard that vanity was the besetting weakness of murderers; it seemed this was true, for she went on, ignoring our situation in the pride of recounting her accomplishments.

'It was a bit risky, to kill him before the whole company like that, but I had to manage something quickly.' Not arsenic, either, to kill like that. I remembered the fiscal's hard blue lips and the numbness of my own where they had touched him. A quick and deadly poison.

And I had thought that Dougal was confessing to an affair with Laoghaire! But in that case, while Callum might be disapproving, there would have been nothing to prevent Dougal marrying the girl. He was a widower, and free.

But an adulterous affair, with the wife of the fiscal? That was a different kettle of fish for all concerned. I seemed to recall that the penalties for adultery were severe. Callum could hardly smooth over an affair of that magnitude, but I couldn't see him condemning his brother to public whipping or banishment. And Geilie might well consider murder a reasonable alternative to being burnt on the face with a hot iron and shut up for several years in a prison, pounding hemp for twelve hours a day.

So she had taken her preventive measures, and Callum had taken his. And here was I, caught up in the middle.

'The child, though?' I asked. 'Surely . . .'

There was a grim chuckle in the blackness. 'Accidents happen, my friend. To the best of us. And once it happened . . .' I felt rather than saw her shrug. 'I meant to get rid of it, but then I thought it might be a way to make him marry me, once Arthur was dead.'

A horrible suspicion struck me.

'But Dougal's wife was still alive, then. Geillis, did you – ?'

Her dress rustled as she shook her head, and I caught a faint gleam from her hair.

'I meant to,' she said. 'But God saved me the trouble. I rather thought that was a sign, you know. And it might all have worked nicely, too, if not for Callum MacKenzie.'

I hugged my elbows against the cold. I was talking now only for distraction.

'Was it Dougal you wanted, or only his position and money?'

'Oh, I had plenty of money,' she said with a note of satisfaction. 'I knew where Arthur kept the key to all his papers and notes, ye ken. And the man wrote a fair hand, I'll say that for him – 'twas simple enough to forge his signature. I'd managed to divert near on ten thousand pounds over the last two years.'

'But what for?' I asked, completely startled.

'For Scotland.'

'What?' For a moment I thought I had misheard. Then I decided that one of us was possibly a trifle unbalanced. And going on the evidence to hand, it wasn't me.

'What do you mean, Scotland?' I asked cautiously, drawing away a bit. I wasn't sure just how unstable she was; perhaps pregnancy had unhinged her mind.

'Ye needna fear; I'm not mad.' The cynical amusement in her voice made me flush, grateful for the darkness.

'Oh, no?' I said, stung. 'By your own admission you've committed fraud, theft and murder. It might be charitable to consider that you're mad, because if you're not – '

'Neither mad nor depraved,' she said decisively. 'I'm a patriot.'

The light dawned. I let out the breath I had been holding in expectation of a deranged attack.

'A Jacobite,' I said. 'Holy Christ, you're a bloody Jacobite!'

She was. And that explained quite a bit. Why Dougal, generally the mirror of his brother's opinions, should have shown such initiative in raising money for the House of Stuart. And why Geillis Duncan, so well equipped to lead any man she wanted to the altar, had chosen two such dissimilar specimens as Arthur Duncan and Dougal MacKenzie. The one for his money and position, the other for his power to influence public opinion.

'Callum would have been better,' she continued. 'A pity. His misfortune is my own, as well. It's him would have been the one I should have had; the only man I've seen could be my proper match. Together, we could . . . well, no help for it. The one man I'd want, and the one man in the world I couldn't touch with the weapon I had.'

'So you took Dougal instead.'

'Oh, aye,' she said, deep in her own thoughts. 'A strong man, and with some power. A bit of property. The ear of the people. But really, he's no more than the legs, and the cock' – she laughed briefly – 'of Callum MacKenzie. It's Callum has the strength. Almost as much as I have.'

Her boastful tone annoyed me.

'Callum has a few small things that you haven't, so far as I can see. Such as a sense of compassion.'

'Ah, yes. "Bowels of mercy and compassion", is it?' She spoke ironically. 'Much good it may do him. Death sits on his shoulder; ye can see it with half an eye. The man may live two years past Hogmanay; not much longer than that.'

'And how much longer will *you* live?' I asked.

The irony turned inwards, but the silver voice stayed steady.

'A bit less than that, I expect. No great matter. I've managed a good deal in the time I had; ten thousand pounds diverted to France, and the district roused for Prince Charles. Come the Rising, I shall know I helped. If I live so long.'

She stood nearly under the hole in the roof. My eyes were sufficiently accustomed to the darkness that she showed as a pale shape in the murk, a premature and unlaid ghost. She turned abruptly towards me.

'Whatever happens with the examiners, I have no regrets, Claire.'

'I regret only that I have but one life to give for my country?' I asked ironically.

'That's nicely put,' she said.

'Isn't it, just?'

We fell silent as it grew darker. The black of the hole seemed a tangible force, pressing cold and heavy on my chest, clogging my lungs with the scent of death. At last I huddled into as close a ball as I could, put my head on my knees, and gave up the fight, lapsing into an uneasy doze on the edge between cold and panic.

'Do ye love the man, then?' Geilie asked suddenly.

I raised my head from my knees, startled.

'Who, Jamie?'

'Who else?' she said dryly. 'It's his name ye call out in your sleep.'

'I didn't know I did that.'

'Well, do ye?' The cold encouraged a sort of deadly drowsiness, but Geilie's prodding voice dragged me a bit further out of my stupor.

I hugged my knees, rocking slightly back and forth. The light from the hole above had faded away to the soft dark of early night. The examiners would arrive within the next day or so. It was getting a bit late for prevarications, either to myself or anyone else. While I still found it difficult to admit that I might be in serious danger of death, I was beginning to understand the instinct that made condemned prisoners seek shriving on the eve of execution.

'Really love him, I mean,' Geilie persisted. 'Not just want to bed him; I know you want that, and he does too. They all do. But do you love him?'

Did I love him? Beyond the urges of the flesh? The hole had the dark anonymity of the confessional, and a soul on the verge of death had no time for lies.

'Yes,' I said, and laid my head back on my knees.

It was silent in the hole for some time, and I was hovering once more on the verge of sleep when I heard her speak once more, as though to herself.

'So it's possible,' she said thoughtfully.

The examiners arrived a day later. From the dankness of the thieves' hole we could hear the stir of their arrival; the shouts of the villagers and the clopping of horses on the

534

stone of the High Street. The bustle grew fainter as the procession passed down the street.

'They've come,' said Geilie, listening to the excitement above.

We clasped hands reflexively, enmities buried in fear.

'Well,' I said with attempted bravado, 'I suppose being burned is better than freezing to death.'

In the event, we continued to freeze. It was not until noon of the next day that the door of our prison slid abruptly back, and we were pulled out of the pit to be taken to trial.

No doubt to accommodate the crowd of spectators, the session was held in the square, before the Duncans' house. I saw Geilie glance up briefly at the diamond-paned windows of her parlour, then turn away, expressionless.

There were two ecclesiastical examiners seated on padded stools behind a table that had been erected in the square. One judge was abnormally tall and thin, the other short and stout. They reminded me irresistibly of an American comic paper I had once seen; not knowing their names, I mentally christened the tall one Mutt and the other Jeff.

Most of the village was there. Looking about, I could see a good many of my former patients. But the inhabitants of the castle were notably absent.

It was John MacRae, lockman of the village of Cranesmuir, who read out the dittay, or indictment, against the persons of one Geillis Duncan and one Claire Fraser, both accused before the Church's court of the crime of witchcraft.

'Stating in evidence whereof the accused did cause the death of Arthur Duncan, by means of witchcraft,' MacRae read in a firm, steady voice. 'And whereas they did procure the death of the unborn child of Janet Robinson, did cause the boat of Thomas MacKenzie to sink, did bring upon the village of Cranesmuir a wasting sickness of the bowels . . .'

It went on for some time. Callum had been thorough in his preparations.

After the reading of the dittay, the witnesses were called. Most of them were villagers I didn't recognize; none of my own patients were among them, a fact for which I was grateful.

While many of the witnesses' testimony was simply absurd, and others had plainly been paid for their services, others had a clear ring of truth to their words. Janet Robinson, for example, who was haled before the court by her father, pale and trembling, with a purple bruise on her cheek, to confess that she had conceived a child by a married man, and sought to rid herself of it, through the offices of Geillis Duncan.

'She gave me a draught to drink, and a charm to say three times, at the rising o' the moon,' the girl mumbled, glancing fearfully from Geillis to her father, unsure which one posed the greater threat. 'She said, 'twould bring my courses on.'

'And did it?' Jeff asked with interest.

'Not at the first, Your Honour,' the girl answered, bobbing her head nervously. 'But I took the draught again, at the waning o' the moon, and then it started.'

'Started?! The lassie near bled to death!' An elderly lady, plainly the girl's mother, broke in. ' 'Twas only because she felt herself to be dyin' as she told me the truth o' the matter.' More than willing to add to the gory details, Mrs Robinson was shut up with some difficulty, in order to make way for the succeeding witnesses.

There seemed to be no one with anything in particular to say about me, aside from the vague accusation that since I had been present at Arthur Duncan's death, and had laid hands on him before he died, clearly I must have had something to do with it. I began to think that Geilie was right; I had not been Callum's target. That being so, I thought it possible that I would escape. Or at least I thought so until the hill woman appeared.

When she came forward, a thin, bowed woman with a yellow shawl, I sensed that we were in serious trouble. She was not one of the villagers, no one I had ever seen before. Her feet were bare, stained with the dust of the road she had walked to come here.

'Have ye a charge to make against either o' the women here?' asked the tall, thin judge.

The woman was afraid; she wouldn't raise her eyes to look at the judges. She bobbed her head briefly, though, and the crowd quieted its murmur to hear her.

Her voice was low, and Mutt had to ask her to repeat herself.

She and her husband had an ailing child, born healthy but then turned puny and unthrifty. Finally deciding that the child was a fairy changeling, they had placed it in the Fairy's Seat on the hill of Croich Gorm. Keeping watch so as to recover their own child when the fairies should return it, they had seen the two ladies standing here go to the Fairy's Seat, pick up the child and speak strange spells over it.

The woman twisted her thin hands together, working them under her apron.

'We watched through the nicht, sirs. And when the dark came, soon after there cam' a great demon, a huge black shape comin' through the shadows wi' no sound, to lean ower the spot where we'd laid the babe.'

There was an awed murmur from the crowd, and I felt the hair on the back of my neck stir slightly, even knowing as I did that the 'great demon' had been Jamie, gone to see whether the child still lived. I braced myself, knowing what was coming next.

'And when the sun rose, my man and I went to see. And there we found the changeling babe, dead on the hill, and no sign of our own wee bairn.' At this she broke, and threw her apron over her face to hide her weeping.

As though the mother of the changeling had been a signal of some sort, the crowd parted and the figure of Peter the drover came out. I groaned inwardly when I saw him. I had felt the emotions of the crowd turn against me as the woman spoke; all I needed now was for this man to tell the court about the waterhorse.

Enjoying his moment of celebrity, the drover drew himself up and pointed dramatically at me.

' 'Tis right ye are to call her witch, My Lords! Wi' my

537

own eyes I saw this woman call up a waterhorse from the waters of the Evil Loch, to do her bidding! A great fearsome creature, sirs, tall as a pine tree, wi' a neck like a great blue snake, an' eyes big as apples, wi' a look in them as would steal the soul from a man.'

The judges appeared impressed with his testimony, and whispered amongst themselves for several minutes, while Peter glared defiantly at me with a 'that'll show *you*!' sort of look.

At length the fat judge broke from the conference and beckoned imperiously to John MacRae, who stood to one side, alert for trouble.

'Lockman!' he said. He turned and pointed at the drover. 'Tak' that man away and shut him up in the pillory for public drunkenness. This is a solemn coort o' law; we'll no ha' the time of the court wasted by frivolous accusations from a sot who sees waterhorses when he's taken too much whisky!'

Peter the drover was so astonished that he did not even resist as the lockman strode firmly forward and took him by the arm. Mouth hanging open, he glared back wildly in my direction as he was led away. I couldn't resist fluttering my fingers in a tiny salute after him.

After this slight break in the tension of the proceedings, though, things got rapidly worse. There was a procession of girls and women to swear that they had bought charms and philtres from Geillis Duncan, for purposes such as causing illness, ridding oneself of an unwanted babe or casting spells of love upon some man. All, without exception, swore that the charms had worked – an enviable record for a general practitioner, I thought cynically. While no one claimed such results for me, there were several to say – truthfully – that they had seen me in Mrs Duncan's herb room, mixing medicines and grinding herbs.

Still, that might not have been fatal; there were an equal number of people to claim that I had healed them, using nothing more than ordinary medicines, with nothing in the way of spells, charms or general hocus-pocus. Given the force of public opinion, it took some nerve for these people to step forward to testify on my behalf, and I was grateful.

My feet were aching from standing so long; while the judges sat in relative comfort, no stools were provided for the prisoners. But when the next witness appeared I entirely forgot my feet.

With an instinct for drama that rivalled Callum's, Father Bain flung wide the door of the church and emerged into the square, limping heavily on a wooden crutch. He advanced slowly to the centre of the square, inclined his head to the judges, then turned and surveyed the crowd, until his steely glare had reduced the noise to a low, uneasy muttering. When he spoke, his voice lashed out like the crack of a whip.

'It's a judgement on ye, ye folk o' Cranesmuir! "Before him went the pestilence, and burning coals went forth with his feet." Aye, ye've allowed yerselves to be seduced from the paths o' righteousness! Ye've sown the wind, and the whirlwind's amongst ye now!'

I stared, somewhat taken aback by this unsuspected gift for rhetoric. Or perhaps he was capable of such flights of oratory only under the stimulus of crisis. The florid voice thundered on.

'The pestilence will come upon ye, and ye shall die o'your sins, unless ye be cleansed! Ye've welcomed the whore of Babylon into yer midst' – that was me, I assumed, from the glare he shot at me – 'ye've sold your soul to your enemies, ye've taken the English viper to your bosom, and now the vengeance o' the Lord God Almighty is on ye. "Deliver thee from the strange woman, even from the stranger that flattereth with her words. For her house inclineth unto death, and her paths unto the dead." Repent, people, before it's too late! Fall to your knees, I say, and pray for forgiveness! Cast out the English whore, and renounce your bargain wi' the spawn o' Satan!' He snatched the rosary from his belt and brandished the large wooden crucifix in my direction.

Entertaining as this all was, I could see Mutt becoming rather restive. Professional jealousy, perhaps.

'Er, Father,' the judge said, with a slight bow in Father Bain's direction, 'have ye evidence to bring as to the charge regarding these women?'

'That I have.' The first explosion of oratory spent, the little priest was calm now. He levelled a menacing forefinger in my direction and I had to brace myself to keep from taking a step backwards.

'At noonday on a Tuesday, these weeks past, I met this woman in the gardens of Castle Leoch. Using unnatural powers, she called down a pack of hounds upon me, such that I fell before them, and was in mortal peril. Bein' wounded grievously in the leg, I made to leave her presence. The woman tried to lure me wi' her sinfulness, to go awa' in private with her, and when I resisted her wiles, she cast a curse upon me.'

'What bloody nonsense!' I said indignantly. 'That's the most ridiculous exaggeration I've ever heard!'

Father Bain's eye, dark and glittering as with fever, swivelled from the examiners and fixed on me.

'Do ye deny, woman, that ye said these words to me? "Come with me now, priest, or your wound shall fester and go putrid"?'

'Well, tone it down a bit, but something to that effect, perhaps,' I admitted.

Jaw clenched in triumph, the priest whipped aside the skirts of his soutane. A bandage stained with dried blood and wet with yellow pus encircled his thigh. The pale flesh of the leg puffed above and below the bandage, with ominous red streaks extending up from the hidden wound.

'Jesus Christ, man!' I said, shocked at the sight. 'You've got blood poisoning. You need it tended, and right now, or you'll die!'

There was a deep murmur of shock from the crowd. Even Mutt and Jeff seemed a bit stunned.

Father Bain shook his head slowly.

'You hear?' he demanded. 'The temerity of the woman kens nae bounds. She curses me wi' death, a man of God, before the judgement seat of the Church itself!'

The excited murmuring of the crowd grew louder. Father

Bain spoke again, raising his voice slightly in order to be heard over the noise.

'I leave ye, gentlemen, wi' the judgement o' your own senses, and the injunction o' the Lord – "Ye shallna suffer a witch to live!" '

Father Bain's dramatic evidence put a stop to the testimony. Presumably no one was prepared to top *that* performance. The judges called a short recess and were brought refreshments from the inn. No such amenities were forthcoming for the accused.

I braced myself and pulled experimentally against my bonds. The leather of the straps creaked a bit, but didn't give an inch. This, I thought cynically, trying to still my panic, was surely where the dashing young hero was meant to ride through the crowd, beating back the cringing townspeople and scooping the fainting heroine up on to his saddle.

But my own dashing young hero was out in the forest somewhere, swilling ale with an ageing poofter of noble blood and slaughtering innocent deer. It was rather unlikely, I thought, gritting my teeth, that Jamie would return in time even to gather up my ashes for ceremonial disposal before I was scattered to the four winds.

Preoccupied with my growing fear, I didn't at first hear the hoofbeats. It was only as the faint murmurs and head-turnings of the crowd attracted my attention that I noticed the rhythmic clopping, ringing from the stones of the High Street.

The murmurs of surprise grew louder, and the fringes of the crowd began to draw apart to admit the rider, still beyond the range of my sight. Despite my earlier despair, I began to feel a faint flicker of illogical hope. What if Jamie had come back early? Perhaps the Duke's advances had been too pressing, or the deer too few and far between. Whatever it might be, I strained on tiptoe to see the face of the approaching rider.

The ranks of the crowd parted reluctantly as the horse, a strong bay, poked its long nose between two sets of shoulders. Before the astonished eyes of everyone – including me – the sticklike figure of Ned Gowan spryly dismounted.

Jeff surveyed the spare, neat form before him with some astonishment.

'And you are, sir?' No doubt his tone of reluctant courtesy was a result of the visitor's silver shoe-buckles and velvet coat – employment with the laird of Leoch was not without its compensations.

'My name is Edward Gowan, Your Lordship,' he said precisely. 'Lawyer.'

Mutt hunched his shoulders and wriggled a bit; the stool he had been provided had no back, and his lengthy torso was no doubt feeling the strain. I stared hard at him, wishing him a herniated lumbar disc. If I were about to be burnt for having an evil eye, I thought, let it count for something.

'Lawyer?' he rumbled. 'What brings you here, then?'

Ned Gowan's grey wig inclined itself in the most precise of formal bows.

'I have come to offer my humble services in the support of Mistress Fraser, My Lords,' he said, 'a most gracious lady, whom I know of my own witness to be as kind and beneficial in the administration of the healing arts as she is knowledgeable in their application.'

Very nice, I thought approvingly. Get a blow in for our side first thing. Looking across the square, I could see Geilie's mouth quirk up in a half-admiring, half-derisive smile. While Ned Gowan wouldn't be everyone's choice as Prince Charming, I was not inclined to be fussy at a time like this. I would take my champions as they came.

With a bow to the judges and another, no less formal, to myself, Mr Gowan drew himself still straighter than his normal upright posture, braced both thumbs in the waist of his breeks, and prepared with all the romanticism of his aged, gallant heart to do battle, fighting with the law's chosen weapon of excruciating boredom.

Boring he most certainly was. With the deadly precision of an automated mincing machine, he arranged each charge of the dittay on the slab of his scrutiny and diced it ruthlessly into shreds with the blade of statute and the cleaver of precedent.

It was a noble performance. He talked. And he talked. And he talked some more, seeming occasionally to pause respectfully for instruction from the bench, but in fact only drawing breath for another onslaught of verbiage.

With my life hanging in the balance and my future entirely dependent on the eloquence of this skinny little man, I should have hung rapt on his every word. Instead, I found myself yawning appallingly, unable to cover my gaping mouth, and shifting from foot to aching foot, wishing fervently that they would burn me at once and end this torture.

The crowd appeared to feel much the same, and as the high excitement of the morning faded into ennui, Mr Gowan's small, tidy voice went on and on and on. People began to drift away, suddenly mindful of beasts that needed milking and floors that wanted sweeping, secure in the surety that nothing of any interest could possibly happen while that deadly voice droned on.

When Ned Gowan finally finished his initial defence, evening had set in; and the squatty judge I had named Jeff announced that the court would reconvene in the morning.

After a short, muttering conference amongst Ned Gowan, Jeff and John MacRae the lockman, I was led off towards the inn between two burly townsmen. Casting a glance over my shoulder, I saw Geilie being moved away in the opposite direction, back straight, refusing to be hurried or, for that matter, to acknowledge her surroundings in any way.

In the dark back room of the inn my bonds were at last removed, and a candle brought. Then Ned Gowan arrived, bearing a bottle of ale and a plate of meat and bread.

'I've but the few minutes with ye, my dear, and that hard-won, so listen closely.' The little man leaned nearer, conspiratorial in the flickering candlelight. His eyes were bright, and save a slight disarrangement of his wig, he gave no hint of exertion or fatigue.

'Mr Gowan, I am so glad to see you,' I said sincerely.

'Yes, yes, my dear,' he said, 'but there's no time for

that now.' He patted my hand in a kindly but perfunctory fashion.

'I've succeeded in getting them to consider your case as separate from that of Mrs Duncan, and that may be of help. It would appear that there was no original intent to arrest you, but that you were taken because of your association with the w – with Mrs Duncan.

'Still,' he continued briskly, 'there is some danger to ye, and I'll not hide it from you. The climate of opinion in the village is none too favourable to ye at present. What possessed ye,' he demanded, with uncharacteristic heatedness, 'to touch that child?'

I opened my mouth to reply, but he waved the question aside impatiently.

'Ah well, it's of no matter now. What we must do is to play upon the fact of your Englishness – and hence your ignorance, ye ken, not your strangeness – and draw matters out so long as we may. Time is on our side, ye see, for the worst of these trials take place in a climate of hysteria, when the soundness of evidence may be disregarded for the sake of satisfyin' blood-hunger.'

Blood-hunger. That captured completely the feeling of the emotion I had felt emanating from the faces of the mob. Here and there I saw some traces of doubt or sympathy, but it was a rare soul who would stand against a crowd, and Cranesmuir was rather lacking in characters of that stamp. Or no, I corrected myself. There was one – this dry little Edinburgh lawyer, tough as the old boot he so strongly resembled.

'The longer we go on,' Mr Gowan continued matter of factly, 'the less inclined anyone will be to take hasty action.

'So,' he said, hands on his knees, 'your part on the morrow is only to keep silent. I shall do all the talkin', and pray God it will be to some effect.'

'That seems sound enough,' I said, with a weary attempt at a smile. I glanced at the door to the front of the inn, where voices were being raised. Catching my look, Mr Gowan nodded.

'Aye, I'll have to leave ye momentarily. I've arranged that

you'll spend the night here.' He glanced around dubiously. A small shed tacked on to the inn, and used mostly for the storage of oddments and spare supplies, it was cold and dark, but an improvement of several-fold over the thieves' hole.

The door to the shed opened, silhouetting the form of the innkeeper, peering into the dark behind the pale waver of a candle flame. Mr Gowan rose to go, but I gripped him by the sleeve. There was one thing I needed to know.

'Mr Gowan – did Callum send you to help me?' He hesitated in his reply, but within the limits of his profession he was a man of irreproachable honesty.

'No,' he said bluntly. A look almost of embarrassment flitted over his withered features, and he added, 'I came for . . . for myself.' He clapped his hat upon his head and turned to the door, wishing me a brief 'Good e'en' before disappearing into the light and bustle of the inn.

There had been little preparation for my accommodation, but a small jug of wine and a loaf of bread – clean, this time – sat on one of the hogsheads, and there was an old blanket folded on the ground at its foot.

I wrapped myself in the blanket and sat down on one of the smaller casks to dine, musing as I munched the sparse fare.

So Callum had not sent the lawyer. Had he known, even, that Mr Gowan intended to come? Chances were that Callum had forbidden anyone to come down to the village, for fear of being caught up in the witch-hunt. The waves of fear and hysteria that swept over the village were palpable; I could feel them beating against the walls of my flimsy shelter.

A noisy outburst from the nearby taproom distracted me from my thoughts. Perhaps it was only deathwatch plus one. But on the edge of destruction, even an extra hour was cause for thanks. I rolled myself up in the blanket, pulled it over my head to shut out the noises from the inn, and tried very hard to feel nothing but gratitude.

After an exceedingly restless night I was roused soon after

dawn and marched back out to the square, though the judges didn't arrive for another hour.

Fine, fat and full of breakfast, they buckled straight down to work. Jeff turned to John MacRae, who had returned to his station behind the accused.

'We find ourselves unable to determine guilt solely on the basis of the evidence presented.' There was a burst of outrage from the regathered crowd, which had made its own determination, but this was quelled by Mutt, who turned a pair of eyes like gimlets on the young workmen in the front row, which quieted their yapping like dogs doused with cold water. Order restored, he turned his angular face back to the lockman.

'Conduct the prisoners to the loch side, if ye please.' There was a gratified sound of expectation at this that roused all my worst suspicions. John MacRae took me by one arm and Geilie by the other, to steer us along, but he had plenty of help. Vicious hands tore at my gown, pinching and pushing as I was yanked along. Some idiot had a drum and was beating out a ragged tattoo. The crowd was chanting in a rough rhythm to the tuck of the drum, something that I didn't catch among the random shouts and cries. I didn't think I wanted to know what they were saying.

The procession flowed down the meadow to the edge of the loch, where a small wooden quay projected into the water. We were pulled out to the end of this, where the two judges had taken up their posts, one at either side of the quay. Jeff turned to the crowd waiting on shore.

'Bring out the cords!' There was a general mutter and expectant looking around from one to another, until someone ran up hastily with a length of thin rope. MacRae took it and approached me rather hesitantly. He stole a glance at the examiners, though, which seemed to harden his resolve.

'Please be so kind as to remove your shoon, ma'am,' he ordered.

'What the he – What for?' I demanded, crossing my arms.

He blinked, plainly unprepared for resistance, but one of the judges forestalled his reply.

' 'Tis the proper procedure for trial by water. The suspected witch shall have the right thumb bound by a cord of hemp to the great toe of the left foot. Likewise, the left thumb shall be bound to the right great toe. And then . . .' He cast an eloquent glance at the waters of the loch. Two fishermen stood barefooted in the mud of the shore, trews rolled above their knees and tied with twine. Grinning insinuatingly at me, one of them picked up a small stone and heaved it out across the steely surface. It skipped once and sank.

'Upon entering the water,' the short judge chimed in, 'a guilty witch will float, as the purity of the water rejects her tainted person. An innocent woman will sink.'

'So I've the choice of being condemned as a witch or being found innocent but drowned, have I?' I snapped. 'No thank you!' I hugged my elbows harder, trying to still the shiver that seemed to have become a permanent part of my flesh.

The short judge puffed himself up like a threatened toad.

'You'll nae speak before this court without leave, woman! Do ye dare to refuse lawful examination?'

'Do I dare refuse to be drowned? Too right I do!' Too late I caught sight of Geilie, frantically shaking her head, so that the fair hair swirled around her face.

The judge turned to MacRae.

'Strip her and skelp her,' he said flatly.

Through a daze of disbelief I heard a collective inhalation, presumably of shocked dismay – in truth, of anticipatory enjoyment. And I realized just what hate really meant. Not theirs. Mine.

They didn't bother taking me back to the village square. So far as I was now concerned, I had little left to lose, and I didn't make it easy for them.

Rough hands jerked me forward, yanking at the edges of skirt and bodice.

'Let go of me, you bloody lout!' I yelled, and kicked one manhandler squarely where it would do most good. He crumpled with a groan, but his doubled form was quickly lost in a boiling eruption of shouting, spitting, glaring faces. More hands seized my arms and hustled me stumbling onwards, half lifting me over bodies fallen in the crush, pushing me bodily through gaps too small to walk through.

Someone hit me in the stomach, and I lost my breath. My bodice was virtually in shreds by this time, so it was with no great difficulty that the remainder was stripped off. I had never suffered from excessive modesty, but standing half naked before the jeers of that crowd of ill wishers, with the prints of sweaty hands on my bare breasts, filled me with a hatred and humiliation I could not even have imagined.

John MacRae bound my hands before me, looping a woven rope about my wrists, leaving a length of several feet. He had the grace to look ashamed as he did it, but would not raise his eyes to mine, and it was clear I could expect neither help nor lenience from that quarter; he was as much at the mercy of the crowd as I was.

Geilie was there, no doubt similarly treated; I caught a glimpse of her platinum hair, flying in a sudden breeze. My arms stretched high above my head as the rope was thrown over the branch of a large pine and hauled tight. I gritted my teeth and held on to my fury; it was the only thing I had to combat my fear. There was an air of breathless expectancy, punctuated by the excited murmurs and shouts from the crowd of watchers.

'Give it 'er, John!' one shouted. 'Get on wi' it!'

John MacRae, sensitive to the theatrical responsibilities of his profession, paused, scourge held level at waist height, and surveyed the crowd. He walked forward and gently adjusted my position, so that I faced the trunk of the tree, almost touching the rough bark. Then he drew back two paces, raised the whip and let it fall.

The shock of it was worse than the pain. In fact, it was only after several blows that I realized the lockman was doing his level best to spare me what he could. Still, one or two blows were hard enough to break the skin; I felt the sharp tingle in the wake of the impact.

I had my eyes shut tight, cheek pressed hard against the wood, trying for all I was worth to be somewhere else. Suddenly, though, I heard something that recalled me at once to the here and now.

'Claire!'

There was now a little slack in the rope that bound my wrists; enough to let me make a lunge that brought me clear around, facing the mob. My sudden escape disconcerted the lockman, who brought his lash down on empty air, stumbled forward off balance, and knocked his head against a limb. This had a very good effect on the mob, who roared insults and started jeering at him.

My hair was in my eyes, stuck to my face with sweat, tears and the filth of confinement. I shook my head to free it, and managed at least a sidelong glance that confirmed what my ears had heard.

Jamie was shoving his way through the hindering crowd, face like thunder, ruthlessly taking advantage of his size and muscle.

I felt very much like General McAuliffe at Bastogne during the Battle of the Bulge, sighting Patton's Third Army in the offing. In spite of the horrible danger to Geilie, to me and now to Jamie himself, I had never been so happy to see anyone.

'The witch's man!' 'Her husband, it is!' 'Stinkin' Fraser! Crowner!' and similar epithets began to be heard among the more general abuse aimed at me and Geilie. 'Take him too!' 'Burn 'em! Burn 'em all!' The crowd's hysteria, temporarily dispersed by the lockman's accident, was rising to fever pitch once more.

Hampered by the clinging forms of the lockman's assistants, who were trying to restrain him, Jamie had come to a dead halt. A man hanging from each arm, he struggled to force his hand towards his belt. Thinking him reaching for a knife, one man punched him hard in the belly.

Jamie doubled slightly, then came up, smashing an elbow to the nose of the man who'd hit him. One arm temporarily freed, he ignored the frantic pawings of the man on the other side. He dipped a hand into his sporran, raised his arm and threw. His shout reached me as the object left his hand.

'Claire! Stand *still!*'

Not much place for me to go, I thought dazedly. There

was a dark blur headed straight for my face, and I started to flinch backwards, but stopped in time. The blur struck my face with a clattering sting and the black beads fell on my shoulders as the jet rosary, flung bola-style, neatly ringed my neck. Or not quite neatly; the strand had caught on my right ear. I shook my head, eyes watering from the blow, and the circle settled into place, crucifix swinging jauntily between my naked breasts.

The faces in the front row were staring at it in a kind of horrified bemusement. Their sudden silence affected those further back, and the roaring seethe of noise subsided. Jamie's voice, customarily soft-spoken, even in anger, rang out in the silence. There was nothing soft about it now.

'Cut her down!'

The hangers-on had dropped away, and the waves of the crowd parted before him as he strode forward. The lockman watched him come, standing gape-jawed and frozen.

'I said, cut her down! Now!' The lockman, freed from his trance by the apocalyptic vision of red-haired death bearing down on him, stirred himself and fumbled hastily for his dirk. The rope, sawn through, let go with a shuddering snap and my arms dropped like bolsters, aching with released strain. I staggered and would have fallen, but a strong, familiar hand caught my elbow and pulled me upright. Then my face was against Jamie's chest, and nothing mattered to me any more.

I may have lost consciousness for a few moments, or only been so overcome with relief that it seemed that way. Jamie's arm was hard around my waist, holding me up, and his plaid had been thrown over me, hiding me at last from the stare of the villagers. There was a confusion of voices all around, but it was no longer the crazed and gleeful blood lust of the mob.

The voice of Mutt – or was it Jeff? – cut through the confusion.

'Who are you? How dare ye to interfere wi' the investigations of the court?'

I could feel, rather than see, the crowd pushing forward, Jamie was large, and he was armed, but he was only one man. I cowered against him under the folds of the plaid. His right arm tightened around me, but his left hand went to the sheath on his hip. The silver-blue blade hissed with menace as it came half out of its scabbard, and those in the forefront of the crowd came to a sudden stop.

The judges were made of somewhat tougher fabric. Peering out from my hiding place, I could see Jeff glaring at Jamie. Mutt appeared more bemused than annoyed at this sudden intrusion.

'Do ye dare to draw arms against the justice of God?' snapped the tubby little judge.

Jamie drew the sword completely, with a flash of steel, then thrust it point-first into the ground, leaving the hilt quivering with the force of the blow.

'I draw it in defence of this woman, and the truth,' he said. 'If any here be against those two, they'll answer to me, and then God, in that order.'

The judge blinked once or twice, as though unable to credit this behaviour, then surged to the attack once more.

'You have no place in the workings o' this court, sir! I'll demand that ye surrender the prisoner at once. Your own behaviour will be dealt with presently!'

Jamie looked the judges over coolly. I could feel his heart hammering beneath my cheek as I clung to him, but his hands were rock steady, one resting on the hilt of his sword, the other on the dirk at his belt.

'As to that, sir, I swore an oath before the altar of God to protect this woman. And if you're tellin' me that ye consider your own authority to be greater than that of the Almighty, then I must inform ye that I'm no of that opinion myself.'

The silence that followed this was broken by an embarrassed titter, echoed here and there by a nervous laugh. While the sympathies of the crowd had not shifted to our side, still the momentum carrying us to disaster had been broken.

Jamie turned me with a hand on my shoulders. I couldn't bear to face the crowd, but I knew I must. I kept my chin as high as I could, and my eyes focused beyond the faces, to a small boat in the centre of the loch. I stared at it till my eyes watered.

Jamie turned back the plaid, holding it around me but letting it drop far enough to show my neck and shoulders. He touched the black rosary and set it swinging gently to and fro.

'Jet will burn a witch's skin, no?' he demanded of the judges. 'Still more, I should think, would the cross of Our Lord. But look.' He dipped a finger under the beads and lifted up the crucifix. My skin beneath was pure white, unmarked save for the smudges of captivity, and there was a gasp and murmur from the crowd.

Raw courage, an ice-cold presence of mind and that instinct for showmanship. Callum MacKenzie had been right to be apprehensive of Jamie's ambitions. And given Callum's fear that I might reveal Hamish's parentage, or what he thought I knew of it, what he had done to me – his not lifting a finger to help me – was understandable too. Understandable, but not forgivable.

The mood of the crowd now swayed to and fro, uncertain. The bloodlust that had driven it earlier was dissipating, but it might still tilt like a cresting wave and crush us. Mutt and Jeff glanced at each other, undecided; taken aback by this last development, the judges had momentarily lost control of the situation.

Geillis Duncan stepped forward into the breach. I do not know whether there was hope for her at that point or not. In any case, she now tossed her fair hair defiantly over one shoulder, and threw her life away.

'This woman is no witch,' she said simply. 'But I am.'

Jamie's show, good as it was, was no match for this. The resulting uproar drowned completely the voices of the judges, questioning and exclaiming.

There was no clue to what she thought or felt, no more than there ever was; her high white brow was clear, the big green eyes gleaming in what might be amusement. She stood straight in her ragged garments, daubed with filth, and stared down her accusers. When the tumult had quieted a bit she began to speak, not deigning to raise her voice but forcing them to quiet themselves to hear her.

'I, Geillis Duncan, do confess that I am a witch, and the mistress of Satan.' This caused another outcry, and she waited again with perfect patience for them to quiet.

'In obedience to my Master, I do confess that I killed my husband, Arthur Duncan, by means of witchcraft.' At this she glanced aside, catching my eye, and the hint of a smile touched her lips. Her eyes rested on the woman in the yellow shawl, but did not soften. 'Of malice, I placed a spell upon the changeling child, that it might die, and the human child it replaced remain with the fairies.' She turned and gestured in my direction.

'I took advantage of the ignorance of Claire Fraser, using her for my purposes. But she had neither part nor knowledge in my doings, nor does she serve my Master.'

The crowd was muttering again, people jostling to get a better look, pushing nearer. She stretched out both hands towards them, palm outwards.

'Stay back!' The clear voice cracked like a whip, to much the same effect. She tilted back her head to the skies and froze, like one listening.

'Hear!' she said. 'Hear the wind of his coming! Beware, ye people of Cranesmuir! For my Master comes on the wings o' the wind!' She lowered her head and screamed, a high, eerie sound of triumph. The large green eyes were fixed and staring, trancelike.

The wind *was* rising; I could see the clouds of the storm rolling across the far side of the loch. People began to look uneasily around; a few souls dropped back from the edge of the crowd.

Geilie began to spin, twirling round and round, hair whipping in the wind, hand gracefully overhead like a maypole dancer's. I watched her in stunned disbelief.

As she turned, her hair hid her face. On the last turn, though, she snapped her head to throw the fair mane to one side and I saw her face clearly, looking at me. The mask of trance had vanished momentarily, and her mouth formed a single word. Then her turn took her around to

face the crowd once more, and she began her eerie screaming again.

The word had been 'Run!'

She stopped her spinning suddenly, and with a look of
mad exultation gripped the remnants of her bodice with
both hands and tore it down the front. Tore it far enough
to show the crowd the secret I had learned, huddled close
beside her in the cold filth of the thieves' hole. The secret
Arthur Duncan had learned, in the hour before his death.
The secret for which he had died. The shreds of her loose
gown dropped away, exposing the swelling bulge of a six-
month pregnancy.

I still stood like a rock, staring. Jamie had no such hesitations. Seizing me with one hand and his sword with the
other, he flung himself into the crowd, knocking people out
of the way with elbows, knees and sword hilt, bulling his
way towards the edge of the loch. He let out a piercing
whistle, through his teeth.

Intent on the spectacle under the pine, few people at first
realized what was happening. Then, as individuals began to
shout and grab at us, there was the sound of galloping
hooves on the hard-packed earth above the shore.

Donas still didn't care much for people, and was all too
willing to show it. He bit the first hand reaching for his
bridle, and a man dropped back, crying out and dripping
blood. The horse reared, squealing and pawing the air, and
the few bold souls still intent on stopping him suddenly lost
interest.

Jamie flung me over the saddle like a sack of meal and
swung up himself in one fluid motion. Clearing a path with
vicious swipes of his sword, he turned Donas through the
hindering mass of the crowd. As people fell back from the
onslaught of teeth, hooves and blade, we picked up speed,
leaving the loch, the village and Leoch behind. Breath
knocked out of me by the impact, I struggled to speak, to
scream to Jamie.

For I hadn't stood frozen at the revelation of Geilie's
pregnancy. It was something else I had seen that chilled me
to the marrow of my bones. As Geilie had spun, white arm

554

stretched aloft, I saw what she had seen when my own clothes were stripped away. A mark on her arm like the one I bore. Here, in this time, the mark of sorcery, the mark of a magus. The small, homely scar of a smallpox vaccination.

Rain pattered on the water, soothing my swollen face and the rope burns on my wrists. I dipped a handful of water from the stream and sipped it slowly, feeling the cold liquid trickle down my throat with gratitude.

Jamie disappeared for a few minutes. He came back with a handful of trailing green plants, chewing something. He spat a glob of macerated green into the palm of his hand, stuffed another wad of leafy stems into his mouth and turned me away from him. He rubbed the chewed leaves gently over my back, and the stinging eased considerably.

'What is that?' I said, making an effort to control myself. I was still shaky and snuffling, but the helpless tears were beginning to ebb.

'Chickweed,' he answered, voice slightly muffled by the leaves in his mouth. He spat them out and applied them to my back. 'You're no the only one knows a bit about grass-cures, Sassenach,' he said, a bit clearer.

'How – how does it taste?' I asked, gulping back the sobs.

'No bad,' he replied laconically. He finished his application and laid the plaid softly back across my shoulders.

'It won't – ' he began, then hesitated, 'I mean, the cuts are not deep. I – I think you'll no be . . . marked.' He spoke gruffly, but his touch was very gentle, and reduced me to tears once more.

'I'm sorry,' I mumbled, dabbing my nose on a corner of the plaid. 'I – I don't know what's wrong with me. I don't know why I can't stop crying.'

He shrugged. 'I dinna suppose anyone's tried to hurt ye on purpose before, Sassenach,' he said. 'It's likely the shock of that, so much as the pain.' He paused, picking up a plaid-end.

'I did just the same, lass,' he said matter of factly. 'Puked after, and cried while they cleansed the cuts. Then I shook.'

555

He wiped my face carefully with the plaid, then put a hand under my chin and tilted my face up to his.

'And when I stopped shaking, Sassenach,' he said quietly, 'I thanked God for the pain, because it meant I was still alive.' He let go, nodding at me. 'When ye get to that point, lassie, tell me; for I've a thing or two I want to be sayin' to ye then.'

He got up and went down to the edge of the burn, to wash out his bloodstained handkerchief in cold water.

'What brought you back?' I asked when he returned. I had managed to stop crying, but I still shook, and huddled deeper into the folds of the plaid.

'Auld Alick,' he said, smiling. 'I told him to watch over ye while I was gone. When the villagers took you and Mistress Duncan, he rode all night and the next day to find me. And then I rode like the Devil himself comin' back. Lord, that's a good horse.' He looked approvingly up the slope to Donas, tethered to a tree at the top of the bank, his wet coat gleaming like copper.

'I'll have to move him,' he said thoughtfully. 'I doubt anyone will follow, but it isna that far from Cranesmuir. Can ye walk now?'

I followed him up the steep slope with some difficulty, small rocks rolling under my feet and bracken and bramble catching my shift. Near the top of the slope was a grove of young alders grown so close together that the lower branches interlaced, forming a green roof over the bracken. Jamie shoved the branches up far enough for me to crawl into the narrow space, then carefully rearranged the crushed bracken before the entrance. He stood back and surveyed the hiding place critically, nodding in satisfaction.

'Aye, that's good. No one will find ye there.' He turned to go, then turned back. 'Try to sleep, if ye can, and don't worry if I'm not back at once. I'll hunt a bit on the way back; we've no food with us, and I dinna want to attract attention by stopping at a cot-house. Pull the tartan up over your head, and make sure it covers your shift; the white shows for a long way.'

Food seemed irrelevant; I felt as though I would never

want to eat again. Sleep was something else again. My back and arms still ached, the rope burns on my wrists were raw, and I felt sore and bruised all over; but worn out with fear, pain and simple exhaustion, I fell asleep almost at once, the pungent scent of ferns rising around me like incense.

I awoke with something gripping my foot. Startled, I sat up straight, crashing into the springy branches. Leaves and sticks showered down around me, and I flailed my arms wildly, trying to disentangle my hair from the snagging twigs. Scratched, dishevelled and irritated, I crawled out of my sanctuary to find an amused Jamie squatting nearby, watching my emergence. It was near sunset; the sun had dropped below the lip of the burn, leaving the rocky glen in shadow. The smell of roasting meat rose from a small fire burning among the rocks near the stream, where two rabbits browned on a makeshift spit made of sharpened green sticks.

Jamie held out a hand to help me down the slope. I haughtily declined and swept down myself, tripping only once on the trailing ends of the plaid. My earlier nausea had vanished, and I fell ravenously on the meat.

'We'll move up into the forest after supper, Sassenach,' Jamie said, tearing a joint from the rabbit carcass. 'I dinna want to sleep near the burn; I canna hear anyone coming over the noise of the water.'

There was not much conversation as we ate. The horror of the morning, and the thought of what we had left behind, oppressed us both. And for me there was a profound sense of mourning. I had lost not only the chance of finding out more about the why and wherefore of my presence here, but a friend as well. My only friend. I was often in doubt as to Geilie's motives, but I had no doubt at all that she had saved my life that morning. Knowing herself doomed, she had done her best to give me a chance of escape. The fire was growing brighter now as darkness filled the glen. I looked into the flames, seeing the crisp skin and browned bones of the rabbits on their spits. A drop of blood from a broken bone fell into the fire, hissing into nothing. Suddenly

557

the meat stuck in my throat. I set it down hastily and turned away, retching.

Still without speaking much, we moved out of the glen and found a comfortable place near the edge of a clearing in the forest. Hills rose in undulant mounds all around us, but Jamie had chosen a high spot, with a good view of the track from the village. The dusk momentarily heightened all the colours of the countryside, lighting the land with jewels; a glowing emerald in the hollows, a lovely shadowed amethyst among the clumps of heather, and burning rubies on the red-berried rowan trees that crowned the hills. Rowan berries, a specific against witchcraft. Far in the distance, the outline of Castle Leoch was still visible at the foot of Ben Aden. It faded quickly as the light died.

Jamie made a fire in a sheltered spot, and sat down next to it. A faint drizzle of rain misted the air and spangled my eyelashes with rainbows when I looked at the flames.

He sat staring into the fire for a long time. Finally he looked up at me, hands clasped around his knees.

'I said before that I'd not ask ye things ye had no wish to tell me. And I'd not ask ye now; but I must know, for your safety as well as mine.' He paused, hesitating.

'Claire, if you've never been honest wi' me, be so now, for I must know the truth. Claire, are ye a witch?'

I gaped at him. 'A witch? You – you can really ask that?' I thought he must be joking. He wasn't.

He took me by the shoulders and gripped me hard, staring into my eyes as though willing me to answer him.

'I *must* ask it, Claire! And you must tell me!'

'And if I were?' I asked through dry lips. 'If you had thought I were a witch? Would you still have fought for me?'

'I would have gone to the stake with you!' he said violently. 'And to hell beyond, if I must. But may the Lord Jesus have mercy on my soul and on yours, tell me the truth!'

The strain of it all caught up with me. I tore myself out of his grasp and ran across the clearing. Not far, only to the edge of the trees; I could not bear the exposure of the open space. I clutched a tree, put my arms around it and dug my fingers hard into the bark, pressed my face to it and shrieked with hysterical laughter.

Jamie's face, white and shocked, loomed up on the other side of the tree. With the dim realization that what I was doing must sound unnervingly like cackling, I made a terrific effort and stopped. Panting, I stared at him for a moment.

'Yes,' I said, backing away, still heaving with gasps of unhinged laughter. 'Yes, I am a witch! To you, I must be. I've never had smallpox, but I can walk through a room full of dying men and never catch it. I can nurse the sick and breathe their air and touch their bodies, and the sickness can't touch me. I can't catch cholera, either, or lockjaw, or the morbid sore throat. And you must think it's an enchantment, because you've never heard of vaccine, and there's no other way you can explain it.

'The things I know – ' I stopped backing away and stood still, breathing heavily, trying to control myself. 'I know about Jonathan Randall because I was told about him. I know when he was born and when he'll die, I know about what he's done and what he'll do, I know about Sandringham because Frank told me. He knew about Randall because he . . . he . . . oh, God!' I felt as though I might be sick, and closed my eyes to shut out the spinning stars overhead.

'And Callum . . . he suspects me because I know Hamish isn't his own son. I know . . . he can't sire children. But he thought I knew who Hamish's father is . . . I thought maybe it was you, but then I knew it couldn't be, and . . .' I was talking faster and faster, trying to keep the vertigo at bay with the sound of my own voice.

'Everything I've ever told you about myself was true,' I said, nodding madly as though to reassure myself. 'Everything. I haven't any people, I haven't any history, because I haven't happened yet.

'Do you know when I was born?' I asked, looking up. I knew my hair was wild and my eyes staring, and I didn't care. 'On the twentieth of October, in the Year of Our Lord nineteen hundred and eighteen. Do you hear me?' I demanded, for he was blinking at me unmoving, as though paying no attention to a word I said. 'I said nineteen eighteen! Nearly two hundred years from now! Do you hear?'

I was shouting now, and he nodded slowly.

'I hear,' he said softly.

'Yes, you hear!' I blazed. 'And you think I'm raving mad. Don't you? Admit it! That's what you think. You have to think so, there isn't any other way you can explain me to yourself. You *can't* believe me, you can't dare to. Oh, Jamie . . .' I felt my face start to crumple. All this time spent hiding the truth, realizing that I could never tell anyone, and now I realized that I could tell Jamie, my beloved husband, the man I trusted beyond all others, and he wouldn't – he *couldn't* believe me either.

'It was the rocks – the fairy hill. The standing stones. Merlin's stones. That's where I came through.' I was gasping, half sobbing, becoming less coherent by the second. 'Once upon a time, but it's really two hundred years. It's always two hundred years, in the stories . . . But in the stories, the people always get back. I couldn't get back.' I turned away, staggering, grasping for support. I sank down on a rock, shoulders slumped, and put my head in my hands. There was a long silence in the wood. It went on long enough for the small night birds to recover their courage and start their noises once again, calling to each other with a thin, high *zeek!* as they hawked for the last insects of the autumn.

I looked up at last, thinking that perhaps he had simply risen and left me, overcome by my revelations. He was still there, though, still sitting, hands braced on his knees, head bowed as though in thought.

The hairs on his arms shone stiff as copper wires in the firelight, though, and I realized that they stood erect, like the bristles on a dog. He was afraid of me.

'Jamie,' I said, feeling my heart break with absolute loneliness. 'Oh, Jamie.'

I sat down and curled myself into a ball, trying to roll myself around the core of my pain. Nothing mattered any longer, and I sobbed my heart out.

His hands on my shoulders raised me, enough to see his face. Through the haze of tears I saw the look he wore in battle, of struggle that had passed the point of strain and become calm certainty.

'I believe you,' he said firmly. 'I dinna understand it a bit – not yet – but I believe you. Claire, I believe you! Listen to me! There's the truth between us, you and me, and whatever ye tell me, I shall believe it.' He gave me a gentle shake.

'It doesna matter what it is. You've told me. That's enough for now. Be still, *mo duinne*. Lay your head and rest. You'll tell me the rest of it later. And I'll believe you.'

I was still sobbing, unable to grasp what he was telling me. I struggled, trying to pull away, but he gathered me up and held me tightly against himself, pushing my head into the folds of his plaid and repeating over and over again, 'I believe you.'

At last, from sheer exhaustion, I grew calm enough to look up and say, 'But you *can't* believe me.'

He smiled down at me. His mouth trembled slightly, but he smiled.

'Ye'll no tell *me* what I canna do, Sassenach.' He paused a moment. 'How old are ye?' he asked curiously. 'I never thought to ask.'

The question seemed so preposterous that it took me a minute to think.

'I'm twenty-seven . . . or maybe twenty-eight,' I added. That rattled him for a moment. At twenty-eight, women in this time were usually on the verge of middle age.

'Oh,' he said. He took a deep breath. 'I thought ye were about my age – or younger.'

He didn't move for a second. But then he looked down and smiled faintly at me. 'Happy birthday, Sassenach,' he said.

It took me completely by surprise and I just stared stupidly at him for a moment. 'What?' I managed at last.

'I said "Happy birthday". It's the twentieth of October today.'

'Is it?' I said dumbly. 'I'd lost track.' I was shaking again, from cold and shock and the force of my tirade. He drew me close against him and held me, smoothing his big hands lightly over my hair, cradling my head against his chest. I began to cry again, but this time with relief. In my state of upheaval it seemed logical that if he knew my real age and still wanted me, then everything would be all right.

Jamie picked me up, and holding me carefully against his shoulder, carried me to the side of the fire where he had laid the horse's saddle. He sat down, leaning against the saddle, and held me, light and close.

A long time later, he spoke.

'All right. Tell me now.'

I told him. Told him everything, haltingly but coherently. I felt numb from exhaustion, but content, like a rabbit that has outrun a fox and found temporary shelter under a log. It isn't sanctuary, but at least it is respite. And I told him about Frank.

'Frank,' he said softly. 'Then he isna dead, after all.'

'He isn't *born*.' I felt another small wave of hysteria break against my ribs, but managed to keep myself under control. 'Neither am I.'

He stroked and patted me back into silence, making his small murmuring Gaelic sounds.

'When I took ye from Randall at Fort William,' he said suddenly, 'you were trying to get back. Back to the stones. And . . . Frank. That's why ye left the grove.'

'Yes.'

'And I beat you for it.' His voice was soft with regret.

'You couldn't know. I couldn't tell you.' I was beginning to feel very drowsy indeed.

'No, I dinna suppose ye could.' He pulled the plaid closer around me, tucking it gently around my shoulders. 'Do ye sleep now, *mo duinne*. No one shall harm ye; I'm here.'

I burrowed into the warm curve of his shoulder, letting my tired mind fall through the layers of oblivion. I forced myself to the surface long enough to ask, 'Do you really believe me, Jamie?'

He sighed and smiled ruefully down at me.

'Aye, I believe ye, Sassenach. But it would ha' been a good deal easier if you'd only been a witch.'

I slept like the dead, awakening some time after dawn with a terrible headache, stiff in every muscle. Jamie had a few handfuls of oats in a small bag in his sporran, and forced me to eat drammach – oats mixed with cold water. It stuck in my throat, but I choked it down.

He was slow and gentle with me, but spoke very little. After breakfast he quickly packed up the small campsite and saddled Donas.

Numb with the shock of recent events, I didn't even ask where we were going. Mounted behind him, I was content to rest my face against the broad slope of his back, feeling the motion of the horse rock me into a state of mindless trance.

We came down from the braes near a lonely loch, pressing through the chilly dawn mist to the edge of a still sheet of grey. Wild ducks began to rise from the reeds in untidy flocks that circled the marshes, quacking and calling to rouse late sleepers below. By contrast, a well-disciplined wedge of geese passed over us, calling of heartbreak and desolation.

The grey fog lifted near midday and a weak sun lighted the meadows filled with heather and yellow gorse. A few miles past the loch we came out on to a narrow track which took us up again, rising into low rolling hills that gave way gradually to tors and crags. We met few travellers on the way, and prudently turned aside into the brush whenever hoofbeats were heard ahead.

The vegetation turned to pine forest. I sniffed deeply, enjoying the crisp resinous air, though it was turning chill towards dusk. We stopped for the night in a small clearing some way from the path, scooped together a nestlike wallow of pine needles and blankets, and huddled close together for warmth, covered by Jamie's plaid.

He woke me some time in the darkness and made love to me, slowly and tenderly, not speaking. I watched stars winking through the lattice of black branches overhead, and fell asleep again with his comforting weight still warm on top of me.

In the morning Jamie seemed more cheerful, or at least more peaceful, as though a difficult decision had been reached. He promised me hot tea for supper, which was small comfort then in the frigid air. Sleepily I followed him back to the path, brushing pine needles and small spiders from my skirt. The narrow path faded during the morning to no more than a faint trace through heather and rough sheep's-fescue, zigzagging around the more prominent rocks.

I had been paying little attention to our surroundings as I dreamily enjoyed the growing warmth of the sun, but suddenly my eye struck a familiar rock formation and I started out of my torpor. I knew where we were. And why.

'Jamie!'

He turned at my exclamation.

'You didna know?' he asked curiously.

'That we were coming here? No, of course not.' I felt mildly sick. The hill of Craigh na Dun was no more than a mile away; I could see the hump-backed shape of it through the last shreds of the morning mist.

I swallowed hard. I had tried for nearly six months to reach this place. Now that I was here at last I wanted to be anywhere else. The standing stones on the hilltop were invisible from below, but they seemed to emanate a subtle terror that reached out for me.

Well below the summit, the footing grew too uncertain for Donas. We dismounted and tethered him to a scrubby pine, continuing on foot.

I was panting and sweating by the time we reached the top; Jamie showed no signs of exertion, save a faint flush rising from the neck of his shirt. It was quiet here above the pines, but with a steady wind whining faintly in the crevices of the rock.

Jamie took my hand to pull me up the last step to the top. He didn't release it but drew me close, looking carefully at me as though memorizing my features. 'Why – ?' I began, gasping for breath.

'It's your place,' he said roughly. 'Isn't it?'

'Yes.' I stared as though hypnotized at the stone circle. 'It looks just the same.'

Jamie followed me into the circle. Taking me by the arm, he marched firmly up to the split rock.

'Is it this one?' he demanded.

'Yes.' I tried to pull away. 'Careful! Don't go too near it!' He glanced from me to the rock, clearly sceptical. Perhaps he was right to be. I felt suddenly doubtful of the truth of my own story.

'I – I don't know anything about it. Perhaps the . . . whatever it is . . . closed behind me. Maybe it only works at certain times of the year. It was at Beltane when I came through last.'

Jamie glanced over his shoulder at the sun, a flat disc hanging in mid-sky behind a thin screen of cloud.

'It's almost Samhain now,' he said. 'All Hallows' Eve. Seems suitable, no?' He shivered involuntarily, in spite of the joke. 'When you . . . came through. What did ye do?'

I tried to remember. I felt ice cold, and I folded my hands under my armpits.

'I walked round the circle, looking at things. Just randomly, though; there was no pattern. And then I came near to the split rock, and I heard a buzzing, like bees – '

It was still like bees. I drew back as though it had been the hiss of a snake.

'It's still here!' I reared in panic, throwing my arms around Jamie, but he set me firmly away from him, his face white, and turned me once again towards the stone.

'What then?' The keening wind was sharp in my ears, but his voice was sharper still.

'I put my hand on the rock.'

'Do it then.' He pushed me closer, and when I did not respond he grasped my wrist and planted my hand firmly against the brindled surface.

Chaos reached out and grabbed me.

The sun stopped whirling behind my eyes at last, and the shriek faded out of my ears. There was another persistent noise, Jamie calling my name.

I felt too sick to sit up or open my eyes, but I flapped my hand weakly, to let him know I was still alive.

'I'm all right,' I said.

'Are ye then? Oh God, Claire!' He clasped me against his chest then, holding me tightly. 'Jesus, Claire, I thought ye were dead, sure. You . . . you began to . . . go, somehow. You had the most awful look on your face, like ye were frightened to death. I – I pulled ye back from the stone. I stopped ye. I shouldna have done so – I'm sorry, lassie.'

My eyes were open enough now to see his face above me, shocked and frightened.

'It's all right.' It was still an effort to speak, and I felt heavy and disorientated, but things were coming clearer. I tried to smile, but felt nothing more than a twitch.

'At least . . . we know . . . it still works.'

'Oh God. Aye, it works.' He cast a glance of fearful loathing at the stone.

He left me long enough to wet a kerchief in a puddle of rainwater that stood in one of the stony depressions. He wet my face, still muttering reassurances and apologies. At last I felt well enough to sit up.

'You didn't believe me after all, did you?' Groggy as I was, I felt somehow vindicated. 'It's true, though.'

'Aye, it's true.' He sat next to me, staring at the stone for several minutes. I rubbed the wet cloth over my face, feeling still faint and dizzy. Suddenly he sprang to his feet, walked to the rock and slapped his hand against it.

Nothing whatsoever happened, and after a minute his shoulders slumped and he came back to me.

'Maybe it's only women it works on,' I said fuzzily. 'It's always women in the legends. Or maybe it's only me.'

'Well, it isna me,' he said. 'Better make sure, though.'

'Jamie! Be careful!' I shouted, to no avail. He marched to the stone, slapped it again, threw himself against it, walked through the split and back again, but it remained no more than a cleft-stone monolith. As for myself, I shuddered at the thought of even approaching that door to madness once again.

And yet. Yet when I had begun to pass into the realm of

chaos this time, I had been thinking of Frank. And I had *felt* him, I was sure of it. Somewhere in the void had been a tiny pinprick of light, and he was in it. I knew. I knew also that there had been another point of light, one that sat still beside me, staring at the stone, cheeks gleaming with sweat in spite of the chill of the day.

At last he turned to me and grasped both my hands. He raised them to his lips and kissed each one formally.

'My lady,' he said softly. 'My ... Claire. It's no use in waiting. I must part wi' ye now.'

My lips were too stiff to speak, but the expression on my face must have been as easily readable as usual.

'Claire,' he said urgently, 'it's your own time on the other side of ... that thing. You've a home there, a place. The things that you're used to. And ... and Frank.'

'Yes,' I said, 'there's Frank.'

Jamie caught me by the shoulders, pulling me to my feet and shaking me gently in supplication.

'There's nothing for ye on this side, lass! Nothing save violence and danger. Go!' He pushed me slightly, turning me towards the stone. I turned back to him, catching his hands.

'Is there really nothing for me here, Jamie?' I held his eyes, not letting him turn away from me.

He pulled himself gently from my grasp without answering and stood back, suddenly a figure from another time, seen in relief upon a background of hazy hills, the life in his face a trick of the shadowing rock, as if flattened beneath layers of paint, an artist's reminiscence of forgotten places and passions turned to dust.

I looked into his eyes, filled with pain and yearning, and he was flesh again, real and immediate, lover, husband, man.

The anguish I felt must have been reflected in my face, for he hesitated, then turned to the east and pointed down the slope. 'Do ye see behind the small clump of pine down there? About halfway.'

I saw the clump, and saw what he was pointing at, the half-ruined cot-house abandoned on the haunted hill.

'I shall go down to the house, and I shall stay there till the evening. To make sure – to be sure that you're safe.' He looked at me, but made no move to touch me. He closed his eyes, as though he could no longer bear to look at me.

'Goodbye,' he said, and turned to go.

I watched him, numb, and then remembered. There was something that I had to tell him. I called after him.

'Jamie!'

He stopped and stood motionless for a moment, fighting to control his face. It was white and strained and his lips were bloodless when he turned back to me.

'Aye?'

'There's something . . . I mean, I have to tell you something before . . . before I go.'

He closed his eyes briefly, and I thought he swayed, but it might have been only the wind tugging at his kilt.

'There's no need,' he said. 'No. Do ye go, lass. Ye shouldna tarry. Go.' He made to turn away, but I clutched him by the sleeve.

'Jamie, listen to me! You must!' He shook his head helplessly, lifting a hand as though to push me away.

'Claire . . . no. I can't.' The wind was bringing the moisture to his eyes.

'It's the Rising,' I said urgently, shaking his arm. 'Jamie, listen. Prince Charlie – his army. Callum is right! Do you hear me, Jamie? Callum is right, not Dougal.'

'Eh? What d'ye mean, lass?' I had his attention now. He rubbed his sleeve across his face and the eyes that looked down at me were sharp and clear. The wind sang in my ears.

'Prince Charlie. There will be a Rising, Dougal's right about that, but it won't succeed. Charlie's army will do well for a bit, but it will end in slaughter. At Culloden, that's where it will end. The – the clans . . .' In my mind's eye I saw the clanstones, the grey boulders that would lie scattered on the field, each stone bearing the single clan name of the butchered men who lay under it. I took a breath and gripped his hand to steady myself. It was cold as a corpse's.

I shuddered and closed my eyes to concentrate on what I was saying.

'The Highlanders – all the clans that follow Charlie – will be wiped out. Hundreds and hundreds of the clansmen will die at Culloden; those that are left will be hunted and killed. The clans will be crushed . . . and they'll not rise again. Not in your time – not even in mine.'

I opened my eyes to find him staring at me, expressionless.

'Jamie, stay out of it!' I begged him. 'Keep your people out of it if you can, but for the Lord's sake . . . Jamie, if you – ' I broke off. I had been going to say 'Jamie, if you love me'. But I couldn't. I was going to lose him forever, and if I could not speak of love to him before, I could not do it now.

'Don't go to France,' I said softly. 'Go to America, or to Spain, to Italy. But for the sake of the people who love you, Jamie, don't set foot on Culloden Field.'

He went on staring at me. I wondered if he had heard.

'Jamie? Did you hear me? Do you understand?'

After a moment he nodded numbly.

'Aye,' he said quietly, so quietly I could hardly hear him beneath the whining of the wind. 'Aye, I hear.' He dropped my hand.

'Go wi' God . . . *mo duinne.*'

He stepped off the top and made his way down the steep incline, bracing his feet against tufts of grass, catching at branches to keep his balance, not looking back. I watched him until he disappeared into the pine clump, walking slowly, like a man wounded, who knows he must keep moving but feels his life ebbing slowly away through the fingers he has clenched over the wound.

My knees were trembling. Slowly I lowered myself to the ground and sat cross-legged. I could just see the roof of the cot-house that now held my past. At my back loomed the cleft stone. And my future.

I sat without moving through the afternoon. I tried to force all emotion from my mind and use reason. Jamie certainly had logic on his side when he argued that I should go back: home, safety, Frank; even the small amenities of life that I sorely missed from time to time, like hot baths and indoor plumbing, to say nothing of larger considerations such as proper medical care and convenient travel.

And yet, while I would certainly admit the inconveniences and outright dangers of this place, I would have also to admit that I had enjoyed many aspects of it. If travel were inconvenient, there were no enormous stretches of road blanketing the countryside, nor any noisy, stinking cars – contrivances with their own dangers, I reminded myself. Life was much simpler, and so were the people. Not less intelligent, but much more direct – with a few sterling exceptions like Callum mac Gibbon MacKenzie, I thought grimly.

Because of Uncle Lamb's work I had lived in a great many places, even cruder and more lacking in amenities than this one. I adapted quite easily to rough conditions, and did not really miss 'civilization' when away from it, though I adapted just as easily to the presence of niceties like electric cookers and hot-water heaters. I shivered in the cold wind, hugging myself as I stared at the rock.

Rationality did not appear to be helping much. I turned to emotion, and began, shrinking from the task, to reconstruct the details of my married lives – first with Frank, then with Jamie. The only result of this was to leave me shattered and weeping, the tears forming icy trails on my face.

Well, if not reason nor emotion, what of duty? I had given Frank a wedding vow, and had meant it with all my heart. I had given Jamie the same, meaning to betray it as soon as possible. And which of them would I betray now? I continued to sit as the sun sank lower in the sky.

As the evening star began to glow among the black pines' branches I concluded that in this situation reason was of little use. I would have to rely on something else; just what, I wasn't sure. I turned towards the split rock and took a step, then another, and another. Pausing, I faced around and tried it in the other direction. A step, then another, and another, and before I even knew that I had decided, I was

570

halfway down the slope, scrabbling wildly at grass clumps, slipping and falling through the patches of scree.

When I reached the cot-house, breathless with fear lest Jamie had left already, I was reassured to see Donas hobbled and grazing nearby. The horse raised his head and eyed me unpleasantly. Walking softly, I pushed the door open.

He was in the front room, asleep on a narrow wooden settle. He slept on his back, as he usually did, hands crossed on his stomach, mouth slightly open. The last rays of daylight from the window behind me limned his face like a metal mask; the silver tracks of dried tears glinted on golden skin, and the copper stubble of his beard gleamed dully.

I stood watching him for a moment, filled with an unutterable tenderness. Moving as quietly as I could, I lay down beside him on the narrow settle and nestled close. He turned to me in sleep as he so often did, gathering me spoon-fashion against his chest and resting his cheek against my hair. Half conscious, he reached to smooth my hair away from his nose; I felt the sudden jerk as he came awake to realize that I was there, and then we overbalanced and crashed together on to the floor, Jamie on top of me.

I didn't have the slightest doubt that he was solid flesh. I pushed a knee into his abdomen, grunting.

'Get off! I can't breathe!'

Instead, he aggravated my breathless condition by kissing me thoroughly. I ignored the lack of oxygen temporarily in order to concentrate on more important things.

We held each other for a long time without speaking. At last he murmured 'Why?' his mouth muffled in my hair.

I kissed his cheek, damp and salty. I could feel his heart beating against my ribs, and wanted nothing more than to stay there for ever, not moving, not making love, just breathing the same air.

'I had to,' I said. I laughed a little shakily. 'You don't know how close it was. The hot baths nearly won.' And I wept then, and shook a little, because the choice was so freshly made, and because my joy for the man I held in my arms was mingled with a tearing grief for the man I would never see again.

Jamie held me tightly, pressing me down with his weight as though to protect me, to save me from being swept away by the roaring pull of the stone circle. At length my tears were spent and I lay exhausted, head against his comforting chest. It had grown altogether dark by this time, but still he held me, murmuring softly as though I were a child afraid of the night. We clung to each other, unwilling to let go even long enough to start a fire.

At length Jamie rose, and picking me up, carried me to the settle, where he sat with me cradled on his lap. The door still hung open, and we could see the stars beginning to burn over the valley below.

'Do you know,' I said drowsily, 'that it takes thousands and thousands of years for the light of those stars to reach us? In fact, some of the stars we see may be dead by now, but we won't know it, because we still see the light.'

'Is that so?' he answered, stroking my back. 'I didna know that.'

I must have fallen asleep, head on his shoulder, but roused briefly when he laid me gently on the floor, on a makeshift bed of blankets from the horse's saddle roll. He lay down beside me and drew me close again.

'Lay your head, lass,' he whispered. 'In the morning I'll take ye home.'

We rose just before dawn and were on the downward trail when the sun rose, eager to leave Craigh na Dun.

'Where are we going, Jamie?' I asked, rejoicing that I could look forward into a future that held him, even as I left behind the last chance of returning to the man who had loved – who would – love me.

Jamie reined in the horse, pausing to look over his shoulder for a moment. The forbidding circle of standing stones was invisible from here, but the rocky hillside seemed to rise impassable behind us, bristling with boulders and gorse bushes. From here, the crumbling husk of the cothouse looked like one more crag, a bony knuckle jutting from the stony fist of the hill.

'I wish I could have fought him for you,' he said abruptly, looking back at me. His blue eyes were dark and earnest.

I smiled at him, touched.

'It wasn't your fight, it was mine. But you won it anyway.' I reached out a hand and he squeezed it.

'Aye, but that's not what I meant. If I'd fought him man to man and won, ye'd not need to feel any regret over it.' He hesitated. 'If ever – '

'There aren't any more ifs,' I said firmly. 'I thought of every one of them yesterday, and here I still am.'

'Thank God,' he said, smiling, 'and God help you.' Then he added, 'Though I'll never understand why.'

I put my arms around his waist and held on as the horse slithered down the last steep slope.

'Because,' I said, 'I bloody well can't do without you, Jamie Fraser, and that's all about it. Now, where are you taking me?'

Jamie twisted in his saddle, to look back up the slope.

'I prayed all the way up that hill yesterday,' he said softly. 'Not for you to stay; I didna think that would be right. I prayed I'd be strong enough to send ye away.' He shook his head, still gazing up the hill, a faraway look in his eyes.

'I said, "Lord, if I've never had courage in my life before, let me have it now. Let me be brave enough not to fall on my knees and beg her to stay." ' He pulled his eyes away from the cot-house and smiled briefly at me.

'Hardest thing I ever did, Sassenach.' He turned in the saddle and reined the horse's head towards the west. It was a rare bright morning, and the early sun gilded everything, drawing a thin line of fire along the edge of the reins, the curve of the horse's neck and the broad planes of Jamie's face and shoulders.

He took a deep breath and nodded across the moor, towards a distant pass between two crags.

'So now I suppose I can do the second-hardest thing.' He kicked the horse gently, clicking his tongue. 'We're going home, Sassenach. To Lallybroch.'

PART FIVE

Lallybroch

26

The Laird's Return

At first we were so happy only to be with each other and away from Leoch than we didn't talk much. Across the flat of the moor, Donas could carry us both without strain, and I rode with my arms about Jamie's waist, glorying in the feel of the sun-warmed muscle shifting under my cheek. Whatever problems we might be facing – and I knew there were plenty – we were together. For ever. And that was enough.

As the first shock of happiness mellowed into the glow of companionship we began to talk again. About the countryside through which we were passing, at first. Then, cautiously, about me, and where I had come from. He was fascinated by my descriptions of modern life, though I could tell that most of my stories seemed like fairy tales to him. He loved especially the descriptions of automobiles, tanks and aeroplanes, and made me describe them over and over, as minutely as I could. By tacit agreement, we avoided any mention of Frank.

As the days passed and we covered more countryside the conversation turned back to our present time; Callum, the castle, then the stag hunt and the Duke.

'He seems a nice chap,' Jamie remarked. As the going became rougher he had dismounted and walked alongside, which made conversation easier.

'I thought so too,' I answered. 'But – '

'Oh, aye, ye canna put too much faith in what a man seems these days,' he agreed. 'Still, we got on, he and I. We'd sit together and talk of an evening, round the fire in the hunting lodge. He's a good bit brighter than he seems, for the one thing; he knows how that voice makes him seem, and I think he uses it to make himself look a bit of a fool, while all the time the mind is there, workin' behind his eyes.'

'Mmm. That's what I'm afraid of. Did you . . . tell him?'

He shrugged. 'A bit. He knew my name, of course, from that time before, at the castle.'

I laughed at the memory of his account of that time. 'Did you, er, reminisce about old times?'

He grinned, the ends of his hair floating about his face in the autumn breeze.

'Oh, just a bit. He asked me once whether I still suffered from stomach trouble. I kept my face straight and answered that as a rule, no, but I thought perhaps I felt a bit of griping coming on just now. He laughed, and said he hoped it did not discommode my beautiful wife.'

I laughed myself. Right now, what the Duke might or mightn't do didn't seem of overwhelming importance. Nevertheless, he might one day be of use.

'I told him a little,' Jamie went on. 'That I was outlawed, but not guilty of the charge, though I'd have precious little chance of proving it. He seemed sympathetic, but I was cautious about telling him the circumstances – let alone the fact that there's a price on my head. I hadna yet made up my mind whether to trust him with the rest of it, when . . . well, when Alick came tearing into the camp like the Devil himself was on his tail, and Murtagh and I left the same way.'

This reminded me. 'Where *is* Murtagh?' I asked. 'He came back with you to Leoch?' I hoped the little clansman hadn't fallen afoul of either Callum or the villagers of Cranesmuir.

'He started back wi' me, but the beast he was riding was no match for Donas. Aye, a bonny wee lad ye are, Donas *mo buidheag.*' He slapped the shimmering sorrel neck, and Donas snorted and ruffled his mane. Jamie glanced up at me and smiled.

'Dinna worry for Murtagh. There's a canty wee bird can mind for himself.'

'Canty? Murtagh?' I knew the word meant 'cheerful',

which seemed incongruous to a degree. 'I don't think I've ever seen him smile. Have you?'

'Oh, aye. At least twice.'

'How long have you known him?'

'Twenty-three years. He's my godfather.'

'Oh. Well, *that* explains a bit. I didn't think he'd bother on my account.'

Jamie patted my leg. 'Of course he would. He likes you.'

'I'll take your word for it.'

Having thus approached the subject of recent events, I took a deep breath and asked something I badly wanted to know.

'Jamie?'

'Aye?'

'Geillis Duncan. Will they . . . will they really burn her?'

He glanced up at me, frowning slightly, and nodded.

'I expect so. Not till after the child is born, though. Is that what troubles ye?'

'One of the things. Jamie, look at this.' I tried to push up the voluminous sleeve, failed, and settled for pulling the neck of the shirt off my shoulder to display my vaccination scar.

'God in heaven,' he said slowly, after I had explained. He looked sharply at me. 'So that's why . . . is she from your own time then?'

I shrugged helplessly. 'I don't know. All I can say is that she was likely born some time after 1920; that's when public inoculation came in.' I looked over my shoulder, but low-lying clouds hid the crags that now separated us from Leoch. 'I don't suppose I ever will know . . . now.'

Jamie took Donas' reins and led him aside, under a small pine grove, on the banks of a stream. He grasped me around the waist and lifted me down.

'Dinna grieve for her,' he said firmly, holding me. 'She's a wicked woman; a murderer, if not a witch. She did kill her husband, no?'

'Yes,' I said, with a shudder, remembering Arthur Duncan's glazed eyes.

'I still dinna understand why she should kill him, though,'

579

he said, shaking his head in puzzlement. 'He had money, a good position. And I doubt he beat her.'

I looked at him in exasperated amazement.

'And that's your definition of a good husband?'

'Well . . . yes,' he said, frowning. 'What else might she want?'

'What *else*?' I was so taken aback I just looked at him for a moment, then slid down on the grass and started to laugh.

'What's funny? I thought this was murder.' He smiled, though, and put an arm around me.

'I was just thinking,' I said, still snorting a bit, 'if your definition of a good husband is one with money and position who doesn't beat his wife . . . what does that make *you*?'

'Oh,' he said. He grinned. 'Well, Sassenach, I never said I was a good husband. Neither did you. "Sadist", I think ye called me, and a few other things that I wouldna repeat for the sake of decency. But not a good husband.'

'Good. Then I won't feel obliged to poison you with cyanide.'

'Cyanide?' He looked down curiously at me. 'What's that?'

'The thing that killed Arthur Duncan. It's a bloody fast, powerful poison. Fairly common in my time, but not here.' I licked my lips meditatively.

'I tasted it on his lips, and just that tiny bit was enough to make my whole face go numb. It acts almost instantly, as you saw. I should have known then – about Geilie, I mean. I imagine she made it from crushed peach kernels or cherry stones, though it must have been the devil of a job.'

'Did she tell ye why she did it, then?'

I sighed and rubbed my feet. My shoes had been lost in the struggle at the loch, and I tended to pick up thorns and cockleburs, my feet not being hardened as Jamie's were.

'That and a good deal more. If there's anything to eat in your saddlebags, why don't you fetch it, and I'll tell you all about it.'

We entered the valley of Broch Tuarach the next day. As

we came down out of the foothills I spotted a solitary rider, some distance away, heading roughly in our direction. He was the first person we had seen since we left Cranesmuir.

The man approaching us was stout and prosperous-looking, with a snowy stock showing at the neck of a serviceable grey serge coat, its long tails covering all but an inch or two of his breeches.

We had been travelling for the best part of a week, sleeping out of doors, washing in the cold, fresh water of the burns and living quite well off such rabbits and fish as Jamie could catch, and such edible plants and berries as I could find. Between our efforts, our diet was better than that in the castle – fresher, and certainly more varied, if a little unpredictable.

But if nutrition were well served by an outdoor life, appearance was another thing, and I took hasty stock of our looks as the gentleman on ponyback hesitated, frowning, then changed direction and trotted slowly towards us to investigate.

Jamie, who had insisted on walking most of the way to spare the horse, was a disreputable sight indeed, hose stained to the knees with reddish dust, spare shirt torn by brambles and a week's growth of beard bristling fiercely from cheek and jaw.

His hair had grown long enough in the last months to reach his shoulders. Usually clubbed into a queue or laced back, it was free now, thick and unruly, with small bits of leaf and stick caught in the disordered coppery locks. Face burned a deep ruddy bronze, boots cracked from walking, dirk and sword thrust through his belt, he looked a wild Highlander indeed.

I was hardly better. Covered modestly enough in the billows of Jamie's best shirt and the remnants of my shift, barefoot and shawled in his plaid, I looked a right ragamuffin. Encouraged by the misty dampness and lacking any restraint in the form of comb or brush, my hair rioted all over my head. It had grown as well during my sojourn at the castle, and floated in clouds and tangles about my shoulders, drifting into my eyes whenever the wind was behind us, as it was now.

Shoving the wayward locks out of my eyes, I watched the cautious approach of the gentleman in grey. Jamie, seeing him, brought Donas to a stop and waited for him to draw near enough for speech.

'It's Jock Graham,' he said to me, 'from up the way at Murch Nardagh.'

The man came within a few yards, reined up and sat looking us over carefully. His eyes, pouched with fat, crinkled and rested suspiciously on Jamie, then suddenly sprang wide.

'Lallybroch?' he said unbelievingly.

Jamie nodded benignly. With a completely unfounded air of proprietorial pride, he laid a hand on my thigh and said, 'And my lady Lallybroch.'

Jock Graham's mouth dropped an inch or two, then was hastily drawn up again into an expression of flustered respect.

'Ah ... my ... lady,' he said, belatedly doffing his hat and bowing in my direction. 'You'll be, er, going home, then?' he asked, trying to keep his fascinated gaze from resting on my leg, bared to the knee by a rent in my shift, and stained with elderberry juice.

'Aye.' Jamie glanced over the man's shoulder, towards the rift in the hill he had told me was the entrance to Broch Tuarach. 'You'll have been there lately, Jock?'

Graham pulled his eyes away from me and looked at Jamie. 'Och? Oh, aye. Aye, I've been there. They're all well. Be pleased to see ye, I expect. Go well, then, Fraser.' And with a hasty dig into his pony's ribs, he turned aside and headed up the valley.

We watched him go. Suddenly, a hundred yards away, he paused. Turning in the saddle, he rose in his stirrups and cupped his mouth to shout. The sound, borne by the wind, reached us thin but distinct.

'Welcome home!'

And he disappeared over a rise.

Broch Tuarach means 'the north-facing tower'. From the side of the mountain above, the broch that gave the small estate its name was no more than another mound of rocks, much like those that lay at the foot of the hills we had been travelling through.

We came down through a narrow, rocky gap between two crags, leading the horse between boulders. Then the going was easier, the land sloping more gently down through the fields and scattered cottages until at last we struck a small winding road that led to the house.

It was larger than I had expected; a handsome three-storey house of harled stone, windows outlined in the natural grey stone, a high slate roof with multiple chimneys, and several smaller whitewashed buildings clustered about it, like chicks about a hen. The old stone broch, situated on a small rise to the rear of the house, rose sixty feet above the ground, cone-topped like a witch's hat, girdled with three rows of tiny arrow slits.

As we drew near there was a sudden terrible racket from the direction of the outbuildings, and Donas shied and reared. No horsewoman, I promptly fell off, landing ignominiously in the dusty road. With an eye for the relative importance of things, Jamie leapt for the plunging horse's bridle, leaving me to fend for myself.

The dogs were almost upon me, baying and growling, by the time I found my feet. To my panicked eyes there seemed to be at least a dozen of them, all with teeth bared and wicked. There was a shout from Jamie.

'Bran! Luke! *Seas!*'

The dogs skidded to a halt within a few feet of me, confused. They milled, growling uncertainly, until he spoke again.

'*Seas, mo maise!* Stand, ye wee heathens!' They did, and the largest dog's tail began gradually to wag, once, and then twice, questioningly.

'Claire. Come take the horse. He'll not let them close, and it's me they want. Walk slowly; they'll no harm ye.' He spoke casually, not to alarm either horse or dogs further. I was not so sanguine, but edged carefully towards him.

Donas jerked his head and rolled his eyes as I took the bridle, but I was in no mood to put up with tantrums, and I yanked the rein firmly down and grabbed the head collar.

The thick velvet lips writhed back from his teeth, but I jerked harder. I put my face close to the big glaring golden eye and glared back.

'Don't try it!' I hissed. 'Or you'll end up as dog's meat, and I won't lift a hand to save you!'

Jamie meanwhile was slowly walking towards the dogs, one hand held out fistlike towards them. What had seemed a large pack was only four dogs: a small brownish rat-terrier, two ruffed and spotted sheepdogs and a huge black and tan monster that could have stood in for the Hound of the Baskervilles with no questions asked.

This slavering creature stretched out a neck thicker than my waist and sniffed gently at the proffered knuckles. A tail like a ship's cable beat back and forth with increasing fervour. Then it flung back its enormous head, baying with joy, and leaped on its master, knocking him flat in the road.

' "In which Odysseus returns from the Trojan War and is recognized by his faithful hound," ' I remarked to Donas, who snorted briefly, giving his opinion either of Homer or of the undignified display of emotion going on in the roadway.

Jamie, laughing, was ruffling the fur and pulling the ears of the dogs, who were all trying to lick his face at once. Finally he beat them back sufficiently to rise, keeping his feet with difficulty against their ecstatic demonstrations.

'Well, *someone's* glad to see me, at any rate,' he said, grinning, as he patted the beast's head. 'That's Luke' – he pointed to the terrier – 'and Elphin and Mars. Brothers, they are, and bonny sheepdogs. And this' – he laid an affectionate hand on the enormous black head, which slobbered in appreciation – 'is Bran.'

'I'll take your word for it,' I said, cautiously extending a knuckle to be sniffed. '*What* is he?'

'A staghound.' He scratched the pricked ears, quoting,

> *'Thus Fingal chose his hounds:*
> *Eye like sloe, ear like leaf,*
> *Chest like horse, hough like sickle*
> *And the tail joint far from the head.'*

'If those are the qualifications, then you're right,' I said, inspecting Bran. 'If his tail joint were any further from his head, you could ride him.'

'I used to, when I was small – not Bran, I don't mean, but his grandfather, Nairn.'

He gave the hound a final pat and straightened, gazing towards the house. He took the restive Donas's bridle and turned him downhill.

' "In which Odysseus returns to his home, disguised as a beggar . . ." ' he quoted in Greek, having picked up my earlier remark. 'And now,' he said, straightening his collar with some grimness, 'I suppose it's time to go and deal with Penelope and her suitors.'

When we reached the double doors, the dogs panting at our heels, Jamie hesitated.

'Should we knock?' I asked, a bit nervous. He looked at me in astonishment.

'It's my home,' he said, and pushed the door open.

He led me through the house, ignoring the few startled servants we passed, past the entrance hall and through a small gun room, into the drawing room. It boasted a wide hearth with a polished mantel, and bits of silver and glass gleamed here and there, capturing the late-afternoon sun. For a moment I thought the room was empty. Then I saw a faint movement in one corner near the hearth.

She was smaller than I had expected. With a brother like Jamie, I had imagined her at least my height, or even taller, but the woman by the fire barely reached five feet. Her back was to us as she reached for something on the shelf of the china cabinet, and the ends of her dress sash dipped close to the floor.

Jamie froze when he saw her.

'Jenny,' he said.

The woman turned and I caught an impression of brows

black as ink, and blue eyes wide in a white face before she launched herself at her brother.

'Jamie!' Small as she was, she jarred him with the impact of her embrace. His arms went about her shoulders in reflex and they clung for a moment, her face tight against his shirtfront, his hand tender on the nape of her neck. On his face was an expression of such mingled uncertainty and yearning joy that I felt almost an intruder.

Then she pressed herself closer to him, murmuring something in Gaelic, and his expression dissolved in shock. He grasped her by the arms and held her away from him, looking down.

The faces were much alike; the same oddly slanted dark blue eyes and broad cheekbones. The same thin, blade-bridged nose, just a trifle too long. But she was dark where Jamie was fair, with cascades of black curly hair, bound back with green ribbon.

She was beautiful, with clear-drawn features and alabaster skin. She was also clearly in a state of advanced pregnancy.

Jamie had gone white at the lips. 'Jenny,' he whispered, shaking his head. 'Oh, Jenny. *Mo cridh.*'

Her attention was distracted just then by the appearance of a small child in the doorway, and she pulled away from her brother without noticing his discomposure. She took the little boy's hand and led him into the room, murmuring encouragement. He hung back a little, thumb in mouth for comfort, peering up at the strangers from behind his mother's skirts.

For his mother she plainly was. He had her mop of thick, curly black hair and the square set of her shoulders, though the face was not hers.

'This is wee Jamie,' she said, looking proudly down at the lad. 'And this is your Uncle Jamie, *mo cridh*, the one you're named for.'

'For me? You named him for me?' Jamie looked like a fighter who has just been punched very hard in the stomach. He backed away from mother and child until he blundered into a chair, and sank into it as though the strength had gone from his legs. He hid his face in his hands.

His sister by this time was aware that something was amiss. She touched him tentatively on the shoulder.

'Jamie? What is it, my dearie? Are ye ill?'

He looked up at her then, and I could see his eyes were full of tears.

'Did ye have to do that, Jenny? Do ye think that I've not suffered enough for what happened – for what I let happen – that ye must name Randall's bastard for me, to be a reproach to me so long as I live?'

Jenny's face, normally pale, lost all vestiges of colour.

'Randall's bastard?' she said blankly. 'Jonathan Randall, ye mean? The redcoat captain?'

'Aye, the redcoat captain. Who else would I mean, for God's sake! You'll remember him, I suppose?' Jamie was recovering enough of his customary poise for sarcasm.

Jenny eyed her brother closely, one arched brow lifted in suspicion.

'Have ye lost your senses, man?' she inquired. 'Or have ye taken a drop too much along the way?'

'I should never have come back,' he muttered. He rose then, stumbling slightly, and tried to pass without touching her. She stood her ground, however, and gripped him by the arm.

'Correct me, brother, if I'm wrong,' Jenny said slowly, 'but I've the strong impression you're saying I've played the whore to Captain Randall, and what I'm askin' myself is what maggots you've got in your brain to make ye say so?'

'Maggots, is it?' Jamie turned to her, mouth twisted in bitterness. 'I wish it were so; I'd rather I was dead and in my grave than to see my sister brought to such a pass.' He seized her by the shoulders and shook her slightly, crying out, 'Why, Jenny, why? To have ye ruin yourself for me was shame enough to kill me. But this . . .' He dropped his hands then, with a gesture of despair that took in the protruding belly, swelling accusingly under the light smocking.

He turned abruptly towards the door, and an elderly

587

woman, who had been listening avidly with the child clinging to her skirts, drew back in alarm.

'I should not have come. I'll go.'

'You'll do no such thing, Jamie Fraser,' his sister said sharply. 'Not before you've listened to me. Sit yourself down, then, and I'll tell ye about Captain Randall, since ye want to know.'

'I *don't* want to know! I don't want to hear it!' As she advanced towards him he turned sharply away to the window that looked out over the yard.

She followed him, saying, 'Jamie . . .' but he repelled her with a violent gesture.

'No! Don't talk to me! I've said I canna bear to hear it!'

'Och, is that a fact?' She eyed her brother, standing at the window with his legs braced wide apart, hands on the sill and back stubbornly set against her. She bit her lip and a calculating look came over her face. Quick as lightning, she stooped and her hand shot under his kilt like a striking snake.

Jamie let out a roar of sheer outrage and stood bolt upright with shock. He tried to turn, then froze as she apparently tightened her grip.

'There's men as are sensible,' she said to me, with a wicked smile, 'and beasts as are biddable. Others ye'll do nothing with, unless ye have 'em by the bollocks. Now, ye can listen to me in a civil way,' she said to her brother, 'or I can twist a bit. Hey?'

He stood still, red-faced, breathing heavily through clenched teeth. 'I'll listen,' he said. 'And then I'll wring your wee neck, Jenny! Let me go!'

No sooner did she oblige than he whirled on her.

'What in hell d'ye think you're doing?' he hissed. 'Tryin' to shame me before my own wife?' Jenny was not fazed by his outrage. She rocked back on her heels, viewing her brother and myself sardonically.

'Weel, and if she's your wife, I expect she's more familiar wi' your balls than what I am. I havena seen them myself since ye got old enough to wash alone. Grown a bit, no?'

Jamie's face went through several alarming transformations as the dictates of civilized behaviour struggled with the primitive impulse of a younger brother to clout his sister over the head. Civilization at length won out, and he said through his teeth, with what dignity he could summon, 'Leave my balls out of it. And then, since you'll not rest till ye make me hear it, *tell* me about Randall. Tell me why ye disobeyed my orders and chose to dishonour yourself and your family instead.'

Jenny put her hands on her hips and drew herself to her full height, ready for combat. Slower than he to lose her temper; still she had one, no doubt of that.

'Oh, disobey your orders, is it? That's what eats at ye, Jamie, isn't it? You know best, and we'll all do as ye say, or we'll come to rack and ruin, nae doubt.' She flounced angrily. 'And if I'd done as *you* said, that day, you'd ha' been dead in the dooryard, Faither hanged or in prison for killing Randall and the lands gone forfeit to the Crown. To say nothing of me, wi' my home and family gone, needing to beg in the byroads to live.'

Not pale at all now, Jamie was flushed with anger.

'Aye, so ye chose to sell yourself rather than beg! I'd sooner have died in my blood and seen Father and the lands in hell along with me, and well ye know it!'

'Aye, I know it! You're a ninny, Jamie, and always have been!' his sister returned in exasperation.

'Fine thing for *you* to say! You're not content wi' ruining your good name and my own, ye must go on with the scandal, and flaunt your shame to the whole neighbourhood!'

'You'll not speak to me in that way, James Fraser, brother or no! What d'ye mean, "my shame"? Ye great fool, you – '

'What I *mean*? When you're goin' about swelled out to here like a mad toad?' He mimicked her belly with a contemptuous swipe of the hand.

She took one step back, drew back her hand and slapped him with all the force she could muster. The impact jarred his head back and left a white outline of her fingers printed on his cheek. He slowly raised a hand to the mark, staring at his sister. Her eyes were glittering dangerously and her bosom heaved. The words spilled out in a torrent between clenched white teeth.

'Toad, is it? Stinking coward – ye've no more courage than to leave me here, thinking ye dead or imprisoned, wi' no word from one day to the next, and then ye come strolling in one fine day – with a wife, no less – and sit in my drawing room calling me toad and harlot and – '

'I didna call ye harlot, but I should! How can ye – '

Despite the differences in their heights, brother and sister were almost nose to nose, hissing at one another in an effort to keep their carrying voices from ringing through the house. The effort was largely wasted, judging from the glimpses I caught of various interested faces peeping discreetly from kitchen, hall and window. The laird of Broch Tuarach was having an interesting homecoming, to be sure.

I thought it best to let them have it out without my presence, and so I stepped quietly into the hall, with an awkward nod to the elderly woman, and continued into the yard. There was a small arbour there with a bench, on which I seated myself, looking about with interest.

Besides the arbour there was a small walled garden, blooming with the last of the summer roses. Beyond it was what Jamie referred to as 'the dovecote'; or so I assumed, from the assorted pigeons that were fluttering in and out of the pierced-work opening at the top of the building.

I knew there was a stable and a shed for silage; these must be to the other side of the house, with the farm's granary and the henyard, kailyard and disused chapel. Which still left a small stone building on this side unaccounted for. The light autumn wind was from that direction; I sniffed deeply, and was rewarded with the rich smell of hops and yeast. That was the brewhouse, then, where the beer and ale for the estate were made.

The track past the gate led up and over a small hill. As I looked, a small group of men appeared at the crest, silhouetted in the evening light. They seemed to hover a moment, as though taking leave of each other. This appeared to be the case, for only one came down the hill towards the house, the others striking off through the fields towards a clump of cottages in the distance.

As the single man came down the hill I could see that he limped badly. When he came through the gate the reason for it was apparent. The right leg was missing below the knee, and he wore a wooden peg in replacement.

In spite of the limp he moved youthfully. In fact, as he drew near to the arbour, I could see that he was only in his twenties. He was tall, nearly as tall as Jamie, but much narrower through the shoulder, thin, in fact, nearly to the point of skinniness.

He paused at the entrance to the arbour, leaning heavily on the lattice, and looked in at me with interest. Thick brown hair fell smoothly over a high brow, and deep-set brown eyes held a look of patient good humour.

The voices of Jamie and his sister had risen while I waited outside. The windows were open to the warm weather, and the disputants were quite audible from the arbour, though not all the words were clear.

'Interfering, nosy bitch!' came Jamie's voice, loud on the soft evening air.

'Havena the decency to . . .' His sister's reply was lost in a sudden breeze.

The newcomer nodded easily towards the house.

'Ah, Jamie's home, then.'

I nodded in reply, not sure whether I should introduce myself. It didn't matter, for the young man smiled and inclined his head to me.

'I'm Ian Murray, Jenny's husband. And I imagine ye'll be . . . ah . . .'

'The Sassenach wench Jamie's married,' I finished for him. 'My name is Claire. Did you know about it, then?' I asked, as he laughed. My mind was racing. Jenny's *husband*?

'Oh, aye. We heard from Joe Orr, who'd got it from a tinker in Ardraigh. Ye canna keep anything secret long in the Highlands. You should know that, even if you've been wed but a few months. Jenny's been wondering for weeks what you'd be like.'

'Whore!' Jamie bellowed from inside the house. Jenny's

husband didn't turn a hair, but went on examining me with friendly curiosity.

'You're a bonny lass,' he said, looking me over frankly. 'Are ye fond of Jamie?'

'Well . . . yes. Yes, I am,' I answered, a bit taken aback. I was becoming accustomed to the directness that characterized most Highlanders, but it still took me unawares from time to time.

He pursed his lips and nodded as though satisfied, and sat down beside me on the bench.

'Better let them have a few minutes longer,' he said with a wave at the house, where the shouting had now turned to Gaelic. He seemed completely unconcerned as to the cause of the battle. 'Frasers dinna listen to anything when they've their danders up. I've been acquent' wi' those two all my life, and I know. When they've shouted themselves out, sometimes ye can make them see reason, but not till then.'

'Yes, I noticed,' I said dryly, and he laughed.

'So you've been wed long enough to find that out, eh? We heard as how Dougal made Jamie wed ye,' he said, ignoring the battle and concentrating his attention on me. 'But Jenny said it would take more than Dougal MacKenzie to make Jamie do something he didna care to. Now that I see ye, of course I can see why he did it.' He lifted his brows, inviting further explanation, but politely not forcing it.

'I imagine he had his reasons,' I said, my attention divided between my companion and the house, where the sounds of combat continued. 'I don't want . . . I mean, I hope . . .' Ian correctly interpreted my hesitations and my glance towards the drawing-room windows.

'Oh, I expect you've something to do with it. But she'd take it out of him whether you were here or not. She loves Jamie something fierce, ye know, and she worried a lot while he was gone, especially with her father goin' so sudden. Ye'll know about that?' The brown eyes were sharp and observant, as though to gauge the depth of confidence between me and Jamie.

'Yes, Jamie told me.'

'Ah.' He nodded towards the house. 'Then, of course, she's wi' child.'

'Yes, I noticed that too,' I said.

'Hard to miss, is it no?' Ian answered with a grin, and we both laughed. 'Makes her fractious,' he explained. 'Not that I'd blame her. But it would take a braver man than me to cross words wi' a woman in her ninth month.' He leaned back, stretching his wooden leg out in front of him.

'Lost it in France with Fergus nic Leodhas,' he explained. 'Grapeshot. Aches a wee bit towards the end of the day.' He rubbed the flesh just above the leather cuff that attached the peg to his stump.

'Have you tried rubbing it with camomile lotion?' I asked. 'Fresh water-pepper or stewed rue might help too.'

'I've not tried the water-pepper,' he answered, interested. 'I'll ask Jenny does she know how to make it.'

'Oh, I'd be glad to make it for you,' I said, liking him. I looked towards the house again. 'If we stay long enough,' I added doubtfully.

We chatted inconsequentially for a little, both listening with one ear to the confrontation going on beyond the window, until Ian hitched forward, carefully settling his artificial limb under him before rising.

'I imagine we should go in now. If either of them stops shouting long enough to hear the other, they'll be hurting each other's feelings.'

'I hope that's all they hurt.'

Ian chuckled. 'Oh, I dinna think Jamie would strike her. He's used to forbearance in the face of provocation. As for Jenny, she might slap his face, but that's all.'

'She already did that.'

'Weel, the guns are locked up and all the knives are in the kitchen, except what Jamie's wearing. And I don't suppose he'll let her close enough to get his dirk away from him. Nay, they're safe enough.' He paused at the door. 'Now, as for you and me . . .' He winked solemnly. 'That's a different matter.'

Inside, the maids started and flitted nervously away at Ian's approach. The housekeeper, though, was still hovering by the drawing-room door in fascination, drinking in the scene within, Jamie's namesake cradled against her capacious bosom. Such was her concentration that when Ian spoke to her, she jumped as though he had run a pin into her, and put a hand to her palpitating heart.

Ian nodded politely to her, took the little boy in his arms and led the way into the drawing room. We paused just inside the door to survey the scene. Brother and sister had paused for breath, both still bristling and glaring like a pair of angry cats.

Small Jamie, spotting his mother, struggled and kicked to get down from Ian's arms, and once on the floor, made for her like a homing pigeon. 'Mama!' he cried. 'Up! Jamie up!' Turning, she scooped up the little boy and held him like a weapon against her shoulder.

'Can ye tell your uncle how old ye are, sweetheart?' she asked him, throttling her voice down to a coo – under which the sound of clashing steel was still all too apparent. The boy heard it; he turned and burrowed his face into his mother's neck. She patted his back mechanically, still glaring at her brother.

'Since he'll not tell ye, I will. He's two, come last January. And if you're bright enough to count – which I take leave to doubt – you'll see he was conceived six months past the time I last saw yon Randall, which was in our own dooryard, beating the living daylights out of my brother with a sabre.'

'That's so, is it?' Jamie glowered at his sister. 'I've heard a bit differently. It's common knowledge you've taken the man to your bed; not the once, but as your lover. That child's his.' He nodded contemptuously at his namesake, who had turned to peer under his mother's chin at this big, loud stranger. 'I believe ye when ye say the new bastard you're carrying is not; Randall was in France till this March. So you're not only a whore, but an unchoosy one too. Who fathered this last Devil's spawn on ye?'

The tall young man beside me coughed apologetically, breaking the tension in the room.

'I did,' he said mildly. 'That one too.' Advancing stiffly

on his wooden leg, he took the little boy from his fuming wife and set him in the crook of his arm. 'Favours me a bit, some say.'

In fact, seen side by side, the faces of man and boy were nearly identical, allowing for the round cheeks of the one and the crooked nose of the other. The same high brow and narrow lips. The same feathery brows arched over the same deep, liquid-brown eyes. Jamie, staring at the pair of them, looked rather as though he'd been hit in the small of the back with a sandbag. He closed his mouth and swallowed once, clearly having no idea what to do next.

'Ian,' he said a little weakly. 'You're married, then?'

'Oh, aye,' his brother-in-law said cheerfully. 'Wouldn't do, otherwise, would it?'

'I see,' Jamie murmured. He cleared his throat and bobbed his head at his newly discovered brother-in-law. 'It's, er, it's kind of ye, Ian. To take her, I mean. Most kind.'

Feeling that he might be in need of some moral support at this point, I moved to Jamie's side and touched his arm. His sister's eyes lingered on me speculatively, but she said nothing. Jamie looked around and seemed startled to find me there, as though he had forgotten my existence. And no wonder if he had, I thought. But he seemed relieved by the interruption, at least, and put out a hand to draw me forward.

'My wife,' he said rather abruptly. He nodded towards Jenny and Ian. 'My sister, and, her, ah . . .' He trailed off, as Ian and I exchanged polite smiles.

Jenny was not to be distracted by social niceties.

'What d'ye mean, it's kind of him to take me!' she demanded, ignoring the introductions. 'As if I didna ken!' Ian looked inquiringly at her, and she waved a disdainful hand at Jamie. 'He means it was kind of ye to wed me in my soiled condition!' She gave a snort that would have done credit to someone twice her size. 'Bletherer!'

'Soiled condition?' Ian looked startled, and Jamie suddenly leaned forward and grasped his sister hard about the upper arm.

'Did ye not tell him about Randall?' He sounded truly shocked. 'Jenny, how could ye do such a thing?'

Only Ian's hand on Jenny's other arm restrained her from flying at her brother's throat. Ian drew her firmly behind him, and turning, set small Jamie in her arms so that she was forced to grasp the child to save him falling. Then Ian put an arm about Jamie's shoulders and tactfully steered him a safe distance away.

'It's hardly a matter for the drawing room,' he said, low-voiced and deprecating, 'but ye might be interested to know that your sister was virgin on her wedding night. I was, after all, in a position to say.'

Jenny's wrath was now more or less evenly divided between brother and husband.

'How dare ye to say such things in my presence, Ian Murray?' she flamed. 'Or out of it, either! My wedding night's no one's business but mine and yours – sure it's not *his*! Next you'll be showing him the sheets from my bridal bed!'

'Weel, if I did now, it would shut him up, no?' said Ian soothingly. 'Come now, *mi dubh*, ye shouldna worry yourself, it's bad for the babe. And the shouting troubles wee Jamie too.' He reached out for his son, who was whimpering, not sure yet whether the situation required tears. Ian jerked his head at me and rolled an eye in Jamie's direction.

Taking my cue, I grabbed Jamie by the arm and dragged him to an armchair in a neutral corner. Ian had Jenny likewise installed on the loveseat, a firm arm across her shoulders to keep her in place.

'Now, then.' In spite of his unassuming manner, Ian Murray had an undeniable authority. I had my hand on Jamie's shoulder, and could feel the tension begin to go out of it.

I thought that the room looked a bit like the ring of a boxing match, with the fighters twitching restlessly in the corners, each awaiting the signal for action under the soothing hand of a manager.

Ian nodded at his brother-in-law, smiling. 'Jamie. It's good to see ye, man. We're pleased you're home, and your wife with ye. Are we not, *mi dubh?*' he demanded of Jenny, his fingers tightening perceptibly on her shoulder.

She was not one to be forced into anything. Her lips compressed into a thin tight line as though forming a seal, then opened reluctantly to let one word escape.

'Depends,' she said, and shut them tight again.

Jamie rubbed a hand over his face, then raised his head, ready for a fresh round.

'I saw ye go into the house with Randall,' he said stubbornly. 'And from things he said to me later – how comes he to know you've a mole on your breast, then?'

She snorted violently. 'Do ye remember all that went on that day, or did the Captain beat it out of ye wi' his sabre?'

'Of course I remember! I'm no likely to forget it!'

'Then perhaps you'll remember that I gave the Captain a fair jolt in the crutch wi' my knee at one point in the proceedings?'

Jamie hunched his shoulders, wary. 'Aye, I remember.'

Jenny smiled in a superior manner.

'Weel then, if your wife here – ye could tell me her name at least, Jamie, I swear you've no manners at all – anyway, if she was to give ye similar treatment – and richly you deserve it, I might add – d'ye think you'd be able to perform your husbandly duties a few minutes later?'

Jamie, who had been opening his mouth to speak, suddenly shut it. He stared at his sister for a long moment, then one corner of his mouth twitched slightly.

'Depends,' he said. The mouth twitched again. He had been sitting hunched forward in his chair, but sat back now, looking at her with the half-sceptical expression of a younger brother listening to a sister's fairy tales, feeling himself too old to be amazed, but half believing still against his will.

'Really?' he said.

Jenny turned to Ian. 'Go and fetch the sheets, Ian,' she ordered.

Jamie raised both hands in surrender. 'No. No, I believe ye. It's just, the way he acted after . . .'

Jenny sat back, relaxed in the curve of Ian's arm, her son

597

cuddling as close as the bulk of her belly would permit, gracious in victory.

'Weel, after all he'd said outside, he could hardly admit in front of his own men to being incapable, now could he? He'd have to seem as though he'd done as he promised, no? And,' she admitted, 'I'll have to say the man was verra unpleasant about it all; he did strike me and tear my gown. In fact, he knocked me half senseless trying, and by the time I'd come to myself and got decently covered again, the English had gone, taking you along with them.'

Jamie gave a long sigh and closed his eyes briefly. His broad hands rested on his knees and I covered one of them with a gentle squeeze. He took my hand and opened his eyes, giving me a faint smile of acknowledgement before turning back to his sister.

'All right,' he said. 'But I want to know, Jenny; did ye know when ye went with him that he'd not harm you?'

She was silent for a moment, but her gaze was steady on her brother's face, and at last she shook her head, a slight smile on her lips.

She put out a hand to stop Jamie's protest, and the gull-winged brows rose in a graceful arc of inquiry. 'And if your life is a suitable exchange for my honour, tell me why my honour is not a suitable exchange for your life?' The brows drew together in a scowl, the twin of the one adorning her brother's face. 'Or are you telling me that I may not love you as much as you love me? Because if ye are, Jamie Fraser, I'll tell ye right now, it's not true!'

Opening his mouth to reply before she was finished, Jamie was taken suddenly at a loss by this conclusion. He closed his mouth abruptly as his sister pressed her advantage.

'Because I do love ye, for all you're a thick-headed, slack-witted, lack-brained gomerel. And I'll no have ye dead in the road at my feet just because you're too stubborn to keep your mouth shut for the once in your life!'

Blue eyes glared into blue eyes, shooting sparks in all directions. Swallowing the insults with difficulty, Jamie struggled for a rational reply. He seemed to be making up his mind to something. Finally he squared his shoulders, resigned to it.

'All right, then, I'm sorry,' he said. 'I was wrong, and I'll beg your pardon.'

He and his sister sat staring at each other for a long moment, but whatever pardon he was expecting from her was not forthcoming. She examined him closely, biting her lip, but said nothing. Finally he grew impatient.

'I've said I'm sorry! What more d'ye want of me?' he demanded. 'Do ye want me to go on my knees to ye? I'll do it if I must, but tell me!'

She shook her head slowly, lip still caught between her teeth.

'No,' she said at last, 'I'll not have ye on your knees in your own house. Stand up, though.'

Jamie stood, and she set the child down on the loveseat and crossed the room to stand in front of him.

'Take off your shirt,' she ordered.

'I'll not!'

She jerked the shirt tail out of his kilt and reached for the buttons. Short of forcible resistance, clearly he was going to obey or submit to being undressed. Retaining as much dignity as he could, he backed away from her and, tight-lipped, removed the disputed garment.

She circled behind him and surveyed his back, her face displaying the same carefully blank expression I had seen Jamie adopt when concealing some strong emotion. She nodded, as though confirming something long suspected.

'Weel, and if you've been a fool, Jamie, it seems you've paid for it.' She laid her hand gently on his back, covering the worst of the scars.

'It looks as though it hurt.'

'It did.'

'Did you cry?'

His fists clenched involuntarily at his sides. 'Yes!'

Jenny walked back around to face him, pointed chin lifted and slanted eyes wide and bright. 'So did I,' she said softly. 'Every day since they took ye away.'

The broad-cheeked faces were once more mirrors of

each other, but the expression that they wore was such that both Ian and I rose and stepped quietly through the kitchen door to leave them alone. As the door swung to behind us I saw Jamie catch hold of his sister's hands and say something huskily in Gaelic. She stepped into his embrace, and the rough bright head bent to the dark.

27

The Last Reason

We ate like wolves at supper, retired to a large airy bedroom and slept like logs. The sun would have been high by the time we rose in the morning, save that the sky was covered in clouds. I could tell it was late by the bustling feel of the house, as of people going cheerfully about their business, and by the tempting aromas that drifted up the stairs.

After breakfast the men prepared to go out, visiting tenants, inspecting field walls, mending carts and generally enjoying themselves. As they paused in the hall to don their coats, Ian spotted Jenny's large basket resting on the table beneath the hall mirror.

'Shall I fetch home some apples from the orchard, Jenny? 'Twould save ye walking so far.'

'Good idea,' said Jamie, casting an appraising eye at his sister's expansive frontage. 'We dinna want her to drop it in the road.'

'I'll drop *you* where ye stand, Jamie Fraser,' she retorted, calmly holding up the coat for Ian to shrug into. 'Be useful for the once, and take this wee fiend outside wi' ye. Mrs Crook's in the washhouse; ye can leave him there.' She moved her foot, dislodging small Jamie, who was clinging to her skirts and chanting 'up, up' monotonously.

His uncle obediently grabbed the wee fiend around the middle and swept him out the door, upside down and shrieking with delight.

'Ah,' Jenny sighed contentedly, bending to inspect her appearance in the gold-framed mirror. She wet a finger and smoothed her brows, then finished doing up the buttons at her throat. 'Nice to finish dressing wi'out someone clinging to your skirts or wrapped round your knees. Some days I can scarce go to the privy alone, or speak a single sentence wi'out being interrupted.'

Her cheeks were slightly flushed and her dark hair gleamed against the blue silk of her dress. Ian smiled at her, warm brown eyes glowing at the blooming picture she presented.

'Weel, you'll have time to talk wi' Claire, perhaps,' he suggested. He cocked one eyebrow in my direction. 'I expect she's mannerly enough to listen, but for God's sake, dinna tell her any of your poems or she'll be on her way to London before Jamie and I get back.'

Jenny snapped her fingers under his nose, unperturbed by the teasing.

'I'm none too worried, man. Get on wi' ye; Jamie's waiting.'

While the men went about their business, Jenny and I spent the day in the parlour, she stitching, I winding up stray bits of yarn and sorting the coloured silks.

Outwardly friendly, we circled each other cautiously in conversation, watching each other from the corners of our eyes. Jamie's sister, Jamie's wife; Jamie was the central point, unspoken, about which our thoughts revolved.

Their shared childhood linked them for ever, like the warp and the weft of a single fabric, but the patterns of their weave had been loosened, by absence and suspicion, then by marriage. Ian's thread had been present in their weaving since the beginning, mine was a new one. How would the tensions pull in this new pattern, one thread against another?

Our conversation ran on casual lines, but with the words unspoken clearly heard beneath.

'You've run the house here alone since your mother died?'

'Oh, aye. Since I was ten.'

I had the nurturing and the loving of him as a boy. What will you do with the man I helped make?

'Jamie says as you're a rare fine healer.'

'I mended his shoulder for him when we first met.'

Yes, I am capable, and kind. I will care for him.

602

'I hear ye married very quickly.'

Did you wed my brother for his land and money?

'Yes, it was quick. I didn't even know Jamie's true surname until just before the ceremony.'

I didn't know he was laird of this place; I can only have married him for himself.

And so it went through the morning, a light luncheon, and into the hours of the afternoon, as we exchanged small talk, tidbits of information, opinions, small and hesitant jokes, taking each other's measure. A woman who had run a large household since the age of ten, who had managed the estate since her father's death and her brother's disappearance, was not a person to be lightly esteemed. I did wonder what she thought of me, but she seemed as capable as her brother of hiding her thoughts when she chose to.

As the clock on the mantelpiece began to strike five, Jenny yawned and stretched, and the garment she had been mending slid down the rounded slope of her belly on to the floor.

She began clumsily to reach for it, but I dropped to my knees beside her.

'No, I'll get it.'

'Thank ye . . . Claire.' Her first use of my name was accompanied by a shy smile, and I returned it.

Before we could return to our conversation, we were interrupted by the arrival of Mrs Crook, the housekeeper, who poked a long nose into the parlour and inquired worriedly whether we had seen wee Master Jamie.

Jenny laid aside her sewing with a sigh.

'Got away again, has he? Nay worry, Lizzie. He's likely gone wi' his da or his uncle. We'll go and see, shall we, Claire? I could use a breath of air before supper.'

She rose heavily to her feet and pressed her hands against the small of her back. She groaned and gave me a wry smile.

'Three weeks, about. I canna wait.'

We walked slowly through the grounds, Jenny pointing out the brewhouse and the chapel, explaining the history of the estate and when the different bits had been built.

As we approached the corner of the dovecote we heard voices in the arbour.

'There he is, the wee rascal!' Jenny exclaimed. 'Wait till I lay hands on him!'

'Wait a minute.' I laid a hand on her arm, recognizing the deeper voice that underlaid the little boy's.

'Dinna worry yourself, man,' said Jamie's voice. 'You'll learn. It's a bit difficult, isn't it, when your cock doesna stick out any further than your belly button?'

I stuck my head around the corner, to find him seated on a chopping block, engaged in converse with his namesake, who was struggling manfully with the folds of his smock.

'What are you doing with the child?' I inquired cautiously.

'I'm teachin' young James here the fine art of not pissing on his feet,' he explained. 'Seems the least his uncle could do for him.'

I raised one eyebrow. 'Talk is cheap. Seems the least his uncle could do is show him.'

He grinned. 'Well, we've had a few practical demonstrations. Had a wee accident last time, though.' He exchanged accusatory looks with his nephew. 'Dinna look at *me*,' he said to the boy. 'It was all your fault. I *told* ye to keep still.'

'Ahem,' said Jenny dryly, with a look at her brother and a matching one at her son. The smaller Jamie responded by pulling the front of his smock up over his head, but the larger one, unabashed, grinned cheerfully and rose from his seat, brushing wood chips from his breeks. He set a hand on his nephew's swathed head and turned the little boy towards the house.

' "To everything there is a season," ' he quoted, ' "and a time for every purpose under heaven." First we work, wee James, and then we wash. And *then* – thank God – it's time for supper.'

The most pressing matters of business attended to, Jamie took time the next afternoon to show me over the house. Built in 1702, it was indeed modern for its time, with such innovations as porcelain stoves for heating, and a great brick oven built into the kitchen wall, so that bread was no longer baked in the ashes of the hearth. The ground floor hallway, the stairwell and the drawing room walls were lined with pictures. Here and there was a pastoral landscape, or an animal study, but most were of the family and their connections.

I paused before a picture of Jenny as a young girl. She sat on the garden wall, a red-leaved vine behind her. Lined up in front of her along the top of the wall was a row of birds: sparrows, a thrush, a lark and even a pheasant, all jostling and sidling for position before their laughing mistress. It was quite unlike most of the formally posed pictures, in which one ancestor and another glared out of their frames as though their collars were choking them.

'My mother painted that,' Jamie said, noting my interest. 'She did quite a few of the ones in the stairwell, but there are only two of hers in here. She always liked that one best herself.' A large, blunt finger touched the surface of the canvas gently, tracing the line of the red-leaved vine. 'Those were Jenny's tame birds. Any time there was a bird wi' a lame leg or a broken wing, whoever found it would bring it along, and in days she'd have it healed, and eatin' from her hand. That one always reminded me of Ian.' The finger tapped above the pheasant, wings spread to keep its balance, gazing at its mistress with dark, adoring eyes.

'You're awful, Jamie,' I said, laughing. 'Is there one of you?'

'Oh, aye.' He led me to the opposite wall, near the window.

Two red-haired, tartan-clad little boys stared solemnly out of the frame, seated with an enormous staghound. That must be Nairn, Bran's grandfather, Jamie, and his older brother Willy, who had died of the smallpox at eleven. Jamie could not have been more than two when it was painted, I thought; he stood between his elder brother's knees, one hand resting on the dog's head.

Jamie had told me about Willy during our journey from Leoch, one night by the fire at the bottom of a lonely glen.

605

I remembered the small snake, carved of cherrywood, that he had drawn from his sporran to show me.

'Willy gave it me for my fifth birthday,' he had said, finger gently stroking the sinuous curves. It was a comical little snake, body writhing artistically, and its head turned back to peer over what would have been its shoulder, if snakes had shoulders.

Jamie handed me the little wooden object, and I turned it over curiously.

'What's this scratched on the underside? S-a-w-n-y. Sawny?'

'That's me,' Jamie said, ducking his head as though mildly embarrassed. 'It's a pet name, like, a play on my second name, Alexander. It's what Willy used to call me.'

The faces in the picture were very much alike; all the Fraser children had that forthright look that dared you to take them at less than their own valuation of themselves. In this portrait, though, Jamie's cheeks were rounded and his nose still snubbed with babyhood, while his brother's strong bones had begun to show the promise of the man within, a promise never kept.

'Were you very fond of him?' I asked softly now, laying a hand on his arm. He nodded, looking away into the flames on the hearth.

'Oh, aye,' he said with a faint smile. 'He was five years older than me, and I thought he was God, or at least Christ. Used to follow him everywhere; or everywhere he'd let me, at least.'

He turned away and wandered towards the bookshelves. Wanting to give him a moment alone, I stayed, looking out of the window.

From this side of the house I could see dimly through the rain the outline of a rocky, grass-topped hill in the distance. It reminded me of the fairies' dun where I had stepped through a rock and emerged from a rabbit hole. Only six months. But it seemed like a very long time ago.

Jamie had come to stand beside me at the window. He was silent for a long time, and I made no effort to engage him in conversation, thinking that perhaps his thoughts were still on his dead brother. But apparently they had shifted. Staring absently out at the rain, he abruptly said, 'I told ye once I'd tell you the other reason. Do ye want to know?'

'Reason?' I said stupidly, taken by surprise.

'Why I married you.'

'Which was?' I don't know what I expected him to say, perhaps some further revelation of his family's contorted affairs. What he did say was more of a shock, in its way.

'Because I wanted you.' He turned from the window to face me. 'More than I ever wanted anything in my life,' he added softly.

I continued staring at him, dumbstruck. Whatever I had been expecting, it wasn't this. Seeing my openmouthed expression, he continued lightly. 'When I asked my da how ye knew which was the right woman, he told me when the time came, I'd have no doubt. And I didn't. When I woke in the dark on the way to Leoch, with you sitting on my chest, cursing me for bleeding to death, I said to myself, "Jamie Fraser, for all ye canna see what she looks like, and for all she weighs as much as a good draught horse, this is the woman." '

I started towards him and he backed away, talking rapidly. 'I said to myself, "She's mended ye twice in as many hours, me lad; life amongst the MacKenzies being what it is, it might be as well to wed a woman as can stanch a wound and set broken bones." And I said to myself, "Jamie, lad, if her touch feels so bonny on your collarbone, imagine what it might feel like lower down . . ." '

He dodged around a chair. 'Of course, I thought it might ha' just been the effects of spending four months in a monastery, without benefit of female companionship, but then that ride through the dark together' – he paused to sigh theatrically, neatly evading my grab at his sleeve – 'with that lovely broad arse wedged between my thighs' – he ducked a blow aimed at his left ear and sidestepped, getting a low table between us – 'and that rock-solid head thumping me in the chest' – a small metal ornament bounced off his own head and went clanging to the floor – 'I said to myself . . .'

He was laughing so hard at this point that he had to gasp for breath between phrases. 'Jamie . . . I said . . . for all she's a Sassenach bitch . . . with a tongue like an adder's . . . with a bum like that . . . what does it matter if she's a f-face like a sh-sh-sheep?'

I tripped him neatly and landed on his stomach with both knees as he hit the floor with a crash that shook the house.

'You mean to tell me that you married me out of love?' I demanded. He raised his eyebrows, struggling to draw in breath.

'Have I not . . . just been . . . saying so?'

Grabbing me round the shoulders with one arm, he wormed the other hand under my skirt and proceeded to inflict a series of merciless pinches on that part of my anatomy he had just been praising.

Returning to pick up her embroidery basket, Jenny sailed in at this point and stood eyeing her brother with some amusement. 'And what are *you* up to, young Jamie me lad?' she inquired, one eyebrow up.

'I'm makin' love to my wife,' he panted, breathless between giggling and fighting.

'Well, ye could find a more suitable place for it,' she said, raising the other eyebrow. 'That floor'll give ye splinters in your arse.'

If Lallybroch was a peaceful place, it was also a busy one. Everyone in it seemed to stir into immediate life at cock-crow, and the farm then spun and whirred like a complicated bit of clockwork until after sunset, when one by one the cogs and wheels that made it run began to fall away, rolling off into the dark to seek supper and bed, only to reappear like magic in their proper places in the morning.

So essential did every last man, woman and child seem to the running of the place that I could not imagine how it had fared these last few years, lacking its master. Now not only Jamie's hands, but mine as well, were pressed into full employment. For the first time I understood the stern Scottish strictures against idleness that had seemed like mere quaintness before – or after, as the case might be.

Idleness would have seemed not only a sign of moral decay but an affront to the natural order of things.

There were moments, of course. Those small spaces of time, too soon gone, when everything seems to stand still and existence is balanced on a perfect point, like the moment of change between the dark and the light, when both and neither surround you.

I was enjoying such a moment on the evening of the fourth day following our arrival at the farmhouse. Sitting on the wall behind the house, I could see tawny fields to the edge of the cliff past the broch, and the mesh of trees on the hills, dimming to black before the pearly glow of the sky. Objects near and far away seemed to be at the same distance, as their long shadows melted into the dusk.

The air was chilly with a hint of the coming frost and I thought I must go in soon, though I was reluctant to leave the still beauty of the place. I wasn't aware of Jamie approaching until he slid the heavy folds of a cloak around my shoulders. I hadn't realized quite how cold it was until I felt the contrasting warmth of the thick wool.

Jamie's arms came around me with the cloak, and I nestled back against him, shivering slightly.

'I could see ye shivering from the house,' he said, taking my hands in his. 'Catch a chill, if you're not careful.'

'And what about you?' I twisted about to look at him. Despite the increasing bite of the air he looked completely comfortable in nothing but shirt and kilt, with no more than a slight reddening of the nose to show it was not the balmiest of spring evenings.

'Ah, well, I'm used to it. Scotsmen are none so thin-blooded as ye blue-nosed Southrons.' He tilted my chin up and kissed my nose, smiling. I took him by the ears and adjusted his aim downwards.

It lasted long enough for our temperatures to have equalized by the time he released me, and the warm blood sang in my ears as I leaned back, balancing on the wall. The breeze blew from behind me, fluttering strands of hair across my face. He brushed them off my shoulders, spreading the ruffled locks out with his fingers, so the setting sun shone through the strands.

'You look like you've a halo, with the light behind ye that way,' he said softly. 'An angel crowned with gold.'

'And you,' I answered softly, tracing the edge of his jaw where the amber light sparked from his sprouting beard. 'Why didn't you tell me before?'

He knew what I meant. One eyebrow went up and he smiled, half his face lit by the glowing sun, the other half in shadow.

'Well, I knew ye didna want to wed me. I'd no wish to burden you or make myself foolish by telling you then, when it was plain you'd lie with me only to honour vows you'd rather not have made.' He grinned, teeth white in the shadow, forestalling my protest. 'The first time, at least. I've my pride, woman.'

I reached out and drew him to me, pulling him close, so that he stood between my legs as I sat on the wall. Feeling the faint chill of his skin, I wrapped my legs around his hips and enfolded him with the wings of my cloak. Under the sheltering fabric, his arms came tight around me, pressing my cheek against the smudged cambric of his shirt.

'My love,' he whispered. 'Oh, my love. I do want ye so.'

'Not the same thing, is it?' I said. 'Loving and wanting, I mean.'

He laughed a little huskily. 'Damn close, Sassenach, for me, at least.' I could feel the strength of his wanting, hard and urgent. He stepped back suddenly and, stooping, lifted me from the wall.

'Where are we going?' We were headed away from the house, towards the cluster of sheds in the shadow of the elm grove.

'To find a hay loft.'

28

Kisses and Drawers

I gradually found my own place in the running of the estate. As Jenny could no longer manage the long walk to the tenants' cottages, I took to visiting them myself, accompanied sometimes by a stable lad, sometimes by Jamie or Ian. I took food and medicines with me, treated the sick as best I could, and made suggestions as to the improvement of health and hygiene, which were received with varying degrees of grace.

At Lallybroch itself I poked about the house and grounds, making myself useful wherever I could, mostly in the gardens. Besides the lovely little ornamental garden the house had a small herb garden and an immense kitchen garden or kailyard that supplied leeks, cabbages and vegetable marrows.

Jamie was everywhere; in the study with the account books, in the fields with the tenants, in the stable with Ian, making up for lost time. There was something more than duty or interest in it, too, I thought. We would have to leave soon; he wanted to set things running in a direction that would continue while he was gone, until he – until *we* – could return for good.

I knew we would have to leave, yet surrounded by the peaceful house and grounds of Lallybroch and the cheerful company of Jenny, Ian and small Jamie, I felt as though I had come home at last.

After breakfast one morning Jamie rose from the table, announcing that he thought he would go as far as the head of the valley to see a pony that Martin Mack had for sale.

Jenny turned from the sideboard, brows drawn together.

'D'ye think it safe, Jamie? There's been English patrols all through the district the last month or so.'

He shrugged, taking his coat from the chair where he had laid it.

'I'll be careful.'

'Oh, Jamie,' said Ian, coming in with an armful of firewood for the hearth. 'I meant to ask – can ye gang up to the mill this morning? Jock was up yestere'en to say something's gone amiss wi' the wheel. I had a quick look, but he and I together couldna shift it. I think there's a bit o' rubbish stuck in the works outside, but it's well under the water.'

He stamped his wooden leg lightly, smiling at me.

'I can still walk, thank God, and ride as well, but I canna swim. I just thrash about, and gang in circles like a spider wi' four legs.'

Jamie laid the coat back on the chair with a smile at his brother-in-law's description.

'None so bad, Ian, if it keeps ye from havin' to spend the morning in a freezing millpond. Aye, I'll go.' He turned to me.

'Care to walk up wi' me, Sassenach? It's a fine morning, and ye can bring your wee basket.' He cocked an ironic eye at the enormous withy basket I used for gathering. 'I'll go and change my sark. Be wi' ye in a moment.' He headed for the staircase and bounded athletically up the steps, three at a time.

Ian and I exchanged smiles. If there was any regret that such feats were now beyond him, it was hidden beneath his pleasure in seeing Jamie's exuberance.

'It's good to have him back,' he said.

'I only wish we could stay,' I said with regret.

The soft brown eyes filled with alarm. 'Ye'll no be going at once, surely?'

I shook my head. 'No, not at once. But we'll need to leave well before the snow comes.' Jamie had decided that our best course was to go to Beauly, seat of Clan Fraser. Perhaps his grandfather, Lord Lovat, could be of help; if not, he might at least arrange us passage to France.

Ian nodded, reassured. 'Oh, aye. But you've a few weeks yet.'

*

It was a beautiful bright autumn day, with air like cider and a sky so blue you could drown in it. We walked slowly so that I could keep an eye out for mushrooms, chatting casually.

'It's Quarter Day next week,' Jamie remarked. 'Will your new gown be ready then?'

'I expect so. Why, is it an occasion?'

He smiled down at me, taking the basket while I stooped to pull up a stalk of tansy.

'Oh, in a way. Nothing like Callum's great affairs, to be sure, but all the Lallybroch tenants will come to pay their rents – and their respects to the new Lady Lallybroch.'

'I expect they'll be surprised you've married an English-woman.'

'I reckon there are a few fathers might be disappointed at that; I'd courted a lass or two hereabouts before I got arrested and taken to Fort William.'

'Sorry you didn't wed a local girl?' I asked coquettishly.

'If ye think I'm going to say "yes", and you standin' there holding a pruning knife,' he remarked, 'you've less opinion of my good sense than I thought.'

I dropped the pruning knife, which I'd taken to dig with, stretched my arms out and stood waiting. When he released me at last, I stooped to pick up the knife again, saying teasingly, 'I always wondered how it was you stayed a virgin so long. Are the girls in Lallybroch all plain, then?'

'No,' he said, squinting up into the morning sun. 'It was mostly my father was responsible for that. We'd stroll over the fields in the evenings, sometimes, he and I, and talk about things. And once I got old enough for such a thing to be a possibility, he told me that a man must be responsible for any seed he sows, for it's his duty to take care of a woman and protect her. And if I wasna prepared to do that, then I'd no right to burden a woman with the consequences of my own actions.'

He glanced behind us towards the house. And towards the small family graveyard, near the foot of the broch, where his parents were buried.

'He said the greatest thing in a man's life is to lie wi' a

woman he loves,' he said softly. He smiled at me, eyes blue as the sky overhead. 'He was right.'

I touched his face lightly, tracing the broad sweep downwards from cheek to jaw.

'Rather hard on you, though, if he expected you to wait so long to marry,' I said.

Jamie grinned, kilt flapping round his knees in the brisk autumn breeze.

'Well, the Church does teach that self-abuse is a sin, but my father said he thought that if it came to a choice between abusin' yourself or some poor woman, a decent man might choose to make the sacrifice.'

When I stopped laughing I shook my head and said, 'No. No, I won't ask. You did stay a virgin, though.'

'Strictly by the grace of God and my father, Sassenach. I dinna think I thought much about anything but the lasses, once I turned fourteen or so. But that was when I was sent to foster wi' Dougal at Beannachd.'

'No girls there?' I asked. 'I thought Dougal had daughters.'

'Aye, he has. Four. The two younger are no much to look at, but the eldest was a verra handsome lassie. A year or two older than me, Molly was. And not much flattered by my attention, I dinna think. I used to stare at her across the supper table, and she'd look down her nose at me and ask did I have the catarrh? Because if so, I should go to bed, and if not, she would be much obliged if I'd close my mouth, as she didna care to look at my tonsils while she was eating.'

'I begin to see how you stayed a virgin,' I said, hiking my skirts to climb a stile. 'But they can't all have been like that.'

'No,' he said reflectively, giving me a hand over the stile. 'No, they weren't. Molly's younger sister, Tabitha, was a bit friendlier.' He smiled reminiscently.

'Tibby was the first girl I kissed. Or perhaps I should say the first girl who kissed me. I was carrying two pails of milk for her, from the barn to the dairy, plotting all the way how I'd get her behind the door, where there wasna room to get away, and kiss her there. But my hands were full, and she had to open the door for me to go through. So it was me ended up behind the door, and Tib who walked up to me, took me by both ears and kissed me. Spilled the milk, too,' he added.

'Sounds a memorable first experience,' I said, laughing.

'I doubt I was *her* first,' he said, grinning. 'She knew a lot more about it than I did. But we didna get much practice; a day or two later her mother caught us in the pantry. She didna do more than give me a sharpish look and tell Tibby to go and set the table for dinner, but she must have told Dougal about it.'

If Dougal MacKenzie had been quick to resent an insult to his sister's honour, I could only imagine what he might have done in defence of his daughter.

'I shudder to think,' I said, grinning.

'So do I,' said Jamie, shuddering. He shot me a sidelong glance, looking shy.

'You'll know that young men in the morning, sometimes they wake up with . . . well, with' – he was blushing.

'Yes, I know,' I said. 'So do old men of twenty-three. You think I don't notice? You've brought it to my attention often enough.'

'Mmmphm. Well, the morning after Tib's mother caught us, I woke up just at dawn. I'd been dreaming about her – Tib, I mean, not her mother – and I wasna surprised to feel a hand on my cock. What was surprising was that it wasn't mine.'

'Surely it wasn't Tibby's?'

'Well, no, it wasna. It was her father's.'

'Dougal?! Whatever – ?'

'Well, I opened my eyes wide and he smiled down at me, verra pleasant. And then he sat on the bed and we had a nice little chat, uncle and nephew, foster-father to foster-son. He said how much he was enjoying my being there, him not having a son of his own, and all that. And how his family was all so fond of me, and all. And how he would hate to think that there might be any advantage taken of such fine, innocent feelings as his daughters might have

615

towards me, but how of course he was so pleased that he could trust me as he would his own son.

'And all the time he was talking and me lying there, he had his one hand on his dirk, and the other resting on my fine young balls. So I said yes, Uncle, and no, Uncle, and when he left, I rolled myself up in the quilt and dreamed about pigs. And I didna kiss a girl again until I was sixteen, and went to Leoch.'

He looked over at me, smiling. His hair was laced back with a leather thong, but the shorter ends were sticking up at the crown as usual, glimmering red and gold in the brisk, clear air. His skin had darkened to a golden bronze during our journey from Leoch and Craigh na Dun, and he looked like an autumn leaf, swirling joyfully wind-borne.

'And what of you, my bonny Sassenach?' he asked, grinning. 'Did ye have the wee laddies panting at your heels, or were ye shy and maidenly?'

'A bit less than you,' I said circumspectly. 'I was eight.'

'Jezebel. Who was the lucky lad?'

'The dragoman's son. That was in Egypt. He was nine.'

'Och, well, you're no to blame then. Led astray by an older man. And a bloody heathen, no less.'

The mill came into sight below, picture-pretty, with a deep-red vine glowing up the side of the harled yellow wall, and shutters standing open to the daylight, tidy in spite of the worn green paint. The water gushed happily down the sluice under the idle water-wheel into the millpond. There were even ducks on the pond, teal and goldeneye.

'Look,' I said, pausing at the top of the hill, putting a hand on Jamie's arm to stop him. 'Isn't it lovely?'

'Be a sight more lovely if the water-wheel were turnin',' he said practically. Then he glanced down at me and smiled.

'Aye, Sassenach. It's a bonny place. I used to swim here when I was a lad – there's a wide pool round the bend of the stream.'

A little further down the hill, the pool became visible through the screen of willows. So did the boys. There were four of them, sporting and splashing and yelling, all naked as jays.

'Brr,' I said, watching them. The weather was fine for autumn, but there was enough of a nip in the air to make me glad of the shawl I'd brought. 'It makes my blood run cold, just to see them.'

'Och?' Jamie said. 'Well, let me warm it for ye then.'

With a glance down at the boys in the stream he stepped back into the shade of a big tree, put his hands about my waist and drew me into the shadow after him.

'Ye werena the first lass I kissed,' he said softly. 'But I swear you'll be the last.' And he bent his head to my upturned face.

Once the miller had emerged from his lair, and hasty introductions were made, I retired to the bank of the millpond while Jamie spent several minutes listening to an explanation of the problem. As the miller went back into the millhouse, to try turning the stone from within, Jamie stood a moment, staring into the dark, weedy depths of the millpond. Finally, with a shrug of resignation, he began to strip off his clothes.

'No help for it,' he remarked to me. 'Ian's right; there's something stuck in the wheel under the sluice. I'll have to go down and – ' Stopped by my gasp, he turned around to where I sat on the bank with my basket.

'And what's amiss wi' *you*?' he demanded. 'Have ye no seen a man in his drawers before?'

'Not . . . not like . . . *that*!' I managed to get out, between sputters. Anticipating possible submergence, he had donned beneath his kilt a short garment of incredible elderliness, originally of red flannel, now patched with a dazzling array of colours and textures. Obviously this pair of drawers had originally belonged to someone several inches more around the middle than Jamie. They hung precariously from his hipbones, the folds drooping in Vs over his flat belly.

'Your grandfather's?' I guessed, making a highly unsuccessful effort to suppress my giggling. 'Or your grandmother's?'

'My father's,' he said coldly, looking down his nose at me. 'Ye dinna expect me to be swimming bare as an egg before my wife and my tenants, do ye!'

617

With considerable dignity he gathered the excess material up in one hand and waded into the millpond. Treading water near the wheel, he took his bearings, then with a deep breath, upended and submerged, my last sight of him the ballooning bottom of the red flannel drawers. The miller, leaning out of the millhouse window, shouted encouragement and directions whenever Jamie's wet head broke the surface for air.

The pond bank was crowded with plants, and I foraged with my digging stick, finding the roots of coltsfoot and butterbur, dandelion and soapwort. I had half the basket filled when I heard a polite cough behind me.

She was a very old lady indeed, or at least she looked it. She leaned on a hawthorn stick, enveloped in garments she must have worn twenty years before, now much too voluminous for the shrunken frame inside them.

'Good morn to ye,' she said, nodding a head like a bobbin. She wore a starched white kertch that hid most of her hair, but a few wisps of iron grey peeped out beside cheeks like withered apples.

'Good morning,' I said and started to scramble up, but she advanced a few steps and sunk down beside me with surprising grace. I hoped she could get up again.

'I'm – ' I started, but had barely opened my mouth when she interrupted.

'Ye'll be the new lady, o' course. I'm Mrs MacNab – Grannie MacNab, they call me, along o' my daughters-in-law all bein' Mrs MacNabs as weel.' She reached out a skinny hand and pulled my basket towards her, peering into it.

'Coltsfoot root – ah, that's good for cough.' She pulled the basket on to her lap and pawed expertly through the remaining plants, while I watched with a mixture of amusement and irritation. At last, satisfied, she handed it back.

'Weel, you're none sae foolish, for a Sassenach lassie,' she remarked. 'Ye ken caraway from cowbane, at least.' She cast a glance towards the pond, where Jamie's head appeared briefly, sleek as a seal, before disappearing once again beneath the millhouse. 'I see Lallybroch didna wed ye for your face alone.'

'Thank you,' I said, choosing to construe this as a compliment. The old lady's eyes, sharp as needles, were fastened on my midsection.

'Not wi' child yet?' she demanded. 'Raspberry leaves, that's the thing. Steep a handful wi' rosehips and drink it when the moon's waxing, from the quarter to the full.'

'Oh,' I said. 'Well – '

'I'd a bit of a favour to ask your man,' the old lady went on. 'But as I see he's a bit occupied at present, I'll tell *you* about it.'

'All right,' I agreed weakly, not seeing how I could stop her anyway.

'It's my grandson,' she said, fixing me with small grey eyes the size and shininess of marbles. 'My grandson Rabbie, that is; I've sixteen altogether, and the three o' them named Robert, but the one's Bob and t'other Rob, and the wee one's Rabbie.'

'Congratulations,' I said politely.

'I want Lallybroch to take the lad on as stable lad,' she went on.

'Well, I can't say – '

'It's his father, ye ken,' she said, leaning forward confidentially. 'Not as I'll say there's aught wrong wi' a bit o' firmness; spare the rod and spoil the child, I've said often enough, and the good Lord kens weel enough that boys were meant to be smacked, or he'd not ha' filled 'em sae full o' the De'il. But when it comes to layin' a child out on the hearth, and a bruise on his face the size o' my hand, and for naught more than takin' an extra bannock from the platter, then – '

'Rabbie's father beats him, you mean?' I interrupted.

The old lady nodded, pleased with my ready intelligence. 'To be sure. Is that no what I've been sayin'?' She held up a hand. 'Now, in the regular way, o' course I'd not interfere. A man's son's his ain to do as he sees fit wi', but . . . weel, Rabbie's a bit of a favourite o' mine. And it's no the lad's fault as his father's a drunken sot, shameful as 'tis for his own mother to say such a thing.'

She raised an admonitory finger like a stick. 'Not but what Ronald's father didna take a drop too much from time to time. But lay a hand on me or the bairns he never did – not after the first time, at any rate,' she added thoughtfully. She twinkled suddenly at me, little cheeks round and firm as summer apples, so I could see what a very lively and attractive girl she must have been.

'He struck me the once,' she confided, 'and I snatched the girdle off the fire and crowned him wi' it.' She rocked back and forth, laughing. 'Thought I'd kilt him for sure, and me wailin' and holdin' of his heid in my lap, thinkin' what would I do, a widow wi' twa bairns to feed? But he came round,' she said matter of factly, 'and ne'er laid a hand on me or the bairns again. I bore thirteen, ye ken,' she said proudly. 'And raised ten.'

'Congratulations,' I said, meaning it.

'Raspberry leaves,' she said, laying a confiding hand on my knee. 'Mark me, lassie, raspberry leaves will do it. And if not, come to see me, and I'll make ye a bittie drink that'll draw yer man's seed straight up into the womb, ye ken, and you'll be swellin' like a ewe wi' triplets by Easter.'

I coughed, growing a bit red in the face. 'Mmmphm. And you want Jamie, er, Lallybroch I mean, to take your grandson into his house as stable lad, to get him away from his father?'

'Aye, that's it. Now he's a braw wee worker, is Rabbie, and Lallybroch will no be – '

The old lady's face froze in the midst of her animated conversation. I turned to look over my shoulder, and froze as well. Redcoats. Dragoons, six of them, on horseback, making their way carefully down the hill towards the mill-house.

With admirable presence of mind Mrs MacNab stood up and sat down again on top of Jamie's discarded clothes, her spreading skirts hiding everything.

There was a splash and an explosive gasp from the mill-pond behind me as Jamie surfaced again. I was afraid to call out or move, for fear of attracting the dragoons' attention to the pond, but the sudden dead silence behind me told me he had seen them. The silence was broken by a single word travelling across the water, softly spoken, but heartfelt in its sincerity.

'*Merde*,' he said.

The old lady and I sat unmoving, stone-faced, watching the soldiers come down the hill. At the last moment, as they made the final turn around the millhouse path, she turned swiftly to me and laid a stick-straight finger across her withered lips. I mustn't speak and let them hear that I was English. I didn't have time even to nod in acknowledgement before the mud-caked hooves came to a halt a few feet away.

'Good morrow to you, ladies,' said the leader. He was a corporal, but not, I was pleased to see, Corporal Hawkins. A quick glance showed me that none of the men were among those I had seen at Fort William, and I relaxed my grip on the handle of my basket just a fraction.

'We saw the mill from above,' the dragoon said, 'and thought perhaps to purchase a sack of meal?' He divided a bow between us, not sure who to address.

Mrs MacNab was frosty, but polite.

'Good morrow,' she said, inclining her head. 'But if ye've come for meal, I fear me ye'll be sair disappointit. The millwheel's nae workin' just now. Perhaps next time ye come this way.'

'Oh? What's amiss, then?' The corporal, a short young man with a fresh complexion, seemed interested. He walked down to the edge of the pond to peer at the wheel. The miller, popping up in the mill to report the latest progress with the millstone, saw him and hastily popped back down out of sight.

The corporal called to one of his men. Climbing up the slope, he gestured to the other soldier, who obligingly stooped to let the corporal climb on his back. Reaching up, he managed to catch the edge of the roof with both hands, and squirmed up on to the heather thatch. Standing, he could barely reach the edge of the great wheel. He reached out and rocked it with both hands. Bending down, he shouted through the window to the miller to try turning the millstone by hand.

I willed myself to keep my eyes away from the bottom of the sluice. I wasn't sufficiently familiar with the workings of waterwheels to know for sure, but I was afraid that if the wheel gave way suddenly, anything near the underwater works might be crushed. Apparently this was no idle fear, for Mrs MacNab spoke sharply to one of the soldiers near us.

'Ye should ca' your master doon now, laddie. He'll do no good tae the mill or himsel'. Ye shouldna meddle wi' things as ye dinna understand.'

'Oh, you've no cause for worry, missus,' said the soldier casually. 'Corporal Silvers' father has a wheat mill in Hampshire. What the corporal doesn't know about waterwheels would fit in me shoe.'

Mrs MacNab and I exchanged looks of alarm. The corporal, after a bit more clambering up and down and exploratory rockings and pokings, came down to where we sat. He was perspiring freely, and wiped his red face with a large, grubby handkerchief before addressing us.

'I can't move it from above, and that fool of a miller doesn't seem to speak any English at all.' He glanced at Mrs MacNab's sturdy stick and gnarled limbs, then at me. 'Perhaps the young lady could come and talk to him for me?'

Mrs MacNab stretched out a protective hand, gripping me by the sleeve.

'Ye'll hae to pardon my daughter-in-law, sir. She's gone sair saft in the heid, ever syne her last babe was stillborn. Hasna spoke a word in ower a year, puir lassie. And I canna leave her for a minute, for fear she'll throw hersel' intae the water in her grief.'

I did my best to look soft-headed, no great effort in my present state of mind.

The corporal looked disconcerted. 'Oh,' he said. 'Well . . .' He wandered down to the edge of the pond and stood frowning into the water. He looked just as Jamie had an hour before, and apparently for the same reason.

'No help for it, Collins,' he said to the old trooper. 'I'll have to go under and see what's holding it.' He took off his scarlet coat and began to unfasten the cuffs of his shirt. I exchanged looks of horror with Mrs MacNab. While there might be sufficient air under the millhouse for survival, certainly there was not room to hide very effectively.

I was considering, not very optimistically, the chances of throwing a convincing epileptic fit, when the great wheel suddenly creaked overhead. With a sound like a tree being murdered, the big arc made a swooping half-turn, stuck for a moment, then rolled into a steady revolution, scoops merrily pouring bright streamlets into the sluice.

The corporal paused in his undressing, admiring the arc of the wheel.

'Look at that, Collins! Wonder what was stuck in it?'

As though in answer, something came into sight at the top of the wheel. It hung from one of the scoops, sodden red folds dripping. The scoop hit the stream now churning down the sluice, the object came loose, and Jamie's father's erstwhile drawers floated majestically out on to the waters of the millpond.

The elderly trooper fished them out with a stick, presenting them gingerly to his commander, who plucked them off the stick like a man obliged to pick up a dead fish.

'Hm,' he said, holding up the garment critically. 'Wonder where on earth *that* came from? Must have been caught around the shaft. Curious that something like that could cause so much trouble, isn't it, Collins?'

'Yessir.' The trooper plainly did not consider the interior workings of a Scottish millwheel to be of absorbing interest, but answered politely.

After turning the cloth over a time or two, the corporal shrugged and used it to wipe the dirt from his hands.

'Decent bit of flannel,' he said, wringing out the sopping cloth. 'It'll do to polish tack, at least. Something of a souvenir, eh, Collins?' And with a polite bow to Mrs MacNab and me, he turned to his horse.

The dragoons had barely disappeared from sight over the brow of the hill when a splashing from the millpond heralded the rising from the depths of the resident water sprite.

He was the bloodless white, blue-tinged, of Carrera marble, and his teeth chattered so hard that I could barely make out his first words, which were, in any case, in Gaelic.

Mrs MacNab had no trouble making them out, and her ancient jaw dropped. She snapped it shut, though, and made a low reverence towards the emergent laird. Seeing her, he stopped his progress towards the shore, the water still lapping modestly about his hips. He took a deep breath, clenching his teeth to stop the chattering, and plucked a streamer of duckweed off his shoulder.

'Mrs MacNab,' he said, bowing to his elderly tenant.

'Sir,' she said, bowing back once again. 'A fine day, is it no?'

'A bit b-brisk,' he said, casting an eye at me. I shrugged helplessly.

'We're pleased to see ye back in yer home, sir, and it's our hope, the lads and mysel', as you'll soon be back to stay.'

'Mine too, Mrs MacNab,' Jamie said courteously. He jerked his head at me, glaring. I smiled blandly.

The old lady, ignoring this by-play, folded her gnarled hands in her lap and settled back with dignity.

'I've a wee favour I was wishin' to ask of you,' she began, 'havin' tae do wi – '

'Grannie MacNab,' Jamie interrupted, advancing a menacing half step through the water, 'whatever your wish is, I'll do it. Provided only that ye'll give me back my shirt before my parts fall off wi' cold.'

29

More Honesty

In the evenings, when supper was cleared away we generally sat in the drawing room with Jenny and Ian, talking companionably of this and that or listening to Jenny's stories.

Tonight, though, it was my turn, and I held Jenny and Ian rapt as I told them about Mrs MacNab and the redcoats.

'God kens well enough that boys need to be smacked, or he'd no fill them sae full o' the De'il.' My imitation of Grannie MacNab brought down the house.

Jenny wiped tears of laughter from her eyes.

'Lord, it's true enough. And she'd know it too. What has she got, Ian, eight boys?'

Ian nodded. 'Aye, at least. I canna even remember all their names; seemed like there was always a couple of MacNabs about to hurt or fish or swim with, when Jamie and I were younger.'

'You grew up together?' I asked. Jamie and Ian exchanged wide, complicitous grins.

'Oh, aye, we're familiar,' Jamie said, laughing. 'Ian's father was the factor for Lallybroch, like Ian is now. On a number of occasions during my reckless youth, I've found myself standing elbow to elbow with Mr Murray there, explaining to one or other of our respective fathers how appearances can be deceiving, or failing that, why circumstances alter cases.'

'And failin' *that*,' said Ian, 'I've found myself on the same number of occasions, bent over a gate alongside Mr Fraser there, listenin' to him yell his heid off while waitin' for my own turn.'

'Never!' replied Jamie indignantly. 'I never yelled.'

'Ye call it what ye like, Jamie,' his friend answered, 'but ye were awful loud.'

'Ye could hear the both of ye for miles,' Jenny interjected. 'And not only the yelling. Ye could hear Jamie arguing all the time, right up to the gate.'

'Aye, ye should ha' been a lawyer, Jamie. But I dinna ken why I always let you do the talking,' said Ian, shaking his head. 'You always got us in worse trouble than we started.'

Jamie began to laugh again. 'You mean the broch?'

'I do.' Ian turned to me, motioning towards the west, where the ancient stone tower rose from the hill behind the house.

'One of Jamie's better arguments, that was,' he said, rolling his eyes upwards. 'He told Brian it was uncivilized to use physical force in order to make your point of view prevail. Corporal punishment was barbarous, he said, and old-fashioned, to boot. Thrashing someone just because they had committed an act with whose ram – ramifications, that was it – with whose ramifications ye didn't agree was not at a' a constructive form of punishment . . .'

All of us were laughing by this time.

'Did Brian listen to all of this?' I asked.

'Oh, aye.' Ian nodded. 'I just stood there wi' Jamie, nodding whenever he'd stop for breath. When Jamie finally ran out of words, his father sort of coughed a bit and said "I see". Then he turned and looked out of the window for a little, swinging the strap and nodding his head, as though he were thinking. We were standing there, elbow to elbow like Jamie said, sweating. At last Brian turned about and told us to follow him to the stables.'

'He gave us each a broom, a brush and a bucket, and pointed us in the direction of the broch,' said Jamie, taking up the story. 'Said I'd convinced him of my point, so he'd decided on a more "constructive" form of punishment.'

Ian's eyes rolled slowly up, as though following the rough stones of the broch upwards.

'That tower rises sixty feet from the ground,' he told me, 'and it's thirty feet in diameter, wi' three floors.' He heaved a sigh. 'We swept it from the top to the bottom,' he said, 'and scrubbed it from the bottom to the top. It took five

626

days, and I can taste rotted oat-straw when I cough, even now.'

'And you tried to kill me on the third day,' said Jamie, 'for getting us into that.' He touched his head gingerly. 'I had a wicked gash over my ear, where ye hit me wi' the broom.'

'Oh, weel,' Ian said comfortably, 'that was when ye broke my nose the second time, so we were even.'

'Trust a Murray to keep score,' Jamie said, shaking his head.

'Let's see,' I said, counting on my fingers. 'According to you, Frasers are stubborn, Campbells are sneaky, MacKenzies are charming but sly, and Grahams are stupid. What's the Murrays' distinguishing characteristic?'

'Ye can count on them in a fight,' said Jamie and Ian together, then laughed.

'Ye can too,' said Jamie, recovering. 'You just hope they're on your side.' And both men went off into fits again.

Jenny shook her head disapprovingly at spouse and brother.

'And we havena even had any wine yet,' she said. She put down her sewing and heaved herself to her feet. 'Come wi' me, Claire; we'll see has Mrs Crook made any biscuits to have wi' the port.'

As we were coming back down the hall a quarter of an hour later with trays of refreshments, I heard Ian say, 'You'll not mind then, Jamie?'

'Mind what?'

'That we wed without your consent – me and Jenny, I mean.'

Jenny, walking ahead of me, came to a sudden stop outside the drawing-room door.

There was a brief snort from the loveseat where Jamie lay sprawled, feet propped on a hassock. 'Since I didna tell ye where I was, and ye had no notion when – if ever – I'd come back, I can hardly blame ye for not waiting.'

I could see Ian in profile, leaning over the log basket. His long, good-natured face wore a slight frown.

'Weel, I didna think it right, especially wi' me being crippled . . .'

There was a louder snort.

'Jenny couldna have a better husband, if you'd lost both legs and your arms as well,' Jamie said gruffly. Ian's pale skin flushed slightly in embarrassment. Jamie coughed and swung his legs down from the hassock, leaning over to pick up a scrap of kindling that had fallen from the basket.

'How did ye come to wed anyway, given your scruples?' he asked, one side of his mouth curling up.

'Gracious, man,' Ian protested, 'ye think I had any choice in the matter? Up against a Fraser?' He shook his head, grinning at his friend.

'She came up to me out in the field one day, while I was tryin' to mend a cart that sprang its wheel. I crawled out, all covered wi' muck, and found her standin' there looking like a bush covered wi' butterflies. She looks me up and down and she says – ' He paused and scratched his head. 'Weel, I don't know exactly *what* she said, but it ended with her kissing me, muck notwithstanding, and saying, "Fine, then, we'll be married on St Martin's Day." ' He spread his hands in comic resignation. 'I was still explaining why we couldna do any such thing, when I found myself in front of a priest, saying, "I take thee, Janet" . . . and swearing to a lot of verra improbable statements.'

Jamie rocked back in his seat, laughing.

'Aye, I ken the feeling,' he said. 'Makes ye feel a bit hollow, no?'

Ian smiled, embarrassment forgotten. 'It does and all. I still get that feeling, ye know, when I see Jenny sudden, standing against the sun on the hill, or holding wee Jamie, not lookin' at me. I see her, and I think, *God, man, she can't be yours, not really.*' He shook his head, brown hair flopping over his brow. 'And then she turns and smiles at me . . .' He looked up at his brother-in-law, grinning.

'Weel, ye know yourself. I can see it's the same wi' you and your Claire. She's . . . something special, no?'

Jamie nodded. The smile didn't leave his face, but altered somehow.

'Aye,' he said softly. 'Aye, she is that.'

Over the port and biscuits Jamie and Ian reminisced further about their shared boyhood, and their fathers. Ian's father, William, had died just the past spring, leaving Ian to run the estate alone.

'You remember when your father came on us down by the spring, and made us go wi' him to the smithy to see how to fix an axletree?'

'Aye, and he couldna understand why we kept squirming and shifting about – '

'And he kept asking ye did ye need to go to the privy – '

Both men were laughing too hard to finish the story, so I looked at Jenny.

'Toads,' she said succinctly. 'The two o' them each had five or six toads inside his shirt.'

'Oh, Lord,' said Ian. 'When the one crawled up your neck and hopped out of your shirt into the forge, I thought I'd dic.'

'I cannot imagine why my father didna wring my neck on several occasions,' said Jamie, shaking his head. 'It's a wonder I ever grew up.'

Ian looked consideringly at his own offspring, industriously engaged in piling wooden blocks on top of each other by the hearth. 'I don't quite know how I'm goin' to manage it, when the time comes I have to beat my own son. I mean . . . he's, well, he's so *small.*' He gestured helplessly at the sturdy little figure, tender neck bent to his task.

Jamie eyed his small namesake cynically. 'Aye, he'll be as much a devil as you or me, give him time. After all, I suppose even *I* must ha' looked small and innocent at one point.'

'You did,' said Jenny unexpectedly, coming to set a glass of port in her husband's hand. She patted her brother on the head.

'You were verra sweet as a baby, Jamie. I remember standing with Mother over your cot. Ye canna ha' been more than two, asleep wi' your thumb in your mouth, and we agreed we'd never seen a prettier lad. You had fat round cheeks and the dearest red curls.'

The pretty lad turned an interesting shade of rose, and drained his port at one gulp, avoiding my glance.

'Didna last long, though,' Jenny said, flashing white teeth in a mildly malicious smile at her brother. 'How old were ye when ye got your first thrashing, Jamie? Seven?'

'No, eight,' Jamie said, thrusting a new log into the fire. 'Christ, that hurt. Twelve strokes full across the bum, and he didna let up a bit, beginning to end. He never did.' He sat back on his heels, rubbing his nose with the knuckles of one hand. His cheeks were flushed and his eyes bright from the exertion.

'Once it was over, Father went off a bit and sat down on a rock while I settled myself. Then when I'd ceased howling and got down to a sort of wet snuffle, he called me over to him. Now that I think of it, I can remember just what he said. Maybe you can use it on young Jamie, Ian, when the time comes.' Jamie closed his eyes, recalling.

'He stood me between his knees and made me look him in the face, and said, "That's the first time, Jamie. I'll have to do it again, maybe a hundred times, before you're grown to a man." He laughed a bit then and said, "My father did it to me at least that often, and you're as stubborn and cockle-headed as ever I was."

'He said, "Sometimes, I daresay I'll enjoy thrashing you, depending what you've done to deserve it. Mostly I won't. But I'll do it, nonetheless. So remember it, lad. If your head thinks up mischief, your backside's going to pay for it." Then he gave me a hug and said, "You're a braw lad, Jamie. Go away to the house now and let your mother comfort ye." I opened my mouth to say something to that, and he said, quick-like, "No, I know you don't need it, but *she* does. Get on wi' ye." So I came down and Mother fed me bread with jam on it.'

Jenny suddenly started to laugh. 'I just remembered,' she said, 'Da used to tell that story about you, Jamie, about thrashing you, and what he said to you. He said when he sent ye back to the house after, you came halfway down, then all of a sudden stopped and waited for him.

'When he came down to ye, you looked up at him and said, "I just wanted to ask, Faither – did ye enjoy it this time?" And when he said "no", you nodded and said, "Good. I didna like it much either." '

We all laughed for a minute together, then Jenny looked up at her brother, shaking her head. 'He loved to tell that story. Da always said you'd be the death of him, Jamie.'

The merriment died out of Jamie's face, and he looked down at the big hands resting on his knees.

'Aye,' he said quietly. 'Well, and I was, then, wasn't I?'

Jenny and Ian exchanged glances of dismay, and I looked down at my own lap, not knowing what to say. There was no sound for a moment but the crackling of the fire. Then Jenny, with a quick look at Ian, set down her glass and touched her brother on the knee.

'Jamie,' she said. 'It wasna your fault.'

He looked up at her and smiled a little bleakly.

'No? Who else's, then?'

She took a deep breath and said, 'Mine.'

'What?' He stared at her in blank astonishment.

She had gone a little paler even than usual, but remained composed.

'I said it was my fault, as much as anyone's. For – for what happened to you, Jamie. And Father.'

He covered her hand with his own and rubbed it gently.

'Dinna talk daft, lass,' he said. 'Ye did what ye did to try to save me; you're right, if ye'd not gone wi' Randall, he'd likely have killed me here.'

She studied her brother's face, a troubled frown wrinkling her rounded brow.

'No, I dinna regret taking Randall to the house – not even if he'd . . . well, no. But that wasn't it.' She drew a deep breath again, steeling herself.

'When I took him inside, I brought him up to my room. I – I didna ken quite what to expect – I'd not . . . been wi' a man. He seemed verra nervous, though, all flushed and as though he were not certain himself, which seemed strange to me. He pushed me on to the bed, and then he stood there, rubbing himself. I thought at first I'd really damaged him wi' my knee, though I knew I hadna struck him so hard, really.' The colour was creeping up her cheeks, and she stole a sidelong glance at Ian before looking hastily back at her lap.

'I ken now that he was trying to – to make himself ready. I didna mean to let him know I was frightened, so I sat up straight on the bed and stared at him. That seemed to anger him, and he ordered me to turn round. I wouldna do it, though, and just kept looking at him.'

Her face was the colour of one of the roses by the doorstep. 'He ... unbuttoned himself, and I ... well, I laughed at him.'

'You did what?' Jamie said incredulously.

'I laughed. I mean – ' Her eyes met her brother's with some defiance. 'I kent well enough how a man's made. I'd seen you naked often enough, and Willy and Ian as well. But he – ' A tiny smile appeared on her lips, despite her apparent efforts to suppress it. 'He looked so funny, all red in the face, and rubbing himself so frantic, and yet still only half – '

There was a choked sound from Ian, and she bit her lip, but went on bravely.

'He didna like it when I laughed, and I could see it, so I laughed some more. That's when he lunged at me and tore my dress half off me. I smacked him in the face, and he struck me across the jaw, hard enough to make me see stars. Then he grunted a bit, as though that pleased him, and started to climb on to the bed wi' me. I had just about sense enough left to laugh again. I struggled up on to my knees, and I – I taunted him. I told him I kent he was no a real man, and couldna manage wi' a woman. I – '

She bent her head still further, so the dark curls swung down past her flaming cheeks. Her words were very low, almost a whisper.

'I ... spread the pieces of my gown apart, and I ... taunted him wi' my breasts. I told him I knew he was afraid o' me, because he wasna fit to touch a woman, but only to sport wi' beasts and young lads . . .'

'Jenny,' said Jamie, shaking his head helplessly.

Her head came up to look at him. 'Weel, I did then,' she said. 'It was all I could think of, and I could see that he was fair off his head, but it was plain too that he . . . couldn't. And I stared right at his breeches and I laughed again. And then he got his hands round my throat, throttling me, and I cracked my head against the bedpost, and . . . and when I woke he'd gone, and you wi' him.'

There were tears standing in her lovely blue eyes as she grasped Jamie's hands.

'Jamie, will ye forgive me? I know if I'd not angered him that way he wouldna have treated you as he did, and then Faither – '

'Oh, Jenny, love, *mo cridh*, don't.' He was kneeling beside her, pulling her face into his shoulder. Ian, on her other side, looked as though he had been turned to stone.

Jamie rocked her gently as she sobbed. 'Hush, little dove. Ye did right, Jenny. It wasna your fault, and maybe not mine either.' He stroked her back.

'Listen, *mo cridh*. He came here to do damage, under orders. And it would ha' made no difference who he'd found here, or what you or I might have done. He meant to cause trouble, to rouse the countryside against the English, for his own purposes – and those of the man that hired him.'

Jenny stopped crying and sat up, looking at him in amazement.

'To rouse folk against the English? But why?'

Jamie made an impatient gesture with one hand. 'To find out the folk that might support Prince Charles, should it come to another Rising. But I dinna ken yet which side Randall's employer is on – if he wants to know so those that follow the Prince can be watched, and maybe have their property seized, or if it's that he – Randall's employer – means to go wi' the Prince himself, and wants the Highlands roused and ready for war when the time comes. I dinna ken, and it isna important now.' He touched his sister's hair, smoothing it back from her brow.

'All that's important is that you're not harmed, and I am home. Soon I'll come back to stay, *mo cridh*. I promise.'

She raised his hand to her lips and kissed it, her face glowing. She fumbled in her pocket for a handkerchief and blew her nose. Then she looked at Ian, still frozen by her side, a look of hurt anger in his eyes.

She touched him gently on the shoulder.

'You think I should ha' told you.'

He didn't move, but went on looking at her. 'Aye,' he said quietly. 'I do.'

She put the handkerchief down in her lap and took him by both hands.

'Ian, man, I didna tell ye because I didna wish to lose you too. My brother was gone, and my father. I didna mean to lose my own heart's blood as well. For you are dearer to me even than home and family, love.' She cast a lopsided smile at Jamie. 'And that's saying quite a bit.'

She looked into Ian's eyes, pleading, and I could see love and hurt pride struggling for mastery on his face. Jamie rose then and touched me on the shoulder. We left the room quietly, leaving them together before the dying fire.

It was a clear night, and the moonlight fell in floods through the tall casements. I could not fall asleep myself, and I thought perhaps it was the light also that kept Jamie awake; he lay quite still, but I could tell by his breathing that he was not asleep. He turned on to his back and I heard him chuckle softly under his breath.

'What's funny?' I asked quietly.

He turned his head towards me. 'Oh, did I wake ye, Sassenach? I'm sorry. I was only remembering about things.'

'I wasn't asleep.' I moved closer. The bed had obviously been made for the days when a whole family slept together on one mattress; the gigantic featherbed must have consumed the entire productivity of hundreds of eider ducks, and navigating through the drifts was like crossing the Alps without a compass. 'What were you remembering?' I asked, once I had safely reached his side.

'Oh, about my father, mostly. Things he said.'

He folded his arms behind his head, staring musingly at the thick beams that crossed the low ceiling. 'It's strange,' he said, 'when he was alive I didna pay him much heed. But once he was dead, the things he'd told me had a good deal more influence.' He chuckled briefly again. 'What I was thinking about was the last time he thrashed me.'

'Funny, was it?' I said. 'Anyone ever told you that you have a very peculiar sense of humour, Jamie?' I fumbled through the quilts for his hand, then gave up and pushed them back. He began to stroke my back, and I snuggled next to him, making small noises of pleasure.

'Didn't your uncle beat you, then, when you needed it?' he asked curiously. I smothered a laugh at the thought.

'Lord, no! He would have been horrified at the thought. Uncle Lamb didn't believe in beating children – he thought they should be reasoned with, like adults.' Jamie made a Scottish noise in his throat, indicating derision at this ludicrous idea.

'That accounts for the defects in your character, no doubt,' he said, patting my bottom. 'Insufficient discipline in your youth.'

'What defects in my character?' I demanded. The moonlight was bright enough for me to see his grin.

'Ye want me to list them all?'

'No.' I dug an elbow into his ribs. 'Tell me about your father. How old were you then?' I asked.

'Oh, thirteen – fourteen maybe. Tall and skinny, with spots. I canna remember why I was being thrashed; at that point, it was more often something I'd said than something I'd done. All I remember is we were both of us boiling mad about it. That was one of the times he enjoyed beating me.' He pulled me to him and settled me closer against his shoulder, his arm around me. I stroked his flat belly, toying with his navel.

'Stop that, it tickles. D'ye want to hear, or no?'

'Oh, I want to hear. What are we going to do if we ever

635

have children – reason with them, or beat them?' My heart raced a little at the thought, though there was no sign that this would ever be more than an academic question. His hand trapped mine, holding it still over his belly.

'That's simple. You reason with them, and when you're through I'll take them out and thrash them.'

'I thought you *liked* children.'

'I do. My father liked *me*, when I wasna being an idiot. And he loved me, too – enough to beat the daylights out of me when I *was* being an idiot.'

I flopped on to my stomach. 'All right, then. Tell me about it.'

Jamie sat up and wadded the pillows more comfortably before lying back down, folded arms behind his head again.

'Well, he sent me up to the gate, as usual – he always made me go up first, so I could experience the proper mixture of terror and remorse while I waited for him, he said – but he was so angry, he was right behind me. I was bent over and taking it, then, gritting my teeth and determined I'd make no noise about it – damned if I'd let him know how much it hurt. I was digging my fingers into the wood of the gate rail as hard as I could – hard enough to leave splinters behind – and I could feel my face turnin' red from holding my breath.' He drew a deep breath, as though making up for it, and let it out slowly.

'Usually I'd know when it was going to be over, but this time he didn't stop. It was all I could do to keep my mouth shut; I was grunting wi' each stroke and I could feel the tears starting, no matter how much I blinked, but I held on for dear life.' He was uncovered to the waist, almost glowing in the moonlight, frosted with tiny silver hairs. I could see the pulse beat just below his breastbone, a steady throb just under my hand.

'I don't know how long it went on,' he continued. 'Not that long, likely, but it seemed like a long time to me. At last he stopped a moment and shouted at me. He was beside himself wi' fury, and I was so furious myself I could barely make out what he said at first, but then I could.

'He roared, "Damn you, Jamie! Can ye no cry out? You're

636

grown now, and I dinna mean to beat you ever again, but I want one good yelp out of ye, lad, before I quit, just so I'll think I've made some impression on ye at last!" ' Jamie laughed, disturbing the even movement of his pulse beat.

'I was so upset at that, I straightened up and whirled round and yelled at him, "Weel, why did ye no say so in the first place, ye auld fool! OUCH!!"

'Next thing I knew I was on the ground, wi' my ears ringing and a pain in my jaw where he'd clouted me. He was standing over me, panting, and wi' his hair and his beard all on end. He reached down and got my hand and hauled me up.

'Then he patted my jaw and said, still breathing hard, "That's for calling your father a fool. It may be true, but it's disrespectful. Come on, we'll wash for supper." And he never struck me again. He still shouted at me, but I shouted back, and it was mostly man to man, after that.'

He laughed comfortably, and I smiled into the warmth of his shoulder.

'I wish I'd known your father,' I said. 'Or maybe it's better not,' I said, struck by a thought. 'He might not have liked you marrying an Englishwoman.'

Jamie hugged me closer and pulled the quilts up over my bare shoulders. 'He'd have thought I'd got some sense at last.' He stroked my hair. 'He'd have respected my choice, whoever it was, but you' – he turned his head and kissed my brow gently – 'he would have liked you verra much, my Sassenach.' And I recognized it for the accolade it was.

30

Conversations by the Hearth

Whatever rift Jenny's revelations had caused between her and Ian, it seemed to have healed. We sat for a short time after supper in the parlour next evening, Ian and Jamie talking over the farm's business in the corner, accompanied by a decanter of elderberry wine, while Jenny relaxed at last with her swollen ankles propped on a hassock. I tried to write down some of the receipts she had tossed over her shoulder at me as we whizzed through the day's work, consulting her for details as I scribbled.

TO TREAT CARBUNCLES, I headed one sheet.

Three iron nails, to be soaked for one week in sour ale. Add one handful of cedarwood shavings, allow to set. When shavings have sunk to the bottom, mixture is ready. Apply three times daily, beginning on the first day of a quarter moon.

BEESWAX CANDLES began another sheet.

Drain honey from the comb. Remove dead bees, so far as possible. Melt comb with a small amount of water in a large cauldron. Skim bees, wings and other impurities from surface of water. Drain water, replace. Stir frequently for half an hour, then allow to settle. Drain water, keep for use in sweetening. Purify with water twice more.

My hand was getting tired, and I had not even reached the twisting of wicks and the hanging of candles to dry.

'Jenny,' I called, 'how long does it take to make candles, counting everything?'

She laid her stitching in her lap, considering.

'Half a day to gather the combs, two to drain the

honey – one if it's hot – one day to purify the wax, unless there's a lot or it's verra dirty – then two. Half a day to make the wicks, half a day to melt the wax, pour the moulds and hang them to dry. Say near a week altogether.'

The dim lamplight and the spluttering quill were too much to contend with after the day's labours. I sat down next to Jenny and admired the tiny garment she was embroidering with nearly invisible stitches.

Her rounded stomach suddenly heaved as the inhabitant shifted position. I watched, fascinated. I had never been close for a prolonged period to someone pregnant, and hadn't realized the amount of activity that went on inside.

'Would you like to feel it?' Jenny offered, seeing me staring at her middle.

'Well . . .' She took my hand and placed it firmly on her mound.

'Right there. Just wait a moment; he'll kick again soon. They don't like ye lying back like this, ye know. It makes them restless and they start to squirm.'

Sure enough, a surprisingly vigorous push raised my hand by several inches.

'Goodness! He's strong!' I exclaimed.

'Aye.' Jenny patted her stomach with a touch of pride. 'He'll be bonny, like his brother and his da.' She smiled across at Ian, whose attention had momentarily wandered from the breeding records of ponies to his wife and child-to-be.

'Or even like his good-for-nothing red-heided uncle,' she added, raising her voice slightly and nudging me.

'Hey?' Jamie looked up, distracted from his accounts. 'Were ye speaking to me?'

'I wonder was it the "red-heided" or the "good-for-nothing" that caught his attention,' Jenny said to me, sotto voce, with another nudge.

To Jamie she said sweetly, 'Nothing at all, *mo cridh*. We were just speculating on the possibility that the new one would have the misfortune to resemble his uncle.'

The uncle in question grinned and came across to sit on

the hassock, Jenny amiably moving her feet, then replacing them in his lap.

'Rub them for me, Jamie,' she begged. 'You're better at it than Ian.'

He obliged, and Jenny leaned back and closed her eyes in bliss. She dropped the tiny shirt on her central mound, which continued to heave as though in protest. Jamie stared entranced at the movements, just as I had.

'Isn't it uncomfortable?' he asked. 'Havin' someone turn somersaults in your belly?'

Jenny opened her eyes and grimaced as a long swell arced across her abdomen.

'Mmm. Sometimes I feel my liver's black and blue from bein' kicked. But mostly it's a good feeling, instead. It's like . . .' She hesitated, then grinned at her brother. 'It's hard to describe to a man, you not having the proper parts. I don't suppose I could tell ye what carrying a child feels like, no more than you could tell me what it's like to be kicked in the bollocks.'

'Oh, I could tell ye that.' He promptly doubled up, clasping himself, and rolled his eyes back in his head with a hideous gurgling groan.

'Is that not right, Ian?' he asked, turning his head towards the stool where Ian sat laughing, wooden leg propped on the hearth.

His sister put a delicate foot on his chest and pushed him upright. 'All right then, clown. In that case, I'm glad I havena got any.'

Jamie straightened up and brushed the hair out of his eyes. 'No, really,' he said, interested, 'is it just that the parts are different? Could you describe it to Claire? After all, she's a woman, though she's not borne a child yet.'

Jenny eyed my midriff appraisingly, and I felt that small pang once more.

'Mmm, perhaps.' She spoke slowly, thinking. 'You feel as though your skin is verra thin all over. You feel everything that touches you, even the rubbing of your clothes, and not just on your belly, but over your legs and flanks and breasts.' Her hands went to them unconsciously, curving the lawn over the swelling rounds. 'They feel heavy and full . . . and they're verra sensitive just at the tips.' The small, blunt thumbs slowly circled the breasts and I saw the nipples rise against the cloth.

'And of course you're big and you're clumsy.' Jenny smiled ruefully, rubbing the spot on her hip where she had bumped against the table earlier. 'You take up more room than you're used to.

'Here, though' – her hands rose protectively to the top of her abdomen – 'that's where you feel things most, of course.' She caressed the rounded bulge as though it were her child's skin she stroked, rather than her own. Ian's eyes followed her hands as they moved from top to bottom of the curving hillock, over and over, smoothing the fabric again and again.

'In the early days, it's a bit like belly-gas,' she said, laughing. She poked a toe into her brother's midsection. 'Just there – like little bubbles rippling through your belly. But then later, you feel the child move, and it's like a fish on your line and then gone – like a quick tug, but so soon past you're not sure you felt it.' As though in protest at this description, her unseen companion heaved to and fro, making her abdomen bulge on one side, then the other.

'I imagine you're sure, by this time,' Jamie remarked, following the movement with fascination.

'Oh, aye.' She placed a hand on one bulge, as though to quiet it. 'They sleep, ye know, for hours at a time. Sometimes ye fear they've died, when there's no movement for a long time. Then you try to wake them' – her hand pushed in sharply at the side, and was rewarded immediately by a strong push in the opposite direction – 'and you're happy when they kick again. But it's not just the babe itself. You feel swollen all over, near the end. Not painful . . . just so ripe you could burst. It's as though you need to be touched, verra lightly, all over.' Jenny was no longer looking at me. Her eyes held her husband's, and I knew she was no longer aware of me or her brother. There was an air of intimacy between her and Ian as though this were a story often told, but one of which they never tired.

Her voice was lower now, and her hands rose again to her breasts, heavy and compelling under the light bodice.

'And in the last month or so, the milk begins to come in. You feel yourself filling, just a wee bit at a time, a little each time the child moves. And then suddenly, everything comes up hard and round.' She cupped her belly again. 'There's no pain, then, just a breathless feeling, and then your breasts tingle as though they'll explode if they're not suckled.' She closed her eyes and leaned back, stroking her massive belly, over and over, with a rhythm like the invocation of a spell. It came to me, watching her, that if ever there were such a thing as a witch, then Janet Fraser was one.

The smoky air was filled with the trance over the room; the feeling that lies at the root of lust, the terrible yearning need to join, and create. I could have counted every hair on Jamie's body without looking at him, and knew each one stood erect.

Jenny opened her eyes, dark in the shadows, and smiled at her husband, a slow, rich curve of infinite promise.

'And late in bearing, when the child moves a lot, sometimes there's a feeling like when you've your man inside ye, when he comes to ye deep and pours himself into you. Then, then when that throbbing starts deep inside ye along with him, it's like that, but it's much bigger; it ripples all through the walls of your womb and fills all of you. The child's quiet then, and it's as though it's him you've taken inside you instead.'

Suddenly she turned to me, and the spell was broken. 'That's what they want sometimes, ye know,' she said quietly, smiling into my eyes. 'They want to come back.'

Some time later Jenny rose, floating towards the door with a glance back that pulled Ian after her like iron to true north. She paused near the door for him, looking back at her brother who sat still by the fire hearth.

'You'll see to the fire, Jamie?' She stretched, arching her back, and the curve of her spine echoed the strangely sinuous curve of her belly. Ian's knuckles pressed hard along the length of her back, and ground into the base of her spine, making her groan. And then they were gone.

I stretched too, arms upwards, feeling the pleasant pull of tired muscles. Jamie's hands ran down my sides and rested on the swell of my hips. I leaned back into him, drawing his hands forward, imagining them cupping the gentle curve of an unborn child.

As I turned my head to kiss him I noticed the small form curled in the corner of the settle.

'Look. They've forgotten small Jamie.' The little boy customarily slept on a truckle bed in his parents' room. Tonight he had fallen asleep by the fire while we sat talking over the wine, but no one had remembered to carry him up to his bed. My own Jamie turned me to face him, smoothing my hair away from his nose.

'Jenny never forgets anything,' he said. 'I expect she and Ian do not care for company just now.' His hands went to the fastening at the back of my skirt. 'He'll do where he is for the present.'

'But what if he wakes up?'

The roving hands came up under the now-loose edge of the bodice. Jamie cocked an eyebrow at the recumbent form of his small nephew.

'Aye well. He'll have to learn his job some time, won't he? Ye don't want him to be as ignorant as his uncle was.' He tossed several cushions to the floor before the fire and lowered himself, carrying me with him.

The firelight gleamed on the silvery scars on his back, as though he were in fact the iron man I had once accused him of being, the metal core showing through rents in the fragile skin. I traced the lashmarks one by one, and he shivered under my touch.

'Do you think Jenny's right?' I asked later. 'Do men really want to come back inside? Is that why you make love to us?' A breath of laughter stirred the hair by my ear.

'Well, it's no usually the first thing in my mind when I take ye to bed, Sassenach. Far from it. But then . . .' His hands cupped my breasts softly and his lips closed on one nipple. 'I'd no just say she was completely wrong either.

Sometimes . . . aye, sometimes it would be good, to be inside again, safe and . . . one. Knowing we cannot, I suppose, is what makes us want to beget. If we cannot go back ourselves, the best we can do is to give that precious gift to our sons, at least for a little while . . .' He shook himself suddenly, like a dog flinging water from its coat.

'Pay me no mind, Sassenach,' he murmured. 'I get verra maudlin, drinking elderberry wine.'

31

Quarter Day

There was a light knock on the door and Jenny stepped in, carrying a folded blue garment over her arm and a hat in one hand. She looked her brother over critically, then nodded.

'Aye, the shirt's well enough. And I've let out your best coat for ye; you've grown a bit through the shoulders since I saw ye last.' She cocked her head to one side, considering. 'Ye've done a braw job of it today – up to the neck, at least. Sit ye down over there, and I'll tend to your hair.' She pointed to the stool by the window.

'My hair? What's wrong wi' my hair?' Jamie demanded, putting a hand up to check. Grown now to shoulder length, it was as usual laced back with a leather thong to keep it out of his face.

Wasting no time on chat, his sister pushed him down on to the stool, yanked the thong loose and began to brush him vigorously with two tortoiseshell brushes.

'What's wrong wi' your hair?' she asked rhetorically. 'Weel, now. There's cockleburs in it, for one thing.' She plucked a small brown object delicately from his head and dropped it on the dresser. 'And bits of oak leaf. Where *were* ye yesterday – rootling under the trees like a hog? And more tangles than a skein of washed yarn – '

'Ouch!'

'Be still, *ruadh*.' Frowning with concentration, she picked up a comb and teased out the tangles, leaving a smooth, shining mass of auburn, copper, cinnamon and gold, all gleaming together in the morning sun from the window. Jenny spread it in her hands, shaking her head over it.

'I canna think why the good Lord should waste hair like

645

that on a man,' she remarked. 'Like a red-deer's pelt, in places.'

'It is wonderful isn't it?' I agreed. 'Look, where the sun's bleached it on top, he's got those lovely blond streaks.' The object of our admiration glowered up at us.

'If ye both dinna stop it, I shall shave my head.' He stretched out a threatening hand towards the dresser, where his razor rested. His sister, deft in spite of the enormous bulge of pregnancy, reached out and smacked his wrist with a hairbrush. He yelped, then yelped again as she yanked the hair back into a fistful.

'Keep still,' she ordered. She began to separate the hair into three thick strands. 'I'll make ye a proper cockernonny,' she declared with satisfaction. 'I'll no have ye goin' down to your tenants looking like a savage.'

Jamie muttered something rebellious but subsided under his sister's ministrations. Dexterously tucking in stray bits here and there, she plaited the hair into a thick formal queue, tucking the ends under and binding them securely with thread. Then she reached into her pocket, pulled out a blue silk ribbon and triumphantly tied it in a bow.

'There!' she said. 'Bonny, no?' She turned to me for confirmation, and I had to admit it. The closely bound hair set off the shape of his head and the bold modelling of his face. Clean and orderly, in snowy linen and grey breeches, he cut a wonderful figure.

'Especially the ribbon,' I said, suppressing an urge to laugh. 'The same colour as his eyes.'

Jamie glared at his sister.

'No,' he said shortly. 'No ribbons. This isna France, nor yet King Geordie's court! I dinna care if it's the colour of the Virgin's cloak – no ribbons, Janet!'

'Oh, all right then, fusspot. There.' She pulled the ribbon loose and stood back.

'Aye, ye'll do,' she said with satisfaction. Then she turned her penetrating blue eyes on me.

'Hm,' she said, tapping her foot thoughtfully.

As I had arrived more or less in rags, it had been necessary to make me two new gowns as quickly as possible; one of homespun for daily use, and one of silk for occasions of state such as this. Better at stitching wounds than cloth, I had helped with the cutting and pinning, but been obliged to leave the design and sewing to Jenny and Mrs Crook.

They had done a beautiful job and the primrose yellow silk fitted my torso like a glove, with deep folds rolling back over the shoulders and falling behind in panels that flowed into the luxuriant drape of the full skirt. Bowing reluctantly to my absolute refusal to wear corsets, they had instead ingeniously reinforced the upper bodice with whalebone stays ruthlessly stripped from an old corset.

Jenny's eyes travelled slowly upwards from my feet to my head, where they lingered. With a sigh, she reached for a hairbrush.

'You, too,' she said.

I sat, face burning, avoiding Jamie's eyes as she carefully removed small twigs and bits of leaf from my curls, depositing them on the dresser next to those seined from her brother's hair. Eventually my hair was combed out and pinned up, and she reached into her pocket and pulled out a small lace cap.

'There,' she said, pinning it firmly to the top of my pile of curls. 'Kertch and all. Verra respectable ye look, Claire.'

I assumed this was meant as a compliment, and murmured something in reply.

'Have ye any jewellery, though?' Jenny asked.

I shook my head. 'No, I'm afraid not. All I had were the pearls Jamie gave me for our wedding, and those – ' Under the circumstances of our departure from Leoch, pearls had been the last thing on my mind.

'Oh!' Jamie exclaimed, suddenly reminded. He dug in the sporran resting on the dresser and triumphantly pulled out the string of pearls.

'Where on earth did you get those?' I asked in amazement.

'Murtagh brought them, early this morning,' he answered. 'He went back to Leoch during the trial and got everything he could carry – thinking that we'd need it if we got away. He looked for us on the way here, but of course we'd gone to . . . to the hill, first.'

'Is he still here?' I asked.

Jamie stood behind me to fasten the necklace.

'Oh, aye. He's downstairs eating everything in the kitchen and devilling Mrs Crook.'

Aside from his songs, I had heard the wiry little man say less than three dozen words throughout the course of our acquaintanceship, and the thought of his 'devilling' anyone was incongruous. He must feel remarkably at home at Lallybroch, I thought.

'Who *is* Murtagh?' I asked. 'Besides being your godfather, I mean; is he related to you as well?'

Jamie and Jenny both looked surprised.

'Oh, aye,' the latter replied. She turned to her brother. 'He's – what, Jamie? – Father's second cousin's uncle?'

'Nephew,' he corrected. 'Ye dinna remember? Old Leo had the two boys, and then – '

I put my hands over my ears in a marked manner. This seemed to remind Jenny of something, for she clapped her hands together.

'Earbobs!' she exclaimed. 'I think I've some pearl ones that will just do with that necklace! I'll fetch them directly.' She vanished with her usual light speed.

'Why does your sister call you Roy?' I asked curiously, watching as he tied his stock before the looking glass. He wore the customary expression of a man doing battle with a mortal enemy, common to all men adjusting their neckwear, but he unclamped his lips to grin at me.

'Och, that. It isna the English name Roy. It's a pet name in Gaelic; the colour of my hair. The word's *ruadh* – means red.' He had to spell the word and say it over several times before I could catch any difference.

'Sounds the same to me, Roy,' I said, shaking my head.

Jamie picked up his sporran and began tucking in the loose bits of things that had come out when he pulled out the pearls. Finding a tangled length of fishing line, he upended the bag over the bed, dumping everything in a pile. He began to sort through it, painstakingly winding up the bits of line and string, finding loose fish-hooks and firmly re-embedding them in the piece of cork where they normally rested. I moved over to the bed and inspected the array.

'I've never seen so much rubbish in my life,' I observed. 'You're a regular jackdaw, Jamie.'

'It isna rubbish,' he said, stung. 'I've uses for all these things.'

'Well, the fish lines and the hooks, yes. And the string for snares. Even, stretching a point, the pistol wadding and the balls – you do carry a pistol now and again. And the little snake Willy gave you, I understand that. But the stones? And a snail shell? And a piece of glass? And . . .' I bent closer to peer at a dark, furry mass of *something*.

'What is – it isn't, is it? Jamie, why on earth are you carrying a dried mole's foot in your sporran?'

'Against rheumatism, of course.' He snatched the object from under my nose and stuffed it back in the pouch.

'Oh, of course,' I agreed, surveying him with interest. His face was mildly flushed with embarrassment. 'It must work; you don't creak anywhere.' I picked a small Bible out of the remaining rubble and thumbed through it, while he stowed away the rest of his valuable equipment.

'Alexander William Roderick MacGregor.' I read aloud the name on the flyleaf. 'You said there was a debt owing him, Jamie. What did you mean by that?'

'Oh, that.' He sat down beside me on the bed, took the small book from me and gently flipped the pages.

'I told ye this belonged to a prisoner who'd died at Fort William, no?'

'Yes.'

'I didna know the lad myself; he died a month before I came there. But the doctor who gave it to me told me about him, while he tended my back. I think he needed to tell someone about it, and he couldna speak to anyone in the garrison.' He closed the book, holding it on his knee, and stared out the window at the gay November sunshine.

Alick MacGregor, a lad of eighteen or so, had been arrested for the common offence of cattle-lifting. A fair, quiet lad, he had seemed likely to serve his sentence and be released without incident. A week before his release, though, he had been found hanging in the stable.

'There was no doubt he'd done it himself, the doctor said.' Jamie caressed the leather cover of the small book, drawing one large thumb along the binding. 'And he did not exactly *say* what he thought, himself. But he did say that Captain Randall had had a private conversation with the lad a week before.'

I swallowed, suddenly cold despite the sunshine.

'And you think – '

'No.' His voice was soft and certain. 'I dinna think. I *know*, and so did the doctor. And I imagine the sergeant knew for certain, and that's why he died.' He spread his hands flat on his knees, looking down at the long joints of his fingers. Large, strong and capable; the hands of a farmer, the hands of a warrior. He picked up the small Bible and put it into the sporran.

'I'll tell ye this, *mo duinne*. One day Black Jack Randall will die at my hands. And when he is dead, I shall send back that book to the mother of Alick MacGregor, with word that her son is avenged.'

The air of tension was broken by the sudden reappearance of Jenny, now resplendent in blue silk and her own lace kertch, holding a large box of worn red morocco leather.

'Jamie, the Currans are come, and Willy Murray and the Jeffries. You'd best go down and have a second breakfast with them – I've put out fresh bannocks and salt herring, and Mrs Crook's doing fresh jam cakes.'

'Oh, aye. Claire, come down when you're ready.' Rising hastily, he paused long enough to gather me up for a brief but thorough kiss, and disappeared. His footsteps clattered down the first flight of stairs, slowing on the second to the more sedate pace suitable to a laird's entrance as he neared the ground floor.

Jenny smiled after him, then turned her attention to me. Placing the box on the bed she threw back the lid, revealing a jumbled array of jewels and baubles. I was surprised to see it; it seemed unlike the neat, orderly Jenny Murray whose iron hand kept the household running smoothly from dawn to dusk.

She stirred a finger through the bright clutter, then as though picking up my thought, looked up and smiled at me.

'I keep thinking I must sort all these things one day. But when I was small, my mother would let me rummage in her box sometimes, and it was like finding magic treasure – I never knew what I'd pick up next. I suppose I think if it were all orderly, the magic would go somehow. Daft, no?'

'No,' I said, smiling back at her. 'No, it isn't.'

We rummaged slowly through the box, holding the cherished bits and pieces of four generations of women.

'That was my grandmother Fraser's,' Jenny said, holding up a silver brooch. It was in the shape of a fretworked crescent moon, a small single diamond shining above the tip like a star.

'And this – ' she pulled out a slender gold band, with a ruby surrounded by brilliants. 'That's my wedding ring. Ian spent half a year's wages on it, though I told him he was foolish to do it.' The fond look on her face suggested that Ian had been anything but foolish. She polished the stone on the bosom of her dress and admired it once more before replacing it in the box.

'I'll be happy once the babe is born,' she said, patting her bulge with a grimace. 'My fingers are so swollen in the mornings I can scarcely do up my laces, let alone wear my rings.'

I caught a strange nonmetallic gleam in the depths of the box, and pointed. 'What's that?'

'Oh, those,' she said, dipping into the box again. 'I've never worn them; they don't suit me. But you could wear them – you're tall and queenly, like my mother was. They were hers, ye ken.'

They were a pair of bracelets. Each made from the curving, almost-circular tusk of a wild boar, polished to a deep ivory glow, the ends capped with silver tappets, etched with flowered tracery.

'Lord, they're gorgeous! I've never seen anything so . . . so wonderfully barbaric.'

651

Jenny was amused. 'Aye, that they are. Someone gave them to Mother as a wedding gift, but she never would say who. My father used to tease her now and then about her admirer, but she wouldna tell him, either, just smiled like a cat that's had cream to its supper. Here, try them.'

The ivory was cool and heavy on my arm. I couldn't resist stroking the deep yellow surface, grained with age.

'Aye, they suit ye,' Jenny declared. 'And they go wi' that yellow gown as well. Here are the earbobs – put these on, and we'll go down.'

Murtagh was seated at the kitchen table, industriously eating ham off the end of his dirk. Passing behind him with a platter, Mrs Crook dexterously bent and slid three fresh hot bannocks on to his plate, hardly breaking her stride.

Jenny peered over Murtagh's shoulder at his rapidly emptying plate.

'Don't stint yourself, man,' she remarked. 'There's another hog in the pen, after all.'

'Begrudge a kinsman a bite, do ye?' he asked, not interrupting his chewing.

'Me?' Jenny put both hands on her hips. 'Heavens, no! After all, ye've only had the four helpings so far. Mrs Crook,' she called to the departing housekeeper, 'when you've done wi' the bannocks, fix this starveling man a bowl of parritch to fill in the chinks with. We dinna want him fainting on the doorstep, ye ken.'

When he saw me standing in the doorway he promptly choked on a bite of ham.

'Mmmphm,' he said, by way of greeting, after Jenny had pounded him helpfully on the back.

'Nice to see you too,' I replied, sitting down opposite him. 'Thank you by the way.'

'Mmmphm?' The question was muffled by half a bannock, spread with honey.

'For fetching my things from the castle.'

'Mmp.' He dismissed any notion of thanks with a wave that ended in a reach for the butter dish.

'I brought your wee bits of plant and such as well,' he

said with a jerk of the head at the window. 'Out in the yard, in my saddlebags.'

'You've brought my medicine box? That's wonderful!' I was delighted. Some of the medicinal plants were rare, and had taken no little trouble to find and prepare properly.

'But how did you manage?' I asked. Once I had recovered from the horror of the witchcraft trial, I often wondered how the occupants of the castle had taken my sudden arrest and escape. 'I hope you didn't have any difficulty.'

'Och, no.' He took another healthy bite but waited until it had made its leisurely way down his throat before replying further.

'Mrs Fitz had them put away, like, packed up in a box already. I went to her at the first, ye ken, for I wasna sure what reception I'd get.'

'Very sensible. I don't imagine Mrs Fitz would scream at sight of you,' I agreed. The bannocks were steaming gently in the cool air, and smelt heavenly. I reached for one, the heavy boar's-tooth bracelets clinking together on my wrist. I saw Murtagh's eyes on them and adjusted them so he could see the engraved silver end pieces.

'Aren't they lovely?' I said. 'Jenny said they were her mother's.'

Murtagh's eyes dropped to the bowl of parritch that Mrs Crook had thrust unceremoniously under his nose.

'They suit ye,' he mumbled. Then, returning suddenly to the earlier subject, he said, 'No, she wouldna summon help against me. I was well acquent' wi' Glenna FitzGibbons, some time ago.'

'Oh, a long-lost love of yours, was she?' I teased, enjoying the incongruous thought of him entwined in amorous embrace with the ample Mrs Fitz.

Murtagh glanced up coldly from his parritch.

'That she wasna, and I'll thank ye to keep a civil tongue when ye speak of the lady. Her husband was my mother's brother. And she was sore grieved for ye, I'll ha' ye to know.'

I lowered my eyes, abashed, and reached for the honey to cover my embarrassment. The stone jar had been set in a pot of hot water to liquify the contents, and it was comfortingly warm to the touch.

'I'm sorry,' I said, drizzling the sweet golden fluid over the bannock, watching carefully so as not to spill it. 'I wondered, you know, what she felt like, when . . . when I . . .'

'They didna realize at the first ye were gone,' the little man said matter of factly, ignoring my apology. 'When ye didna come in to dinner, they thought maybe you'd stayed late in the fields and gone up to your bed without eating; your door was closed. And the next day, when there was all the outcry over the taking of Mistress Duncan, no one thought to look for ye. There was no mention of you, only of her, when the news came, and in all the excitement no one thought to look for ye.'

I nodded thoughtfully. No one would have missed me, save those seeking medical treatment; I had spent most of my time in Callum's library while Jamie was away.

'What about Callum?' I asked. I was more than idly curious; had he really planned it, as Geilie thought?

Murtagh shrugged. He scanned the table for further victuals, apparently spotted nothing to his liking, and leaned back, folding his hands comfortably over his lean midriff.

'When he had the news from the village he had the gates closed at once, and forbade anyone from the castle to go down, for fear of being caught up in the moil.' He leaned further back, eyeing me speculatively.

'Mrs Fitz thought to find ye, the second day. She said that she asked all the maids if they'd laid eyes on ye. No one had, but one of the girls said she thought perhaps ye'd gone to the village – maybe you'd taken shelter in a house there.' One of the girls, I thought cynically. The one that knew bloody well where I was.

He belched softly, not bothering to stifle the sound.

'I heard Mrs Fitz turned the castle upside down, then, and made Callum send down a man to the village, once she was sure ye werena to be found. And when they learned what had happened . . .' A faint look of amusement lighted the dark face.

'She didna tell me everything, but I gathered she made Himself's life more of a misery to him than it usually is, naggin' ·at him to send down and free ye by force of arms – and not the least bit of use, him arguin' that it had gone well beyond the point where he could do that, and now it was in the hands o' the examiners, and one thing and another. It must ha' been something to see,' he said reflectively, 'twa wills like that, set one against the other.'

And in the end, it seemed, neither had either triumphed nor given way. Ned Gowan, with his lawyer's gift for compromise, had found the way between them by offering to go himself to the trial, not as representative of the laird but as an independent advocate.

I took a deep breath, almost fearing to ask what must come next. I had tried as hard as I could to forget those last moments near the loch, but the memory of Geillis Duncan was impossible to escape. A murderous woman, and plainly mad, but courageous nonetheless, and linked to me in a way that could not be denied, no matter what I felt for Geillis herself.

'And . . . Mrs Duncan?' I asked softly. Murtagh paused for a moment, long enough to scratch one stubbled cheek, then bent his attention to mopping up the last dribble of honey on his plate with a blunt forefinger.

'Imprisoned,' he said briefly. 'Till the babe's born.'

'Imprisoned? You don't mean . . . not the thieves' hole?' The thought of anyone spending weeks and months in frigid darkness, let alone a pregnant woman, was appalling. The ivory bracelets clicked softly together as I clasped my hands in my lap.

Murtagh shook his head, still not looking at me.

'Nay. In the castle. Callum will keep her under ward, until the time to deliver her to the examiners.' He glanced at me then, with what might be a flicker of compassion.

'Dinna fret yourself; Mrs Fitz will care for her – and the wean, when it's born. She'll find it a good home.'

This thought was a comfort, if a small one. I would trust Mrs Fitz with my own wean, if I had one.

655

'Did she believe I was a witch – Mrs Fitz, I mean?' I asked curiously. Murtagh snorted briefly.

'I've yet to see the auld woman believes in witches, nor the young one, neither. It's men think there must be ill wishes and magic in women, when it's only the natural way of the creatures.'

'I begin to see why you've never married,' I said.

'Do ye, then?' He pushed back his chair abruptly and rose, pulling the plaid forward over his shoulders.

'I'll be off. Gie my respects to the laird,' he said to Jenny as she reappeared from the front hall where she had been greeting tenants. 'He'll be busy, I've nae doubt.'

Jenny handed him a large cloth sack, tied in a knot at the mouth and plainly holding enough provisions for a week.

'A wee bite for the journey home,' she said, dimpling at him. 'Might last ye at least out of sight o' the house.'

He tucked the knot of the sack snugly into his belt and nodded briefly, turning towards the door.

'Aye,' he said, 'and if not, ye'll see the corbies gatherin' just beyond the rise, come to pick my bones.'

'A lot of good they'd get from it,' she answered cynically, eyeing his scrawny frame. 'I've seen more sound flesh on a broomstick.'

Murtagh's dour face remained unchanged, but a faint gleam showed in his eye nonetheless.

'Oh, aye?' he said. 'Weel, I'll tell ye, lass . . .' The voices passed down the hall, mingling in amiable insult and argument, vanishing at last in the echoes of the front hall.

I sat at the table for a moment longer, idly caressing the warm ivory of Ellen MacKenzie's bracelets. At the far-off slam of the door, I shook myself and stood up to take my place as the Lady of Lallybroch.

Usually a busy place, on Quarter Day the manor house simply bristled with activity. Tenants came and went all day. Many came only long enough to pay their rents; some stayed all day, wandering about the estate, visiting with friends, taking refreshment in the parlour. Jenny, blooming in blue silk, and Mrs Crook, starched in white linen, flitted back and forth between kitchen and parlour, overseeing the two maidservants, who staggered to and fro under enormous platters of oatcake, fruitcake, 'crumbly' and other sweets.

Jamie, having introduced me with ceremony to the tenants present in dining room and parlour, then retired into his study with Ian to receive the tenants singly, to confer with them over the needs of the spring planting, to consult over the sale of wool and grain, to note the activities of the estate and to set things in order for the next quarter of the year.

I puttered cheerfully about the place, talking with tenants, lending a hand with the refreshments when needed, sometimes just drifting into the background to watch the comings and goings.

Recalling Jamie's promise to the old woman by the millpond, I waited with some curiosity for the arrival of Ronald MacNab.

He came shortly past noon, riding a slip-jointed garron, with a small boy clinging to his belt behind. I viewed them covertly from the parlour door, wondering just how accurate his mother's assessment had been.

I decided that while 'drunken sot' might be overstating things slightly, Grannie MacNab's general perceptions were acute. Ronald MacNab's hair was long and greasy, carelessly tied back with twine, and his collar and cuffs were grey with dirt. While surely a year or two younger than Jamie, he looked at least fifteen years older, the bones of his face submerged in bloat, small grey eyes dulled and bloodshot.

As for the child, he also was scruffy and dirty. Worse, so far as I was concerned, he slunk along behind his father, keeping his eyes on the floor, cringing when Ronald turned and spoke sharply to him. Jamie, who had come to the door of his study, saw it too, and I saw him exchange a sharp look with Jenny, who was bringing a fresh decanter in answer to his call.

She nodded fractionally and handed over the decanter. Then, taking the child firmly by the hand she towed him towards the kitchen, saying, 'Come along wi' me now, laddie. I believe we've a crumbly or two going wantin'. Or what about a slice of fruitcake?'

Jamie nodded formally to Ronald MacNab, standing aside as the man went into the study. Reaching out to shut the door, Jamie caught my eye and nodded towards the kitchen. I nodded back and turned to follow Jenny and young Rabbie.

I found them engaged in pleasant converse with Mrs Crook, who was ladling punch from the big cauldron into a bowl. She tipped a bit into a wooden cup and offered it to the lad, who hung back, eyeing her suspiciously, before finally accepting it. Jenny went on chatting casually to the lad as she loaded platters, receiving little more than grunts in return. Still, the half-wild little creature seemed to be relaxing a bit.

'Your sark's a bit grubby, lad,' she observed, leaning forward to turn back the collar. 'Take it off, and I'll give it a bit of a wash before ye go.' Grubby was a gross understatement, but the boy pulled back defensively. I was behind him, though, and at a gesture from Jenny, grabbed him by the arms before he could dart away.

He kicked and yowled, but Jenny and Mrs Crook closed in on him as well, and between the three of us we peeled the filthy shirt off his back.

'Ah.' Jenny drew in her breath sharply. She was holding the boy's head firmly under one arm, and the scrawny back was fully exposed. Welts and scabs scored the flesh on either side of the knobby backbone, some freshly healed, some so old as to be only faded shadows lapping the prominent ribs. Jenny took a good grip on the back of the boy's neck, speaking soothingly to him as she released his head. She jerked her head in the direction of the hall, looking at me.

'You'd better tell him.'

I knocked tentatively at the study door, holding a plate of honeyed oatcakes as excuse. At Jamie's muffled bidding I opened the door and went in.

My face as I served MacNab must have been sufficient, for I didn't have to ask to speak privately with Jamie. He

658

stared meditatively at me for a moment, then turned back to his tenant.

'Well then, Ronnie, that will do for the grain allotment. There's the one other thing I meant to speak wi' you about, though. You've a likely lad named Rabbie, I understand, and I'm needing a boy of that size to help in the stables. Would ye be willing for him to come?' Jamie's long fingers played with a goose-quill on the desk. Ian, seated at a smaller table to one side, propped his chin on his fists, staring at MacNab with frank interest.

MacNab glowered belligerently. I thought he had the irritable resentment of a man who isn't drunk but wishes he were.

'No, I've need of the lad,' he said curtly.

'Mm.' Jamie lounged back in his chair, hands folded across his middle. 'I'd pay ye for his services, of course.'

The man grunted and shifted in his chair.

'My mother's been at ye, eh? I said no, and I meant no. The lad's my son, and I'll deal wi' him as I see fit. And I see fit to keep him to hame.'

Jamie eyed MacNab thoughtfully, but turned his attention back to the ledgers without further argument.

Late in the afternoon, as the tenants repaired to the warmer reaches of kitchen and parlour for refreshment before departing, I spotted Jamie from the window, strolling in leisurely fashion towards the cowshed, arm slung about the scruffy MacNab in comradely style. The pair disappeared behind the shed, presumably to inspect something of agricultural interest, and reappeared within a minute or two, coming towards the house.

Jamie's arm was still about the shorter man's shoulders, but seemed now to be supporting him. MacNab's face was an unhealthy grey, slicked with sweat, and he walked very slowly, seeming unable to straighten up all the way.

'Weel, that's good, then,' Jamie remarked cheerfully as they came within earshot. 'Reckon your missus will be glad of the extra money, eh, Ronald? Ah, here's your animal for you – fine-looking beast, is he no?' The moth-eaten garron that had brought the MacNabs to the farm shambled out of the yard where it had been enjoying the hospitality of the estate. A wisp of hay still protruded from the corner of its mouth, jerking irregularly as the beast chewed.

Jamie gave MacNab a hand under the foot to assist him to his seat; much-needed help, by the look of it. MacNab did not speak or wave in response to Jamie's voluble 'God-speeds' and 'safe journeys', but only nodded in a dazed way as he left the yard at a walk, seemingly intent on some secret trouble that absorbed his attention.

Jamie stood leaning on the wall, exchanging pleasantries as other tenants wended their ways homeward, until the untidy figure of MacNab was out of sight over the crest of the hill. He straightened, gazing down the road, then turned and gave a whistle. A small figure in a torn but clean smock and stained kilt crept out from under a hay cart.

'Weel then, young Rabbie,' said Jamie genially. 'Looks as though your father's given his permission for ye to be a stable lad after all. I'm sure as you'll be a hard worker and a credit to him, eh?' Round, bloodshot eyes stared up dumbly out of the dirty face, and the boy made no response at all until Jamie reached out and, grasping him gently by the shoulder, turned him towards the water trough.

'There'll be some supper waiting for ye in the kitchen, laddie. Go and wash a bit first, though; Mrs Crook's a fussy woman. Oh, and Rabbie' – he leaned down to whisper to the lad – 'mind your ears, or she'll do 'em for ye. She scrubbed mine for me this morning.' He put his hands behind his ears and flapped them solemnly at the boy, who broke into a shy smile and fled towards the trough.

'I'm glad you managed it,' I said, taking Jamie's arm to go in to supper. 'With little Rabbie MacNab, I mean. How did you do it, though?'

He shrugged. 'Took Ronald back of the cowshed and fisted him once or twice in the soft parts. Asked him did he want to part wi' his son or his liver.' He glanced down at me, frowning.

'It wasna right, but I couldn't think what else to do. And I didna want the lad to go back wi' him. It wasn't only I'd promised his grannie, either. Jenny told me about the lad's

660

back.' He hesitated. 'I'll tell ye, Sassenach. My father whipped me as often as he thought I needed it, and a lot oftener than I thought I did. But I didna cower when he spoke to me. And I dinna think young Rabbie will lie in bed with his wife one day and laugh about it.'

He hunched his shoulders with that odd half shrug, something I hadn't seen him do in months.

'He's right; the lad's his own son, he can do as he likes. And I'm not God; only the laird, and that's a good bit lower down. Still . . .' He looked down at me with a crooked half smile.

'It's a damn thin line between justice and brutality, Sassenach. I only hope I've come down on the right side of it.'

I put an arm around his waist and hugged him.

'You did right, Jamie.'

'Ye think so?'

'Yes.'

We strolled back towards the house, arms about each other. The whitewashed farm buildings glowed amber in the setting sun. Instead of going into the house, though, Jamie steered me up the slight rise behind it. Here, sitting on a field wall, we could see the whole of the home farm laid out before us.

I laid my head on Jamie's shoulder and sighed. He squeezed me gently in response.

'This is what you were born to do, isn't it, Jamie?'

'Perhaps, Sassenach.' He looked out over the fields and buildings, then looked down, a smile suddenly curving the wide mouth.

'And you, my Sassenach? What were you born for? To be Lady of Lallybroch, or to sleep in the fields like a gypsy? To be a healer, or a don's wife or an outlaw's lady?'

'I was born for you,' I said simply, and held out my arms to him.

'Ye know,' he observed, letting go at last, 'you've never said it.'

'Neither have you.'

'I have. The day after we came. I said I wanted you more than anything.'

'And *I* said that loving and wanting weren't necessarily the same thing,' I countered.

He laughed. 'Perhaps you're right, Sassenach.' He smoothed the hair from my face and kissed my brow. 'I wanted ye from the first I saw ye – but I loved ye when you wept in my arms and let me comfort you, that first time at Leoch.'

The sun sank below the line of black pines, and the first stars of the evening came out. It was mid-November, and the evening air was cold, though the days still kept fine. Standing on the opposite side of the wall, Jamie bent his head, putting his forehead against mine.

'You first.'

'No, you.'

'Why?'

'I'm afraid.'

'Of what, my Sassenach?' The darkness was rolling in over the fields, filling the land and rising up to meet the night. The light of the new crescent moon marked the ridges of brow and nose, crossing his face with light.

'I'm afraid if I start I shall never stop.'

He cast a glance at the horizon, where the sickle moon hung low and rising. 'It's nearly winter, and the nights are long, *mo duinne*.' He leaned across the wall, reaching, and I stepped into his arms, feeling the heat of his body and the beat of his heart.

'I love you.'

32

Hard Labour

A few days later, near sunset, I was on the hill behind the house, digging up the tubers of a small patch of corydalis I had found. Hearing the rustle of footsteps approaching through the grass, I turned, expecting to see Jenny or Mrs Crook come to call me to supper. Instead it was Jamie, hair spiked with dampness from his pre-supper ablutions, still in his shirt, which was knotted together between his legs for working in the fields. He came up behind me and put his arms around me, resting his chin on my shoulder. Together we watched the sun sinking behind the pines, robed in gold and purple glory. The landscape faded quietly around us but we stayed where we were, wrapped in contentment. Finally, as it began to grow dark, I could hear Jenny calling from the house below.

'We'd better go in,' I said, reluctantly stirring.

'Mmm.' Jamie didn't move but merely tightened his hold, still gazing into the deepening shadows as though trying to fix each stone and blade of grass in memory.

I turned to him and slipped my arms around his neck.

'What is it?' I asked quietly. 'Must we leave soon?' My heart sank at the prospect of leaving Lallybroch, but I knew that it was dangerous for us to stay too much longer; another visit from the redcoats could happen at any time, with much more sinister results.

'Aye. Tomorrow, or the day after, at latest. There are English at Knockchoilum; it's twenty miles from here, but that's only two days' ride in fine weather.' I started to turn for the house, but Jamie slid an arm under my knees and lifted me, holding me against his chest.

I could feel the heat of the sun still in his skin and smell the warm dusty scent of sweat and oat grass. He had been helping with the last of the harvesting, and the smell reminded me of a supper the week before, when I knew that Jenny, always friendly and polite, had finally accepted me fully as a member of the family.

Harvesting was gruelling work, and Ian and Jamie were often nodding by the end of supper. On one occasion I had left the table to fetch a brose pudding for dessert, and returned to find both of them sound asleep, and Jenny laughing quietly to herself amid the remains of supper. Ian lay slumped in his chair, chin resting on his chest, breathing heavily. Jamie had laid his cheek on his folded arms and sprawled forward across the table, snoring peacefully between the platter and the peppermill.

Jenny took the pudding from me and served us both, shaking her head at the slumbering men.

'They were yawning so much I wondered, ye know,' she said, 'what would happen if I stopped talking. So I kept quiet, and sure enough, two minutes later they were out, the both of them.' She smoothed Ian's hair tenderly off his forehead.

'That's why there's so few babies born in August here,' she said, with a wicked cock of the eyebrow at me. 'The men can't keep awake long enough in November to start one.' It was true enough, and I laughed. Jamie stirred and snorted next to me, and I laid a hand on the back of his neck to soothe him. His lips curved at once in a soft, reflexive smile, then relaxed into sleep once more.

Jenny, watching him, said, 'That's funny, that is. I've not seen him do that since he was quite small.'

'Do what?'

She nodded. 'Smile in his sleep. He used always to do it, if ye came by and petted him in his cradle, or even later, in his truckle bed. Sometimes Mother and I would take it in turns to stroke his head and see could we make him smile; he always would.'

'That's odd, isn't it?' I experimented, running a hand gently down the back of his head and neck. Sure enough, I was rewarded at once by a singularly sweet smile that lingered for a moment before the lines of his face relaxed once more into the rather stern expression he presented when asleep.

'I wonder why he does that?' I said, watching him in fascination. Jenny shrugged and smiled at me.

'I imagine it means he's happy.'

In the event, we did not leave next day. In the middle of the night I was wakened by low conversation in the room. Rolling over, I saw Ian bending over the bed, holding a candle.

'The babe's on its way,' said Jamie, seeing me awake. He sat up, yawning. 'A bit early, Ian?'

'Ye never know. Small Jamie was late. Better early than late, I reckon.' Ian's smile was quick and nervous.

'Sassenach, can ye deliver a child? Or had I best go for the midwife?' Jamie turned to me, questioning. I didn't hesitate in my answer.

I shook my head. 'Get the midwife.' I had seen only three births during my training; all conducted in a sterile operating room, the patient draped and anaesthetized, nothing visible save the grotesquely swelling perineum and the suddenly emergent head.

Having seen Jamie on his way to fetch the midwife, Mrs Martins, I went up the stairs.

Jenny was sitting in a chair near the window, leaning comfortably back. She had put on an old nightgown, stripped the bed and spread an aged quilt over the feather mattress, and was now just sitting. Waiting.

Ian, hovering nervously over her, was glad to see me. Jenny smiled too, but with a distracted inward look, as though listening to something far off which only she could hear. Ian, fully dressed, fidgeted about the room, picking things up and putting them down, until Jenny at last ordered him to leave.

'Go downstairs and rouse Mrs Crook, Ian,' she said, smiling to ease the dismissal. 'Tell her to get things ready for Mrs Martins. She'll ken what to do.' She drew in her breath sharply then, and put both hands on her distended abdomen. I stared, seeing her belly draw up suddenly tight and round. She bit her lip and breathed heavily for a moment, then relaxed. Her belly had resumed its normal shape, a slightly pendant teardrop, rounded at both ends.

Ian put his hand hesitantly on her shoulder and she covered it with her own, smiling up at him.

'Then tell her to feed ye, man. You and Jamie will be needing a bite to eat. They say the second babe comes faster than the first; maybe by the time you're done wi' breakfast, I'll be ready for a bite myself.'

He squeezed her shoulder tightly and kissed her, murmuring something in her ear before turning to go. He hesitated in the doorway, looking back, but she waved him firmly away.

It seemed a very long time before Jamie arrived with the midwife, and I became more nervous as the contractions grew stronger. Second babies *were* said to be faster, as a rule. What if this one decided to arrive before Mrs Martins?

At first Jenny carried on light conversation with me, only pausing to bend forward slightly, holding her belly, as the contractions tightened their grip. But she quickly lost the urge to talk, and lay back, resting quietly in between the increasingly powerful pains. Finally, after one that almost bent her double in her chair, she rose to her feet, staggering.

'Help me walk a bit, Claire,' she said. Unsure what was the proper procedure, I did as she said, grasping her tightly under the arm to help her stand upright. We made several slow circuits of the room, pausing when a contraction struck, going on when it eased. Shortly before the midwife arrived, Jenny made her way to the bed and lay down.

Mrs Martins was a reassuring-looking person; tallish and thin, she had wide shoulders and muscular forearms, and the sort of kind, down-to-earth expression that invited confidence. Two vertical creases between her iron-grey brows, always visible, deepened when she was concentrating.

They stayed shallow as she made her preliminary examination. Everything normal so far, then. Mrs Crook had produced a pile of clean, ironed sheets for our use and Mrs Martins took one of these, still folded, and pushed it under

Jenny. I was startled to see the dark stain of blood between her thighs as she raised herself slightly.

Seeing my look, Mrs Martins nodded reassuringly.

'Aye. Bloody show, it's called. It's all right. It's only when the blood is bright red, and a terrible lot all at once, that ye worry. There's nothing wrong.'

We all settled down to wait. Mrs Martins talked quietly and comfortingly to Jenny, rubbing the small of her back, pressing hard during the contractions. As the pains became more frequent Jenny began to clamp her lips together and snort heavily through her nose. Often, there was a deep, faint groan as the full force of the pain came on.

Jenny's hair was soaked with perspiration by this time, and her face bright red with the strain. Watching her, I realized fully why it was called labour. Giving birth was bloody hard work.

Over the next two hours little progress appeared to be made, except that the pains grew obviously stronger. Able at first to answer questions, Jenny stopped responding, lying panting at the end of each contraction, face fading from red to white in a matter of seconds.

She clamped her lips through the next one, beckoning me to her side as it eased.

'If the child lives . . .' she said, gasping for air, 'and it's a girl . . . her name is Margaret. Tell Ian . . . name her Margaret Ellen.'

'Yes, of course,' I soothed. 'But you'll be able to tell him yourself. It won't be long now.'

She only shook her head in determined negation and clenched her teeth as the next pain came. Mrs Martins took me by the arm, steering me away.

'Dinna mind it, lassie,' she said matter of factly. 'They always think they're goin' to die about now.'

'Oh,' I said, mildly relieved.

'Mind ye,' she said, in a lower voice, 'sometimes they do.'

Even Mrs Martins seemed a trifle worried as the pains went on with no appreciable progress. Jenny was tiring badly; as each pain eased, her body went slack, and she even dozed off as though seeking escape in small intervals of sleep. Then as the remorseless fist grasped her once again she would wake fighting and groaning with effort, writhing to the side to curl protectively over the rigid lump of the unborn child.

'Could the child be backwards?' I asked in a low voice, shy about suggesting such a thing to an experienced midwife. Mrs Martins seemed not at all offended by the suggestion, though; the lines between her brows merely deepened as she looked at the straining woman.

When the next pain eased, Mrs Martin flung back the sheet and nightgown, and went rapidly to work, pressing here and there on the huge mound with quick, skilled fingers. It took several tries, as the probing seemed to incite the pains, and examination was impossible during the relentlessly powerful contractions.

At last she drew back, thinking, tapping one foot abstractedly as she watched Jenny writhe through two more of the spine-wrenching pains. As she jerked on the sheets, one of the strained linens parted suddenly with a rending tear.

As though this had been a signal, Mrs Martins started forward with decision, beckoning to me.

'Lean her back a bit, lass,' she instructed me, not at all disconcerted by Jenny's cries. I supposed she had heard her share of screaming.

At the next relaxation Mrs Martins plunged into action. Grasping the child through the momentarily flaccid walls of the womb, she heaved, trying to turn it. Jenny screamed and jerked my arms as another contraction started.

Mrs Martins tried again. And again. And again. Unable to keep from pushing, Jenny was wearing herself far past the point of exhaustion, her body struggling past the bounds of ordinary strength as it strove to force the child into the world.

Then it worked. There was a sudden strange fluid shifting, and the amorphous bulk of the child turned under Mrs Martins' hands. All at once the shape of Jenny's belly was altered and there was an immediate sense of getting down to business.

'Now push.' She did, and Mrs Martins dropped to her knees beside the bed. Apparently she saw some sign of progress, for she rose and hastily snatched a small bottle from the table where she had put it when she came in. She poured a small amount of what looked like oil on her fingertips, and began to rub it gently between Jenny's legs.

Jenny made a deep and vicious sound of protest at being touched as the next pain came on, and Mrs Martins took her hand away. Jenny sagged into inertness and the midwife resumed her gentle massage, crooning to her patient, telling her everything was well, just to rest, and now . . . push!

During the next contraction Mrs Martins put her hand on top of Jenny's belly and pushed down strongly. Jenny shrieked, but the midwife kept pushing until the contraction eased.

'Push with me on the next one,' the midwife said. 'It's almost here.'

I put my hands above Mrs Martins' on Jenny's belly, and at her signal all three of us pushed together. There was a deep, victorious grunt from Jenny, and a slimy blob swelled suddenly between her thighs. She straightened her legs against the mattress and pushed once more, and Margaret Ellen Murray shot into the world like a greased pig.

A little later I straightened from wiping Jenny's smiling face with a damp rag and glanced out the window. It was nearly sunset.

'I'm all right,' Jenny said. 'Quite all right.' The broad grin of delight with which she had greeted the delivery of her daughter had turned into a small, permanent smile of deep contentment. She reached up with an unsteady hand and touched my sleeve.

'Go and tell Ian,' she said. 'He'll be worrit.'

To my cynical eyes, it didn't look it. The scene in the study, where Ian and Jamie had taken refuge, strongly resembled a premature celebratory debauch. An empty decanter stood on the sideboard accompanied by several bottles, and a strong alcoholic fume hung over the room like a cloud.

The proud father appeared to have passed out, head

669

resting on the laird's desk. The laird himself was still conscious but bleary-eyed, leaning back against the panelling and blinking like an owl.

Outraged, I stamped over to the desk and gripped Ian by the shoulder, shaking him roughly and ignoring Jamie, who pushed himself upright, saying, 'Sassenach, wait . . .'

Ian was not quite unconscious. His head came up reluctantly and he looked at me with a set, rigid face, eyes bleak and pleading holes. I realized suddenly that he thought I had come to tell him that Jenny was dead.

I relaxed my grip and patted him gently instead.

'She's all right,' I said softly. 'You have a daughter.'

He laid his head down on his arms again and I left him, his thin shoulders shaking as Jamie patted his back.

The survivors now revived and cleaned up, the Murray–Fraser families gathered in Jenny's room for a celebratory supper. Little Margaret, tidied for inspection and swaddled in a small blanket, was given to her father, who received his new offspring with an expression of beatific reverence.

'Hello, wee Maggie,' he whispered, touching the tiny button of a nose with one fingertip.

His new daughter, unimpressed by the introduction, closed her eyes in concentration, stiffened, and urinated on her father's shirt.

During the brief bustle of hilarity and repair occasioned by this lapse of good manners, small Jamie succeeded in escaping from the clutches of Mrs Crook and flung himself on to Jenny's bed. She grunted slightly in discomfort, but put out a hand and gathered him in, waving at Mrs Crook to let him be.

'*My* mama!' he declared, burrowing into Jenny's side.

'Well, who else?' she asked reasonably. 'Here, laddie.' She hugged him and kissed the top of his head, and he relaxed, reassured, and snuggled against her. She gently pushed his head down, stroking his hair.

'Lay your head then, man,' she said. 'Past your bedtime. Lay your head.' Comforted by her presence, he put a thumb in his mouth and fell asleep.

Given a turn to hold the baby, Jamie proved remarkably

competent, cupping the small fuzzy skull in the palm of one hand. He seemed reluctant to hand the child back to Jenny, who cuddled her against her breasts, crooning soft endearments.

At last we made our way to our own room, which seemed silent and empty in contrast to the warm family scene we had just left, Ian kneeling by his wife's bed, hand resting on small Jamie as Jenny nursed the new baby. I was conscious for the first time of just how tired I was; it was nearly twenty-four hours since Ian had roused me.

Jamie closed the door quietly behind him. Without speaking he came behind me and undid the fastenings of my gown. His hands reached around me and I lay back gratefully against his chest. Then he bent his head to kiss me and I turned, putting my own arms around his neck. I felt not only very tired but very tender, and not a little sad.

'Perhaps it's as well,' Jamie said slowly, as though to himself.

'What's as well?'

'That you're barren.' He couldn't see my face, buried in his chest, but he must have felt me stiffen.

'Aye, I knew that long ago. Geillis Duncan told me, soon after we wed.' He stroked my back gently. 'I regretted it a bit at first, but then I began to think it was as well; living as we must, it would be verra difficult if you were to get with child. And now' – he shivered slightly – 'now I think I am glad of it; I wouldna want ye to suffer that way.'

'I wouldn't mind,' I said after a long while, thinking of the rounded, fuzzy head and tiny fingers.

'I would.' He kissed the top of my head. 'I saw Ian's face; it was like his own flesh was being torn, each time Jenny screamed.' My arms were around him, stroking the ridged scars on his back. 'I can bear pain, myself,' he said softly, 'but I couldna bear yours. That would take more strength than I have.'

33

The Watch

Jenny recovered rapidly after Margaret's birth, insisting on coming downstairs the day following the delivery. At the combined insistence of Ian and Jamie, she reluctantly refrained from doing any work, only supervising from the sofa in the parlour where she reclined, baby Margaret sleeping in her cradle alongside.

Not content to sit idle, though, within a day or two she had ventured as far as the kitchen, and then the back garden. Sitting on the wall, the well-wrapped baby in a carrying sling, she was keeping me company as I simultaneously pulled dead plants and kept an eye on the enormous cauldron in which the household's laundry was boiled. Mrs Crook and the maids had already removed the clean wash to be hung and dried; now I was waiting for the water to cool sufficiently to be dumped out.

Small Jamie was 'helping' me, yanking out plants with mad abandon and flinging bits of stick in all directions. I called a warning as he ventured too near the cauldron, then raced after him as he ignored me. Luckily the pot had cooled quickly; the water was no more than warm. Warning him to keep back with his mother, I grasped the pot and tilted it away from the iron contrivance that held it and kept it from falling.

I sprang back out of the way as the dirty water cascaded over the lip of the pot, steaming in the chilly air. Young Jamie, squatting beside me on his heels, splatted his hands joyfully in the warm mud, and black droplets flew all over my skirts.

His mother slid down from the wall, yanked him up by the collar and dealt him a smart clout on the backside.

'Have ye no sense, *gille*? Look at ye! There's your shirt'll have to go and be washed again! And look what ye've done to your auntie's skirt, ye wee heathen!'

'It doesn't matter,' I protested, seeing the miscreant's lower lip quiver.

'Weel, it matters to me,' said Jenny, giving her offspring the benefit of a gimlet eye. 'Say "sorry" to your auntie, laddie, then get ye into the house and have Mrs Crook give ye a bit of a wash.' She patted his bottom, gently this time, and gave him a push in the direction of the house.

We were turning back to the cauldron when the sound of hoofbeats came from the road.

'That'll be Jamie back, I expect,' I said, listening. 'He's early, though.'

Jenny shook her head, peering intently towards the road. 'Not his horse.'

The pony, when it appeared at the crest of a hill, was not one she knew, to judge from her frown. The man aboard, though, was no stranger. She stiffened beside me, then began to run towards the gate, wrapping both arms around the baby to hold it steady.

'It's Ian!' she called to me.

He was tattered and dusty and bruised about the face, as he slid off his pony. One bruise on his forehead was swollen, with a nasty split that went through the eyebrow. Jenny caught him under the arm as he hit the ground, and it was only then I saw that his wooden leg was gone.

'Jamie,' he gasped. 'We met the Watch near the mill. Waiting for us. They knew we were coming.'

My stomach lurched. 'Is he alive?'

He nodded, panting for breath. 'Aye. Not wounded, either. They took him off with them.

Jenny's fingers were exploring his face.

'Are ye bad hurt, man?'

He shook his head. 'No. They took my pony and my leg; they didna need to kill me to stop me following.'

Jenny glanced at the horizon, where the sun lay just above the trees. Maybe five o'clock, I estimated. Ian followed her gaze and anticipated her question.

'We met them near midday. It took me over two hours to get to a place that had a mount.'

She stood still for a moment, calculating, then turned to me with decision.

'Claire. Help Ian to the house, will ye, and if he needs aught in the way of doctoring, do it as fast as ye can. I'll give the babe to Mrs Crook and fetch the ponies.'

She was gone before either of us could protest.

'Does she mean . . . but she can't!' I exclaimed. 'She can't mean to leave the baby!'

Ian was leaning heavily on my shoulder as we made our way slowly up the path to the house. He shook his head.

'Maybe not. But I dinna think she means to let the English hang her brother, either.'

It was growing dark by the time we reached the spot where Jamie and Ian had been ambushed. Jenny slid off her horse and cast about through the bushes like a small terrier, pushing branches out of her way and muttering things under her breath that sounded suspiciously like some of her brother's better curses.

'East,' she said, finally coming out of the trees, scratched and dirty. She beat dead leaves from her skirt and took her pony's reins from my numbed hands. 'We canna follow in the dark, but at least I know which way to go, come the dawn.'

We made a simple camp, hobbling the horses and building a small fire. I admired the efficiency with which Jenny had done it, and she smiled.

'I used to make Jamie and Ian show me things, when they were young. How to build fires, and climb trees – even how to skin things. And how to track.' She glanced again in the direction taken by the Watch.

'Dinna worry, Claire.' She smiled at me and sat down by the fire. 'Twenty horses canna go far through the brush, but two ponies can. The Watch will be taking the low road, by the looks of it. We can cut over the hills and catch them up.'

Her nimble fingers were tugging at the bodice of her

gown. I stared in amazement as she spread the folds of cloth and pulled down the top of her underblouse to show her breasts. They were very large and looked hard, swollen with milk. In my ignorance I had not thought to wonder what a nursing mother does if deprived of her nursling.

'I canna leave the babe for long,' she said in answer to my thoughts, grimacing as she cupped one breast from beneath. 'I'll burst.' In response to the touch, milk had begun to drip from the engorged nipple, thin and bluish. Pulling a large kerchief from her pocket, Jenny tucked it beneath her breast. There was a small pewter cup on the ground beside her, one she had taken from the saddlebag. Pressing the lip of the cup just below the nipple, she gently stroked the breast between two fingers, squeezing gently towards the nipple. The milk dripped faster in response, then suddenly the areola around the nipple contracted and the milk spurted out in a tiny jet of surprising force.

'I didn't know it did that!' I blurted, staring in fascination.

Jenny moved the cup to catch the stream, and nodded. 'Oh, aye. The babe's sucking starts it, but once the milk lets down, all the child need do is swallow. Oh, that feels better.' She closed her eyes briefly in relief.

She emptied the cup on to the ground, remarking, 'Shame to waste it, but there isn't much to do wi' it, is there?' Switching hands, she placed the cup again and repeated the process with the other breast.

'It's a nuisance,' she said, looking up to see me still watching. 'Everything to do wi' bairns is a nuisance, almost. Still, ye'd never choose not to have them.'

'No,' I answered softly. 'You wouldn't choose that.'

She looked across the fire at me, face kind and concerned.

'It isna your time yet,' she said. 'But you'll have bairns of your own one day.'

I laughed a little shakily. 'First we'd better find the father.'

She emptied the second cup and began readjusting her dress.

'Oh, we'll find them. Tomorrow. We have to, for I canna stay away from wee Maggie much longer than that.'

'And once we've found them?' I asked. 'What then?'

She shrugged and reached for the blanket rolls.

'That depends on Jamie. And on how much he's made them hurt him.'

Jenny was right; we did find the Watch the next day. We left our campsite before full day, pausing only long enough for her to express more milk. She seemed to be able to find trails where none existed, and I followed her without question into a heavily wooded area. Quick travel was impossible through the brushy undergrowth, but she assured me that we were taking a much more direct route than the one the Watch would have to follow, bound as they were to tracks by the size of their group.

We came on them near noon. I heard the jingle of harness and the casual voices I had heard once before, and put out a hand to stop Jenny, who was following me for the moment.

'There's a ford in the stream below,' she whispered to me. 'It sounds as though they've stopped there to water the horses.' Sliding down, she took both sets of reins and tethered our ponies, then, beckoning to me to follow, she slid into the undergrowth like a snake.

From the vantage point to which she led me, on a small ledge overlooking the ford, we could see almost all of the men of the Watch, mostly dismounted and talking in casual groups, some sitting on the ground eating, some leading the horses in groups of two and three to the water. What we couldn't see was Jamie.

'Do you suppose they've killed him?' I whispered in panic. I had counted every man twice, to be sure I had missed no one. There were twenty men and twenty-six horses; all in plain view, so far as I could see. But no hint of a prisoner, and no telltale gleam of sun on red hair.

'I doubt it,' Jenny answered. 'But there's only one way to find out.' She began to squirm backwards from the ledge.

'What's that?'

'Ask.'

The track narrowed as it left the ford, becoming little more than a dusty trail through dense stands of pine and alder on either side. The trail was not wide enough for the Watch to ride two abreast; each man would have to pass down it in single file.

As the last man in the line approached a bend in the trail, Jenny Murray stepped suddenly out in the road ahead of him. His horse shied, and the man struggled to rein it in, cursing. As he opened his mouth to demand indignantly what she meant by this behaviour, I stepped out of the bush behind and whacked him solidly behind the ear with a fallen branch.

Taken completely by surprise, he lost his balance as the horse shied again, and fell off on to the path. He wasn't stunned; the blow had only knocked him over. Jenny remedied this deficiency with the assistance of a good-sized rock.

She grabbed the horse's reins and gestured violently to me.

'Come on!' she whispered. 'Get him off the road before they notice he's gone.'

So it was that when Robert MacDonald of the Glen Elrive Watch recovered consciousness it was to find himself securely tied to a tree, looking down the barrel of a pistol held by the steely-eyed sister of his erstwhile prisoner.

'What have ye done wi' Jamie Fraser?' she demanded.

MacDonald shook his head dazedly, obviously thinking her a figment of his imagination. An attempt to move put paid to this notion, and after an allowance for the statutory amount of cursing and threatening, he at last reconciled himself to the idea that the only way to get loose was to tell us what we wanted to know.

'He's dead,' MacDonald said sullenly. Then, as Jenny's finger tightened ominously on the trigger he added in sudden panic, 'It wasna me! It was his own fault!'

Jamie, he said, had been mounted double, arms bound with a leather strap, behind one of the Watch, riding between two other men. He had seemed docile enough, and they had taken no particular precautions when fording the river six miles from the mill.

'Damn fool threw himself off the horse and into the deep water,' said MacDonald, shrugging as well as he could with his hands tied behind him. 'We fired at him. Must have hit him, for he didna come up again. But the stream's swift just below the ford, and it's deep. We searched a bit, but no body. Must ha' been carried downstream. Now, for God's sake, ladies, will ye no untie me!'

After repeated threats from Jenny had elicited no further details or changes in his story, we decided to accept it as true. Declining to free MacDonald altogether, Jenny did at least loosen his bonds, so that given time he might struggle out of them. Then we ran.

'Do you think he's dead?' I puffed as we reached the tethered ponies.

'I don't. Jamie swims like a fish, and I've seen him hold his breath for three minutes at a time. Come on. We're going to search the river bank.'

We cast up and down the banks of the river, stumbling on rocks, splashing in the shallows, scratching our hands and faces on the willows that trawled their branches in the pools.

At last Jenny gave a triumphant shout and I splashed my way across, balancing precariously on the mossy rocks that lined the bottom of the river, shallow at this spot.

She was holding a leather strap, still fastened in a circle. A smear of blood discoloured one side.

'Wriggled out of it here,' she said, bending the circlet between her hands. She looked back in the direction we had come, down that jagged fall of tangled rocks, deep pools and foaming rapids, and shook her head.

'However did ye manage, Jamie?' she said, half to herself.

We found an area of flattened grass, not far from the verge, where he had evidently lain to rest. I found a small brownish smudge on the bark of an aspen nearby.

'He's hurt,' I said.

'Aye, but he's moving,' Jenny answered, looking at the ground as she paced back and forth.

'Are you good at tracking?' I asked hopefully.

'I'm no much of a hunter,' she replied, setting off with me close behind, 'but if I canna follow something the size of Jamie Fraser through dry bracken, then I'm daft as well as blind.'

Sure enough, a broad track of crushed brown fern led up the side of the hill and disappeared into a thick clump of heather. Circling around this point turned up no further evidence, nor did calling produce any answer.

'He'll be gone,' Jenny said, sitting down on a log and fanning herself. I thought she looked pale, and realized that kidnapping and threatening armed men was no pursuit for a woman who had given birth less than a week before.

'Jenny,' I said, 'you have to go back. Besides, he might return to Lallybroch.'

She shook her head. 'No, that he wouldna. Whatever MacDonald told us, they're no likely to give up so easy, not with a reward at hand. If they havena hunted him down yet, it's because they couldn't. But they'll have sent someone back to keep an eye on the farm, just in case. No, that's the one place he wouldna go.' She pulled at the neck of her gown. The day was cold, but she was sweating slightly, and I could see growing dark stains on the bosom of her dress, from leaking milk.

She saw me looking and nodded. 'Aye, I'll have to go back soon. Mrs Crook's nursing the lassie wi' goat's milk and sugar water, but she canna do without me much longer, nor me without her. I hate to leave ye alone, though.'

I didn't much care for the thought of having to hunt alone through the Scottish Highlands for a man who might be anywhere, either, but I put a bold face on it.

'I'll manage,' I said. 'It could be worse. At least he's alive.'

'True.' She glanced at the sun, low over the horizon. 'I'll stay wi' ye through the night, at least.'

Huddled around the fire at night, we didn't talk much. Jenny was preoccupied with thoughts of her abandoned child, me with thoughts of just how I was to proceed on my own, with no real knowledge of geography or Gaelic.

Suddenly Jenny's head snapped up, listening. I sat up and listened myself, but heard nothing. I peered into the dark woods in the direction Jenny was looking, but saw no gleaming eyes in the depths, thank God.

When I turned back to the fire, Murtagh was sitting on the other side, calmly warming his hands at the blaze. Jenny snapped round at my exclamation, and uttered a short laugh of surprise.

'I could ha' cut both your throats before ye ever looked in the right direction,' the little man observed.

'Oh, could ye then?' Jenny was sitting with her knees drawn up, hands clasped near her ankles. With a lightning dart, her hand went under her skirt and the blade of a tiny knife flashed in the firelight.

'None sae bad,' Murtagh agreed, nodding sagely. 'Is the wee Sassenach that good?'

'No,' said Jenny, restoring her blade to her stocking. 'So it's good you'll be with her. Ian sent for ye, I expect?'

The little man nodded. 'Aye. Did ye find the Watch yet?'

We told him of our progress to date. At the news that Jamie had escaped I could have sworn that a muscle twitched near the corner of his mouth, but it would have been stretching matters to call it a smile.

At length Jenny rose, folding her blanket.

'Where are you going?' I asked in surprise.

'Home.' She nodded at Murtagh. 'He'll be wi' ye now; you don't need me, and there's others that do.'

Murtagh looked up at the sky. The waning moon was faintly visible behind a haze of cloud, and a soft spatter of rain whispered in the pine boughs above us.

'The morning will do. The wind's risin', and no one will move far tonight.'

Jenny shook her head and went on tucking her hair beneath her kerchief.

'I know my way. And if none will move tonight, there's none will hinder me on the way, no?'

Murtagh sighed impatiently. 'You're stubborn as your ox of a brother, beggin' your pardon. Little reason to hurry back, so far as I can see – I doubt your good man will ha' taken a doxy to his bed in the time ye've been gone.'

'You see as far as the end o' your nose, *duine*, and that's short enough,' Jenny answered sharply. 'And if ye've lived so long without knowing better than to stand between a nursing mother and a hungry child, you've not sense enough to hunt hogs, let alone find a man in the heather.'

Murtagh raised his hands in surrender. 'Oh, aye, ye'll take your own way. I didna ken I was tryin' to talk sense to a wild sow. Get a tush through the leg for my trouble, I expect.'

Jenny laughed unexpectedly, dimpling. 'I expect ye might at that, ye auld rogue.' She bent and heaved the heavy saddle up on her knee. 'See that ye take care with my good-sister, then, and send word when ye've found Jamie.'

As she turned to saddle the pony, Murtagh added, 'By the bye, ye'll reckon to find a new kitchen-maid when ye reach home.'

She paused and eyed him, then slowly set the saddle on the ground. 'And who might that be?' she asked.

'The Widow MacNab,' he replied with deliberation.

She was still for a moment, nothing moving but the kerchief and cloak that stirred in the rising wind.

'How?' she asked at last.

Murtagh bent to pick up the saddle. He heaved it up and secured the girth with what seemed like one effortless motion.

'Fire,' he said, giving a final tug to the stirrup leather. 'Watch your way as ye pass the high field; the ashes will still be warm.'

He cupped his hands to give her a foot up, but she shook her head and took the reins instead, beckoning to me.

'Walk wi' me to the top of the hill, Claire, if ye will.'

The air was cold and heavy, away from the fire. My skirts were damp from sitting on the ground, and clung to my legs as I walked. Jenny's head was bent against the wind, but I could see her profile, lips pale and set with chill.

'It was McNab that gave Jamie to the Watch?' I asked at last. She nodded slowly.

'Aye. Ian will have found out, or one of the other men; it doesna matter which.'

It was late November, well past Guy Fawkes day, but I had a sudden vision of a bonfire, flames leaping up walls and sprouting in the thatch like the tongues of the Holy Ghost, while the fire within roared its prayers for the damned. And inside, the guy, an effigy crouched in ash on his own hearthstone, ready to fall into black dust at the next blast of cold wind to sweep through the shell of his home. *There is a fine line sometimes, between justice and brutality.*

I realized Jenny was looking full at me, questioning, and I returned her gaze with a nod. We stood together, in this case at least, on the same side of that grim and arbitrary line.

We paused at the top of the hill, Murtagh a dark speck by the fire below. Jenny rummaged for a moment in the side pocket of her skirt, then pressed a small wash-leather bag into my hand.

'The rents from Quarter Day,' she said. 'Ye might need it.'

I tried to give the money back, insisting that Jamie would not want to take money that was needed for the running of the estate, but she would have none of it. And while Janet Fraser was half her brother's size, she more than matched his stubbornness.

Outclassed, I gave up at last, and tucked the money safely away in the recesses of my own costume. At Jenny's insistence I took also the small knife she pressed upon me.

'It's Ian's, but he has another,' she said. 'Put it into your stocking top, and hold it with your garter. Don't leave it off, even when ye sleep.'

She paused a moment, as though there were something else she meant to say. Apparently there was.

'Jamie said,' she said carefully, 'that ye might . . . tell me things sometimes. And he said that if ye did, I was to do as ye said. Is there . . . anything ye wish to tell me?'

Jamie and I had discussed the necessity for preparing Lallybroch and its inhabitants against the coming disasters of the Rising. But we had thought then that there was time.

Now I had no time, or at most a few minutes, in which to give this new sister I held dear enough information to guard Lallybroch against the coming storm.

Being a prophet was a very uncomfortable occupation, I thought, not for the first time. I felt considerable sympathy with Jeremiah and his Lamentations. I also realized exactly why Cassandra was so unpopular. Still, there was no help for it. On the crest of a Scottish hill, the night wind of an autumn storm whipping my hair and skirts like the sheets of a banshee, I turned my face to the shadowed skies and prepared to prophesy.

'Plant potatoes,' I said.

Jenny's mouth dropped slightly open, then she firmed her jaw and nodded briskly. 'Potatoes. Aye. There's none closer than Edinburgh, but I'll send for them. How many?'

'As many as you can. They're not planted in the Highlands now, but they will be. They're a root crop that will keep for a long time, and the yield is better than oats or barley. Put as much ground as you can into crops that can be stored. There's going to be a famine, a bad one, in two years. If there's land or property that's not productive now, sell it, for gold. There's going to be a war, and slaughter. Men will be hunted, here and everywhere through the Highlands.' I thought for a moment. 'Is there a priest-hole in the house?'

'No, it was built well after the Protector's time.'

'Make one then, or some safe place to hide. I hope Jamie won't need it' – I swallowed hard at the thought – 'but someone may.'

'All right. Is that all?' Her face was serious and intent in the half light. I blessed Jamie for his forethought in warning her, and her for her trust in her brother. She didn't ask me how, or why, but only took careful note of what I said, and I knew my hasty instructions would be followed.

'That's all. All I can think of just now, anyway.' I tried to smile, but the effort seemed unconvincing, even to me.

Hers was better. She touched my cheek briefly in farewell.

'God go wi' ye, Claire. We'll meet again – when ye bring my brother home.'

PART SIX

The Search

34

Dougal's Story

Whatever the disadvantages of civilization, I reflected grimly, the benefits were undeniable. Take telephones, for example. For that matter, take newspapers, which were popular in such metropolitan centres as Edinburgh or Perth, but completely unknown in the wilderness of the Scottish Highlands.

With no such methods of mass communication, news spread from one person to the next at the speed of a man's stride. People generally found out what they needed to know, but with a delay of several weeks. Consequently, faced with the problem of finding exactly where Jamie was, there was little to rely on except the possibility of someone encountering him and sending word back to Lallybroch. That was a process that might take weeks. And the winter would set in shortly, making travel impossible. I sat feeding sticks to the fire, pondering the possibilities.

Which way would Jamie have gone from the point of his escape? Not back to Lallybroch, to be sure, and almost certainly not north, into the MacKenzie lands. South to where he might meet again with his earlier rough companions? No, most likely northeast, towards Leoch. But if I could figure that out, so could the men of the Watch.

Murtagh returned from his gathering, dumping an armload of sticks on the ground. He sat down crosslegged on a fold of his plaid, wrapping the rest around himself to keep out the chill. He cast an eye towards the sky, where the moon glowed behind racing clouds.

'It willna snow just yet,' he said, frowning. 'Another week, maybe two. We might reach Leoch before then.' Well, nice to have confirmation of my deductions, I supposed.

'You think he'll be there?'

The little clansman shrugged, hunching his plaid higher around his shoulders.

'No tellin'. The travel will no be as easy for him, lyin' hid during the day, and staying off the tracks. And he hasna got a mount.' He scratched his stubbled chin thoughtfully. 'We canna find him; we'd best let him find us.'

'How? Send up flares?' I suggested sarcastically. One thing about Murtagh; no matter what incongruous thing I said, he could be counted on to behave as though I hadn't spoken.

'I've brought your wee packet of medicines,' he said, nodding towards the saddlebags on the ground. 'And you've enough of a reputation near Lallybroch; you'll be known as a healer through most of the countryside near.' He nodded to himself. 'Aye, that'll do well enough.' And without further explanations, he lay down, rolled up in his plaid and went calmly to sleep, ignoring the wind in the trees, the light patter of rain, and me.

I found out soon enough what he meant. Travelling openly – and slowly – along the main tracks, we stopped at every cot-house and village and hamlet we came to. There he would make a quick survey of the local populace, round up anyone suffering from illness or injury, and bring them to me for treatment. Physicians being few and far between in these parts, there was always someone ailing to attend to.

While I was occupied with my tonics and salves he would chat idly with the friends and relatives of the afflicted, taking care to describe the path of our journey towards Leoch. If by chance there were no patients to be seen in a place, we would pause nonetheless for the night, seeking shelter at a cottage or pot-house. In these places Murtagh would sing to entertain our hosts and earn our supper, stubbornly insisting that I preserve all the money I had with me in case it should be needed when we found Jamie.

Not naturally inclined towards conversation, he taught me some of his songs, to pass the time as we plodded on from place to place.

'Ye've a decent voice,' he observed one day after a moderately successful attempt at 'The Dowie Dens of Yarrow'. 'Not well trained, but strong and true enough. Try it once more and ye'll sing it wi' me tonight. There's a wee alehouse over the hill.'

'Do you really think this will work?' I asked. 'What we're doing, I mean?'

He shifted about in the saddle before answering. No natural horseman, he always looked like a monkey trained to ride a pony, but still managed to dismount fresh as a daisy at day's end, while I could barely manage to hobble my mount before staggering off to collapse.

'Oh, aye,' he said at last. 'Sooner or later. You're seein' more sick folk these days, no?'

This was true, and I admitted as much.

'Well, then,' he said, proving his point, 'that means word o' your skill is spreading. And that's what we want. But we could maybe do better. That's why you'll sing tonight. And perhaps . . .' He hesitated, as though reluctant to suggest something.

'Perhaps what?'

'Know anything about fortune-telling, do ye?' he asked warily. I understood the reason for his hesitancy; he had seen the frenzy of the witch-hunt at Cranesmuir.

I smiled. 'A bit. You want me to try it?'

'Aye. The more we can offer, the more folk will come to see us – and go back to tell others. And word will spread till the lad hears of us. And that's when we'll find him. Game to try, are ye?'

I shrugged. 'If it will help, why not?'

I made my debut as singer and fortune-teller that night at Limraigh, with considerable success. I found that Mrs Graham had been right in what she had told me – it was the faces, not the hands, that gave you the necessary clues.

Our fame spread, little by little, until by the next week people were running out of their cottages to greet us as we rode into a village, and showering us with pennies and small gifts as we rode away.

'You know, we could really make something of this,' I remarked one evening, stowing the night's takings away.

'Too bad there's no theatre anywhere near – we could do a proper music-hall turn: Magical Murtagh and His Glamorous Assistant, Gladys.'

Murtagh treated this remark with his usual taciturn indifference, but it was true; we really did quite well together. Perhaps it was because we were united in our quest, despite our very basic personality differences.

The weather grew increasingly bad and our pace even slower, but there was as yet no word from Jamie. Outside Belladrum one night, in a driving rain, we met with a band of real gypsies.

I blinked disbelievingly at the tiny cluster of dingy caravans in the clearing near the road. It looked something like a camp of the gypsy bands that came to Hampstead Heath every year.

The people looked the same, too: swarthy, cheerful, loud and welcoming. At the jingle of our harness, a woman's head poked out of the window of one caravan. She looked us over for a moment, then gave a shout, and the ground under the trees was suddenly alive with grinning brown faces.

'Gie me your purse for safekeeping,' said Murtagh, unsmiling, watching the young man swaggering towards us with a gay disregard of the rain soaking his colourful shirt. 'And dinna turn your back on anyone.'

I was cautious, but we were welcomed with expansive motions and invited to share the gypsies' supper. It smelt delicious – some sort of stew – and I eagerly accepted the invitation, ignoring Murtagh's dour speculations as to the basic nature of the beast that had provided the stewmeat.

They spoke little English, and less Gaelic; we conversed largely in gestures, and a sort of bastard tongue that owed its parentage largely to French. It was warm and companionable in the caravan where we ate; men and women and children all ate casually from bowls, sitting wherever they could find space, dipping the succulent stew up with chunks of bread. It was the best food I had had in days, and I ate until my sides creaked. I could barely muster breath to sing,

690

but did my best, humming along in the difficult spots and leaving Murtagh to carry the tunes.

Our performance was greeted with rapturous applause, and the gypsies reciprocated, a young man singing some sort of wailing lament to the accompaniment of an ancient fiddle. His performance was punctuated by the crashing of a tambourine, wielded with some gravity by a little girl of about eight.

While Murtagh had been circumspect in his inquiries in the villages and farms we visited, with the gypsies he was entirely open. To my surprise he told them bluntly who we sought: a big man, with hair like fire and eyes like the summer skies. The gypsies exchanged glances up and down the aisle of the caravan, but there was a unanimous shaking of regretful heads. No, they had not seen him. But . . . and here the leader, the purple-shirted young man who had welcomed us, pantomimed the sending of a messenger, should they happen across the man we sought.

I bowed, smiling, and Murtagh in turn pantomimed the handing across of money for information received. This bit of business was greeted with smiles, but also with gazes of speculation. I was glad when Murtagh declared that we could not stay the night but must be on our way, thank ye just the same. He shook out a few coins from his sporran, taking care to exhibit the fact that it held only a small handful of coppers. Distributing these by way of thanks for the supper, we made our exit, followed by voluble protestations of farewell, gratitude and good wishes – at least that's what I assumed they were.

They might actually have been promising to follow us and cut our throats, and Murtagh behaved rather as though this had been the case, leading the ponies at a gallop to a track crossing two miles distant, then ducking aside into the vegetation for a substantial detour before re-emerging on to the track.

Murtagh glanced up and down the road, empty in the fading, rain-soaked dusk.

'Do you really think they followed us?' I asked curiously.

'I dinna ken, but since there's twelve o' them and no but

the twa o' us, I thought we'd best act as though they did.'
This seemed sound reasoning, and I followed him without
question through several more evasive manoeuvres, arriving
at last in Rossmoor, where we found shelter in a barn.

Snow fell the next day. Only a light fall, enough to dust
the ground with a white like the flour on the millhouse
floor, but it worried me. I didn't like to think of Jamie, alone
and unsheltered in the heather, braving winter's storms in
nothing but the shirt and plaid he had been wearing at his
capture by the Watch.

Two days later, the messenger came.

The sun was still above the horizon, but it was evening
already in the rock-walled glens. The shadows lay so deep
under the leafless trees that the path – what there was of
one – was nearly invisible. Fearful of losing my guide in
the gathering dark, I walked so closely behind him that once
or twice I actually trod on the trailing hem of his cloak. At
last, with an impatient grunt, he turned and thrust me ahead
of him, steering me through the dusk with a heavy hand on
my shoulder.

It felt as though we had been walking for a long time. I
had long since lost track of our turnings amid the towering
boulders and thick dead undergrowth. I could only hope
that Murtagh was somewhere behind, keeping within earshot if not within sight. The man who had come to the
tavern to fetch me, a middle-aged gypsy with no English,
had flatly refused to have anyone but me accompany him,
pointing emphatically first at Murtagh and then the ground,
to indicate that he must stay put.

The night chill came on fast at this time of year, and my
heavy cloak was barely enough protection against the sudden
gusts of icy wind that met us in the open spaces of the
clearings. I was torn between dismay at the thought of Jamie
lying through the cold, wet nights of late autumn without
shelter, and excitement at the thought of seeing him again.
A shiver ran up my spine that had nothing to do with the
cold.

At last my guide pulled me to a halt, and with a precautionary squeeze of my shoulder, stepped off the path and disappeared. I stood, as patiently as could be managed, hands folded under my arms for warmth. I was sure my guide – or someone – would return; I hadn't paid him, for one thing. Still, the wind rattled through the dead brambles like the passing of a deer's ghost still in panic-stricken flight from the hunter. And the damp was seeping through the seams of my boots; the tallow waterproofing had worn away, and I'd had no chance to reapply it.

My guide reappeared as suddenly as he had left, making me bite my tongue as I stifled a squeak of surprise. With a jerk of his head he bade me follow him, and pressed aside a screen of alders for me to pass.

The cave entrance was narrow. There was a lantern burning on a ledge, silhouetting the tall figure that turned towards the entrance to meet me.

I flung myself forward, realizing even before I touched him that it was not Jamie. Disappointment struck me like a blow in the stomach, and I had to step back and swallow several times to choke back the heavy bile that rose in my throat.

I clenched my hands at my sides, digging my fists into my thighs until I felt calm enough to speak.

'Rather out of your territory, aren't you?' I said in a voice that surprised me by its coolness.

Dougal MacKenzie had watched my struggle for control, not without some sympathy on his dark face. Now he took my elbow and led me farther into the cave. There were a number of bundles piled against the far side, many more than a single horse could carry. He wasn't alone, then. And whatever he and his men carried, it was something he preferred not to expose to the curious gaze of innkeepers and stable lads.

'Smuggling, I suppose?' I said with a nod towards the bundles. Then I thought better and answered my own question. 'No, not exactly smuggling – goods for Prince Charles, hm?'

He didn't bother to answer but sat down on a boulder opposite me, hands on his knees.

'I've news,' he said abruptly.

I took a deep breath, bracing myself. News – and not good news, from the expression on his face. I took another breath, swallowed hard and nodded.

'Tell me.'

'He's alive,' he said, and the largest of the ice lumps in my stomach dissolved. Dougal cocked his head to one side, watching intently. To see whether I were going to faint? I wondered dimly. It didn't matter; I wasn't.

'He was taken two weeks ago,' Dougal said, still watching me. 'Not his fault; poor luck. He met six dragoons face to face round a turn in the path, and one recognized him.'

'Was he hurt?' My voice was still calm but my hands were beginning to shake. I pressed them flat against my legs to still them.

Dougal shook his head. 'Not as I heard.' He paused a moment. 'He's in Wentworth Prison,' he said reluctantly.

'Wentworth,' I repeated mechanically. Wentworth Prison. Originally one of the mighty Highland fortresses, it had been built some time in the late sixteenth century, and added to at intervals over the next hundred and fifty years. The sprawling pile of rock now covered nearly two acres of ground, sealed behind ten-foot walls of weathered granite. But even granite walls have gates, I thought. I looked up to ask a question, and saw the reluctance still stamped on Dougal's features.

'What else?' I demanded. The hazel eyes met mine, unflinching.

'He stood his trial three days ago,' Dougal said. 'And was condemned to hang.'

The ice lump was back, with company. I closed my eyes.

'How long?' I asked. My voice seemed rather far off to my own ears and I opened my eyes again, blinking to refocus them in the flickering lantern light. Dougal was shaking his head.

'I dinna ken. Not long, though.'

My breath was coming a little easier now, and I was able to unclench my fists.

694

'We'd better hurry, then,' I said, still calmly. 'How many men are with you?'

Instead of answering, Dougal rose and came over to me. Reaching down, he took my hands and pulled me to my feet. The look of sympathy was back, and a deep grief lurking in his eyes frightened me more than anything he'd said so far. He shook his head slowly.

'Nay, lass,' he said gently. 'There's nothing we can do.'

Panicked, I tore my hands away from him.

'There is!' I said. 'There must be! You said he was still alive!'

'And I said "Not long!" ' he retorted sharply. 'The lad's in Wentworth Prison, not the thieves' hole at Cranesmuir! They may hang him today, or tomorrow, or not till next week, for all I know o' the matter, but there is no way on earth that ten men can force a way into Wentworth Prison!'

'Oh, no?' I was trembling again, but with rage this time. 'You don't know that – you don't know what might be done! You're just not willing to risk your skin, or your miserable . . . profit!' I flung an arm accusingly at the piled bundles.

Dougal grappled with me, seizing my flailing arms. I hammered his chest in a frenzy of grief and rage. He ignored the blows and put his arms around me, pulling me tight against him and holding me until I ceased struggling.

'Claire.' It was the first time he had ever used my first name, and it frightened me still further.

'Claire,' he said again, loosening his grip so that I could look up at him, 'do ye not think I'd do all I could to free the lad, did I think there was the slightest chance? Damn it, he's my own foster-son! But there is no chance – none!' He shook me slightly to emphasize his words.

'Jamie wouldna have me throw away good men's lives in a vain venture. Ye know that as well as I do.'

I could keep back the tears no longer. They burned down my icy cheeks as I pushed against him, seeking to free myself. He held me tighter, though, trying to force my head against his shoulder.

'Claire, my dear,' he said, voice gentler. 'My heart's sore

for the lad – and for you. D'ye come away wi' me. I'll take ye safe. To my own house,' he added hastily, feeling me stiffen. 'Not to Leoch.'

'To your house?' I said slowly. A horrible suspicion was beginning to form in my mind.

'Aye,' he said. 'Ye dinna think I'd take ye back to Cranesmuir, surely?' He smiled briefly before the stern features relaxed back into seriousness. 'Nay. I'll take ye to Beannachd. You'll be safe there.'

'Safe?' I said. 'Or helpless?' His arms dropped away at the tone of my voice.

'What d'ye mean?' The pleasant voice was suddenly cold.

I felt rather cold myself, and pulled my cloak together as I moved away from him.

'You kept Jamie away from his home by telling him his sister had borne a child to Randall,' I said, 'so that you and that precious brother of yours would have a chance to lure him into your camp. But now the English have him, you've lost any chance of controlling the property through Jamie.' I backed up another step, swallowing.

'You were party to your sister's marriage contract. It was by your insistence – yours and Callum's – that Broch Tuarach might be held by a woman. You think that if Jamie dies, Broch Tuarach will belong to me – or to you, if you can seduce or force me into marrying you.'

'What?!' His voice was incredulous. 'Ye think . . . ye think this is all some plot? Saint Agnes! Do ye think I'm lying to ye?'

I shook my head, keeping my distance. I didn't trust him an inch.

'No, I believe you. If Jamie weren't in prison, you'd never dare to tell me he was. It's too easy to check that. Nor do I think you betrayed him to the English – not even you could do something like that to your own blood. Besides, if you had, and word of it ever reached your men, they'd turn on you in a second. They'd tolerate much in you, but not treachery against your own kinsman.' As I spoke I was reminded of something.

'Was it you who attacked Jamie in the Lowlands last year?'

The heavy brows rose with surprise.

'Me? No! I found the lad near death, and saved him! Does that sound as though I meant him harm?'

Under cover of my cloak I ran my hand down my thigh, feeling for the comforting shape of my dagger.

'If it wasn't you, who was it?'

'I dinna ken.' The handsome face was wary, but not hiding anything. ''Twas one of three men – broken men, outlaws – that hunted wi' Jamie then. All of them accused each other, and there was no way of findin' out the truth o' the matter, not then.' He shrugged, the travelling cloak falling back from one broad shoulder.

'It doesna matter much now; twa of the men are dead, and the third in prison. Over another matter, but it makes little difference, do ye think?'

'No, I don't suppose so.' It was in a way a relief to find that he wasn't a murderer, whatever else he might be. He had no reason to lie to me now; so far as he knew, I was completely helpless. Alone, he could compel me to do whatever he wished. Or at least he likely thought so. I took a grip on the handle of my dirk.

The light was poor in the cave but I was watching carefully, and I could see indecision flicker momentarily across his face as he chose his next move. He stepped towards me, hand out, but stopped when he saw me flinch away.

'Claire. My sweet Claire.' The voice was soft now, and he ran an insinuating hand lightly down my arm. So he had decided to try seduction rather than compulsion.

'I know why ye talk so cold to me, and why ye think ill of me. You know that I burn for ye, Claire. And it's true – I've wanted ye since the night of the Gathering, when I kissed your sweet lips.' He had two fingers resting lightly on my shoulder, inching towards my neck. 'If I'd been a free man when Randall threatened ye, I'd ha' wed ye myself on the spot, and sent the man to the Devil for ye.' He was moving his body gradually closer, crowding me against the stone wall of the cavern. His fingertips moved to my throat, tracing the line of my cloak-fastening.

He must have seen my face then, for he stopped his advance, though he left his hand where it was, resting lightly above the rapid pulse that beat in my throat.

'Even so,' he said, 'even feeling as I do – for I'll hide it from ye no longer – even so, ye couldna imagine I'd abandon Jamie if there were any hope of saving him? Jamie Fraser is the closest thing I've got to a son!'

'Not quite,' I said. 'There's your real son. Or perhaps two, by now?' The fingers on my throat increased their pressure, just for a second, then dropped away.

'What d'ye mean?' And this time all pretence, all games, were dispensed with. The hazel eyes were intent and the full lips a grim line in the russet beard. He was very large, and very close to me. But I had gone too far already for caution.

'It means I know who Hamish's father really is,' I said. He had been half expecting it and had his face well under control, but the last weeks spent telling fortunes had not been in vain. I saw the tiny flicker of shock that widened his eyes and the sudden panic, swiftly quelled, that tightened the corners of his mouth.

Bull's-eye. In spite of the danger, I knew a moment's fierce exultation. I had been right, then, and the knowledge might just possibly be the weapon I needed.

'Do ye, then?' he said softly.

'Yes,' I said, 'and I imagine Callum knows as well.'

That stopped him for a moment. The hazel eyes narrowed and I wondered for an instant whether he were armed.

'He thought it was Jamie for a time, I think,' I said, staring directly into his eyes. 'Because of the rumours. You must have started those, feeding them to Geillis Duncan. Why? Because Callum got suspicious of Jamie and started to question Letitia? She couldn't hold out for long against him. Or was it that Geilie thought you were Letitia's lover, and you told her it was Jamie to quiet her suspicions? She's a jealous woman, but she can't have any reason to protect you now.'

Dougal smiled cruelly. The ice never left his eyes.

'No, she can't,' he agreed, still speaking softly. 'The witch is dead.'

'Dead!' The shock must have shown as plainly on my face as in my voice. His smile broadened.

'Oh, aye,' he said. 'Burnt. Stuck feet first in a barrel of pitch and heaped about with dry peats. Bound to a stake and lit like a torch. Sent to the Devil in a pillar of flame, under the branches of a rowan tree.'

'I thought she wasn't to . . . die until after the baby was born.'

He glanced at me, still smiling, but I noticed the trickle of sweat making its way down the side of his neck.

'It's come. The wean was birthed afore time. Small, but a bonny boy nonetheless; strong and kicking, and yelling for the breast at once. He's his mother's eyes, the wee devil.'

I thought at first this merciless recitation of detail was meant to impress me, but I was wrong. I shifted to one side, and as the light shone fresh on his face I could see the lines of grief etched around his eyes. It wasn't a catalogue of horror, then, but a lashing of himself. I felt no pity for him, under the circumstances.

'So you were fond of her,' I said coldly. 'Much good it did her. Or the child. What did you do with that?'

He shrugged. 'Saw it placed in a good home. It was a healthy babe, and there are folk who've lost their own who would give it a place, for all its mother was a witch and an adulteress.'

'And its father an adulterer and a betrayer,' I snapped. 'Your wife, your mistress, your nephew, your brother – is there anyone you haven't betrayed and deceived? You . . . you . . .' I choked on the words, quite sick with loathing. 'I don't know why I'm surprised,' I said, trying to speak calmly. 'If you've no loyalty to your king I suppose there's no reason to think you'd feel it for your nephew or your brother, either.'

His head snapped round and he glared at me. He raised his thick dark brows, the same shape as Callum's, as Jamie's, as Hamish's. The deep-set eyes, the broad cheekbones, the beautifully shaped skull. Old Jacob MacKenzie's legacy was a strong one.

A big hand clamped hard on my shoulder.

'My brother? You think I'd betray my brother?' For some reason that had stung him; his face was dark with anger.

'You've just admitted that you did!' and then I realized.

'The both of you,' I said slowly. 'You did it together, you and Callum. Together, as you've always done things.' I pulled his hand off my shoulder and flung it back at him.

'Callum couldn't be chieftain, unless you would go to war for him. He couldn't hold the clan together, without you to travel for him, to collect the rents and settle the claims. He couldn't ride, he couldn't travel. And he couldn't father a son, to pass the chieftainship on to. And you had no son by Maura. You swore to be his arms and legs' – I was beginning to feel a little hysterical by this time – 'why shouldn't you be his cock, as well?'

Dougal had lost his anger; he stood watching me speculatively for a moment. Deciding that I was going nowhere, he sat down on one of the bales of goods and waited for me to finish.

'So you did it with Callum's knowledge. Was Letitia willing?' Knowing by now just what sort of ruthlessness they possessed, I wouldn't put it past the brothers MacKenzie to have forced her.

Dougal nodded. His anger had evaporated.

'Oh, aye, willing enough. She didna fancy me particularly, but she wanted a child – enough to take me to her bed for the three months it took to start Hamish. A boring damn job it was too,' Dougal added reflectively, scraping a bit of mud from his boot heel. 'I'd as soon swive a warm bowl of milk pudding.'

'And did you tell Callum that?' I asked. Hearing the edge in my voice, he looked up. He regarded me levelly for a moment, then a faint smile lightened his face.

'No,' he said quietly. 'No, I didna tell him that.' He

looked down at his hands, turning them over as though looking for some secret hidden in the lines of his palms.

'I told him,' he said softly, not looking at me, 'that she was tender and sweet as a ripe peach, and all that a man could want in a woman.'

He closed his hands abruptly and looked up at me, that momentary glimpse of Callum's brother submerged once more in the sardonic eyes of Dougal MacKenzie.

'Tender and sweet is not precisely what I'd say of *you*,' he observed. 'But all that a man could want . . .' The deep-set hazel eyes travelled slowly downwards over my body, lingering on the roundness of breast and hip that showed through my open cloak. One hand moved unconsciously back and forth, stroking lightly across the muscles of his thigh as he watched me.

'Who knows?' he said, as though to himself. 'I might have yet another son – legitimate, this time. True' – he tilted his head appraisingly, looking at my midsection – 'it hasna happened yet wi' Jamie. You may be barren. But I'll take the chance. The property is worth it, at any rate.'

He stood suddenly and took a step towards me.

'Who knows?' he said again, very softly. 'If I were to plough that pretty brown-haired furrow and seed it deep each day . . .' The shadows on the cavern wall shifted suddenly as he took another step.

'Well, you took your bloody time about it,' I said crossly.

A look of incredulous shock spread across his features before he realized that I was looking beyond him towards the cave mouth.

'It didna seem mannerly to interrupt,' said Murtagh, advancing into the cave behind a loaded pair of snaphance pistols. He held one trained on Dougal, using the other to gesture with.

'Unless ye mean to accept that last proposal here and now, I'd suggest ye leave. And if ye *do* mean to accept it, then *I'll* leave.'

'Nobody's leaving yet,' I said shortly. 'Sit down,' I said to Dougal. He was still standing, staring at Murtagh as though at an apparition.

'Where's Rupert?' he demanded, finding his voice.

'Oh, Rupert.' Murtagh scratched his chin thoughtfully with the muzzle of one pistol. 'He's likely made it to Belladrum by now. Should be back before dawn,' he added helpfully, 'wi' the keg of rum he thinks ye sent him to fetch. The rest o' your men are still asleep in Quinborough.'

Dougal had the grace to laugh, if a little grudgingly. He sat down again, hands on his knees, and glanced from me to Murtagh and back again. There was a momentary silence.

'Well?' Dougal inquired. 'Now what?'

That, I realized, was rather a good question. Surprised at finding Dougal instead of Jamie, shocked by his revelations and infuriated at his consequent proposals, I had had no time to think of what ought to be done. Luckily, Murtagh was better prepared. Well, after all, *he* hadn't been occupied in fighting off lecherous advances.

'We'll need money,' he said promptly. 'And men.' He cast an eye appraisingly over the bundles stacked against the wall. 'Nay,' he said thoughtfully. 'That'll be for King James. But we'll take what ye've got on your person.' The small black eyes swivelled back to Dougal and the muzzle of one pistol gestured gently in the vicinity of his sporran.

One thing to be said for life in the Highlands was that it apparently gave one a certain fatalistic attitude. With a sigh Dougal reached into the sporran and tossed a small purse at my feet.

'Twenty gold pieces and thirty-odd shillings,' he said, lifting one brow in my direction. 'Take it and welcome.'

Seeing my look of scepticism, he shook his head.

'Nay, I mean it. Think what ye like of me. Jamie's my sister's son, and if ye can free him, then God be wi' ye. But ye can't.' His tone was final.

He looked at Murtagh, still holding his pistols steady.

'As to the men, no. If you and the lass mean to commit suicide I canna stop ye. I'll even offer to bury ye, one on either side of Jamie. But you'll not take my men to hell with ye, pistols or no.' He crossed his arms and leaned back against the cavern wall, calmly watching us.

702

Murtagh's hands didn't waver from his aim. His eyes flickered towards me, though. Did I wish him to shoot?

'I'll make a bargain,' I said.

Dougal raised one brow.

'You're in a bit better position to bargain than I am at present,' he said. 'What's your offer?'

'Let me talk to your men,' I said. 'And if they'll come with me of their own accord, then let them. If not, we'll go as we came – and we'll hand back your purse as well.'

One side of his mouth came up in a lopsided smile. He looked me over carefully, as though assessing my persuasiveness and my skills as an orator. Then he sat back, hands on his knees. He nodded once.

'Done,' he said.

In the event we left the glen of the cave with Dougal's purse and five men, in addition to Murtagh and myself: Rupert, John Whitlow, Willy MacMurtry, and the twin brothers Rufus and Geordie Coulter. It was Rupert's decision that swayed the others; I could still see – with a feeling of grim satisfaction – the look on Dougal's face when his squat, black-bearded lieutenant eyed me speculatively, then patted the dags at his belt and said, 'Aye, lass, why not?'

Wentworth Prison was thirty-five miles away. A half-hour's ride in a fast car over good roads. Two days' hard slog over half-frozen mud by ponyback. *Not long.* Dougal's words echoed in my ears and kept me in my saddle long past the point where I might have dropped from fatigue.

My body was pushed to its limits to keep to the saddle through the long weary miles, but my mind was free to worry. To keep it from thoughts of Jamie I spent the time remembering my interview in the cave with Dougal.

And the last thing he had said to me. Standing outside the small cave, waiting as Rupert and his companions brought their ponies down from a hiding place higher up the glen, Dougal had turned to me abruptly.

'I've a message for ye,' he had said. 'From the witch.'

'From Geilie?' To say I was startled was the least of it.

703

I couldn't make out his face in the dark, but I saw his head tilt in affirmation.

'I saw her the once,' he said softly, 'when I came to take the child.' Under other circumstances I might have felt some sympathy for him, parting for the last time from his mistress who was condemned to the stake, holding the child they had made together, a son whom he could never acknowledge. As it was, my voice was icy.

'What did she say?'

He paused; I wasn't sure if it were merely the disinclination to reveal information, or if he were trying to make sure of his words. Apparently it was the latter, for he spoke carefully.

'She said if ever I saw you again, I was to tell you two things, just as she told them to me. The first was: "I think it is possible, but I do not know." And the second – the second was just numbers. She made me say them over, to be sure I had them right, for I was to tell them to you in a certain order. The numbers were one, nine, six and seven.' The tall figure turned towards me in the dark, inquiring.

'Mean anything to ye?'

'No,' I said, and turned away to my mount. But it did, of course, mean something to me.

'I think it is possible.' There was only one thing she could mean by that. She thought, though she did not know, that it was possible to go back, through the circle of stone, to my proper place. Clearly she hadn't tried it herself, but had chosen – to her cost – to stay. Likely she had had her own reasons. Dougal, perhaps?

As for the numbers, I thought I knew what those meant, too. She had told them to him separately, for the sake of secrecy which must have gone bone deep in her by that time, but they were all part of one number, really. One, nine, six, seven. Nineteen-sixty-seven. The year of *her* disappearance into the past.

I felt a small thrill of curiosity, and deep regret. What a pity that I had not seen the vaccination mark on her arm until it was too late! And yet, had I seen it sooner, would

I have gone back to the circle of stone, perhaps with her help, and never have married Jamie?

Jamie. The thought of him was a leaden weight in my mind, a pendulum swinging slowly at the end of a rope. *Not long.* The track stretched endless and dreary before us, sometimes petering out altogether into frozen marshes or open sheets of water that had once been meadows and moors. In a freezing drizzle that would soon turn to snow, we reached our goal near evening of the second day.

The building loomed up black against the overcast sky. Built in the shape of a gigantic cube, four hundred feet on a side, with a tower on each corner, it could house three hundred prisoners, plus the forty soldiers of the garrison and their commander, the civilian governor and his staff, and the four dozen cooks, servants, grooms and other menials necessary for the running of the establishment. Wentworth Prison.

I looked up at the menacing walls of greenish granite, two feet thick at the base. Tiny windows pierced the walls here and there. A few were beginning to wink with light. Others, serving what I assumed were the prisoners' cells, stayed dark. I swallowed. Seeing the massive edifice, with its impenetrable walls, its monumental gate and its red-coated guards, I began to have doubts.

'What if' – my mouth was dry and I had to stop and lick my lips – 'what if we can't do it?'

Murtagh's expression was the same as always: grim-mouthed and dour, narrow chin receding into the grimy neck of his shirt. It didn't alter as he turned to me.

'Then Dougal will bury us wi' him, one on either side,' he answered. 'Come on, there's work to be done.'

PART SEVEN

Sanctuary

35

Wentworth Prison

Sir Fletcher Gordon was a short and portly man whose striped silk waistcoat fitted him like a second skin. Slope-shouldered and paunch-bellied, he looked rather like a large ham seated in the governor's wheel-backed chair.

The bald head and rich pinkish colour of his complexion did little to dispel this impression, though few hams boasted such bright blue eyes. He turned over the sheaf of papers on his desk with a slow, deliberate forefinger.

'Yes, here it is,' he said after an interminable pause to read a page. 'Fraser, James. Convicted of murder. Sentenced to hang. Now, where's the Warrant of Execution?' He paused again, shuffling nearsightedly through the papers. I dug my fingers deep into the satin of my reticule, willing my face to remain expressionless.

'Oh, yes. Date of execution, twenty-third December. Yes, we still have him.'

I swallowed, relaxing my hold on my bag, torn between exultation and panic. He was still alive, then. For another two days. And he was nearby, somewhere in the same building with me. The knowledge surged through my veins with a rush of adrenalin and my hands trembled.

I sat forward in the visitor's chair, trying to look winsomely appealing.

'May I see him, Sir Fletcher? Just for a moment, in case he . . . he might wish me to convey a message to his family?'

In the guise of an English friend of the Fraser family I had found it reasonably easy to gain admittance to Wentworth, and to the office of Sir Fletcher, civilian governor of the prison. It was dangerous to ask to see Jamie; not knowing my cover story, he might well give me away if he saw me suddenly without warning. For that matter, I might give myself away; I was not at all sure that I could maintain my precarious self-control if I saw him. But the next step was clearly to find out where he was; in this huge stone rabbit warren the chances of finding him without direction were almost nil.

Sir Fletcher frowned, considering. Plainly he found this request from a mere family acquaintance a nuisance, but he was not an unfeeling man. Finally he shook his head reluctantly.

'No, my dear. No, I'm afraid I really cannot allow that. We are rather crowded at present, and haven't sufficient facilities to permit private interviews. And the man is presently in' – he consulted his pile of papers again – 'in one of the large cells in the west block, with several other condemned felons. It would be extremely perilous for you to visit him there – or at all. The man is a dangerous prisoner, you understand; I see here that we have been keeping him in chains since his arrival.'

I gripped my bag again; this time to keep from striking him.

He shook his head again, plump chest rising and falling with his laboured breathing. 'No, if you were an immediate member of his family, perhaps . . .' He looked up, blinking. I clamped my jaw tightly, determined to give nothing away. Surely a slight show of agitation was reasonable, under the circumstances.

'But perhaps, my dear . . .' He seemed struck by sudden inspiration. He got ponderously to his feet and went to an inner door, where a uniformed soldier stood on guard. He murmured to the man, who nodded once and vanished.

Sir Fletcher came back to his desk, pausing on the way to retrieve a decanter and glasses from the top of a cabinet. I accepted his offer of claret; I needed it.

We were both halfway through the second glass by the time the guard returned. He marched in without invitation, placed a wooden box on the desk at Sir Fletcher's elbow and turned to march out again. I caught his eye lingering on me and modestly lowered my own gaze. I was wearing a gown borrowed from a lady of Rupert's acquaintance in

710

the nearby town, and from the scent that saturated the dress and its matching reticule I had a reasonably good idea just what this particular lady's profession was. I hoped the guard didn't recognize the gown.

Draining his glass, Sir Fletcher set it down and pulled the box towards him. It was a plain, square box of unfinished wood, with a sliding lid. There were letters chalked on the lid. I could read them, even upside down. FRASER, they read.

Sir Fletcher slid back the lid, peered inside for a moment, then closed the box and pushed it towards me.

'The prisoner's personal effects,' he explained. 'Customarily, we send them to whomever the prisoner designates as next of kin, after execution. This man, though' – he shook his head – 'has refused altogether to say anything about his family. Some estrangement, no doubt. Not unusual, of course, but regrettable under the circumstances. I hesitate to make the request, Mrs Beauchamp, but I thought that perhaps, since you are acquainted with the family, you would consider taking it upon yourself to convey his effects to the appropriate person?'

I didn't trust myself to speak, but nodded and buried my nose in my glass of claret.

Sir Fletcher seemed relieved, either at disposing of the box or at the thought of my imminent departure. He sat back, wheezing slightly, and smiled expansively at me.

'That is very kind of you, Mrs Beauchamp. I know such a thing cannot but be a painful duty to a young woman of feeling, and I am most sensible of your kindness in undertaking it, I do assure you.'

'N-not at all,' I stammered. I managed to stand up and to gather up the box. It measured about eight inches by six, and was four or five inches deep. A small, light box to hold the remains of a man's life.

I knew the things it held. Three fishing lines, neatly coiled; a cork stuck with fish-hooks; a flint and steel; a small piece of broken glass, edges blunt with wear; various small stones that looked interesting or had a good feel between the fingers; a dried mole's foot carried as a charm

711

against rheumatism. A Bible – or perhaps they had let him keep that? I hoped so. A ruby ring, if it hadn't been stolen. And a small wooden snake, carved of cherry wood, with the name SAWNY scratched on its underside.

I paused at the door, gripping the frame with my fingers to steady myself.

Sir Fletcher, following courteously to see me out, was at my side in a moment.

'Mrs Beauchamp! Are you feeling faint, my dear? Guard, a chair!'

I could feel the prickles of a cold sweat breaking out along the sides of my face, but I managed to smile and wave away the proffered chair. I wanted more than anything to get out of there – I needed fresh air, in large quantities. And I needed to be alone to cry.

'No, I'm quite all right,' I said, trying to sound convincing. 'It's only . . . a bit close in here, perhaps. No, I shall be perfectly all right. My groom is waiting outside, in any case.'

Forcing myself to stand up straight and smile, I had a thought. It might not help, but it couldn't hurt.

'Oh, Sir Fletcher . . .'

Still worried by my appearance, he was all gallantry and attention.

'Yes, my dear?'

'It occurred to me. . . . How sad for a young man in this situation to be estranged from his family. I thought perhaps . . . if he wished to write to them – a letter of reconciliation, perhaps? I would be pleased to deliver it to – to his mother.'

'You are thoughtfulness itself, my dear.' Sir Fletcher was jovial, now that it seemed I was not going to collapse on his rug after all. 'Of course. I will inquire. Where are you staying, my dear? If there is a letter, I shall have it sent to you.'

'Well' – I was doing better with the smile, though it felt pasted on my face – 'that is rather uncertain at the moment. I have several relatives and close acquaintances in the town, with whom I fear I shall be obliged to stay in turn, in order to avoid offending anyone, you see.' I managed a small laugh.

'So if it does not disturb you too much, perhaps my groom could call to inquire for the letter?'

'Of course, of course. That will do excellently, my dear. Excellently!'

And with a quick glance back at his decanter, he took my arm to escort me to the gate.

'Better, lassie?' Rupert pushed back the curtain of my hair to peer at my face. 'Ye look like an ill-cured pork belly. Here, better have a bit more.'

I shook my head at the proffered whisky flask and sat up, wiping my face with the damp rag he had brought.

'No, I'm all right now.' Escorted by Murtagh, who was disguised as my groom, I had barely made it out of sight of the prison before sliding off my pony and being sick in the snow. There I remained, weeping, with Jamie's box clutched to my bosom, until Murtagh had gathered me up bodily, forced me to mount and led me to the small inn in Wentworth town where Rupert had found lodgings. We were in an upper room, from which the bulk of the prison was barely visible in the gathering dusk.

'Is the lad dead then?' Rupert's broad face, half obscured by his beard, was grave and kind, lacking any of its usual clowning.

I shook my head and took a deep breath. 'Not yet.'

After hearing my story Rupert paced slowly around the room, pushing his lips in and out as he thought. Murtagh sat still, as usual, no sign of agitation on his features. He would have made a wonderful poker player, I thought.

Rupert returned, sinking down on the bed beside me with a sigh.

'Weel, he's alive still, and that's the most important thing. Damned if I see what to do next, though. We've no way to get into the place.'

'Aye, we have.' Murtagh said, suddenly. 'Thanks to the wee lassie's thought about the letter.'

'Mmmphm. One man, though. And only so far as the

713

governor's office. But aye, it's a start.' Rupert drew his dirk and idly scratched his thick beard with the point. 'It's a damn big place to search.'

'I know where he is,' I said, feeling better with the planning and the knowledge that my companions weren't giving up, no matter how hopeless our enterprise seemed. 'At least I know which wing he's in.'

'Do ye, then? Hmm.' He replaced the dirk and resumed his pacing, stopping to demand, 'How much money have ye, lass?'

I fumbled in the pocket of my gown. I had Dougal's purse, the money Jenny had forced me to take, and my string of pearls. Rupert rejected the pearls, but took the purse, pouring a stream of coins into the palm of one capacious hand.

'That'll do,' he said, jingling them experimentally. He cocked an eye at the Coulter twins. 'You twa laddies and Willy – come wi' me. John and Murtagh can stay here wi' the lassie.'

'Where are you going?' I asked.

He poured the coins into his sporran, keeping back one, which he tossed meditatively in the air.

'Och,' he said vaguely. 'Happen there's another inn, the other side of the town. The guards from the prison go there when they're off duty, for it's closer, and the drink's a penny cheaper.' He flipped the coin with his thumb, and turning his hand, caught it between the two knuckles.

I watched it, with a growing idea of what he intended.

'Is that so?' I said. 'I wouldn't suppose they play cards there, too, would you?'

'I wouldna ken, lassie, wouldna ken,' he answered. He tossed the coin once more and clapped his hands together, trapping it, then spread his hands apart, to show nothing but thin air. He smiled, teeth white in the black beard.

'But we might go and see, no?' He snapped his fingers, and the coin appeared once more between them.

Shortly past two o'clock on the following afternoon I passed again beneath the spiked portcullis that had guarded the gate of Wentworth since its construction in the late sixteenth century. It had lost very little of its forbidding aspect in the succeeding years, and I touched the dagger in my pocket for courage.

Sir Fletcher should now be well dug in at his midday repast, according to the information Rupert and his assistant spies had extracted from the prison guards during their foray the evening before. They had staggered in, red-eyed and reeking of ale, just before dawn. All Rupert would say in response to my questions was 'Och, lassie, all it takes to win is luck. It takes *skill* to lose!' He curled up in the corner then and went soundly to sleep, leaving me to pace the floor in frustration, as I had been doing all night.

He woke an hour later, though, clear-eyed and clear-headed, and laid out the rudiments of the plan I was about to put into execution.

'Sir Fletcher doesna allow anyone or anything to disturb his meals,' he said. 'Anyone wantin' him then must just go on wantin' until he's done wi' his food and drink. And after the midday meal, it's his habit to retire to his quarters for a wee sleep.'

Murtagh, in the character of my groom, had arrived a quarter of an hour previously and been admitted without difficulty. Presumably he would be shown to Sir Fletcher's office and asked to wait. While there, he was to search the office, first for a plan of the west wing, and then, on the off-chance, for keys that might open the cells.

I hung back a bit, glancing at the sky to judge the time. If I arrived before he had sat down, I might be invited to join Sir Fletcher for dinner, which would be highly inconvenient. But Rupert's card-playing acquaintances among the guards had assured him that the governor's habits were invariable; the bell for dinner was rung promptly at one, and the soup served five minutes later.

The guard on duty at the entrance was the same as the day before. He looked surprised, but greeted me courteously.

'So vexing,' I said, 'I had meant my groom to bring a small present for Sir Fletcher, as some return for his kindness to

715

me yesterday. But I found that the silly man had ridden off without it, and so I was obliged to follow with it myself, hoping to catch him up. Has he arrived already?' I displayed the small package I carried and smiled, thinking that it would help if I had dimples. Since I hadn't, I settled for a brilliant display of teeth.

It seemed to be sufficient. I was admitted and led through the corridors of the prison towards the governor's office. Though this part of the castle was decently furnished, there was little mistaking the place for anything other than a prison. There was a smell about it, which I imagined as the smell of misery and fear, though I supposed it was no more than the niff of ancient squalor and a shortage of drains.

The guard allowed me to precede him down the hall, following discreetly so as not to step on my cloak. And a damn good thing he did, for I rounded the corner towards Sir Fletcher's office a few feet ahead of him just in time to see Murtagh through the open door, dragging the unconscious form of the office guard behind the enormous desk.

I took one step back and dropped my package on to the stone floor. There was a shattering of glass, and the air was filled with the smothering aroma of peach brandy.

'Oh, dear,' I said, 'what *have* I done?'

While the guard was calling for a prisoner to clear up the mess I tactfully murmured something about waiting for Sir Fletcher in his private office, slipped in, and hastily shut the door behind me.

'What the bloody hell have you done?' I hissed at Murtagh. He looked up from his rummaging of the body, unconcerned at my tone.

'Sir Fletcher doesna keep keys in his office,' he informed me in a low voice, 'but *this* wee laddie has a set.' He pulled the huge ring free of the man's coat, careful to keep the keys from jingling.

I dropped to my knees behind him. 'Oh, well done!' I said. I cast an eye over the prostrate soldier; still breathing, at least. 'What about a plan of the prison?'

He shook his head. 'Not that either, but my friend here told me a bit while we waited. The condemned cells are on

716

the same floor as this, in the middle of the west corridor. There're three cells, though, and I couldna ask more than that – he was a bit suspicious as it was.'

'It's enough – I hope. All right, give me the keys and get out.'

'Me? It's *you* should leave, lassie, and right smart too.' He glanced at the door, but there was no sound on the other side.

'No, it has to be me,' I said, reaching again for the keys. 'Listen,' I said impatiently. 'If they find you wandering round the prison with a bunch of keys, and the guard here laid out like a mackerel, we're both done for, because why didn't I cry out for help?' I snatched the keys and crammed them in my pocket, with some difficulty.

Murtagh was still sceptical, but had risen to his feet.

'And if *you're* caught?' he demanded.

'I swoon,' I said crisply. 'And when I recover – eventually – I say that I saw you apparently murdering the guard and fled in terror, with no idea where I was going. I lost my way looking for help.'

He nodded slowly. 'Aye, all right.' He moved towards the door, then stopped.

'But why did I – oh.' He crossed swiftly to the desk and pulled out one drawer after another, stirring the contents with one hand and tossing items on to the floor with the other.

'Theft,' he explained, coming back to the door. He opened it a crack, looking out.

'If it's theft, shouldn't you take something?' I suggested, looking about for something small and portable. I picked up an enamelled snuffbox. 'This, perhaps?'

He made an impatient gesture to me to put it down, still peering through the crack.

'Nay, lass! If I'm found wi' Sir Fletcher's property, that's a hanging offence. Attempted theft is only flogging or mutilation.'

'Oh.' I put the snuffbox down hastily and stood behind him, peering over his shoulder. The hall seemed empty.

'I go first,' he said. 'If I meet anyone, I'll draw 'em off.

Wait to the count of thirty, then follow. We'll meet ye in the small wood to the north.' He opened the door, then paused and turned back.

'If you're caught, mind ye throw the keys awa'.' Before I could speak he was through the door like an eel and down the corridor, moving silently as a shadow.

It seemed to take an eternity to find the west wing, dodging through the corridors of the old castle, peering around corners and hiding behind columns. I saw only one guard on my way, though, and managed to avoid him by diving back around a corner, pressing myself to the wall with hammering heart until he passed.

Once I found the west wing, though, I had little doubt that I was in the right place. There were three large doors in the corridor, each with a tiny barred window from which I could catch no more than a frustrating glimpse of the room behind it.

'Eenie, meenie, minie, mo,' I muttered to myself, and headed for the centre cell. The keys on the ring were unlabelled, but of different sizes. Clearly only one of three big ones would fit the lock before me. Naturally, it was the third one. I took a deep breath as the lock clicked, then wiped my sweating hands on my skirt and shoved the door open.

I sorted frantically through the stinking mass of men in the cell, stepping over outstretched feet and legs, pushing past heavy bodies that moved with maddening sluggishness out of my way. The stir occasioned by my abrupt entrance had spread; those who had been asleep amid the filth on the floor began to sit up, roused by the rippling murmur of astonishment. Some were manacled to the walls; the chains grated and clanked in the half light as they moved. I grabbed one of the standing men, a brown-bearded clansman in ragged yellow and green tartan. The bones of his arm under my hand were frighteningly near the skin; the English wasted little extra food on their prisoners.

'James Fraser! A big, redheaded man! Is he in this cell? Where is he?'

He was already moving towards the door with the others who were not chained, but paused a moment to glance down at me. The prisoners by now had seized the idea, and were pouring through the open door in a shuffling flood, peering and murmuring to each other.

'Who? Fraser? Och, they took him awa' this mornin'.' The man shrugged and pushed at my hands, trying to shake me off.

I took hold of his belt with a grip that halted him in his tracks. 'Where did they take him? Who took him?'

'I dinna ken where; was yon Captain Randall took 'im – a pinch-faced snark, he is.' With an impatient wrench he freed himself and headed for the door with a step born of long-nourished purpose.

Randall. I stood stunned for a moment, jostled by the escaping men, deaf to the shouts of the chained. Finally I shook myself from my stupor and tried to think. Geordie had watched the castle since dawn. No one had left in the morning save a small kitchen party going to fetch supplies. So they were still here, somewhere.

Randall was a captain; likely no one ranked higher in a prison garrison, save Sir Fletcher himself. Presumably Randall could thus command the castle's resources so as to provide him with some suitable spot in which to torture a prisoner at his leisure.

And torture it surely was. Even if it was meant to end in hanging, the man I had seen at Fort William was a cat by nature. He could no more resist the chance to play with this particular mouse than he could alter his height or the colour of his eyes.

I took a deep breath, resolutely shoving aside thoughts of what might have happened since morning, and charged out the door myself, colliding full force with an English redcoat rushing in. The man reeled backwards, staggering with tiny running steps to keep his balance. Thrown off balance myself, I crashed heavily into the door jamb, numbing my left side and banging my head. I clutched the door post for support, the ringing in my ears chiming with the echoes of Rupert's voice: *Ye have a moment of surprise, lass. Use it!*

It was open to question, I thought dizzily, who was more surprised. I groped madly for the pocket that held my dagger, cursing my stupidity for not having entered the cell with it already drawn.

The English soldier, balance recovered, was staring at me with his mouth agape, but I could feel my precious moment of surprise already slipping away. Abandoning the elusive pocket, I stooped and drew the dagger from my stocking in a move that continued upward with all the force I could muster. The knifepoint took the advancing soldier just under the chin as he reached for his belt. His hands rose halfway to his throat, then with a look of surprise he staggered back against the wall and slid down it in slow motion as the life drained away from him. Like me he had come to investigate without bothering to draw his weapon first, and that small oversight had just cost him his life. The grace of God had saved me from this mistake; I could afford no more. Feeling very cold, I stepped over the twitching body, careful not to look.

I dashed back the way I had come, as far as the turning by the stairs. There was a spot here by the wall where I would be sheltered from view from both directions. I leaned against the wall and indulged myself in a moment of trembling nausea.

Wiping my sweaty hands on my skirt, I dredged the dirk from its hidden pocket. It was now my only weapon; I'd had neither time nor stomach enough to retrieve my sock-knife. Perhaps that was as well, I thought, rubbing my fingers on my bodice; there had been surprisingly little blood, and I shrank from the thought of the gush that would follow if I pulled the knife free.

Dagger now safely in hand, I peered cautiously out into the corridor. The prisoners I had inadvertently released had gone to the left. I had no idea what they were set on doing, but they would likely occupy the English while they were doing it. With no reason to pick one direction over another for my search, it made sense to move away from whatever commotion they caused.

The light from the high slit windows fell aslant behind me; this was the west side of the castle, then. I must keep my bearings as I moved, since Rupert would be waiting for me near the south gate.

Stairs. I forced my numbed mind to think, trying to reason my way to the spot I was looking for. If you wanted to torture someone, presumably you wanted both privacy and soundproofing. Both considerations pointed to an isolated dungeon as the most likely spot. And the dungeons in castles such as this were customarily underground, where tons of earth muffled any cries, and darkness hid all cruelty from the eyes of those responsible.

The wall rounded into a curve at the end of the corridor; I had reached one of the four corner towers – and the towers had stairs.

The spiral stair opened around another curve, the wedge-shaped steps plunging down in dizzying flights that deceived the eye and twisted the ankles. The plunge from the relative light of the corridor into the gloom of the stairwell made it even harder to judge the distance from one stair to the next, and I slipped several times, barking my knuckles and skinning my palms on the stone walls as I caught myself.

The stairway yielded one benefit. From a narrow window let in to save the stairwell from total darkness I could see the main courtyard. At least I could now orient myself. A small group of soldiers was drawn up in neat red lines for inspection, but not, apparently, to witness the summary punishment of a Scottish rebel. There was a gibbet in the courtyard, black and foreboding, but unoccupied. The sight of it was like a blow in the stomach. Tomorrow morning. I clattered down the stairs, heedless of scraped elbows and stubbed toes.

Hitting the bottom in a swish of skirts, I stopped to listen. Dead silence all around, but at least this part of the castle was in use; there were torches in the wall sconces, dyeing the granite blocks in pools of flickering red, each pool ebbing into darkness at its edges before the pool of the next torch leached into light again. Smoke from the torches hung in grey swirls along the vaulted roof of the corridor.

There was only one way to go from this point. I went, dagger still gripped at the ready. It was eerie to be pacing softly down this corridor. I had seen similar dungeons before, as a day-tripper, visiting historic castles with Frank. But then the massive granite blocks had been stripped of their menace by the glare of electric lights hung from the arches of the cavernous ceiling. I remembered recoiling from the small, dank chambers, even in those days when they had been in disuse for over a century. Seeing the remnants of old and horrible ways, the thick doors and the rusting manacles on the wall, I had been able, I thought, to imagine the torments of those imprisoned in these forbidding cells. I would have laughed now at my naivety. There were some things, as Dougal said, that the imagination was simply not equal to.

I tiptoed past bolted doors six inches thick; thick enough to smother any sound from inside. Bending close to the floor, I checked for a strip of light at the base of each door. Prisoners might be left to rot in darkness, but Randall would need to see what he was doing. The floor here was gummy with ancient dirt, covered with a thick layer of loose dust. Apparently this part of the prison was not in current use. But the torches showed that *someone* was down here.

The fourth door in the corridor showed the light I was looking for. I listened, kneeling on the floor with my ear pressed against the crack, but heard nothing more than the thin crackle of a fire.

The door was unlocked. I pushed it open a small crack and peered cautiously within. Jamie was there, sitting on the floor against one wall, curled into himself with his head between his knees. He was alone.

The room was small but well lit, with a rather homely looking brazier in which burned a cheery fire. For a dungeon it was remarkably cosy; the stone flags were halfway clean, and a small camp bed leaned against one wall. The room was further furnished with two chairs and a table, on which sat a number of objects including a large pewter flask and horn cups. It was an astonishing sight, after my visions of dripping walls and scuttling rats. It occurred to me that perhaps the garrison officers had furnished this snuggery as a refuge in which to entertain such female companionship as they could induce to visit them within the prison; clearly it had the advantage of privacy over the barracks.

'Jamie!' I called softly. He didn't raise his head or answer me, and I felt a thrill of fear. Pausing only long enough to shut the door behind me, I crossed rapidly to him and touched his shoulder.

'Jamie!'

He looked up then; his face was dead white, unshaven and sheened with a cold sweat that had soaked his hair and shirt. The room stank of fear and vomit.

'Claire!' he said, speaking hoarsely through lips cracked with dryness. 'How did you – ye must get out of here at once. He'll be back soon.'

'Don't be ridiculous.' I was assessing the situation as rapidly as I could, hoping that concentration on the job at hand would ease the choking sensation and help melt the large ball of ice in the pit of my stomach.

He was chained by the ankle to a bolt in the wall, but otherwise unfettered. A coil of rope among the rubble of objects on the table had plainly been used, though; there were raw marks on his wrists and elbows.

I was puzzled by his condition. He was clearly dazed and every line of his body was eloquent with pain, but I could see no obvious damage. There was no blood and no wound visible. I dropped to my knees and began methodically to try the keys of my ring on the manacle around his ankle.

'What has he done to you?' I asked, keeping my voice low for fear of Randall's return.

Jamie swayed where he sat, eyes closed, the sweat beading in hundreds of tiny pearls on his skin. Plainly he was near to fainting, but opened his eyes for a moment at my voice. Moving with exquisite care, he used his left hand to lift the object he had been cradling in his lap. It was his right hand, almost unrecognizable as a human appendage. Grotesquely swollen, it was now a bloated bag, blotched with red and purple, the fingers dangling at crazy angles. A white shard of bone poked through the torn skin of the middle finger, and a trickle of blood stained the knuckles, puffed into shapeless dimples.

The human hand is a delicate marvel of engineering, an intricate system of joints and pulleys, served and controlled by a network of millions of tiny nerves, exquisitely sensitive to touch. A single broken finger is enough to sink a strong man to his knees with nauseated pain.

'Payment,' Jamie said, 'for his nose – with interest.' I stared at the sight for a moment, then said in a voice that I didn't recognize as mine, 'I'm going to kill him for this.'

Jamie's mouth twitched slightly as a flicker of humour forced its way through the mask of pain and dizziness. 'I'll hold your cloak, Sassenach,' he whispered. His eyes closed again and he sagged against the wall, too far gone to protest my presence further.

I went back to work on the lock, glad to see that my hands were no longer shaking. The fear was gone, replaced by a glorious rage.

I had gone through the complete ring of keys twice, and still found none that would turn the lock. My hands were growing sweaty and the keys slid through my fingers like minnows as I began to try the most likely ones again. My muttered cursing roused Jamie from his stupor and he leaned down slowly to look at what I was doing.

'Ye needn't find a key will turn it,' he said, bracing a shoulder on the wall to keep upright. 'If one will fit to the length of the barrel, you can spring the lock wi' a good bash on the head of it.'

'You've seen this kind of lock before?' I wanted to keep him awake and talking; he was going to have to walk if we were to leave here.

'I've been in one. When they brought me here they chained me in a big cell with a lot of others. A lad named Reilly was chained next to me; a Leinsterman – said he'd been in most of the jails in Ireland and decided to try Scotland for a change o' scenery.' Jamie was struggling to talk; he realized as well as I that he must rouse himself. He

724

managed a feeble smile. 'He told me a good bit about locks and such, and showed me how we could break the ones we were wearing, *if* we'd had a spare bit of straight metal, which we didn't.'

'Tell me, then.' The effort of talking was making him sweat freely, but he seemed more alert. Concentrating on the problem of the lock seemed to help.

Following his directions, I found a suitable key and thrust it in as far as it would go. According to Reilly, a solid blow straight in on the end of the key would force the other end hard against the tumblers and spring them loose. I looked around for a suitable instrument for bashing.

'Use the mallet on the table, Sassenach,' said Jamie. Caught by a grim note in his voice I glanced from his face to the table, where a medium-sized wooden mallet lay, the handle wrapped with tarred twine.

'Is that what – ' I began, aghast.

'Aye. Brace the manacle against the wall, lass, before ye hit it.'

Grasping the handle gingerly, I picked up the mallet. It was awkward to get the iron manacle correctly positioned so that one side was braced by the wall, as this required that Jamie cross the manacled leg under the other and press his knee to the wall on the far side.

My first two blows were too weak and timorous. Gathering determination about me like a cloak, I smashed the rounded end of the key as hard as I could. The mallet slipped off the key and caught Jamie a glancing but hard blow on the ankle. Recoiling, he lost his precarious balance and fell, instinctively reaching out his right hand to save himself. He let out an unearthly moan as his right arm crumpled beneath him and his shoulder hit the floor.

'Oh, damn,' I said wearily. Jamie had fainted, not that I could blame him. Taking advantage of his momentary immobility, I turned his ankle so that the manacle was well braced, and banged doggedly on the embedded key, with little apparent effect. I was thinking grim thoughts about Irish locksmiths when the door beside me swung suddenly open.

725

Randall's face, like Frank's, seldom showed what he was thinking, presenting instead a bland and impenetrable facade. At the moment, though, the Captain's customary poise had deserted him and he stood in the doorway with his jaw agape, looking not unlike the man who accompanied him. A very large man in a stained and ragged uniform, this assistant had the sloping brow, flat nose and loose prominent lips characteristic of some types of mental retardation. His expression did not change as he peered over Randall's shoulder, showing no particular interest either in me or the unconscious man on the floor.

Recovering, Randall walked into the room and reached down to prod the manacle around Jamie's ankle. 'Been damaging the Crown's property, I see, my girl. That's an offence punishable by law, you know. To say nothing of attempting to aid a dangerous prisoner in escaping.' His pale grey eyes held a spark of amusement. 'We'll have to arrange something suitable for you. In the meantime . . .' He jerked me to my feet and pulled my arms behind me, twisting his stock around my wrists.

Struggle was plainly fruitless, but I stamped on his toes as hard as I could, purely to vent some of my own frustration.

'Ouch!' He turned me and gave me a hard shove, so that my legs hit the bed and I fell, half lying on the rough blankets. Randall surveyed me with grim satisfaction, rubbing the scuffed toe of his boot with a linen handkerchief. I glared back at him and he gave a short laugh.

'You're no coward, I'll give you that. In fact, you're a fit match for him' – he nodded at Jamie, who was beginning to stir a bit – 'and I can't give you a better compliment than that.' He tenderly fingered his throat, where a darkening bruise showed in the open neck of his shirt. 'He tried to kill me, one-handed, when I untied him. And damned near managed it too. Pity I didn't realize he was left-handed.'

'How unreasonable of him,' I said.

'Quite,' said Randall, with a nod. 'I don't suppose you'd be so impolite, do you? Still, on the off-chance . . .' He turned to the large servant, who was simply standing in the doorway, shoulders sloped, waiting for orders.

'Marley,' said Randall, 'come here and search this woman for weapons.' He watched with some amusement as the man groped clumsily about my person, eventually coming upon and extracting my dirk.

'You don't care for Marley?' asked the Captain, watching me try to avoid the thick fingers that prodded me all too intimately. 'Rather a pity; I'm sure he's quite taken with you.

'Poor Marley hasn't much luck with women,' the Captain went on, a malicious gleam in his eye. 'Have you, Marley? Even the whores won't have him.' He fixed me with a designing sort of look, smiling wolfishly. 'Too big, they say.' He raised one eyebrow. 'Which is quite a judgement, coming from a whore, is it not?' He raised the other brow, making his meaning quite clear.

Marley, who had begun to pant rather heavily during the search, stopped and wiped a thread of saliva from the side of his mouth. I moved as far away as I could manage, disgusted.

Randall, watching me, said, 'I imagine Marley would like to entertain you privately in his quarters, once we've finished our conversation. Of course he might decide later on to share his good fortune with his friends, but that's up to him.'

'Oh, you don't want to watch?' I asked sarcastically.

Randall laughed, truly amused.

'I may have what are called "unnatural tastes" myself, as I imagine you know by this time. But give me credit for some aesthetic principles.' He glanced at the immense servant, slouched in his filthy clothes, paunch straining over his belt. The loose, blubbery lips chewed and mumbled constantly, as though seeking some fragment of food, and the short, thick fingers worked nervously against the crotch of the stained breeches. Randall shuddered delicately.

'No,' he said. 'You're a very lovely woman, shrewish tongue notwithstanding. To see you with Marley – no, I don't believe I want to watch that. Appearances aside, Marley's personal habits leave quite a lot to be desired.'

'So do yours,' I said.

'That's as may be. At any rate, they'll not concern you much longer.' He paused, looking down at me. 'I would still like to know who you are, you know. A Jacobite, plainly, but whose? The Earl Marischal's? Seaforth's? Lovat's, most likely, since you're with the Frasers.' Randall nudged Jamie gently with a polished boot-toe, but he still lay inert. I could see his chest rising and falling regularly; perhaps he had merely slipped from unconsciousness into sleep. The smudges under his eyes gave evidence that he had had little rest of late.

'I've even heard from some that you're a witch,' the Captain went on. His tone was light but he watched me closely, as though I might suddenly turn myself into an owl and flap away. 'There was some kind of trouble at Cranesmuir, wasn't there? A death of some kind? But no doubt that's all superstitious nonsense.'

Randall eyed me speculatively. 'I might be persuaded to make a bargain with you,' he said abruptly. He leaned back, half sitting on the table, inviting me.

I laughed bitterly. 'I can't say I'm in either a position or a mood to bargain at the moment. What can you offer me?'

Randall glanced at Marley. The idiot's eyes were fixed on me and he was mumbling under his breath.

'A choice, at least. Tell me – and convince me – who you are and who sent you to Scotland. What you're doing and what information you've sent to whom. Tell me that, and I'll take you to Sir Fletcher instead of giving you to Marley.'

I kept my eyes firmly away from Marley. I had seen the rotting stumps of teeth embedded in pustulant gums, and the thought of him kissing me, let alone – I choked the thought off. Randall was right; I wasn't a coward. But neither was I a fool.

'You can't take me to Sir Fletcher,' I said, 'and I know it as well as you do. Take me to him and risk my telling him about *this*?' My nod took in the snug little room, the cosy fire, the bed I sat on and Jamie lying at my feet. 'Whatever his shortcomings, I don't imagine Sir Fletcher would stand, officially, for his officers torturing prisoners. Even the English army must have *some* standards.'

Randall raised both eyebrows. 'Torture? Oh, that.' He waved negligently at Jamie's hand. 'An accident. He fell in his cell and was trampled by the other prisoners. It's rather crowded in those cells, you know.' He smiled derisively.

I was silent. While Sir Fletcher might or might not believe the damage to Jamie's hand was an accident, he was most unlikely to believe anything *I* said, once I was unmasked as a Scottish spy.

Randall was watching me, eyes alert for any signs of weakening. 'Well? The choice is yours.'

I sighed and closed my eyes, tired of looking at him. The choice *wasn't* mine, but I could hardly tell him why not.

'It doesn't matter,' I said wearily. 'I can't tell you anything.'

'Think it over for a moment.' He stood up and stepped carefully over Jamie's unconscious form, taking a key from his pocket. 'I may need Marley's help for a bit, but then I'll send him back to his quarters – and you with him, if you don't mean to cooperate.' He stooped, unlocked the manacle, and heaved the inert body up with an impressive display of strength for one so slightly built. The muscles of his forearms ridged the cloth of his snowy shirt as he carried Jamie, head lolling, to a stool in the corner. He nodded at the bucket standing nearby.

'Rouse him,' he directed the silent hulk curtly. Cold water splashed from the stones in the corner and puddled on the floor, making a filthy pool underneath. 'Once more,' Randall said, inspecting Jamie, who was moaning slightly, head stirring against the stones of the wall. He flinched and coughed under the second drenching shower.

Randall strode forward and took him by the hair, yanking his head back, shaking it like a drowned animal, so that drops of fetid water spattered on the walls. Jamie's eyes were dull slits. Randall threw Jamie's head back in disgust, wiping his hand down the side of his trousers as he turned away. His eye must have caught the flicker of movement because he began to turn back, but not in time to brace himself against the big Scot's sudden lunge.

Jamie's arms went around Randall's neck. Lacking the use of his right hand, he gripped his right wrist with the able left and pulled, forearm braced on the Englishman's windpipe. As Randall turned purple and began to sag, Jamie loosed his left hand long enough to drive it into the captain's kidney. Even weakened as Jamie was, the blow was enough to make Randall give at the knees.

Dropping the limp captain, Jamie whirled to face the hulking servant, who had been watching events so far without the slightest flicker of interest on his slack-jawed face. Although his expression remained rather inert, he did move, picking up the mallet from the table as Jamie came towards him holding the stool by one leg in his good left hand. A certain dull wariness came into the man's face as the two circled each other slowly, looking for an opening.

Better-armed, Marley tried first, swinging the mallet at Jamie's ribs. Jamie whirled away and feinted with the stool, forcing the man back towards the door. The next attempt, a murderous blow downwards, would have split Jamie's skull had it landed on target. As it was, the stool split instead, one leg and the seat sheared away.

Impatiently Jamie smashed the stool against the wall with his next swing, reducing it to a smaller but more manageable club; a two-foot length of wood with a ragged, splintered end.

The air in the cell, made stifling with smoke from the torches, was still except for the gasping breath of the two men and the occasional bruising thud of wood on flesh. Afraid to speak for fear of disturbing Jamie's precarious concentration, I pulled my feet up on to the bed and shrank back against the wall, trying to stay out of the way.

It was plain to me – and by his faint smile of anticipation, to the servant also – that Jamie was tiring rapidly. Amazing enough that he was on his feet at all, let alone fighting. It was clear to all three of us that the fight couldn't last much longer; if he was to have any chance at all, he must move soon. With short, hard jabs of the stool leg, he advanced cautiously on Marley, forcing the bigger man into the corner where the arc of his swing would be restricted. Realizing this by some instinct, Marley came out with a vicious horizontal swing, expecting to force Jamie back.

Instead of stepping back, Jamie stepped forward into the swing, taking the full brunt of the blow in the left side as he brought his club down full force on Marley's temple. Intent on the scene before me, I had paid no attention to Randall's prone body on the floor near the door. But as Marley tottered, eyes glazing, I heard the scraping sounds of boots on stone, and a laboured breathing rasped in my ear.

'Nicely fought, Fraser.' Randall's voice was hoarse from the choking, but as composed as ever. 'Cost you a few ribs, though, didn't it?'

Jamie leaned against the wall, breathing in sobbing gasps, still holding the club, elbow pressed hard to his side. His eyes dropped to the floor, measuring the distance.

'Don't try it, Fraser.' The light voice was bland. 'She'll be dead before you get two steps.' The thin cool knife blade slid past my ear; I could feel the point gently pricking the corner of my jaw.

Jamie surveyed the scene with dispassionate eyes for a moment, still braced by the wall. With a sudden effort he straightened painfully and stood swaying. The club clanked hollowly on the stone floor. The knifepoint pricked infinitesimally harder, but otherwise Randall stood motionless as Jamie slowly crossed the few feet to the table, stooping carefully on the way to pick up the twine-wrapped mallet. He held it dangling in two fingers in front of him, his non-offensive intent apparent.

The mallet clattered on the table in front of me, the handle spinning hard enough to carry the weighty head nearly to the edge. It lay dark and heavy on the oak, a homely, solid tool. A reed basket of large nails to go with it lay in the jumble of objects at the far end of the table; something perhaps left behind by the carpenters who had furnished the room. Jamie's good hand, the fine straight fingers rimmed with gold in the light, gripped the table

731

edge hard. With an effort I could only guess at he lowered himself slowly into a chair and deliberately spread both hands flat before him on the scarred wood surface, the mallet within easy reach.

His gaze had been locked with Randall's during the painful trip across the room, and did not waver now. He nodded briefly in my direction without looking at me and said, 'Let her go.'

The knife-hand seemed to relax a trifle. Randall's voice was amused and curious. 'Why should I?'

Jamie seemed now in complete command of himself, despite his white face and the sweat that ran unregarded down his face like tears.

'You cannot hold a knife on two people at once. Kill the woman or leave her side, and I'll kill you.' He spoke softly, a steely thread beneath the quiet Scots accent.

'And what's to stop me killing both of you, one at a time?'

I would have called the expression on Jamie's face a smile only because his teeth were showing. 'What, and cheat the hangman? Bit hard to explain, come morning, no?' He nodded briefly at the unconscious hulk on the floor. 'You'll recall that ye had to have your wee helper bind me wi' rope before ye broke my hand.'

'So?' The knife stayed steady at my ear.

'Your helper is no going to be much good to ye awhile yet.' This was undeniably true; the monstrous servant was lying on his face in the corner, breathing in ragged, stertorous snores. Severe concussion, I thought mechanically. Possible cerebral haemorrhage. I couldn't care less if he died before my eyes.

'You can't take me alone, one-handed or no.' Jamie shook his head slowly, appraising Randall's size and strength. 'No. I'm bigger, and far the better fighter, hand to hand. Did ye not have the woman there, I would take that wee knife from ye and cram it down your throat. And you know it, which is why you've not harmed her.'

'But I do have her. You could leave yourself, of course. There's a way out, quite near. That would leave your wife – you did say she's your wife? – to die, of course.'

732

Jamie shrugged. 'And myself as well. I'd not get far, with the whole garrison hunting me. To be shot in the open might be preferable to being hanged in here, but not enough to make a difference.' A brief grimace of pain crossed his face and he held his breath for a moment. When he breathed again it was in shallow, panting gulps. Whatever shock had been protecting him from the worst of the pain, it was apparently wearing off.

'So we seem to be at an impasse.' Randall's well-bred English tones were casual. 'Unless you have a suggestion?'

'I have. You want me.' The cool Scottish voice was matter of fact. 'Let the woman go, and ye can have me.' The knifepoint moved slightly, nicking my ear. I felt a sting and the warm ooze of blood.

'Do what ye wish to me. I'll not struggle, though I'll allow you to bind me if ye think it needful. And I'll not speak of it, come tomorrow. But first you'll see the woman safe from the prison.' My eyes were on Jamie's ruined hand. A small pool of blood under the middle finger was growing, and I realized with a shock that he was deliberately pressing the finger into the table, using the pain as a spur to stay conscious. He was bargaining for my life using the only thing he had left – himself. If he fainted now, that single chance was gone.

Randall had relaxed completely; the knife lay carelessly on my right shoulder as he thought it through. I was there before him. Jamie was meant to hang in the morning. Sooner or later he would be missed, and the castle would be searched. While a certain amount of brutality might be tolerated among officers and gentlemen – I was sure it would extend to a broken hand or a flayed back – Randall's other inclinations were not so lightly to be overlooked. No matter what Jamie's status as a condemned prisoner, if he stood at the foot of the gallows come morning and claimed abuse at the hands of Randall, his claims would be investigated. And if physical examination proved them true, Randall's career was at an end, and possibly his life as well. But with Jamie sworn to silence . . .

'You'll give me your word?'

733

Jamie's eyes were like blue matchflames in the parchment of his face. After a moment he nodded slowly. 'In return for yours.'

The attraction of a victim at once completely unwilling and completely compliant was irresistible.

'Done.' The knife left my shoulder and I heard the susurrus of sheathed metal. Randall walked slowly past me, around the table, picking up the mallet as he went. He held it up, ironically questioning, 'You'll allow me a brief test of your sincerity?'

'Aye.' Jamie's voice was as steady as his hands, flat and motionless on the table. I tried to speak, to utter some protest, but my throat had dried to a sticky silence.

Moving without haste, Randall leaned past Jamie to pluck a large nail delicately from the reed basket. He positioned the point with care and brought the mallet down, driving the nail through Jamie's right hand into the table with four solid blows. The broken fingers twitched and sprang straight, like the legs of a spider pinned to a collection board.

Jamie groaned, his eyes wide and blank with shock. Randall set the mallet down with care. He took Jamie's chin in his hand and turned his face up. 'Now kiss me,' he said softly, and lowered his head to Jamie's unresisting mouth.

Randall's face when he rose was dreamy, eyes gentle and faraway, long mouth quirked in a smile. Once upon a time I had loved a smile like that, and that dreamy look had roused me in anticipation. Now it sickened me. Tears ran into the corner of my mouth, though I didn't remember starting to cry. Randall stood a moment in his trance, gazing down at Jamie. Then he stirred, remembering, and drew the knife once more from its sheath.

The blade slashed carelessly through the binding around my wrists, grazing the skin. I hardly had time to rub the circulation back into my hands before he was urging me up with a hand beneath my elbow, pushing me towards the door.

'Wait!' Jamie spoke behind us and Randall turned impatiently.

'You'll allow me to say goodbye?' It was a statement more than a question, and Randall hesitated only briefly before nodding and giving me a shove back towards the motionless figure at the table.

Jamie's good arm was tight around my shoulders and my wet face was buried in his neck.

'You can't,' I whispered. 'You can't. I won't let you.'

His mouth was warm against my ear. 'Claire, I'm to hang in the morning. What happens to me between now and then doesna matter to anyone.' I drew back and stared at him.

'It matters to me!' The strained lips quivered in what was almost a smile, and he raised his free hand and laid it against my wet cheek.

'I know it does, *mo duinne*. And that's why you'll go now. So I'll know there is someone still who minds for me.' He drew me close again, kissed me gently and whispered in Gaelic, 'He will let you go because he thinks you are helpless. I know you are not.' Releasing me, he said in English, 'I love you. Go now.'

Randall paused as he ushered me out the door. 'I'll be back very shortly.' It was the voice of a man taking reluctant leave of his lover, and my stomach heaved.

Silhouetted in red by the torch behind him, Jamie inclined his head gracefully towards the pinioned hand. 'I expect you'll find me here.'

Black Jack. A common name for rogues and scoundrels in the eighteenth century. A staple of romantic fiction, the name conjured up charming highwaymen, dashing blades in plumed hats. The reality walked at my side.

One never stops to think what underlies romance. Tragedy and terror, transmuted by time. Add a little art in the telling, and *voilà!* a stirring romance, to make the blood run fast and maidens sigh. My blood was running fast, all right, and never a maiden sighed like Jamie, cradling his mangled hand.

'This way.' It was the first time he had spoken since we had left the cell. He indicated a narrow alcove in the wall, unlighted by torches. The way out, of which he had spoken to Jamie.

By now I had sufficient command of myself to speak, and I did so. I stepped back a pace so that the torchlight fell full on me, for I wanted him to remember my face.

'You asked me, Captain, if I were a witch,' I said, my voice low and steady. 'I'll answer you now. Witch I am. Witch, and I curse you. You will marry, Captain, and your wife will bear a child, but you shall not live to see your firstborn. I curse you with knowledge, Jonathan Randall – I give you the hour of your death.'

His face was in shadow, but the gleam of his eye told me he believed me. And why should he not? For I spoke the truth, and I knew it. I could see the lines of Frank's genealogical chart as though they were drawn on the mortar lines between the stones of the wall, and the names listed by them. 'Jonathan Wolverton Randall,' I said softly, reading it from the stones. 'Born third September 1705. Died – ' He made a convulsive movement towards me, but not fast enough to prevent me from speaking.

A narrow door at the back of the alcove crashed open with a squeal of hinges. Expecting further darkness, my eyes were dazzled by a blinding flash of light on snow. A quick shove from behind sent me staggering headlong into the drifts, and the door slammed to behind me.

I was lying in a ditch of sorts, behind the castle. The drifts around me covered heaps of something – the prison's refuse, most likely. There was something hard beneath the drift I had fallen into; wood, perhaps. Looking up at the sheering wall above me, I could see streaks and runnels down the stone, marking the path of rubbish tipped from a sliding door forty feet above. That must be the kitchen quarters.

I rolled over, bracing myself to rise, and found myself looking into a pair of wide blue eyes. The face was nearly as blue as the eyes, and hard as the log of wood I had mistaken him for. I stumbled to my feet, choking, and staggered back against the castle wall.

Head down, breathe deep, I told myself firmly. You are

not going to faint, you have seen dead men before, lots of them, you are not going to faint – God, he has blue eyes like – *you are not going to faint, damn it!*

My breathing slowed at last, and with it my racing pulse. As the panic receded I forced myself back to that pathetic figure, wiping my hands convulsively on my skirt. I don't know whether it was pity, curiosity or simple shock that made me look again. Seen without the suddenness of surprise, there was nothing frightening about the dead man; there never is. No matter how ugly the manner in which a man dies, it's only the presence of a suffering human soul that is horrifying; once gone, what is left is only an object.

The blue-eyed stranger had been hanged. He was not the only inhabitant of the ditch. I didn't bother to excavate the drift, but now that I knew what it contained, I could plainly see the outline of frozen limbs and the softly rounded heads under the snow. At least a dozen men lay there, waiting either for a thaw that would make their burial easier, or for a cruder disposal by the beasts of the nearby forest.

The thought startled me out of my pensive immobility. I had no time to waste in graveside meditation, or one more pair of blue eyes would stare sightless up into falling snow.

I had to find Murtagh and Rupert. That hidden postern door could be used, perhaps. Clearly it was not fortified or guarded like the main gates and other entrances to the prison. But I needed help, and I needed it quickly.

I glanced up at the rim of the ditch. The sun was quite low, burning through a haze of cloud just above the treetops. The air felt heavy with moisture. Likely it would snow again by nightfall; the haze was thick across the sky in the east. There was perhaps an hour of light left.

I began to follow the ditch, not wanting to climb the steep rocky sides until I had to. The ravine curved away from the prison quite soon and looked as though it would lead down towards the river; presumably the runoff of melting snow carried the prison's refuse away. I was nearly to the corner of the soaring wall when I heard a faint sound behind me. I whirled. The sound had been made by a rock falling from the lip of the ditch, dislodged by the foot of a large wolf.

As an alternative to the items under the snow, I had certain desirable characteristics, from a wolf's point of view. On the one hand I was mobile, harder to catch, and posed the possibility of resistance. On the other, I was slow, clumsy and, above all, not frozen stiff, thus offering no danger of broken teeth. I also smelled of fresh blood, temptingly warm in this frozen waste. Were I a wolf, I thought, I wouldn't hesitate. The animal made up his mind at the same time I came to my own decision regarding our future relations.

There had been a Yank at Pembroke Hospital, name of Charlie Marshall. He was a pleasant chap, friendly as all the Yanks were, and most entertaining on his pet subject. His pet subject was dogs; Charlie was a sergeant in the K–9 Corps. He had been blown up, along with two of his dogs, by a mine outside a small village near Arles. He grieved for his dogs, and often told me stories about them when I would sit with him during the odd slack moments in my shift.

More to the immediate point, he had also once told me what to do, and not do, should I ever be attacked by a dog. I felt it was stretching a point to call the eerie creature picking its delicate way down the rocks a dog, but hoped that it might yet share a few basic character traits with its tame descendants.

'Bad dog,' I said firmly, staring it in one yellow eyeball. 'In fact,' I said backing very slowly towards the prison wall, 'you are a perfectly horrible dog.' (*Speak firmly and loudly*, I heard Charlie saying.) 'Probably the worst I've ever seen,' I said, firmly and loudly. I continued to back up, one hand feeling behind me for the stones of the wall, and once there I sidled towards the corner some ten yards away.

I pulled the ties at my throat and began to fumble at the brooch fastening my cloak, still telling the wolf firmly and loudly what I thought of him, his ancestors and his immediate family. The beast seemed interested in the diatribe, tongue lolling in a doggy grin. He was in no hurry; he limped slightly, I could see as he drew nearer, and was thin and mangy. Perhaps he had trouble hunting, and infirmity

738

was what drew him to the prison midden to scavenge. I certainly hoped so; the more infirm, the better.

I found my leather gloves in the pocket of my cloak and put them on. Then I wrapped the heavy cloak several times around my right forearm, blessing the weight of the velvet. 'They'll go for the throat,' Charlie had instructed me, 'unless their trainer tells them otherwise. Keep looking him in the eye; you'll see it when he makes up his mind to jump. That's your moment.'

I could see a number of things in that wicked yellow orb, including hunger, curiosity and speculation, but not yet a decision to leap.

'You disgusting creature,' I told it, 'don't you *dare* leap at my throat!' I had other ideas. I had wrapped the cloak in several loose folds about my arm, leaving the bulk of it dangling, but providing enough padding, I hoped, to keep the beast's teeth from sinking through.

The wolf was thin, but not emaciated. I judged it to weigh perhaps eighty or ninety pounds; less than me, but not enough to give me any great advantage. The leverage was definitely in the animal's favour; four legs against two gave better balance on the slippery crust of snow. I hoped bracing my back against the wall would help.

A certain feeling of emptiness at my back told me I had reached the corner. The wolf was some twenty feet away. This was it. I scraped enough snow from under my feet to give good footing, and waited.

I didn't even see the wolf leave the ground. I could swear I had been watching its eyes, but if the decision to leap had registered there, it had been followed by action too swiftly to note. It was instinct, not thought, that raised my arm as a whitish-grey blur hurtled towards me.

The teeth sank into the padding with a force that bruised my arm. It was heavier than I thought; I was unprepared for the weight, and my arm sagged. I had planned to throw the beast against the wall, perhaps stunning it. Instead, I heaved myself at the wall, squashing the wolf between the stone blocks and my hip. I struggled to wrap the loose cloak around it. Claws shredded my skirt and scraped my thigh.

I drove a knee viciously into its chest, eliciting a strangled yelp. Only then did I realize that the odd, growling whimpers were coming from me and not the wolf.

Strangely enough I was not at all frightened now, though I had been terrified watching the wolf stalk me. There was room in my mind for only one thought: I would kill this animal, or it would kill me. Therefore, I was going to kill it.

There comes a turning point in intense physical struggle where one abandons oneself to a profligate usage of strength and bodily resource, ignoring the costs until the struggle is over. Women find this point in childbirth; men in battle.

Past that certain point you lose all fear of pain or injury. Life becomes very simple then; you will do what you are trying to do, or die in the attempt, and it does not really matter much which.

I had seen this sort of struggle during my training on the wards, but never had I experienced it before. Now all my concentration was focused on the jaws locked around my forearm and the writhing demon tearing at my body.

I managed to bang the beast's head against the wall, but not hard enough to do much good. I was growing tired rapidly; had the wolf been in good condition I would have had no chance. I hadn't much now, but took what there was. I fell on the animal, pinning it under me and knocking the wind from it in a gust of carrion breath. It recovered almost immediately and began squirming beneath me, but the second's relaxation enabled me to get it off my arm, one hand clamped under its wet muzzle.

By forcing my fingers back into the corners of its mouth I managed to keep them out from between the scissoring carnassial teeth. Saliva drizzled down my arm. I was lying flat on top of the wolf. The corner of the prison wall was perhaps eighteen inches ahead of me. Somehow I must get there, without releasing the fury that heaved and squirmed under me.

Scrabbling with my feet, pressing down with all my might, I pushed myself forward inch by inch, constantly straining to keep the fangs from my throat. It cannot have taken more than a few minutes to move those eighteen inches, but it seemed I had lain there most of my life, locked in battle with this beast whose hind claws raked my legs, seeking a good ripping purchase in my belly.

At last I could see around the corner. The blunt angle of stone was directly in front of my face. Now was the tricky part. I must manoeuvre the wolf's body to allow me to get both hands under the muzzle; I would never be able to exert the necessary force with one.

I rolled abruptly away and the wolf slithered at once into the small clear space between my body and the wall. Before it could rise to its feet I brought my knee up as hard as I could. The wolf grunted as my knee drove into its side, pinning it, however fleetingly, against the wall.

I had both hands beneath its jaw now. The fingers of one hand were actually in its mouth. I could feel a crushing sting across my gloved knuckles, but ignored it as I forced the hairy head back, and back, and back again, using the angle of the wall as a fulcrum for the lever of the beast's body. I thought my arms would break, but this was the only chance.

There was no audible noise, but I *felt* the reverberation through the whole body as the neck snapped. The straining limbs – and the bladder – at once relaxed. The intolerable strain on my arms now released, I dropped, as limp as the dying wolf. I could feel the beast's heart, the only part still capable of a death struggle, fibrillating beneath my cheek. The stringy fur stank of ammonia and soggy hair. I wanted to move away, but could not.

I think I must have slept for a moment, odd as that sounds, cheek pillowed on the corpse. I opened my eyes to see the greenish stone of the prison wall a few inches in front of my nose. Only the thought of what was transpiring on the other side of that wall got me to my feet.

I stumbled down the ditch, cloak dragged over one shoulder, tripping on stones hidden in the snow, banging my shins painfully on half-buried tree branches. Subconsciously I must have been aware that wolves usually run in packs, because I do not recall being surprised by the howl that wavered out of the forest above and behind me. If I felt anything it was black rage at what seemed a conspiracy to thwart and delay me.

Wearily I turned to see where the sound had come from. I was in the open away from the prison by this time; no wall to brace my back against, and no weapon to hand. It had been luck as much as anything that helped me with the first wolf; there was not a chance in a thousand that I could kill another animal bare-handed – and how many more might there be? The pack I had seen feeding in the moonlight in the summer had had at least ten wolves. I could hear in memory the sounds of their teeth scraping and the crack of breaking bones. The only question now was whether I bothered to fight at all or whether I would rather just lie down in the snow and give up. That option seemed remarkably attractive, all things considered.

Still, Jamie had given up his life, and considerably more than that, to get me out of the castle. I owed it to him at least to try.

Once more I backed slowly away, moving farther down the ditch. The light was fading; soon the ravine would be filled with shadow. I doubted that that would help me. The wolves undoubtedly had better night sight than I did.

The first of the hunters appeared on the rim of the ditch as the other had; a shaggy figure, standing motionless and alert. It was with something of a shock that I realized two more were already in the ravine with me, trotting slowly almost in step with each other. They were almost the same colour as the snow in the twilight – dirty grey – and almost invisible, though they moved with no attempt at concealment.

I stopped moving. Flight was clearly useless. Bending, I freed a dead pine branch from the snow. The bark was black with the wet, and rough even through my gloves. I waved the branch around my head and shouted. The animals stopped moving towards me but did not retreat. The closest one flattened its ears, as though objecting to the noise.

'Don't like it?' I screeched. 'Too bloody bad! Back off,

you fucking sod!' Scooping up a half-buried rock, I hurled it at the wolf. It missed, but the beast scooted to one side. Encouraged, I began to fling missiles wildly: rocks, twigs, handfuls of snow, anything I could grab one-handed. I shrieked until my throat was raw with cold air, howling like the wolves themselves.

At first I thought one of my missiles had scored a hit. The nearest wolf yelped and seemed to convulse. The second arrow passed within a foot of me and I caught the tiny blur of motion before it thudded home in the chest of the second wolf. That animal died where it stood. The first, struck less vitally, kicked and struggled in the snow, no more than a heaving lump in the glowing dusk.

I stood stupidly staring at it for some time, then looked up by instinct to the lip of the ravine. The third wolf, wisely choosing discretion, had vanished back into the trees, from whence a shivering howl went up.

I was still looking up at the dark trees when a hand clutched my elbow. I whirled with a gasp to find myself looking up into the face of a stranger. Narrow-jawed and with a weak chin ill disguised by a scabby beard, he was a stranger indeed, but his plaid and his dirk marked him a Scot.

'Help,' I said, and fell forward into his arms.

36

MacRannoch

It was dark in the cottage and there was a bear in the corner of the room. In panic I recoiled against my escort, wanting nothing more to do with wild beasts. He shoved me strongly forward into the cottage. As I staggered towards the fire, the hulking shape turned to me, and I realized belatedly that it was merely a large man in a bearskin.

A bearskin cloak, to be exact, fastened at the neck with a silver-gilt brooch as large as the palm of my hand. It was made in the shape of two leaping stags, backs arched and heads meeting to form a circle. The locking pin was a short, tapered fan, the head of it shaped like the tail of a fleeing deer.

I noticed the brooch in detail because it was directly in front of my nose. Looking up, I briefly considered the possibility that I had been wrong; perhaps it really *was* a bear.

Still, bears presumably did not wear brooches or have eyes like blueberries; small, round and a dark, shiny blue. They were sunk in heavy cheeks whose lower slopes were forested with silver-shot black hair. Similar hair cascaded over thick-set shoulders to mingle with the hair of the cloak, which, in spite of its new use, was still pungently redolent of its former owner.

The shrewd little eyes flickered over me, evaluating both the bedraggled state of my attire and the good basic quality of it, including the two wedding rings, gold and silver. The bear's address was formulated accordingly.

'You seem to have had some difficulty, mistress,' he said formally, inclining a massive head still spangled with melting snow. 'Perhaps we might assist ye?'

I hesitated over what to say. I desperately needed this

man's help, yet I would be suspect immediately my speech revealed me to be English. The archer who had brought me here forestalled me.

'Found her near Wentworth,' he said laconically. 'Fightin' wolves. An English lassie,' he added, with an emphasis that made my host's blueberry eyes fix on me with a rather unpleasant speculation in their depths. I pulled myself up to my full height and summoned as much of the Matron attitude as I could.

'English by birth, Scots by marriage,' I said firmly. 'My name is Claire Fraser. My husband is a prisoner in Wentworth.'

'I see,' said the bear slowly. 'Weel, my own name is MacRannoch, and ye're presently on my land. I can see by your dress as you're a woman of some family; how come ye to be alone in Eldridge Wood on a winter night?'

I caught at the opening; here was some chance to establish my bona fides, as well as to find Murtagh and Rupert.

'I came to Wentworth with some clansmen of my husband's. As I was English, we thought I could gain entrance to the prison and perhaps find some way of, er, removing him. However, I – I left the prison by another way. I was looking for my friends when I was set upon by wolves – from which this gentleman kindly rescued me.' I tried a grateful smile on the raw-boned archer, who received it in stony silence.

'Ye've certainly met *something* wi' teeth,' MacRannoch agreed, eyeing the gaping rents in my skirt. Suspicion yielded temporarily to the demands of hospitality.

'Are ye hurt, then? Just a bit scratched? Weel, you're cold, nae doubt, and a wee bit shaken, I imagine. Sit here by the fire. Hector will fetch ye a sup of something, and then ye can tell me a bit more about these friends of yours.' He pulled a rough three-legged stool up with one foot, and sat me firmly on it with a massive hand on my shoulder.

Peat fires give little light but are comfortingly hot. I shuddered involuntarily as the blood started to flow back into my frozen hands. A couple of gulps from the leather

745

flask grudgingly provided by Hector started the blood flowing internally again as well.

I explained my situation as well as I could, which was not particularly well. My brief description of my exit from the prison and subsequent hand-to-hand encounter with the wolf was received with particular scepticism.

'Given that ye did manage to get into Wentworth, it doesna seem likely that Sir Fletcher would allow ye to wander about the place. Nor if this Captain Randall had found ye in the dungeons, he would merely ha' shown ye the back door.'

'He – he had reasons for letting me go.'

'Which were?' The blueberry eyes were implacable.

I gave up and put the matter baldly; I was much too tired for delicacy or circumlocutions.

MacRannoch appeared semi-convinced, but still reluctant to take any action.

'Aye, I see your concern,' he argued, 'still, that may not be so bad.'

'Not so bad!' I sprang to my feet in outrage.

He shook his head as though plagued by horseflies. 'What I mean,' he explained, 'is that if it's the lad's arse he's after, he's none so likely to hurt him badly. And, savin' your presence, ma'am' – he cocked a bushy eyebrow in my direction – 'bein' buggered has seldom killed anyone.' He held up placating hands the size of soup plates.

'Now, I'm no sayin' he'll enjoy it, mind, but I do say it's not worth a major set-to with Sir Fletcher Gordon, just to save the lad a sore arse. I've a precarious position here, ye know, verra precarious.' And he puffed out his cheeks and beetled his brows at me.

Not for the first time I regretted the fact that there were no real witches. Had I been one, I would have turned him into a toad on the spot. A big fat one, with warts.

I choked down my rage and tried reason yet again.

'I rather think his arse is beyond saving by this time; it's his neck I'm concerned with. The English mean to hang him in the morning.'

MacRannoch was muttering to himself, twisting back and

forth like a bear in a too-small cage. He stopped abruptly in front of me and thrust his nose to within an inch of my own. I would have recoiled, had I not been so exhausted. As it was, I merely blinked.

'And if I said I'd help ye, what good would that do?' he roared. He resumed his turning and pacing, two steps to one wall, hurling around in a fling of fur, and two steps to the other. He spoke as he paced, words keeping time to the steps, pausing to puff as he turned.

'If I were to go to Sir Fletcher myself, what would I say? Ye've a captain here who's engaged in torturin' the prisoners in his spare time? And when he asks how I know that, I tell him a stray Sassenach wench my men found wanderin' in the dark told me this man's been makin' indecent advances to her husband, who's an outlaw wi' a price on his head, and a condemned murderer to boot?'

MacRannoch stopped and thumped one paw on the flimsy table. 'And as for takin' men into the place! If, and mind ye, I say *if* we could get in – '

'You could get in,' I interrupted. 'I can show you the way.'

'Mmmphm. That's as may be. *If* we could get in, what happens when Sir Fletcher finds my men wanderin' about his fortress? He sends Captain Randall round next mornin' with a brace of cannon and levels Eldridge Hall to the ground, that's what!' He shook his head again, making the black locks fly.

'Nay, lass, I canna see – '

He was interrupted by the sudden flinging open of the cottage door to admit another bowman, this one pushing Murtagh in front of him at knifepoint. MacRannoch stopped and stared in amazement.

'What *is* this?' he demanded. 'Ye'd think 'twas May Day, and the lads and lassies all out gatherin' flowers in the wood, not the dead o' winter and snow comin' on!'

'This is my husband's clansman,' I said. 'As I told you – '

Murtagh, undisturbed by the less-than-cordial greeting, was eying the bearskin-clad figure closely, as though mentally stripping hair and years away.

'MacRannoch, is it no?' he said in a tone almost accusing. 'Ye'll have been at a Gathering, I think, some time ago at Castle Leoch?'

MacRannoch was more than startled. 'Some time ago, I should say! Why, that must ha' been near on thirty year ago. How d'ye know that, man?'

Murtagh nodded, satisfied. 'Och, I thought so. I was there. And I remember that Gathering, likely for the same reason ye do yourself, Sir Marcus.'

MacRannoch was studying the wizened little man, trying to subtract thirty years from the seamed countenance.

'Aye, I know ye,' he said at last. 'Or not the name, but you. Ye killed a wounded boar single-handed with a dagger, during the tinchel. A gallant beast too. That's right, the MacKenzie gave ye the tushes – a bonny set, almost a complete double curve. Lovely work that, man.' A look perilously close to gratification creased Murtagh's pitted cheek momentarily.

I started, remembering the magnificent, barbaric bracelets I had worn at Lallybroch. *My mother's*, Jenny had said, *given to her by an admirer*. I stared at Murtagh in disbelief. Even allowing for the passage of thirty years he did not seem a likely candidate for the tender passion.

Thinking of Ellen MacKenzie, I remembered her pearls which I was still carrying, sewn into the seam of my pocket. I groped for the free end, pulling them out into the firelight.

'I can pay you,' I said. 'I wouldn't expect your men to risk themselves for nothing.'

Moving a good deal faster than I would have thought possible, MacRannoch snatched the pearls from my hand. He stared at them disbelievingly.

'Where did ye get these, woman?' he demanded. 'Fraser, did ye say your name is?'

'Yes.' Tired as I was, I drew myself up straight. 'And the pearls are mine. My husband gave them to me on our wedding day.'

'Did he, then?' The hoarse voice was suddenly hushed. He turned to Murtagh, still holding the pearls.

'Ellen's son? Is this lass's husband Ellen's son?'

'Aye,' Murtagh said, unemphatic as ever. 'As ye'd ken at once if ye saw him; he's the spit of her.'

Mindful at last of the pearls he was clutching, MacRannoch unfolded his hand and gently stroked the shining gems.

'I gave these to Ellen MacKenzie,' he said. 'For a wedding gift. I would ha' given them to her as my wife, but as she'd chosen elsewhere – well, I'd thought of them so often, around her bonny throat, I told her I couldna see them elsewhere. So I bade her keep them, and only think of me when she wore them. Hm!' He snorted briefly at some memory, then handed the pearls carefully back to me.

'So they're yours now. Well, wear them in good health, lassie.'

'I'll stand a much better chance of doing so,' I said, trying to control my impatience at these sentimental displays, 'if you'll help me to get my husband back.'

The small rosy mouth, which had been smiling slightly at its owner's thought, tightened suddenly.

'Ah,' said Sir Marcus, pulling at his beard. 'I see. But I've told ye, lassie, I canna see how it can be done. I've a wife and three weans at home. Aye, I'd do a bit for Ellen's lad. But it's a bit much ye're askin'.'

Suddenly my legs gave way altogether and I sat down with a thump, letting my shoulders sag and my head droop. Despair dragged at me like an anchor, pulling me down. I closed my eyes and retreated to some dim place within, where there was nothing but an aching grey blankness and where the sound of Murtagh's voice, still arguing, was no more than a faint yapping.

It was the bawling of cattle that roused me from my stupor. I looked up to see MacRannoch swirl out of the cottage. As he opened the door a blast of winter air came in, thick with the lowing of cattle and yelling of men. The door thumped shut behind the vast hairy figure, and I turned to ask Murtagh what he thought we should do next.

The look on his face stopped me, wordless. I had seldom seen him with anything more than a sort of patient dourness showing on his features, but now he positively glowed with suppressed excitement.

I caught at his arm. 'What is it? Tell me quickly!'

He had time only to say, 'The kine! They're MacRannoch's!' before MacRannoch himself plunged back into the cottage, pushing a lanky young man before him.

With a last shove he brought the young man flat up against the wall of the cottage. Apparently MacRannoch found confrontation effective; he tried the same nose-to-nose technique he had used on me earlier. Less poised, or less tired than I, the young man hunched nervously back against the wall as far as he could go.

MacRannoch started out being sweetly reasonable. 'Absalom, man, I sent ye out three hours ago to bring in forty head of cattle. I told ye it was important to find them, because there's about to be a damn awfu' snowstorm.' The nicely modulated voice was rising. 'And when I heard the sound of kine bellowin' outside, I said to meself, Ah, Marcus, there's Absalom gone and found all the cattle, what a good lad, now we can all go home and thaw ourselves by the fire, with the kine safe in their byres.'

One ham-fist had fastened itself on to Absalom's jacket. The material, gathered between those stubby fingers, began to twist.

'And then I go out to congratulate you on a good job done, and begin to count the beasts. And how many do I count, Absalom, my bonny wee lad?' The voice had risen to a full-powered roar. While not possessed of a particularly deep voice, Marcus MacRannoch had enough lung-power for three ordinary-sized men.

'Fifteen!' he shouted, jerking the unfortunate Absalom to his tiptoes. 'Fifteen beasts he finds, out of forty! And where are the rest o' them? Where? Out loose in the snow, to freeze to death!'

Murtagh had faded quietly back into the shadows in the corner while all this was going on. I was watching his face, though, and saw the sudden gleam of amusement in his eyes at these words. Suddenly I realized what he had started to tell me, and I knew where Rupert was now. Or, if not precisely where he was, at least what he was doing. And I began to hope a little.

It was full dark. The castle's lights below shone weakly through the snow like the lamps of a drowned ship. Waiting under the trees with my two companions I mentally reviewed for the thousandth time everything that could go wrong.

Would MacRannoch carry out his part of the bargain? He'd have to, if he expected to get his prized purebred Highland cattle back. Would Sir Fletcher believe MacRannoch and order a search of the basement dungeons at once? Likely – the baronet wasn't a man to be taken lightly.

I had seen the cattle disappear, one shaggy beast at a time, down the ditch that led to the hidden postern door, under the expert driving of Rupert and his men. But would they be able to force the cattle through that door, singly or not? And if so, what would they do once inside; half-wild cattle, trapped suddenly in a stone corridor lit with glaring torchlight? Well, perhaps it would work. The corridor itself would be not unlike their stone-floored byre, including torches and the scent of humans. If they got so far, the plan might succeed. Randall himself was unlikely to call for help in the face of the invasion, for fear of having his own little games uncovered.

The handlers were to get away from the castle as fast as possible, once the beasts were well and truly launched on their chaotic path, and then to ride hell for leather for the MacKenzie lands. Randall didn't matter; what could he do alone, in the circumstances? But what if the noise attracted the rest of the prison garrison too soon? If Dougal had been reluctant to try to break his nephew *out* of Wentworth, I could imagine his choler if several MacKenzie men were arrested for breaking *into* the place. I didn't want to be responsible for that, either, though Rupert had been more than willing to take the risk. I bit my thumb and tried to comfort myself, thinking of the tons of solid, sound-muffling granite that separated the dungeons from the prison quarters above.

Most worrying of all, of course, was the fear that everything might work, and might be still too late. Waiting hangman or no, Randall might go too far. I knew too well, from stories told by returning soldiers from POW camps, that nothing is easier than for a prisoner to die by 'accident', and the body be conveniently disposed of before embarrassing official questions can be asked. Even if questions *were* asked, and Randall found out, it would be small comfort to me – and to Jamie.

I had been resolutely keeping myself from imagining the possible uses of the homely objects on the table of that room. But I could not keep from seeing over and over the bone-ends of that shattered finger pressing into the table. I rubbed my own knuckles hard against the saddle leather, trying to erase the image. I felt a slight burning, and pulled off the glove to examine the grazes left across my hand by the wolf's teeth. Not bad, no more than a few scratches, with one small puncture where a cusp had penetrated the leather. I licked the wound absently. It was little use telling myself that I had done my best. I had done the only possible thing, but knowing it didn't make the waiting easier.

At last we heard a faint, confused shouting from the direction of the prison. One of the MacRannoch men put a hand on the bridle of my pony and motioned towards the shelter of the trees. The snow was much lighter on the ground and the flurries diminished under the interlaced branches of the grove, thin lines of snow stark and sudden on the rocky leaf-strewn ground. While the snow fell less thickly in here, visibility was still so poor that tree trunks a few feet away loomed surprisingly as I walked my mount restlessly around the small clearing, trunks springing up black in the pinkish light.

Muffled by the heavy snow, the approaching hoofbeats were almost upon us before we heard them. The two MacRannoch men drew their pistols and reined their ponies up close to the trees, waiting, but I had picked up the dull lowing of cattle, and spurred my pony forward out of the grove.

Sir Marcus MacRannoch, distinguishable by his piebald mount and his bearskin cloak, was leading the way up the slope, snow spurting in small explosions from under the hooves of his pony. He was followed by several men, all in good humour, from the sound of it. More of his men rode further back, chivvying the milling herd of cattle from behind, driving the band of bewildered beasts around the base of the hill towards their well-earned shelter in the MacRannoch byres.

MacRannoch reined up beside me, laughing heartily. 'I've to thank ye Mistress Fraser,' he shouted through the snow, 'for a most entertaining evening.' His earlier suspicion had vanished, and he greeted me with the utmost geniality. His eyebrows and moustache coated with snow, he looked like Father Christmas on a spree. Taking my bridle, he led my pony back into the quieter air of the grove. He waved my two companions down the hill to help with the cattle, then dismounted and swung me down from my saddle, still laughing to himself.

'Ye should ha' seen it!' he chortled, hugging himself in ecstasy. 'Sir Fletcher went red as a robin's breast when I pushed in in the midst of his supper, shouting that he was concealing stolen property on his premises. And then when we got below-stairs and he heard the beasts bellowin' like thunder, I thought he'd dirtied his breeches. He – ' I shook his arm impatiently.

'Never mind Sir Fletcher's breeches. Did you find my husband?'

MacRannoch sobered a bit, wiping his eyes with his sleeve. 'Oh, aye. We found him.'

'Is he all right?' I spoke calmly, though I wanted to scream.

MacRannoch nodded towards the trees behind me and I whirled to see a rider making his way carefully through the branches, a bulky cloth-covered shape draped across the saddlebow in front of him. I dashed forward, followed by MacRannoch, explaining helpfully.

'He's no deid, or at least he wasn't when we found him. Been mistreated a good bit though, poor laddie.' I had pushed aside the cloth over Jamie's head and was anxiously examining him as best I could, with the pony fidgeting from

753

the excitement of the cold ride and the extra burden. I could see dark bruises and feel stiff patches of blood in the rumpled hair, but could tell little more in the dim light. I thought I could feel a pulse in the icy neck, but wasn't sure.

MacRannoch caught my elbow and pulled me away. 'We'll do best to get him inside quick, lass. Come with me. Hector will bring him along to the house.'

In the main drawing room of Eldridge Hall, MacRannoch's home, Hector humped his burden on to the rug before the fire. Seizing one corner of the blanket he unrolled it carefully, and a limp, naked figure flopped out on to the pink and yellow flowers of Lady Annabelle MacRannoch's pride and joy.

To do the Lady Annabelle credit, she didn't seem to notice the blood soaking into her expensive Aubusson rug. A birdlike woman in her early forties, arrayed like a canary in a sunburst of yellow silk dressing gown, she had servants bustling in all directions with a brisk clap of her hands; blankets, linen, hot water and whisky appeared at my elbow almost before I had my cloak off.

'Best turn him on his belly,' advised Sir Marcus, pouring out two large whiskys. 'He's had his back flayed, and it must feel fierce to lie on it. Not that he looks like he feels anything, much,' he added, peering closely at Jamie's ashen face and sealed, bluish eyelids. 'You're sure he's still alive?'

'Yes,' I answered shortly, hoping I was right. I struggled to pull Jamie over. Unconsciousness seemed to have tripled his weight. MacRannoch lent a hand and we got him positioned on a blanket, back to the fire.

A rapid triage having established that he was in fact alive, missing no body parts, and not in immediate danger of bleeding to death, I could afford to make a less hurried inventory of the damage.

'I can send for a physician,' said Lady Annabelle, looking dubiously at the corpselike figure on her hearth, 'but I doubt he can get here in under an hour; it's snowing something fierce out.' The reluctance in her tone was only partly on account of the snow, I thought. A physician would make one more dangerous witness to the presence of an escaped criminal in her home.

'Don't bother,' I said absently, 'I am a physician.' Disregarding the looks of surprise from both MacRannochs, I knelt beside what was left of my husband, covered him with blankets and began to apply cloths soaked in hot water to the outlying parts. My chief concern was to get him warm; the blood from his back was a slow ooze which could be dealt with later.

Lady Annabelle faded into the distance, her high finch's voice summoning, beckoning and arranging. Her spouse sank down on his haunches beside me and began to rub Jamie's frozen feet in a businesslike way between large blunt-fingered hands, pausing occasionally to sip his whisky.

Turning back the blankets in bits, I surveyed the damage. He had been finely striped from nape to knees with something like a coachwhip, the weals crisscrossing neatly like hemstitching. The sheer orderliness of the damage, speaking as it did of a deliberation that revelled in each punishing stroke, made me feel sick with rage.

Something heavier, perhaps a cane, had been used with less restraint across his shoulders, cutting so deeply in spots that a gleam of bone showed over one shoulderblade. I pressed a thick pad of lint gently over the worst of the mess and went on with the examination.

The spot on his left side where the mallet had struck was an ugly contused swelling, a black and purple patch bigger than Sir Marcus' hand. Broken ribs there for sure, but those too could wait. My attention was caught by the livid patches on neck and breast, where the skin was puckered, reddened and blistered. The edges of one such patch were charred, rimmed with white ash.

'What in hell did that?' Sir Marcus had completed his ministrations and was looking over my shoulder with deep interest.

'A hot poker.' The voice was weak and indistinct; it was a moment before I realized that it was Jamie who had spoken. He raised his head with an effort, showing the

755

reason for his difficult speech; the lower lip was badly bitten on one side and puffed like a bee sting.

With considerable presence of mind Sir Marcus put a hand behind Jamie's neck and pressed the beaker of whisky to his lips. Jamie winced as the spirit stung his torn mouth, but drained the beaker before laying his head down again. His eyes slanted up at me, slightly filmed with pain and whisky, but alight with amusement nonetheless. 'Cows?' he asked. 'Was it really cows, or was I dreaming?'

'Well, it was all I could manage in the time,' I said, beaming in my relief at seeing him alive and conscious. I placed a hand on his head, turning it to inspect a large bruise over the cheekbone. 'You look bloody awful. How do you feel?' I asked, from force of long-held habit.

'Alive.' He struggled up on to one elbow to accept with a nod a second beaker of whisky from Sir Marcus.

'Do you think you should drink so much all at once?' I asked, trying to examine his pupils for signs of concussion. He foiled me by closing his eyes and tilting his head back.

'Yes,' he said, handing back the empty beaker to Sir Marcus, who bore it back in the direction of the decanter.

'Now, that'll be enough for the present, Marcus.' Lady Annabelle, reappearing like the sun in the east, stopped her husband with a commanding chirp. 'The lad needs hot strong tea, not more whisky.' The tea followed her processionally in a silver pot, borne by a maidservant whose air of natural superiority was unimpaired by the fact that she was still attired in her nightdress.

'Hot strong tea with plenty of sugar in it,' I amended.

'And perhaps a wee tot of whisky as well,' said Sir Marcus, neatly removing the lid of the teapot as it passed and adding a generous dollop from his decanter. Accepting the steaming cup gratefully, Jamie raised it in mute tribute to Sir Marcus before cautiously bringing the hot liquid to his mouth. His hand shook badly, and I wrapped my own around his fingers to guide the cup.

More servants were bringing in a portable camp bed, a mattress, more blankets, more bandages and hot water, and a large wooden chest containing the household's medical supplies.

'I thought we had best work here before the fire,' Lady Annabelle explained in her charming bird voice. 'There's more light, and it's far the warmest place in the house.'

At her direction two of the larger manservants each seized an end of the blanket under Jamie and transferred it smoothly, contents and all, to the camp bed, now set up before the fire, where another servant was industriously poking the night-banked coals and feeding the growing blaze. The maid who had brought in the tea was efficiently lighting the wax tapers in the branched candelabra on the sideboard. Despite her songbird appearance, the Lady Annabelle plainly had the soul of a sergeant major.

'Yes, now that he's awake, the sooner the better,' I said. 'Have you a flat board about two feet long,' I asked, 'a stout strap, and perhaps some small straight flat sticks, about so long?' I held my fingers apart, measuring a length of four inches or so. One of the servants disappeared into the shadows, flicking out of sight like a djinn to do my bidding.

The whole house seemed magical, perhaps because of the contrast between the howling cold outside and the luxurious warmth within, or maybe only because of the relief of seeing Jamie safe, after so many days of fear and worry.

Heavy dark furniture gleamed with polish in the lamplight, silver shone on the sideboard and a collection of delicate glass and china ornamented the mantelpiece, in bizarre contrast to the bloody, bedraggled figure before it.

No questions were asked. We were Sir Marcus' guests, and Lady Annabelle behaved as though it were an everyday occurrence to have people come and bleed on the rug at midnight. It occurred to me for the first time that such a visit might have happened before.

'Verra nasty,' said Sir Marcus, examining the smashed hand with an expertise born of the battlefield. 'And wretched painful, too, I expect. Still, it's no going to kill ye, is it?' He straightened up and addressed me in confidential tones.

'I thought it might be worse than this, given what ye told

me. Except the ribs and hand, there's no bones broken, and the rest will heal fine. I'd say maybe ye were lucky, lad.'

There was a faint snort from the recumbent figure on the bed.

'I suppose ye could call it luck. They meant to be hanging me in the morning.' He moved his head restlessly on the pillow, trying to look up at Sir Marcus. 'Did ye know that . . . sir?' he added, catching sight of Sir Marcus' embroidered waistcoat with its coat of arms worked in silver stitchery among the pigeons and roses.

MacRannoch waved a hand, dismissing this minor detail.

'Weel, if he meant to be keepin' ye presentable for the hangman, he went a bit far on your back, then,' Sir Marcus remarked, removing the soaked lint and replacing it with a fresh pad.

'Aye. He lost his head a bit when . . . when he . . .' Jamie struggled to get the words out, then gave it up as a bad job and turned his face to the fire, eyes closed. 'God, I'm tired,' he said.

We let him rest until the manservant materialized by my elbow with the splints I had requested. Then I carefully picked up the smashed right hand, bringing it into the candlelight for examination.

It would have to be set, and as soon as possible. The injured muscles were already clawing the fingers inwards. I felt hopeless as I saw the full extent of the damage. But if he was ever to have any use of the hand again it would have to be attempted.

Lady Annabelle had hung back during my examination, watching interestedly. When I set the hand down she stepped forward and opened the chest of medical supplies.

'I suppose you'll be wanting the boneset, and perhaps the willow bark. I don't know . . .' She eyed Jamie doubtfully. 'Leeches, do you think?' Her well-kept hand hovered over a small lidded jar filled with murky liquid.

I shuddered and shook my head. 'No, I don't think so; not just now. What I could really use . . . do you by chance have any sort of opiate?' I sank to my knees beside her to pore over the contents of the box.

'Oh, yes!' Her hand went unerringly to a small green flask. 'Flowers of laudanum,' she read from the label. 'Will that do?'

'Perfect.' I accepted the flask gratefully.

'All right, then,' I said briskly to Jamie, pouring a small amount of the odorous liquid into a glass, 'you'll need to sit up just long enough to swallow this. Then you'll go to sleep and stay that way for a good long time.' In fact I had some doubts as to the advisability of administering laudanum on top of such a quantity of whisky, but the alternative – reconstructing that hand while he was conscious – was unthinkable. I tipped the bottle to pour a bit more.

Jamie's good hand on my arm stopped me.

'I don't want that,' he said firmly. 'Just perhaps a wee drop more of whisky' – he hesitated, tongue touching the bitten lip – 'and maybe something to bite down on.'

Sir Marcus, hearing this, crossed to the lovely glowing walnut desk in the corner and began to rummage. He returned in a moment with a small piece of well worn leather. Looking more closely, I could see the dozens of overlapping semicircular indentations in the thick leather – toothmarks, I realized with a shock.

'Here,' Sir Marcus said helpfully. 'I used this myself at St Simone; got me through it while I had a musket ball dug out of my leg.'

I looked on, open-mouthed, as Jamie took the leather with a nod of thanks, smoothing his thumb over the marks. I spoke slowly, stunned.

'You actually expect me to set nine broken bones while you're *awake*?'

'Yes,' he said briefly, placing the leather between his teeth and biting down experimentally. He shifted it back and forth, seeking a comfortable grip.

Overcome by the sheer theatricality of it, the precarious control I had been hoarding suddenly snapped.

'Will you stop being such a goddamned frigging hero!' I blazed at Jamie. 'We all know what you've done, you don't have to prove how much you can stand! Or do you think we'll all fall apart if you're not in charge, telling everyone

759

what to do every minute? Who in bloody hell do you think you are, frigging John Wayne!?'

There was an awkward silence. Jamie looked at me, open-mouthed. Finally he spoke.

'Claire,' he said softly, 'we're perhaps two miles from Wentworth Prison. I'm meant to hang in the morning. No matter what's happened to Randall, the English are soon going to notice I'm gone.'

I bit my lip. What he said was true. My inadvertent release of the other prisoners might confuse the issue for a time, but eventually a tally would be made, and a search begun. And thanks to the flamboyant method of escape I had chosen, attention was bound to be focused on Eldridge Hall in short order.

'If we're lucky,' the quiet voice continued, 'the snow will delay a search till we've gone. If not . . .' He shrugged, staring into the flames. 'Claire, I'll not let them take me back. And to be drugged, to lie here helpless if they come, and maybe wake up chained in a cell again . . . Claire, I couldna bear it.'

There were tears blurring on my lower lashes. I stared wide-eyed at him, not wanting to blink and let them run down my cheeks.

He closed his eyes against the fire's heat. The glow lent a spurious look of ruddy health to the white cheeks. I could see the long muscles in his throat work as he swallowed.

'Don't cry, Sassenach,' he said, so softly I could hardly hear him. He reached out and patted my leg with his good hand, trying to be reassuring. 'I imagine we're safe enough, lass. If I thought likely we'd be captured, I'd certainly no waste one of my last hours having you mend a hand I'd not be going to need. Go and fetch Murtagh for me. Then bring me a drink and we'll get on wi' it.'

Busy at the table with the medical preparations, I couldn't hear what he said to Murtagh, but I saw the two heads close together for a moment, then Murtagh's sinewy hand gently touch the younger man's ear – one of the few unin-jured spots available.

With a brief nod of farewell Murtagh sidled towards the

door. Like a rat, I thought, darting along the wainscoting, not to be noticed. I was behind him as he went out into the hall, and grabbed him by the plaid just before he escaped altogether through the front door.

'What did he tell you?' I demanded fiercely. 'Where are you going?'

The dark stringy little man hesitated for a moment, but answered evenly, 'I'm to go wi' young Absalom towards Wentworth and keep watch in that direction. If any redcoats are headin' this way I'm to beat them here, and if there's time I'm to see you and him both hidden, then ride off with three ponies, to draw followers away from the house. There's a cellar, it might do for hiding, if the search isna too thorough.'

'And if there isn't time to hide?' I eyed him narrowly, daring him not to answer.

'Then I'm to kill him, and take you wi' me,' he answered promptly. 'Willing or no,' he added with an evil grin, and turned to go.

'Just a minute!' I spoke sharply and he stopped. 'Do you have an extra dirk?'

His scruffy brows shot upwards, but his hand went to his belt without hesitation.

'Do ye need one? Here?' His glance took in the opulence and serenity of the entrance hall, with its painted plaster ceiling and linenfold panelling.

My dagger-pocket was shredded beyond use. I took the proffered dagger and slid it between kirtle and bodice in the back, as I had seen the gypsy women do.

'One never knows, does one?' I said evenly.

Preparations complete, I probed as gently as possible, assessing harm, deciding what must be done. Jamie drew in his breath sharply when I touched an especially bad spot, but kept his eyes closed as I felt my way slowly along each separate bone and joint, noting the position of each fracture and dislocation. 'Sorry,' I murmured.

I took his good hand as well, and felt carefully down each finger of both the good hand and the injured, making comparisons. With neither X-rays nor experience to guide me, I would have to depend on my own sensitivity to find and realign the smashed bones.

The first joint was all right, but the second phalange was cracked, I thought. I pressed harder to determine the length and direction of the crack. The damaged hand stayed motionless in my fingers, but the good one made a small, involuntary clenching gesture.

'I'm sorry,' I murmured once more.

The good hand pulled suddenly out of my grasp as Jamie raised himself on one elbow. Spitting out the leather gag, he regarded me with an expression between amusement and exasperation.

'Sassenach,' he said, 'if you apologize each time ye hurt me, it's going to be a verra long night – and it's lasted some time already.'

I must have looked stricken, because he started to reach towards me, then stopped, wincing at the movement. He controlled the pain, though, and spoke firmly. 'I know you dinna wish to hurt me. But you've no more choice about it than I have, and there's no need for more than one of us to suffer for it. You do what's needed, and I'll scream if I have to.'

Replacing the leather strip, he bared his clenched teeth ferociously at me, then slowly and deliberately crossed his eyes. This made him look so like an addlepated tiger that I burst into half-hysterical laughter before I could stop myself.

I clapped my hands over my mouth, cheeks flaming as I saw the astonished looks on the faces of Lady Annabelle and the servants, who, standing behind Jamie, naturally could see nothing of his face. Sir Marcus, who had caught a brief glimpse from his seat at the bedside, grinned in his spade-shaped beard.

'Besides,' said Jamie, spitting out the leather once more, 'if the English turn up after *this*, I expect I'll beg them to take me back.'

I picked up the leather, put it between his teeth and pushed his head down again.

'Clown,' I said. 'Know-all. Sodding hero.' But he had relieved me of a burden, and I worked more calmly. If I still noticed every twitch and grimace, at least I no longer felt it as well.

I began to lose myself in the concentration of the job, directing all my awareness to my fingertips, assessing each point of damage and deciding how best to draw the smashed bones back into alignment. Luckily the thumb had suffered least; only a simple fracture of the first joint. That would heal clean. The second knuckle on the third finger was completely gone; I felt only a pulpy grating of bone chips when I rolled it gently between my own thumb and forefinger, making Jamie groan. Nothing could be done about that, save splint the joint and hope for the best.

The compound fracture of the middle finger was the worst to contemplate. The finger would have to be pulled straight, drawing the protruding bone back through the torn flesh. I had seen this done before – under general anaesthesia, with the guidance of X-rays.

To this point it had been more a mechanical problem than a real one, deciding how to reconstruct a smashed, disembodied hand. I was now smack up against the reason that physicians seldom treat members of their own families. Some jobs in medicine require a certain ruthlessness to complete successfully; detachment is necessary to inflict pain in the process of effecting a healing.

Quietly, Sir Marcus had brought up a stool by the side of the bed. He settled his bulk comfortably as I finished the strapping, and gripped Jamie's good hand with his own.

'Squeeze all ye like, lad,' he said.

Divested of the bearskin, and with his grizzled locks neatly clubbed and laced back, MacRannoch was no longer the intimidating wildman of the forest, but appeared as a soberly clad man of late middle age, with a neatly trimmed spade-beard and a military bearing. Nervous at what I was about to attempt, I found his solid presence comforting.

I drew a deep breath and prayed for detachment.

It was a long, horrible, nerve-wracking job, though not

without its fascination. Some parts, such as the splinting of the two fingers with simple fractures, went quite easily. Others did not. Jamie did scream – loudly – when I set his middle finger, exerting the considerable force necessary to draw the ends of splintered bone back through the skin. I hesitated for an instant, unnerved, but 'Go on, lass!' Sir Marcus said with quiet urgency.

I remembered suddenly what Jamie had said to me the night Jenny's baby was born: *I can bear pain, myself, but I couldna bear yours. That would take more strength than I have.* He was right; it did take strength; I hoped that each of us had enough.

Jamie's face was turned away from me but I could see the jaw muscles bunch as he clenched his teeth harder on the leather strip. I clenched my own teeth and did go on; the sharp bone end slowly disappeared back through the skin and the finger straightened with agonizing reluctance, leaving us both trembling.

As I worked I began to lose consciousness of anything outside the job I was doing. Jamie groaned occasionally, and we had to stop twice briefly in order for him to be sick, retching up mostly whisky, as he had taken little food in prison. For the most part, though, he kept up a low, constant muttering in Gaelic, forehead pressed hard against Sir Marcus' knees. I couldn't tell through the leather gag whether he was cursing or praying.

All five digits eventually lay straight as new pins, stiff as sticks in their bandaged splints. I was afraid of infection, particularly from the torn middle finger, but otherwise was fairly sure they would heal well. By good luck, only the one joint had been badly damaged. It would likely leave him with a stiff ring finger, but the others might function normally – in time. There was nothing I could do about the cracked metacarpal bones or the puncture wound except apply an antiseptic wash and a poultice and pray against a tetanus infection. I stepped back, shaking in every limb from the strain of the night, my bodice soaked with sweat from the fire's heat at my back.

Lady Annabelle was at my side at once, guiding me to a

chair and pressing a cup of tea, laced with whisky, into my shaking hands. Sir Marcus, as good an operating-room assistant as any physician could have, was unfastening Jamie's captive arm and rubbing the marks where the strap had bitten deep into straining flesh. The older man's hand was red, I saw, where Jamie had gripped it.

I was not aware of having nodded off, but suddenly jerked, my head snapping on my neck. Lady Annabelle was urging me upwards, soft hand under my elbow. 'Come along, my dear. You're all in; you must have your own hurts seen to, and sleep a bit.'

I shook her off as politely as possible. 'No, I can't. I must finish . . .' My words trailed off into the fuzziness of my mind as Sir Marcus smoothly took the vinegar bottle and rag from my hand.

'I'll take care of the rest,' he said. 'I've some experience wi' battle wounds, ye understand.' Flipping back the blankets, he began to swab the blood from the whip cuts, moving with a brisk gentleness that was impressive. Catching my eye, he grinned, beard tilted jauntily. 'I've cleansed a good many stripes in my time,' he said. 'And applied a few too. These are naught, lass; they'll heal in a few days.' Knowing he was right, I walked up to the head of the cot. Jamie was awake, grimacing slightly at the sting of the antiseptic solution on the raw cuts, but his eyelids were heavy and the blue eyes darkened with pain and weariness.

'Go to sleep, Sassenach. I'll do.'

Whether he would or not, I didn't know. It was clear, however, that I wouldn't do, or not for much longer. I was swaying with exhaustion and the scratches on my legs were beginning to burn and ache. Absalom had cleansed them for me at the cottage, but they needed salving.

I nodded numbly and turned in response to Lady Annabelle's gently insistent pressure on my elbow.

Halfway up the stairs, I remembered that I had forgotten to tell Sir Marcus how to bandage the cuts. The deep wounds over the shoulders would have to be bound and padded, to allow for wearing a shirt over them when we made our escape. But the lighter lash-marks should be left

765

in the open air to scab over. I took a quick look at the guest room Lady Annabelle showed me, then excused myself with a word and stumbled back down the stairs towards the drawing room.

I paused in the shadowed doorway, Lady Annabelle behind me. Jamie's eyes were closed; apparently he had fallen into a doze brought on by whisky and fatigue. The blankets were thrown back, rendered unnecessary by the heat of the fire. Sir Marcus casually rested a hand on Jamie's bare rump as he reached across the bed for a rag. The effect was electric. Jamie's back arched sharply, the muscles of his buttocks clenched tightly as he let out an involuntary sound of protest, flinging himself backwards in spite of the shattered ribs to glare up at Sir Marcus with startled, dazed eyes. Startled himself, Sir Marcus stood stock-still for a second, then leaned forward and took Jamie by the arm, gently settling him face down once more. Thoughtfully he drew a finger very gingerly across Jamie's flesh. He rubbed his fingers together, leaving an oily sheen visible in the firelight.

'Oh,' he said matter of factly. The old soldier drew the blanket up to Jamie's waist and I saw the tense shoulders relax slightly.

Sir Marcus seated himself companionably near Jamie's head and poured another pair of whiskys. 'At least he had the consideration to grease ye a bit beforehand,' he observed, handing one beaker to Jamie, who heaved himself laboriously up on his elbows to accept it.

'Aye, well. I dinna think it was so much for *my* convenience,' he said dryly.

Sir Marcus took a gulp of his drink and smacked his lips meditatively. There was no sound for a moment save the crackle of flames, but neither Lady Annabelle nor I made any motion to enter the room.

'If it's any comfort to ye,' Sir Marcus said suddenly, eyes fixed on the decanter, 'he's dead.'

'You're sure?' Jamie's tone was unreadable.

'I dinna see how anybody could live after bein' trampled flat by thirty quarter-ton beasts. He peeked out into the corridor to see what was causin' the noise, then tried to go back when he saw. A horn caught him by the sleeve and pulled him out, and I saw him go down next to the wall. Sir Fletcher an' I were on the stair, keepin' out o' the way. O' course Sir Fletcher was rare excited, and sent some men after 'im, but they couldna get anywhere near, with all the horns pokin' and beasts shovin', and the torches shook down from the wall wi' the ruckus. Christ, man, ye should ha' seen it!' Sir Marcus hooted at the memory, clutching the decanter by the neck. 'Your wife's a rare lass, and no mistake, lad!' Snorting, he poured out another glass and gulped, choking a bit as the laugh interfered with the swallow.

'Anyway,' he resumed, pounding himself on the chest, 'by the time we'd cleared the cattle out, there was no much left but a rag doll rolled in blood. Sir Fletcher's men carried him awa', but if he was still livin' then, he didna last long. A bit more, lad?'

'Aye, thanks.'

There was a short silence, broken by Jamie. 'No, I canna say it's much comfort to me, but thank ye for tellin' me.' Sir Marcus looked at him shrewdly.

'Mmmphm. Ye're no goin' to forget it,' he said abruptly. 'Don't bother to try. If ye can, let it heal like the rest o' your wounds. Don't pick at it, and it'll mend clean.' The old warrior held up a knotted forearm, from which the sleeve had been pushed back during his ministrations, to show the scar of a jagged tear running from elbow to wrist. 'Scars are nothin' to trouble ye.'

'Aye, well. Some scars, maybe.' Apparently reminded of something, Jamie struggled to turn on to his side. Sir Marcus set down his beaker with an exclamation.

'Here, lad, be careful! Ye'll get a rib-end through the lung, next thing.' He helped Jamie balance on his right elbow, wadding a blanket behind to prop him there.

'I need a wee knife,' said Jamie, breathing heavily. 'A sharp one, if it's handy.' Without question Sir Marcus lumbered to the gleaming French walnut sideboard and rummaged through the drawers with a prodigious clatter, emerging at last with a pearl-handled fruit knife. He thrust it into Jamie's sound left hand and sat down again with a grunt, resuming his glass.

'Ye don't think ye have enough scars?' he inquired. 'Going to add a few more?'

'Just one.' Jamie balanced precariously on one elbow, chin pressed on his chest as he awkwardly aimed the razor-sharp knife under his left breast. Sir Marcus' hand shot out, a bit unsteadily, and gripped Jamie's wrist.

'Best let me help ye, man. Ye'll fall on it in a moment.' After a moment's pause Jamie reluctantly surrendered the knife and lay back against the wadded blanket. He touched his chest an inch or two below the nipple.

'There.' Sir Marcus reached to the sideboard and snagged a lamp, setting it on the stool he had vacated. At this distance I couldn't see what he was peering at; it looked like a small red burn, roughly circular in shape. He took another deliberate pull at his whisky, then set it down next to the lamp and pressed the tip of the knife against Jamie's chest. I must have made an involuntary movement, because the Lady Annabelle clutched my sleeve with a murmured caution. The knife point pressed in and twisted suddenly, flicking away in the motion one uses to cut a bad spot out of a ripe peach. Jamie grunted, once, and a thin stream of red ran down the slope of his belly to stain the blanket. He rolled on to his stomach, stanching the wound against the mattress.

Sir Marcus laid down the fruit knife. 'As soon as ye're able, man,' he advised, 'take your wife to bed, and let her comfort ye. Women like to do that,' he said, grinning towards the shadowed doorway, 'God knows why.'

Lady Annabelle said softly, 'Come away now, dear. He's better alone for a bit.' I decided that Sir Marcus could manage the bandaging by himself, and stumbled after her up the narrow stair to my room.

I woke with a start from a dream of endless winding stairs, with horror lurking at the bottom. Tiredness dragged at my back and my legs ached, but I sat up in my borrowed nightdress and groped for the candle and flintbox. I felt uneasy, so far from Jamie. What if he needed me? Worse, what if the English did come while he was alone below, unarmed? I pressed my face against the cold casement, reassured by the steady hiss of snow against the panes. While the storm continued we were likely safe. I pulled on a bedgown, and picking up candle and dirk, made my way to the stairs.

The house was quiet save for the fire's crackle. Jamie was asleep, or at least had his eyes closed, face turned to the fire. I sat down on the hearthrug, quietly, so as not to wake him. This was the first time we had been alone together since those few desperate minutes in the dungeon of Wentworth Prison. It felt as though that were many years ago. I studied Jamie carefully, as though inspecting a stranger.

He seemed not too bad physically, all things considered, but I worried nonetheless. He had had enough whisky during the surgery to fell a draught horse, and a good bit of it was plainly still inside him, despite the retching.

Jamie was not my first hero. The men moved too quickly through the field hospital, as a rule, for the nurses to become well acquainted with them, but now and again you would see a man who talked too little or joked too much, who held himself more stiffly than pain and loneliness would account for.

And I knew, roughly, what could be done for them. If there was time, and if they were the kind who talked to keep the dark at bay, you sat with them and listened. If they were silent, you touched them often in passing, and watched for the unguarded moment when you might draw them outside of themselves and hold them while they exorcised their demons. If there were time. And if there wasn't, then you jabbed them with morphine and hoped they would manage to find someone else to listen, while you passed on to a man whose wounds were visible.

Jamie would talk to someone, sooner or later. There was time. But I hoped it wouldn't be me.

He was uncovered to the waist and I leaned forward to

examine his back. It was a remarkable sight. Barely a hand's thickness separated the welted cuts, inflicted with a regularity that boggled the mind. He must have stood like a guardsman while it was done. I stole a quick glance at his wrists – unmarked. He had kept his word then, not to struggle. And had stood unmoving through the ordeal, paying the ransom agreed on for my life.

I rubbed my eyes on my sleeve. He wouldn't thank me, I thought, for blubbering over his prostrate form. I shifted my weight with a soft rustle of skirts. He opened his eyes at the sound, but did not seem particularly haunted. He gave me a smile, faint and tired, but a real one. I opened my mouth, and suddenly realized I had no idea what to say to him. 'How do you feel?' was ridiculous; obviously he felt like hell. While I considered, he spoke first.

'Claire? Are you all right, love?'

'Am *I* all right? My God, Jamie!' Tears stung my eyelids and I blinked hard, sniffing. He raised his good hand slowly, as though it were weighted with chains, and stroked my hair. He drew me towards him, but I pulled away, conscious for the first time what I must look like, face scratched and covered with tree sap, hair stiff with blotches of various unmentionable substances.

'Come here,' he said. 'I want to hold ye a moment.'

'But I'm covered with blood and vomit,' I protested, making a vain effort to tidy my hair.

He wheezed, the faint exhalation that was all his broken ribs would permit in the way of laughter. 'Mother of God, Sassenach, it's my blood and my vomit. Come here.'

His arm was comforting around my shoulders. I rested my head on the pillow next to his and we sat in silence by the fire, drawing strength and peace from one another. His fingers gently touched the small wound under my jaw.

'I did not think ever to see ye again, Sassenach.' His voice was low and a bit hoarse from whisky and screaming. 'I'm glad you're here.'

I sat up. 'Not see me again! Why? Did you think I wouldn't get you out?'

He smiled, one-sided. 'Weel, no, I didn't expect ye

would. I thought if I said so, though, ye might get stubborn and refuse to go.'

'*Me* get stubborn!' I said indignantly. 'Look who's talking!'

There was a pause, which grew slightly awkward. There were things I should ask, necessary from the medical point of view, but rather touchy from the personal aspect. Finally, I settled for 'How do you feel?'

His eyes were closed, shadowed and sunken in the candlelight, but the lines of the broad back were tense. The wide, bruised mouth twitched, somewhere between a smile and a grimace.

'I don't know, Sassenach. I've never felt like this. I seem to want to do a number of things, all at once, but my mind's at war wi' me and my body's turned traitor. I want to get out of here at once and run as fast and as far as I can. I want to hit someone. God, I want to hit someone! I want to burn Wentworth Prison to the ground. I want to sleep.'

'Stone doesn't burn,' I said practically. 'Maybe you'd better sleep instead.'

His good hand groped for mine and found it, and the mouth relaxed somewhat, though his eyes stayed closed.

'I want to hold you hard to me and kiss you, and never let you go. I want to take you to my bed and use you like a whore, till I forget that I exist. And I want to put my head in your lap and weep like a child.'

The mouth turned up at one corner and a blue eye opened slitwise.

'Unfortunately,' he said, 'I can't do any but the last of those without fainting or being sick again.'

'Well, then, I suppose you'll just have to settle for that, and put the rest under the heading of future business,' I said, laughing a little.

It took a bit of shifting, and he nearly was sick again, but at last I was seated on his cot, my back against the wall, and his head resting on my thigh.

'What was it Sir Marcus cut from your breast?' I asked. 'A brand?' I said softly, as he gave me no reply. The bright head moved slightly in affirmation.

'A signet, with his initials.' Jamie laughed shortly. 'It's enough I'll carry his marks for the rest of my life, without letting him sign me like a bloody painting.'

His head lay heavy on my thigh and his breathing eased at last in drowsy exhalations. The white bandages on his hand were ghostly against the dark blanket. I gently traced a burn mark on his shoulder, gleaming faintly with sweet oil.

'Jamie?'

'Mmm?'

'Are you badly hurt?' Awake, he glanced from his bandaged hand to my face. His eyes closed and he began to shake. Alarmed, I thought I had triggered some unbearable memory, until I realized that he was laughing, hard enough to force tears from the corners of his eyes.

'Sassenach,' he said at length, gasping, 'I've maybe six square inches of skin left that are not bruised, burned or cut. Am I *hurt*?' And he shook again, making the chaff-filled mattress rustle and squeak.

Somewhat crossly, I said, 'I *meant* – ' but he stopped me by putting his good hand over mine and bringing it to his lips.

'I know what ye meant, Sassenach,' he said, turning his head to look up at me. 'Never worry, the six inches that are left are all between my legs.'

I appreciated the effort it took to make the joke, feeble as it was. I slapped his mouth lightly. 'You're drunk, James Fraser,' I said. I paused a moment. 'Six, eh?'

'Aye, well. Maybe seven, then. Oh, God, Sassenach, dinna make me laugh again, my ribs won't stand it.' I wiped his eyes with a fold of my skirt and fed him a sip of water, holding his head up with my knee.

'That isn't what I meant, anyway,' I said.

Serious then, he reached for my hand again and squeezed it.

'I know,' he said. 'Ye needna be delicate about it.' He drew a cautious breath and winced at the results. 'I was right, it did hurt less than flogging.' He closed his eyes. 'But it was much less enjoyable.' A quick flash of bitter humour stirred one corner of his mouth. 'At least I'll not be costive for a bit.' I flinched, and he gritted his teeth, breathing in short, reedy gasps.

'I'm sorry, Sassenach. I ... didna think I'd mind it so much. What you mean – that – it's all right. I'm not damaged.'

I made an effort to keep my own voice steady and matter of fact. 'You don't have to tell me about it, if you don't want to. If it might ease you, though ...' My voice trailed off in embarrassed silence.

'I don't *want* to.' His voice was suddenly bitter and emphatic. 'I don't want ever to think about it again, but short of cutting my throat I think I have no choice about it. Nay, lass, I dinna want to tell ye about it, any more than ye want to hear it ... but I think I am going to have to drag it all out before it chokes me.' The words came out now in a burst of bitterness.

'He wanted me to crawl and beg, and by Christ, I did so. I told ye once, Sassenach, ye can break anyone if you're willing to hurt them enough. Well, he was willing. He made me crawl, and he made me beg; he made me do worse things than that, and before the end he made me want verra badly to be dead.'

He was silent for a long moment, looking into the fire, then heaved a deep sigh, grimacing at the pain.

'I wish ye could ease me, Sassenach, I do wish it most fervently, for I've little of ease in me now. But it's not like a poisoned thorn, where if ye found the right grip ye could draw it clean out.' His good hand rested on my knee. He flexed the fingers and spread them flat, ruddy in the firelight. 'It's not even like a brokenness anywhere. If ye could mend it bit by bit, like ye did my hand, I'd stand the pain gladly.' He bunched the fingers into a fist and rested it on my leg, frowning at it.

'It's ... difficult to explain. It's ... it's like ... I think it's as though everyone has a small place inside themselves, maybe, a private bit that they keep to themselves. It's like a little fortress, where the most private part of you lives – maybe it's your soul, maybe just that bit that makes you yourself and not anyone else.' His tongue probed his swollen lip unconsciously as he thought.

'You don't show that bit of yourself to anyone, usually, unless sometimes to someone that ye love greatly.' The hand relaxed, curling around my knee. Jamie's eyes were closed again, lids sealed against the light.

'Now, it's like . . . like my own fortress has been blown up with gunpowder – there's nothing left of it but ashes and a smoking rooftree, and the little naked thing that lived there once is out in the open, squeaking and whimpering in fear, tryin' to hide itself under a blade of grass or a bit o' leaf, but . . . but not . . . makin' m-much of a job of it.' His voice broke, and he turned his head so that his face was hidden in my skirt. Helpless, I could do nothing but stroke his hair.

He suddenly raised his head, face strained as though it would break apart along the seams of the bones. 'I've been close to death a few times, Claire, but I've never really *wanted* to die. This time I did. I . . .' His voice cracked and he stopped speaking, clutching my knee hard. When he spoke again his voice was high and oddly breathless, as though he had been running a long way.

'Claire, will you – I just – Claire, hold on to me. If I start to shake again now, I canna stop it. Claire, hold me!' He was in fact beginning to tremble violently, the shivering making him moan as it caught the splintered ribs. I was afraid to hurt him, but more afraid to let the shaking go on.

I crouched over him, wrapped my arms around his shoulders and held on as tightly as I could, rocking to and fro as though the comforting rhythm might break the racking spasms. I got one hand on the back of his neck and dug my fingers deep into the pillared muscles, willing the clenching to relax as I massaged the deep groove at the base of the skull. Finally the trembling eased and his head fell forward on to my thigh, exhausted.

'I'm sorry,' he said a minute later, in his normal voice. 'I didna mean to go on so. The truth is I do hurt verra bad, and I am most awfully damn drunk. I'm no in much control of mysel'.' For a Scot to admit, even privately, to being drunk, was some indication, I thought, of just how badly he did hurt.

'You need sleep,' I said softly, still rubbing the back of his neck. 'You need it badly.' I used my fingers as best I could, gentling and pressing, and managed to ease him back into drowsiness.

'I'm cold,' he murmured. There was a good fire, and several blankets on the bed, but his fingers were chilly to the touch.

'You're in shock,' I said practically. 'You've lost a hell of a lot of blood.' I looked around, but MacRannochs and servants alike had all disappeared to their own beds. Murtagh, I assumed, was still out in the snow, keeping an eye out in the direction of Wentworth in case of pursuit. With a mental shrug for anyone's opinion of the proprieties, I stood up, stripped off the nightdress and bedgown, and crawled under the blankets.

As gently as possible I eased against him, giving him my warmth. He turned his face into my shoulder like a small boy. I stroked his hair, gentling him, rubbing the ridged columns of muscle at the back of his neck, avoiding the raw places. 'Lay your head, then, man,' I said, remembering Jenny and her boy.

Jamie gave a small grunt of amusement. 'That's what my mother used to say to me,' he murmured. 'When I was a bairn.

'Sassenach,' he said against my shoulder, a moment later. 'Mm?'

'Who in God's name is John Wayne?'

'You are,' I said. 'Go to sleep.'

37

Escape

His colour was better in the morning, though the bruises had darkened through the night and now mottled a good part of his face. He sighed deeply, then stiffened with a groan and let his breath out much more cautiously.

'How do you feel?' I laid a hand on his head. Cool and damp. No fever, thank God.

He grimaced, eyes still closed. 'Sassenach, if I've got one, it hurts.' He extended his good hand, groping. 'Help me up; I'm stiff as pudding.'

The snow stopped at mid-morning. The sky was still grey as wool, threatening further flurries, but the threat of search from Wentworth was greater yet, so we set out from Eldridge Hall just before noon, heavily cloaked against the weather. Murtagh and Jamie bristled with arms beneath their cloaks. I carried nothing but my dagger, and that well hidden. Much against my own will, I was to pose as a kidnapped English hostage, should the worst happen.

'But they've seen me at the prison,' I had argued. 'Sir Fletcher already knows who I am.'

'Aye.' Murtagh was carefully loading the pistols, an array of balls, wadding, powder, patches, rods and pouches neatly spread on Lady Annabelle's polished table, but looked up to nail me with a black glance. 'That's just the point, lass. We must keep ye out o' Wentworth, no matter what. Do no one any good to have ye in there along wi' us.'

He rammed a short rod down the mouth of a scroll-butted dag, punching the wad into place with hard, economical strokes. 'Sir Fletcher willna be doin' his own huntin', not on a day like this. Any redcoats we meet will likely not know ye. If we're found out, ye mun' say we forced ye along wi' us unwillin', and convince the redcoats ye've nothin' to do wi' a pair o' Scottish scalawags like me an' yon ragtag.' He nodded at Jamie, who was balancing gingerly on a stool with a bowl of warm bread and milk.

Sir Marcus and I had padded Jamie's hips and thighs as thickly as we could with linen bandages under a pair of worn breeches and hose, dark in colour to hide any telltale blood spots that might seep through. Lady Annabelle had split one of her husband's shirts down the back to accommodate the breadth of Jamie's shoulders and the thickness of the bandage across them. Even so, the shirt would not meet across the front, and the strapping around his chest peeked through. He had refused to comb his hair, on the grounds that even his scalp was sore, and he looked a wild and woolly sight, red spikes sticking up above a swollen purple face with one eye squeezed disreputably shut.

'If ye're taken,' Sir Marcus chipped in, 'tell them ye're a guest of mine, kidnapped while riding near the estate. Make them bring ye to Eldridge for me to identify. That should convince 'em. We'll tell 'em you're a friend of Annabelle's, from London.'

'And then get you safely out of here before Sir Fletcher comes round to offer his regards,' Annabelle added practically.

Sir Marcus had offered us Hector and Absalom as escorts, but Murtagh pointed out that this would certainly implicate Eldridge should we meet any English soldiers. So there were only the three of us, bundled against the cold, on the road towards the coast. I carried a fat purse and a note from the Master of Eldridge, one or both of which should insure our passage across the North Sea.

It was hard going through the snow. Less than a foot deep, the treacherous white stuff hid rocks, holes and other obstacles, making footing for the ponies slippery and dangerous. Clods of snow and mud flew up with each step, spattering bellies and hocks, and clouds of pony-breath vanished steaming into the frozen air.

Murtagh led the way, following the faint depression that marked the track. I rode beside Jamie, to help if he should lose consciousness, though he was, at his own insistence,

777

tied to his mount. Only his left hand was free, resting on the pistol looped to the saddle bow, concealed under his cloak.

We passed a few scattered bothies, smoke rising from the thatched roofs, but the inhabitants and their beasts seemed all within, secured against the cold. Here and there a lone man passed from cot to byre, carrying buckets or hay, but the road was deserted for the most part.

Two miles from Eldridge we passed under the shadow of Wentworth Prison, a grim bulk set in the hillside. The road was trampled here; traffic in and out did not cease even in the worst of weathers.

Our passage had been timed to coincide with the midday meal, in hopes that the sentries would be immersed in their pasties and ale. We plodded slowly past the short road that led to the gate, just a party of travellers with the ill luck to be abroad on such a miserable day.

Once past the prison we paused to rest the ponies for a moment in the shelter of a small pine grove. Murtagh bent to peer under the slouch hat that masked Jamie's telltale hair.

'All right, lad? Ye're quiet.'

Jamie lifted his head. His face was pale, and trickles of sweat ran down his neck despite the icy wind, but he managed a half-hearted grin.

'I'll do.'

'How do you feel?' I asked, anxious. He sat slumped in the saddle, without much sign of his usual erect grace. I got the other half of the grin.

'I've been trying to decide which hurts worse – my ribs, my hand or my arse. Tryin' to choose among them keeps my mind off my back.' He took a deep pull from the flask which Sir Marcus had thoughtfully provided, shuddered, and passed it to me. It was a good deal better than the raw spirit I had drunk on the road to Leoch, but every bit as potent. We rode on, a small cheerful fire burning in my stomach.

The ponies were labouring up a modest slope, snow spurting from their hooves, when I saw Murtagh's head jerk up. Following the direction of his gaze I saw the redcoat soldiers, four of them on horseback, at the top of the slope.

There was no help for it. We had been seen, and a shouted challenge echoed down the hill. There was no place to run. We were going to have to try to bluff it out. Without a backward glance Murtagh spurred forward to meet them.

The corporal with the group was a middle-aged career soldier, erect in his winter greatcoat. He bowed politely to me, then turned his attention to Jamie.

'Your pardon, sir, madam. We have orders to stop all parties travelling this road, to inquire for details of prisoners lately escaped from Wentworth Prison.'

Prisoners. So I *had* managed to release more than Jamie yesterday. I was glad of it, on various grounds. For one, they would dilute the search somewhat. Four against three was better odds than we might have expected.

Jamie didn't reply, but slouched further forward, letting his head loll. I could see the gleam of his eyes beneath the hat brim; he wasn't unconscious. These must be men he knew; his voice would be recognized. Murtagh was edging his mount forward, between me and the soldiers.

'Aye, the master's a bit the worse for illness, sir, as ye can see,' he said, obsequiously tugging his forelock. 'Perhaps ye could point out the coast road to me? I'm no convinced that we're headed right.'

I wondered what on earth he was up to, until I caught his eye. His glance flickered back and down, then back to the soldier, so fast that the soldier would assume him to have been listening with rapt attention all the time. Was Jamie in danger of falling from the saddle? Pretending to adjust my bonnet, I glanced casually over my shoulder in the direction he had indicated, and nearly froze with shock.

Jamie was sitting upright, head bent to shadow his face. But blood was dripping gently from the tip of the stirrup under his foot, pocking the snow with gently steaming red pits.

Murtagh, pretending vast stupidity, had succeeded in drawing the soldiers ahead to the crest of the hill, so that they could point out that our track was the only one in sight, running down towards the coast, still three miles away.

I slid hastily to the ground, yanking feverishly at my pony's girth strap. Floundering through the drifts, I kicked enough snow under the belly of Jamie's mount to obliterate the telltale drops. A quick look showed the soldiers apparently still engaged in argument with Murtagh, though one of them glanced down the hill at us to ensure that we had not wandered off. I gave a cheery wave, then as soon as the soldier turned his head, stooped and ripped off one of the three petticoats I was wearing. I whipped Jamie's cloak aside and stuffed the wadded petticoat under his thigh, ignoring his exclamation of pain. The cloak flipped back in place just in time for me to dash back to my own pony and be discovered fiddling with the girth when Murtagh and the Englishmen arrived.

'It seems to have worked its way loose,' I explained guilelessly, batting my eyes at the nearest redcoat.

'Oh? And why are you not helping the lady?' he said to Jamie.

'My husband's not well,' I said. 'I can manage it myself, thank you.'

The corporal seemed interested. 'Sick, eh? What's the matter with you, then?' He urged his beast forward, staring closely under the slouch hat at Jamie's pale face. 'Don't look well, I'll say that much. Take your hat off, fellow. What's the matter with your face?'

Jamie shot him through the folds of his cloak. The redcoat was no more than six feet away, and he toppled sideways out of the saddle before the stain on his chest grew bigger than my hand.

Murtagh had a pistol in each hand before the corporal hit the ground. One bullet went wild as his pony shied away from the sudden noise and movement. The second found its mark, ripping through a soldier's upper arm leaving a tuft of shredded fabric flapping from a rapidly reddening sleeve. The man kept his saddle, though, and was tugging at his sabre, one-handed, as Murtagh plunged beneath his cloak for fresh weapons.

One of the two remaining soldiers turned his horse, slipping in the snow, and spurred away, back towards the prison, presumably in search of help.

'Claire!' The shout came from above. I looked up, startled, to see Jamie waving after the fleeing figure. 'Stop him!' He had time to toss me a second pistol, then turned back, drawing his sword to meet the charge of the fourth soldier.

My mount was battle-trained; his ears were laid flat against his head and he stamped and pawed at the noise, but he hadn't run at the sound of shots, and he stood his ground as I groped for the saddle iron. Glad to be leaving the fight behind, he dug in as soon as I was mounted, and we made off at good speed after the fleeing figure.

The snow hampered our going nearly as much as his, but mine was the better animal, and we had the advantage of the rough path the soldier's flight had ploughed through the fresh snow. We gained slowly on him, but I could see that it wouldn't be enough. He had a rise ahead of him, though; if I cut to the right, perhaps I could make better time on the flat and meet him coming down the other side. I jerked the rein and leaned hard to keep my seat as the pony slithered into a messy turn, found his feet and plunged ahead.

I didn't quite catch him up, but I had cut the distance between us to no more than ten yards. Given unlimited distance I could probably catch him, but I didn't have that luxury; the prison wall loomed less than a mile ahead. Much closer, and we would be seen from the walls.

I pulled up and slid off. Battle-trained or not, I didn't know what the pony would do if I fired a pistol from his back. Even if he stood like a statue, I didn't think my own aim was up to it. I knelt in the snow, bracing my elbow on my knee, the gun across my forearm as Jamie had showed me. 'Brace it here, aim there, fire it *here*,' he had said. I did.

Much to my amazement, I hit the fleeing horse. It went into a skid, dropped to one knee and rolled in a flurry of snow and legs. My arm was numb from the pistol's recoil; I stood rubbing it, watching the fallen soldier.

He was injured; he struggled to rise, then fell back in the snow. His horse, bleeding from the shoulder, stumbled away, reins dangling.

I didn't realize until later what I had been thinking, but I knew when I approached him that I could not let him live. Near as we were to the prison, and with other patrols out seeking escaped prisoners, he was sure to be found before too long. And if he were found alive, he could not only describe us – so much for our hostage story in that case! – but tell which way we were travelling. We had still three miles to go to the coast; two hours' travel in the heavy snow. And a boat to find, once there. I simply could not take the chance of allowing him to tell anyone about us.

He struggled to his elbows as I approached. His eyes widened in surprise as he saw me, then relaxed. I was a woman. He wasn't afraid of me.

A more experienced man might have been apprehensive, my sex notwithstanding, but this was a boy. No more than sixteen, I thought with a sense of sick shock. His spotty cheeks still held the last round curves of childhood, though his upper lip sported the fuzz of a hopeful moustache.

He opened his mouth, but only groaned in pain. He pressed his hand to his side and I could see blood soaking through his tunic and coat. Internal injuries, then; the horse must have rolled on him.

It was possible, I thought, that he would die in any case. But that wasn't something I could count on.

The dirk in my right hand was hidden under my cloak. I laid my left hand on his head. Just so I had touched the heads of hundreds of men, comforting, examining, steadying them for whatever lay ahead. And they had looked up at me much as this boy did: with hope and trust.

I couldn't cut his throat. I sank to my knees beside him and turned his head gently away from me. Rupert's techniques for swift killing had all assumed resistance. There was no resistance as I bent his head forward, as far as I could, and plunged the dirk into his neck at the base of his skull.

I left him lying face down in the snow and went to join the others.

Our unwieldy cargo stowed under blankets on a bench below, Murtagh and I met on the *Cristabel*'s deck to survey the storm-tossed skies.

'Looks like a fair, steady wind,' I said hopefully, holding a wet finger aloft.

Murtagh gloomily scanned the clouds, hanging black-bellied over the harbour, their freight of snow wastefully melting into the frigid waves. 'Aye, well. We'll hope for a smooth crossing. If not, we'll likely get there wi' a corpse on our hands.'

Half an hour later, launched on the choppy waters of the North Sea, I discovered what he had meant by this remark.

'Seasick?' I said incredulously. 'Scotsmen aren't seasick!'

Murtagh was testy. 'Then mayhap he's a red-heided Hottentot. All I know is he's green as a rotten fish and pukin' his guts out. Are ye goin' to come down and help me stop him puttin' his ribs out through his chest?'

'Damn it,' I said to Murtagh as we hung over the rail for fresh air during a brief hiatus in the unpleasantness below decks, 'if he knows he's going to be seasick, why in the name of God did he insist on travelling to France?'

The basilisk stare was unwinking. 'Because he knows bluidy well we'd never go far on land wi' him in the state he's in, and he'd no stay at Eldridge for fear o' bringin' the English down on MacRannoch.'

'So he's going to kill himself quietly at sea, instead,' I said bitterly.

'Aye. He figures this way he'll only kill himself, and no take anyone else along wi' him. Unselfish, see. Nothin' quiet about it, though,' added Murtagh, heading for the companionway in response to unmistakable sounds from below.

'Congratulations,' I said to Jamie an hour or two later, pushing dank wisps away from my cheeks and forehead. 'I believe you're going to make medical history by being the only documented person ever actually to die of seasickness.'

'Oh, good,' he mumbled into the wreck of pillows and blankets, 'I'd hate to think it was all a waste.' He heaved himself suddenly to one side. 'God, here it comes again.' Murtagh and I sprang once more to our stations. The job of holding a large man immobile while he succumbs to merciless spasms of retching is not one for the weak.

Afterwards I took his pulse yet again, and rested a hand briefly on the clammy forehead. Murtagh read my face and followed me unspeaking up the gangway to the top deck. 'He's no doin' verra well, is he?' he said quietly.

'I don't know,' I said helplessly, shaking out my sweat-drenched hair in the sharp wind. 'I've honestly never heard of anyone dying of seasickness, but he's bringing up blood now.' The little man's hands tightened on the rail, knuckles knifing through the sun-speckled skin. 'I don't know if he's damaged himself internally with the sharp rib ends, or if it's just that his stomach is raw with the vomiting. Either way, it's not a good sign. And his pulse is much weaker, and irregular. It's a strain on his heart, you know.'

'He's a heart like a lion.' It was quietly said, and I wasn't sure I'd heard it at first. It might only have been the salt wind making the tears stand in his eyes. He turned abruptly to me. 'And a hide like an ox. Have ye any o' that laudanum left that Lady Annabelle gave ye?'

'Yes, all of it. He wouldn't take it; doesn't want to sleep, he said.'

'Aye, well. For most folk, what they want and what they get are no the same thing; I dinna see why he should be any different. Come on.'

I followed him anxiously back below decks. 'I don't think he can keep it down.'

'Leave that to me. Get the bottle and help me sit him up.'

Jamie was half unconscious as it was, an unwieldy burden who protested being manhandled upright against the bulk-head. 'I'm going to die,' he said weakly but precisely, 'and the sooner the better. Go away and let me do it in peace.'

Taking firm hold of Jamie's blazing hair, Murtagh forced his head up and applied the flask to his lips. 'Swallow this, me bonny wee dormouse, or I'll break yer neck. And forbye ye'll keep it down, too. I'm goin' to hold shut yer nose and yer mouth; if ye bring it up, it comes out yer ears.'

By the concerted force of our wills we transferred the contents of the flask slowly but inexorably into the young laird of Lallybroch. Choking and gagging, Jamie manfully drank as much as he could manage before subsiding, green-faced and gasping, against the bulkhead. Murtagh forestalled each threatened explosion of nausea by vicious nose-pinching, an expedient not uniformly successful, but one which allowed a gradual accumulation of the opiate in the patient's bloodstream. At length we laid him slack on the bed, the vivid flames of hair, brows and lashes the only colour on the pillow.

Murtagh came up beside me on deck a bit later. 'Look,' I said pointing. The dim light of sunset, shining in fugitive rays beneath the clouds, gilded the rocks of the French coast ahead. 'The master says we'll be ashore in three or four hours.'

'And not before time,' said my companion, wiping lank brown hair out of his eyes. He turned and gave me the closest thing I had ever seen to a smile on his dour countenance.

And so at length, following the prostrate body of our charge, laid on a board between two stout monks, we passed through the looming gates of the Benedictine Abbey of Ste Anne de Beaupré.

38

The Abbey

The abbey was an enormous twelfth-century edifice, walled to resist both the smashing of sea storms and the onslaughts of land-based invaders. Now, in more peaceful times, its gates stood open to allow easy traffic with the nearby village, and the small stone cells of its guest wing had been softened by the addition of tapestries and comfortable furniture.

I rose from the padded chair in my own chamber, not sure exactly how one greeted an abbot; did one kneel and kiss his ring, or was that only for popes? I settled for a respectful curtsy.

Jamie's slanted cat-eyes *did* come from the Fraser side. Likewise the solid jaw, though the one facing me was somewhat obscured by a black beard.

Abbot Alexander's slanted blue eyes remained cool and speculative as he greeted me with a pleasant, warm smile. He was a good deal shorter than Jamie, about my height, and stocky. He wore the robe of a priest, but walked with a warrior's stride. I thought it likely he had been both in his time.

'You are welcome, *ma nièce*,' he said, inclining his head. I was a little startled at the greeting, but bowed back.

'I'm grateful for your hospitality,' I said, meaning it. 'Have – have you seen Jamie?' The monks had taken Jamie away to be bathed, a process in which I thought I had better not assist.

The Abbot nodded. 'Oh, aye,' he said, a faint Scots accent showing through the cultured English. 'I've seen him. I've set Brother Ambrose to tend his wounds.' I must have looked dubious at this, for he said, a bit dryly, 'Do not worry, madam; Brother Ambrose is most

786

competent.' He looked me over with an air of frank appraisal disturbingly like that of his nephew.

'Murtagh said that you are an accomplished physician yourself.'

'I am,' I said bluntly.

This provoked a real smile. 'I see that you do not suffer from the sin of false modesty,' he observed.

'I have others,' I said, smiling back.

'So do we all,' he said. 'Brother Ambrose will be eager to converse with you, I'm sure.'

'Has Murtagh told you . . . what happened?' I asked hesitantly.

The wide mouth tightened. 'He has. So far as he *knows* what happened.' He waited, as though expecting further contributions from me, but I stayed silent.

It was clear that he would have liked to ask questions, but he was kind enough not to press me. Instead he raised his hand in a gesture of benediction and dismissal.

'You are welcome,' he said once more. 'I will send a serving brother to bring you some food.' He looked me over yet again. 'And some facilities for washing.' He made the sign of the cross over me, in farewell or possibly as an exorcism of filth, and left in a swirl of skirts.

Suddenly realizing how tired I was, I sank down on the bed, wondering whether I could stay awake long enough to both eat *and* wash. I was still wondering when my head hit the pillow.

I was having a dreadful nightmare. Jamie was on the other side of a solid stone wall without a door. I could hear him screaming, over and over, but couldn't reach him. I pounded desperately on the wall, only to see my hands sink into the stone as if it were water.

'Ouch!' I sat up in the narrow cot, clutching the hand I had smashed against the unyielding wall next to my bed. I rocked back and forth, squeezing the throbbing hand between my thighs, then realized that the screaming was still going on.

It stopped abruptly as I ran into the hall. The door to

787

Jamie's room was open, flickering lamplight flooding the corridor.

A Franciscan friar I had not seen before was with Jamie, holding him tightly. A seepage of fresh blood stained the bandages on Jamie's back, and his shoulders shook as though with chill.

'A nightmare,' the friar said in explanation, seeing me in the doorway. He relinquished Jamie into my arms and went to the table for a cloth and the water jug.

Jamie was still trembling and his face was glossy with sweat. His eyes were closed and he breathed heavily, with a hoarse, gasping sound. The monk sat down beside me and began to swab Jamie's face with a gentle hand, smoothing the heavy, wet hair away from his temples.

'You would be his wife, of course,' he said to me. 'I think he'll be better presently.'

The trembling did begin to ease within a minute or two, and Jamie opened his eyes with a sigh.

'I'm all right,' he said. 'Claire, I'm all right, now. But for God's sake, get rid of that stink!'

It was only then that I consciously noticed the scent in the room – a light, spicy, floral smell, so common a perfume that I had thought nothing of it. Lavender. A scent for soaps and toilet water. I had last smelled it in the dungeons of Wentworth Prison, where it anointed the linen or the person of Captain Jonathan Randall.

The source of the scent was a small metal cup filled with herb-scented oil, suspended from a heavy, rose-bossed iron base and hung over a candle flame. Meant to soothe the mind, its effects were plainly not as intended. Jamie was breathing more easily, sitting up by himself and holding the cup of water the friar had given him. But his face was still white and the corner of his mouth twitched uneasily.

I nodded at the Franciscan to do as he said, and the monk quickly muffled the hot cup of oil in a folded towel, then carried it away down the hall.

Jamie heaved a long sigh of relief, then winced, ribs hurting.

'You've opened up your back a bit,' I said, turning him slightly to get at the bandages. 'Not bad, though.'

'I know. I must have rolled on to my back in my sleep.' The thick wedge of folded blanket meant to keep him propped on one side had slipped to the floor. I retrieved it and laid it on the bed beside him.

'That's what made me dream, I think. I dreamt of being flogged.' He shuddered, took a sip of the water, then handed me the cup. 'I need something a bit stronger, if it's handy.'

As though on cue our helpful visitor came through the door with a jug of wine in one hand and a small flask of poppy syrup in the other.

'Alcohol or opium?' he asked Jamie with a smile, holding up the two flasks. 'You may have your choice of oblivions.'

'I'll have the wine, if ye please. I've had enough of dreams for one night,' Jamie said with a lopsided answering smile. He drank the wine slowly as the Franciscan helped me to change the stained bandages, smoothing fresh marigold ointment over the wounds. Not until I had resettled Jamie for sleep, back firmly propped and coverlet drawn up, did the visitor turn to go.

Passing the bed, he bent over Jamie and sketched the sign of the Cross above his head. 'Rest well,' he said.

'Thank ye, Father,' Jamie answered drowsily, clearly half asleep already. Seeing that Jamie would probably not need me now until morning, I touched him on the shoulder in farewell and followed the visitor out into the corridor.

'Thank you,' I said. 'I'm most grateful for your help.'

The friar waved a graceful hand, dismissing my thanks.

'I was pleased to be able to assist you,' he said, and I noticed that he spoke excellent English, though with a faint French accent. 'I was passing through the guest wing on my way to the chapel of St Giles when I heard the screaming.'

I winced at the memory of that screaming, hoarse and dreadful, and hoped I would not hear it again. Glancing at the window at the end of the corridor, I saw no sign of dawn behind the shutter.

'To the chapel?' I said, surprised. 'But I thought Prime

was sung in the main church. And it's surely a bit early, in any case.'

The Franciscan smiled. He was fairly young, perhaps in his early thirties, but his silky brown hair was threaded with grey. It was short and neatly tonsured.

'Very early, for Prime,' he agreed. 'I was on my way to the chapel because it is my turn for the Perpetual Adoration of the Blessed Sacrament at this hour.' He glanced back into Jamie's room, where a clock candle marked the time as half past two.

'I'm very late,' he said. 'Brother Bartolome will be wanting his bed.' Raising his hand, he quickly blessed me, turned on a sandalled heel, and was through the swinging door at the end of the corridor before I could muster wits enough to ask his name.

I stepped into the room and bent to check Jamie. He was asleep again, breathing lightly, with a slight frown creasing his brow. Experimentally I ran my hand lightly over his hair. The frown eased a bit, and then resumed. I sighed and tucked the blankets more securely around him.

I felt much better in the morning, but Jamie was hollow-eyed and queasy after the broken night. He emphatically rejected any suggestion of caudle or broth for breakfast, and snapped irritably at me when I tried to check the dressings on his hand.

'For Christ's sake, Claire, will ye no leave me alone! I dinna want to be poked at any more!'

He yanked his hand away, scowling. I turned away without speaking and went to busy myself with tidying the small pots and packets of medicines on the side table. I arranged them into small groups, sorted by function: marigold ointment and alder balm for soothing, willow bark and camomile for teas, Saint John's wort, garlic and yarrow for disinfection.

'Claire.' I turned back to find him sitting on the bed, looking at me with a shamefaced smile.

'I'm sorry, Sassenach. My bowels are griping, and I've a

damn evil temper this morning. But I've no call to snarl at ye. D'ye forgive me?'

I crossed to him swiftly and hugged him lightly.

'You know there's nothing to forgive. But what do you mean, your bowels are griping?' Not for the first time, I reflected that intimacy and romance are not synonymous.

He grimaced, bending forward slightly and folding his arms over his abdomen. 'It means,' he said, 'that I'd like ye to leave me to myself for a bit. If ye dinna mind?' I hastily complied with his request, and went to find my own breakfast.

Returning a bit later, I spotted a trim figure in the robes of a Franciscan, crossing the courtyard towards the cloister. I hurried to catch up with him.

'Father!' I called, and he turned, smiling when he saw me.

'Good morning,' he said. 'Madame Fraser; is that the name? And how is your husband this morning?'

'Better,' I said, hoping it was true. 'I wanted to thank you again for last night. You left before I could even ask your name.'

Clear hazel eyes sparkled as he bowed to me, hand over his heart. 'François Anselm Mericoeur d'Armagnac, madame,' he said. 'Or so I was born. Known now only as Father Anselm.'

'Anselm of the Merry Heart?' I asked, smiling. He shrugged, a completely Gallic gesture unchanged for centuries.

'One tries,' he said with an ironic twist of the mouth.

'I don't wish to keep you,' I said, glancing towards the cloister. 'I only wanted to thank you for your help.'

'You do not detain me in the least, madame. I was delaying going to my work, in fact, indulging most sinfully in idleness.'

'What is your work?' I asked, intrigued. Plainly this man was a visitor to the monastery, his Franciscan robes altogether conspicuous among those of the Benedictines. There were several such visitors, or so Brother Polydore, one of the serving brothers, had told me. Most of them were scholars, here to consult the works stored in the abbey's renowned library. Anselm, it seemed, was one of these. He was, as he had been for several months, engaged in the translation of some of the works by St Jerome.

'Have you seen the library?' he asked. 'Come, then,' he said, seeing me shake my head. 'It is really most impressive, and I am sure the Abbot your uncle would have no objection.'

I was both curious to see the library and reluctant to go back at once to the isolation of the guest wing, so I followed him without hesitation.

The library was beautiful, high-roofed, with soaring columns that joined in ogives in the multi-chambered roof. Full-length windows filled the spaces between columns, letting an abundance of light into the library. Most were of clear glass, but some had deceptively simple-looking stained-glass parables. Tiptoeing past the bent forms of studying monks, I paused to admire one of *The Flight into Egypt*.

Some of the bookshelves looked like those I was used to, the books nestling side by side. Other shelves held the books laid flat, to protect the ancient bindings. There was even one glass-fronted bookshelf holding a number of rolled parchments. Overall, the library held a hushed exultation, as though the cherished volumes were all singing soundlessly within their covers. I left the library feeling soothed, and strolled slowly across the main courtyard with Father Anselm.

I tried again to thank him for his help the night before, but he shrugged off my thanks.

'Think nothing of it, my child. I hope that your husband is better today?'

'So do I,' I said. Not wanting to dwell on that subject, I asked, 'What exactly is Perpetual Adoration? You said that was where you were going last night.'

'You are not a Catholic?' he asked in surprise. 'Ah, but I forgot, you are English. So of course, I suppose you would be a Protestant.'

'I'm not sure that I'm either one, in terms of belief,' I said. 'But technically, at least, I suppose I am a Catholic.'

'Technically?' The smooth eyebrows shot up in astonishment. I hesitated, cautious after my experiences with Father Bain, but this man did not seem the sort to start waving crucifixes in my face.

'Well,' I said, bending to pull a small weed from between the paving stones, 'I was baptised as a Catholic. But my parents died when I was five, and I went to live with an uncle. Uncle Lambert was . . .' I paused, recalling Uncle Lambert's voracious appetite for knowledge, and that cheerfully objective cynicism that regarded all religion merely as one of the earmarks by which a culture could be catalogued. 'Well, he was everything and nothing, I suppose, in terms of faith,' I concluded. 'Knew them all, believed in none. So nothing further was ever done about my religious training. And my . . . first husband was Catholic, but not very observant, I'm afraid. So I suppose I'm really rather a heathen.'

I eyed him warily, but rather than being shocked by this revelation he laughed heartily.

'Everything and nothing,' he said, savouring the phrase. 'I like that very much. But as for you, I am afraid not. Once a member of Holy Mother Church, you are eternally marked as her child. However little you know about your faith, you are as much a Catholic as our Holy Father the Pope.' He glanced at the sky. It was cloudy, but the leaves of the alder bushes near the church hung still.

'The wind has dropped. I was going for a short stroll to clear my brain in the fresh air. Why do you not accompany me? You need air and exercise, and I can perhaps make the occasion spiritually beneficial as well, by enlightening you as to the ritual of Perpetual Adoration as we go.'

'Three birds with one stone, eh?' I said dryly. But the prospect of air, if not light, was enticing, and I went to fetch my cloak without demur.

With a glance at the form within, head bent in prayer, Anselm led me past the quiet darkness of the chapel entrance and down the cloister, out to the edge of the garden.

Beyond the possibility of disturbing the monks within the chapel, he said, 'It's a very simple idea. You recall the Bible, and the story of Gethsemane, where our Lord waited out the hours before his trial and crucifixion, and his friends, who should have borne him company, all fell fast asleep?'

'Oh,' I said, understanding all at once. 'And he said, "Can you not watch with me one hour?" So that's what you're doing – watching with him for that hour – to make up for it.' I liked the idea, and the darkness of the chapel suddenly seemed inhabited and comforting.

'Oui, madame,' he agreed. 'Very simple. We take it in turns to watch, and the Blessed Sacrament on the altar here is never left alone.'

'Isn't it difficult, staying awake?' I asked curiously. 'Or do you always watch at night?'

He nodded, a light breeze lifting the silky brown hair. The patch of his tonsure needed shaving; short bristly hairs covered it like moss.

'Each watcher chooses the time that suits him best. For me, that is two o'clock in the morning.' He glanced at me, hesitating as though wondering how I would take what he was about to say.

'For me, in that moment . . .' He paused. 'It's as though time has stopped. All the humours of the body, all the blood and bile and vapours that make a man; it's as though just at once all of them are working in perfect harmony.' He smiled. His teeth were slightly crooked, the only defect in his otherwise perfect appearance.

'Or as though they've stopped altogether. I often wonder whether that moment is the same as the moment of birth, or of death. I know that its timing is different for each man . . . or woman, I suppose,' he added with a courteous nod to me.

'But just then, for that fraction of time, it seems as though all things are possible. You can look across the limitations of your own life and see that they are really nothing. In that moment when time stops, it is as though you know you could undertake any venture, complete it and come back to yourself to find the world unchanged, and everything just as you left it a moment before. And it's as though . . .' He hesitated for a moment, carefully choosing words.

'As though, knowing that everything is possible, suddenly nothing is necessary.'

'But . . . do you actually *do* anything?' I asked. 'Er, pray, I mean?'

'I? Well,' he said slowly, 'I sit, and I look at God.' A wide smile stretched the fine-drawn lips. 'And he looks at me.'

Jamie was sitting up when I returned to the room, and essayed a short trip up and down the hall, leaning on my shoulder. But the effort left him pale and sweating, and he lay down without protest when I turned back the coverlet for him.

I offered him a little soup and milk, but he shook his head wearily. 'I've no appetite, Sassenach. If I take anything, I think I shall be sick again.'

I didn't press the matter, but took the soup away in silence.

At dinner I was more insistent, and succeeded in persuading him to try a few spoonfuls of soup. He managed quite a bit of it, but didn't succeed in keeping it down.

'I'm sorry, Sassenach,' he said afterwards. 'I'm disgusting.'

'It doesn't matter, Jamie, and you are not disgusting.' I set the basin outside the door and sat down beside him, smoothing back the tumbled hair from his brow.

'Don't worry. It's only that your stomach is still irritated from the seasickness. Perhaps I've pushed you too fast to eat. Let it rest and heal.'

He closed his eyes, sighing under my hand.

'I'll be all right,' he said, without interest. 'What did ye do today, Sassenach?'

He was obviously restless and uncomfortable, but eased a bit as I told him about my explorations of the day; the library, the chapel, the winepress and finally the herb garden, where I had at last met the famous Brother Ambrose.

'He's amazing,' I said enthusiastically. 'Oh, but I forgot, you've met him.' Brother Ambrose was tall – even taller than Jamie – and cadaverous, with the long drooping face of a basset hound. And ten long, skinny digits, every one of them bright green.

'He seems to be able to make *anything* grow,' I said. 'He's got all the normal herbs there, and a greenhouse so tiny that he can't even stand up straight inside it, with things that shouldn't grow at this season, or shouldn't grow in this part of the world, or just shouldn't grow. Not to mention the imported spices and drugs.'

The mention of drugs reminded me of the night before, and I glanced out of the window. The winter twilight set in early, and it was already full dark outside, the lanterns of the monks who tended the stables and outdoor work bobbing to and fro as they passed on their rounds.

'It's getting dark. Do you think you can sleep by yourself? Brother Ambrose has a few things that might help.'

His eyes were smudged with tiredness, but he shook his head.

'No, Sassenach. I dinna want anything. If I fall asleep . . . no, I think I'll read for a bit.' Anselm had brought him a selection of philosophical and historical works from the library, and he stretched out a hand for a copy of Tacitus that lay on the table.

'You need sleep, Jamie,' I said gently, watching him. He opened the book before him, propped on the pillow, but continued to stare at the wall above it.

'I didna tell ye what I dreamed,' he said suddenly.

'You said you dreamed of being flogged.' I didn't like the look on his face; already pale under the bruises, it was lightly sheened with dampness.

'That's right. I could look up and see the ropes, cutting into my wrists. My hands had gone almost black, and the rope scraped bone when I moved. I had my face pressed against the post. Then I could feel the lead plummets at the ends of the lashes, cutting through the flesh of my shoulders.

'The lashes kept coming, long past when they should have stopped, and I realized that he didn't mean to stop. The tips of the cords were biting out small chunks of my flesh. The blood . . . my blood was running down my sides and my back, soaking into my kilt. I was very cold.

'Then I looked up again, and I could see that the flesh had begun to fall away from my hands, and the bones of my fingers were scrabbling at the wood, leaving long raw scratches behind. The bones of my arms were bare, and only the ropes were holding them together. I think that's when I began to scream.

'I could hear a strange rattling noise when he hit me, and after a time I realized what it was. He'd stripped all the flesh off my bones, and the plummets of the whip were rattling on my dry rib bones. And I knew that I was dead, but it didn't matter. He would go on and on, and it would never stop, he would go on until I began to fall to pieces and crumble away from the post, and it would never stop, and . . .'

I moved to take hold of him and make him hush, but he had already stopped himself, gripping the edge of the book with his good hand. His teeth were set hard in the torn flesh of his lower lip.

'Jamie, I'll stay with you tonight,' I said. 'I can lay a pallet on the floor.'

'No.' Weak as he was, there was no mistaking the basic stubbornness. 'I'll do best alone. And I'm not sleepy now. Do ye go and find your own supper, Sassenach. I'll . . . just read for a bit.' He bent his head over the page. After a minute of helplessly watching him, I did as he said, and left.

I was becoming more and more worried by Jamie's condition. The nausea lingered; he ate almost nothing, and what he did eat seldom stayed with him. He grew paler and more listless, showing little interest in anything. He slept a great deal in the daytime, because of sleeping so little at night. Still, whatever his fears of dreaming, he would not allow me to share his chamber, so that his wakefulness need not impair my own rest.

Not wishing to hover over him, even if he would have allowed it, I spent much of my time in the herbarium or the drying shed with Brother Ambrose, or wandering idly through the abbey's grounds, engaged in conversation with Father Anselm. He took the opportunity to engage in a gentle catechism, trying to instruct me in the basics of Catholicism, though I had assured him over and over of my basic agnosticism.

'*Ma chère*,' he said at last, 'do you recall the conditions necessary for the commission of sin, that I told you yesterday?'

There was nothing wrong with my memory, whatever my moral shortcomings might be.

'First, that it be wrong, and secondly, that you give full consent to it,' I parroted.

'That you give full consent to it,' he repeated. 'And that, *ma chère*, is the condition for grace to occur, as well.' We were leaning on the wall of the abbey pigsty, watching several large brown hogs huddling together in the weak winter sun. He turned his head, resting his face on his forearms, folded on the wall.

'I don't see how I can,' I protested. 'Surely grace is something you have or you don't. I mean' – I hesitated, not wishing to seem rude – 'to you, the thing on the altar in the chapel is God. To me, it's a bit of bread, no matter how lovely the holder it's in.'

He sighed with impatience and straightened up, stretching his back.

'I have observed, on my way to my nightly watch, that your husband does not sleep well,' he said. 'And consequently, neither do you. Since you are not asleep in any case, I invite you to come with me tonight. Join me in the chapel for an hour.'

I eyed him narrowly. 'Why?'

He shrugged. 'Why not?'

I had no difficulty in waking up for my appointment with Anselm, largely because I had not been asleep. Neither had Jamie. Whenever I poked my head out into the corridor I could see the flicker of candlelight from the half-open door of his room, and hear the flip of pages and the occasional grunt of discomfort as he shifted his position.

Unable to rest, I had not bothered to undress, and so was ready when a tap at my door announced Anselm's presence.

The monastery was quiet, in the way that all large institutions grow quiet at night; the rapid pulse of the day's activities has dropped, but the heartbeat goes on, slower, softer, but unending. There is always someone awake, moving quietly through the halls, keeping watch, keeping things alive. And now it was my turn to join the watch.

The chapel was dark except for the burning of the red sanctuary lamp and a few of the clear white votive candles, flames rising straight in still air before the shadowed shrines of saints.

I followed Anselm down the short centre aisle, genuflecting in his wake. The slight figure of Brother Bartolome knelt towards the front, head bowed. He didn't turn at the faint noise of our entrance but stayed motionless, bent in adoration.

The Sacrament itself was almost obscured by the magnificence of its container. The huge monstrance, a sunburst of gold more than a foot across, sat serenely on the altar, guarding the humble bit of bread at its centre.

Feeling somewhat awkward I took the seat Anselm indicated, near the front of the chapel, and heard the faint creak of a lowered seat behind me as Anselm found his place.

'But what shall I do?' I had asked him, voice lowered in respect of night and silence as we had approached the chapel.

'Nothing, *ma chère*,' he had replied simply. 'Only be.'

So I sat, listening to my own breathing and the tiny sounds of a silent place; the almost inaudible things normally hidden in other sounds. The settling of stone, the creak of wood. The hissing of the tiny, unquenchable flames. A faint skitter of some small creature, wandered from its place into the home of majesty.

It was a peaceful place, I would grant Anselm that. In spite of my own fatigue and my worry over Jamie I gradually felt myself relaxing, the tightness of my mind gently unwinding like the relaxation of a clock spring. Strangely I didn't feel at all sleepy, despite the lateness of the hour and the strains of the last few days and weeks.

After all, I thought, what were days and weeks in the presence of eternity? And that's what this was, to Anselm and Bartolome, to Ambrose, to all the monks, up to and including the formidable Abbot Alexander.

It was in a way a comforting idea; if there were all the time in the world, then the happenings of a given moment became less important. I could see, perhaps, how one could draw back a little, seek some respite in the contemplation of an endless Being, whatever one conceived its nature to be.

The red of the sanctuary lamp burned steadily, reflected in the smooth gold. The flames of the white candles before the statues of St Giles and the Blessed Mother flickered and jumped occasionally, as the burning wicks yielded an occasional imperfection, a momentary sputter of wax or moisture. But the red lamp burned serene, with no unseemly waver to betray its light.

And if there were eternity, or even the idea of it, then perhaps Anselm was right; all things were possible. And all love? I wondered. I had loved Frank; I still did. And I loved Jamie, more than my own life. But bound in the limits of time and flesh, I could not keep them both. Beyond, perhaps? Was there a place where time no longer existed, or where it stopped? Anselm thought so. A place where all things were possible. And none were necessary.

And was there love there? Beyond the limits of flesh and time, was all love possible? Was it necessary?

The voice of my thoughts seemed to be Uncle Lamb's. My family, and all I knew of love as a child. A man who had never spoken love to me, who had never needed to, for I knew he loved me, as surely as I knew I lived. For where all love is, the speaking is unnecessary. It is all. It is undying. And it is enough.

Time passed without my awareness of it, and I was startled by the sudden appearance of Anselm before me, coming through the small door near the altar. Surely he had been sitting behind me? I glanced behind, to see one of the young monks whose name I didn't know genuflecting near the rear entrance. Anselm bowed low before the altar, then motioned to me with a nod towards the door.

'You left?' I said, once outside the chapel. 'But I thought you weren't supposed to leave the, er, the Sacrament, alone?'

He smiled tranquilly. 'I didn't, *ma chère*. You were there.'

I repressed the urge to argue that I didn't count. After all, I supposed, there was no such thing as a Qualified Official Adorer. You only had to be human, and I imagined I was still that, though I barely felt it at times.

Jamie's candle still burned as I passed his door, and I caught the rustle of turning pages. I would have stopped but Anselm went on, to leave me at the door of my own chamber. I paused there to bid him goodnight, and to thank him for taking me to the chapel.

'It was . . . restful,' I said, struggling to find the right word.

He nodded, watching me. 'Oui, madame. It is.' As I turned to go, he said, 'I told you that the Blessed Sacrament was not alone, for you were there. But what of you, *ma chère*? Were you alone?'

I stopped, and looked at him for a moment before answering.

'No,' I said. 'I wasn't.'

39

To Ransom a Man's Soul

In the morning I went as usual to check Jamie, hoping that he had managed some breakfast. Just short of his room, Murtagh slid out of a wall alcove, barring my way.

'What is it?' I said abruptly. 'What's wrong?' My heart began to beat faster and my palms were suddenly wet.

My panic must have been obvious, for Murtagh shook his head in reassurance. 'Nay, he's all right.' He shrugged. 'Or as much all right as he's been.' He turned me with a light hand under the elbow and began to walk me back down the corridor. I thought with a moment's shock that this was the first time Murtagh had ever deliberately touched me; his hand on my arm was light and strong as a pelican's wing.

'What's the matter with him?' I demanded. The little man's seamed face was as expressionless as usual, but the crinkled eyelids twitched at the corners.

'He doesna want to see ye just yet,' he said.

I stopped dead and pulled my arm from his grasp.

'Why not?' I demanded.

Murtagh hesitated as though choosing his words carefully. 'Weel, it's just . . . he's decided as it would be best for ye to leave him here and go back to Scotland. He – '

The rest of what he was saying was lost as I pushed my way rudely past him.

The heavy door swung shut with a soft thump behind me. Jamie was dozing, face down on the bed. He was uncovered, clad only in a novice's short gown; the charcoal brazier in the corner made the room comfortably warm, if smoky.

He started violently when I touched him. His eyes, still glazed with sleep, were sunk deep and his face was haunted by dreams. I took his hand between both of mine, but he wrenched it away. With a look of near despair he shut his eyes and buried his face in the pillow.

Trying not to exhibit any outward sign of disturbance, I quietly pulled up a stool and sat down near his head. 'I won't touch you,' I said, 'but you must talk to me.' I waited for several minutes while he lay unmoving, shoulders hunched defensively. At last he sighed and sat up, moving slowly and painfully, swinging his legs over the edge of the cot.

'Aye,' he said flatly, not looking at me, 'aye, I suppose I must. I should have done so before . . . but I was coward enough to hope I need not.' His voice was bitter and he kept his head bowed, hands clasped loosely around his knees. 'I didna use to think myself a coward, but I am. I should have made Randall kill me, but I did not. I had no reason to live, but I was not brave enough to die.' His voice dropped and he spoke so softly I could hardly hear him. 'And I knew I would have to see you one last time . . . to tell you . . . but . . . Claire, my love . . . oh, my love.'

He picked up the pillow from the bed and hugged it to him as though for protection, a substitute for the comfort he could not seek from me. He rested his forehead on it for a moment, gathering strength.

'When ye left me there at Wentworth, Claire,' he said quietly, head still bowed, 'I listened to your footsteps, going away on the flags outside, and I said to myself: I'll think of her now. I'll remember her; the feel of her skin and the scent of her hair and the touch of her mouth on mine. I'll think of her until that door opens again. And I'll think of her tomorrow, when I stand on the gallows, to give me courage at the last. Between the time the door opens and the time I leave this place to die' – the big hands clenched briefly and relaxed – 'I will not think at all,' he finished softly.

In the small dungeon room he had closed his eyes and sat waiting. The pain was not bad, so long as he sat still, but he knew it would grow worse soon. Fearing pain, still he had dealt with it often before. He knew it and his own response to it well enough that he was resigned to endurance, hoping only that it would not exceed his strength too soon. The prospect of physical violation, too, was only a matter of mild revulsion now. Despair was in its own way an anaesthetic.

There was no window in the room by which to judge the time. It had been late morning when he was brought to the dungeon, but his sense of time was unreliable. How many hours could it be until dawn? Six, eight, ten? Until the end of everything. He thought with grim humour that Randall at least had done him the favour of rendering death welcome.

When the door opened he had looked up, expecting – what? There was only a man, slightly built, handsome and a little dishevelled, linen shirt torn and hair disarranged, leaning against the wood of the door, watching him.

After a moment Randall had crossed the room unspeaking and stood beside him. He rested a hand briefly on Jamie's neck, then bent and freed the trapped hand with a jerk of the nail that brought Jamie to the edge of fainting. A glass of brandy was set before him and a firm hand raised his head and helped him to drink it.

'He lifted my face then, between his hands, and he licked the drops of brandy from my lips. I wanted to pull back from him, but I'd given my word, so I just sat still.'

Randall had held Jamie's head for a moment looking searchingly into his eyes, then released him and sat down on the table next to him.

'He sat there for quite a time, not saying anything, just swinging one leg back and forth. I had no idea what he wanted, and wasn't disposed to guess. I was tired and feeling a bit sick from the pain in my hand. So after a time I just laid my head down on my arms and turned my face away.' He sighed heavily.

'After a moment I could feel a hand on my head, but I didn't move. He began to stroke my hair, very gently, over and over. There wasn't any sound but the big fellow's hoarse breathing and the crackle of the fire in the brazier, and I think . . . I think I went to sleep for a few moments.'

When he woke, Randall was standing in front of him.

'Are you feeling a bit better?' Randall had asked in a remote, courteous tone.

Wordless, Jamie had nodded and stood up. Randall had stripped him, careful of the wounded hand, and led him to the bed.

'I'd given my word not to struggle, but I did not mean to help, either, so I just stood, as though I were made of wood. I thought I would let him do as he liked, but I'd take no part in it – I would keep a distance from him, in my mind at least.' Randall had smiled then, and gripped Jamie's right hand, hard enough to make him sink on to the bed, sick and dizzy with the sudden stab of pain. Randall had knelt then on the floor before him, and taught him, in a few shattering minutes, that distance is an illusion.

'When he rose up, he took the knife and drew it across my chest, from one side to the other. It was not a deep cut, but it bled a bit. He watched my face a moment, then reached out a finger and dipped it in the blood.' Jamie's voice was unsteady, tripping and stammering from time to time. 'He licked my blood off his finger, with little flicks of his tongue, like a c-cat washing itself. He smiled a bit, then – very kind, like – and bent his head to my chest. I was not bound at all, but I could not have moved. I just . . . sat there, while he used his tongue to . . . It did not hurt, precisely, but it felt verra queer. After a time he stood up and cleaned himself careful with a towel.'

I watched Jamie's hand. With his face turned away, it was the best indicator of his feelings. It clenched convulsively on the edge of the cot as he went on.

'He – told me that . . . I was delicious. The cut had almost stopped bleeding, but he took the towel and scrubbed it hard over my chest to open the wound again.' The knuckles of the clenched hand were knobs of bloodless bone. 'He unbuttoned his breeches then, and smeared the fresh blood on himself, and said it was my turn now.'

Afterwards Randall held his head and helped him to be sick, wiped his face gently with a wet cloth and gave him brandy to cleanse his mouth of foulness. And so, by turns vicious and tender, bit by bit, using pain as his weapon, he had destroyed all barriers of mind and body.

I wanted to stop Jamie, to tell him that he didn't need to go on, must not go on, but I bit my lip hard to keep from speaking and clasped my own hands tight together to keep from touching him.

He told me the rest of it, then; the slow and deliberate whipstrokes, interspersed with kisses. The shocking pain of burns, administered to drag him from the brink of a desperately sought unconsciousness to face further degradations. He told me everything, with hesitations, sometimes with tears, much more than I could bear to hear, but I heard him out, silent as a confessor. He glanced quickly up at me, then away.

'I could have stood being hurt, no matter how bad it was. I expected to be . . . used, and I thought I could stand that too. But I couldn't . . . I . . . he . . .' I dug my nails fiercely into my palms in the struggle to keep quiet. He shook soundlessly for a time, then his voice came again, thick, but desperately steady.

'He did not just hurt me, or use me. He made love to me, Claire. He hurt me – hurt me badly – while he did it, but it was an act of love to him. And he made me answer him – damn his soul! He made me rouse to him!' The hand bunched into a fist and struck the bedframe with an impotent rage that made the whole bed tremble.

'The . . . first time, he was verra careful with me. He used oil, and took a long time, rubbing it all over me . . . touchin' me gentle in all my parts. I could no more stop myself rising to his touch than I could stop myself bleeding when he cut me.' Jamie's voice was weary and wretched with despair. He paused and looked directly at me for the first time since I had come in.

'Claire, I did not want to think of you. I couldna bear to be there, naked, and . . . like that . . . and to remember loving you. It was blasphemy. I meant to wipe you from my mind, and only to . . . exist, so long as I must. But he would not allow it.' Wetness shone on his cheeks, but he was not crying now.

806

'He talked. All during it, he talked to me. Partly it was threats, and partly it was love talk, but often it was you.'

'Me?' My voice, unused for so long, came out of my strained throat as little more than a croak. He nodded, looking down at the pillow again.

'Aye. He was most terribly jealous of you, you know.'

'No. No, I didn't know.'

He nodded again. 'Oh, yes. He would ask me – while he touched me – he would ask, "Does *she* do this for you? Can your woman r-rouse you like this?" ' His voice trembled. 'I wouldna answer him – I couldn't. And then, he'd ask how I thought you would feel to see me . . . to see me . . .' He bit his lip hard, unable to go on for a moment.

'He'd hurt me a bit, then stop and love me till I began to rouse . . . and then he'd hurt me fierce and take me in the midst of the hurting. And all the time he would talk of you, and keep you before my eyes. I fought, in my mind . . . I tried to keep myself from him, to keep my mind apart from my body, but the pain broke through, again and again, past every barrier I could put up. I tried, Claire – God, I tried so hard, but . . .'

He sank his head in his hand, fingers digging hard into his temples. He spoke abruptly. 'I know why young Alick MacGregor hanged himself. I'd do the same, did I not know it to be mortal sin. If he's damned me in life, he'll not do so in heaven.' There was a moment's silence while he struggled to control himself. I noticed automatically that the pillow on his knees was blotched with dampness, and wanted to get up and change it for him. He shook his head slowly, still gazing down at his feet.

'The . . . it's all linked for me now. I canna think of you, Claire, even of kissing you or touching your hand, without feeling the fear and the pain and the sickness come back. I lie here feeling that I will die without your touch, but when you touch me I feel as though I will vomit with shame and loathing of myself. I canna even see you now without . . .' His forehead rested on knotted fists, knuckles dug hard into his eye sockets. The tendons of his neck were sharply etched with strain, and his voice came half muffled.

'Claire, I want you to leave me. Go back to Scotland, to Craigh na Dun. Go back to your place, to your . . . husband. Murtagh will take you safe, I've told him.' He was silent for a moment and I did not move.

He looked up again with desperate bravery and spoke very simply.

'I will love you as long as I live, but I cannot be your husband any longer. And I will not be less to you.' His face began to break apart. 'Claire, I want you so badly that my bones shake in my body, but God help me, I am afraid to touch you!'

I started up to go to him, but he stopped me with a sudden motion of his hand. He was half doubled up, face contorted with internal struggle, and his voice was strangled and breathless.

'Claire . . . please. Please go. I'm going to be verra sick, and I don't want you to see it. Please.'

I heard the pleading in his voice and knew I must spare him this one indignity, at least. I rose and for the first time in my professional life left a sick man to his own devices, helpless and alone.

I left his chamber, numbed, and leaned against the white stone wall outside, cooling my flushed cheek against the unyielding blocks, ignoring the stares of Murtagh and Brother William. *God help me*, he had said. *God help me, I am afraid to touch you*.

I straightened and stood alone. Well, why not? Surely there was no one else.

At the hour when time began to slow, I genuflected in the aisle of the chapel of St Giles. Anselm was there, elegant shoulders straight beneath his habit, but no other. He neither moved nor looked around, but the living silence of the chapel embraced me.

I remained on my knees for a moment, reaching out to the quiet darkness, staying my mind from its hurry. Only when I felt my heart slow to the rhythms of the night did I slide into a seat near the back.

I sat rigid, lacking the form and ritual, the liturgical courtesies that eased the brothers into the depths of their sacred conversation. I did not know how to begin. Finally I said, silently, bluntly: I need help. Please.

And then I let the silence fall back in waves around me, lapping me like the folds of a cloak, comforting against the cold. And I waited, as Anselm had told me, and the minutes passed by uncounted.

There was a small table at the back of the chapel, covered with a linen cloth, bearing the stoup of holy water, and beside it a Bible and two or three other inspirational works. For use by adorers for whom the silence was too much, I supposed.

It was becoming too much for me, and I rose and took the Bible, bringing it back to the prie-dieu with me. I was hardly the first person to have recourse to it in time of confusion or trouble. There was sufficient light from the candles for me to read, turning the flimsy pages carefully and squinting over the lines of fine black type.

'. . . and he smote them with emerods, and they were very sore.' No doubt they were, I thought. What the hell were emerods? Try Psalms, instead.

'But I am a worm, and no man . . . I am poured out like water, and all my bones are out of joint: my heart is like wax; it is melted in the midst of my bowels.' Well, yes, a competent diagnosis, I thought with some impatience. But was there some treatment?

'But be not thou far from me, O Lord: O my strength, haste thee to help me. Deliver my soul from the sword; my darling from the power of the dog.' Hmm.

I turned to the Book of Job, Jamie's favourite. Surely if anyone was in a position to offer helpful advice . . .

'But his flesh upon him shall have pain, and his soul within him shall mourn.' Mmm, yes, I thought, and turned the page.

'He is chastened also with pain upon his bed, and the multitude of his bones with strong pain . . . His flesh is consumed away, that it cannot be seen; and his bones that were not seen stick out.' Spot on, I thought. What next?

'Yea, his soul draweth near unto the grave, and his life to the destroyers.' Not so good, but the next bit was more heartening. 'If there be a messenger with him, an interpreter, one among a thousand, to shew unto man his uprightness: Then he is gracious unto him, and saith, Deliver him from going down to the pit: I have found a ransom. His flesh shall be fresher than a child's: he shall return to the days of his youth.' And what was the ransom, then, that would buy a man's soul, and deliver my darling from the power of the dog?

I closed the book and my eyes. The words muddled together, blurring with my urgent need. An overriding misery struck me when I spoke Jamie's name. And yet there was some small peace there, a lessening of tension when I said, as I did over and over again, 'O Lord, into thy hands I commend the soul of your servant James.'

The thought came to me that perhaps Jamie would be better off dead; he had said he wanted to die. I was morally sure that if I left him as he wished, he would be dead soon, whether from the aftereffects of torture and illness, from hanging, or in some battle. And I was in no doubt that he knew it as well. Ought I to do as he said? Damned if I will, I said to myself. *Damned* if I will, I said fiercely to the sunburst on the altar, and opened the book again.

It was some time before I became aware that my thread of petition was no longer a monologue. In fact, I knew it only when I realized that I had just answered a question I had no memory of asking. In my trance of sleepless misery something had been asked of me, I wasn't sure just what, and I had answered without thinking, 'Yes, I will.'

I stopped all thought abruptly, listening to the ringing silence. And then, more cautiously, repeated, voiceless, 'Yes. Yes, I will,' and thought fleetingly, *The conditions of sin are these . . . you must give your full consent to it . . . And the conditions of grace as well*, came an echo of Anselm's quiet voice.

There was a feeling, not sudden, but complete, as though I had been given a small object to hold unseen in my hands. Precious as opal, smooth as jade, weighty as a river stone, more fragile than a bird's egg. Infinitely still, live as the root of Creation. Not a gift, but a trust. Fiercely to cherish, softly to guard. The words spoke themselves and disappeared into the groined shadows of the roof.

I genuflected to the Presence then, and left the chapel, never doubting, in the eternity of the moment when time stops, that I had an answer, but having no idea what that answer was. I knew only that what I held was a human soul; my own or another's, I could not tell.

It did not appear to be an answer to prayer, when I woke to the resumption of ordinary time in the morning to find a lay brother standing over me, telling me that Jamie was burning with fever.

'How long has he been like this?' I asked, laying a practised hand on brow and back, armpit and groin. No trace of relieving sweat; only the dry stretched skin of persistent parching, fiery with heat. He was awake, but heavy-eyed and groggy. The source of the fever was plain. The shattered right hand was puffy, with a foul-smelling ooze soaking the bandages. Ominous red streaks ran up the wrist. A bloody infection, I thought to myself. A filthy, suppurating, blood poisoning, a life-threatening infection.

'I found him so when I came to look in on him after Matins,' replied the brother who had come to fetch me. 'I gave him water, but he began to vomit just after dawn.'

'You should have fetched me at once,' I said. 'Still, never mind. Bring me hot water, raspberry leaves and Brother Ambrose, as quickly as possible.' He left with the assurance that he would see some breakfast was brought for me as well, but I waved such amenities aside, reaching for the pewter jug of water.

By the time Brother Ambrose appeared I had tried the internal application of water, only to have it violently rejected, and was applying it externally instead, soaking the sheets and wrapping them loosely over the hot skin.

Simultaneously I set the infected hand to soak in fresh-boiled water, as hot as could be stood without burning the skin. Lacking sulpha drugs or penicillin, heat was the only defence against a bacterial infection. The patient's body was doing its best to supply that heat by means of high fever, but the fever itself posed a serious danger, wasting muscle and damaging brain cells. The trick was to apply sufficient local heat to destroy the infection while keeping the rest of the body cool enough to prevent damage, and sufficiently hydrated to maintain its normal functions. A bloody three-tier balancing act, I thought bleakly.

Neither Jamie's state of mind nor his physical discomfort was relevant any longer. It was a straightforward struggle to keep him alive until the infection and the fever ran their course; nothing else mattered.

In the afternoon of the second day he began to halluci-nate. We tied him to the bed with soft rags to prevent his hurling himself to the floor. Finally, as a desperate measure to break the fever, I sent one of the lay brothers out to bring in a basket of snow, which we packed around him. This resulted in a violent shivering fit that left him drained and exhausted, but did briefly bring his temperature down.

Unfortunately the treatment had to be repeated at hourly intervals. By sunset the room looked like a swamp, with puddles of melted snow standing on the floor, tussocks of sodden sheeting mounded among them, and steam like marsh gas rising from the brazier in the corner. Brother Ambrose and myself were sodden too, soaked with sweat, chilled with snow water and near to exhaustion, in spite of the helpful assistance of Anselm and the lay brothers. Febrifuges such as burdock, thistle, bogbean and yarrow had been tried, without effect. Willow-bark tea, which might have helped with its content of salicylic acid, could not be consumed in amounts large enough to matter.

In one of his increasingly rare lucid intervals, Jamie asked me to let him die. I answered curtly, as I had the night before, 'Damned if I will,' and went on with what I was doing.

As the sun went down there was a stir of approaching men in the corridor. The door opened and the Abbot, Jamie's Uncle Alick, came in accompanied by Brother Anselm and three other monks, one carrying a small cedar-

812

wood box. The Abbot came over to me and blessed me briefly, then took one of my hands in his.

'We are going to anoint the lad,' he said, his deep voice kind. 'Do not be frightened.'

He turned towards the bed and I looked wildly to Anselm for explanation.

'The sacrament of Extreme Unction,' he explained, moving close so that his low tones would not disturb the monks gathered around the bed. 'The Last Anointing.'

'Last Anointing! That's for people who are dying!'

'Ssh.' He drew me farther away from the bed. 'It might more properly be called anointing of the sick, though in fact it is usually reserved for those in danger of death.' The monks had turned Jamie gently on to his back, arranging him tenderly so that he might lie with the least hurt to his raw shoulders.

'The purpose of the sacrament is twofold,' Anselm went on, murmuring in my ear as the preparations went on. 'First, it is intended as a sacrament of healing; we pray that the sufferer may be restored to health, if that be God's will for him. The chrism, the consecrated oil, is used as a symbol of life and healing.'

'And the second purpose?' I asked, already knowing.

Anselm nodded. 'If it is not God's will that he should recover, then he is given absolution of sins and we commend him to God, that his soul may depart in peace.' He saw me tighten in protest, and laid a warning hand on my arm.

'These are the last rites of the Church. He is entitled to them, and to whatever peace they may bring him.'

The preparations were complete. Jamie lay on his back, a cloth modestly draped across his loins, with lighted candles at the head and the foot of the bed that reminded me most unpleasantly of grave lights. Abbot Alexander sat at the bedside, accompanied by a monk who held a tray with a covered ciborium, two small silver bottles containing holy water and chrism, and a white cloth draped across both forearms. Like a bloody wine steward, I thought crossly. The whole procedure unnerved me.

The rites were conducted in Latin, the soft antiphonal

murmuring soothing to the ear, though I did not understand the meaning. Anselm whispered softly to me the meaning of some parts of the service; others were self-explanatory. At one point the Abbot motioned to Ambrose, who stepped forward and held a small vial under Jamie's nose. It must have contained spirits of ammonia or some other stimulant, because he jerked and turned his head away sharply, eyes still closed.

'Why are they trying to wake him?' I whispered.

'If possible, the person should be conscious in order to give assent to the statement that he is sorry for any sins committed during his life. Also, if he is capable of receiving it, the Abbot will give him the Blessed Sacrament.'

The Abbot stroked Jamie's cheek softly, turning his head back to the vial, speaking quietly to him. He had dropped from Latin into the broad Scots of their family, and his voice was gentle.

'Jamie! Jamie, lad! It's Alick, lad. I'm here wi' ye. Ye must wake a bit now, only for a bit. I shall be givin' ye the absolution now, and then the Blessed Sacrament of Our Lord. Take a wee sup, now, so ye can answer me when ye must.' The monk called Polydore held the cup against Jamie's lips, carefully pouring the water a drop at a time until the parched tongue and throat could take more. His eyes were open, still heavy with fever, but alert enough.

The Abbot went on then, the questions in English, but pitched so low that I could scarcely catch them. 'Do ye renounce Satan and all his works?' 'Do ye believe in the Resurrection of Our Lord Jesus Christ?' and so on. To each one, Jamie answered 'Aye' in a scratchy whisper.

Once the sacrament had been given, Jamie lay back with a sigh, closing his eyes once more. I could see his ribs as the deep-sprung chest moved with his breathing. He had wasted dreadfully, between the sickness and the fever. The Abbot, taking the vials of holy water and chrism in turn, made the sign of the Cross on his body, anointing forehead, lips, nose, ears and eyelids. Then, in turn, he made the sign of the Cross with the holy oil in the hollow of the chest over the heart, on the palm of each hand and the arch of each foot. He lifted the injured hand with infinite care, brushing the oil across the wound lightly and laying the hand back on Jamie's chest, where it lay below the livid slash of the knife scar.

The anointing was quick and immeasurably gentle, a feather touch by the Abbot's rapidly moving thumb. *Superstitious magic*, said the rational side of my brain, but I was deeply moved by the love on the faces of the monks as they prayed. Jamie's eyes were open once more, but very calm, and his face was peaceful for the first time since we had left Lallybroch.

The ceremony concluded with a brief prayer in Latin. Laying his hand on Jamie's head, the Abbot said in English, 'Lord, into thy hands we commend the soul of your servant, James. Heal him, we pray, if that be thy will, and strengthen his soul, that he may be filled with grace, and know thy peace throughout eternity.'

'Amen,' replied the other monks. And so did I.

By dark, the patient had lapsed into semiconsciousness again. As Jamie's strength waned it was all we could do to rouse him for the sips of water that were keeping him alive. His lips were cracked and peeling, and he could no longer talk, though he would still open glazed eyes when shaken roughly. He no longer recognized us; his eyes stared fixedly, then gradually closed as he turned his head away, moaning.

I stood by the bed looking down at him, so exhausted from the rigours of the day that I felt no more than a sort of dull despair. Brother Ambrose touched me gently, bringing me out of my daze.

'You cannot do any more for him now,' he said, leading me firmly away. 'You must go and rest.'

'But – ' I began, then stopped. He was right, I realized. We had done everything possible. Either the fever would break soon of itself, or Jamie would die. Even the strongest body could not endure the consuming ravages of high fever for more than a day or two, and Jamie had little strength left to see him through such a siege.

'I will stay with him,' Ambrose said. 'Go to your bed. I'll

summon you if . . .' He didn't finish the sentence, but waved me gently in the direction of my own chamber.

I lay sleepless on my cot, staring at the beamed ceiling. My eyes were dry and hot and my throat ached as though I were coming down with a fever as well. Was this the answer to my prayer, that we would die here together?

At last I rose and took up the jug and basin from the table by the door. I set the heavy pottery dish in the centre of the floor and filled it carefully, letting the water swell up over the thickened rim into a trembling bubble.

I had made a short detour to Brother Ambrose's stillroom on the way to my chamber. I undid the small packets of herbs and scattered the contents into my brazier, where the myrrh leaves gave off a fragrant smoke and the crumbs of camphor flamed with tiny blue tongues between the red glow of the charcoal sticks.

I set the candlestick behind my reflecting pool, took my place before it, and sat down to summon a ghost.

The stone corridor was cold and dark, lit at intervals by dimly flickering oil lamps hung from the ceiling. My shadow stretched forward under my feet as I passed beneath each one, lengthening until it seemed to dive headfirst and disappear into the dark ahead.

In spite of the cold I was barefoot and wearing only a coarse white cotton nightrobe. A small envelope of warmth moved with me under the robe, but the chill from the stones crept up my feet and legs.

I knocked once, softly, and pushed open the heavy door without waiting for an answer.

Brother Roger was with him, sitting by the bed, telling beads with bowed head. The wooden rosary rattled as he looked up, but his lips continued to move silently for a few seconds, finishing the Ave Maria before acknowledging my presence.

He met me near the door, speaking quietly though it was clear that he could have shouted without disturbing the motionless figure on the bed.

'No change. I've just put fresh water in the hand bath.'

A few drops gleamed on the sides of the small pewter kettle on the brazier, freshly filled.

I nodded and put a hand on his arm in thanks. It was startlingly solid and warm after the imaginations of the last hour, and somehow comforting.

'I'd like to stay with him alone, if you don't mind.'

'Of course. I'll go to the chapel – or should I stay near in case . . .' His voice trailed off, hesitant.

'No.' I tried to smile reassuringly. 'Go to the chapel. Or better yet, go to bed. I can't sleep; I'll stay here till morning. If I need help, I'll send for you.'

Still dubious, he glanced back at the bed. But it was very late and he was tired; there were shadows under the kind brown eyes.

The heavy door squeaked on its hinges, and I was alone with Jamie. Alone and afraid, and very, very doubtful about what I proposed to do.

I stood at the foot of the bed, watching him for a moment. The room was dimly lit by the glow of the brazier and by two enormous candlesticks, each nearly three feet tall, that stood on the table at the side of the room. He was naked, and the faint light seemed to accentuate the hollows left by the wasting fever. The multicoloured bruise over the ribs stained the skin like a spreading fungus.

A dying man takes on a faint greenish tinge. At first just a touch at the edge of the jaw, this pallor spreads gradually, over the face and down the chest as the force of life begins to ebb. I had seen it many times. A few times, I had seen that deadly progress arrested and reversed, the skin flush with blood once more, and the man live. More often . . . I shook myself vigorously and turned away.

I brought my hand out of the folds of my robe and laid on the table the objects I had collected in a surreptitious visit to Brother Ambrose's darkened workshop. A vial of spirits of ammonia. A packet of dried lavender. Another of valerian. A small metal incense burner, shaped like an open blossom. Two pellets of opium, sweet scented and sticky with resin. And a knife.

The room was close and stuffy with smoke from the

817

brazier. The only window was covered with a heavy tapestry, one showing the execution of St Sebastian. I eyed the saint's upturned face and arrow-punctured torso, wondering afresh at the mentality of the person who had chosen this particular decoration for a sickroom.

Indifferently rendered as it was, the tapestry was of heavy silk and wool, and excluded all but the strongest draughts. I lifted the lower edge and flapped it, urging the charcoal smoke out through the stone arch. The cold, damp air that streamed in was refreshing, and did something to calm the throbbing that had started in my temples as I stared into the reflecting water, remembering.

There was a faint moan behind me, and Jamie stirred in the draught. Good. He was not deeply unconscious, then.

Letting the tapestry fall back over the window, I next took up the incense burner. I fixed an opium pellet on the spike and lighted it with one of the wax tapers for the candlesticks. I placed it on the small table near Jamie's head, careful not to inhale the sickly fumes myself.

There was not much time. I must finish my preparations quickly, before the opium smoke drove him too far under to be roused.

I unlaced the front of my robe and rubbed my body quickly with handfuls of the lavender and valerian. It was a pleasant, spicy smell, distinctive and richly evocative. A smell that, to me, conjured the shade of the man who wore its perfume, and the shade of the man behind him; shades that evoked confusing images of present terror and lost love. A smell that, to Jamie, must recall the hours of pain and rage spent wrapped in its waves. I rubbed the last of it vigorously between my palms and dropped the fragrant shreds on the floor.

With a deep breath for courage I picked up the vial of ammoniacal spirits. I stood by the bed a moment holding it, looking down at the gaunt, stubbled face. At most he might last a day; at least, only a few more hours.

'All right, you bloody Scottish bastard,' I said softly. 'Let's see how stubborn you really are.' I lifted the injured hand, dripping, from the water and set the soaking dish aside.

818

I opened the vial and waved it closely under his nose. He snorted and tried to turn his head away, but didn't open his eyes. I dug my fingers into the hair on the back of his head to prevent his turning away and brought the vial back to his face. He shook his head slowly, swinging it from side to side like an ox roused from slumber, and his eyes came open just a crack.

'Not done yet, Fraser,' I whispered in his ear, trying as best I could to catch the rhythm of Randall's clipped consonants.

Jamie moaned and hunched his shoulders. I grasped him by both shoulders and shook him roughly. His skin was so hot I nearly let go.

'Wake up, you Scottish bastard! I'm not done with you yet!' He began to struggle up on to his elbows with a pitiful effort at obedience that nearly broke my heart. His head was still shaking back and forth and the cracked lips were muttering something that sounded like 'please not yet' over and over again.

Strength failing, he rolled to one side and collapsed face down on the pillow again. The room was beginning to fill with opium smoke and I felt mildly dizzy.

I gritted my teeth and plunged my hand between his buttocks, gripping one curving round. He screamed, a high breathy sound, and rolled painfully sideways, curling into a ball with his hands clasped between his legs.

I had spent the hour in my chamber, hovering over my pool of reflection, conjuring memories. Of Black Jack Randall and of Frank, his six-times-great-grandson. Such very different men, but with such startling physical similarities.

It tore me to think of Frank, to recall his face and voice, his mannerisms, his style of lovemaking. I had tried to obliterate him from my mind, once my choice was made in the circle of stone, but he was always there, a shadowy figure in the recesses of my mind.

I felt sick with betrayal of him, but in the extremity I had forced my mind to clear as Geilie had shown me, concentrating on the flame of the candle, breathing the astringency of the herbs, calming myself until I could bring him from the shadows, see the lines of his face, feel once more the touch of his hand without weeping.

There had been another man in the shadows, with the same hands, the same face. Eyes filled with the candle flame, I had brought him forward too, listening, watching, seeing the likenesses and the differences, building a – a what? A simulacrum, a persona, an impression, a masquerade. A shaded face, a whispered voice and a loving touch that I might bring to deceive a mind adrift in delirium. And I left my chamber at last, with a prayer for the soul of the witch Geillis Duncan.

Jamie was on his back now, writhing slightly against the pain of his wounds. His eyes were fixed and staring, with no sign of recognition.

I caressed him in the way I knew so well, tracing the line of his ribs from breastbone to back, lightly as Frank would have done, pressing hard on the aching bruise, as I was sure the other would have. I leaned forward and ran my tongue slowly around his ear, tasting and probing, and whispered, 'Fight me! Fight back, you filthy scut!'

His muscles tightened and his jaw clenched, but he continued to stare upwards. No choice, then. I would have to use the knife after all. I knew the risk I was taking in this, but better to kill him myself, I thought, than to sit quietly by and let him die.

I took the knife from the table and drew it firmly across his chest, along the path of the freshly healed scar. He gasped with the shock of it, and arched his back. Seizing a towel, I scrubbed it briskly over the wound. Before I could falter, I forced myself to run my fingers over his chest, scooping up a gout of blood which I rubbed savagely over his lips. There was one phrase that I didn't have to invent, having heard it myself. Bending low over him, I whispered, 'Now kiss me.'

I was not at all prepared for it. He hurled me half across the room as he came up off the bed. I staggered and fell against the table, making the giant candlesticks sway. The shadows darted and swung as the wicks flared and went out.

The edge of the table had struck me hard across the back, but I recovered in time to dodge away as he lunged for me. With an inarticulate growl he came after me, hands outstretched.

He was both faster and stronger than I expected, though he staggered awkwardly, bumping into things. He cornered me for a moment between the brazier and the table, and I could hear his breath rasping harshly in his throat as he grabbed for me. He smashed his left hand towards my face; had his strength and reflexes been anything like normal, the blow would have killed me. Instead I jerked to one side and his fist glanced off my forehead, knocking me to the floor, mildly stunned.

I crawled under the table. Reaching for me, he lost his balance and fell against the brazier. Glowing coals scattered across the stone floor of the chamber. He howled as his knee crunched heavily into a patch of hot coal. I seized a pillow from the bed and beat out a smouldering nest of sparks in the trailing bedcover. Preoccupied with this, I didn't notice his approach until a solid clout across the head knocked me sprawling.

The cot overturned as I tried to pull myself up with a hand on the frame. I lay sheltering behind it for a moment, trying to get my senses back. I could hear Jamie hunting me in the semidarkness, breath rasping between incoherent phrases of Gaelic cursing. Suddenly he caught sight of me and flung himself over the bed, eyes mad in the dim light.

It is difficult to describe in detail what happened next, if only because everything happened a number of times, and the times all overlap in my memory. It seems as though Jamie's burning hand closed on my neck only once, but that once went on for ever. In fact, it happened dozens of times. Each time I managed to break his grip and throw him off, to retreat once more, dodging and ducking around the wrecked furniture. And once again he would follow, a man pulled by rage from the edge of death, swearing and sobbing, staggering and flailing wildly.

Deprived of the sheltering brazier, the coals died quickly, leaving the room black as pitch and peopled with demons. In the last flickers of light I saw him crouched against the wall, maned in fire and mantled in blood, penis stiff against the matted hair of his belly, eyes blue murder in a skull-white face. A Viking berserker. Like the northern devils who burst from their dragon-ships into the mists of the ancient Scottish coast, to kill and plunder and burn. Men who would kill with the last ounce of their strength. Who would use that last strength to rape and sow their violent seed in the bellies of the conquered. The tiny incense burner gave no light, but the sickly smell of opium clogged my lungs. Though the coals were out I saw lights in the darkness, coloured lights that floated at the edge of my vision.

Movement was becoming harder; I felt as though I were wading through water thigh-deep, pursued by monstrous fish. I lifted my knees high, running in slow motion, feeling the water splash against my face.

I shook off the dream, to realize that there was in fact wetness on my face and hands. Not tears, but blood, and the sweat of the nightmare creature I grappled with in the dark.

Sweat. There was something I should remember about sweat, but I couldn't recall it. A hand tightened on my upper arm and I pulled away, a slick film left on my skin.

Around and around the mulberry bush, the monkey chased the weasel. But something was wrong, it was the weasel chasing me, a weasel with sharp white teeth that pierced my forearm. I hit out at it and the teeth let go, but the claws . . . around and around the mulberry bush . . .

The demon had me up against the wall; I could feel stone behind my head and stone beneath my grasping fingers, and a stone-hard body pressing hard against me, bony knee between my own, stone and bone, between my own . . . legs, more stony hardness . . . ah. A softness amidst the hardness of life, pleasant coolness in the heat, comfort in the midst of woe . . .

We fell locked together to the floor, rolling over and over, tangled in the folds of the fallen tapestry, washed in the draughts of cold air from the window. The mists of madness began to recede.

We bashed into some piece of furniture and both lay still. Jamie's hand was locked on my breasts, fingers digging bruisingly into the flesh. I felt the plop of dampness on my face – sweat or tears, I couldn't tell, but opened my eyes to see. Jamie was looking down at me, face blank in the moony light, eyes wide, unfocused. His hand relaxed. One finger gently traced the outline of my breast, from slope to tip, over and over. His hand moved to cup the breast, fingers spread like a starfish, soft as the grip of a nursing child.

'M-mother?' he said. The hair stood up on the back of my neck. It was the high, pure voice of a young boy. 'Mother?'

The cold air laved us, whirling the unhealthy smoke away in a drift of snowflakes. I reached up and laid the palm of my hand along his cold cheek.

'Jamie, love,' I said, whispering through a bruised throat, 'come then, come lay your head, man.' The mask trembled then and broke, and I held the big body hard against me, the two of us shaking with the force of his sobbing.

It was, by considerable good luck, the unflappable Brother William who found us in the morning. I woke groggily to the sound of the door opening, and snapped to full consciousness when I heard him clear his throat emphatically before saying 'Good morning to ye' in his soft Yorkshire drawl.

The heavy weight on my chest was Jamie. His hair had dried in bronze streaks and whorled over my breasts like the petals of a Chinese chrysanthemum. The cheek pressed against my sternum was warm and slightly sticky with sweat, but the back and arms I could touch were as cold as my thighs, chilled by the winter air gusting in on us.

Daylight streaming through the uncurtained window revealed the full extent of the wreckage I had only dimly realized the night before; smashed furniture and crockery littered the room, and the massive paired candlesticks lay like fallen logs in the midst of a tangle of torn hangings and scattered bedclothes. From the pattern of indentations impressing itself painfully into my back, I thought I must be lying on the indifferently executed tapestry of St Sebastian the Human Pincushion; no great loss to the monastery, if so.

Brother William stood motionless in the doorway, jug and basin in hand. With great precision he fixed his eyes on Jamie's left eyebrow and inquired, 'And how do you feel this morning?'

There was a rather long pause, during which Jamie considerately remained in place, blanketing most of me from view. At last, in the hoarse tones of one to whom a revelation has been vouchsafed, he replied, 'Hungry.'

'Oh, good,' said Brother William, still staring hard at the eyebrow, 'I'll go and tell Brother Josef.' The door closed soundlessly behind him.

'Nice of you not to move,' I remarked. 'I shouldn't like us to be responsible for giving Brother William impure thoughts.'

Dense blue eyes stared down at me. 'Aye, well,' he said judiciously, 'a view of *my* arse is no going to corrupt anyone's Holy Orders; not in its present condition. Yours, though . . .' He paused to clear his throat.

'What *about* mine?' I demanded.

The bright head lowered slowly to plant a kiss on my shoulder. 'Yours,' he said, 'would compromise a bishop.'

'Mmmphm.' I was, I felt, getting rather good at Scottish noises myself. 'Be that as it may, perhaps you should move now. I don't suppose even Brother William's tact is infinite.'

Jamie lowered his head next to mine with some care, laying it on a fold of tapestry, from which he peered sideways at me. 'I dinna know how much of last night I dreamed and how much was real.' His hand unconsciously strayed to the cut across his chest. 'But if half what I thought happened really happened, I should be dead now.'

'You're not. I looked.' With some hesitation I asked, 'Do you want to be?'

He smiled slowly, eyes half closing. 'No, Sassenach, I

don't.' His face was gaunt and shadowed with illness and fatigue, but peaceful, the lines around his mouth smoothed out and the blue eyes clear. 'But I'm damned close to it, want to or not. The only reason I think I'm not dying now is that I'm hungry. I wouldna be hungry if I were about to die, do ye think? Seems a waste.' One eye closed altogether, but the other stayed half open, fixed on my face with a quizzical expression.

'You can't stand up?'

He considered carefully. 'If my life depended on it, I might possibly lift my head again. But stand up? No.'

With a sigh I wriggled out from under him and righted the bed before trying to lever him into a vertical position. He managed to stand for only a few seconds before his eyes rolled back and he fell across the bed. I groped frantically for the pulse in his neck and found it, slow and strong, just below the three-cornered scar at the base of his throat. Simple exhaustion. After weeks of imprisonment and another week of intense physical and mental stress, starvation, injury, sickness and high fever, even that vigorous frame had finally come to the end of its resources.

'The heart of a lion,' I said, shaking my head, 'and the head of an ox. Too bad you haven't also got the hide of a rhinoceros.' I touched a freshly bloodied weal on his shoulder.

He opened one eye. 'What's a rhinoceros?'

'I thought you were unconscious!'

'I was. I am. My head's spinning like a top.'

I drew a blanket up over him. 'What you need now is food and rest.'

'What *you* need now,' he said, 'is clothes.' And shutting the eye again, he fell promptly asleep.

40

Absolution

I had no memory of finding my way to bed, but I must have done so because I woke up there. Anselm was sitting by the window, reading.

I sat bolt upright in bed.

'Jamie?' I croaked.

'Asleep,' he said, putting the book aside. He glanced at the hour-candle on the table. 'Like you. You have been with the angels for the last thirty-six hours, *ma belle*.' He filled a cup from the earthenware jug and held it to my lips. At one time I would have considered drinking wine in bed before brushing one's teeth to be the last word in decadence. Performed in a monastery, in company with a robed Franciscan, the act seemed somewhat less degenerate. And the wine did cut through the mossy feeling in my mouth.

I swung my feet over the side of the bed, and sat swaying. Anselm caught me by the arm and eased me back on to the pillow. He seemed suddenly to have four eyes, and altogether more noses and mouths than strictly necessary.

'I'm a bit dizzy,' I said, closing my eyes. I opened one. Somewhat better. At least there was only one of him, if a trifle blurry around the edges.

Anselm bent over me, concerned.

'Shall I fetch Brother Ambrose or Brother Polydore, madame? I have little skill in medicine, unfortunately.'

'No, I don't need anything. I just sat up too suddenly.' I tried again, more slowly. This time the room and its contents stayed relatively still. I became aware of numerous bruises and sore spots earlier submerged in the dizziness. I tried to clear my throat and discovered that it hurt. I grimaced.

'Really, *ma chère*, I think perhaps . . .' Anselm was poised by the door, ready to fetch assistance. He looked quite alarmed. I reached for the looking glass on the table and then changed my mind. I really wasn't ready for that. I grasped the wine jug instead.

Anselm came slowly back into the room and stood watching me. Once convinced that I wasn't going to collapse after all, he sat down again. I sipped the wine slowly as my head cleared, trying to shake off the aftereffects of opium-induced dreams. So we were alive, after all. Both of us.

My dreams had been chaotic, filled with violence and blood. I had dreamed over and over that Jamie was dead or dying. And somewhere in the fog had been the image of the boy in the snow, his surprised round face overlying the image of Jamie's bruised and battered one. Sometimes the pathetic, fuzzy moustache seemed to appear on Frank's face. I distinctly remembered killing all three of them. I felt as though I had spent the night in stabbing and butchery, and I ached in every muscle with a sort of dull depression.

Anselm was still there, patiently watching me, hands on his knees.

'There is something you could do for me, Father,' I said.

He rose at once, eager to help, reaching for the jug.

'Of course? More wine?'

I smiled wanly.

'Yes, but later. Right now, I want you to hear my confession.'

He was startled, but quickly gathered his professional self-possession around him like his robes.

'But of course, *chère madame*, if you wish it. But really, would it not be better to fetch Father Gerard? He is well known as a confessor, while I' – he gave a Gallic shrug – 'I am allowed to hear confessions, of course, but in truth I seldom do so, being only a poor scholar.'

'I want you,' I said firmly. 'And I want to do it now.'

He sighed in resignation and went to fetch his stole. Arranging it about his neck so that the purple silk lay straight and shimmering down the front of his habit, he took a seat on the stool, blessed me briefly and sat back, waiting.

827

And I told him. Everything. Who I was and how I came there. About Frank, and about Jamie. And about the young English dragoon with the pale, spotty face, dying against the snow.

He showed no change of expression while I spoke, except that the round hazel eyes grew rounder still. When I finished he blinked once or twice, opened his mouth, closed it again and shook his head as though to clear it.

'No,' I said patiently. I cleared my throat again; I croaked like a bullfrog. 'You haven't been hearing things. And you're not imagining it, either. Now you see why I wanted you to hear it under the seal of confession?'

He nodded, a bit abstractedly.

'Yes. Yes, to be sure. If . . . but yes. Of course, you wished me to tell no one. And also, since you tell it to me under the seal of the sacrament, then you expect that I must believe it. But . . .' He scratched his head, then looked up at me. A wide smile spread slowly across his countenance.

'But how marvellous!' he exclaimed softly. 'How extraordinary, and how wonderful!'

'Wonderful isn't precisely the word I would have chosen,' I said dryly, 'but extraordinary is all right.' I coughed and reached for more wine.

'But it is . . . a miracle,' he said, as though to himself.

'If you insist,' I said, sighing. 'But what I want to know – what ought I to do? Am I guilty of murder? Or adultery, for that matter? Not that there's much to be done about it in either case, but I'd like to know. And since I *am* here, how ought I to act? Can I – *should* I, I mean – use what I know to . . . change things? I don't even know if such a thing is possible. But if it is, have I the right?'

He rocked back on his stool, considering. Slowly he raised both index fingers, placed them tip to tip and stared at them for a long time. Finally he shook his head and smiled at me.

'I don't know, *chère madame*. It is not, you will appreciate, a situation one is prepared to encounter in the confessional. I will have to think, and to pray. Yes, assuredly to pray. Tonight I will contemplate your situation when I hold my watch before the Blessed Sacrament. And tomorrow perhaps I can advise you.'

He motioned me gently to kneel.

'But for now, my child, I will absolve you. Whatever your sins might be, have faith that they will be forgiven.'

He lifted one hand in blessing, placing the other on my head, *'Te absolvo, in nomine Patri, et Filii . . .'*

Rising, he lifted me to my feet.

'Thank you, Father,' I said. Unbeliever that I was, I had used confession only to force him to take me seriously, and was somewhat surprised to feel a lightening of the burden on my spirits. Perhaps it was only the relief of telling someone the truth.

He waved a hand in dismissal. 'I will see you tomorrow, *chère madame.* For now, you should rest more, if you can.'

He headed for the door, winding his stole up neatly into a square. At the doorway he paused for a moment, turning to smile at me. A childlike excitement lighted his eyes.

'And perhaps tomorrow . . .' he said, 'perhaps you could . . . tell me what it is like?'

I smiled back.

'Yes, Father. I'll tell you.'

After he left I staggered down the hall to see Jamie. I had seen any number of corpses in much better condition, but his chest rose and fell regularly, and the sinister green tinge had faded from his skin.

'I've been waking him every few hours, just long enough to swallow a few spoonfuls of soup.' Brother Roger was at my elbow, speaking softly. He moved his gaze from the patient to me, and recoiled noticeably at my appearance. I should probably have combed my hair. 'Er, perhaps you would . . . like some?'

'No, thank you. I think . . . I think perhaps I will sleep a bit more, after all.' I no longer felt weighed down by guilt and depression, but a drowsy, contented heaviness was spreading through my limbs. Whether it was due to the effects of confession or of wine, I found to my surprise that I was looking forward to bed and to oblivion.

I leaned forward to touch Jamie. He was warm, but with

no trace of fever. I gently stroked his head, smoothing the tumbled red hair. The corner of his mouth stirred briefly and fell back into place. But it had turned up. I was sure of it.

The sky was cold and damp, filling the horizon with a grey blankness that blended into the grey mist of the hills and the grimy cover of last week's snow, so that the abbey seemed wrapped inside a ball of dirty cotton. Even inside the cloister, the winter's silence weighed on the inhabitants. The chanting from the Hours of Praise in the chapel was muted, and the thick stone walls seemed to absorb all sound, swaddling the bustle of daily activity.

Jamie slept for nearly two days, waking only to take a little soup or wine. Once awake he began to heal in the usual fashion of a normally healthy young man, suddenly deprived of the strength and independence usually taken for granted. In other words he enjoyed the cosseting for approximately twenty-four hours and then became in turn restive, restless, testy, irritable, cranky, fractious and extremely bad tempered.

The cuts on his shoulders ached. The scars on his legs itched. He was sick of lying on his belly. The room was too hot. His hand hurt. The smoke from the brazier made his eyes burn so that he could not read. He was sick of soup, posset and milk. He wanted meat.

I recognized the symptoms of returning health, and was glad of them, but was prepared to put up with only so much of this. I opened the window, changed his sheets, applied marigold salve to his back and rubbed his legs with aloe juice. Then I summoned a serving brother and ordered more soup.

'I don't want any more of this slop! I need food!' He pushed the tray irritably away, making the soup splash on to the napkin cradling the bowl.

I folded my arms and stared down at him. Imperious blue eyes stared right back. He was thin as a rail, the lines of jaw and cheekbone bold against the skin. Though he was mending well, the raw nerves of his stomach would take a little longer to heal. He still could not always keep down the soup and milk.

'You'll get food when I say you can have it,' I informed him, 'and not before.'

'I'll have it now! D'ye think you can tell me what I'm to eat?'

'Yes, I bloody well do! I'm the doctor here, if you've forgotten.'

He swung his feet over the edge of the bed, clearly intending to take steps. I put a hand on his chest and shoved him back.

'Your job is to stay in that bed and do as you're told, for once in your life,' I snapped. 'You're not fit to be up, and you're not fit for solid food yet. Brother Roger said you vomited again this morning.'

'Brother Roger can mind his own business, and so can you,' he said through his teeth, struggling back up. He reached out and got a hold on the table edge. With considerable effort he made it to his feet and stood there, swaying.

'Get back in bed! You're going to fall down!' He was alarmingly pale, and even the small effort of standing had made him break out in a cold sweat.

'I'll not,' he said. 'And if I do, it's my own concern.'

I was really angry by this time.

'Oh, is it! And who do you think saved your miserable life for you, anyway? Did it all by yourself, did you?' I grabbed his arm to steer him back to bed, but he jerked it away.

'I didna ask ye to, did I? I told ye to leave me, no? And I canna see why ye bothered to save my life anyway, if it's only to starve me to death – unless ye enjoy watching it!'

This was altogether too much.

'Bloody ingrate!'

'Shrew!'

I drew myself to my full height and pointed menacingly at the cot. With the authority learned in years of nursing, I said, 'Get back in that bed this instant, you stubborn, mulish, idiotic – '

'Scot,' he finished for me succinctly. He took a step

towards the door and would have fallen, had he not caught hold of a stool. He plumped heavily down on it and sat swaying, his eyes a little unfocused with dizziness. I clenched my fist and glared at him.

'Fine,' I said. 'Bloody fine! I'll order bread and meat for you, and after you vomit on the floor you can just get down on your hands and knees and clean it up yourself! I won't do it, and if Brother Roger does, I'll skin him alive!'

I stormed into the hall and slammed the door behind me, just before the porcelain wash basin crashed into it from the other side. I turned to find an interested audience, no doubt attracted by the racket, standing in the hall. Brother Roger and Murtagh stood side by side, staring at my flushed face and heaving bosom. Roger looked disconcerted, but a slow smile spread over Murtagh's craggy countenance as he listened to the string of Gaelic obscenities going on behind the door.

'He's feeling better, then,' he said contentedly. I leaned against the corridor wall and felt an answering smile spread slowly across my own face.

'Well, yes,' I said, 'he is.'

On my way back to the main building from a morning spent in the herbary I met Anselm coming from the cloister near the library. His face lighted when he saw me, and he hurried to join me in the courtyard. We walked together through the abbey grounds, talking.

'Yours is an interesting problem, to be sure,' he said, breaking a stick from a bush near the wall. He examined the winter-tight buds critically, then tossed it aside and glanced up at the sky, where a feeble sun poked its way through the light cloud layer.

'Warmer, but a good way to go until the spring,' he observed. 'Still, the carp should be lively today – let us go down to the fish pools.'

Far from being the delicate ornamental structures I had imagined them to be, the fish pools were little more than utilitarian rock-lined troughs, placed conveniently near to the kitchens. Stocked with carp, they provided the necessary food for Fridays and fast days, when the weather was too rough to permit ocean fishing for the more customary haddock, herring and flounder.

True to Anselm's word the fish were lively, the fat fusiform bodies gliding past each other, white scales reflecting the clouds overhead, the vigour of their movements occasionally stirring up small waves that sloshed against the sides of their rocky prison. As our shadows fell on the water, the carp turned to us like compass needles surging towards the north.

'They expect to be fed, when they see people,' Anselm explained. 'It would be a shame to disappoint them. One moment, *chère madame*.'

He darted into the kitchens, returning shortly with two loaves of stale bread. We stood on the lip of the pool, tearing crumbs from the loaves and tossing them to the endlessly hungry mouths below.

'You know, there are two aspects to this curious situation of yours,' Anselm said, absorbed in tearing bread. He glanced aside at me, a sudden smile lighting his face. He shook his head in wonderment. 'I can scarcely believe it still, you know. Such a marvel! Truly God has been good, to show me such things.'

'Well, that's nice,' I said, a bit dryly, 'I don't know whether he's been quite so obliging to me.'

'Really? *I* think so.' Anselm sank down on his haunches, crumbling bread between his fingers. 'True,' he said, 'the situation has caused you no little personal inconvenience – '

'That's one way of putting it,' I muttered.

'But it may also be regarded as a signal mark of God's favour,' he went on, disregarding my interruption. The bright hazel eyes regarded me speculatively.

'I prayed for guidance, kneeling before the Blessed Sacrament,' he went on, 'and as I sat in the silence of the chapel I seemed to see you as a shipwrecked traveller. And it seems to me that that is a good parallel to your present situation, is it not? Imagine such a soul, madame, suddenly cast away in a strange land, bereft of friends and familiarity, without resources save what the new land can provide. Such a happening is disaster, truly, and yet may be the opening for great opportunity and blessings. What if the new land shall be rich? New friends may be made, and a new life begun.'

'Yes, but – ' I began.

'So' – he said authoritatively, holding up a finger to hush me – 'so, if you have been deprived of your earlier life, perhaps it is only that God has seen fit to bless you with another, that may be richer and fuller.'

'Oh, it's full, all right,' I agreed. 'But – '

'Now, from the standpoint of canon law,' he said, frowning, 'there is no difficulty regarding your marriages. Both were valid marriages, consecrated by the Church. And strictly speaking, your marriage to the young chevalier in there antedates your marriage to Monsieur Randall.'

'Yes, strictly speaking,' I agreed, getting to finish a sentence for once. 'But not in *my* time. I don't believe canon law was constructed with such contingencies in mind.' Anselm laughed.

'More than true, *ma chère*, more than true. All that I meant was that, considered from a strictly legal standpoint, you have committed neither sin nor crime in what you have done regarding these two men. Those were the two aspects of your situation, of which I spoke earlier: what you have done, and what you *will* do.' He reached up a hand and took mine, tugging me down to sit beside him, so our eyes were on a level.

'That is what you asked me when I heard your confession, is it not? What have I done? And what shall I do?'

'Yes, that's it. And you're telling me that I haven't done anything wrong? But I've – '

He was, I thought, nearly as bad as Dougal MacKenzie for interrupting.

'No, you have not,' he said firmly. 'It is possible to act in strict accordance with God's law and with one's conscience, you comprehend, and still to encounter difficulties and tragedy. It is the painful truth that we still do not know why *le bon Dieu* allows evil to exist, but we have his word for it that this is true. "I created good," he says in the Bible, "and I created evil." Consequently, even good people

834

sometimes, I think, *especially* good people,' he added meditatively, 'may encounter great confusion and difficulties in their lives. For example, take the young boy you were obliged to kill. No,' he said, raising a hand against my interruption, 'make no mistake. You were obliged to kill him, given the exigencies of your situation. Even Holy Mother Church, which teaches the sanctity of life, recognizes the need for defence of oneself and of one's family. And having seen the earlier condition of your husband' – he cast a look back at the guest wing – 'I have no doubt that you were obliged to take the path of violence. That being so, you have nothing with which to reproach yourself. You do, of course, feel pity and regret for the action, for you are, madame, a person of great sympathy and feeling.' He gently patted the hand that rested on my drawn-up knees.

'Sometimes our best actions result in things that are most regrettable. And yet you could not have acted otherwise. We do not know what God's plan for the young man was – perhaps it was his will that the boy should join him in heaven at that time. But you are not God, and there are limits to what you can expect of yourself.'

I shivered briefly as a cold wind came round the corner, and drew my shawl closer. Anselm saw it, and motioned towards the pool.

'The water is warm, madame. Perhaps you would care to soak your feet?'

'Warm?' I gaped incredulously at the water. I hadn't noticed before, but there were no broken sheets of ice in the corners of the trough, as there were on the holy water fonts outside the church, and small green plants floated in the water, sprouting from the cracks between the rocks that lined the pool.

In illustration, Anselm slipped off his own leather sandals. Cultured as his face and voice were, he had the square, sturdy hands and feet of a Norman peasant. Hiking the skirt of his habit to his knees, he dipped his feet into the pool. The carp dashed away, turning almost at once to nose curiously at this new intrusion.

'They don't bite, do they?' I asked, viewing the myriad voracious mouths suspiciously.

'Not flesh, no,' he assured me. 'They have no teeth to speak of.'

I shed my own sandals and gingerly inserted my feet into the water. To my surprise it was pleasantly warm. Not hot, but a delightful contrast to the damp, chilly air.

'Oh, that's nice!' I wiggled my toes with pleasure, causing considerable consternation among the carp.

'There are several mineral springs near the abbey,' Anselm explained. 'They bubble hot from the earth, and the waters hold great healing powers.' He pointed to the far end of the trough, where I could see a small opening in the rocks, half obscured by the drifting water plants.

'A small amount of the hot mineral water is piped here from the nearest spring. That is what enables the cook to maintain live fish for the table at all seasons; normally the winter weather would be too bitter for them.'

We paddled our feet in congenial silence for a time, the heavy bodies of the fish flicking past, occasionally bumping into our legs with a surprisingly weighty impact. The sun came out again, bathing us in a weak but perceptible warmth. Anselm closed his eyes, letting the light wash over his face. He spoke again without opening them.

'Your first husband – Frank was his name? – he too, I think, must be commended to God as one of the regrettable things that you can do nothing about.'

'But I could have done something,' I argued. 'I could have gone back – perhaps.'

He opened one eye and regarded me sceptically.

'Yes, perhaps,' he agreed. 'And perhaps not. You need not reproach yourself for hesitating to risk your life.'

'It wasn't the risk,' I said, flicking my toes at a big black-and-white-splotched carp. 'Or not entirely. It was – well, it was partly fear, but mostly it was that I – I couldn't leave Jamie.' I shrugged helplessly. 'I – simply couldn't.'

Anselm smiled, opening both eyes.

'A good marriage is one of the most precious gifts from God,' he observed. 'If you had the good sense to recognize

836

and accept the gift, it is no reproach to you. And consider . . .' He tilted his head to one side, like a brown sparrow.

'You have been gone from your place for most of a year. Your first husband will have begun to reconcile himself to your loss. Much as he may have loved you, loss is common to all men, and we are given means of overcoming it for our good. He will have started, perhaps, to build a new life. Would it do good for you to desert the man who needs you so deeply, and whom you love, to whom you are united in the bonds of holy matrimony, to return and disrupt this new life? And in particular, if you were to go back from a sense of duty, but feeling that your heart is given elsewhere – no.' He shook his head decisively.

'No man can serve two masters, and no more can a woman. Now, if that were your only valid marriage, and this' – he nodded again towards the guest wing – 'merely an irregular attachment, then your duty might lie elsewhere. But you were bound by God, and I think you may honour your duty to the chevalier.

'Now, as to the other aspect – what you shall do. That may require some discussion.' He pulled his feet from the water and dried them on the skirt of his habit.

'Let us adjourn this meeting to the abbey kitchens, where perhaps Brother Eulogius may be persuaded to provide us with a warming drink.'

Finding a stray bit of bread on the ground, I tossed it to the carp and stooped to put my sandals on.

'I can't tell you what a relief it is to talk to someone about it,' I said. 'And I still can't get over the fact that you really do believe me.'

He shrugged, gallantly offering me an arm to hold while I slipped the rough straps of the sandals over my instep.

'*Ma chère*, I serve a man who multiplied the loaves and fishes' – he smiled, nodding at the pool, where the swirls of the carps' feeding were still subsiding – 'who healed the sick and raised the dead. Shall I be astonished that the master of eternity has brought a young woman through the stones of the earth to do his will?'

Well, I reflected, it was better than being denounced as the whore of Babylon.

The kitchens of the abbey were warm and cavelike, the arching roof blackened with centuries of grease-filled smoke. Brother Eulogius, up to his elbows in a vat of dough, nodded a greeting to Anselm and called in French to one of the lay brothers to come and serve us. We found a seat out of the bustle and sat down with two cups of ale and a plate containing a hot pastry of some kind. I pushed the plate towards Anselm, too preoccupied to be interested in food.

'Let me put it this way,' I said, choosing my words carefully. 'If I knew that some harm was going to occur to a group of people, should I feel obliged to try to avert it?'

Anselm rubbed his nose reflectively on his sleeve; the heat of the kitchen was beginning to make it run.

'In principle, yes,' he agreed. 'But it would depend also upon a number of other things – what is the risk to yourself, and what are your other obligations? Also what is the chance of your success?'

'I haven't the faintest idea. Of any of those things. Except obligation, of course – I mean, there's Jamie. But he's one of the group who might be hurt.'

He broke off a piece of pastry and passed it to me, steaming. I ignored it, studying the surface of my ale. 'The two men I killed,' I said, 'either of them might have had children, if I hadn't killed them. They might have done' – I made a helpless gesture with the cup – 'who knows what they might have done? I may have affected the future ... no, I *have* affected the future. And I don't know how, and that's what frightens me so much.'

'Um.' Anselm grunted thoughtfully and motioned to a passing lay brother, who hastened over with a fresh pastry and more ale. He refilled both cups before speaking.

'If you have taken life, you have also preserved it. How many of the sick you have treated would have died without your intervention? They also will affect the future. What if a person you have saved should commit an act of great evil? Is that your fault? Should you on that account have let that person die? Of course not.' He rapped his pewter mug on the table for emphasis.

'You say that you are afraid to take any actions here for fear of affecting the future. This is illogical, madame. *Everyone's* actions affect the future. Had you remained in your own place, your actions would still have affected what was to happen, no less than they will now. You have still the same responsibilities that you would have had then – that any man has at any time. The only difference is that you may be in a position to see more exactly what effects your actions have – and then again, you may not.' He shook his head, looking steadily across the table.

'The ways of the Lord are hidden to us, and no doubt for good reason. You are right, *ma chère*, the laws of the Church were not formulated with situations such as yours in mind, and therefore you have little guidance other than your own conscience and the hand of God. I cannot tell you what you should do, or not do.

'You have free choice; so have all the others in this world. And history, I believe, is the cumulation of all those actions. Some individuals are chosen by God to affect the destinies of many. Perhaps you are one of those. Perhaps not. I do not know why you are here. You do not know. It is likely that neither of us will ever know.' He rolled his eyes comically. 'Sometimes I don't even know why *I* am here!' I laughed and he smiled in return. He leaned towards me across the rough planks of the table, intense.

'Your knowledge of the future is a tool, given to you as a shipwrecked castaway might find himself in possession of a knife or a fishing line. It is not immoral to use it, so long as you do so in accordance with the dictates of God's law, to the best of your ability.'

He paused, drew a deep breath, and blew it out in an explosive sigh. He smiled.

'And that, *ma chère madame*, is all I can tell you – no more than I can tell any troubled soul who comes to me for advice: put your trust in God, and pray for guidance.'

He shoved the fresh pastry towards me.

'But whatever you are to do, you will require strength for it. So take one last bit of advice: when in doubt, eat.'

When I came into Jamie's room in the evening he was asleep, head pillowed on his forearms. The empty soup bowl sat virtuously on the tray, the untouched platter of bread and meat beside it. I looked from the innocent, dreaming face to the platter and back. I touched the bread. My finger left a slight depression in the moist surface. Fresh.

I left him asleep and went in search of Brother Roger, whom I found in the buttery.

'Did he eat the bread and meat?' I demanded without preliminaries.

Brother Roger smiled. 'Yes.'

'Did he keep it down?'

'No.'

I eyed him narrowly. 'You didn't clean up after him, I hope.'

He was amused, the round cheeks pink. 'Would I dare? No, he took the precaution of having a basin ready, in case.'

'Damn wily Scot,' I said, laughing despite myself. I returned to his chamber and kissed him lightly on the forehead. He stirred but didn't wake. Heeding Father Anselm's advice, I took the platter of fresh bread and meat back to my chamber for my own supper.

Thinking I would give Jamie time to recover, both from pique and indigestion, I stayed in my own room most of the next day, reading a herbal Brother Ambrose had provided me. After lunch I went to check on my recalcitrant patient. Instead of Jamie, though, I found Murtagh, sitting on a stool tilted back against the wall, wearing a bemused expression.

'Where is he?' I said, looking blankly around the room.

Murtagh jerked a thumb towards the window. It was a cold, dark day and the lamps were lit. The window was uncovered and the chill draught set the little flame fluttering in its dish.

'He went *out?*' I asked incredulously. 'Where? Why? And what on earth is he wearing?' Jamie had remained largely naked over the last several days, since the room was warm and any pressure on his healing wounds was painful. He had worn a monk's outer robe when leaving his room on necessary short excursions, with the support of Brother Roger, but the robe was still present, neatly folded at the foot of the bed.

Murtagh rocked his stool forward and regarded me owlishly.

'How many questions is that? Four?' He held up one hand, index finger point up.

'One: Aye, he went out.' The second finger rose. 'Two: Where? Damned if I know.' The third finger joined its companions. 'Three: Why? He said he was tired of bein' cooped up indoors.' The little finger waggled briefly. 'Four: Also damned if I know. He wasna wearin' anything at all last time I saw him.'

Murtagh folded all four fingers and stuck out his thumb. 'Ye didna ask me, but he's been gone an hour or so.'

I fumed, at a loss as to what to do. Since the offender wasn't available I snapped at Murtagh instead.

'Don't you know it's near freezing out there, and snow coming on? Why didn't you stop him? And what do you mean he isn't wearing anything?'

The diminutive clansman was tranquil. 'Aye, I know it. Reckon he does, too, not bein' blind. As for stoppin' him, I tried.' He nodded at the robe on the bed.

'When he said he was goin' out, I said he wasna fit for it, and you'd have my head, did I let him go. I snatched up his gown and set my back against the door, and told him he wasna leavin' unless he was prepared to go through me.'

Murtagh paused, then said irrelevantly, 'Ellen MacKenzie had the sweetest smile I ever saw; would warm a man to the backbone just to see it.'

'So you let her fat-headed son go out and freeze to death,' I said impatiently. 'What's his mother's smile to do with it?'

Murtagh rubbed his nose meditatively. 'Weel, when I

said I wouldna let him pass, young Jamie just looked at me for a moment. Then he gave me a smile looked just like his ma's, and stepped out of the window in naught but his skin. By the time I got to the window he was gone.'

I rolled my eyes heavenwards.

'Reckoned I should let ye know where he'd gone,' Murtagh continued, 'so ye'd no be worrit for him.'

'So I'd no be worrit for him!' I muttered under my breath as I strode towards the stables. '*He'd* better be worrit, when I catch up to him!'

There was only one main lane heading inland. I rode along it at a good pace, keeping an eye on the fields as I passed. This part of France was a rich farming area, and luckily most of the forest had been cleared; wolves and bears would not be as much a danger as they might be further inland.

As it happened I found him barely a mile beyond the gates of the monastery, sitting on one of the ancient Roman mile-markers that dotted the roads.

He was barefoot, but otherwise clad in a short jerkin and thin breeches, the property of one of the stable lads, to judge from the stains on them.

I reined up and stared at him for a moment, leaning on the pommel. 'Your nose is blue,' I remarked conversationally. I glanced downwards. 'And so are your feet.'

He grinned and wiped his nose on the back of his hand.

'So are my balls. Want to warm them for me?' Cold or not, he was plainly in good spirits. I slid off the horse and stood in front of him, shaking my head.

'It's no use at all, is it?' I said.

'What isn't?' He rubbed his hand on the ragged breeches.

'Being angry with you. You don't care a bit whether you give yourself pneumonia, or get eaten by bears, or worry me half to death, do you?'

'Well, I'm no much worrit about bears. They sleep in the winter, ye know.'

I lost my temper and swung my hand at him, intending to slap his ear through the side of his head. He caught my wrist and held it without difficulty, laughing at me. After a moment's fruitless struggle I gave up and laughed too.

'Are you coming back, now?' I asked. 'Or have you got anything else to prove?'

He gestured back along the road with his chin. 'Take the horse back to that big oak tree and wait for me there. I'll walk that far. Alone.'

I bit my tongue to repress the several remarks I felt bubbling to the surface, and mounted. At the oak tree I got off and looked down the road. After a moment, though, I found I couldn't bear to watch his laboured progress. When he fell the first time, I clutched the reins in my gloved hands, then resolutely turned my back and waited.

We barely made it back to the guest wing, but managed, staggering through the corridor, his arm looped over my shoulder for support. I spotted Brother Roger, anxiously lurking in the hall, and sent him scampering for a warming pan while I steered my awkward burden into the chamber and dumped him on to the bed. He grunted at the impact but lay still, eyes closed, as I proceeded to strip the filthy rags off him.

'All right; in you get.'

He rolled obediently under the covers I held back for him. I thrust the warming pan hastily between the sheets at the foot of the bed and shoved it back and forth. When I removed it, he stretched his long legs down and relaxed with a blissful sigh as his feet touched the pocket of warmth.

I went quietly about the room, picking up the discarded clothes, straightening the trifling disorder on the table, putting fresh charcoal in the brazier, adding a pinch of elecampane to sweeten the smoke. I thought he was asleep, and was startled when he spoke behind me.

'Claire.'

'Yes?'

'I love you.'

'Oh.' I was mildly surprised, but undeniably pleased. 'I love you too.'

He sighed, and opened his eyes halfway.

'Randall,' he said. 'Towards the end. That's what he

843

wanted.' I was even more startled by this, and replied cautiously.

'Oh?'

'Aye.' His eyes were fixed on the open window where the snow clouds filled the space with a deep, even grey.

'I was lying on the floor, and he was lying next to me. He was naked by then, too, and both of us were smeared with blood – and other things. I remember trying to lift my head, and feeling my cheek stuck to the stone of the floor with dried blood.' He frowned, a distant look in his eyes as he conjured the memory.

'I was far gone by then; so far that I didna even feel much pain – I was just terribly tired, and everything seemed far away and not very real.'

'Just as well,' I said with some asperity, and he smiled briefly.

'Aye, just as well. I was drifting a bit, half-fainted, I expect, so I don't know how long we both lay there, but I came awake to find him holding me and pressing himself to me.' He hesitated, as though the next part were difficult to say.

'I'd not fought him till then. But I was so tired, and I thought I couldna bear it again . . . anyway, I started to squirm away from him, not really fighting, just pulling back. He had his arms round my neck, and he pulled on me and buried his face in my shoulder, and I could feel he was crying. I couldna tell what he was saying for a bit, and then I could; he was saying "I love you, I love you", over and over, with his tears and his spittle running down my chest.' Jamie shuddered briefly, from cold or memory. He blew out a long breath, disturbing the cloud of fragrant smoke that swirled near the ceiling.

'I canna think why I did it. But I put my arms about him and we just lay still for a bit. He stopped crying, finally, and kissed me and stroked me. Then he whispered to me, "Tell me that you love me." ' He paused in the recital, smiling faintly.

'I would not do it. I dinna know why. By then I would ha' licked his boots and called him the King of Scotland,

844

if he'd wanted it. But I wouldna tell him that. I don't even remember thinking about it; I just – wouldn't.' He sighed and his good hand twitched, gripping the coverlet.

'He used me again – hard. And he kept on saying it: "Tell me that you love me, Alick. Say that you love me." '

'He called you Alick?' I interrupted, not able to hold back.

'Aye. I remember I wondered how he knew my second name. Did not occur to me to wonder why he'd use it, even if he knew.' He shrugged.

'Anyway, I didna move or say a word, and when he'd finished he jumped up as though he'd gone mad, and started to beat me with something – I could not see what – cursing and shouting at me, saying "You know you love me! Tell me so! I know it's true!" I got my arms up over my head to protect it, and after a bit I must have fainted again, because the pain in my shoulders was the last I remember, except for sort of a dream about bellowing kine. Then I woke, jouncing along belly-down on a horse for a few moments, and then nothing again till I came round on the hearthside at Eldridge, with you looking down on me.' He closed his eyes again. His tone was dreamy, almost unconcerned.

'I think . . . if I had told him that . . . he would have killed me.'

Some people have nightmares peopled by monsters. I dreamed of genealogical trees, thin black branches bearing clusters of dates on every stem. The lines like snakes, with death between the brackets of their jaws. Once again I heard Frank's voice, saying *He became a soldier, a good choice for a second son. There was a third brother who became a curate, but I don't know much about him . . .* I didn't know much about him, either. Only his name. There were the three sons listed on that chart; the sons of Joseph and Mary Randall. I had seen it many times: the oldest, William; and the second, Jonathan; and the third, Alexander.

Jamie spoke again, summoning me from my thoughts.

'Sassenach?'

'Yes?'

'Ye know the fortress I told ye of, the one inside me?'

'I remember.'

He smiled without opening his eyes, and reached out a hand for me.

'Well, I've a lean-to built, at least. And a roof to keep out the rain.'

I went to bed tired but peaceful, and wondering. Jamie would recover. When that had been in doubt, I had looked no further than the next hour, the next meal, the next administration of medicine. But now I needed to look further.

The abbey was a sanctuary, but only a temporary one. We could not stay here indefinitely, no matter how hospitable the monks. Scotland and England were too dangerous by far; unless Lord Lovat could help – a remote contingency, under the circumstances. Our future must lie on this side of the sea. Knowing what I now knew about Jamie's seasickness, I understood his reluctance to consider emigration to America – three months of nausea was a daunting prospect to anyone. So what was left?

France was the most likely. We both spoke French fluently. While Jamie could do as well in Spanish, German or Italian, I was not so linguistically blessed. Also, the Fraser family was rich in connections here; perhaps we could find a place on an estate owned by a relative or friend, and live peacefully in the country. The idea held considerable attractions.

But there remained, as always, the question of time. It was the beginning of 1744 – the New Year was but two weeks past. And in 1745 Bonnie Prince Charlie would take ship from France to Scotland, the Young Pretender come to claim his father's throne. With him would come disaster; war and slaughter, the crushing of the Highland clans, and with them the butchery of all that Jamie – and I – held dear.

And between now and then there lay one and a half years – a time when things might happen. When steps might be taken to prevent disaster. How, and by what means? I had no idea, but neither had I any doubts about the consequences of inaction.

Could events be changed? Perhaps. My fingers stole to my left hand and idly caressed the gold ring on my third finger. I thought of what I had said to Jonathan Randall, burning with rage and horror in the dungeons under Wentworth Prison.

'I curse you,' I had said, 'with the hour of your death.' And I had told him when he would die. Had told him the date written on the genealogical tree, in Frank's fine black calligraphic script – 16 April 1746. Jonathan Randall was to die at the battle of Culloden, caught up in the slaughter that the English would create. But he didn't. He had died instead a few hours later, trampled beneath the hooves of my revenge.

And he had died a childless bachelor. Or at least I thought so. The chart – that cursed chart! – had given the date of his marriage, some time in 1744. And the birth of his son, Frank's five-times-great-grandfather, soon after. If Jonathan Randall was dead and childless, how would Frank be born? And yet his ring was still upon my hand. He had existed, would exist. I comforted myself with the thought, rubbing the ring in the darkness as though it contained a djinn that could advise me.

I woke out of a sound sleep some time later with a half scream.

'Ssh. 'Tis only me.' The large hand lifted from my mouth. With the candle out, the room was pitch black. I groped blindly until my hand struck something solid.

'You shouldn't be out of bed!' I exclaimed, still groggy with sleep. My fingers slid over smooth cold flesh. 'You're freezing!'

'Well, of course I am,' he said somewhat crossly. 'I havena got any clothes on, and it's perishing in the corridor. Will ye let me in bed?'

I wriggled as far over as I could in the narrow cot, and he slid in naked beside me, clutching me for warmth. His breathing was uneven, and I thought his trembling was from weakness as much as from cold.

'God, you're warm.' He snuggled closer, sighing. 'It feels good to hold ye, Sassenach.'

I didn't bother asking what he was doing there; that was becoming quite plain. Nor did I ask whether he was sure. I had my own doubts, but would not voice them for fear of making self-fulfilling prophecies. I rolled to face him, mindful of the injured hand.

There was that sudden startling moment of joining, that quick gliding strangeness that at once becomes familiar. Jamie sighed deeply, with satisfaction and, perhaps, relief. We lay still for a moment, as though afraid to disturb our fragile link by moving. Jamie's good hand caressed me slowly, feeling its way in the dark, fingers spread like a cat's whiskers, sensitive to vibration. He moved against me, once, as though asking a question, and I answered him in the same language.

We began a delicate game of slow movements, a balancing act between his desire and his weakness, between pain and the growing pleasure of the body. Somewhere in the dark, I thought to myself that I must tell Anselm that there was another way to make time stop, and then thought perhaps not, as it was not a way open to a priest.

I held Jamie steady, with a light hand on his scarred back. He set our rhythm, but let me carry the force of our movement. We were both silent save our breathing, until the end. Feeling him tiring, I grasped him firmly and pulled him to me, rocking my hips to take him deeper, forcing him towards a climax. 'Now,' I said softly, 'come to me. Now!' He put his forehead hard against mine and yielded himself to me with a quivering sigh.

The Victorians called it 'the little death', and with good reason. He lay so limp and heavy that I would have thought him dead if not for the slow thump of his heart against my ribs. It seemed a long time before he stirred and mumbled something against my shoulder.

'What did you say?'

He turned his head so his mouth was just below my ear. I felt warm breath on my neck. 'I said,' he answered softly, 'my hand doesna hurt at all just now.'

The good hand gently explored my face, smoothing away the wetness on my cheeks.

'Were ye afraid for me?' he said.

'Yes,' I said. 'I thought it was too soon.'

He laughed softly in the dark. 'It was; I almost killed myself. Aye, I was afraid too. But I woke with my hand painin' me and couldna go back to sleep. I was tossing about, feeling lonely for ye. The more I thought about ye, the more I wanted ye, and I was halfway down the corridor before I thought to worry about what I was going to do when I got here. And once I thought . . .' He paused, stroking my cheek. 'Well, I'm no verra good, Sassenach, but I'm maybe not a coward, after all.'

I turned my head to meet his kiss. His stomach rumbled loudly.

'Don't laugh, you,' he grumbled. 'It's your fault, starving me. It's a wonder I could manage at all, on nothing but soup and ale.'

'All right,' I said, still laughing. 'You win. You can have an egg for your breakfast tomorrow.'

'Ha,' he said, in tones of deep satisfaction. 'I knew ye'd feed me, if I offered ye a suitable inducement.'

We fell asleep face to face, locked in each other's arms.

41

From the Womb of the Earth

Over the next two weeks Jamie continued to heal, and I continued to wonder. Some days I would feel that we must go to Rome, site of the Pretender's court, and do . . . what? Other times, I wanted with all my heart only to find a safe and isolated spot, to live our lives in peace.

It was a warm, bright day and the icicles hanging from the gargoyles' noses dripped incessantly, leaving deep ragged pits in the snow beneath the eaves. The door of Jamie's room had been left ajar and the window uncovered, to clear out some of the lingering vapours of smoke and illness.

I poked my head cautiously around the jamb, not wishing to wake him if he were asleep, but the narrow cot was empty. He was seated by the open window, turned half away from the door so that his face was mostly hidden.

He was desperately thin still, but the shoulders were broad and straight beneath the rough fabric of the novice's habit, and the grace of his strength was returning; he sat solidly without a tremor, back straight and legs curled back beneath the stool, the lines of his body firm and harmonious. He was holding his right wrist with his sound left hand, slowly turning the right hand in the sunlight.

There was a small pile of cloth strips on the table. He had removed the bandages from the injured hand and was examining it closely. I stood in the doorway, not moving. From here I could see the hand clearly as he turned it back and forth, probing gingerly.

The stigma of the nail wound in the palm of the hand was quite small, and well healed, I was glad to see; no more than a small pink knot of scar tissue that would gradually fade. On the back of the hand the situation was not so favourable. Eroded by infection, the wound there covered an area the size of a sixpence, still patched with scabs and the rawness of a new scar.

The second finger, too, showed a jagged ridge of pink scar tissue running from just below the first joint almost to the knuckle. Released from their splints, the thumb and index finger were straight, but the little finger was badly twisted; that one had had three separate fractures, I remembered, and apparently I had not been able to set them all properly. The ring finger was set oddly, so that it protruded slightly upwards when he laid the hand flat on the table, as he did now.

Turning the hand palm upwards, he began to manipulate the fingers gently. None would bend more than an inch or two; the ring finger not at all. As I had feared, the second joint was probably permanently frozen.

He turned the hand to and fro, holding it before his face, watching the stiff, twisted fingers and the ugly scars, mercilessly vivid in the sunlight. Then he suddenly bent his head, clutching the injured hand to his chest, covering it protectively with the sound one. He made no sound, but the wide shoulders trembled briefly.

'Jamie.' I crossed the room swiftly and knelt beside him, putting my hand softly on his knee.

'Jamie, I'm sorry,' I said. 'I did the best I could.'

He looked down at me in astonishment. The thick auburn lashes sparkled with tears in the sunlight, and he dashed them hastily away with the back of his hand.

'What?' he said, gulping, clearly taken aback by my sudden appearance. 'Sorry? For what, Sassenach?'

'Your hand.' I reached out and took it, lightly tracing the crooked lines of the fingers, touching the sunken scar on the back.

'It will get better,' I assured him anxiously. 'Really it will. I know it seems stiff and useless right now, but that's only because it's been splinted so long, and the bones haven't fully knitted yet. I can show you how to exercise and massage. You'll get back a good deal of the use of it, honestly – '

He stopped me by laying his good hand along my cheek.

'Did you mean . . . ?' He started, then stopped, shaking his head in disbelief. 'You thought . . . ?' He stopped once more and started again.

'Sassenach,' he said, 'ye didna think that I was grieving for a stiff finger and a few more scars?' He smiled a little crookedly. 'I'm a vain man, maybe, but it doesna go that deep, I hope.'

'But you – ' I began. He took both my hands in both of his and stood up, drawing me to my feet. I reached up and smoothed away the single tear that had rolled down his cheek. The tiny smear of moisture was warm on my thumb.

'I was crying for joy, my Sassenach,' he said softly. He reached out slowly and took my face between his hands. 'And thanking God that I have two hands. That I have two hands to hold you with. To serve you with, to love you with. Thanking God that I am a whole man still, because of you.'

I put my own hands up, cupping his.

'But why wouldn't you be?' I asked. And then I remembered the butcherous assortment of saws and knives I had seen among Beaton's implements at Leoch, and I knew. Knew what I had forgotten when I had been faced with the emergency. That in the days before penicillin, the usual – the only – cure for an infected extremity was an amputation of the limb.

'Oh, Jamie,' I said. I was weak-kneed at the thought, and sat down on the stool rather abruptly.

'I never thought of it,' I said, still stunned. 'I honestly never thought of it.' I looked up at him. 'Jamie, if I'd thought of it, I probably would have done it. To save your life.'

'It's not how . . . they don't do it that way, then, in . . . your time?'

I shook my head. 'No. There are drugs to stop infections. So I didn't even think of it,' I marvelled. I looked up suddenly. 'Did you?'

He nodded. 'I was expecting it. It's why I asked you to let me die, that once. I was thinking of it, in between the bouts of muzzy-headedness, and – just for that one moment – I didna think I could bear to live like that. It's what happened to Ian, ye know.'

'No, really?' I was shocked. 'He told me he'd lost it by grapeshot, but I didn't think to ask about the details.'

'Aye, a grapeshot wound in the leg went bad. The surgeons took it off to keep it from poisoning his blood.' He paused.

'Ian does verra well, all things considered. But' – he hesitated, pulling on the stiff ring finger – 'I knew him before. He's as good as he is only because of Jenny. She ... keeps him whole.' He smiled sheepishly at me. 'As ye did for me. I canna think why women bother.'

'Well,' I said softly, 'women like to do that.'

He laughed quietly and drew me close. 'Aye. God knows why.'

We stood entwined for a bit, not moving. My forehead rested on his chest, my arms around his back, and I could feel his heart beating, slow and strong. Finally he stirred and released me.

'I've something to show ye,' he said. He turned and opened the small drawer of the table, removing a folded letter which he handed to me.

It was a letter of introduction, from Abbot Alexander, commending his nephew, James Fraser, to the attention of the Chevalier St George – otherwise known as His Majesty King James of Scotland – as a most proficient linguist and translator.

'It's a place,' Jamie said, watching as I folded the letter. 'And we'll need a place to go, soon. But what ye told me on the hill at Craigh na Dun – that was true, no?'

I took a deep breath and nodded. 'It's true.'

He took the letter from me and tapped it thoughtfully on his knee.

'Then this' – he waved the letter – 'is not without a bit of danger.'

'It could be.'

He tossed the parchment into the drawer and sat staring after it for a moment. Then he looked up and the dark blue eyes held mine. He laid a hand along my cheek.

'I meant it, Claire,' he said quietly. 'My life is yours. And it's yours to decide what we shall do, where we go next. To

Italy, or stay in France, or even back to Scotland. My heart has been yours since first I saw ye, and you've held my soul and body between your two hands here, and kept them safe. We shall go as ye say.'

There was a light knock at the door and we sprang apart like guilty lovers. I dabbed hastily at my hair, thinking that a monastery, while an excellent convalescent home, lacked something as a romantic retreat.

A lay brother came in at Jamie's bidding, and dumped a large leather saddlebag on the table. 'From MacRannoch of Eldridge Hall,' he said with a grin. 'For my lady Broch Tuarach.' He bowed then and went, leaving a faint breath of seawater and cold air behind.

I unbuckled the leather straps, curious to see what MacRannoch might have sent. Inside were three things: a note, unaddressed and unsigned, a small package addressed to Jamie, and the cured skin of a wolf, smelling strongly of the tanner's arts.

The note read: 'For a virtuous woman is a pearl of great price, and her value is greater than rubies.'

Jamie had opened the other parcel. He held something small and glimmering in one hand and was quizzically regarding the wolf pelt.

'A bit odd, that. Sir Marcus has sent ye a wolf pelt, Sassenach, and me a pearl bracelet. Perhaps he's got his labels mixed?'

The bracelet was a lovely thing, a single row of large baroque pearls set between twisted gold chains.

'No,' I said, admiring it. 'He's got it right. The bracelet goes with the necklace you gave me when we wed. He gave that to your mother, did you know?'

'No, I didn't,' he answered softly, touching the pearls. 'Father gave them to me for my wife, whoever she was to be' – and a quick smile tugged at his mouth – 'but he didna tell me where they came from.'

I remembered Sir Marcus' help on the night we had burst so unceremoniously into his house, and the look on his face when we had left him next day. I could see from Jamie's face that he also was remembering the baronet who might have been his father. He reached out and took my hand, fastening the bracelet about my wrist.

'But it's not for me!' I protested.

'Aye, it is,' he said firmly. 'It isna suitable for a man to send jewellery to a respectable married woman, so he gave it to me. But clearly it's for you.' He looked at me and grinned. 'For one thing, it won't go round my wrist, even scrawny as I am.'

He turned to the bundled wolfskin and shook it out.

'Why ever did MacRannoch send ye this, though?' He draped the shaggy wolfhide about his shoulders and I recoiled with a sharp cry. The head had been carefully skinned and cured as well; equipped with a pair of yellow glass eyes, it was glaring nastily at me from Jamie's left shoulder.

'Ugh!' I said. 'It looks just like it did when it was alive!'

Jamie, following the direction of my glance, turned his head and found himself suddenly face to face with the snarling countenance. With a startled exclamation he jerked the skin off and flung it across the room.

'Jesus God,' he said, and crossed himself. The skin lay on the floor, glowering balefully in the candlelight.

'What d'ye mean, when it was alive, Sassenach? A personal friend, was it?' Jamie asked, eyeing it narrowly.

I told him then the things I had had no chance to tell him; about the wolf, and the other wolves, and Hector, and the snow, and the cottage with the bear, and the argument with Sir Marcus, and the appearance of Murtagh, and the cattle, and the long wait on the hillside in the pink mist of the snow-swept night, waiting to see whether he were dead or alive.

Thin or not, his chest was broad and his arms warm and strong. He pressed my face into his shoulder and rocked me while I sobbed. I tried for a bit to control myself, but he only hugged me harder and said small and gentle things into the cloud of my hair, and I finally gave up and cried with the complete abandon of a child, until I was worn to utter limpness and hiccupping exhaustion.

'Come to think of it, I've a wee gift for ye myself, Sassenach,' he said, smoothing my hair. I sniffed and wiped my nose on my skirt, having nothing else handy.

'I'm sorry I haven't got anything to give you,' I said, watching as he stood up and began to dig through the tumbled bedclothes. Probably looking for a handkerchief, I thought, sniffing some more.

'Aside from such minor gifts as my life, my manhood and my right hand?' he said dryly. 'They'll do nicely, *mo duinne*.' He straightened up with a novice's robe in one hand. 'Undress.'

My mouth fell open. 'What?'

'Undress, Sassenach, and put this on.' He handed me the robe, grinning. 'Or do ye want me to turn my back first?'

Clutching the rough homespun around me, I followed Jamie down yet another flight of dark stairs. This was the third, and the narrowest yet; the lantern he held lit the stone blocks of walls no more than eighteen inches apart. It felt rather like being swallowed up into the earth as we went further and further down the narrow black shaft.

'Are you sure you know where you're going?' I asked. My voice echoed in the stairwell, but with a curiously muffled sound as though I were speaking underwater.

'Well, there's no much chance of taking the wrong turning, now is there?'

We had reached another landing, but true enough, the way ahead lay in only one direction – down.

At the bottom of this flight of steps, though, we came to a door. There was a small landing, carved out of the solid side of a mountain, from the looks of it, and a wide, low door made of oak planks and brass hinging. The planks were grey with age, but still solid, and the landing swept clean. Plainly this part of the monastery was still in use, then. The wine cellar perhaps?

There was a sconce near the door that held a torch, half burnt from previous use. Jamie paused to light it with a paper spill from the pile that lay ready nearby, then pushed open the unlocked door and ducked beneath the lintel, leaving me to follow.

At first I could see nothing at all inside but the glow of Jamie's lantern. Everything was black. The lantern bobbed along, moving away from me. I stood still, following the blob of light with my eyes. Every few feet he would stop, then continue, and a slow flame would rise up in his wake to burn in a small red glow. As my eyes slowly accustomed themselves, the flames became a row of lanterns, situated on rock pillars, shining into the black like beacons.

It was a cave. At first I thought it was a cave of crystals, because of the odd black shimmer beyond the lanterns. But I stepped forward to the first pillar and looked beyond, and then I saw it.

A clear black lake. Transparent water, shimmering like glass over fine black volcanic sand, giving off red reflections in the lantern light. The air was damp and warm, humid with the steam that condensed on the cool cavern walls, running down the ribbed columns of rock.

A hot spring. The faint scent of sulphur bit at my nostrils. A hot mineral spring, then. I remembered Anselm's mentioning the springs that bubbled up from the ground near the abbey, renowned for their healing powers.

Jamie stood behind me, looking out over the gently steaming expanse of jet and rubies.

'A hot bath,' he said proudly. 'Do ye like it?'

'Jesus H. Roosevelt Christ,' I said.

'Oh, ye do,' he said, grinning at the success of his surprise. 'Come in, then.'

He dropped his own gown and stood glowing dimly in the darkness, patched with red in the glimmering reflections off the water. The arched ceiling of the cave seemed to swallow the light of the lanterns, so that the glow reached only a few feet before being engulfed.

A little hesitantly I let the novice's robe drop from my arms.

'How hot is it?' I asked.

'Hot enough,' he answered. 'Dinna worry, it won't burn

ye. But stay over an hour or so, and it might cook the flesh off your bones like soupmeat.'

'What an appealing idea,' I said, discarding the robe.

Following his straight, slender figure I stepped cautiously into the water. There were steps cut in the stone, leading down underwater, with a knotted rope fastened along the wall to provide handholds.

The water flowed up over my hips, and the flesh of my belly shivered in delight as the heat swirled through me. At the bottom of the steps I stood on clean black sand, the water just below the level of my shoulders, my breasts floating like glass fisher-floats. My skin was flushed with the heat, and small prickles of perspiration were starting on the back of my neck, under the heavy hair. It was pure bliss.

The surface of the spring was smooth and waveless, but the water wasn't still; I could feel small stirrings, currents running through the body of the pool like nerve impulses. It was that, I suppose, added to the incredible soothing heat, that gave me the momentary illusion that the spring was alive – a warm, welcoming entity that reached out to soothe and embrace. Anselm had said that the springs had healing powers, and I wasn't disposed to doubt it.

Jamie came up behind me, tiny wavelets marking his passage through the water. He reached around me to cup my breasts, softly smoothing the hot water over the upper slopes.

'Do ye like it, *mo duinne?*' He bent forward and planted a kiss on my shoulder.

I let my feet float out from under me, resting against him.

'It's wonderful! It's the first time I've been warm all the way through since August.' He began to tow me, backing slowly through the water; my legs streamed out in the wake of our passage, the amazing warmth passing down my limbs like caressing hands.

He stopped, swung me around and lowered me gently on to hard wood. I could see planks set into a rocky niche, half visible in the shadowy underwater light. He sat down on the bench beside me, stretching his arms out on the rocky ledge behind us.

'Brother Ambrose brought me down here the other day to soak,' he said. 'To soften the scars a bit. It does feel good, doesn't it?'

'More than good.' The water was so buoyant that I felt I might float away if I loosed my hold on the bench. I looked upwards into the black shadows of the roof.

'Does anything live in this cave? Bats, I mean? Or fish?'

He shook his head. 'Nothing but the spirit of the spring, Sassenach. The water bubbles up from the earth through a narrow crack back there' – he nodded towards the Stygian blackness at the back of the cave – 'and trickles out through a dozen tiny openings in the rock. But there's no real opening to the outside, save the door into the monastery.'

'Spirit of the spring?' I said, amused. 'Sounds rather pagan, to be hiding under a monastery.'

He stretched luxuriously, long legs wavering under the glassy surface like the stems of water plants.

'Well, whatever ye wish to call it, it's been here a good deal longer than the monastery.'

'Yes, I can see that.'

The walls of the cave were of smooth, dark volcanic rock, almost like black glass, slick with the moisture of the spring. The whole chamber looked like a gigantic bubble, half filled with that curiously alive but sterile water. I felt as though we were cradled in the womblike centre of the earth, and that if I pressed my ear to the rock I would hear the infinitely slow beat of a great heart nearby.

We were very quiet for a long time then, half floating, half dreaming, brushing now and then against each other as we drifted in the unseen currents of the cave.

When I spoke at last my voice seemed slow and drugged. 'I've decided.'

'Ah. Will it be Rome, then?' Jamie's voice seemed to come from a long way away.

'Yes. I don't know, once there – '

'It doesna matter. We shall do what we can.' His hand

859

reached for me, moving so slowly I thought it would never touch me.

He drew me close until the sensitive tips of my breasts rubbed across his chest. The water was not only warm but heavy, almost oily to the touch, and his hands floated down my back to cup my buttocks and lift me.

The intrusion was startling. Hot and slippery as our skins were, we drifted over each other with barely a sensation of touching or pressure, but his presence within me was solid and intimate, a fixed point in a watery world, like an umbilical cord in the random driftings of the womb. I made a brief sound of surprise at the small inrush of hot water that accompanied his entrance, then settled firmly on to my fixed point of reference with a little sigh of pleasure.

'Oh, I like that one,' he said appreciatively.

'Like what?' I asked.

'That sound that ye made. The little squeak.'

It wasn't possible to blush; my skin was already as flushed as it could get. I let my hair swing forward to cover my face, the curls relaxing as they dragged the surface of the water.

'I'm sorry; I didn't mean to be noisy.'

He laughed, the deep sound echoing softly in the columns of the roof.

'I said I liked it. And I do. It's one of the things I like the best about bedding ye, Sassenach, the small noises that ye make.'

He pulled me closer, so my forehead rested against his neck. Moisture sprang up at once between us, slick as the sulphur-laden water. He made a slight movement with his hips and I drew in my breath in a half-stifled gasp.

'Yes, like that,' he said softly. 'Or . . . like that?'

'Urk,' I said. He laughed again, but kept doing it.

'That's what I thought most about,' he said, drawing his hands slowly up and down my back, cupping, curving, tracing the swell of my hips. 'In prison at night, chained in a room with a dozen other men, listening to the snoring and farting and groaning. I thought of those small tender sounds that ye make when I love you, and I could feel ye there next to me in the dark, breathing soft and then faster, and the little grunt that ye give when I first take you, as though ye were settling yourself to your job.'

My breathing was definitely coming faster. Supported by the dense, mineral-saturated water, I was buoyant as an oiled feather, kept from floating away only by my grip on the curved muscles of his shoulders and the snug, firm clasp I kept of him lower down.

'Even better' – his voice was a hot murmur in my ear – 'when I come to ye fierce and wanting, and ye whimper under me, and struggle as though you wanted to get away, and I know it's only that you're struggling to come closer, and I'm fighting the same fight.'

His hands were exploring, gently, slowly as tickling a trout, sliding deep into the rift of my buttocks, gliding lower, groping, caressing the stretched and yearning point of our joining. I quivered and the breath went from me in an unwilled gasp.

'Or when I come to you needing, and ye take me into you with a sigh and that quiet hum like a hive of bees in the sun, and ye carry me wi' you into peace with a little moaning sound.'

'Jamie,' I said hoarsely, my voice echoing off the water. 'Jamie, please.'

'Not yet, *mo duinne*.' His hands came hard around my waist, settling and slowing me, pressing me down until I did groan.

'Not yet. We've time. And I mean to hear ye groan like that again. And to moan and sob, even though you dinna wish to, for ye canna help it. I mean to make you sigh as though your heart would break, and scream with the wanting, and at last to cry out in my arms, and I shall know that I've served ye well.'

The rush began between my thighs, shooting like a dart into the depths of my belly, loosening my joints so that my hands slipped limp and helpless off his shoulders. My back arched and the slippery firm roundness of my breasts pressed flat against his chest. I shuddered in hot darkness, Jamie's steadying hands all that kept me from drowning.

Resting against him I felt boneless, like a jellyfish. I didn't know – or care – what sort of sounds I had been making, but I felt incapable of coherent speech. Until he began to move again, strong as a shark under the dark water.

'No,' I said. 'Jamie, no. I can't bear it like that again.' The blood was still pounding in my fingertips and his movement within me was an exquisite torture.

'You can, for I love ye.' His voice was half muffled in my soaking hair. 'And you will, for I want ye. But this time, I go wi' you.'

He held my hips firm against him, carrying me beyond myself with the force of an undertow. I crashed formless against him, like breakers on a rock, and he met me with the brutal force of granite, my anchor in the pounding chaos.

Boneless and liquid as the water around us, contained only by the frame of his hands, I cried out, the soft, bubbling half-choked cry of a sailor sucked beneath the waves. And heard his own cry, helpless in return, and knew I had served him well.

We struggled upwards out of the womb of the world, damp and steaming, rubber-limbed with wine and heat. I fell to my knees at the first landing, and Jamie, trying to help me, fell down next to me in an untidy heap of robes and bare legs. Giggling helplessly, drunk more with love than with wine, we made our way side by side, on hands and knees up the second flight of steps, hindering each other more than helping, jostling and caroming softly off one another in the narrow space, until we collapsed at last in each other's arms on the second landing.

Here an ancient oriel window opened glassless to the sky, and the light of the hunter's moon washed us in silver. We lay clasped together, damp skins cooling in the winter air, waiting for our racing hearts to slow and breath to return to our heaving bodies.

The moon above was a January moon, so large as almost to fill the empty window. It seemed no wonder that the tides of sea and woman should be subject to the pull of that stately orb, so close and so commanding.

But my own tides moved no longer to that chaste and sterile summons, and the knowledge of my freedom raced like danger through my blood.

'I have a gift for you too,' I said suddenly to Jamie. He turned towards me and his hand slid, large and sure, over the plane of my still-flat stomach.

'Have you now?' he said.

And the world was all around us, new with possibility.

Author's Note

While most of the historical details and backgrounds in *Cross Stitch* are based on published historical sources, and are accurate so far as is possible, some minor events and details have been altered slightly, as required by the demands of the story. For example, the last recorded witch-burning in Scotland occurred in 1722. When I mentioned this difficulty to my husband, he stared at me and said, 'You have a book in which you start right off expecting people to believe Stonehenge is a time machine, you meet the Loch Ness monster, and you're upset because your witches are twenty years too late?'

'You've got a point,' I said. So, I have taken history both as foundation and as jumping-off point, and trust this admission will discommode no one.

I would also like to note that while the botanical preparations noted in the story were historically used for the medicinal purposes indicated, this fact shouldn't be taken as an indication that such preparations are necessarily either effective for such purposes, or harmless. Many herbal preparations are toxic if used improperly or in excess dosage, and should be administered only by an experienced practitioner.

**READ ON FOR AN EXTRACT FROM
THE SECOND NOVEL IN THE BESTSELLING
OUTLANDER SERIES**

For twenty years Claire Randall has kept her secrets. But now she is returning with her grown daughter to the majesty of Scotland's mist-shrouded hills. Here Claire plans to reveal a truth as stunning as the events that gave it birth: about the mystery of an ancient circle of standing stones, about a love that transcends the boundaries of time, and about James Fraser, a warrior whose gallantry once drew the young Claire from the security of her century to the dangers of his.

Mustering the Roll

Roger Wakefield stood in the center of the room, feeling surrounded. He thought the feeling largely justified, insofar as he *was* surrounded: by tables covered with bric-a-brac and mementos, by heavy Victorian-style furniture, replete with antimacassars, plush and afghans, by tiny braided rugs that lay on the polished wood, craftily awaiting an opportunity to skid beneath an unsuspecting foot. Surrounded by twelve rooms of furniture and clothing and papers. And the books – my God, the books!

The study where he stood was lined on three sides by bookshelves, every one crammed past bursting point. Paperback mystery novels lay in bright, tatty piles in front of calf-bound tomes, jammed cheek by jowl with book-club selections, ancient volumes pilfered from extinct libraries, and thousands upon thousands of pamphlets, leaflets, and hand-sewn manuscripts.

A similar situation prevailed in the rest of the house. Books and papers cluttered every horizontal surface, and every closet groaned and squeaked at the seams. His late adoptive father had lived a long, full life, a good ten years past his biblically allotted threescore and ten. And in eighty-odd years, the Reverend Mr. Reginald Wakefield had never thrown anything away.

Roger repressed the urge to run out of the front door, leap into his Morris Minor, and head back to Oxford, abandoning the manse and its contents to the mercy of weather and vandals. Be calm, he told himself, inhaling deeply. You can deal with this. The books are the easy part; nothing more than a matter of sorting through them and then calling someone to come and haul them away. Granted, they'll need a lorry the size of a railcar, but it can be done. Clothes – no problem. Oxfam gets the lot.

He didn't know what Oxfam was going to do with a lot of vested black serge suits, circa 1948, but perhaps the deserving poor weren't all that picky. He began to breathe a little easier. He had taken a month's leave from the History department at Oxford in order to clear up the Reverend's affairs. Perhaps that would be enough, after all. In his more depressed moments, it had seemed as though the task might take years.

He moved toward one of the tables and picked up a small china dish. It was filled with small metal rectangles; lead 'gaberlunzies,' badges issued to eighteenth-century beggars by parishes as a sort of license. A collection of stoneware bottles stood by the lamp, a ramshorn snuff mull, banded in silver, next to them. Give them to a museum? he thought dubiously. The house was filled with Jacobite artifacts; the Reverend had been an amateur historian, the eighteenth century his favorite hunting ground.

His fingers reached involuntarily to caress the surface of the snuff mull, tracing the black lines of the inscriptions – the names and dates of the Deacons and Treasurers of the Incorporation of Tailors of the Canongate, from Edinburgh, 1726. Perhaps he should keep a few of the Reverend's choicer acquisitions . . . but then he drew back, shaking his head decidedly. 'Nothing doing, cock,' he said aloud, 'this way lies madness.' Or at least the incipient life of a pack rat. Get started saving things, and he'd end up keeping the lot, living in this monstrosity of a house, surrounded by generations of rubbish. 'Talking to yourself, too,' he muttered.

The thought of generations of rubbish reminded him of the garage, and he sagged a bit at the knees. The Reverend, who was in fact Roger's great uncle, had adopted him at the age of five when his parents had been killed in World War II; his mother in the Blitz, his father out over the dark waters of the Channel. With his usual preservative instincts, the Reverend had kept all of Roger's parents' effects, sealed in crates and cartons in the back of the garage. Roger knew for a fact that no one had opened one of those crates in the past twenty years.

Roger uttered an Old Testament groan at the thought of pawing through his parents' memorabilia. 'Oh, God,' he said aloud. 'Anything but that!'

868

The remark had not been intended precisely as prayer, but the doorbell pealed as though in answer, making Roger bite his tongue in startlement.

The door of the manse had a tendency to stick in damp weather, which meant that it was stuck most of the time. Roger freed it with a rending screech, to find a woman on the doorstep.

'Can I help you?'

She was middle height and very pretty. He had an overall impression of fine bones and white linen, topped with a wealth of curly brown hair in a sort of half-tamed chignon. And in the middle of it all, the most extraordinary pair of light eyes, just the color of well-aged sherry.

The eyes swept up from his size-eleven plimsolls to the face a foot above her. The sidelong smile grew wider. 'I hate to start right off with a cliché,' she said, 'but my, how you have grown, young Roger!'

Roger felt himself flushing. The woman laughed and extended a hand. 'You *are* Roger, aren't you? My name's Claire Randall; I was an old friend of the Reverend's. But I haven't seen you since you were five years old.'

'Er, you said you *were* a friend of my father's? Then, you know already. . . .'

The smile vanished, replaced by a look of regret.

'Yes, I was awfully sorry to hear about it. Heart, was it?'

'Um, yes. Very sudden. I've only just come up from Oxford to start dealing with . . . everything.' He waved vaguely, encompassing the Reverend's death, the house behind him, and all its contents.

'From what I recall of your father's library, that little chore ought to last you 'til next Christmas,' Claire observed.

'In that case, maybe we shouldn't be disturbing you,' said a soft American voice.

'Oh, I forgot,' said Claire, half-turning to the girl who had stood out of sight in the corner of the porch. 'Roger Wakefield -- my daughter, Brianna.'

Brianna Randall stepped forward, a shy smile on her face. Roger stared for a moment, then remembered his manners. He stepped back and swung the door open wide, momentarily wondering just when he had last changed his shirt.

'Not at all, not at all!' he said heartily. 'I was just wanting a break. Won't you come in?'

He waved the two women down the hall toward the Reverend's study, noting that as well as being moderately attractive, the daughter was one of the tallest girls he'd ever seen close-to. She had to be easily six feet, he thought, seeing her head even with the top of the hall stand as she passed. He unconsciously straightened himself as he followed, drawing up to his full six feet three. At the last moment, he ducked, to avoid banging his head on the study lintel as he followed the women into the room.

'I'd meant to come before,' said Claire, settling herself deeper in the huge wing chair. The fourth wall of the Reverend's study was equipped with floor-to-ceiling windows, and the sunlight winked off the pearl clip in her light-brown hair. The curls were beginning to escape from their confinement, and she tucked one absently behind an ear as she talked.

'I'd arranged to come last year, in fact, and then there was an emergency at the hospital in Boston – I'm a doctor,' she explained, mouth curling a little at the look of surprise Roger hadn't quite managed to conceal. 'But I'm sorry that we didn't; I would have liked so much to see your father again.'

Roger rather wondered why they had come now, knowing the Reverend was dead, but it seemed impolite to ask. Instead, he asked, 'Enjoying a bit of sightseeing, are you?'

'Yes, we drove up from London,' Claire answered. She smiled at her daughter. 'I wanted Bree to see the country; you wouldn't think it to hear her talk, but she's as English as I am, though she's never lived here.'

'Really?' Roger glanced at Brianna. She didn't really look English, he thought; aside from the height, she had thick red hair, worn loose over her shoulders, and strong, sharp-angled bones in her face, with the nose long and straight – maybe a touch too long.

'I was born in America,' Brianna explained, 'but both Mother and Daddy are – were – English.'

'Were?'

'My husband died two years ago,' Claire explained. 'You knew him, I think – Frank Randall.'

'*Frank* Randall! Of course!' Roger smacked himself on the forehead, and felt his cheeks grow hot at Brianna's giggle. 'You're going to think me a complete fool, but I've only just realized who you are.'

The name explained a lot; Frank Randall had been an eminent historian, and a good friend of the Reverend's; they had exchanged bits of Jacobite arcana for years, though it was at least ten years since Frank Randall had last visited the manse.

'So – you'll be visiting the historical sites near Inverness?' Roger hazarded. 'Have you been to Culloden yet?'

'Not yet,' Brianna answered. 'We thought we'd go later this week.' Her answering smile was polite, but nothing more.

'We're booked for a trip down Loch Ness this afternoon,' Claire explained. 'And perhaps we'll drive down to Fort William tomorrow, or just poke about in Inverness; the place has grown a lot since I was last here.'

'When was that?' Roger wondered whether he ought to volunteer his services as tour guide. He really shouldn't take the time, but the Randalls had been good friends of the Reverend's. Besides, a car trip to Fort William in company with two attractive women seemed a much more appealing prospect than cleaning out the garage, which was next on his list.

'Oh, more than twenty years ago. It's been a long time.' There was an odd note in Claire's voice that made Roger glance at her, but she met his eyes with a smile.

'Well,' he ventured, 'if there's anything I can do for you, while you're in the Highlands . . .'

Claire was still smiling, but something in her face changed. He could almost think she had been waiting for an opening. She glanced at Brianna, then back to Roger.

'Since you mention it,' she said, her smile broadening.

'Oh, Mother!' Brianna said, sitting up in her chair. 'You don't want to bother Mr. Wakefield! Look at all he's got to do!' She waved a hand at the crowded study, with its overflowing cartons and endless stacks of books.

'Oh, no bother at all!' Roger protested. 'Er . . . what is it?'

Claire shot her daughter a quelling look. 'I wasn't planning to knock him on the head and drag him off,' she said tartly. 'But he might well know someone who could help. It's a small historical project,' she explained to Roger. 'I need someone who's fairly well versed in the eighteenth-century Jacobites – Bonnie Prince Charlie and all that lot.'

Roger leaned forward, interested. 'Jacobites?' he said. 'That period's not one of my specialties, but I do know a bit – hard not to, living so close to Culloden. That's where the final battle was, you know,' he explained to Brianna. 'Where the Bonnie Prince's lot ran up against the Duke of Cumberland and got slaughtered for their pains.'

'Right,' said Claire. 'And that, in fact, has to do with what I want to find out.' She reached into her handbag and drew out a folded paper.

Roger opened it and scanned the contents quickly. It was a list of names – maybe thirty, all men. At the top of the sheet was a heading: 'JACOBITE RISING, 1745 – CULLODEN'

'Oh, the '45?' Roger said. 'These men fought at Culloden, did they?'

'They did,' Claire replied. 'What I want to find out is – how many of the men on this list survived that battle?'

Roger rubbed his chin as he perused the list. 'That's a simple question,' he said, 'but the answer might be hard to find. So many of the Highland clansmen who followed Prince Charles were killed on Culloden Field that they weren't buried individually. They were put into mass graves, with no more than a single stone bearing the clan name as a marker.'

'I know,' Claire said. 'Brianna hasn't been there, but I have – a long time ago.' He thought he saw a fleeting shadow in her eyes, though it was quickly hidden as she reached into her handbag. No wonder if there was, he thought. Culloden Field was an affecting place; it brought tears to his own eyes, to look out over that expanse of moorland and remember the gallantry and courage of the Scottish Highlanders who lay slaughtered beneath the grass.

She unfolded several more typed sheets and handed them to him. A long white finger ran down the margin of one

872

sheet. Beautiful hands, Roger noted; delicately molded, carefully kept, with a single ring on each hand. The silver one on her right hand was especially striking; a wide Jacobean band in the Highland interlace pattern, embellished with thistle blossoms.

'These are the names of the wives, so far as I know them. I thought that might help, since if the husbands were killed at Culloden, you'd likely find these women remarrying or emigrating afterward. Those records would surely be in the parish register? They're all from the same parish; the church was in Broch Mordha – it's a good bit south of here.'

'That's a very helpful idea,' Roger said, mildly surprised. 'It's the sort of thing an historian would think of.'

'I'm hardly an historian,' Claire Randall said dryly. 'On the other hand, when you live with one, you do pick up the occasional odd thought.'

'Of course.' A thought struck Roger, and he rose from his chair. 'I'm being a terrible host; please, let me get you a drink, and then you can tell me a bit more about this. Perhaps I could help you with it myself.'

Despite the disorder, he knew where the decanters were kept, and quickly had his guests supplied with whisky. He'd put quite a lot of soda in Brianna's, but noticed that she sipped at it as though her glass contained ant spray, rather than the best Glenfiddich single malt. Claire, who took her whisky neat by request, seemed to enjoy it much more.

'Well.' Roger resumed his seat and picked up the paper again. 'It's an interesting problem, in terms of historical research. You said these men came from the same parish? I suppose they came from a single clan or sept – I see a number of them were named Fraser.'

Claire nodded, hands folded in her lap. 'They came from the same estate; a small Highland farm called Broch Tuarach – it was known locally as Lallybroch. They were part of clan Fraser, though they never gave a formal allegiance to Lord Lovat as chief. These men joined the Rising early; they fought in the Battle of Prestonpans – while Lovat's men didn't come until just before Culloden.'

'Really? That's interesting.' Under normal eighteenth-century conditions, such small tenant-farmers would have died where they lived, and be filed tidily away in the village churchyard, neatly docketed in the parish register. However, Bonnie Prince Charlie's attempt to regain the throne of Scotland in 1745 had disrupted the normal course of things in no uncertain terms.

In the famine after the disaster of Culloden, many Highlanders had emigrated to the New World; others had drifted from the glens and moors toward the cities, in search of food and employment. A few stayed on, stubbornly clinging to their land and traditions.

'It would make a fascinating article,' Roger said, thinking aloud. 'Follow the fate of a number of individuals, see what happened to them all. Less interesting if they all *were* killed at Culloden, but chances were that a few made it out.' He would be inclined to take on the project as a welcome break even were it not Claire Randall who asked.

'Yes, I think I can help you with this,' he said, and was gratified at the warm smile she bestowed on him.

'Would you really? That's wonderful!' she said.

'My pleasure,' Roger said. He folded the paper and laid it on the table. 'I'll start in on it directly. But tell me, how did you enjoy your drive up from London?'

The conversation became general as the Randalls regaled him with tales of their transatlantic journey, and the drive from London. Roger's attention drifted slightly, as he began to plan the research for this project. He felt mildly guilty about taking it on; he really shouldn't take the time. On the other hand, it was an interesting question. And it was possible that he could combine the project with some of the necessary clearing-up of the Reverend's material; he knew for a fact that there were forty-eight cartons in the garage, all labeled JACOBITES, MISCELLANEOUS. The thought of it was enough to make him feel faint.

With a wrench, he tore his mind away from the garage, to find that the conversation had made an abrupt change of subject.

'Druids?' Roger felt dazed. He peered suspiciously into his glass, checking to see that he really had added soda.

'You hadn't heard about them?' Claire looked slightly disappointed. 'Your father – the Reverend – he knew about them, though only unofficially. Perhaps he didn't think it worth telling you; he thought it something of a joke.'

Roger scratched his head, ruffling the thick black hair. 'No, I really don't recall. But you're right, he may not have thought it anything serious.'

'Well, I don't know that it is.' She crossed her legs at the knee. A streak of sunlight gleamed down the shin of her stockings, emphasizing the delicacy of the long bone beneath.

'When I was here last with Frank — God, that was twenty-three years ago! — the Reverend told him that there was a local group of — well, modern Druids, I suppose you'd call them. I've no idea how authentic they might be; most likely not very.' Brianna was leaning forward now, interested, the glass of whisky forgotten between her hands.

'The Reverend couldn't take official notice of them — paganism and all that, you know — but his housekeeper, Mrs. Graham, was involved with the group, so he got wind of their doings from time to time, and he tipped Frank that there would be a ceremony of some kind on the dawn of Beltane — May Day, that is.'

Roger nodded, trying to adjust to the idea of elderly Mrs. Graham, that extremely proper person, engaging in pagan rites and dancing round stone circles in the dawn. All he could remember of Druid ceremonies himself was that some of them involved burning sacrificial victims in wicker cages, which seemed still more unlikely behavior for a Scottish Presbyterian lady of advanced years.

'There's a circle of standing stones on top of a hill, fairly nearby. So we went up there before dawn to, well, to spy on them,' she continued, shrugging apologetically. 'You know what scholars are like; no conscience at all when it comes to their own field, let alone a sense of social delicacy.' Roger winced slightly at this, but nodded in wry agreement.

'And there they were,' she said. 'Mrs. Graham included, all wearing bedsheets, chanting things and dancing in the midst of the stone circle. Frank was fascinated,' she added, with a smile. 'And it *was* impressive, even to me.'

She paused for a moment, eyeing Roger rather speculatively.

'I'd heard that Mrs. Graham had passed away a few years ago. But I wonder . . . do you know if she had any family? I believe membership in such groups is often hereditary; maybe there's a daughter or granddaughter who could tell me a bit.'

'Well,' Roger said slowly. 'There is a granddaughter – Fiona's her name, Fiona Graham. In fact, she came to help out here at the manse after her grandmother died; the Reverend was really too elderly to be left all on his own.'

If anything could displace his vision of Mrs. Graham dancing in a bedsheet, it was the thought of nineteen-year-old Fiona as a guardian of ancient mystic knowledge, but Roger rallied gamely and went on.

'She isn't here just now, I'm afraid. I could ask her for you, though.'

Claire waved a slender hand in dismissal. 'Don't trouble yourself. Another time will do. We've taken up too much of your time already.'

To Roger's dismay, she set down her empty glass on the small table between the chairs and Brianna added her own full one with what looked like alacrity. He noticed that Brianna Randall bit her nails. This small evidence of imperfection gave him the nerve to take the next step. She intrigued him, and he didn't want her to go, with no assurance that he would see her again.

'Speaking of stone circles,' he said quickly. 'I believe I know the one you mentioned. It's quite scenic, and not too far from town.' He smiled directly at Brianna Randall, registering automatically the fact that she had three small freckles high on one cheekbone. 'I thought perhaps I'd start on this project with a trip down to Broch Tuarach. It's in the same direction as the stone circle, so maybe . . . aaagh!'

With a sudden jerk of her bulky handbag, Claire Randall had bumped both whisky glasses off the table, showering Roger's lap and thighs with single malt whisky and quite a lot of soda.

'I'm terribly sorry,' she apologized, obviously flustered. She bent and began picking up pieces of shattered crystal, despite Roger's half-coherent attempts to stop her.

Brianna, coming to assist with a handful of linen napkins seized from the sideboard, was saying 'Really, Mother, how they ever let you do surgery, I don't know. You're just not safe with anything smaller than a bread-box. Look, you've got his shoes soaked with whisky!' She knelt on the floor, and began busily mopping up spilled Scotch and fragments of crystal. 'And his pants, too.'

Whipping a fresh napkin from the stack over her arm, she industriously polished Roger's toes, her red mane floating deliriously around his knees. Her head was rising, as she peered at his thighs, dabbing energetically at damp spots on the corduroy. Roger closed his eyes and thought frantically of terrible car crashes on the motorway and tax forms for the Inland Revenue and the Blob from Outer Space – anything that might stop him disgracing himself utterly as Brianna Randall's warm breath misted softly through the wet fabric of his trousers.

'Er, maybe you'd like to do the rest yourself?' The voice came from somewhere around the level of his nose, and he opened his eyes to find a pair of deep blue eyes facing him above a wide grin. He rather weakly took the napkin she was offering him, breathing as though he had just been chased by a train.

Lowering his head to scrub at his trousers, he caught sight of Claire Randall watching him with an expression of mingled sympathy and amusement. There was nothing else visible in her expression; nothing of that flash he thought he'd seen in her eyes just before the catastrophe. Flustered as he was, it was probably his imagination, he thought. For why on earth should she have done it on purpose?

'Since when are you interested in Druids, Mama?' Brianna seemed disposed to find something hilarious in the idea; I had noticed her biting the insides of her cheeks while I was chatting with Roger Wakefield, and the grin she had been hiding then was now plastered across her face. 'You going to get your own bedsheet and join up?'

'Bound to be more entertaining than hospital staff meetings every Thursday,' I said. 'Bit drafty, though.' She hooted with laughter, startling two chickadees off the walk in front of us.

877

'No,' I said, switching to seriousness. 'It isn't the Druid ladies I'm after, so much. There's someone I used to know in Scotland that I wanted to find, if I can. I haven't an address for her – I haven't been in touch with her for more than twenty years – but she had an interest in odd things like that: witchcraft, old beliefs, folklore. All that sort of thing. She once lived near here; I thought if she was still here, she might be involved with a group like that.'

'What's her name?'

I shook my head, grabbing at the loosened clip as it slid from my curls. It slipped through my fingers and bounced into the deep grass along the walk.

'Damn!' I said, stooping for it. My fingers were unsteady as I groped through the dense stalks, and I had trouble picking up the clip, slippery with moisture from the wet grass. The thought of Geillis Duncan tended to unnerve me, even now.

'I don't know,' I said, brushing the curls back off my flushed face. 'I mean – it's been such a long time, I'm sure she'd have a different name by now. She was widowed; she might have married again, or be using her maiden name.'

'Oh.' Brianna lost interest in the topic, and walked along in silence for a little. Suddenly she said, 'What did you think of Roger Wakefield, Mama?'

I glanced at her; her cheeks were pink, but it might be from the spring wind.

'He seems a very nice young man,' I said carefully. 'He's certainly intelligent; he's one of the youngest professors at Oxford.' The intelligence I had known about; I wondered whether he had any imagination. So often scholarly types didn't. But imagination would be helpful.

'He's got the grooviest eyes,' Brianna said, dreamily ignoring the question of his brain. 'Aren't they the greenest you've ever seen?'

'Yes, they're very striking,' I agreed. 'They've always been like that; I remember noticing them when I first met him as a child.'

Brianna looked down at me, frowning.

'Yes, Mother, really! Did you have to say "My, how you've grown!" when he answered the door? How embarrassing!'

I laughed.

'Well, when you've last seen someone hovering round your navel, and suddenly you find yourself looking up his nose,' I defended myself, 'you can't help remarking the difference.'

'*Mother!*' But she fizzed with laughter.

'*He has a very nice bottom, too,*' I remarked, just to keep her going. '*I noticed when he bent over to get the whisky.*'

'*Mo-THERRR! They'll* hear *you!*'

We were nearly at the bus stop. There were two or three women and an elderly gentleman in tweeds standing by the sign; they turned to stare at us as we came up.

'*Is this the place for the Loch-side Tours bus?*' I asked, scanning the bewildering array of notices and advertisements posted on the signboard.

'*Och, aye,*' one of the ladies said kindly. '*The bus will be comin' along in ten minutes or so.*' She scanned Brianna, so clearly American in blue jeans and white windbreaker. The final patriotic note was added by the flushed face, red with suppressed laughter. '*You'll be going to see Loch Ness? Your first time, is it?*'

I smiled at her. '*I sailed down the loch with my husband twenty-odd years ago, but this is my daughter's first trip to Scotland.*'

'*Oh, is it?*' This attracted the attention of the other ladies and they crowded around, suddenly friendly, offering advice and asking questions until the big yellow bus came chugging round the corner.

Brianna paused before climbing the steps, admiring the picturesque drawing of green serpentine loops, undulating through a blue-paint lake, edged with black pines.

'*This will be fun,*' she said, laughing. '*Think we'll see the monster?*'

'*You never know,*' I said.

Roger spent the rest of the day in a state of abstraction, wandering absently from one task to another. The books to be packed for donation to the Society for the Preservation of Antiquities lay spilling out of their carton, the Reverend's ancient flatbed lorry sat in the drive with its bonnet up, halfway through a motor check, and a cup of tea sat half-drunk and milk-scummed at his elbow as he gazed blankly out at the falling rain of early evening.

What he should do, he knew, was get at the job of dismantling the heart of the Reverend's study. Not the books; massive as that job was, it was only a matter of deciding which to keep himself, and which should be dispatched to the SPA or the Reverend's old college library.

No, sooner or later he would have to tackle the enormous desk, which had papers filling each huge drawer to the brim and protruding from its dozens of pigeonholes. And he'd have to take down and dispose of all of the miscellany decorating the cork wall that filled one side of the room; a task to daunt the stoutest heart.

Aside from a general disinclination to start the tedious job, Roger was hampered by something else. He didn't *want* to be doing these things, necessary as they were; he wanted to be working on Claire Randall's project, tracking down the clansmen of Culloden.

It was an interesting enough project in its way, though probably a minor research job. But that wasn't it. No, he thought, if he were being honest with himself, he wanted to tackle Claire Randall's project because he wanted to go round to Mrs. Thomas's guesthouse and lay his results at the feet of Brianna Randall, as knights were supposed to have done with the heads of dragons. Even if he didn't get results on that scale, he urgently wanted some excuse to see her and talk with her again.

It was a Bronzino painting she reminded him of, he decided. She and her mother both gave that odd impression of having been outlined somehow, drawn with such vivid strokes and delicate detail that they stood out from their background as though they'd been engraved on it. But Brianna had that brilliant coloring, and that air of absolute physical presence that made Bronzino's sitters seem to follow you with their eyes, to be about to speak from their frames. He'd never seen a Bronzino painting making faces at a glass of whisky, but if there had been one, he was sure it would have looked precisely like Brianna Randall.

'Well, bloody hell,' he said aloud. 'It won't take a lot of time just to look over the records at Culloden House tomorrow, will it? You,' he said, addressing the desk and its multiple burdens, 'can wait for a day. So can you,' he said to the wall, and defiantly plucked a mystery novel from the shelf. He glanced around belligerently, as though daring any of the furnishings to object, but there was no sound but the whirring of the electric fire. He switched it off and, book under his arm, left the study, flicking off the light.